D1076256

NO LONGER THE
PROPERTY OF
UNIVERSITY LIBRARY

THE

VIRGINIA COMEDIANS

JOHN ESTEN COOKE

THE

VIRGINIA COMEDIANS:

OR,

OLD DAYS IN THE OLD DOMINION.

JOHN ESTEN COOKE

Come wealth or want, come good or ill,
Let young and old accept their part,
And bow before the Awful Will,
And bear it with an honest heart.
Who misses or who wins the prize?
Go, lose or conquer, as you can;
But if you fail, or if you rise,
Be each, pray God, a gentleman.
THACKERAY.

Two Volumes in One

THE GREGG PRESS / RIDGEWOOD, N. J.

First published in 1854 by D. Appleton & Co.
Republished in 1968 by
The Gregg Press Incorporated
171 East Ridgewood Avenue
Ridgewood, New Jersey, U.S.A.

Library of Congress Catalog Card Number: 68-23717

Printed in United States of America

AMERICANS IN FICTION

In the domain of literature the play may once have been the chief abstract and chronicle of the times, but during the nineteenth and twentieth centuries the novel has usurped the chief place in holding the mirror up to the homely face of society. On this account, if for no other, the Gregg Press series of reprints of American fiction merits the attention of all students of Americana and of librarians interested in building up adequate collections dealing with the social and literary history of the United States. Most of the three score and ten novels or volumes of short stories included in the series enjoyed considerable fame in their day but have been so long out of print as to be virtually unobtainable in the original editions.

Included in the list are works by writers not presently fashionable in critical circles—but nevertheless well known to literary historians—among them Joel Chandler Harris, Harriet Beecher Stowe, Thomas Bailey Aldrich, and William Gilmore Simms. A substantial element in the list consists of authors who are known especially for their graphic portrayal of a particular American setting, such as Gertrude Atherton (California), Arlo Bates (Boston), Alice Brown (New England), Edward Eggleston (Indiana), Mary Wilkins Freeman (New England), Henry B. Fuller (Chicago), Richard M. Johnston (Georgia), James Lane Allen (Kentucky), Mary N. Murfree (Tennessee), and Thomas Nelson Page (Virginia). There is even a novel by Frederic Remington, one of the most popular painters of the Western cowboy and Indian—and another, and impressive minor classic on the early mining region of Colorado, from the pen of Mary Hallock Foote. The professional student of American literature will rejoice in the opportunity afforded by the collection to extend his reading of fiction belonging to what is called the "local-color movement"—a major current in the development of the national belles-lettres.

Among the titles in the series are also a number of famous historical novels. Silas Weir Mitchell's *Hugh Wynne* is one of the very best fictional treatments of the American Revolution. John Esten Cooke is the foremost Southern writer of his day who dealt with the Civil War. The two books by Thomas Dixon are among the most famous novels on the Reconstruction Era, with sensational disclosures of the original Ku Klux Klan in action. They supplied the grist for the first great movie "spectacular"—*The Birth of a Nation* (1915).

Paul Leicester Ford's *The Honorable Peter Stirling* is justly ranked among the top American novels which portray American politics in action—a subject illuminated by other novelists in the Gregg list—A. H. Lewis, Frances H. Burnett, and Alice Brown, for example. Economic problems are forcefully put before the reader in works by Aldrich, Mrs. Freeman, and John Hay, whose novels illustrate the ominous concern over the early battles between labor and capital. From the sweatshops of Eastern cities in which newly arrived immigrants toiled for pittances, to the Western mining camps where the laborers packed revolvers, the working class of the times enters into various other stories in the Gregg list. The capitalist class, also, comes in for attention, with an account of a struggle for the ownership of a railroad in Samuel Merwin's *The Short-Line War* and with the devastating documentation of the foibles of the newly rich and their wives in the narratives of David Graham Phillips. It was Phillips whose annoying talent for the exposure of abuses led Theodore Roosevelt to put the term "muck-raker" into currency.

While it is apparent that local-color stories, the historical novel, and the economic novel have all been borne in mind in choosing the titles for this important series of reprints, it is evident that careful consideration has also been given to treatments of various minority elements in the American population. The Negro, especially, but also the Indian, the half-breed, Creoles, Cajuns—and even the West Coast Japanese—appear as characters in various of these novels or volumes of short stories and sketches. Joel Chandler Harris's *Free Joe* will open the eyes of readers who know that author solely as the creator of humorous old Uncle Remus. And there is a revelatory volume of dialect tales, written by a Negro author, *The Conjure Woman* by Charles W. Chesnutt.

In literary conventions and the dominating attitudes toward life, the works in the Gregg series range from the adventurous romance illustrated so well by Mayne Reid or the polite urbanity of Owen Wister to the mordant irony of Kate Chopin and the grimmer realism of Joseph Kirkland's own experiences on bloody Civil War battlefields or the depressing display of New York farm life by Harold Frederic. In short, the series admirably illustrates the general qualities of the fiction produced in the United States during the era covered, just as it generously mirrors the geographical regions, the people, and the problems of the times.

PROFESSOR CLARENCE GOHDES
Duke University
Durham, North Carolina

December, 1967

JOHN ESTEN COOKE

John Esten Cooke was one of the few first-rate imaginative writers which the Civil War era produced. He was born in 1830 near Winchester, Virginia, the son of one of Virginia's First Families, educated at Charlestown Academy, and later studied law, but wanted to be a professional writer, and successfully submitted several of his early stories to *Harper's Magazine*. During the War, Cooke rose from the rank of private, served on J. E. B. Stuart's staff as captain, and with General Lee after Stuart's death at Richmond. He was in charge of a cannon at Bull Run, knew all of the generals of the Army of Northern Virginia, and saw most of the great battles in which Lee's army participated. After the war Cooke married Mary Francis Page, and settled at "The Briers," Clarke County, Virginia, where he remained until his death in 1886. Cooke, like Thomas Nelson Page and William Gilmore Simms, wrote in the tradition of James Fenimore Cooper, combining a vivid historical sense of the American past with love of an adventure story *per se*. He had the additional advantage of war experiences and first-hand knowledge of the people and geography which he described.

The critic and poet Richard Henry Stoddard said of Cooke: "His books have the charm of elegant comedy, the pathos of pastoral tragedy, sparkles of wit, flashes of humor, and everywhere the amenities of high breeding."

And Cooke said of his work: "My aim has been to paint the Virginia phase of American society, to do for the Old Dominion what Cooper has done for the Indians, Simms for the Revolutionary drama in South Carolina, Irving for the Dutch Knickerbockers, and Hawthorne for the weird Puritan life of New England." In spite of his sympathy for the Southern cause, he never harbored bitterness toward the North.

Cooke wrote in 1855 that the *Virginia Comedians* was "intended to be a picture of our curiously graded Virginia society just before the Revolution. The book is profoundly democratic, and American — the aristocracy whom I don't like getting the worst of it." Patrick Henry, "that great agitator of ideas," is the leading character in this dramatic narrative set in a society in which were heard "On all sides murmurs, mutterings as of an approaching storm! Men doubtful of the ground they walk on — new ideas dazzling them — old institutions crumbling . . . (England) has given to Lord Culpeper the whole territory from the mouth of the Rappahannock to the sources of the Potomac — enthroned him a prince and king over us!" Cooke, like his great contemporary William Gilmore Simms, is a vigorous, robust writer, with a strong sense of the freshness of nature and the joys of physical action. The style is manly, direct, simple, and natural. *The Virginia Comedians* is filled with descriptions of the hunt, field sports, wine, music, the table, dancing, the theater, and love. Cooke's descriptions of festivals, and fox-hunts rival those of Fielding's *Tom Jones,* and if the aristocrats get "the worst of it," their *carpe diem* way of life is painted in the most brilliant and glowing of colors, and the squire-owners of Effingham Hall are as gallant, witty, and fearless as the English nobility whose manners they imitated. Cooke's feminine portraits are vivid and realistic, particularly that of Beatrice, the actress. Although the setting is romantic, the characters are drawn realistically; they are flesh and blood, and act out of sordid motives as well as idealistic ones.

The plot is quite complicated: An English repertory company, "The Virginia Company of Comedians," is performing at Williamsburg in 1763. Champ Effingham, a young Virginian aristocrat, falls in love with Beatrice, the leading lady, and joins the company to be near her, though she loves another young man, who is more stable and sincere. Beatrice and Charley, her true love, leave Williamsburg, but are pursued by the hot-headed Effingham, who stabs Charley and leaves him for dead. Effingham flees to Europe, Charley recovers and marries Beatrice. Two years later the romantic intrigue resumes, when Champ, older and wiser, returns to marry his cousin Clare. The book ends with the Stamp Act rebellion.

PRINCIPAL WORKS: Novels — *Leather Stocking and Silk,* 1854; *The Virginia Comedians,* 1854; *Ellie,* 1855; *The Last of the Foresters,* 1856; *Henry St. John: Gentleman,* 1859; *Surry of Eagle's Nest,* 1866; *Mohun,* 1868; *Fairfax,* 1868; *Hilt to Hilt,* 1869; *The Heir of Gaymount,* 1870; *Dr. Paul Vandike,* 1872; *Her Majesty the Queen,* 1873; *Pretty Mrs. Gaston and Other Stories,* 1874; *Canolles,* 1877; *Stories of the Old Dominion,* 1879; *The Maurice Mystery,* 1885; *My Lady Pokahontas,* 1885. History and Biography: *The Youth of Jefferson,* 1854; *Stonewall Jackson,* 1863; *Wearing of the Gray,* 1867; *Hammer and Rapier,* 1870; *Life of General Robert E. Lee,* 1871; *Life of Samuel J. Tilden,* 1876; *Virginia: A History of the People,* 1883.

F. C. S.

PREFACE.

THE design of this book will plainly appear from the most cursory perusal. The writer can only trust that the curiosity to discover its true intent and meaning may be universal.

That strange Virginia of 1765, with its passions, humors, and anomalies of every description, afforded a broad field for dramatic narrative, and the author has endeavored to embody some of its peculiarities in this rapid and shifting panorama. The period was one of transition. England was attacking—the Colonies were resisting. The Stamp Act hung over America like a gathering cloud, and men's minds were agitated by the breath of a coming storm—that storm which was to swell into the hurricane of the Revolution.

But the aim of this book is scarcely to follow the course of public events, or reflect the political spirit of the period. True, many pages are dedicated to that great agitator of ideas, who more than any other single man, aroused the tornado; and those intellectual giants who stood shoulder to shoulder in the after-struggle once or twice appear. But these men of whom history has spoken so clearly, are not the real personages of the narrative—and the writer has indeed scarcely named them. The historic muse was far too noble to be invoked on such an occasion; and the simple design he proposed to himself was a rapid delineation of some social peculiarities in their passionate and humorous development. The merely passionate, however, yields to the bright and hopeful—and if the Chorus sings of far-away events, when the real narrative is ended the song is not a bitter song, as the tears of the singers are not bitter tears—rather of hope and joy. Every where the writer has endeavored to preserve the traits of the period, and above all to make his characters flesh and blood. A herculean labor! For surely it is no slight task to accurately delineate that wonderful machine called man, made up of such innumerable wheels and levers—some of them too ponderous for a giant to move, others so minute that the little finger of a child may shatter them. The summits of Art rise to view often as the poor writer passes onward; but only the Titans—Shakspeare and the rest—can scale them.

But to descend from these generalities. The author's wish was simply to depict some Virginia scenes and personages ten years before the Revolution. He trusts his picture is at least truthful, as far as it extends. If some pages are painful and bitter, more, he trusts, are bright and hopeful, as life is, with all its sufferings and trials. If the dissection of that impulsive and fiery nature, the incidents of whose wild career absorb the greater portion of the first part, is unpleasant; the author indulges the hope, that in the jovial utterances of the worthy soldier, and in the songs and laughter of another personage—a child—the reader may find something more agreeable. That child is scarcely a figment of the imagination. Every man must have been thrown in contact at some time with one of these pure and tender creatures, who, like stars, hover long above the rosy fields of youth, and seem to fill the air with the gay music of their laughter and the radiance of their eyes.

One word more. In the sketch of the parson of the Established Church first introduced, the writer has endeavored to preserve the fidelity of history with the most sedulous care. Here, as on all important occasions, imagination has yielded to history: fancy, to recorded fact. That hundreds of such men were sent to Virginia to act as spiritual guides to our ancestors, there can, unhappily, be no reason to doubt. So far from the sketch in this history being a mere caricature, the writer could bring, were he disposed to clog the narrative with notes, the most irrefragable records, to support the assertion that the picture is much less harsh than he had the right to make it. He has no desire to cast odium on that former church, by depicting one of her unworthy followers—God forbid. Did he not feel perfectly well convinced that the sketch was truthful—if any thing, too favorable—he would erase every line. Unhappily, the church was cursed with just such men, and she suffered. The blot was ere long removed, however, and with it those other excrescences which lowered her standing and diminished her usefulness. It was a source of real regret, that the length to which the narrative had extended, rendered it impossible for the writer to give that prominence to the true follower, which he has accorded to the false. But it is difficult to introduce a new thread into the tangled web of a narrative dealing with so many personages, and this must be his excuse.

Every book should be judged, first for its purity and healthfulness: afterwards for what it contains of novel character, incident, or idea. The writer trusts that in the first particular these pages are irreproachable: he is too well aware of his deficiencies on the remaining point.

But the subject does not suffer:—the field remains. Some day that strange past will attract the eye of the man who will possess the intellect to master its ideas—the heart to comprehend its spirit and interpret its mystery. When that day comes, the world will have a volume which will live for ever—a book in which the Revolution will speak in its grand, eloquent voice of thunder, lightning, and tempest. When that day comes, as it will, the master-mind may possibly find in these poor pages of the obscure writer of to-day, some hint to arouse his genius—some word may set his thoughts in motion.

If this hope should be fulfilled, the book now offered to the world will not have been written wholly in vain.

CONTENTS OF VOL. I.

BOOK I.

CONTENTS OF VOL. II.

BOOK II.

CONTENTS OF VOL. II.

THE VIRGINIA COMEDIANS.

BOOK I.

PROLOGUE.

THE memories of men are full of old romances: but they will not speak—our skalds. King Arthur lies still wounded grievously, in the far island valley of Avilyon: Lord Odin in the misty death realm: Balder the Beautiful, sought long by great Hermoder, lives beyond Hela's portals, and will bless his people some day when he comes. But when? King Arthur ever *is to* come: Odin will one day wind his horn and clash his wild barbaric cymbals through the Nordland pines as he returns, but not in our generation: Balder will rise from sleep and shine again the white sun god on his world. But always these things will be: Arthur and the rest are meanwhile sleeping.

Romance is history: the illustration may be lame—the truth is melancholy. Because the men whose memories hold this history will not speak, it dies away with them: the great past goes deeper and deeper into mist: becomes finally a dying strain of music, and is no more remembered forever.

Thinking these thoughts I have thought it well to set

down here some incidents which took place on Virginia soil, and in which an ancestor of my family had no small part: to write my family romance in a single word, and also, though following a connecting thread, a leading idea, to speak briefly of the period to which these memories, as I may call them, do attach.

That period was very picturesque: illustrated and adorned, as it surely was, by such figures as one seldom sees now on the earth. Often in my evening reveries, assisted by the partial gloom resulting from the struggles of the darkness and the dying firelight, I endeavor, and not wholly without success, to summon from their sleep these stalwart cavaliers, and tender, graceful dames of the far past. They rise before me and glide onward—manly faces, with clear eyes and lofty brows, and firm lips covered with the knightly fringe: soft, tender faces, with bright eyes and gracious smiles and winning gestures; all the life and splendor of the past again becomes incarnate! How plain the embroidered doublet, and the sword-belt, and the powdered hair, and hat adorned with its wide floating feather! How real are the ruffled breasts and hands, the long-flapped waistcoats, and the buckled shoes! And then the fairer forms: they come as plainly with their looped-back gowns all glittering with gold and silver flowers, and on their heads great masses of curls with pearls interwoven! See the gracious smiles and musical movement—all the graces which made those dead dames so attractive to the outward eye—as their pure faithful natures made them priceless to the eyes of the heart.

If fancy needed assistance, more than one portrait hanging on my walls might afford it. Old family portraits which I often gaze on with a pensive pleasure. What a tender maiden grace beams on me from the eyes of Kate Effingham yonder; smiling from the antique frame and blooming like a radiant summer—she was but seventeen when it was taken—under the winter of her snow-like powder, and bright diamond pendants, glittering like icicles! The canvas is discolored, and even cracked in places, but the little face laughs merrily still—the eyes fixed peradventure upon another portrait hanging opposite. This is a picture of Mr. William Effingham, the brave soldier of the Revolution, taken in his younger days, when he had just returned from College. He is most preposterously dressed in flowing periwig and enormous ruffles; and his coat is heavy with embroidery in gold thread: he is a handsome young fellow, and excepting some pomposity in his air, a simple-looking excellent, honest face.

Over my fireplace, however, hangs the picture which I value most—a portrait of my ancestor, Champ Effingham, Esq. The form is lordly and erect; the face clear and pale; the eyes full of wondrous thought in their far depths. The lips are chiselled with extraordinary beauty, the brow noble and imaginative—the whole face plainly giving indication of fiery passion, and no less of tender softness. Often this face looks at me from the canvas, and I fancy sometimes that the white hand, covered as in Vandyke's pictures with its snowy lace, moves from the book it holds and raises slowly the forefinger and points toward its owner's breast. The lips then seem to say, "Speak of me as I was: nothing extenuate: set down nought in malice!"—then the fire-light leaping up shows plainly that this all was but a dream, and the fine pale face is again only canvas, the white hand rests upon its book:—my dream ends with a smile.

But still I fancy I hear my ancestor calling to me from the dead past and saying, "Speak!" and other voices, loud and low, rough, hearty, laughing, tender voices of all possible descriptions, do command that I speak of them. How can I resist? Though in that great art of speaking with the pen I am a mere tyro, still I find myself compelled to speak—to place here all I know, to write down what is in my memory and my heart. The serene friendly stars are yonder in the sky—the nights are still:—my friends look down upon me from their shelves, and the twigs in the fireplace are crackling merrily.

Yes, yes! I shall obey that dreamy voice which but now spoke to me. I shall obey the injunction of the portrait, whose soft eyes smile on me as I write these lines. Here in the quiet country with the winds around me I will write it all:—for I have heard all the family history. It shall be done honestly at least, and every other portrait shall be painted with such accuracy and truth as I possess—I trust with perfect truth. Then some day when I go away, my friend will find these MSS., and he has my full permission to make them public.

Now I will begin.

Thus far the author of the MS. The worthy gentleman gave us his full permission to edit it in such manner as seemed to us best calculated to present incidents and personages clearly: and this has been the labor of the last two months. The sequence of events has been somewhat altered, to give more artistic point to certain pages—since art is all in all after honesty—and many moral digressions of the worthy gentleman have been omitted, as unnecessary and superfluous. Still a number of these passages have been retained—but always when they bore directly upon the narrative.

The work is now given to the world in obedience to his last request.

CHAPTER I.

AN INTERIOR WITH PORTRAITS.

On a splendid October afternoon, in the year of our Lord 1763, two persons who will appear frequently in this history were seated in the great dining-room of Effingham Hall.

But let us first say a few words of this old mansion. Effingham Hall was a stately edifice not far from Williamsburg, whi h, as every body knows, was at that period the capital city of the colony of Virginia. The hall was constructed of elegant brick brought over from England: and from the great portico in front of the building a beautiful rolling country of hills and valleys, field and forest, spread itself pleasantly before the eye, bounded far off along the circling belt of woods by the bright waters of the noble river.

Entering the large hall of the old house, you had before you, walls covered with deers' antlers, fishing-rods, and guns: portraits of cavaliers, and dames and children: even carefully painted pictures of celebrated race-horses, on whose speed and bottom many thousands of pounds had been staked and lost and won in their day and generation.

On one side of the hall a broad staircase with oaken balustrade led to the numerous apartments above: and on the opposite side, a door gave entrance into the great dining-room.

The dining-room was decorated with great elegance:—the carved oak wainscot extending above the mantelpiece in an unbroken expanse of fruits and flowers, hideous laughing faces, and long foamy surges to the cornice. The furniture was in the Louis Quatorze style, which the reader is familiar with, from its reproduction in our own day; and the chairs were the same low-seated affairs, with high carved backs, which are now seen. There were Chelsea figures, and a sideboard full of plate, and a Japan cabinet, and a Kidderminster carpet, and huge andirons. On the andirons crackled a few twigs lost in the great country fireplace.

On the wall hung a dozen pictures of gay gallants, brave warriors, and dames, whose eyes outshone their diamonds:—and more than one ancestor looked grimly down, clad in cuirass and armlets, and holding in his mailed hand the sword which had done bloody service in its time. The lady portraits, as an invariable rule, were decorated with sunset clouds of yellow lace—the bright locks were powdered, and many little black patches set off the dazzling fairness of the rounded chins. Lapdogs nestled on the satin laps: and not one of the gay dames but seemed to be smiling, with her head bent sidewise fascinatingly on the courtly or warlike figures ranged with them in a long glittering line.

These portraits are worth looking up to, but those which we promised the reader are real.

In one of the carved chairs, if any thing more uncomfortable than all the rest, sits, or rather lounges, a young man of about twenty-five. He is very richly clad, and in a costume which would be apt to attract a large share of attention in our own day, when dress seems to have become a mere covering, and the prosaic tendencies of the age are to despise every thing but what ministers to actual material pleasure.

The gentleman before us lives fortunately one hundred years before our day: and suffers from an opposite tendency in costume. His head is covered with a long flowing peruke, heavy with powder, and the drop curls hang down on his cheeks ambrosially: his cheeks are delicately rouged, and two patches, arranged with matchless art, complete the distinguished tout ensemble of the handsome face. At breast, a cloud of lace reposes on the rich embroidery of his figured satin waistcoat, reaching to his knees:—this lace is *point de Venise* and white, that fashion having come in just one month since. The sleeves of his rich doublet are turned back to his elbows, and are as large as a bushel—the opening being filled up, however, with long ruffles, which reach down over the delicate jewelled hand. He wears silk stockings of spotless white, and his feet are cased in slippers of Spanish leather, adorned with diamond buckles. Add velvet garters below the knee:—a little muff of leopard-skin reposing near at hand upon a chair—not omitting a snuff-box peeping from the pocket, and Mr. Champ Effingham, just from Oxford and his grand tour, is before you with his various surroundings.

He is reading the work which some time since attained to such extreme popularity, Mr. Joseph Addison's serial, "The Spectator,"—collected now for its great merits, into bound volumes. Mr. Effingham reads with a languid air, just as he sits, and turns over the leaves with an ivory paper cutter, which he brought from Venice with the plate glass yonder on the sideboard near the silver baskets and pitchers. This languor is too perfect to be wholly affected, and when he yawns, as he does frequently, Mr. Effingham applies himself to that task very earnestly.

In one of these paroxysms of weariness the volume slips from his hand to the floor.

"My book," he says to a negro boy, who has just brought in some dishes. The boy hastens respectfully to obey—crossing the whole width of the room for that purpose. Mr. Effingham then continues reading.

Now for the other occupant of the apartment. She sits near the open window, looking out upon the lawn and breathing the pure delicious air of October as she works. She is clad in the usual child's costume of the period (she is only eleven or twelve), namely, a sort of half coat, half frock, reaching scarcely below the knees; an embroidered undervest; scarlet silk stockings with golden clocks, and little rosetted shoes with high red heels. Her hair is unpowdered, and hangs in curls upon her neck and bare shoulders. Her little fingers are busily at work upon a piece of embroidery which represents or is to represent a white water dog upon an intensely emerald back-ground, and she addresses herself to this occupation with a business air which is irresistibly amusing, and no less pleasant to behold. There is about the child, in her movements, attitude, expression, every thing, a freshness and innocence which is only possessed by children. This is Miss Kate Effingham, whose parents died in her infancy, for which reason the little sunbeam was taken by the squire, her father's brother.

Kate seems delighted with the progress she has made in delineating Carlo, as she calls him, and pauses a moment to survey her brilliant handiwork. She then opens her ivory decorated work-box to select another shade of silk, holding it on her lap by the low-silled open window.

But disastrous event! Just as she had found what she wanted, just as she had procured the exact shade for Carlo's ears, just as she closed the pretty box, full of all manner of little elegant instruments of needle-work—she heard an impatient exclamation of weariness and disdain, something fluttered through the air, and this something striking the handsome box delicately balanced on Kate's knees, precipitated it, with its whole contents, through the window to the lawn beneath.

The explanation of this sudden event is, that Mr. Effingham has become tired of the "Spectator," hurled it sidewise from him without looking; and thus the volume has, after its habit, produced a decided sensation, throwing the work-box upon the lawn, and Kate into utter despair.

CHAPTER II.

A SERIES OF CATASTROPHES, ENDING IN A FAMILY TABLEAU.

Kate, spite of her great age and near approach to womanhood, is almost ready to cry:

"Oh cousin Champ!" she says, "how could you!"

Mr. Effingham yawns.

"Did you speak to me, Katy?" he says languidly.

"Yes!"

"Why, what's the matter?"

"You've ruined my work-box!"

"I!"

"Yes, you knocked it out of the window with your book—and I think it was not kind," Kate says, pouting, and leaning out of the window to gaze at the prostrate work-box.

Mr. Effingham sees the catastrophe at a glance, and apparently smitten with remorse, tries to ascertain the extent of the injury. But the morning seems an unlucky one for him. As he places his heel upon the carpet, he unfortunately treads with his whole weight upon the long silky ear of his sister's favorite lapdog Orange, who is about the size of the fruit from which he takes his name.

Orange utters a yell sufficiently loud to arouse from their sleep the seven champions of Christendom.

Drawn by his successive yells, a lady appears at the door and enters the apartment hurriedly.

Miss Alethea, only sister of Mr. Effingham, is a lady of about thirty, with a clear complexion, serene eyes, her hair trained back into a tower; and with an extremely stately and dignified expression. She looks like the president of a benevolent society, and the very sight of her erect head, the very rustle of her black silk dress has been known to strike terror into evil-doers.

"Who has hurt Orange?" she says, severely; "here, poor fellow!—some one has hurt him!"

Orange yells much louder, seeing his defender.

"What in the world is the matter with him, Champ?" she says; "please answer me!"

Mr. Effingham regales his nostrils with a pinch of snuff, and replies indifferently:

"Probably Orange has an indigestion, or perhaps he is uttering those horrible sounds because I stepped upon his ear."

"Stepped on his ear!"

Mr. Effingham nods serenely.

"Really, you are too careless!" Miss Alethea exclaims, and her black silk rustling, she goes to Orange and takes him in her arms.

But in brushing by Mr. Effingham her ample sleeve chances to strike that gentleman's snuff-box, and the contents of the useful article are discharged over little Kate, who coughing, sneezing, crying and laughing, perfects the scene.

"See what you have done, Alethea!" says Mr. Effingham, reproachfully, and yawning as he speaks; "you have thrown my snuff upon Kate."

And turning to the child:

"Never mind, Kate!" he says, "it's excellent snuff. It won't hurt you—now don't—"

With such observations Mr. Effingham is quieting the child, when another addition is made to the company.

This is in the person of a young gentleman of thirteen or fourteen—Master Willie Effingham, Mr. Champ's brother, and a devoted admirer of Kate.

Will, seeing his sweetheart in tears, bustles up, upon his little rosetted shoes, flirting his little round-skirted coat, and fiercely demands of the company at large:

"Who made Kate cry!"

"Oh, the snuff! the snuff!" says Kate, crying and laughing.

"Whose snuff!" says Will, indignantly.

"Mine," replies Mr. Effingham; "there are no excuses to be made; arrange the terms of the combat."

"For shame, Champ!" says Miss Alethea, with stately dignity; "you jest at Willie, but I think his behavior very honorable."

"Ah!" you are an advocate of duelling, then, my dear madam?" drawls Mr. Effingham.

"No, I am not; but your snuff made Kate cry."

"Deign to recall the slight circumstance that your sleeve discharged it from my hand."

"Never mind, I think Will right."

Will raises his head proudly.

"Kate is his favorite and playmate—"

"As Orange is yours," says Mr. Effingham, languidly, the lapdog having uttered an expiring howl. "Well, well, don't let us argue; I am ready to make the amende to my little Kate—we are all dear to each other—so here is my lace handkerchief, *ma mignonette*, to wipe away the snuff—"

Kate laughs.

"And here's a kiss, to make friends for the snuff and the work-box."

Kate wrung her hands, and says, laughing and pouting; "Oh my box! my box!"

"Your box!" says Will, who has been looking daggers at Mr. Effingham for kissing the child.

"Yes! my poor box!"

"Never mind, Katy," says Mr. Effingham, smiling as he passes his hand caressingly over the little head; "I unfortunately broke it, but you shall have one twice as handsome; I saw one in Williamsburg yesterday, which I thought of getting for Clare Lee—but you shall have it."

"Oh, thankee!" cries Kate, "but I oughtn't to take cousin Clare's, you know! And there's papa! he's got my box!"

Kate springs forward to meet the squire—the head of the house—who enters at the door.

The squire is a gentleman of fifty-five or sixty, with an open frank face, clear, honest eyes, and his carriage is bold, free, and somewhat pompous. He is clad much more simply than his eldest son, his coat having upon it not a particle of embroidery, and his long plain waistcoat buttoning up to the chin: below which a white cravat and an indication only of frill are visible. His limbs are cased in thick, strong and comfortable cloth, and woollen, and he wears boots, very large and serviceable, to which strong spurs are attached. His broad, fine brow, full of intelligence and grace, is covered by an old cocked hat, which, having lost the loops which held it in the three-cornered shape, is now rolled up upon each side; and his manner in walking, speaking, arguing, reading, is much after the description of his costume—plain, straightforward, and though somewhat pompous, destitute of finery and ornament. He is the head of a princely establishment, he has thousands of acres, and hundreds of negroes, he is a justice, and has sat often in the House of Burgesses: he is rich, a dignitary, every body knows it,—why should he strive to ape elegancies, and trouble himself about the impression he produces? He is simple and plain, as he conceives, because he is a great proprietor and can afford to wear rough clothes, and talk plainly.

His pomposity is not obtrusive, and it is tempered with

so much good breeding and benevolence that it does not detract from the pleasant impression produced by his honest face. As he enters now that face is brown and red with exercise upon his plantation—and he comes in with cheerful smiles; his rotund person, and long queue gathered by a ribbon smiling no less than his eyes.

In his hand is the unfortunate work-box, which has not, however, sustained any injury.

"Here 'tis, puss!" says the squire, "nothing hurt—I picked up the scissors and the vest: and the grass was as soft as a cushion."

With which words the worthy squire sits down and wipes his brow.

"Oh, thank'ee, papa," says Kate—this is the child's name for him:—and she runs and takes his hat, and then climbs on his lap, and laughingly explains how cousin Champ hadn't meant to throw the box out—"because you know me and cousin Champ are great favorites of each other's: and I am his pet."

Having achieved this speech, which she utters with a rush of laughter in her voice, Kate hugs her box, and returns to Carlo.

"Well, Champ," says the planter, "whither go you this afternoon—any where?"

"I believe not," says Mr. Effingham.

"Still enamored of your ease, you jolly dog!"

"The Epicurean philosophy is greatly to my taste," says Mr. Effingham, "riding wearies me."

"Every thing does."

"Ah?"

"Yes, sir: you are the finest fine gentleman in the Colony."

This half compliment produces no effect upon Mr. Effingham, who yawns.

"Why not go and see Clare Lee?—Clary's the most bewitching little creature in the world," says the squire, unfolding a copy of the "Virginia Gazette," which he draws from his pocket.

"Clare Lee?" says Mr. Effingham.

"Yes, sir: she's a little beauty."

"Well, so she is."

"And as good as an angel."

"Hazardous, that, sir."

"No, sir!" exclaims the squire, "it is true! Zounds! she's too good for any mortal man."

"Consequently, as I am a mortal man—I draw the inference," says Mr. Effingham.

"Well, she's too good for you, sir: you had better go and see her: it may improve you."

Mr. Effingham relents.

"I think that is very desirable, sir," he says, "and on my word, I'll go. Please ring that bell."

The squire without protest takes up the small silver bell and rings it. Mr. Effingham orders his horse—descends soon in boots and riding gloves, and mounting, sets forth towards the abode of the angel—Miss Clare Lee.

CHAPTER III.

SOMETHING LIKE AN ADVENTURE.

Leaving the group which we have seen assemble in the drawing-room of Effingham Hall, let us follow the worthy whose misdeeds in connection with the work-box and lapdog caused the dramatic assemblage.

Mr. Effingham, elegantly clad in a riding costume, perfect in its appointment, and mounted on a splendid courser which he had appropriated from his father's stud, took his way through the fresh woods towards Riverhead, the residence of Mr. Lee and his two daughters, Henrietta and Clare. But Mr. Effingham was much too sensible a gentleman to bore himself, as we say to-day, with the fine scenery of October—the fair blue skies, with their snowy clouds floating on like ships towards the clear horizon—the variegated woods full of singing birds—the streams dancing in the sun—and all the myriad attractions of an autumn afternoon. His taste had been shaped in London, and the glare of lights, the noise of revelry, and gay encounter of bright wits and beauty, had long since deprived him of the faculty of admiring such an insipid thing as simple nature. There was little affectation about the worthy gentleman in reality: he was really and truly worn out. Accustomed for some length of time to every species of dissipation, his character had been seriously injured—his freshness was gone, and he sought now for nothing so much as *emotions*. We shall see if he was fortunate in his search.

At times, as he went along, Mr. Effingham indulged in a sort of silent, well-bred laughter, at the scene he had just witnessed at the Hall.

"What a farce the world is," he said, philosophically, "we all run after something—one has his literary ambition, another political aspiration: this young lady wishes to marry a lord: that young gentleman's highest hope in life is, that his comedy may not be damned for its want of freedom—the polite word now I understand. It's all weariness: I really begin to think that little Katy and Alethea, with their embroidery and lapdogs, are the most sensible after all. Embroidery and lapdogs cost less, and——"

Mr. Effingham drew up suddenly—so suddenly, that his horse rose on his haunches, and tossed his head aloft.

The meaning of this movement was simply that he saw before him in the centre of the road he was following, a lady, who apparently awaited his approach.

The lady was mounted upon a tall white horse, which stood perfectly quiet in the middle of the road, and seemed to be docility itself, though the fiery eyes contradicted this first impression. Rather would one acquainted with the singular character of horses have said that this animal was subdued by the gentle hand of his rider, and so laid aside from pure affection, all his waywardness.

This rider was a young girl about eighteen, and of rare and extraordinary beauty. Her hair—so much as was visible beneath her hood—seemed to be dark chestnut, and her complexion was dazzling. The eyes were large, full, and dark—instinct with fire and softness, feminine modesty, and collected firmness—the firmness, however, predominating. But the lips were different. They were the lips of a child—soft, guileless, tender, confiding; they were purity and innocence itself, and seemed to say, that however much the brain might become hard and worldly, the heart of this young woman never could be other than the tender and delicately sensitive heart of a child.

She was clad in a riding-dress of pearl color—and from the uniformity of this tint, it seemed to be a favorite with her. The hood was of silk, and the delicately-gloved hand held a little ivory-handled riding whip, which now dangled at her side. The other gloved hand supported her cheek; and in this position the unknown lady calmly awaited Mr. Effingham's approach still nearer, though he was already nearly touching her.

Mr. Effingham took off his hat and bowed with elegant courtesy. The lady returned this inclination by a graceful movement of her head.

"Would you be kind enough to point out the road to the town of Williamsburg, sir?" she said, in a calm and clear voice.

"With great pleasure, madam," replied Mr. Effingham, "you have lost your way!"

"Yes, sir, very strangely, and as evening drew on, was afraid of being benighted."

"You have but to follow this road until you reach Effingham Hall, madam," he said—"the house in the distance yonder: then turn to the left, and you are in the highway to town."

"Thanks, sir," the young girl said, with another calm inclination of her head: and she touched her horse with the whip.

"But cannot I accompany you?" asked Mr. Effingham, whose curiosity was greatly aroused, and found his eyes, he knew not why, riveted to the rare beauty of his companion's face, "do you not need me as a guide?"

"Indeed, I think not, sir," she said, with the same calmness, your direction is very plain, and I am accustomed to ride by myself."

"But really," began Mr. Effingham, somewhat piqued, "I know it is intrusive—I know I have not the honor——"

She interrupted him with her immovable calmness.

"You would say you do not know me, and that your offer is intrusive, I believe, sir. I do not consider it so—it is very kind: but I am not a fearful girl, and need not trouble you at all."

And she bowed.

"One moment, madam," said Mr. Effingham; "I am really dying with curiosity to know you. 'Tis very rude to say so, of course—but I am acquainted with every lady in the neighborhood, and I do not recall any former occasion upon which I had the pleasure—"

"It is very easily explained, sir," the young girl said.

"Madam—?"

"I do not live in the neighborhood—"

"Ah?—no?"

"And I am not a lady, sir: does not that explain it?"

Mr. Effingham scarcely believed his ears: these astounding words were uttered with such perfect calmness that there was no possible room to suppose that they were meant for a jest. What then? He could not speak: he only looked at her.

"You are surprised, sir," the young girl said, quite simply and gravely.

"Upon my word, madam—never have I—really—"

"Your surprise will not last long, sir."

"How, madam?"

"Do you ever visit the town of Williamsburg?"

"Frequently."

"Well, sir, I think you will see me again. Now I must continue my way, having returned you my very sincere thanks for your kindness."

With which words—words uttered in that wondrous voice of immovable calmness—the young girl again inclined her sumptuous head, touched her white horse with the whip, and slowly rode out of sight.

Mr. Effingham remained for several moments motionless, in the middle of the road, gazing with wide and astonished eyes after the beautiful equestrian. He was endeavoring by a tremendous mental exertion to solve the astounding problem of her identity. Vain was all his pondering—nothing came of all his thought, his knit brows, his lip gnawed ferociously, as he mused. Mr. Effingham was confident that he knew, at least by sight, every young lady at Williamsburg, and within a circuit of twenty miles, but this face was wholly unknown to him. He had certainly never seen her before, and then the strange fact of her riding out alone: her self-possession: "she was accustomed to ride alone"—"she was not a lady"—"they should probably meet again"—what in the name of Fate, was the meaning of all this?

"May the fiend seize me, if the days of wandering knights and forlorn damsels, haunted castles and giants have not returned!" exclaimed Mr. Effingham, emphatically. And having thus disburdened his mind, he rode on—but still his mind dwelt on the strange lady, and her more singular words.

Not a lady!" what could she mean? was there ever since the days of the Sphinx so complete a puzzle! In face, person, dress, and carriage she was every inch a lady—why then utter that astounding observation, enunciate that startling intelligence? who could she be, however? Mr. Effingham ran over in his mind, the whole of his friends and acquaintances, and could recollect no one whose face bore the slightest resemblance to that of the unknown lady. He gave up in despair, finally, and struck his spurs into the noble animal he rode, with unusual vigor. The horse started forward, and in half an hour he had reached Riverhead.

CHAPTER IV.

THE ROSE AND THE VIOLET.

Two young ladies were walking upon the smooth-shaven lawn, which stretched unbroken save by a few noble oaks and clumps of shrubbery, from the fine old mansion to the woodland on each side and the enclosure in front.

One of the ladies was tall and brilliant: her superb figure undulating with every movement would have graced a palace, and her bright eyes and merry lips were full of life and fire. She was clad with extreme richness, and the fine silks and velvets which she wore shone brilliantly in the clear October sunlight as she moved. This sheen of silk seemed her appropriate accompaniment, and the diamond necklace which she wore was not observed. Her eyes and brilliant expression threw the silk and velvet and all jewels in the background. She looked the incarnation of aristocracy, using that term in its colloquial sense, and seemed to brim with mirth and merry witticisms from a pure sentiment of life and superiority to every one.

Her companion was smaller in stature, and plainly younger—apparently about nineteen. Her figure was more delicate, her beauty more pensive and aerial. The squire's criticism, or abandonment of all criticism, did not seem at all extravagant. A profusion of golden hair, blue eyes full of deep tenderness and instinct with a species of quiet happy pensiveness—these, added to a complexion as fair as a lily and as transparent as a fresh stream, made up a countenance of exquisite beauty.

The first lady was Miss Henrietta Lee:—the second was her sister, Miss Clare Lee, between whom and Mr. Effingham a sort of undeveloped courtship existed.

Mr. Effingham approached the ladies, trailing the feather of his hat upon the grass.

"Ah! Mr. Effingham!" cried Henrietta, with a merry laugh, "and as weary-looking as ever!"

"Still jesting, Miss Henrietta—or cousin Henrietta, as you agree I may in future call you; have I presumed, and may I address you by that pleasant name?"

"Certainly you may," said the laughing girl, "though I believe the cousinship is rather distant."

"To my regret."

"Your regret?—truly?"

"In sober truth," replied Mr. Effingham, languidly twirling his cocked hat: "near cousins, you know, have many agreeable privileges. Have they not, Miss Clare?"

Clare turned her soft, frank eyes on the young man and smiled.

"That is enough," continued Mr. Effingham, "when a lady smiles she always means yes."

"A hasty conclusion!" said Henrietta, "many a gay cavalier on his knees before a lady has been laughed at."

"True, true: though I am most happy to say that I

have never had the bad fortune to verify the truth of your observation."

And smoothing gently the ruffles at his breast, Mr. Effingham yawned. Henrietta burst into laughter, and her brilliant eyes flashed mischievously.

Mr. Effingham looked round in apparent astonishment.

"If I may be permitted to inquire, Miss Henrietta, or cousin Henrietta, as I shall beg leave henceforth to call you——"

"Oh, certainly!"

"What were you laughing at, pray?"

"Shall I tell you?'

"If you please."

"At you, then!"

"At me?"

"At you."

"I am glad to find my company so agreeably entertaining: true, I am in unusually excellent spirits."

"Spirits! you? Why you yawned most portentously this moment!"

"All habit—a bad habit, I confess: and to prove that I am not weary, I have an adventure to relate."

"An adventure?"

"Yes."

And Mr. Effingham, in an elegant, *petit maitre* manner, narrated his adventure, as he was pleased to call it, with the unknown horsewoman.

"Who could it have been?" said Clare.

"Who, indeed!" echoed Henrietta.

"Upon my soul, I don't know. Some wandering queen, or fairy, I suppose—this Virginia is the land of romance and magic. I think it very fortunate that she did not bid me dismount, seat myself behind her, and go off thus to fairyland with her. In which case," continued Mr. Effingham, gallantly, "I should not have experienced the happiness of gazing at your pleasant and beautiful countenances, cousins Henrietta and Clare."

"You are too kind!" laughed Henrietta.

"And not very sincere," said Clare, smiling.

"Not sincere?"

And Mr. Effingham's glance dwelt for a moment almost

tenderly on the face of Clare, who looked like a pure angel, in the bright crimson light of sunset.

"If you thought us so pleasant you would come oftener," she said, with a flitting blush.

"My poor society would only weary you, I fear," he said, ostensibly addressing both of the sisters, but looking at Clare, "I am a poor visitor."

Clare turned away and pulled a rose.

"It is not so far," she murmured, refusing plainly to accept the excuse, and speaking in so low a tone that Henrietta, who had taken some steps to meet her approaching father, did not hear the words.

"And if I came?" whispered Mr. Effingham.

Clare turned away to hide her confusion.

"Could I hope, dear cousin Clare—dearest Clare!—"

Mr. Effingham was getting on. But Henrietta and Mr. Lee approached.

"That you could—could—"

"Good evening, Champ," said Mr. Lee, a fine portly old gentleman, coming up arm in arm with Henrietta, "glad to see you."

Mr. Effingham bowed, and Clare bent down to examine, with profound curiosity, the rosebud which she held in her little hand.

"The evening was so fine, that I thought I could not spend it more agreeably than in a ride to Riverhead, sir," said Mr. Effingham.

"Delightful!—these August days are excellent for the corn; what news?"

"Nothing, sir—I have not seen the 'Gazette.'"

"Oh, the 'Gazette' never contains any intelligence: sometimes, it is true, we hear what is going on in Parliament, but it never condescends to afford us any news from Virginia. The tobacco on the south side may be all gone to the devil for any thing you read in the 'Gazette.' Here it is—an abominable sheet! Ah! I see we are to have a theatrical performance in Williamsburg next week," added the old gentleman, glancing over the paper, "Mr. Hallam and his 'Virginia Company of Comedians'—very politic, that addition of 'Virginia!'—are to perform *The Merchant of Venice*, by permission of his worship the Mayor, at the Old Theatre near the Capitol, he announces. Truly we are improving: really becoming civilized, in this barbarous *terra incognita.*

Mr. Effingham winced; he had more than once expressed a similar opinion of Virginia in good faith—not ironically—and the old gentleman's words seemed directed at himself. A moment's reflection, however, persuaded him that this could not be the case; he had not visited Riverhead a dozen times since his return from Oxford and London—and on those occasions had never touched upon the subject of Virginia and its dreadful deficiencies.

"A play?" he said, "that is really good news:—but the 'Merchant of Venice' is not one of my acquaintances."

"Ah, you young men are wrong in giving up Will Shakespeare for the Steeles, Addisons, and Vanbrughs. Mr. Addison's essays are very pleasant and entertaining reading, and sure, there never was a finer gentleman than Sir Roger;—but in the drama, Will Shakespeare distances him all to nothing."

"Let us go to see the play, papa," said Henrietta.

"Oh, yes," said Clare.

The old gentleman tenderly smoothed the bright golden hair.

"Certainly, if you wish it," he said.

"And may I request permission to accompany the party, ladies?" said Mr. Effingham, languidly.

"How modest!" said Henrietta, laughing; "certainly you may go, sir. You will tell us when to hiss or applaud, you know, as you are just from London!"

"What a quick tongue she has!" said Mr. Lee, fondly; "well, we will all go, and see what the 'Virginia Company of Comedians' is like: not much, I fear."

"Oh, we'll have a delightful time," cried Clare, glancing at Mr. Effingham softly and frankly.

That young gentleman's languor melted like snow in the sunshine, and as he placed the little hand upon his arm to lead its owner in to supper, he pressed it tenderly, and whispered:

"I know I shall, for you will be with me, dearest Clare:—don't be offended, for you know—"

The whisper of the leaves around them, drowned the end of the sentence, but the red sunset lighting up Clare's soft warm cheek might very well have spared its crimson!

CHAPTER V.

POLITICS AND COURTSHIP.

"We cannot rationally doubt it, sir," said the squire, admiring the excellent glass of claret which he held between his eye and the window; "there must be classes, scales of refinement, culture and authority: to state the proposition proves it."

The squire uttered these oracular words at his dinner-table on the day after Mr. Champ Effingham's visit to Riverhead. That gentleman was seated in a lounging attitude, ever and anon moistening his lips with a glass of wine. In one corner of the room Miss Alethea prosecuted some darling household work, her favorite Orange lying comfortably coiled up in her lap: in another, Master Willie and little Kate were having a true-love quarrel as to the proper shade of silk to be used on Carlo's nose in the famous embroidery. But we have omitted in this catalogue of personages a gentleman sitting at the table on the squire's right hand, and whom we now beg leave to briefly introduce to the reader as Mr. Tag, the parson of the parish. The parson was a rosy, puffy-looking individual of some fifty years, and in his person, carriage, and tone of voice betrayed a mingled effrontery and awkwardness: having formerly served as a common soldier, then lived by his wits, as an adventurer, he had finally, perforce of the influence of a noble patron for whom he had performed some secret service, been presented to a benefice in the colony of Virginia. We cannot dwell on the worthy gentleman's character, and can only add here that he was a regular visitor at Effingham Hall about dinner time, and that he had no religious scruples against taking a hand at tictac or other games of chance, any more than he was opposed to the good old English divertisement of fox-hunting.

To the squire's oracular dogma laying down the laws of social organization, the parson replied between two gulps of claret:

"Certainly — oh, certainly."

"The men of education and lineage not only *must* always rule," continues his host, "but ought to; to trust the reins of power in the hands of common men, who have comparatively no stake in the community, no property, no family, is absurd—a doctrine too monstrous to require refutation."

The parson shook his head.

"I very much fear, squire, that these good old sentiments are becoming obsolete. We men of position and rank in society, born in high social station, will have to yield, I fear.—They are seriously talking, I understand, of giving every man in the colony a vote."

"Every man a vote! who speaks of it? who broaches such an absurdity?"

"A parcel of hair-brained young men, who will yet get themselves into trouble. As a minister of the Established Church, I hold it my duty to warn them, and after that have no further concern with them. I have pointed them out to the authorities, and I now call your worship's attention to the subject."

"Who are they?"

"First and foremost, a young man called Waters—son of the fisherman on the river there near Williamsburg. He had the audacity to intrude upon a conversation I was holding with some gentlemen of my parish in town a day or two since, and he uttered opinions over and above what I have called to your attention, which will bring him to the gallows if he does not beware."

"Other opinions?"

"He spoke of the *oppressions* of the Home Government, said that Virginians would not always be slaves, and actually broached a plan for thoroughly educating the lower classes."

"A statesman in short clothes," said the squire, with a sneer—"the wine stays with you, sir—a colonial *patriot!* faugh! Educate the lower classes! *Educate* my indented servant, and the common tradesman and farmer, and have the knave talking to me of the 'rights of men,' and all the wretched stuff and foolery of Utopian castle-builders! you are right, sir, that young man must be watched. Good heavens! how has the Home Government oppressed us? I grant you, there are some laws I would have altered—and others refused us, passed—but is this oppression? Damn my blood!" added the squire, with great indignation, "I now feel the truth of Will Shakespeare's words, that 'the age is grown so picked, the toe of the peasant comes near the heel of the courtier and galls his 'kibe,' or to that effect. The direct consequence of these fooleries is to abolish our rank—follow these doctrines, and where will be our gentlemen?"

"Where, indeed?"

"Even the very parsons will go to the devil," here interposed Mr. Champ Effingham, with an evident desire to yawn.

The squire greeted this sally of his son with a laugh.

"You are irreverent, young sir," the parson said, making an effort to look dignified.

"I irreverent!" replied Mr. Effingham, coolly; "by no means, most reverend sir. I think my respect for you is sufficiently shown by attending church punctually every Sunday, and respectably going to sleep under the effect of your admirable homilies."

"You jest at my homilies——"

"Oh, no."

"But you should understand, young man, that a minister of the Church of England is not a public haranguer——"

"Precisely."

"And dishonors his high place and position by appealing to the passions and feelings of his hearers instead of giving them good wholesome doctrine."

And Parson Tag drew himself up, with a hauteur which badly assorted with his puffy face and figure.

"You are right," replied Mr. Effingham, with languid indifference; "nothing is so disagreeable as these appeals to the feelings which you speak of, most reverend sir. How could you bend your excellent mind to ombre and tictac after such performances; or, exhausted by such unnecessary exertion as a 'rousing appeal' demands, join in the delightful pursuit of a grey fox on the following Monday?"

The squire laughed again, at the crestfallen parson, and said:

"Come, no tongue-fencing at the dinner-table; we have wandered from the subject which we commenced with."

"What was the subject?" asked Mr. Effingham, languidly.

"What! was all the parson's eloquence thrown away on you?"

"Perfectly; I was not listening, with the exception of a moment, when you closed your address."

"We were speaking of classes, and the necessity which every gentleman is under to preserve his rank."

"I suppose it's true; but I never busy myself with these matters."

"You should, sir; the estate of Effingham falls to you as eldest son."

"I trust, respected sir, that I shall worthily comport myself in that station in life to which it hath pleased Heaven to call me," drawled Mr. Effingham.

"Never jest with the forms of the Established Church, sir," said his father, with some asperity; for however willing the squire was to applaud a jest at the parson's expense, one directed at the church itself was a very different matter. "I hold every thing connected with the Liturgy of the Holy Church as sacred."

Mr. Effingham assented, with a careless inclination of his head.

"This spirit of free speaking and thinking is worse than the other," continued the planter; "those abominable New Lights!"

"Wretched, misguided fools," chimed in the parson, whose equanimity several glasses of wine had restored by this time perfectly.

"I cordially hate and despise them," said the planter, "and consider it my duty to do so. I hope the representative of my family will share my sentiments."

This observation being directed at Mr. Effingham, that gentleman replied indifferently:

"Of course—of course."

"Champ," said the old planter, "you are really becoming worse than ever. Where will your indifference to every thing end, I should like much to know? You seem to have no aim in life, no thought of advancement, no opinions, even."

"True, sir; that is a pretty fair statement of the truth. This subject of rank and classes, gentlemen and commoners, advancement, ambition, and all that, never troubles me."

"Sunt quos curriculo pulverem Olympicum,
Collegisse juvat metaque fervidis
Evitata rotis,"

or something of that sort. It's Horace, I believe, and the scanning strikes me as correct. I mean, respected sir, that I am not ambitious, and have no very fervid desire to get dusty in the arena, or race-course, I should more properly say—dust soils the ruffles so abominably."

The squire always ended by laughing at his son's *petit maitre* airs, though he had sagacity enough to perceive that there was little real affectation in the young gentleman's weariness and indifference. He argued, however, that this would disappear in time, and knowing that any argument would be useless on the present occasion, turned the conversation by taking wine with the parson.

Let us see what the youthful members of the company were saying now. Human nature, under all guises, and in every possible degree of development, is worthy of attention. Master Will, who had been making assiduous love to Kate, engaged now on Carlo's nose, caught Mr. Effingham's Latin, and betook himself to a *sotto voce* criticism on the speaker.

"Just listen to brother Champ, how learned he is! He's just from Oxford, and thinks that Latin mighty fine——to be kissing you the other day!" added this young scion of the house of Effingham, thus betraying the disinterested and impartial character of his criticism.

"Why, I didn't care—I like to kiss cousin Champ," says Kate, with a coquettish little twinkle of the eye, "he's always so nice, you know."

"Nice! he nice?"

"Why, yes."

"He aint!"

"That's your gallantry: to contradict a lady," says Kate, with the air of a duchess.

"I'm nicer than he is," says Will, eluding like a skilful debater the charge of want of gallantry. "I don't stuff my nose full of snuff and sneeze all the powder off my hair."

"Ha! ha!" laughs Kate.

"What are you laughing at?'

"You hav'n't any powder!"

" Never mind : I mean to."

" When ? "

" Never mind ! "

" Why you'd look ridiculous, Willie."

" Ridiculous ! me ridiculous ! Hav'n't I high-heeled shoes—"

" So have I—I'm a girl."

" And silk stockings."

" So have I, sir."

" And ruffles, and sword, and all.'

" Oh, what a fine cavalier."

Master Will looks mortified.

" Now, Willie," says Kate, " don't pout, for you know I was only jesting."

" Give me a kiss, then."

" A young lady kiss a gentleman ? Indeed ! "

The flattering word " gentleman " completely restores Master Will's good humor : and essaying to conquer a " salute," as they said in those honest courteous old times, Kate's needle pricks his finger, which circumstance causes the youthful cavalier to utter a shrill cry of pain.

" What's the matter, Will ? " asks the squire, breaking off in the middle of a sentence addressed to the parson.

" Nothing much," says Mr. Champ Effingham, who has watched the assault of his younger brother with philosophic interest, " merely an illustration of the truth of my views."

" Your views—what views ?"

" Will was ambitious to 'collect the Olympic dust'—in other words to kiss Katy, and the needle ran into his finger. So much for ambition. Moral : never meddle with the ladies."

Master Will listens to this languidly-uttered speech with many indications of dissatisfaction—uttering more than one expressive " humph ! " that little monosyllable which conveys so much. At Mr. Effingham's " moral," however, he boiled over.

" Never meddle with ladies, indeed ! " he said, " that's pretty, coming from you, brother Champ. when old June from Riverhead says he saw you yesterday courting cousin Clare ! "—old June having, indeed, retailed to Cato that evening, in Master Will's hearing, the fact that he " spec they'd be a marridgin *somewheres* 'fore long 'sidering how Mas' Champ Efnum and Mis' Clary was agwyin' on ! "

The squire burst into a hearty laugh, and rallied Mr. Effingham without mercy. That gentleman, though for a moment disconcerted, quickly regained his nonchalance, and raising his glass languidly, said with a delightful drawl, an exaggeration of his usual languor :

" Of course it's all true, sir ; but why laugh at me for following your respectable advice ? "

" Clare's much too good for you, Champ," said Miss Alethea, taking a pin from her mouth and affixing therewith some indescribable garment to her knee, the better to set to work on it.

" Ah ! " said Mr. Effingham, indifferently, " well, I think so too."

" A thousand times," said Master Will.

" Come, Will, recollect Champ is your elder brother," said the old planter, laughing merrily.

" Brother Champ laughed at me," said Master Will.

" True, I did, and am justly punished—but correct the word, Will : say I philosophized upon the result of your assault to steal the kiss. I never laugh."

" There's no harm in my kissing Kate," says Master Will, with great dignity.

" None—none ! "

" Because we are engaged," adds Will, with the air of an emperor.

Kate suddenly fires up at these words, and exclaims indignantly :

" My goodness ! aint you ashamed, Willie ? "

" Not engaged ! " cries Will.

" No—never," says Kate, with a charming little pout, " and if we were, do you think I would acknowledge it, and have the servants talking about me like cousin Clare ? "

At which speech the whole company burst into laughter ; and a smile is even observed to wander over Mr. Effingham's face.

" I see," says that gentleman, " that Miss Clare is given to me by universal consent :—I forgive you, Katy—"

" Oh, cousin Champ, I didn't mean—" commences Kate, remorsefully.

"No matter," concludes Mr. Effingham, yawning, "I have only to observe that I am willing to take Miss Clare or any other agreeable young lady for my wedded wife:—and now, as I feel drowsy, I beg leave of you, parson, and you, respected sir, to excuse me; I am going to take a nap."

With which words Mr. Effingham saunters through the door, and slowly ascends the broad stairs to his chamber. Miss Alethea continues to sew: the children to play: the parson and his host to converse over their wine.

CHAPTER VI.

HOW THEY WENT TO THE PLAY.

The reader will recollect that Mr. Lee had promised his daughters to go with them to Williamsburg, to witness the performance of the "Merchant of Venice" by those newly-arrived Virginia Comedians, of whom every one was talking. Mr. Champ Effingham had asked permission to be one of the party, it will be remembered, and that permission had been granted by Miss Henrietta with the merry speech we have recorded.

So on the appointed day, Mr. Effingham, in his most becoming riding suit, and mounted on his handsomest courser, made his appearance at Riverhead.

The young ladies came down to him, already dressed for their excursion to town—as Williamsburg was called, just as they called London "the Town" in England—and Miss Henrietta commenced immediately her accustomed amusement of bantering their visitor. She was radiant in a dress of surpassing elegance—flowered satin, yellow lace, jewels, powdered hair, pearl pendants, and rich furbelows—and the bright beauty of her laughing face well assorted with her flashing and glittering costume. As for Clare, her dress was much more subdued, just as her manner was more quiet, than that of her sister. But Mr. Effingham, gazing at her quietly, with little care for Miss Henrietta's sky-rockets, thought he had never seen a more enchantingly beautiful face; so soft and tender was it, with the bright hair gathered back from the temples, and strewed all over with its pearly powder; so warm and red were the girlish lips; so clear and mild the large melting eyes. Mr. Effingham began to think seriously of having in future a distinct aim in life—to make his own this fairy creature, who had thus moved his worn-out heart, making him feel once more some of the light and joy and enthusiasm of his boyhood—that time passed from him, it really seemed, long ages ago.

Clare did not return his gaze, but busied herself in turning over the leaves of a new book from England, with an affectation of interest which was the merest failure.

Really all my wit is thrown away upon Mr. Effingham," said Henrietta suddenly, with a beautiful pout; "he has not done me the honor to listen, I believe—my last question waiting a reply from him."

Mr. Effingham waked up, so to speak, and turned round.

"What did you say, my dear cousin?" he asked indifferently.

"I say that my cousin, Mr. Effingham, is the most affected personage I have ever known."

"I affected! You have made that charge once before. But what was your question?"

"I asked where you procured that ridiculous little muff there on the settee, which you threw down so carelessly on entering."

"In London," said Mr. Effingham, concisely.

"And are the London gallants such apers of the ladies as to wear them?"

"I don't know; they are used."

"And you imitate them?"

"I imitate nobody, my dear cousin Henrietta; it is too troublesome. I do not wear a coat, or powder my hair, or use ruffles from a desire to imitate any one."

"I don't think you do; for I never saw such preposterous ruffles in my life."

"Eh?" said Mr. Effingham, with languid indiffernece.

"Or such red cheeks."

"What of them?"

"They are as rosy as a girl's."

"Your own are more so, and I think cousin Clare's more so still," returned Mr. Effingham; "but let us dismiss the subject of ruffles and roses, and come to the play. Do you anticipate much pleasure?"

"Oh, it will be delightful!" exclaimed Miss Henrietta, always ready to run off upon any subject which afforded her an opportunity to pour out her spirits and gayety.

"And you, cousin Clare—do you think these Virginia Comedians, as they call themselves, will afford you a very pleasant entertainment?"

"Oh, yes—I'm sure I shall be pleased,—you know I have never seen a play."

"But read a plenty?"

"Oh yes: and I like the 'Merchant of Venice' very much. The character of *Portia* is so delicate and noble."

"Quite true—an excellent criticism: better than anything in Congreve, I think, though I should hesitate to advance such an opinion in London."

"Who will act Portia?"

"I don't know: but can tell you without much difficulty. Here is a play-bill which I sent to town for yesterday."

And Mr. Effingham drew daintily from his coat pocket a small roughly-printed handbill, which he spread out before the eyes of Clare.

"'Virginia Company of Comedians,'" he read, "'by permission of his worship the Mayor—in the Old Theatre near the Capitol, Thursday evening—a tragedy called "The Merchant of Venice," by Mr. William Shakespeare—boxes seven shillings sixpence—vivat Rex et Regina—' here it is: —'*Shylock*, Mr. Pugsby—*Portia*, Miss Beatrice Hallam:' The part of Portia is to be performed by Miss Beatrice Hallam—I have never seen or heard of her."

"Which means," said Henrietta, laughing, "that Miss Beatrice cannot be very well worth going to see, as Mr. Champ Effingham, just from London, and conversant with all the celebrities there, has never heard of her existence."

"My dear cousin Henrietta," said Mr. Effingham, languidly, "you really seem to sit in judgment on my wearisome conversation. I do not profess to know any thing about celebrities: true, I very frequently lounged into the theatres in London, but I assure you, took very little interest in the plays or performers. Life itself is enough of a comedy for me, and I want nothing more. I know nothing of Miss Hallam—she may be a new witch of Endor, or as beautiful as Cleopatra, queen of Egypt, for all that I know. That I have not heard of her proves nothing—the best actors and actresses are often treated with neglect and indifference."

"Well," said Clare, smiling, "we shall soon see for ourselves, for there is papa coming, all ready dressed to go, and I hear the wheels of the chariot."

Mr. Effingham took up his muff.

"Oh," cried Henrietta, "how do you carry that funny little thing while riding?—it's smaller than mine."

"I swing it on my arm," replied Mr. Effingham, indifferently.

"Let me relieve you of it—all the girls will then be admiring my new London muff."

"No, thank you. I will not trouble you."

"Oh, here is papa," said Clare. Mr. Lee entered.

"Good morning, Champ," he said, in his strong, hearty voice, "how is your good father? have you dined? Yes? Then let us get on to town. We have no time to lose, as the play commences, I am informed, at seven."

With which words the worthy gentleman led the way to the door, where the large chariot, with its four pawing horses and liveried coachman, awaited them. Mr. Effingham assisted the ladies in with great elegance and gallantry. After performing this social duty, he made a slight bow, and was going toward his horse.

"Come, take a place in the chariot," said Mr. Lee.

"Oh, yes," cried the lively Henrietta, "don't go prancing along out there, where I can't get at you to tease you. There's room enough for a dozen in here."

"No, no, my horse would get impatient."

Mr. Effingham was waiting for Clare to invite him to enter, and no one who looked at his face, and witnessed his tell-tale gaze could doubt it. Clare stole a glance at him, and said, with a slight blush,

"There's plenty of room."

Mr. Effingham took two steps toward the chariot.

"But my horse," he said.

Mr. Lee called to a servant, and ordered him to take the

animal to the stable. Mr. Effingham then yielded—he only wanted the excuse, indeed—and entering the chariot, was about to sit down by the old gentleman, opposite the young girls.

"Ah ! take care !" cried Mr. Lee, with a hearty and sudden laugh, " my glasses are on the seat ! "

Henrietta laughed too, and said, moving near to her side of the carriage, and making room,

" Come ! you may ride between us—mayn't he, Clary ? there's plenty of room for a bodkin."

Mr. Effingham plainly had no objection, and, as before, in the matter of riding within or without, waited for Clare's manifesto on the subject. This time he would have been satisfied with a simple glance granting him permission—so very reasonable was this gentleman at bottom—but unfortunately Clare did not invite him, either with her lips or eyes. The consequence was that Mr. Effingham refused Henrietta's invitation, with a graceful wave of his muff-ornamented arm, and the glasses of the old gentleman having been transferred from the seat to his nose, gently subsided into the softly-cushioned space left free for him, smoothing his ruffles, and arranging delicately the drop-curls of his powdered peruke.

The chariot rolled on, then, with dignified slowness, toward " Town "—that is to say, the imperial metropolis of Virginia, then, and now, known as Williamsburg.

CHAPTER VII.

THE OLD THEATRE NEAR THE CAPITOL.

THE " old Theatre near the Capitol," discoursed of in the manifesto issued by Mr. Manager Hallam, was so far *old*, that the walls were well-browned by time, and the shutters to the windows of a pleasant neutral tint between rust and dust color. The building had no doubt been used for the present purpose in bygone times, before the days of the " Virginia Gazette," which is our authority for many of the facts here stated, and in relation to the "Virginia Company of Comedians"—but of the former companies of "players," as my lord Hamlet calls them, and their successes or misfortunes, printed words tell us nothing, as far as the researches of the present Chronicle extend. That there had been such companies before, however, we repeat, there is some reason to believe; else why that addition "old" applied to the "Theatre near the Capitol." The question is submitted to the future social historians of the Old Dominion.

Within, the play-house presented a somewhat more attractive appearance. There was "box," "pit," and "gallery," as in our own day; and the relative prices were arranged in much the same manner. The common mortals—gentlemen and ladies—were forced to occupy the boxes raised slightly above the level of the stage, and hemmed in by velvet-cushioned railings,—in front, a flower-decorated panel, extending all around the house,—and for this position were moreover compelled to pay an admission fee of seven shillings and sixpence. The demigods—so to speak—occupied a more eligible position in the "pit," from which they could procure a highly excellent view of the actors' feet and ankles, just on a level with their noses: to conciliate the demigods, this superior advantage had been offered, and the price for them was, further still, reduced to five shillings. But "the gods" in truth were the real favorites of the manager. To attract them, he arranged the high upper "gallery"—and left it untouched, unincumbered by railing or velvet cushions, or any other device: all was free space, and liberal as the air: there were no troublesome seats for "the gods," and three shillings and nine pence was all that the managers would demand. The honor of their presence was enough.

From the boxes a stairway led down to the stage, and some rude scenes, visible at the edges of the green curtain, completed the outline.

When Mr. Lee and his daughters entered the box which had been reserved for them, next to the stage, the house was nearly full, and the neatness of the edifice was lost sight of in the sea of brilliant ladies' faces, and strong forms of cavaliers, which extended—like a line of glistening foam—

around the semicircle of the boxes. The pit was occupied by well-dressed men of the lower class, as the times had it, and from the gallery proceeded hoarse murmurs and the unforgotten slang of London.

Many smiles and bows were interchanged between the parties in the different boxes; and the young gallants, following the fashion of the day, gathered at each end of the stage, and often walked across, to exchange some polite speech with the smiling dames in the boxes nearest.

Mr. Champ Effingham was, upon the whole, much the most notable fop present; and his elegant, languid, *petit maître* air, as he strolled across the stage, attracted many remarks, not invariably favorable. It was observed, however, that when the Virginia-bred youths, with honest plainness, called him "ridiculous," the young ladies, their companions, took Mr. Effingham's part, and defended him with great enthusiasm. Only when they returned home, Mr. Effingham was more unmercifully criticised than he would otherwise have been.

A little bell rang, and the orchestra, represented by three or four foreign-looking gentlemen, bearded and moustached, entered with trumpet and violin. The trumpets made the roof shake, indifferently, in honor of the *Prince of Morocco*, or *King Richard*, or any other worthy whose entrance was marked in the play-book "with a flourish." But before the orchestra ravished the ears of every one, the manager came forward, in the costume of *Bassanio*, and made a low bow. Mr. Hallam was a fat little man, of fifty or fifty-five, with a rubicund and somewhat sensual face, and he expressed extraordinary delight at meeting so many of the "noble aristocracy of the great and noble colony of Virginia," assembled to witness his very humble representation. It would be the chief end and sole ambition of his life, he said, to please the gentry, who so kindly patronized their servants —himself and his associates—and then the smiling worthy concluded by bowing lower than before. Much applause from the pit and gallery, and murmurs of approbation from the well-bred boxes, greeted this address, and, the orchestra having struck up, the curtain slowly rolled aloft. The young gallants scattered to the corners of the stage—seating themselves on stools or chairs, or standing, and the "Merchant of Venice" commenced. *Bassanio* having assumed a dignified and lofty port, criticised *Gratiano* with courteous and lordly wit: his friend *Antonio* offered him his fortune with grand magnanimity, in a loud singing voice, worthy the utmost commendation, and the first act proceeded on its way in triumph.

CHAPTER VIII

IN THE SQUIRE'S BOX.

THE first act ended without the appearance of *Portia* or *Nerissa;* the scene in which they hold their confidential—though public and explanatory—interview having been omitted. The audience seemed to be much pleased, and the actors received a grateful guerdon of applause.

In the box opposite that one occupied by Mr. Lee and his daughters, sat the squire, Will, and Kate, and—*proh pudor!*—no less a personage than Parson Tag. Let us not criticise the worthy parson's appearance in a play-house, too severely, however. Those times were not our times, nor those men, the men of to-day. If parsons drank deep then, and hunted Reynard, and not unwillingly took a hand at cards,—and they did all this and more—why should they not also go and see the "good old English drama?" Certain are we, that when the squire proposed to the parson a visit to town, for the purpose of witnessing the performance of the "Merchant of Venice,"—that worthy made no sort of objection:—though it must be said, in justice to him, also, that he expressed some fears of finding his time thrown away. He now sat on the front seat beside the squire, with solemn gravity, and rubicund nose, surveying from his respectable position the agitated pit. Miss Alethea had remained at home: but, beside the squire, Will and Kate were exchanging criticisms on the splendid novelty they had just witnessed. They remembered it for years afterwards—this, their beautiful, glittering, glorious, magical first play!

"Not so bad as you predicted—eh, parson?" said the squire. "I don't think that fellow *Antonio* acts so badly."

"Very well—very well," replied the parson, who was in the habit of echoing the squire's opinions.

"And the audience seem delighted. Look at that scamp of a son of mine, strutting up to friend Lee's box, and smoothing those enormous ruffles like a turkey-cock."

"Harmless devices of youth, sir."

"Yes, and innocent, at least: he'll reform in time, sir, I tell you."

"Beyond all doubt."

"There's good in Champ."

"A most amiable young man."

"Who abused your homilies," laughed the squire.

"Oh! that is forgotten, my respected friend—a mere youthful jest—the words of a thoughtless youth."

The parson was evidently in a most Christian state of mind, and had plainly left his usual severity at home. The fact was, that the worthy man felt no little complaisance at being seen the honored companion of "one of the aristocracy," as Mr. Hallam would have said, in that public place. It flattered him—he thought he heard the gallery say to the pit, "Who is that fine-looking gentleman in Squire Effingham's box?"—and the pit audibly replied, "That is the Reverend Mr. Tag, the distinguished clergyman."

The parson was, therefore, in a forgiving state of mind, and at that moment would not have refused to agree with the squire if that gentleman had stated his opinion that Mr. Effingham's natural genius and moral purity were sublime.

Suddenly, however, the parson's face clouded over, and catching hold of the squire's arm, he said:

"There, sir! look there! That is the young man I spoke of, Charles Waters—below us!"

"What of him?"

"Have you forgotten, sir?"

"Perfectly," said the good-humored squire. "Oh, yes! now I recollect, the young man who—"

"Has been propagating those treasonable opinions, sir—one of the lower classes turned statesman, as you very eloquently observed! What business has he to be there?—

the gallery is his place, among the servants and laborers. I wonder he is not in the boxes, by us gentlemen!"

The squire followed the indignant finger of the parson, and saw beneath them in the pit a young man clad in gray cloth, and gazing with a thoughtful and fixed look upon the curtain. Plainly, however, he was unconscious of thus staring out of countenance the poor curtain—his own thoughts, it was evident, pre-occupied his mind. He was apparently twenty-two or three, and his countenance was full of truth and nobility:—the hair short, chestnut-colored and unpowdered—the eyes large and clear,—the mouth firm, but somewhat sorrowful. Altogether, the face of this young man would have attracted much attention from close observers of character; and it was not without its effect on the generous mind of the squire.

"You may say what you please of young Waters, parson," he said, "but he's no fool; you may see that in his countenance."

"I fear he is much more knave than fool, honored sir," said his companion.

"If what you said of him is true, he's both," said the bluff squire, suddenly recollecting the young man's alleged opinions on education, "but let him go—we came here to be amused—and I shall not talk politics. Come, let us question the juveniles here. How did you like the play, Kate, was it pretty?"

Kate clapped her hands, and said:

"Oh, lovely, papa!"

"And you, Will?"

"Pretty good," said Master Will, endeavoring to smooth his modest ruffles after the manner of his brother Champ, whom he secretly admired and venerated as the model of a gentleman and cavalier. "I think it's pretty well, sir—but not up to my anticipations—hum!"

"My goodness, Willie!" cried Kate, in the midst of the squire's laughter at this magniloquent speech, "you just said to me a minute ago that you were delighted."

"I said so to satisfy you," said Master Will, grandly.

"To satisfy me, indeed!"

"Yes. I never argue with women."

The squire seemed much delighted with this speech, and

endeavoring to command his risible muscles, asked Kate "what she had to reply to that?"

"He says he never argues with women!" answered Kate, pouting and shaking her little fresh-looking head up and down, "never mind! I'll catch him at it before long. Never argues with women!" adds Kate, "as if he was not arguing with me all the time 'most!"

"Let us dismiss the subject," says Will, gently caressing his upper lip as Mr. Champ was doing opposite, "if that's the way you're going on when we are married, I'll have a time of it."

"I won't marry you!" says Kate, "to be quarrelling all the time—"

"I quarrel!"

"Yes!" pouts Kate, wiping her eyes.

"Well, I won't any more," says Will, descending from his heroics, and endeavoring to make friends; "don't cry, Kate. You know how devoted I am to you—"

"I won't be friends!"

"Now, Kate!"

"You needn't be squeezing my hand."

"I'll get you the silk for Carlo's foot."

"Will you?"

"Yes, from cousin Clare."

"To-morrow?"

"This very night."

"Then," says Kate, smiling, "I won't quarrel: and you musn't."

"I? never!"

"How pretty Carlo will be!"

"Lovely—and we're engaged?"

"Oh, yes!" says Kate, absorbed in the imaginary contemplation of Carlo's foot, "but hush! Willie, they are going on with the play, and you musn't be making love to me, you know, where every body can hear you!"

"Never!" says Will, with Roman dignity and firmness.

The audience utter a prolonged "Sh-h-h-h!" and the curtain rises.

CHAPTER IX.

IN MR. LEE'S BOX.

LET us return for a moment to the box occupied by Mr. Lee and his daughters. At the end of the first act Mr. Effingham left his companions, with whom he had been interchanging remarks during the performance, to the great disgust of the pit, and sauntered to the side of Miss Clare Lee, who sat nearest the stage. Clare was radiant with pleasure: she had never seen a play before, and it was therefore as much of a novelty to her as to little Kate. Never had she looked more beautiful, with her bright eyes and soft rosy cheeks— and this fact probably occurred to Mr. Effingham: for his gaze betrayed unmistakable admiration. No one, however, would have discovered it from his manner, which was as full of languor as ever.

"How does my fair cousin relish the performance?" he asked.

"Oh! I was never more pleased with any thing," said Clare, "and how do you like it?"

"Tolerably: but I never had a very great relish for these things—"

"Because, to wit, life itself is a comedy," said Henrietta, laughing.

"Yes," said Mr. Effingham, "and a very brilliant one it would be, if all the world were Miss Henriettas. I hope, my dear cousin, that compliment is sufficiently broad."

"Thank you, sir—I know how to take your fine speeches: don't think they deceive me."

"There! you have it, Champ," said Mr. Lee, who turned round to greet a neighbor who had just entered.

"I'm rather a poor hand at compliments," replied Mr. Effingham, "but really it is hard to do you the injustice, my fair cousin, of withholding them. Come! no reply, for I see cousin Clare is going to say something more flattering than what you are about to utter."

Clare laughed, and said, blushing slightly:

"Oh, no! I was going to say only that *Shylock* really frightened me."

"It was very well done, much like Shuter at Castle Garden," said Mr. Effingham, "how did you like it, cousin Henrietta? Come, your criticism."

"Oh, what could you expect from a mere country girl like me? Besides, there is Mr. Hamilton, my devoted admirer, coming to speak to me."

Mr. Hamilton, the fox-hunter, entered and took his seat, and Henrietta was now engaged in a laughing and animated conversation.

"How I envy them," said Mr. Effingham, applying to his nostrils, with a listless air, a delicate pinch of snuff, "they are so gay."

"Why are you not gay, cousin Champ?" said Clare, in a timid voice, "you have no reason to be sad."

"No—I do not say I have any reason. But I am out of sorts."

"Why are you?"

Mr. Effingham leaning over the velvet cushion, and speaking in a tone audible to no one besides himself and Clare, replied:

"I am out of sorts, because I am rusting."

"Rusting!"

"Yes, more than rusting. I take interest in scarcely any thing—I am wearied to death with every thing—what is life worth? Here are some hundreds of persons, and they all seem delighted with this play, which tires me to death. I take no interest in it. Shylock and Antonio strut and spout without amusing me—I am already weary, and every body else seems to be impatient for the reappearance of those wonders. Why are they so much amused? For my part, I am sick of all this, and only stay," Mr. Effingham added, lowering his voice, "because *you* stay. The nearest approach to happiness I make, is in your presence."

Clare blushed this time in earnest, and yet, gathering self-possession, looked into Mr. Effingham's face and smiled.

"How beautiful you are!" he said, with profound earnestness.

"Oh," said Clare, the color of a peony, "you are jesting with me."

"I am not jesting."

"Well, don't say any thing to make me feel so again—I feel as if my face was as red as fire."

There was so much childlike frankness in the tone with which these words were uttered, that Mr. Effingham felt his heart leaving him, and going quickly into the possession of the owner of the red cheeks. Yet strange to say, he felt no pain, but rather pleasure.

"I really believe I am growing less tired of the play, and all," he said to himself, with a smile: then added aloud:

"I really think you could charm away my misanthropy and melancholy, if you desired, cousin."

"How, pray?"

"By smiling at me."

Clare smiled:

"There," she said, "be merry, then. Indeed, cousin, you could become gay again, if you chose. Do not determine to find fault with every thing—and think every thing wearisome. Seek novelty: you say that all here seem to take pleasure in the play, while you do not. They are pleased because it is new to them.—I have never seen a play, and I am highly pleased. If you have been often to theatres, there is nothing strange in your thinking this poor one excellent—though it seems beautiful to me. But you will find novelty and interest in other things. Try it, now, and see if my philosophy is not true."

The softness and earnestness in the tender voice of the young girl, and the interest in himself betrayed by her tone, was so plain that Mr. Effingham felt his languid heart beat.

"I know but one means," he said.

"What is that?"

"To have a companion."

"A companion?"

His meaning suddenly flashed upon her, and she turned away her head.

"To have the philosopher always near me" said Mr. Effingham, imprisoning in his own the hand which rested on the railing.

The head was turned further away.

"Clare!—dearest Clare!" he whispered, "if you take such a tender interest in my welfare—why not—"

"Sh—h—h—h!" came in a long murmur from the audience.

"True," muttered Mr. Effingham, turning away, "how ridiculous, here in the theatre!"

Suddenly his eyes fell upon one of the actresses, and he almost uttered an exclamation. It was the unknown lady of the wood.

CHAPTER X.

ACTRESS AND GENTLEMAN.

THE unknown lady was no gentle Virginia maiden, no "lady," as she had said, with perfect calmness, at their meeting in the wood—only one of the company of Comedians. Her singular expression when she uttered the words, "I think you will see me again," occurred to the young man, and he wondered that this easy solution of the riddle had not occurred to him at once.

What was her name? Mr. Effingham drew forth his bill, and saw opposite the name of Portia, *Miss Beatrice Hallam.*

"Ah, yes," he said, carelessly, "the same we were speculating upon, this morning. Let us see how Portia looks, and what change the foot-lights work in her face."

He sat down in the corner of the stage upon a wicker chair, and scanned Portia critically. Her costume was faultless. It consisted of a gown and underskirt of fawn-colored silk, trimmed with silver, and a single band of gold encircled each wrist, clearly relieved against the white, finely-rounded arm. Her hair, which was a beautiful chestnut, had been carried back from the temples and powdered, after the fashion of the time, and around her beautiful, swan-like neck, the young woman wore a necklace of pearls of rare brilliance. Thus the costume of the character defied criticism, and Mr. Effingham passed on to the face and figure. These we have already described. The countenance of Beatrice Hallam wore the same simple, yet firm and collected expression, which Mr. Effingham had observed in their first interview, and her figure had the same indefinable grace and beauty. Every movement which she made might have suited a royal palace, and in her large brilliant eyes Mr. Effingham in vain sought the least trace of confusion. She surveyed the audience, while the Prince of Morocco was uttering his speech, with perfect simplicity, but her eyes not for a single moment rested on the young men collected at the corners of the stage. For her they seemed to have no existence, and she turned to the Prince again. That gentleman having uttered his prescribed number of lines, Portia advanced graciously toward him, and addressed him. Her carelessness was gone; she no longer displayed either indifference or coldness. She was the actress, with her rôle to sustain. She commenced in a voice of noble and queen-like courtesy, a voice of pure music, and clear utterance, so to speak, such as few lips possess the power of giving forth. Every word rang and told; there was no hurry, no slurring, no hesitation; it was not an actress delivering a set speech, but the noble Portia doing the honors of her beautiful palace of Belmont. The scene ended with great applause—the young woman had evidently produced a most favorable impression on the audience. But she seemed wholly unconscious of this compliment, and made her exit quite calmly.

A buzz ran through the theatre: the audience were discussing the merits of Portia. On the stage, too, she was the subject of many comments; and this continued until Lancelot made his appearance and went through his speech. Then Portia's reappearance with the Prince was greeted with great applause.

Mr. Effingham leaned forward and touched the young woman's sleeve.

"Come," he said, with easy carelessness, and scarcely moderating his voice, "come, fair Portia, while that tiresome fellow is making his speech, talk to me a little. We are old acquaintances—and you are indebted to me for directing you home."

"Yes, sir," said Beatrice, turning her head slightly, "but pardon me—I have my part to attend to."

"I don't care."

"Excuse me, sir—but I do."

"Really, madam, you are very stiff for an actress. Is it so very unusual a thing to ask a moment's conversation?"

"I know that it is the fashion in London and elsewhere, sir, but I dislike it. It destroys my conception of the character," she said, calmly.

Mr. Effingham laughed.

"Come here and talk to me," he said, "did you not say we should meet again?"

"Yes, sir. And I also said that I was not a lady."

"Well—what is the meaning of that addition?"

"It means, sir, that being an actress, I am not at liberty to amuse myself here as I might were I a lady in a drawing-room. Pardon me, sir," she added calmly, "I am neglecting what I have engaged to do, play Portia."

And the young woman quietly disengaging her sleeve from Mr. Effingham's fingers, moved away to another portion of the stage.

"Here is a pretty affair," said Mr. Effingham to himself, as he fell back, languidly, into the chair, from which, however, he had not deigned to rise wholly when addressing the young actress, "what are things coming to when an actress treats a gentleman in this manner. I really believe the girl thinks I am not good enough for her: 'Pardon me, sir!' was there ever such insufferable prudery and affectation! No doubt she wishes to catch me, and commences with this piquant piece of acting. Or perhaps," added the elegant young gentleman, smoothing his frill, "she fell in love with me the other day, when we met, and is afraid she will betray herself. Not talk when I desire to talk with her, indeed—and yonder all those people have seen her cavalier treatment of me, and are laughing at me. Fortunately I am proof against their jeers—come, come, let us see if Miss Portia will treat me as badly next time."

Portia entered next with the Prince of Arragon, and while that gentleman was addressing the caskets, Mr. Effingham again applied himself to the task of forcing the young woman to converse with him.

"Why did you treat me so, just now?" he said, with abrupt carelessness.

"How, sir?"

"You refused to talk to me."

"I had my part to perform."

"That is no excuse."

"Besides, sir," added the young woman, surveying Mr. Effingham with an indifferent glance, "I know you only very slightly."

"Know me only slightly," cried Mr. Effingham, affecting surprise.

"A chance meeting is very slight acquaintance, sir; but I offer this as no apology for refusing to do what I am now doing—converse with you on the stage."

"Really, one would say you were a queen speaking to a subject, instead of an actress—"

"Honored with the attentions of a gentleman, you would add, sir," she interrupted, quite calmly.

"As you please."

"Pray, speak to me no more, sir—I forget my part. And the audience are looking at you."

"Let them."

"I see some angry faces," said the young woman, looking at Charles Waters, "they do not understand the fashions of London, sir."

"What care I."

"Please release my sleeve, sir—that is my line."

The gallery uttered a prolonged hiss as Portia disengaged her arm. Mr. Effingham turned round disdainfully, and looked up to the gallery from which the hiss came. This glance of haughty defiance might have provoked another exhibition of the same sort, but Portia at that moment commenced her speech.

Thereafter the young woman came no more near Mr. Effingham, and treated that gentleman's moody glances with supreme disregard. What was going on in Mr. Effingham's mind, and why did he lose some of his careless listlessness when, clasping her beautiful hands, the lovely girl, raising her eyes to heaven, like one of the old Italian pictures, uttered that sublime discourse on the "quality of mercy"? and how did it happen that, when she sobbed, almost, in that tender, magical voice,—

> "But mercy is *above* this sceptered sway,
> It is enthroned in the *hearts* of kings—
> It is an attribute of God himself!"—

how did it chance that Mr. Effingham led the enthusiastic applause, and absolutely rose erect in the excess of his enthusiasm ?

As she passed him in going out, he made her a low bow, and said, " Pardon me ! you are a great actress ! " A single glance, and a calm movement of the head, were the only reply to this speech ; and with this Mr. Effingham was compelled to remain content.

He returned to the side of Clare, thoughtful and preoccupied.

" What were they hissing for ? " asked Clare, from whom the scene we have related had been concealed by the projection of the wall, and the group of young men. Indeed, scarcely any portion of the audience had witnessed it, the gallery excepted, which overlooked the whole stage from its great height.

" Some folly which deserved hissing, probably," returned Mr. Effingham, wondering at his own words as he spoke ; " but here are the actors again."

The play proceeded, and ended amid universal applause. Mr. Hallam led out Portia, in response to uproarious calls, and thanked the audience for their kindness to his daughter. Beatrice received all the applause with her habitual calmness ; and, inclining her head slightly, disappeared.

Mr. Effingham's eyes dwelt upon her to the last, and even Clare spoke to him in vain.

" Bah ! she's a mere scheming jade ! " he said, at last, disdainfully, and almost aloud ; " come, cousin Clare, the chariot is ready at the door. Take my arm."

And so the audience separated, rolling, well pleased, to their homes. But why did Mr. Effingham preserve such inexplicable silence in the chariot ? Why did Henrietta tell him that the performance must have made him sleepy ? Why did he push his horse angrily as he galloped back from Riverhead to Effingham Hall ? Was he thinking of that strange Portia ?

CHAPTER XI.

MR. EFFINGHAM CRITICISES THE COMEDY, BETRAYING GREAT CONSISTENCY.

That night Mr. Effingham paced his room for more than an hour in moody thought, troubled and out of humor, it seemed, at something which had recently occurred. He kicked out of his way every obstacle, and betrayed other unmistakable evidences of ill-humor. At last, this annoyed state of mind took to itself words and he muttered:

"An actress, forsooth, to so treat a gentleman! making him the laughing-stock of every body by her insolent airs of superiority! As if it were not a high compliment for me to address her at all—a common *Comedienne!* One would really say that it was presumption in me to speak to one so much my superior. 'Pardon me, sir—I have my part to attend to!' and then those stupid country bumpkins around me tittering! Let 'em! I thank heaven that their mirth does not affect me—how insolent it was! And that hiss from the knaves in the gallery. Presume to hiss a gentleman! And who caused all this? By heaven! she shall repent her insulting hauteur. Who is this woman who conducts herself in such a manner toward a gentleman? Some low woman, the daughter of that vulgar fellow Hallam: no lady, a common actress! Suppose she did act well, and I don't mean to say or think she is not a superior artist. Common justice requires me to acknowledge her genius. But what of that? Her attitude in the trial scene was fine!" continued Mr. Effingham, thoughtfully, forgetting for a moment his indignation, and returning in thought to the theatre. "How tender and noble her countenance! what music in her voice! Never have I seen such purity and truth upon the stage. By heaven! she's no common actress! and I had to tell her so as she went out! But how did she receive my high compliment," he said, returning to his grievances, "how did that respectful address, 'You are a great actress,' affect her? She looked at me as carelessly and indifferently as if I had said 'good morning,' and inclined her head with the coldness of a princess speaking to her subject. Damn my blood!" said Mr. Effingham, with unusual vehemence, "I'll make her repent it, and she shall suffer for causing me this annoyance. It is ridiculous, pitiable, silly: I, Mr. Champ Effingham, of Effingham Hall, to annoy myself about a common actress—to be treated with contemptuous indifference by a woman of her grade!"

And Mr. Champ Effingham, of Effingham Hall, sent an unfortunate cricket which stood in his path, flying across the room. The cricket struck against a table which supported a tall silver candlestick, and all came down with a crash. The incident served the purpose of a partial vent to the young man's irritation, and after some more growling and imprecations he went to bed.

He made his appearance at the breakfast-table on the next morning two hours after the squire had left it, and received a remonstrance from Miss Alethea on his late rising, with great indifference. Entering the library thereafter, he found the squire, who had just returned, reading the "Virginia Gazette."

"Good morning, Champ, lazy as usual, I see," said the squire, good-humoredly; "but you were late returning from Riverhead, which is a good excuse. How did you like the play? we have not met, you know, since."

"I was charmed with it," said Mr. Effingham, "all but *Portia* acted their parts excellently, I thought."

"All but *Portia!*"

Mr. Effingham nodded.

"Why," continued the squire, "I thought her acting excellent."

"Poor, sir—poor—very."

"What fault did you find—come, Mr. London critic?"

"It was overacted."

"How?"

"It took up too much room in the piece."

"Why Portia is a chief character in the play."

"Yes—but not the only one."

"You are very critical."

"I always was."

"And what other fault did you find? Was Miss Hallam ugly?"

"No—not ugly, exactly—but dreadfully affected and stiff."

"I do not agree with you."

"You liked her, then?"

"Exceedingly," said the honest squire; "I thought her a young woman of rare beauty—'

"Bah!"

"And great talents."

"Well," said Mr. Effingham, "tastes proverbially differ. I thought her abominable."

"Were you not speaking to her at one time?"

"Speaking to Portia?"

"Yes. I could not see very well through the group around her, but thought I saw her speaking to you."

"She did speak to me."

"Do you know her?"

"At least she says we are not acquainted."

"Here's a mystery!"

"Not at all. I met her some days since riding out. She had lost her way, and I directed her to Williamsburg."

"I hope you treated her with courtesy."

"As courteously as a subject could a queen, and got snubbed last night for my pains," said Mr. Effingham, with a bad affectation of indifference.

The squire laughed, which caused Mr. Effingham to frown.

"Most insulting treatment," he said.

"Come, come—your ideas are too English and not sufficiently Virginian," said the squire. "This young woman is not degraded by her profession; and though not exactly a lady, is worthy of respect if she conducts herself properly. For my part, I was vastly pleased with her, and I believe every one but yourself who witnessed her acting thought as I did."

"Well, sir," said Mr. Effingham, "I am sorry to find we disagree. In my eyes, her acting, costume, voice, and general style were inappropriate, stilted, and in bad taste."

"You are offended at her refusal to converse with you," laughed the squire, "and so are a prejudiced witness. Hey!" he added, looking through the window, "there's the parson come over to dine."

Mr. Effingham was glad to be thus relieved from the dilemma into which he had fallen, and he greeted the parson with a bow, due to him as deliverer.

"A fine morning, squire," said Parson Tag; "how does your worship find yourself after the late sitting last night?"

"Quite fresh—sit down. How did you like the acting?" Every body is asking that question now."

"Well, well," said the parson, dubiously. "It was tolerably good, but much of it was overdone—overdone, sir, much overdone."

"What part? But excuse me for a moment. I have a word to say to Alethea, and must have your horse taken: you will stay to dinner?"

"No, I think not. I have an engagement—but perhaps —well, I suppose—"

The squire, well accustomed to this formula, was already out of the room, and the first thing he did was to order the parson's animal to be led away, as he would spend the remaining portion of the day at the Hall.

"You said the play was overdone, I believe?" said Mr. Effingham, lounging in an easy chair, and drawling out his words. "What part, please inform me, reverend sir?—I repeat my respected governor's question."

"All was overdone—especially the part of that young woman, the daughter of the manager."

"Miss Hallam?"

"Yes, young sir."

"Who acted *Portia?*"

"Precisely. I never saw a greater failure—it was wretched."

"What do you know of acting?" said Mr. Effingham, with indignant disdain, which expression did not escape Mr. Tag.

"You are somewhat abrupt, sir," he said; "but, nevertheless, I will answer you. In my former worldly days, I frequented playhouses much, and have thus some knowledge of them."

"And you think *Portia's* part was overdone?"

"Yes."

"And wretched?"

"Exactly."

"And a failure?"

"Perfect."

"Then, reverend sir," said Mr. Effingham, with insulting carelessness, "I beg leave to inform you, that you know nothing about acting. I have never seen a more beautiful rendering of the character. Miss Hallam—whom I highly esteem, sir, and should be sorry to hear any one insult!—is an artist of rare genius! Her conception and execution are alike uncommon and admirable. If there are persons who are ignorant of what acting exacts, and who do not know when it is of a superior order, so much the worse for them! I repeat, sir, that any competent critic would have approved unconditionally of Miss Hallam's acting last night in the part of Portia, and I feel some surprise at hearing from you a criticism such as you have uttered. The acting of this young lady—and she is a lady in every sense of the word; for do not think that I am of the prejudiced way of thinking which the gentlemen so-called of this colony take pride in—Miss Hallam's acting is of an order superior to any I have ever witnessed. Her costume, style, voice, and whole rendering were worthy of the first comedians of the English stage. And permit me to say, that your former drilling in theatrical criticism, which you have alluded to, must have been very slight and incomplete, if, after attending the performance with which every one was delighted last night, you failed to perceive that this young girl of eighteen—she is not more, sir—is destined to take a rank inferior to no artist who now adorns with her genius or decorates with her beauty and accomplishments that department of art, the histrionic profession!"

Mr. Tag was fairly overwhelmed. His feelings, while this storm of words was being poured out on his devoted head, might have been compared to those of a man whose eyes are dazzled and his ears deafened by lightning and thunders issuing from a cloudless sky. He could muster no reply—words failed him. He essayed once or twice to muster some appropriate indignation, but failed lamentably. The worthy gentleman was accustomed to bully—as we now say—others, not to be bullied; and Mr. Effingham having "stolen his art," that art now failed him.

"Yes, sir," continued the animated and consistent critic, "I shall make it my business to call upon Miss Hallam, and assure her of my high appreciation and admiration of her brilliant genius. I know what acting is, sir!—and when we, the gentlemen of Virginia, are so fortunate as to secure a great *comedienne*, it becomes us to offer her the tribute of our applause! Miss Hallam deserves it—for I again repeat, that in style, dress, voice, and conception, she is far before any actress with whom, in my various experience, I have been thrown in contact."

"Why, Champ!" cried the voice of the squire, at the door, "you are the most consistent of critics, and the most impartial of admirers! You praise and abuse in the same breath."

Mr. Effingham betrayed some slight embarrassment, upon finding that his enthusiastic tribute to Miss Hallam had thus been overheard, by one to whom he had spoken of her so disparagingly. But this soon disappeared, and the versatile young gentleman replied with great coolness.

"All chivalry, sir—pure chivalry. I thought it my duty to espouse Miss Hallam's cause, when she was attacked by so rough a tilter as the reverend gentleman here. Was I wrong, and would you not have done the same?"

This was very adroit in Mr. Effingham, as it diverted attention from himself to the views of the parson.

"The parson attack Portia!" said the squire; "how so?"

"I did nothing of the sort, your worship," said the crest-fallen parson, "I only expressed some dissatisfaction with a portion of her acting:—for which crime, Mr. Effingham has been for some minutes pouring out upon my head the vials of wrath."

"Well, let us say no more," returned Mr. Effingham, subsiding into indifference again; "I'm tired of the subject, and will no longer afflict your reverence. Bring me some Jamaica," he added, to a servant who was passing through the hall: then to the parson, "we'll bury all differences in a flagon," he said, "I'm as thirsty as a fish."

The parson brightened up, and, when he had emptied a fair cup of excellent Jamaica, was ready to forgive Mr. Effingham and all the world—even think well of *Portia*. In due time, that is to say, about noon, dinner was announced and discussed honestly by all, except Mr. Effingham. That gentleman soon rose and ordered his horse, announcing his intention of riding to Williamsburg, where he would probably spend the night.

"Don't sit up for me, Alethea," he added, with a yawn.

"Indeed, I won't," Miss Alethea replied.

Mr. Effingham nodded indifferently, and sauntered from the room.

CHAPTER XII.

THE OLD RALEIGH TAVERN.

The "Raleigh Tavern" in Williamsburg had been selected for a residence by Mr. Hallam and his company of comedians, chiefly on the ground that there was no other hostelry of any size in the good city at the period : and before the Raleigh Mr. Effingham drew rein. A negro took his horse, and, entering the broad doorway, the young man found himself opposite to the manager himself.

"Give me some Jamaica," he said to the portly landlord, who bowed low to his well-known and richly-clad guest, "and you, Mr. Hallam, come here and empty a cup with me. I came to see Madam *Portia*. Where is she at the present moment? I wish to pay her my respects."

So far from displaying any ill-humor at these cavalier words, the red-faced manager bowed as low as the landlord, and expressed his perfect willingness to drink with Mr. Effingham; which, judging from his voice and appearance, he had performed in company with himself a number of times already. He marched up, accordingly, to the sideboard—in those simple times the bottles were set out freely without any obstructing "bar"—and pouring out an abundant supply of the heady rum, swallowed it at a gulp. Mr. Effingham drank his own more leisurely, talking about the performance on the preceding night.

"A fine house, sir! a most enlightened and intellectual

audience, such as I expected to find in this noble colony," said Mr. Hallam.

"What receipts?" asked Mr. Effingham.

"Nearly a hundred pounds, sir; as much as the great Congreve's 'Love for Love' ever brought me."

"I should have thought the amount larger,—cursed dust! I believe it has strangled me!"

"I saw you, sir, and your honorable party."

"The devil you did! that's strange, for Shylock naturally took up your whole attention."

"Shylock was too drunk," said Hallam, quite naturally; "there he is, in the corner, now."

"Let him stay there, then. You have not answered my question."

"Your question?"

"I asked where *Portia* was."

"Oh, Beatrice! she is somewhere about."

"I met and directed her on her way to town the other day.—Send up, and say that Mr. Effingham wishes to see her."

"Certainly, sir."

A messenger was dispatched to Miss Hallam's room, and in a moment returned with the reply, that she was busy studying her part.

"She can see you, though," said Hallam, laughing; "follow me, sir."

Mr. Effingham followed the fat manager, and a flight of stairs brought them to a door, which Hallam knocked at, and a voice bidding him come in, he threw it open. It afforded entrance to a small, neat room, the simple ornaments of which were in perfect taste; the window of this room was open, and at it sat the young girl, whom we have seen twice before; once, in the bright autumn woods, and again on the stage, in the character of Portia. Beatrice was clad in a handsome morning dress of dove color, and her fine hair was secured behind her statue-like head by a bow of scarlet riband. She leaned one hand upon her book,—the other supported her fair brow, and her classic profile was clearly defined against the rich fall forest, visible through the window.

At the noise made by the opening door she raised her

eyes, and for a moment gazed in silence upon the intruders Then apparently resigning herself to her fate, she closed the book and rose.

"I told the servant to say that I was engaged upon my part, father," she said, calmly, to Hallam. "I shall be badly prepared if I am interrupted, sir."

"Oh, plenty of time—and with your genius, child, you can do any thing. She is as quick as lightning, Mr. Effingham," added the manager, discussing the young girl's talents in her hearing without a thought of any indelicacy in such a proceeding, "and when she catches hold of a rôle it's done."

Beatrice was silent.

"Come, now, talk with Mr. Effingham for a quarter of an hour, since he is an acquaintance," continued the manager, smiling, "in that time you will lose nothing." And passing through the door, he descended into the lower part of the tavern.

For a moment the two personages thus left alone surveyed each other in silence. Before Mr. Effingham's bold and careless glance, Beatrice's eyes did not lower for an instant.

"Well, Mr. Effingham," she said, at length, quite calmly, "what would you have?"

"Simply, a little conversation with you, my charming Beatrice," said Mr. Effingham, carelessly.

"I am busy, sir, very. I act Juliet to-night, and am now studying."

"Oh, you can give me a few moments—"

"Well, sir," she said, sitting down and pointing to a chair.

"Especially," continued her visitor, "as you refused to say any thing to me last night."

"That is a reproach, sir?"

"Yes."

"It is unjust, as you know."

"Now, see the difference of opinion," said Mr. Effingham, smoothing his ruffles, daintily, "I think that nothing could be more just. I reproach you justly, because you have nothing but prudery to allege as an excuse for your refusal."

"I told you, sir, then, as I now do, that conversation on the stage destroys my conception of the character I am representing."

"Bah! all theory."

The young girl seemed to be somewhat irritated by the disdainful expression of Mr. Effingham's voice.

"Mr. Effingham," she said, "be pleased not to treat me like your servant. I am no common attaché of the stage, sir, such as you have met with, doubtless, in London frequently. I say this, sir, in no spirit of self-approval, but because it is true."

"Why, Beatrice, you are really about to bowstring me, or put me to some horrible death, I believe."

"See, sir," said the young girl, with noble calmness, "we are very nearly perfect strangers, and you address me as 'Beatrice,' as familiarly as my own father."

"May the devil take it—you quarrel with a mere habit."

"Mr. Effingham," said the young woman, rising, and speaking in a tone of perfect calmness, "I quarrel neither with you nor any one; above all, I do not presume to criticise your habits, except when those habits, as in the present instance, concern myself."

"Bah!" repeated Mr. Effingham, with a laugh, "how, pray?"

"You seem to think, sir, that it is my place to be thankful when you address me intimately, and familiarly, as you have done."

"What harm is there?"

"That question is an insult, sir!"

"May the devil take me, but you are fruitful in imaginary offences, and insults offered you."

"No, sir—I do not exercise my imagination at all. Your tone to me is disagreeable."

"There it is again—you are really going to bite me, I believe. Let us leave the subject, and discuss last night's performance. Your acting was really not bad."

The proud lip of the young woman moved slightly.

"Ah! ah!" said Mr. Effingham, laughing, "I see what you mean by that scornful look. I am a poor critic, you would say."

"I say nothing, sir."

"I have no taste, you would say: though I beg you to observe, that inasmuch as I have praised your acting, that is a false step in you."

Beatrice repressed her rising anger, and bowed coldly.

Mr. Effingham received this exhibition of hauteur with careless nonchalance, and picking up the volume which the young girl had laid down on his entrance, said:

"You act Juliet to-night?"

"I do, sir."

"I shall come."

Beatrice made no reply.

"I beg, now," continued Mr. Effingham, arranging one of his ambrosial drop-curls daintily upon his cheek, "I beg you will not put any of that ferocious feeling you now exhibit into Juliet. The character is essentially tender and poetical, and ranting would kill it."

"I never rant, sir," said Beatrice, apparently resigning herself to the presence of her insulting visitor, and speaking in a tone of utter coldness.

"That's right," replied Mr. Effingham, indifferently; "be subdued, quiet, but intense, and all that. Juliet is deeply in love with Romeo, recollect, and love does not express itself by tirade. Do you think it suits you? Come, answer me."

"I have played it before, sir."

"That is no answer."

"Please leave me to study my part, sir—time is passing."

"Not before giving my views, Beatrice. I don't think you will act Juliet well. It requires a tender, loving nature; and you are minus the heart, it is plain; and you will butcher the part."

"Thanks for your compliment, sir."

"Oh! I never compliment, or any thing of the sort."

"I am losing time, sir."

"Conversing with me, you mean?"

"Yes, sir."

"The conversation, then, is very distasteful to you, my charming Beatrice?"

"Yes, sir!" she said.

"You hate me, perhaps?"

The young girl made no reply.

"Or, perhaps, your ladyship despises me?" added Mr. Effingham, betraying some irritation.

"I do neither, sir—you are indifferent to me."

These words were uttered with so much coldness, that Mr. Effingham's *amour propre* was deeply wounded. He began to get angry.

"You are really a very amiable young lady," he said. "Here I ride all the way from the country for the sole purpose of seeing you."

"And insulting me, sir, add."

"And you receive me," continued Mr. Effingham, taking no notice of the interruption, "as if I were a common clodhopper, instead of a gentleman, paying you a friendly visit."

"Your friendly visits do not please me, sir."

"I see they do not."

"I am an actress, sir, and not of your class."

"Bah! who speaks of classes?"

"You yourself this moment, sir!"

"You choose to misunderstand me I said that my visit was the friendly one of a well-bred man, not the impertinent intrusion of a country bumpkin, like those knaves who hissed me in the gallery, or that clodhopper who presumed to bend his angry glances on me from the pit—Mr. Charles Waters, I know him well—the young reformer, forsooth!"

Beatrice's face flushed.

"I saw no nobler countenance, sir," she said, coldly, "among all your aristocratic friends."

"Ah! your cavalier, I perceive!" said Mr. Effingham, bitterly; "really, I shall become jealous."

"I do not know him, even, sir—your scoff is unjust."

"Your true knight, who wished to run a tilt with me for touching your arm! Perhaps he has but now left you, and before going, devoted my humble self to the infernal gods for daring to address you."

"I repeat," said Beatrice, indignantly, "that I have seen him but once, and on the occasion you allude to."

"Well, I believe you. But let such impertinent bumpkins beware how they criticise my actions in future, even by their looks."

Beatrice sat down, with a mixture of weariness and scorn on her beautiful countenance, and, taking up the book which the young man had laid down, began to study her part. This calmness seemed to enrage Mr. Effingham not a little, and he put on his cocked hat with a flirt of irritation.

"Very well," he said; "that means that you are weary of me—I am not good enough for Miss Hallam—she is too immaculate for me."

"I have my part to study, sir."

And she began to con her character in silence.

Mr. Effingham swung his short sword round angrily, and without further words went hurriedly out of the room. He brushed by Mr. Hallam, who was talking with Shylock, and, mounting his horse, galloped from the town towards the Hall.

The manager's good-humored greeting as he passed had been completely disregarded; and thinking rightly that something had happened to cause this abrupt departure, he went up to his daughter's room.

"Why did the young man go so abruptly, my, child?" he said.

"Because I would not return him my thanks for visiting me," said Beatrice, bitterly.

"Oh," said the manager, laughing, "you are too prudish, Beatrice. You should not complain of these visits, which are customary, and not strange, when you are acquainted—as you are with Mr. Effingham, he says. Your aim in life, as you say you hate the stage so much, should be to marry well—and I much misunderstand this young fellow, if he would not marry you in the face of the world, if he fancied."

"I do not wish to marry him, or any one like him!" said Beatrice, her face flushing, and her beautiful eyes filling with angry tears.

"You are mad!—he is, the landlord tells me, of one of the best and wealthiest families in the colony."

"And because he is," said Beatrice, wiping her eyes, "he thinks he has the right to intrude upon me, and speak in any tone he chooses. Father!" she added, passionately, "I am sick of this eternal persecution!—in London—here—every where. I shall go mad if I remain upon the stage, exposed to this class of persons all my life—my head is hot and burning now, my eyes feel like fire—oh! I wish I was dead!"

Passionate tears followed these words, and Beatrice covered her face with her hands, bending down and sobbing. The good-hearted old fellow, who really had his daughter's good at heart in all things, betrayed some feeling at this explosion of grief; and betook himself to soothing the young girl, with gentle words, and caresses, and assurances of his own unchangeable love.

"Come, come," he said, much affected, "I can't bear to see you so much moved. Don't think too hardly of this young man. He is thoughtless, perhaps, but does not mean any offence. There now!" he said, caressing her disorderd hair, "don't cry, Beatrice. You shall forget all this to-morrow, when, as there will be no performance, we can go and have the sail upon James River, which you said you would like so much—will you go?"

"Yes, sir," said Beatrice, growing calmer, "oh yes! I want to get away from all this tormenting excitement, and breathe the fresh river air. I am happiest in the woods, or on the water. I won't cry any more, sir, and don't fear I will not act my part well. I don't like acting, and at times I feel a weariness and disgust which I cannot subdue: but I will not let any of my bad feelings interfere with your wishes. Indeed, I'll act very well, sir."

"And don't be too angry at the young man—he meant nothing, I know."

"I have forgotten him, sir," said the young girl, with noble calmness.

"A mere thoughtless youth, who admires you highly—I saw that well, when you were speaking in the trial scene last night. Now I will leave you. Good-bye."

"Good-bye, father—kiss me, before you go."

And Mr. Manager Hallam having retired, the young girl growing gradually calm, again applied herself once more to the study of her part.

CHAPTER XIII.

A LOVER, FOX-HUNTER, AND PARSON.

Out of Williamsburg—into the forest—through the forest—and so into the open highway sped Mr. Effingham, as if an avenging Nemesis were behind him, and nothing but the headlong speed he was pushing his noble bay to, could preserve him from the clutches of the pursuer. He made furious gestures, uttered more furious words. The ordinary languor and nonchalance of this gentleman seemed to have passed from him wholly, and a fiery, passionate man, taken the *petit maitre's* place.

Going at this headlong speed, he very nearly ran over, before he was aware of their proximity, a party of gentlemen of his acquaintance, who were riding leisurely toward the bachelor establishment of Mr. Hamilton, visible a few hundred yards ahead. Mr. Hamilton rode in front of the glittering cortege, and became aware of Mr. Effingham's presence, by having his horse nearly driven from beneath him.

"What, the devil!" cried jolly Jack Hamilton.

"It's Effingham, racing for life!" rose in chorus, from the laughing horsemen.

"The devil, Champ! what's the matter?" asked Hamilton, "have you made a bet that you will ride over us, horse, foot and dragoons?"

"Excuse me," said Mr. Effingham, regaining a portion of his habitual calmness, "but the fact is, Hamilton, I am angry enough to gallop to the devil, whom you have twice apostrophized so emphatically."

"What's the matter?"

"I am mad."

"Intellectually, or do you mean that you are merely out of temper?"

"Both, I believe."

"Then, come and sleep with me, and have a fox-hunt with us in the morning."

"No."

"Come, now."

"I cannot."

"Well, at least, let us have the cause of your fury."

Mr. Effingham hesitated, but at last, overcome with rage, said:

"That young actress has been assuming her airs towards me, and has made me as you find me. There it is! I confess I am out of temper."

"What a confession it is!" cried Hamilton, laughing, "I thought you never suffered yourself to be ruffled."

"I seldom do."

"And she offended you?"

"Snubbed me—nothing less. It is really humiliating."

And Mr. Effingham looked as if he believed what he said: his face was flushed, and he looked gloomy.

"How was it?" asked the company.

"Why, just thus. I went to pay her a visit, and complimented her performance in Portia, highly. What reply did I receive, sir?" said Mr. Effingham, indignantly, "why, an insult! 'Please leave me—I must study my part!' that was her reply. And when I declined to avail myself of the privilege, she went on studying, as calmly as if I was not present."

"A perfect she-dragon, by George!" said Hamilton, "but really, that was bad treatment."

"Abominable!" said the chorus.

"She could not have treated a country clown more harshly," added Hamilton; "how could she be guilty of such rudeness. She don't look like it—I thought her very ladylike."

"All acting!" said Mr. Effingham.

"Plainly."

"She shall repent it," blurted out Mr. Effingham, "the insulting girl! I never saw greater rudeness and hauteur. A mere London commedienne of no talents, and bringing her stilted affectations to the colony."

"Come, my dear Effingham, don't be angry. Here we are at the Trap—my respectable bachelor residence: come in, and cool off in some Jamaica"

"No, thank you—I must get on. I am bad company.'

And, leaving the fox-hunters, Mr. Effingham rode on toward the Hall. A quarter of a mile from the house he met Parson Tag, jogging on his cob from the Hall homeward, with broad-brimmed hat, and knees and elbows painfully angular.

"Good evening, sir," said the parson, "you return soon: the dews of evening are scarce falling."

"I thought you were at the Hall, sir, for the evening."

"Why so?"

"Because I was absent," said Mr. Effingham coldly. "We quarrel, I believe, always, and I thought you would remain, as I was away."

Mr. Effingham's irritation and ill-humor must plead his excuse for this irreverent speech.

"The quarrelling is on your side, not on mine, sir," said the parson, endeavoring to be dignified; "I am a man of peace."

"Carrying out which character, you this morning attacked Miss Hallam, sir!"

"Really, you seem to have espoused that young lady's cause against all comers," said the indignant parson. "Take care, young sir; as the parson of your parish, it is my duty to warn you against the snares of Satan. This Jezebel will be your ruin."

"Be pleased to speak respectfully of Miss Hallam, sir," said Mr. Effingham, threateningly, "when you address me on the subject of her character. Though not her knight, I hold myself ready to 'espouse her cause,' as you say, sir, even against the 'parson of my parish!'"

"Here's a pretty mess," returned the pompous gentleman, descending to the vulgate: "you threaten me, forsooth!"

"No, sir: I acknowledge the folly of my words. You wear no sword, and are not responsible for thus slandering my friends—yes, my friends, sir! I say again, that Miss Hallam is one of my friends, and a young lady who has thus far conducted herself with immaculate propriety. Now, go sir, and laugh at me. I value your derision as I value your praise—as nothing."

And Mr. Effingham rode on as furiously as before, without reflecting for an instant on the strange inconsistency of his conduct. Might not a small modicum of self-knowledge have explained to him the truth of the matter? But he was blinded by those dazzling eyes, and saw no inconsistency in his words.

CHAPTER XIV.

HOW MR. EFFINGHAM STAINED HIS RUFFLES WITH BLOOD.

TEN minutes' ride brought him to Effingham Hall, and, throwing his bridle to a negro who ran forward to take it, he entered the hall. Supper was soon served, and Mr. Effingham was plied with questions as to his abrupt return, and moody state of mind. These questions were received with very little good-humor by the young man, who was in a furious ill-humor, and he was soon left to himself. The squire was not present, having some writing to do in the library, whither a cup of chocolate was sent him.

After supper Mr. Effingham sat down moodily, resting his feet on the huge grim-headed andirons, which shone brightly in the cheerful light thrown out by some blazing splinters, for the October evenings were becoming chilly. Miss Alethea, who sat sewing busily, after pouring out tea, endeavored in vain to extract a word from him.

Little Kate, who sat in the corner near Mr. Effingham, on her own little cricket, paused in the midst of her work—Carlo was going on bravely now—to ask cousin Champ what made him feel bad, and was he sick? The child was Mr. Effingham's favorite, and he was always ready to play with her; but on the present occasion he replied that he was not sick, and did not wish to be annoyed.

Kate looked much hurt, and Master Willie, who was pouring over a wonderful book of travels at the table, manifested some disapprobation, on hearing his future wife thus rudely addressed.

"You are not mad with me, cousin Champ?" said little Kate, piteously.

"No—no! I am angry with nobody," said Mr. Effingham, with some impatience, but more softly than before.

Kate, encouraged by these words, laid Carlo down, and pouring some perfume from a bottle into her hand, stole up to Mr. Effingham, and said:

"Oh, I know you've got a headache, cousin Champ! Let me put this on your forehead."

He would have refused, but the little face was so tender, and the small hand so soft, that he could not.

"I have no headache, Katy," he said, "I am only annoyed—no, I believe I am not even annoyed."

And rising abruptly, he said to a servant:

"Order my horse!"

The negro hastened out.

"Why, where in the world can you be going at this hour?" said Miss Alethea, writing busily.

Mr. Effingham either did not hear this question, or deigned to take no notice of it: a circumstance which caused Miss Alethea to toss her head, and preserve a dignified silence.

"Well! my horse?" he said, as the servant re-entered.

"Be round directly, sir,—I told Dick to be quick."

Kate stole up and took his hand.

"Cousin Champ," she said, "it is getting cold. Won't you wear my white comfort? I'll bring it in a minute."

"No, no! I don't need it."

Kate tip-toed, and whispered in his ear:

"I won't like cousin Clare, if she treats you badly."

"Foolish child! for heaven's sake let me alone!"

Then, seeing that the little face looked hurt and mortified, he added gloomily:

"I am not treated badly by any one, Kate: you attach too much importance to my moods. There: I had no intention of hurting your feelings, and I am not going to see anybody in particular."

"Did anybody ever!" said Miss Alethea, raising her hands. "Apologise to a child, when *my* questions are met with insult."

Mr. Effingham treated this apostrophe to the unknown personage, who finds himself called upon to express his sentiments on such astounding occasions, with profound disregard, and went out into the night. A servant held his horse, and he vaulted into the saddle, and set forward at a gallop—toward Williamsburg.

"That woman will be my fate!" he muttered, between his clenched teeth; and with a reckless laugh, "I see the abyss before me, and the mocking glances of the world are plain to me. I, a gentleman, to trouble myself about an actress! I suppose I will end by offering her my hand, and then comes the storm! Married to an actress!—for, by heaven, if I wish to do so, I will do so in spite of fire and tempest! They'll laugh when they read of my wedding—I see them now, leering and smiling, and giggling: the well-bred gentlemen wondering how I could throw myself away so,—the eligible young ladies intensely indignant, at—what? why, at the loss of a visitor and prospective husband. They would scout the idea, truly! but I defy them to deny it—a score of them. Marry an actress!—I am stamped with degradation for ever by it. Well, I'm not fool enough for that, quite yet; but every bound of this horse is a step in my fate. Let it be!"

And digging his spurs into the animal's sides, he fled on through the darkness like the wild huntsman; as furious and fast. The lights of the town soon rose on his sight, and clattering to the "Raleigh," he gave his horse in charge of an ostler, and repaired without brushing the dust from his clothes, or wiping the perspiration from his brow, to the theatre.

The play had commenced nearly an hour before, and it was with great difficulty that the young man—pushing by a number of ladies, his acquaintances—could reach the stage, upon which some dozen or more gentlemen were standing or seated. In the middle box, his excellency, the Governor, and his household, glittered in silk, embroidery and gold.

Just as he reached the stage, Juliet made her appearance in the garden. Beatrice was the very impersonation of the poet's conception—so tender, yet passionate; bold, yet fearful, were her looks and tones, her gestures, and whole rendering of the part. Her dewy eyes burned with a steady and yet changeable flame; were now veiled with thought, then radiant with passionate love, and like two moons, new risen, swayed the quick currents of the blood. The audience greeted her with enthusiastic applause, and Mr. Effingham saw that the favorable impression she had made on the previous night had now been much heightened.

In truth, nothing could be more splendid than her countenance, as she hastened to meet the nurse, bringing her news of her lover: and Mr. Effingham, spite of his agitation and gloom, could not help hanging on her words and glances, drinking in the music of her rare and wonderful voice with greedy ears. A bitter smile distorted his features, however; for with every burst of applause—and no opportunity was allowed by the audience to escape them—he felt more and more how insignificant he was to this young girl, applauded, caressed, overwhelmed with the intoxicating praise lavished on her from a thousand hands—the incense ascending in her honor there before him.

"What does she care for me!" he said, bitterly; "every body praises her—all are delighted—those fools, there, are devouring her with their eyes, and think her an angel of genius and beauty from the skies. I tear my heart in vain."

And with passionate anger Mr. Effingham grasped his breast, and dug his nails into the flesh, until they were stained with blood. The rich lace ruffle, rumpled and torn, revealed in its crimson stain the excess of his rage.

He made no reply to the laughing words addressed to him by his companions, and taking up a position almost behind the scenes, arrested Beatrice in her passage as she went out.

"You do not see me!" he said, abruptly.

"Good evening, sir," said Beatrice, calmly; "I was absorbed in my part."

And she endeavored to pass on.

"Stop," said Mr. Effingham, with a sneering laugh, "you are really too much in a hurry."

"I must look at my next speech, sir—I should have known it but for your interruption this morning."

"You hate me—do you not?" he said, clasping her arm.

"No, sir—please release me."

"Ah! you have merely contempt for me, madam."

"Mr. Effingham," said Beatrice, raising her head with cold dignity, "I despise no one. Your words are probably ironical, as you ask me, an actress, if I despise you, a wealthy gentleman; but I reply to you as if you were in earnest. Now, sir, I must go."

"Not until I have told you that you are a heartless and unfeeling woman—a nature of stone—a cold and unimpressible automaton!"

The young girl looked strangely at him.

"You have despised the honestly-offered courtesy of a man against whom you know nothing. Stop, madam! You have tormented me; yes, tormented me!—the humiliating truth will out!—tormented me by your coldness and contempt—destroyed my temper;—since seeing you I am another man, and a worse one. Look, my ruffle is rumpled and bloody—*your* nails tore my flesh!"

"Oh, sir!" cried the young girl, starting back in horror, "how could you——"

"A mere scratch, madam," said Mr. Effingham, bitterly, "and I used a mere figure of speech in saying that your hand inflicted it. You only caused it!"

"Mr. Effingham, you frighten me. I must go."

"You shall hear me."

"I must go, sir; listen, the audience are becoming impatient. Release my sleeve, sir," she said, coldly and firmly, again; and leaving him, she issued forth upon the stage, and with a voice as firm and steady as ever—so wonderful was her self-control—continued her character. As she passed out after the scene, Mr. Effingham in vain attempted to address her. Failing in this, he ground his teeth, and clutching a second time the unfortunate lace at his bosom, tore it into shreds. He turned, and almost rushed from the theatre. As he brushed through the box, he heard a little cry of astonishment, and a soft voice full of surprise said, "Mr. Effingham!" He turned, and his eyes met those of Clare, fixed on him with trouble and astonishment.

He bowed, said hurriedly something about regretting the necessity of his departure, and left the theatre just as the audience greeted the re-entrance of Beatrice with a burst of applause. He hastened to the "Raleigh," mounted his horse, and fled out into the dark night like a phantom, full of rage and despair, that joyous applause still ringing in his ears.

CHAPTER XV.

THE SAIL-BOAT "NANCY."

"HAVE you never, O friend, who now readest these unworthy lines, abandoned for a time your city life, with its noise and bustle, and eternal striving, and locking up with your ledgers, or your lawbooks, all thoughts of business, gone into that bright lowland, which the James flows proudly through, a band of silver wavering across a field of emerald? Have you never sought a sensation finer, emotions fresher, than city triumphs and delights—and, leaving for a time your absorbing cares and aspirations, trusted yourself to the current, like a bark, which takes no prescribed course, stops at no stated place, but suffers the wind and the stream to bear it whithersoever they will, well knowing that the wind cannot waft it, the tide cannot bear it, where the blue sky will not arch above, the fresh, waving woods will not mirror their tall trunks and fine foliage in the serene surface? Have you never sailed along that majestic river, with its sentinel pines, and wood-embowered mansions, and bright ripples breaking into foam, when the west wind, blowing freshly, strikes against the tide, surging for ever from the sea? Go, on an October day, when the white clouds are shattered by the breezes of the Atlantic—those breezes still redolent with the perfumes of the tropics,—and telling of their long travel over lands of unimagined beauty and undreamed-of splendor—go on one of those clear, sunny days of the early autumn, when the waters ripple like molten silver agitated by the breath of the Deity; when trees are crimson, and blue, and golden, like the myriad silken banners which erewhile flouted the deep heaven before Tamerlane; when the wave laps upon the shore, and silences the whisper of the pines with its monotonous and dreamy music; where the water-fowl sleep upon the surge, or extend their broad wings above the glittering foam, to strike the quick-darting prey their keen eyes have descried;—go on some day when the white sail of some sea-bound bark bellies in the wind, and her prow cuts the silver, dashing into foam the bright sunlit waters; or when glorying in the fine season, and in his momadic, careless lot, the fisherman spreads his small lateen sail, and feels his bark bound beneath him like a sea-gull tossed upon the waves—when, trusting to Providence to guide his course, he drops the paddle he has been plying, carelessly, and with closed eyes, dreams in the broad sunlight of the past and future. Go, on one of these days, and gliding over the swaying billows of the great stream, see if there is not yet some fresh delight in this our human life—

a poetry and romance unstifled in the heart! On such a day did Beatrice Hallam leave the town of Williamsburg, with her father, and bend her steps toward the stream."

Thus far, the author of the MS., in that rhetorical and enthusiastic style which every where characterizes his works. Let us descend from the heights of apostrophe and declamation to the prose of simple narrative.

Beatrice had received the assurance of her father, that she should spend a day upon the waters, with a delight which may readily be imagined. She was a pure child of the wilderness, in spite of the eternal claims which an artificial civilization, an inexorable convention, laid to her time and thoughts. She rejoiced in the forest, and on the hills: —we have seen her riding out fearlessly to drink in the fresh splendor of the autumn—now she anticipated a delightful day upon the river. Mr. Effingham would not be there, with his insulting advances, his intolerable drawl, his irritating airs of superiority and patronage. She would have the whole day to herself. She had no performance to neglect —no rehearsal to go to. She was free for the day wholly.

Beatrice was an excellent rider, and she chose this mode of reaching the river, in preference to the light calash, which the manager suggested. The good-humored old fellow yielded at once, and mounting a stout cob, instead of installing his corpulent person in the comfortable vehicle, they set forth—the young girl riding her favorite white horse. They reached the bank of the stream without incident, and found the boatman, to whom a message had been sent on the night before, ready to receive them. He gathered up his fishing lines with the ease of a practised hand, placed in the pocket of his peajacket the inseparable black flask of rum, and led the way to his little vessel. It was one of those light and airy barks, which obey the hand of the helmsman, as the body of the seabird runs with the movement of the wings, or turns obedient to the red, webbed feet; and soon it was gliding over the water, borne onward by a fresh wind, which filled the small triangular sail, toward the fishing ground.

Beatrice, with clasped hands and dancing eyes, drank in the splendor of the beautiful day. Her cheeks filled with blood, her parted lips assumed an inexpressible softness and delight—she was free as the bright water, and rejoiced like an Indian once more in his native wilds!—never had she looked more beautiful, more fascinating. She laughed, ran on with childlike merriment in her voice and eyes; dipped her fingers with affected shivering in the foam before the prow, and startled the wild sea-gulls with her cries and laughter. She was a child again, and the manager said as much to her.

"Oh!" cried the young girl, her whole countenance radiant with joy aud pleasure, "you can't think, father, how happy I feel out here on the water!" I'm nothing but a child, you know, and I always shall be. Look at that bird with the white wings; how he darts over the waves!"

The manager smiled.

"It's a shame to keep you where there are any houses, child," he said, "you are never half as happy as this—in London, or any where."

"I can't be, sir."

"Why?"

"Oh, I feel so cramped where people are. They stare at me, and make me feel badly; and often when I pass, I hear them say who I am, and laugh."

"That's because you act well."

"Oh, don't talk about acting now, father, please. I don't want to think of it. I'm so happy! Look at the pretty foam!"

"Yes—you love the water."

"Oh, dearly! you didn't know how I spent the evenings on the ocean, while you were playing ombre with Captain Fellowes."

"Commander of the merchant-vessel 'Charming Sally,'" laughed the manager; "but how about your evenings?"

"Oh, I used to go and lean over the—what are they called?"

"Bulwarks."

"Yes, the bulwarks. I used to lean over, and look at the foam, and the great fish tumbling about in the moonlight, for hours It was delightful!"

The fresh face lit up with a childlike delight, as the young girl spoke.

"Very romantic," said Mr. Hallam, smiling.

"Oh, I'm not romantic, sir, I'm the most matter-of-fact person in the world, but I couldn't help liking the foam."

"You are right—but we old fellows like tictac better than moonlight thinking."

"Yes—I used to think: I recollect I did think."

"What of?"

"Of the beautiful land we were coming to—Virginia: the *Virgin Land*, they called it. How pretty that sounds!"

"Yes."

"A fresh, bright land, where the wind was always blowing, the trees always full of leaves and flowers, and no cold winter to chill one."

"A young poet!"

"No, no, father—I must have been born in the south, though. Oh, tell me where I was born. You never told me."

The manager looked somewhat embarrassed, and replied, after a moment's silence: "We were at Malta, then, I believe. But how did you find Virginia in reality?"

The young girl's face assumed a sorrowful expression, and she replied: "Not very different from England, sir; but it is pretty, the forest and all, and this river. Oh!" she cried suddenly, "look at that bird carrying off the fish in his talons—stop, sir, stop!"

Mr. Hallam laughed heartily. "What would they say if they heard *Juliet* calling after a sea-bird so. Mr. Effingham would not believe the account."

"Oh, father!" said Beatrice, returning to her sorrowful expression, "do not talk to me of playing to-day, I feel so happy now, sir; and don't speak of that wild young man; I shall get angry, and then be sorry, and cry—and you know, father, that would spoil our day. Don't speak of Mr. Effingham; he looked at me so, last night, with his eyes on fire, and his frill crumpled and torn—I thought it was stained with blood."

"With blood!"

"He became angry with me for not attending to him on the stage, in the last act, and clutched his breast with his nails. Oh, don't speak of him," she added, growing gloomy, "I do not like that man."

"Well, well," said the manager, "don't think too hard

of him; he is young, and means nothing. I wish you to marry well, much as I will lose in you; and you may find a mate in Virginia. There, don't look so distressed."

"I don't want to marry!" said Beatrice, her face clouded over.

"You don't like playing?"

"Oh, no! but I have you, father, and I don't wish to part from you. I can bear all."

"There now, dear, don't lose your bright smiles, and spoil the day. We will talk no more of these matters. Sink the theatre!" added the manager good-humoredly, "we came out to fish."

"At the ground, squire," said the boatman. "Go it. I'll keep the craft straight."

And soon the bright fish were being drawn up from the water in numbers which would have afforded delight to Isaac Walton, much as that worthy gentleman dwelt upon brook-sides and art in snaring the solitary trout. They spent the greater part of the morning thus, and Beatrice forgot her gloom completely.

About noon the wind began to grow fresher, and large clouds rolled themselves up from the western horizon, and spread their dark curtain over the sun. The boatman looked at them with an experienced eye, then turning to the manager, said: "Look here, squire; seems to me we're goin' to have a storm. Them clouds look like it; and hear the wind!"

In fact the forest on each side of the river began to toss its boughs and roll aloft that wild, surging sound which the wind wakes up in its passage through tall trees. The pines waved in the chill blast, and roared like great organs; and in addition to these threatening sounds, the waves began to roll higher, tossing the little bark like a nutshell, and sprinkling the white lateen sail with snowy foam.

"I believe you are right, and we had better get to shore."

"We're a mile from the cabin, squire, but this west wind will carry us down like a flash. Must I tie the sail?"

"Oh, let's wait a little, father," cried Beatrice, with animated looks and bright eyes, "the wind is so grand. Oh, don't tie the sail yet!"

"The wind'll tear it to tatters if it keeps crackin' it so, miss," said the boatman; "but I'm willin', for I'm goin' to do all I'm wanted to do. I ain't goin' to deny your pretty face any thing."

With which words the honest boatman laid down tranquilly in the stern of the bark, and—first taking a pull at his black flask—applied himself to the task of keeping the craft before the wind. Mr. Hallam had yielded to this arrangement, but was plainly desirous of returning immediately. He opened his mouth to say as much, but Beatrice interrupted him before he could speak.

"Oh, listen, father!" she cried, starting up and steadying herself by clinging to the slight mast; "listen to the woods! The wind roars through them like the cannon we heard at Dover! How sublime it sounds! And look at the waves; they are beginning to grow black, I believe, and they toss us about like a cork! Oh, how the wind sobs and rolls along! It makes me so happy!"

"Take care, miss!" said the boatman; "that mast is unsteady."

"Oh, don't be afraid for me."

"Come, let us get to shore at once," said Mr. Hallam, becoming really alarmed.

"That's easy, sir," said the boatman; "with the sail up the wind'll carry us down in a jiffy. Don't be afraid of upsetting. The Nancy never served me such a trick, and won't now, though there *is* a wind, squire; it's coming worse, too, but there's no danger."

And he caught the rope, which the wind was cracking as a man cracks a whip, and, with a vigorous hand, secured it to the gunwale. The effect was instantaneous. The little bark, which before had merely danced about on the waves, now shot down the stream like lightning, cleaving the waves which struck it, and shipping clouds of foam.

Beatrice hailed this accession of speed with delight. Her ardent and impressible nature rejoiced in the hurly-burly of the wind, the speed of the bark, the foam of the high waves wetting her at every instant.

"Oh, it's delightful, father!" she cried. "I could shout for joy! Look at that little boat, there, with the man in it so quiet and easy—it jumps about like a dry leaf!"

The boat, indeed, which the young girl was looking at, did seem to be of no more strength than a leaf. It was a frail little canoe, scarcely large enough it seemed to hold a child, and beautifully built. The sides were painted with great taste, and the prow ran up in a curving point, which dashed aside the foaming water like a steel blade. In the stern of the canoe a young man was seated, holding in his hand a paddle, with which he both propelled and guided the skiff on its path toward the shore. The young man seemed to be no stranger to such storms as the present, and, without paying any attention to the foam which broke over him, looked intently at the sail-boat.

"Oh, how it darts!" cried Beatrice; "look, the wind struck it then, and it jumped out of the water!"

"Take care, miss!" cried the boatman; "if she veers you'll fall overboard!"

"Take care, my daughter!" echoed Mr. Hallam; "there is a tremendous gust of wind coming right down. Get down!"

"Steady!" cried the boatman; "this is a roarer; take care of the mast, miss! Sit down!"

It was too late. Beatrice made a movement to obey, but before she had regained her seat, and while she yet clung to the mast, the frail pole bent beneath the powerful blast, the sail almost doubled up, and the spar snapping like a reed, precipitated the young girl into the stream. A huge wave bore her ten feet from the bark in an instant, and, passing over her, swallowed the fair form in its gloomy depths. The fat manager was struck motionless with horror, and the boatman, dropping his paddle, leaped into the stream. But another saviour was before him. The young man in the skiff had approached within a stone's throw of the sail-boat, when the gust struck her, and his canoe was darting directly across the wake of the bark when the mast snapped. At the same moment he seemed to have recognized the young woman—and, uttering an exclamation which was drowned in the shrill blast, threw himself into the waves, and catching her half-submerged form as she rose, struck out with the ease of a practised swimmer.

Beatrice was a dead weight on his arm, and he soon felt that exhaustion which the strongest swimmer experiences, struck every moment in the face by surges strong enough to ingulf a giant. The boatman, swimming with the wind and foam blinding him, could not come to his assistance—the two forms struggled with the devouring waves in vain—a huge billow passed over the young man's head, and he sank, clasping to his heart the chill form of the girl. As he rose for the last time, one of those providences which watch over us, giving the lie to chance, was the means of his salvation. His shoulder struck against the boat, which had been swept to the spot by the wind; and, as he caught its gunwale, he felt the body of the young girl weigh less upon him. He was taken into the sail-boat, he knew not how—he saw a woman whom he had saved lying lifeless before him—a rude boatman chafing her temples—a corpulent man weeping and still grasping a billet of wood with which he had plunged into the waves—and then he fell exhausted, overcome.

The first words which he heard when he came to himself, were:

"Well, squire, she's all right now: only a little wetting. Here we are at neighbour Waters', and that's his son, that saved the young woman."

CHAPTER XVI.

SEQUEL TO THE ADVENTURE.

THE fat manager did not know whether to laugh or weep. She was saved! that was all he was conscious of; and he scarcely knew how he got on shore. Beatrice, who had by this time revived wholly, though she still shivered with cold and terror, was borne to dry land by the strong boatman; and the rest following, the whole party was safe from the storm, which raged more furiously still, at thus being forced to give up its prey.

Before them rose a rough but comfortable cottage, which from its bluff, overlooked the river up and down for miles. A walk of ten minutes brought them to the door, and within a cheerful fire was burning, apparently made necessary by the high and exposed situation of the house. The boatman deposited, we may almost say, the young girl on a comfortable chair. She had been supported from the landing between the honest fellow and her father—the young man walking in silence before.

After thus getting rid of his charge, the boatman turned to greet the owner of the mansion, saying:

"Well, neighbour Waters, here's a mess!—the young lady's been overboard and nigh gone."

The host was an old man of sixty-five or more: in every thing about him, the simplicity of his nature was manifest. His open features were almost constantly lit up by a cheerful smile, and his eyes were full of kindness and good-humor. He was clad as the humbler class were almost universally at that day—in a broad-skirted coat of drab cloth, with plain cuffs, but turned back after the fashion of the time: his stockings were of wool, and his waistcoat was of plain serge, with large pockets, and reaching almost to the knees. On his feet he wore heavy, thick-soled shoes; and his gray hair, gathered in a club behind, was free from powder.

To the boatman's address, he replied, cheerily:

"Overboard! how so, neighbor Townes? and in your craft? I never hearn tell of such a thing happenin' to you before. The pretty bird! we must see how to fix her. Sit down, sir: sit down—your daughter, I reckon. Well, well, this is a bad day to be on the water. How does the young lady feel now?"

Beatrice had profited by the cheering blaze, and replied quietly, though with a slight shiver:

"I am a great deal better than I was, sir: I owe you many thanks for your kindness,"

"No kindness in the world," said the old man, "I'm poor and simple, but you're heartily welcome."

"Poor and simple as you say you are, neighbor," here broke in the boatman, "there ain't a squire about here equal to you: and I've been knowin' you this thirty years: and Charley," here he looked at the young man, who had taken his seat in silence, "Charley is a chip of the old block. Ef it hadn't been for him, the young lady'd a been at Davy Jones' locker by now."

"Why, did Charley?"

"Yes, he did so, neighbor; he saved the young 'ooman.

As for me, I'm most nigh 'shamed to say it, but the wind and foam blinded me."

"Well, well—it's what Charley ought 'a done, and there's an end on it. Now we'll see to a room for you, miss," he said to Beatrice; "you musn't move to-day. I don't know you, but you're welcome to any thing old John Waters owns."

"You are very kind, Mr. Waters," said the fat manager, who had been looking around him, "but we had better get back to town. Our horses are down at your house, friend," he added, to the boatman; "couldn't you bring 'em here?"

"Easiest thing in life. Jest give me time to swallow a drop; and that puts me in mind, won't you take somethin' yourself, 'squire, and the young lady? Neighbor Waters drinks nothing but water—he don't."

Mr. Manager Hallam received this proposal with extreme satisfaction, and no doubt reflecting that it was just "what the great Congreve" would have done—a favorite authority with him—emptied nearly half a pint. Beatrice, however, refused the rum, with a shake of her head.

"Now, I'll take Sam, neighbor," said the boatman, "and jog down. There's Lanky onhitchin' him. 'Seems to me the sooner I am back the better."

"Yes, yes; and there's a pistole," said Mr. Hallam.

The boatman received the money doubtfully, hesitated, then pocketed it; finally, mounting Sam, a rough-looking cart-horse, harness and all, clattered off through the whirling leaves of the forest toward his cabin.

"But you ain't goin' to take the young lady away so soon," said old John Waters; "she'll catch the agy, friend. We'll have a room for her—the little place up there—fixed in no time. Lanky's just come from town, and will make a blazing fire."

"I think we had better get back," said Hallam, uneasily; "eh, daughter?"

"Yes, sir; I feel quite strong now, and would like to ride. I never can thank you, sir, and—and your son, enough for what you have done. He saved my life."

"Oh," laughed the old fisherman, "that's his place—you're a weak little thing, and couldn't be expected to take keer of yourself—not a strong woman, either; only a little easy-livin' lady."

"Oh no, sir," said Beatrice, with her lip twitching, "I am only an actress."

"An actress!—what's that? Oh—"

"My name is Beatrice Hallam," said the young girl, regaining her calmness.

"Well! did any one ever!" said the old man, "the young lady that played!—I heard all about you, the other day, and made Charley go to see the playin': and he said a heap in your favor. Charley, you know," said the old fellow, with a smile, "aint much given to these things—and I 'most fear he hurts his health over his books—look through the door, there what a parcel! He works hard, too, in the field, and helps me with the seine, but he's been studyin' too much lately. I told him so: and says I, 'Charley, you'd better go to town and take some rest: go and see the players.' At first he wouldn't hear of it; but he went, and praised you a heap, I can tell you, Miss; though I'm bound to say he didn't say much in favor of young Squire Effin'ham."

Beatrice flushed to her forehead, and stole a glance at the young man. He rose, and seeming to banish with an effort the thoughts which preoccupied his mind, said, in a grave and serious voice:

"I confess, Miss Hallam, that your acting was faultless, as far as I could judge of it; and my father has not misunderstood my opinion of Mr. Effingham's very unworthy conduct toward yourself. But let us dismiss all these matters—you must be greatly fatigued, and not much disposed to listen to conversation. We are very poor, here, as you see, but can give you, and you also, Mr. Hallam, shelter for the night. Remain."

Beatrice gazed a moment furtively at the noble and thoughtful face, allowed the last sound of the clear voice to die away, then replied:

"We had better return, sir—indeed, we should not refuse your kindness, I know: but—"

"Yes, we must return: you have not dried your own clothes even, sir," said the manager, "and we are under sufficient obligation for one day. You saved my daughter's life, sir—God reward you."

"I did nothing but what I should have done, Mr. Hallam. My father has told you that it was my simple duty, and there was little risk. Had there been real risk, I trust I should still have done my duty."

"I know you would, Charley," said the old man proudly, "you'd throw your life away for a child: and I rather think Mr. Effingham would a had a hard time, if you had met after the play!"

"Come—come, father," said the young man, gravely, "do not repeat my follies. I have repented it. Harsh words do no good."

"If what you said was true, he deserved 'em and more," said old Waters: "you can't deny it!"

"Well, yes! he deserved harsh comment! you are right!" said the young man, his face flushing, "for he insulted and annoyed a woman. We cannot go far wrong in saying that the man who annoys a woman or a child, must have a bad heart, and ungenerous and narrow soul!"

The young man's voice, ordinarily grave and simple, changed, as he uttered these words: and his flushed face positively overawed the fat manager, who, feeling his own character of *pater familias* indirectly called in question, was about to speak, and ask Beatrice the particulars of Mr. Effingham's conduct. His tone was so firm and proud—his eye so clear and full of disdain—his attitude so erect and noble, as he uttered these words, that the wide apartment, with its fishing-nets, and rough chairs and tables, seemed to grow brilliant and imposing—mind penetrating matter, and transforming it to its own likeness.

Beatrice Hallam felt her face fill with blood, her heart throb: for the first time in her life she had found the nature which heaven had moulded in the form of her own, and when the young man, apparently regretting his excitement, momentary as it was, returned in silence to his seat, her lustrous glances, brilliant as light itself, but dimmed by a haze of emotion, followed him, and could not withdraw themselves from him.

A few moments afterwards, the boatman returned with the horses, and the manager, who began to feel some embarrassment, rose to go.

"We've treated you very bad considerin'," said the old man, "but the fire here was about the best thing for you, I thought, after the wettin'. Lanky's makin' the fire now for the young lady: but 'sides that, we had in the way o' clothes nothin' much better 'n a peajacket to offer her, and you said the rum was the best thing for *you* after the wettin'."

"All I wanted—all I wanted, sir," said the manager, with a good-humored laugh.

"And I am nearly quite dry now, sir," said Beatrice, with a timid smile; "I shall never forget your kindness to me, Mr. Waters."

And she pressed with her small fingers the huge, hearty hand of the old fisherman, and then held out the same little hand to his son, who pressed it with a sensation at his heart which he could not understand.

"Strange!" he said, as they turned away, "I seem to have met this young girl in some other world—will, well, the common fancy!"

And following Beatrice to the door, he assisted her to mount—which operation was somewhat embarrassed by the long riding dress, brought with the horses from the boatman's cabin—after which the guests set forward toward Williamsburg.

"Waters—Waters? I seem to have heard that name before, father," said Beatrice, "and really seem to have known Mr. Charles."

"It's a very common name," replied the manager, "and we often find these resemblances. How the evening has cleared off. I don't think any rain has fallen; the storm must have passed off to the southward."

Whether Mr. Manager Hallam wished to turn the conversation or not, remains a mystery: but if such was his design, it succeeded perfectly, and Beatrice began to talk about the adventures through which they had passed. Soon the houses of the town came in sight, and they passed along, and drew up before the "Raleigh."

Beatrice changed her wet garments, and felt no bad effects from her accident beyond a slight chill. One would have said that the warmth at her heart vivified her person, and defied the chilly waters of the river. All that evening, while the fat manager was relating the adventures of the day, she sat studying, apparently; but merely her dreamy eyes were fixed upon the page.

Of what was she thinking, and why that flush upon the tender face, that light in the veiled eyes?

CHAPTER XVII.

MR. EFFINGHAM MAKES A FRIENDLY CALL.

On the next morning, just as Beatrice was binding up her hair before the single mirror of her small sitting-room, she heard a knock at the door, and answering, " Come in," she saw through the open door Mr. Champ Effingham, who entered the apartment with a smile.

" Ah, good morning, charming Miss Beatrice ! " he said, with a pleased air, too elaborate indeed not to be somewhat affected ; " how is your ladyship to-day ? "

Beatrice uttered a sigh of despair, with which no little irritation was commingled. She, however, remembered the wish her father had expressed, that she should not receive her visitor harshly, and this consideration silenced the haughty reply which rose to her lips, though it could not subdue the flash in her proud, brilliant eye.

" I am very well, sir," she said.

" For which reason," replied Mr. Effingham, playing with his ruffle, and sitting down languidly, " you receive me very ill."

" No, sir ; my reception is neither the one nor the other ; but you have no right to expect a very friendly reception."

" Why not friendly ? "

" Can you ask, sir ! "

" Certainly."

" I have nothing to reply, then, sir."

" Ah, ah ! " said Mr. Effingham, first smoothing the feather in his cocked hat, then negligently playing with the bright hilt of his short sword ; " ah, you are thinking about my naughty behavior in the theatre the other evening."

" I have forgotten all, sir," she said calmly.

" Well, well, I have come to-day to ask your ladyship to pardon these various exhibitions of ill-humor. My unfortunate ruffle, which you, no doubt, observed, had suffered somewhat in the *melée*, proved to me the next morning that I must have been rather violent. The fact is, I was in a bad humor—out of temper—a most mortifying acknowledgment for a star of fashion and nonchalance like myself; but still true."

Beatrice made no reply.

"Granted! I *was* out of sorts—nervous, in a bad humor; but, this morning, I am in a delightful state of mind. I feel as if I could embrace the whole world, yourself included, with the most fraternal and enthusiastic regard. Am I not in an enviable state of mind? But this is nothing to you. Ah! you take very little interest in my welfare. I am really afraid, and have not forgiven, as such a lovely saint should, what I have been guilty of. Come, my charming Miss Beatrice, exert your amiability, and pardon all."

Beatrice, with her quick eye, easily discerned the painful emotion beneath this raillery—the fire concealed beneath the ashes. For a moment she hesitated, then said:

"I am not revengeful or unforgiving, sir, and the painful ordeal you subjected me to in the theatre is already forgotten. Now, sir, I must go to rehearsal."

"Bah! don't be in a hurry, Beatrice, and, above all, don't *pity* me; I am not a man to be pitied; and, as to rehearsal, that can wait a little, while we have a short conversation. You have a charming voice, and this morning I am really wearied to death. Come, amuse me."

"I have no time to converse, sir; I must leave you."

"Come, come: don't be so unamiable—you may go directly!"

Beatrice sat down, with a sigh of resignation, instead of leaving the room, as she felt tempted to do. Her father's wish made her patient.

"Where were you yesterday?"

"We went to the river, sir, for a sail."

"To the James?"

"Yes, sir."

"Why did you not send me word?"

"Send you word—why, sir?"

"Why, my new sailboat is just launched, and we might have had a delightful day in her."

"We had a very good one."

"Any adventures?"

"I fell into the river, sir."

"The devil! And how did you get to land?"

"A gentleman rescued me."

"A gentleman—who, in heaven's name?"

Beatrice felt her face flush, half with embarassment—half with anger, at this persevering cross-examination. For a moment she hesitated; but her frank and fearless nature made her reply almost instantly,

"Mr. Charles Waters, sir."

"Charles Waters!" cried Mr. Effingham, with a sudden pallor, and a flash of the eye, which revealed the volcano beneath his affected carelessness.

"Mr. Charles Waters," said Beatrice, calmly and firmly, "to him I am indebted for my existence, at this moment."

A flush of hatred passed over Mr. Effingham's brow, and he said, with a sneer:

"Ah, your cavalier! I had forgotten, Madam."

Beatrice felt her heart throb with anger, and a scornful answer arose to her lips: but she repressed these evidences of feeling, and said coldly:

"Mr. Effingham, I will not exchange another word with you, if I am to be insulted thus. Mr. Waters is, as you well know, almost a perfect stranger to me, and I am nothing to him:" with which the lip trembled: "he saved my life yesterday, at the peril of his own, and I owe to him deep gratitude. For this reason, sir, you will understand that I am not the proper sympathizer with your dissatisfaction. Now, sir, I must go."

Mr. Effingham made a powerful effort over himself, and burst into a laugh which was painful to hear.

"Well, well," he said, in a voice which he in vain endeavored to render careless and easy, "we won't quarrel about the Chevalier Waters. I'm sure I am very much obliged to him for restoring to the community so charming an actress; though, as I always had a partiality for heroism, especially being heroic myself, when nothing was to be lost by it, I regret that the present grand effort was not made by myself. Come! don't burn me with your eyes."

"I must go, sir."

"Without pardoning my naughty treatment of you in the theatre? Wasn't it horrible?"

"Yes, sir!" said Beatrice, flushing; "it was unmanly."

"Striking coincidence of opinion, at least. Yes, it was dreadful; and do you know what occurred when I was making my exit, right of centre?—that is the phrase, I believe —why, I very nearly ran over a young lady with whom I am dead in love."

Beatrice looked at the young man with a strange expression. Had she met with a real life actor superior to herself?

"Just so," continued Mr. Effingham, bursting into laughter; "my *chère amie*, you know—one of the most beautiful, highborn, and wealthy young girls in the colony; pretty, fair hair, blue eyes, and all that—just opposed to your style. Did you see her?"

"No, sir," said Beatrice.

"Well, you might have done so. I'm certain she saw you, and possibly had a view of the attack upon my ruffles, when I accidentally scratched myself, you know. In going out, I placed my foot upon her dress, and nearly tore a furbelow away. What horrible awkwardness! I shall never forgive myself."

"Your tone is bitter, sir."

"Bitter? Not at all! I am ready to laugh now, reflecting on the melodrama. After the affair of the furbelow, the hero made his exit—myself, that is to say—and then I rode quietly away, accomplishing the first ten miles in fifteen minutes, I believe."

"Mr. Effingham, you seem to me to be laboring under some bitter emotion; you shock me. If you love a lady, do not, sir, do not abandon her for me. I know not what I say, sir,—I only know that you banish all sunshine from my life. I have not enough to spare, sir. For heaven's sake, leave me."

"You are right," said Mr. Effingham, losing his forced gayety, "I am carried away by my infatuation—I love you."

"Sir! you must not—"

"Bah!" he said, gloomily; "don't let us mince matters."

"I must go, sir."

"Not before giving me one word not altogether harsh."

"I must go, sir—"

"Beatrice Hallam, you are the most bitter and unreasonable of women. You choose to despise me, because I seek you; you are not only unreasonable, you are a woman without heart!"

Beatrice suppressed her emotion, and said:

"No, sir; that is unjust. I am not a woman without heart—I have feelings, deep feelings.'

"I have never discovered them."

"You do not know me, sir."

"Ah, you mistake, madam; I know you well."

"For heaven's sake, go, sir."

"I prefer remaining."

"I must then leave you, sir."

Mr. Effingham rose with a threatening gesture; but, collecting himself, sat down again.

"Ah, madam," he said, with gloomy bitterness; "you are very prudish: you hate me—Mr. Charles Waters takes you in his arms—I cannot approach you."

"Sir!" said Beatrice, indignantly, "I avoid you, because I feel that you are not a proper companion for me. No, sir! I am not prudish—I am no silly girl. My life has been hard and changeable—my fate adverse. I have embraced the profession of the stage from necessity. My father was an actor. I am an actress because I am his daughter. As an actress, I know that I am exposed to a thousand temptations, and a thousand insults. I know very well that we are considered the bond slaves of the public, especially of the aristocratic portion. But I will not accept the questionable attentions of yourself, or any other young gentleman, who is trained to look upon me, and upon persons of my profession as infinitely beneath him—as so many slaves. No, sir! I have chosen to go and exhibit myself in public, that the bread I eat may be honestly procured. After the theatre, I am a woman, and I will not have my name tossed from mouth to mouth unworthily—remember, sir."

The young girl looked so lovely at that moment—her beautiful eyes flashed such vivid lightning—her rosy face was so eloquent with indignation, that Mr. Effingham found words fail him—lost in, overwhelmed as he was by, her splendid and fiery beauty.

"You are a strange actress," he said at length, in a low, deep-toned voice, "and certainly unlike any other I have ever seen. Yes, I have seen many actresses, in France, Italy, England, every where, and I find in you nothing like them. Well: you say you are no common comedienne, and you see that I agree with you. You hint that I would be apt to abuse any friendship you granted me—I do not say you are wrong there. There is some truth in your views, and I find no fault with you. But, at least, I should not scoff at you:—I might bless you, or only mention your name with a curse upon my lip—but I do not think I could do aught else. For you are not indifferent to me. You smile: you think I am very inconsistent. But when I say that I can never treat your name as that of an indifferent woman, I mean this: I mean that from our first meeting in the forest, near the Hall yonder, your image has dwelt in my mind and heart—or if not quite in my heart, to be frank, at least in my memory. At the theatre we met again, and I treated you as gentlemen are accustomed to treat actresses; for I laughed at my feelings. You received that treatment as became you—you are a noble girl—and I went away cursing and loving you almost. I spent a bad night after the play, and worse since—I came here to-day to jeer at you. In place of further jeering, I bow to you, and offer you respect and admiration, if not love, and ask your friendship in return."

Beatrice betrayed some feeling at these earnest words, and no longer looked at the young man so disdainfully.

"I have listened to you, sir," she said, "and I request you to pardon any harshness in what I have but now said. But, let me here say, what you will feel to be true, and no less true than unchangeable—that there can be nothing in common between us. You cannot be my friend—visiting and talking unreservedly with me as friends may—without causing a scandal in the Colony:—a scandal which will be as injurious to yourself as to me. Now, sir, you had better leave me. We may meet again—indeed, I have it not in my power to refuse to meet you—in the theatre. This is not an invitation, for I say again, there cannot and must not be any thing in common between an actress, like myself, and Mr. Effingham. Good evening, sir."

Mr. Effingham stood looking at the young woman in silence, with an expression upon his countenance which she could not understand. At last he said, with a pale lip, and very abruptly:

"Are you acting?"

"No, sir!" said the young girl, indignantly.

"Then you are a prodigy of truth and nobleness," he said, with a lightning-like glance. "Come, come, let me throw aside all this sophistry with which I am trying to deceive myself. I love you!" he said, gloomily.

The young girl drew back.

'You shall love me in return!" he said.

And there was so much haughtiness in his tone that her cheek flushed.

"You are consistent, sir," she said; "just now, your regard for me was slight, you said—at least, I thought so."

"As you please—I do not know whether I love you or not, and am sure I love another. But what I do know is, that there is something about you, which tears me from all else toward you, my beautiful diabolical syren!"

"Mr. Effingham, you really seem to have grown mad: let our interview end here."

"I am mad, and it is you who have driven me crazy. Beatrice! mine is a family of fiery traits—we love or hate strongly, and do nothing by halves. I am not unlike my ancestors. Look at me! I am a *petit maître*—exhausting my life in idleness and ease. Why? Because I need some great passion. Now I have opened my breast to you, and I add, that you will be my passion."

"Mr. Effingham, dismiss all thought of me. I am an actress, sir—an actress: my associates are players, those who are now waiting for me yonder, sir—no other persons: a barrier is raised between me and the world, by my profession. For the hundredth time, I say we can have nothing in common. Even now your presence is causing discussion in the room below, and rude lips jeer me. Oh, sir! leave me, for heaven's sake! If you have any regard for me, go, and end this trying interview!"

He gazed at her for a moment in silence, and then, putting his hat on, left the room, full of gloomy rage, but with a sneering lip. Ten minutes afterwards he left the town.

CHAPTER XVIII.

THE MAN IN THE RED CLOAK.

JUST as Mr. Champ Effingham left Williamsburg, by the western road—his splendid animal careering at full gallop in obedience to his rider's spur—a young man entered the town from the south on foot, and directed his steps toward the Raleigh Tavern. He soon reached the long platform in front of the inn, and entered the ordinary.

He was about to address some question to the portly landlord, when turning his eyes to the opposite side of the room, he saw seated in one of the large leathern chairs, a man whose face seemed to excite some slumbering thought in his mind, for he passed his hand over his brow, and seemed to question his memory. This man, who was reading the last issue of the "Virginia Gazette" with some interest, seemed to be verging on thirty, and did not appear to be above the rank of what then were called yeomen. His crisp hair was curled up beneath the ears, outwardly: his mouth had in it a world of character, though it was rather stern: and his forehead, very broad and high, was tanned and freckled. He was clad in coarse leather breeches, leggings, a long fustian waistcoat, and coat of shaggy cloth, without a particle of ornament, then almost universal in the costume of gentlemen. Over his shoulders was hung loosely an old red cloak, and his slouch hat lay by him on the rude pine table.

The new comer took in all these details with a single glance, and was about to turn away, when, raising his eyes, the stranger saw him looking at him.

He rose, and extended a hard, brown hand, saying:

"Ah, sir! good-day, I believe we are acquaintances, though I fear you have forgotten me."

"No sir," said the new comer, "I recognized you at once."

"Because you found me an agitator of ideas, like yourself on our last meeting—which I believe was also our first. You will recollect we met some days since near the Capitol, when Parson Tag took politely from your hand the 'Gazette,' you had just purchased 'to look at it,' he said: in return for which courtesy you gave him some original ideas."

"I did not obtrude them," said his companion, calmly, "he questioned me, and I replied."

"Yes, and he treated your crudities, as he called them, with well-bred contempt, when he found an opportunity to turn his back on you."

"I was not offended, sir. He had a perfect right to turn to those gentlemen who bowed to him."

"Offended! I should say that would be a loss of time with a parson, not to mention the deadly sin." As he uttered these words, a grim curl of the lip betrayed the irony of the speaker.

"The fact is," he added, "you gave him, as I said, some original views on the subject of education; and he did not seem to relish them from a gentleman clad, like yourself, in drab and fustian."

"Well, well, sir," said the other, "perhaps he was right. Men of my class are not generally worth listening to on matters of policy, as I feel I am not—he is a cultivated scholar."

"Bah!" said the man in the red cloak, good-humoredly, "mind is mind, sir, and it matters little whether the frame be covered with fustian or cut velvet, the head with a gold-laced hat or a slouch, like mine there; the man, weak or strong, remains."

His companion felt again the strange influence of that voice, at once careless and earnest, laughing and grave; a singular sympathy seemed to have already sprung up between these two men, spite of their acquaintance of yesterday.

"Now," said the stranger, wrapping his old cloak about his shoulders, "I find in you a thinking man—you scarcely reflect about classes and dresses, I venture to say. You have walked far this morning?" he added.

"Yes, that is, some miles," replied the young man, somewhat at a loss to understand this abrupt question.

"You are dusty."

"Yes; the sand is dry."

"Well, did you think of that dust as you came along?"

"I believe not, my thoughts were elsewhere."

"Good, that is what I mean. The squire riding in his coach has his book, or takes his nap; you can't read or nap walking—the consequence? why you must think."

The young man sat down to rest; that coarse yet musical voice drew him in spite of himself.

"It remains to tell me what you were thinking of as you came along, friend," added the stranger; "come, let us talk unreservedly. Let us clash our minds together, and see if some sparks do not spring forth. What were you thinking of?"

"Well, I can tell you easily," said his companion; "I was reflecting upon the system of education we spoke of some days since."

"Oh, I recollect. Your free school ideas?"

"Yes."

"Broached to the parson?"

"Yes."

"They were striking, I confess, but wholly out of the question."

"Out of the question?"

"Certainly; is it possible that a man of your clearness of head—let us speak like friends, and as roughly and honestly as we can—is it possible that you could for a moment be in favor of such a doctrine as you stated, that the men of property should put their hands into their pockets to take out money for people they know nothing of, to support free schools; to give a premium for idleness? That, I think, is what you said they were bound to do, the other day."

"Well, sir," said the young man, looking at his interlocutor with some surprise, "I am still of that opinion."

"It is Utopian!"

"Utopian?"

"Yes, as impossible as it is unjust," said the stranger.

"You are then of the past, instead of the future," said his companion, with noble simplicity, "I am sorry that I misunderstood you so completely."

"Of the future? Oh, yes, I understand you. Well, I did take your part, as was natural:" the speaker pronounced this word, *nat'ral*, "but my only end was to draw out the parson. Do not think that, on that account, I a am reformer, as you are, sir."

"Yes, sir: had I the power to make my words felt I would be a reformer."

"Take care, reform is often merely change: and change for the worse. You would reform, what?"

"Nearly every thing; but originate more."

"Ah, we return to the question of education."

"A paramount question."

"Your darling Utopia—above all the rest."

"My thought always—yes."

"Nothing was ever more visionary," said the man in the red cloak, "excuse my plainness: but I do not even see any necessity for such a system, leaving the possibility of founding it entirely out of the question."

"No necessity, sir!"

"There is very little popular ignorance in Virginia—"

"Very little!" interrupted the other with animated looks, "you deceive yourself! It is immense! From the indented servant who drives his master's coach, to the yeoman who toils with the sweat running from his brow, all is ignorance, darkness and gloom. The children grow up like wild beasts, the animal cultivated in place of the soul—the man is but the larger child—as ignorant and more dangerous."

"Dangerous, did you say?"

"Yes, dangerous! dangerous as a wild animal is dangerous to approach: dangerous as a marsh is to tread upon! This mind, which holds so much of richness and God-given, inherent capability of improvement, is a mere morass; tread on it, it will ingulf you!—a morass covered with poisonous flowers, festering with decayed vegetation, lit up only by dancing fires—a dance of death! But, clear this morass:—drain it, expose it to light, and it will fecundate. Light, light is what it wants, what it cries for despairingly; and no answer is vouchsafed to it."

"You wish government to answer it, eh?"

"Yes, I would have government to change the animal into a human being, the wolf into a civilized man."

"Now you make us all wolves," said the man in the red cloak, "how are men animals, sir?"

"Why, who that has opened the records of the world, for an instant even, could controvert it? The normal condition is animal—the spirit is there, God be thanked! but it flickers, glimmers, burns faintly in the poisonous miasma. Still environed by a thousand foes it lives on. Encourage it never so little and it flames aloft in clear heavenly radiance! what a noble field for those who love the race, and have the power to benefit these souls steeped in gloom. For this poor feeble existence is a soul—it will never die!—the responsibility of leaving that soul to struggle alone and unaided against its foes seems to me dreadful, sir! It seems to me that God will some day ask of those men who had the power and did not use it, what he asked of Cain: 'Where is thy brother?' If they have not struck the blow themselves, they have allowed the better part of men to be overcome within them, and this spiritual murder will lie at their doors. That better part moans and mutters its inarticulate despair, the very life-blood arrested in the veins by this nightmare of ignorance and darkness, which, squatting upon its breast, makes it writhe and groan and toss, in the deep darkness. The more I reflect upon this thing, the more dreadful does it seem to me. There are thousands who have never known the means of salvation—pagans in this Virginia of to-day. Christ has wept tears of blood for them in vain: his hands were not pierced for them, they never heard of him—mere heathen men—there within a stone's throw of us. Is it not dreadful?"

The thinker carried away by his excitement, had risen from his seat, and now stood erect before the man in the red cloak, who seemed to regard him with that philosophic interest which a naturalist takes in a new species of animal.

"Well, well," he said, "there is much truth in your views, but they do not convince me. Governments, my friend, are rather selfish, it seems to me; and though we common people here discussing them, pride ourselves upon our fine and noble views, I fancy we should act much after the same fashion were we in power. Good policy would keep us from testing these elevated ideas.

"No, never!" said his companion; "I cannot agree with you. Rather is it a most false and narrow policy to trample thus on the low."

"Why, pray?" said the stranger, who seemed to have no end beyond making the other talk.

"Because ignorance is the most fatal of all curses to rulers. The ignorant soul is the prey of demagogues and false leaders—it is a sea which any wind will lash into foam. The little history which I have read has been read in vain, if it has not shown me that an ignorant and uncultivated people are the most dangerous of all. You see the great mass every day, and do not look at it from your elevation—you are ruler! Well, sir, some day, that great ocean will be agitated by some popular grievance, it will rise in its might—as strong as it is ignorant—and, with its world of fury, it will burst your vain dykes, and bury you and your government for ever."

The stranger looked at the speaker with the same curious expression.

"You have thought much upon this subject, sir," he said.

"Yes," said the other, "often and deeply. I must have wearied you, and I shall now permit you to return to your paper, sir. Free schools—the form in which I would have this vast evil attacked—are not, to all, the absorbing subject of thought which they are to myself."

"Oh, no; you have given me thoughts. I have listened with attention," said the stranger; "I do not live in Williamsburg, and am thankful for the time and society you give me. I am one of the people myself, and, though I have a smattering of Latin, and some reading, feel, in my own person, the truth of many of your remarks."

"I did not mean, believe me—"

"Come, come, don't let us interchange any compliments," said the stranger, with a laugh; "we understand each other—there is something like sympathy etween us."

"Yes, from our first meeting I have felt it."

"You are more of a student than myself, doubtless," said the stranger; "I recognize in you the patient worker. For myself, I am very indolent, and would rather play the violin, or hunt, or fish, than study."

"But you think—reflect."

"Yes," said the stranger, "much."

And his wandering, careless eye became steadfast, and full of steady strength. There was wonderful clearness in it, and that proud and lofty glance peculiar to men born to lead and rule, did not escape the attention of his companion.

It was the eye of the eagle looking down from the clouds upon men and things, the past and present; old things and new; the glance of fire, which, rejecting petty details, and piercing the heaviest mist, caught the central idea, the living fact, then turned to renew itself at the great source of light. The thinker felt that the stranger was greater than he seemed, greater than he even knew himself. He felt that this ungainly man, clad so rudely, and speaking with such a clownish accent, was a born leader of men—a thinker of new thoughts.

"Yes," the stranger added, "I reflect much, and my conclusions would, perhaps, astound the parsons more than your own ideas have done, sir. At a more opportune moment, I hope to interchange thoughts with you upon some of the vital questions which affect this age and country now. I recognize in you a spirit which sympathizes with my own —a nature like my own—for I am a man of the people. You shall give me your ideas—I will give you my own. Who knows that from this collision of thought fire may not dart. You do not know me by name or condition, sir; I know as little of yourself: still, mind speaks to mind, and recognizes its co-worker. And if, in future, occasions shall arise, which require bold hearts and hands, I shall come to you, and claim your aid, without fear of refusal, as without dread of the result."

With which words the man in the red cloak put on his old slouch hat, made an awkward bow, and with a gait, which was half stride, half shamble, went out of the Raleigh, and disappeared. Charles Waters stood, for some moments, looking thoughtfully after him: then, arousing himself, turned to the landlord, and asked for Miss Hallam. The landlord pointed through the door: the young girl was just going up stairs, having returned from rehearsal, and her visitor followed her.

CHAPTER XIX.

BEATRICE AND HER SECOND VISITOR.

He knocked at the door which he saw close behind her, and, being bid to come in, opened it and entered. The young girl was standing in front of the window, which was open, and did not seem to be in a very amiable mood. Her brow was knit, and her firmly closed lips appeared to indicate the expectation on the part of their mistress, of an unwelcome visitor.

No sooner had she caught sight of the young man, however, than this expression of annoyance and ill-humor vanished like magic: and, running forward, with the abandon and fresh grace of a child, she held out her hands, saying:

"Oh, I am very glad to see you!"

Her beautiful face was, at that moment, lit up with such joy, the eyes were so bright and happy looking, the parted lips radiant with a smile of such tenderness and child-like simplicity, that her companion stood, for a full minute, looking at her in silent surprise. She had taken his hand, and pressed it so warmly that, spite of himself, spite of the pre-occupation, caused by the interview which he had just passed, he felt his heart throb with a new and delightful emotion.

"Oh!" said Beatrice, "this is very kind to come and see us: have I kept you waiting?"

"No, madam," he said, "and I am very happy to find you so well. You are right in supposing that my visit was to you and your father. We were all desirous of knowing whether you had suffered any bad effects from your accident."

"I am very well, sir, I believe," replied Beatrice, becoming more calm, "and I only have a slight cough which will go off, I am sure: sit down, sir."

He was on the point of saying that he only called to ask the simple question to which she had just replied: but, in spite of himself, he was swayed by the bright, tender glance of the young girl, and sat down.

"I am afraid I interrupt you," he said, "you are busy."

"Oh no, sir: I have just returned from—from rehearsal. You know I am an actress, sir," she added, with a slight blush; but, at once calling her pride to her assistance, this blush disappeared, and she said calmly, "I have to play to-night."

He saw the blush, and perfectly well understood it.

"You said, 'I am an actress,' with some hesitation," he replied. "I do not find in that fact any thing that you should be ashamed of. It is an honest and worthy employment, when it is pursued worthily, as you pursue it, Miss Hallam."

"All do not think so, sir."

"At least, I do; and do not expect to find in me the mode of thinking which characterizes the wealthier classes of the day. Nothing is derogatory which is undertaken in a pure and elevated spirit—which is honest. It would take much to persuade me that the 'player,' to use the phrase of Shakspeare, who labors honestly and nobly in his vocation, should not rank above the idle gentleman, who consumes merely, without producing any thing. I do not say this in a fault-finding or bitter spirit: it seems simply true to me; and thus I cannot understand why you should hesitate to avow your profession."

"I do not, sir," said Beatrice softly; "but spite of myself, I am affected by the popular opinion of my class, and find all my pride necessary to combat it. Oh yes, sir! it is unjust—indeed it is!" added the young girl, earnestly; "and though I do not like acting, and dread the approach of every night, I cannot think the gentlemen are right in despising us!"

"I am sure they do not think so of you," he said; "and though Mr. Effingham has behaved toward you in a manner most unworthy of an honorable man, I cannot think he meant a deliberate insult to a young girl. That were too base," he added, with the latent flash of the eye which characterized him.

"Ah, sir!" said Beatrice, with the same cloud upon her face, which had warned the manager upon the river, "do not let us speak of Mr. Effingham—he does not treat me as a gentleman should treat all persons, however much beneath him. I feel that I am not beneath him, and I can forget the suffering he causes me. Come! I won't talk of him any more. I see your face becoming gloomy, and your anger rising. Do let us leave all this, and not talk about it any more."

"Well, madam, you teach me a lofty lesson. If I am indignant, I had the right to be; but there is something greater than anger, that is forgiveness. Let this young man, then, be no longer the subject of our thoughts; he is beneath you far enough—I say it with no scoffing, much less to flatter—far enough for you to pardon him."

The face of the young girl flushed with feeling, and her eyes filled.

"Oh! how different from the other," she murmured, turning away; "these words are a balm to me: they make me happy, though I do not deserve his opinion."

And looking at him with happy eyes, bathed in their tender mist, she said softly:

"You are very kind to me, sir; you must have a noble nature to speak thus to a poor young girl like myself."

Never had he seen a more winning countenance--so much purity and simple truth in human eyes. He began to look at her more closely, surveying in turn the noble brow, the soft, melting eyes, the tender, childlike mouth, the maidenly attitude, so full of modesty and grace. She had just called herself a poor girl, and he found himself looking upon her as a princess.

"I am a poor man, too," he said, "much poorer than yourself. You have many things which I have not. How grateful must the applause your genius excites sound to you! I have no such pleasure," he said with a smile at his own sophistry.

"Ah! but you have liberty."

"Have not you?"

"No—that is, I mean not your liberty."

"What is mine?"

"Oh!" cried Beatrice; "you have the forest, the river, and the clouds. Don't smile at me, sir; when I think of them, I am a child again, and forget all my worry and every thing."

"And you love the woods?"

"Oh, dearly!"

"And the water."

"More still."

"Strange that your career has not made these simple things distasteful," he said, regarding her with more and more attention.

"Never could any thing make me dislike them," said Beatrice, with a lovely rose-color in her beautiful cheek. "I must have been born in the country—I never heard from father, and I only recollect London—for it makes me happy to get away among the leaves and flowers. I like autumn especially, and, I believe, I could listen to the woods sighing in the wind for whole days. I have often thought the great trees were men with grand souls, sheltering all that come beneath them, and raising their heads to heaven without fearing the lightning or storms!"

He had not taken his eyes from the animated face.

"And then on the river," added Beatrice, with a happy light in her eyes, "on the water I feel freer than ever. I feel like dancing sometimes, and father was laughing at me for calling after the waterfowl the other day—when you saved me, you know," she said, with a look which went to his heart. He made a movement with his hand.

"I love the water," she said, "and the clouds and waves, and all—the sunlight makes me deeply joyful. I could never have felt it again," she added in a subdued voice, "but for you—and who knows—who knows—"

The impulsive young girl passing, as was her wont, from excitement to quiet, from joy to melancholy, paused, hanging down her head.

"Who knows—you would say?" he asked, taking the little hand which hung at her side, with scarcely a consciousness of doing so.

"I am not fit to die," said Beatrice, with tears in her eyes, and turning away. There was a silence more eloquent than any words. Her hand remained in his, and neither spoke, but once their glances met, and then were withdrawn.

"God alone knows who is prepared for that voyage to eternity," her companion said at length, in a grave, serious voice, releasing her hand as he spoke; "we are mere instruments—as I was—in his hand: mere wood and metal, which cannot see or know any thing—which are wielded by the right hand of the Deity. But I am trespassing on your time, Miss Hallam, and must go."

"Oh no, sir—no."

"Do not rate my service to you too highly," he said, taking no notice of this interruption, and rising; "if you sustain no inconvenience, I need not say I shall be most happy—as I am happy to have been near you when you fell; any debt you owed me has been more than repaid by the pleasure I have felt in this friendly conversation, and now I must go. I fear that I have trespassed too much upon your time."

"Oh no—please sit down: I am not busy," said Beatrice, with all the simplicity of a child, "you know I have been to rehearsal."

"You play to-night?"

"Yes, sir: but will you do me a great favor?"

"Is it very great?" he said, gazing with a soft smile upon the tender face. Beatrice caught the expression, and her own countenance became so radiant and winning, so full of happiness and tender feeling, that he felt his breast heave: "What is the favor?" he added.

"To promise me not to come," said Beatrice.

"To see you?"

"Yes, sir."

"At the theatre?"

"To-night—yes, sir: I would rather you would not come, to-night or ever."

"Tell me why: we are friends, are we not—enough for that?"

"Oh, you please me more than I can tell you, by saying that," said Beatrice; "indeed I wish you to have no worse one than myself. But I cannot tell you why I do not wish to see you ever at the theatre. I hope you will not come to see me."

"Well, I will not," he said with a softness which was uncommon with him, "at least to-night, but I may come and see you here again?"

"Oh, will you?"

"Indeed—if you will permit me."

"Oh, always—I so love to hear you talk."

Beatrice seemed to be carried away by her feelings, and afterwards blamed herself severely for acting in so childlike a manner. Her companion said, as he exchanged a pressure of the hand at parting,

"I will certainly come as often as I can—you have no better friend than myself, believe me."

And with these simple and sincere words, he took his departure, thinking of the bright, fresh face, which seemed to have risen for the first time, like a harvest moon, upon his sight. As for Beatrice, she sat still for half an hour, with her head bent down, pensively, and her eyes veiled with their long lashes. At the end of that time she raised her face, and said, with deep tenderness, and eyes that swam in happy tears, "He is so good and noble!"

CHAPTER XX.

THE EXPLOSION: SCENE, EFFINGHAM HALL.

"When an individual of violent temperament adopts a manner of ease and unconcern, sedulously avoiding every thing calculated to arouse his latent passion, the effect, after a series of years, is undoubtedly beneficial. The character takes the color of its nutriment in a great degree; and if it is nourished upon strong emotions, and critical sensations, will become more and more violent:—if upon quiet pleasures, and moderate delights, the result will be just the reverse. Still, there is this to be observed in such cases. The mind of man is not unlike a river;—it may be directed into a new channel, but scarcely arrested wholly in its course. Build a dam of convention across it—bid it curb its waves, arrest its current, and it will sweep all before it. The higher you build the obstruction, the more violent the rush of the waters, when once they have broken loose. This was the result with my respected ancestor, Mr. Champ Effingham. True, he declared often and believed, that he needed strong emotion—novelty—passion, for his existence; but this was a mistake. His passions were naturally strong enough, and emotion was dangerous to himself and others. The quiet life of his native country had allowed these passions to sleep for a long time, and he fancied that he had none. He was, as I have already declared, very greatly mistaken.

"The first view of young Miss Hallam had stirred up a hurly-burly in his breast; not because she was so much more beautiful than Miss Clare Lee, for whom, as the reader of these pages has perceived, my respected ancestor had begun to have something more than a friendly regard:—not that she was one of those fiery phenomena, who, like Cleopatra or Aspasia, dazzle the eyes, and set the brain and heart on fire. The effect produced upon Mr. Effingham by the young woman was attributable to the novelty and freshness of her character, and the state of his own mind, ripe for some great passion, and dissatisfied with the tranquil affection of the little beauty at Riverhead. Miss Hallam's reception of his advances had blown the vague and dubious spark into a blaze—her favorable smiles would in all probability have extinguished it at once: and no one who has read the human heart attentively, more especially that strange chapter dedicated to *love*, will fail to understand this simple fact. Love, I am convinced, is a mere thing of the imagination at first: the heart seeks something new and strange—something to ponder upon and treasure up, and spend its passionate yearnings upon: tranquil, quiet, unostentatious affection succeeds, and this is love indeed, but the storm precedes the calm.

"These few words will explain what I mean when I add that Mr. Effingham was not, properly speaking, in love with Miss Hallam. He experienced for her a violent, passionate emotion, which had ripened in a few days to full size and vigor, and though many persons may say—if, indeed many read these pages—that his love was 'love at first sight,' and genuine, still I must be permitted to doubt it; and I hope to show conclusively, before ending this narrative, that those views I have stated are correct. I am convinced that it was a sort of infatuation, like that of the drunkard for the draught of fire: if he comes near it, he seizes and swallows it. Miss Hallam declined being swallowed; if I may be permitted to make a very poor witticism; she was offended, and I think very justly, at the manner in which Mr. Effingham uniformly addressed her, and she did not take the trouble to conceal her feelings. She showed him plainly that she did not desire him to visit her, and the consequence was a vast increase of Mr. Effingham's passion. We have seen how inconsistently this violent emotion led him to speak and behave:—now praising, then scoffing at the object of his passion: at one time almost cursing her, as he said, then blessing her, and declaring that she was a noble, high-souled girl. The last interview he had with Miss Hallam, at which the reader has been present, was the capstone to all these passionate interviews; and the state of Mr. Effingham's mind may very correctly be inferred from his mingled mockery and earnestness, sincerity and sarcasm in Miss Hallam's presence. After leaving her he left Williamsburg—just when Mr. Waters entered it as we know—and launched himself, like a flash of lightning, toward the Hall, overwhelmed with rage and despair."

Thus far the writer of the MS., to whom we shall recur whenever his narrative commentary on the events of this narrative elucidates the posture of affairs, or the emotions of the various personages.

Mr. Champ Effingham soon reached Effingham Hall, and, throwing his bridle loose, hurried to his room. He did not make his appearance again that day, sending word in reply to the various messages dispatched to him, that he was unwell, and wished to be left in quiet. The result of two replies of this description to Miss Alethea's messenger, was the desired quiet. The young gentleman made his appearance on the next morning, at the breakfast-table, after the squire's departure to ride over his farm, looking very much out of sorts. The sallow rings beneath his eyes were darker than ever, and he seemed to have spent a bad night, if indeed he had slept at all before morning. Miss Alethea declared her opinion, that he had not slumbered: and asked an explanation of the stamping and striding over her head —the noise of flying chairs, and rattling swords, hurled apparently for amusement on the floor. She worded these questions in such a manner, that the impression left upon all minds, was to the effect that Mr. Champ Effingham was a naughty boy, who had been behaving badly, and deserved a scolding.

The reader will no doubt imagine, without any explanation upon our part, the manner in which Mr. Effingham received these observations. He looked at Miss Alethea, as a mastiff does at a lapdog who is worrying him, and went on with his breakfast. Miss Alethea was a lady of excellent sense, and did not meddle with him any more during the whole day. Mr. Effingham spent the day in gloomy thought —varying this monotonous amusement, by hurling from his path every thing which stood in his way. Orange, Miss Alethea's lapdog, chanced to obstruct his steps as he was passing through the hall, and this unfortunate scion of a royal race, found himself kicked twenty feet across the passage, into the embraces of an astonished tortoise-shell cat, his inveterate enemy. Orange was so completely astounded, and overawed by this summary treatment on the enemy's part, that he did not utter so much as a single whine. He was cowed.

Mr. Effingham spent several days in this manner, scarcely eating any thing, but sitting long after dinner, drinking claret. The squire could extract nothing from him; and soon little Kate, his favorite, was repulsed, to her sorrow and mortification. The child prayed earnestly that night for cousin Champ, and could not get her geography the next day for sorrowing about him. As for Master Will, that young gentleman preserved a rigid silence, and a respectful distance from the irate Achilles, whose sombre mood he regarded with astonishment and awe. He saw with dumb astonishment that Mr. Effingham's hair had remained unpowdered for a whole week, and that his ruffle was torn regularly every evening.

One morning, Mr. Effingham was observed to sit with his head bent down for more than an hour, in gloomy thought; at the end of that time, he rose and ordered his horse. Mounting, he directed his way, with a strange expression on his lips, toward Riverhead. At the stream, which ran across the road, a quarter of a mile from the house, his new cocked-hat, with its magnificent feather, blew off into the water, and was all muddied and draggled; and when, after picking it up, he again mounted, he found that his horse had by some means become suddenly lame.

"Well," he said, bitterly, "fate is against my seeing her. I will not go." And returning to the Hall, he shut himself up in his room, and did not issue forth again until evening. It was the seventh day after the interview with Beatrice Hallam; but it brought him no rest from his harassing and gloomy thoughts. He was growing reckless; burnt up by his complicated emotions, he began to regard things in a mysterious and fateful light. Was this young woman to be his curse, appointed by Heaven to ruin him here in this world, for some dreadful sin he had committed? He felt no penitence, shrank not, but with the same mocking, reckless smile, entered the supper-room, where Miss Alethea was preparing chocolate. He sat down in moody silence, but was not long left to himself.

"Champ!" said Miss Alethea, as she finished the arrangement of the table to her satisfaction, "you really must have something on your mind."

No reply.

"What has made you so moody for several days? I never saw you more disagreeable."

The same silence.

"Have you addressed Clare Lee and been discarded?"

Mr. Effingham's face flushed, and he turned with an irritated look toward Miss Alethea, which that lady understood perfectly.

"Oh, well, sir!" she said. "If you are going to eat me, I will not presume to speak. I should like to know what there was so insulting in my question?" she added, oblivious of her intention not to address the young man further, on any consideration.

"It is no insult," said Mr. Effingham, gloomily, "and I have not seen Miss Clare Lee for a moment since the play, more than a week ago. But I do not desire to have my affairs meddled with."

"Indeed!" replied Miss Alethea, indignant at the tone of the young man, "perhaps they are better not meddled with, they may not bear examination. I believe that that young play-girl has something to do with the matter; and Clare told me the other day, that some gentleman had told her that you had met him in a distracted state of mind, galloping from town. You had better take care, they are already talking about you."

Mr. Effingham's rage on hearing this intelligence, may be better conceived than described. Clare Lee to know of his infatuation! to hear of his acquaintance with Beatrice Hallam! to be told of his violent, infatuated conduct! And that impudent fellow who had dared to meddle with his affairs! Mr. Effingham ground his teeth, and grasped his sword-hilt with ominous meaning. This, then, was what he was coming to be; the gossip of the country side. Clare Lee, even, was one of the laughers, and pitied him, no doubt, if she did not despise him. Pity or contempt! Mr. Effingham's lip curled, and his brow contracted; then his face resumed its gloomy look again, and he said: "Woe to those who busy themselves with me. Who spoke of me to Miss Clare Lee? Come, tell me, madam."

Miss Alethea, though somewhat awed by his manner, replied, that she did not consider herself called upon to cross-examine Clare. The fact was bad enough.

"What fact?" Mr. Effingham said, rudely.

"That you, my brother, sir," replied Miss Alethea, bridling up, "should make yourself the talk of every one:—in love with a common actress!"

"Madam!" said Mr. Effingham, with a flash of the eye.

"You may scowl upon me as much as you choose, sir," said Miss Alethea, now thoroughly aroused, "but I say it is disgraceful."

Mr. Effingham bit his lip until it bled.

"Yes, disgraceful!" continued Miss Alethea, "for you to be making yourself ridiculous—and not only yourself, but me and all—by your infatuation for this woman, who would not be permitted to enter a respectable house. Yes, sir! you imagine because you have been to Europe, that you are at liberty to do just as you choose, and to act without reference to any one's pleasure but your own. Don't think to awe me, Champ, for you cannot. I say it's a shame—a burning shame! and you ought to be ashamed to treat Clare so. You know it will break her heart, but this has no weight with you. *I* don't mean to submit to your scowling and growling, though," added Miss Alethea, "I can tell you, sir."

Mr. Effingham rose and said to a servant who was going out—

"Pack my portmanteau, and order my horse."

And without further words he left the room, and was seen by that lady no more. She half regretted her vehemence, for she was a woman of excellent heart at bottom, but her strong religious feelings, made her intolerant of conduct like that attributed to Mr. Effingham; and the result of an argument held with her conscience, was, that she had not said a word too much.

Those words had put the capstone upon Mr. Effingham's feelings, and he went to his room, pale, and with a sneer upon his lip, which boded no good. Thenceforth he was perfectly reckless.

CHAPTER XXI.

CHAMP EFFINGHAM, ESQ., COMEDIAN.

On the next morning Mr. Champ Effingham made his appearance in Williamsburg, accompanied by a mounted servant, and the two horsemen drew up before the door of the Raleigh Tavern. The portly landlord came forth, cap in hand, to welcome him.

"Well, Master Boniface," said Mr. Effingham, with elegant pleasantry, "is the room my servant engaged—No. 6—ready?"

"Yes, sir—quite ready, sir."

"Carry up my portmanteau," said Mr. Effingham to the negro, who had brought that article behind him, "and then return. Answer no foolish questions asked you do not hear."

"No, Massa Champ," said Tom, with the grin of intelligence peculiar to his race, "not by no means, sir."

"And tell no lies either: if you do, I'll amputate your ears."

Having given this caution, and made this unmistakable promise, which the negro received with a broader grin, as he turned away, Mr. Effingham lounged into the ordinary.

"Where's Hallam?" he asked, sitting down carelessly.

"He's out somewhere, sir—at the theatre, I should say: but this is nearly his rum hour," laughed the landlord.

"Bring me a cup," said Mr. Effingham; "or no, I'll have some claret."

The landlord hastened to bring the wine, and placed the bottle at Mr. Effingham's elbow.

"A cracker!"

The cracker was brought with the same respectful rapidity, or rather a basket of those edibles, placed generally at hand, then as now, to refresh the company. Mr. Effingham then betook himself to the agreeable employment of sipping his claret, one leg being thrown carelessly over the arm of his leather-bottomed chair: and when tired of this monotony, he varied it by dipping a cracker in his wine-glass, and throwing his leg over the other arm. The young gentleman was more than usually splendid: his coat of crimson cut velvet, was ornamented with a mass of the richest embroidery, and had chased gold buttons:—his waistcoat was of yellow silk, with flowers worked in silver thread, and his new cocked hat, just from London, was resplendent with its sweeping feather. At his side dangled the finest of his short swords, and, altogether, Mr. Champ Effingham seemed, to judge from his "outward accoutrement," the very pet of fortune. His manner was not unsuited to his dress: it was, if possible, more nonchalant and indifferent than ever; but any one who would have taken the trouble to scan the handsome face closely, would have perceived a dark shadow under the eyes, which betokened sleepless nights, and a reckless, mocking expression upon the lips, very much at variance with the *petit maître* airs assumed by the young gentleman.

Half an hour passed, and Mr. Effingham was visibly becoming very impatient, when the entrance of the manager caused him to lay down the "stupid gazette" he had been reading and maligning for the last fifteen minutes.

"Ah! there you are at last, Hallam," he said, "what the devil kept you so long?"

The fat manager received this address with great good-humor, and replied, that they had been getting up a play of the "great Congreve" for that night's performance.

"You had better let Congreve alone, and stick to Shakespeare," said Mr. Effingham, "he won't take here among these barbarous Virginians. But come here, and drink some claret with me—I'm tired of it myself: bring me some rum!"

The rum came, and Mr. Manager Hallam sat down.

"Good?" said Mr. Effingham.

"Very excellent indeed, sir," said Hallam, smacking his lips.

"Well, now, let us come to the matter I am thinking about. Hallam, I am going to join the company."

"The company, sir!"

"Yes—*your* company: what, the devil! Is there any thing so astounding in that?"

"Really, sir—really now—you take me quite aback! *You* join the company?"

"Yes! The 'Virginia Company of Comedians.' Is

there any thing strange in a Virginian belonging to that excellent association of his Majesty's, or his Excellency's players?"

"Upon my word, sir," said the manager, laboring under great astonishment, "never in my life—"

"Why, what surprises you?"

"That a gentleman of your wealth and standing should join us."

"Curse my wealth and standing! That is not your look out."

"But it is yours, sir," said the manager, with a troubled look, "if you knew about these things—your family, sir—really a most extraordinary proposal—"

"Come, no humbug! Let us look at the matter. I am a gentleman, you say, and I have a family to affect. That is a mistake—any thing I do will not affect my family: and if it does, I am a free man. Now, on the other side—I rather flatter myself your house would be filled, when Champ Effingham, Esq., was announced in some thrilling and overwhelming part. What do you say to that? Drink there! give me another cup."

"You would really play, sir?" said the manager, surveying his position with a hurried glance, "you would really appear?"

"Bah! you don't know me. Of course I would: and the fact would *appear* to you too, in adding up your receipts. I needn't tell you that when a gentleman takes to the stage, something more is due him than what your common fellow gets—'a beggarly account of empty benches.'"

Hallam hesitated; evidently troubled.

"I would, you know, sir, be more than pleased—it would make my fortune, sir—I feel, sir, that I ought not to hesitate—"

"Bah! don't hesitate, then. Can't you understand that I would make a better *Romeo*, a better any thing, acting with Beatrice, than that stupid fellow Pugsby?"

A light dawned on the muddy brain of Mr. Manager Hallam. Here was the exciting cause: Beatrice was the engine which had produced this extraordinary convulsion in the heart of Mr. Effingham. And with the thought in his mind, the course he ought to pursue became plainer. One of the darling projects of Mr. Manager Hallam was to marry his accomplished and beautiful daughter to some wealthy and high-born youth:—once married, Beatrice would, of course, abandon the stage: that was the loss to him—but the advantages of such connection would vastly outweigh this. The manager was growing old, and getting tired of his nomadic, restless life; tossed from inn to inn, from country to country: and he wished to settle down. Now, if Beatrice married, of course, her husband would not separate the daughter from the father:—the consequence? "I would live in clover all the rest of my life, in a fine house, with plenty to drink, tictac every night, and nothing to do but eat, drink, and sleep," he said to himself. To eat, drink, and sleep was the height of this worthy gentleman's ambition, and he had already conceived the intention of performing those agreeable ceremonies, for the rest of his days, at Effingham Hall, if that were possible in the nature of things.

The reader will now be able to understand the effect produced upon the worthy manager by the mention of Beatrice's name. That explained all. Mr. Effingham was desperately enamored of her—his family no doubt scoffed at the connection—he came to join the company—time would do the rest; and, once married, a few dramatic scenes of father's weeping and relenting—daughter-in-law kneeling in tears—son promising to be immaculate in future, would make all well again. He trusted to his theatrical experience to arrange these little matters, and already dreamed of ending his days tranquilly, in what he seemed to consider the place of happiness—in "clover."

So, when Mr. Effingham had repeated his disdainful question, "Would he not make a better companion for Beatrice, in every thing, than that stupid fellow, Pugsby?" Mr. Manager Hallam melted from his doubtful state of mind into increasing conviction, and said, that "He really felt—hum—he must certainly acknowledge—hum—Pugsby was certainly not what he had been; and, if Mr. Effingham was bent on joining them, he did not feel himself at liberty to refuse his most flattering proposal. As the great Congreve had said to him, on one occasion, such common players as himself could not feel too much flattered when gentlemen condescended to associate with them on terms of equality; and nothing was more reasonable. He could not refuse Mr. Effingham, whom he was proud to call his friend; he had many such distinguished friends; among the most so, the great Congreve. Therefore, if Mr. Effingham was still of the same mind, he would be most proud, most flattered to have him. He would find them a plain, honest set; and the only drawback was on the delicate subject of his remuneration. For, as to salary, he feared——"

"Curse the salary!" said Mr. Effingham, with disdainful carelessness—he had listened to the above tirade with perfect indifference—"I don't want your money, Hallam. You don't think that I would join your set for a few pistoles, do you? No, sir! I have quite sufficient; but what I want is excitement, novelty, jovial society. I'm sick of the well-bred insipidity of good society, and the 'repose' they consider the *summum bonum* and great desideratum of human existence. I'm done with it—tired of it. I am going to pick out a piece to act this very day. Go, and put 'Champ Effingham, Esq.,' on your roll of comedians."

And Champ Effingham, Esq., rising from his seat, went out, and stood at the door of the Raleigh, yawning and frowning, and scowling on such members of that insipid good society as passed in their coaches. He did not take the trouble to return the nods of the gentlemen, or the smiles of the ladies. He felt perfectly reckless, and cared, at that moment, for no human being on earth. Yes, there was one whom he loved and hated, blessed and cursed; and she passed him, coming from the theatre, with a quick step, and an averted face. Why, else, did the frown become deeper, and the glance of the eye grow more gloomy and reckless?

Beatrice hurried up to her room, and Mr. Effingham re-entered, and began again to converse again with the manager, over a second bottle of claret.

CHAPTER XXII.

THE DOOR OF THE "GAZETTE" OFFICE.

After his interview with Beatrice, Charles Waters returned homeward, lost in thought. Was he pondering again upon his system of education, or upon any of his novel political ideas, such as Parson Tag had "called to the attention" of the squire, for their absurd and treasonable character? Was he admiring the beautiful autumn woods, all yellow, and gold, and crimson, through which the fresh fall breezes laughed and sang, from the far surging ocean? None of these things occupied his thoughts; ideas of national politics were as far from his mind as the forest, which his dreamy eye took no note of.

He was thinking of that young girl he had just left; so womanly, yet childlike; so beautiful and attractive in the richness of her great loveliness; yet so like a girl who has never thought to bind up the careless waves of her hair. What an anomaly was here! And was there not food for thought? He had seen her on the stage, and, spite of his total ignorance of what acting was, felt perfectly convinced that she was a great genius; and now this splendid woman, whose magical voice had interpreted every change and phase of passion, glancing from the highest to the lowest tones, with lightning-like rapidity and marvellous ease; whose attitudes were so grand, whose very walk rivetted the attention, and hushed the crowd; this great interpreter of the greatest of human intellects, with whose name the whole colony was ringing, had thrown aside in his presence all this intellect and strength, to take his hand, and laugh merrily, and talk with rapture of the fresh beauty of the river and the forest, and, like a child, plead for another visit from him! Was the scene real or imaginary?

He passed over the whole distance between Williamsburg and his home in a dream, and all that day, and for more than a week thereafter, was plainly busy with some problem that he could not explain to his satisfaction. He would go and work in the field; and, before he knew it, find himself leaning on his spade and murmuring, "Could she have acted all this?" He pored over his books hour after hour, and found he had made no progress; for her image rose in all its fresh and tender beauty between him and the page. Then he became conscious of his preoccupation, and determined to banish it. She was nothing to him—he had other ends in life, and other duties than idle visits. This young woman was, no doubt, very original and striking in every point of view, and he felt a strange sympathy with her—a strange sensation of having seen and known her elsewhere, perhaps in another world—but that was nothing to him. Realities were his food, not fancies—henceforth he would drive from his mind this fit of dreaming.

And he succeeded. This young man had a mind of rare vigor and resolution; he had trained his mind like a courser to obey the bridle, and now he found the effect of this mental discipline. By degrees the young girl's image no longer made his eye brighter, his lip wreath into a tender smile; he returned to his grave, patient labor, and his thoughts on the great questions which absorbed him.

On the day after Mr. Effingham's instalment at the Raleigh, Charles Waters visited Williamsburg again. His business was to procure some little articles for his father, who seldom went to the town—Lanky, the lad we have seen on the day of the river adventure, attending to the sale of fish and other things which old Waters sent to market. Having dispatched his errand, he went to the office of the "Virginia Gazette" to purchase a copy.

As he was coming out with the paper in his had, he felt a touch upon his arm, and turning round, perceived his friend with the red cloak, who had come for the same purpose, it seemed, as he had a copy of the Gazette under his arm.

"We are well met, friend," said the man in the red cloak, "and at a place which is not extraordinary. We might have expected to find each other here."

"How so?" asked Charles Waters, gravely extending his hand, but betraying evident pleasure at the meeting.

"Why," replied his companion, "we are both thinkers."

"Yes, but—"

"And as thinkers must have food for thought," added the man in the red cloak, "we both decided, some moments since, to come and purchase the 'Gazette.' Is it not so?"

"With me—yes."

"Something new is as much your passion, or I greatly mistake, as it is my own. What is new in facts, what is new in ideas?"

"You will search long in this paper for the latter novelty," said the other; "there is generally, however, a good budget of news from Norfolk, York, and—when a vessel arrives—from England."

"Good! That is what we want more than comments on facts. Give me the food—I can myself digest it. I beg leave to decline taking any writer's opinion on the eternal legislation in Parliament on Virginia affairs—the said opinion being invariably favorable to government. I ask for the new act of Parliament—I will light my pipe with the commentary."

"Still the two things might be combined in a gazette."

"Yes, when thought is free."

"It will be, some day."

"Well, I think so, too," said the man in the red cloak. "I hope I shall live to see the day when the public journal will be the great speaker of the time—though I could never express my own ideas with a pen; it freezes me—I dream sometimes of this mingled chronicle and essay you mention: a great daily volume, containing intelligence from every quarter of the world, news upon every subject, comment free from partisan falsehood; and this great organ of thought I sometimes think will, in future, be scattered over the land like the leaves of that autumn forest yonder. When the time comes, mankind will take a great stride onward."

"I scarcely hope to live so long," said his companion.

"Why? The new era comes slowly, but still comes."

"This paper I hold in my hand is a bad commencement of your grand dream, liberty! Yes, liberty will come—but will it be in our day?"

"What do you mean by liberty?" said the stranger, bending his keen eye on his companion; "are men fit for such a thing?"

"Yes."

"Let us see, now—but here we are at the Raleigh Tavern, accompany me to my room, and we will talk; or if not talk, I will play you a tune on the violin, and before you go show you something I have written."

Charles Waters willingly complied, and, passing Beatrice's door, which he merely glanced at, they entered the apartment of the stranger. It was, like most rooms in Virginia taverns, of considerable extent, and of a rather bare appearance. In one corner, a neat bed covered with a white counterpane, stood, with its tall, slender posts; and the rest of the furniture consisted of a rude oaken table and some leather-bottomed chairs. On the table lay a violin and bow, and beneath it an open book. The fire-place had two square stones in place of andirons, and these stones now supported an armful of twigs, which were crackling and blazing pleasantly. The day was not cold, but the stranger seemed to be one of those men who rightly consider a cheerful blaze always pleasant, and he sat down before it, resting his rudely-shod feet on the iron fender. His companion sat down opposite, and for a moment there was silence. It was first broken by the man in the red cloak, who said:

"We are now separated from the outer world; this inn is our castle, and before I amuse you, as my guest, by playing the violin, let us have a few words upon the subject we were speaking of but now."

CHAPTER XXIII.

A THINKER OF THE YEAR OF GRACE, 1763.

Charles Waters sat down, and resting his elbow on the table, leaned his head upon his hand; he seemed to be thinking; but scarcely upon the subject they had adverted to, if one might have formed any opinion from the compression of the lips and the troubled expression of the eyes. The man in the red cloak, whose keen eye nothing seemed to escape, observed this expression, and determined to try the effect of music. The reader will have already perceived, that one of the peculiarities of this strange man, was great curiosity as to the working of the human heart, and the means of affecting men through their feelings. He took up the violin, which was an old battered instrument of little value, but not without much sweetness of tone, and drew the bow across the strings.

"What shall I play?" he said. His companion raised his head at the sound of the stranger's voice, and looked at him inquiringly.

The man in the red cloak repeated his question with a slight smile.

"Any thing," said the other, relapsing into reverie again; he was subject to these fits of thinking, and the stranger seemed to understand the fact; for he commenced playing without taking any notice of his auditor's preoccupation and indifference. His bowing was firm and strong, and playing evidently from his ear wholly, he executed a minuet with great delicacy and force. His whole soul seemed to be absorbed in the grand floating strain, which, with its crescendos and cadences, sweeping onward in full flood, or dying like sinking winds, filled the whole chamber with a gush of harmony. But still his eye was fixed curiously upon his companion, and he noted with great care every change of expression in the lips, the brow, and the eyes veiled with their long dusky lashes. He finished with a vigorous flourish, and Charles Waters raised his head.

"Do you like it?" asked his companion.

"Yes; you are a fine player, sir," he said indifferently.

"Perhaps you would prefer a Virginia reel?"

"No, I prefer the other, which is a minuet, I believe."

"Yes; but listen to this."

And, first tuning a rebellious string, the stranger struck up, with a vigorous and masculine movement of the elbow, one of those merry and enlivening tunes, which seem to fill the air with joy and mirth. His fingers played upon the strings like lightning, the bow rose, and fell, and darted backward and forward; and, throwing his whole heart into the piece, the stranger seemed to imagine himself in the midst of some scene of festivity and laughter, to be surrounded by a crowd of bright forms and merriest faces, running through the dance, and moving in obedience to his magical bow. He wound up with a tumultuous, deafening roar, his eyes flashing, his crisp hair seeming to move with the music:—and then, stopping suddenly, laid down the instrument. Charles Waters raised his head, waked, so to speak, by the silence.

"You play excellently well, sir," he said; "but I am so wholly ignorant of music, that my praise, doubtless, is of little value."

This seemed to afford the stranger much satisfaction: he evidently prided himself upon his proficiency on the instrument.

"It is a very enviable accomplishment," his companion added, "for it affords you the means of easily contributing to harmless enjoyment. Music is a great educator, too. Dancing is one of the most healthful and innocent of pastimes, I am convinced; and the violin is, I believe, the best instrument to dance to."

"Yes—yes: none other is comparable to it, and I confess I do feel satisfaction in knowing that I perform tolerably on this great' instrument. There is but one other superior to it."

"What is that?"

"The human voice."

"Yes—yes, I understand."

"That is, after all, the great master-instrument, constructed by the Deity. The violin is merry and joyous, or mournful and sombre, but the voice is all this, and all else, in a degree ten thousand times more powerful. To move, to agitate, to sway, to bend; what is like it. Ah! my Livy, there, upon the table, gives me the words; but who shall fill my ear with the magical voices, dead and silent? Who shall 'speak the speech,' as Virginius did, when fronting the tyrant Appius, he plunged the dagger into his child? Would I had been there!" added the stranger, with one of those brilliant flashes which seemed, at times, to convert his eyes into flame. But before his companion could reply, this expression had disappeared, and the man in the red cloak took up the open volume of Livy, and, turning over the leaves, carelessly, seemed to have forgotten Virginius and his misfortune, in a moment.

"After all," he said, with one of his adroit turns, and apparently desiring to make the other talk, "after all, I don't know whether Appius was so much worse than other despots: and men have in all ages required to be ruled strongly, and often tyrannically. Despots are disagreeable, but necessary."

Waters looked at his companion with astonishment: he thought he must be jesting: but there was not the least indication of any such thing: his countenance—that index of the mind, ordinarily—betrayed nothing of the sort. Apparently the stranger had spoken these words in perfect good faith.

"Could I have understood you, sir," said the thinker, "and did you really mean that men required despotic rulers?"

"Yes: certainly."

"This, from *you?*"

"Come, come—you may have taken up a wrong impression in regard to my opinions; let us not break into exclamations, companion; rather let us sift opinions and compare ideas. Is it not undeniable that men in all ages have been weak and faltering, preferring rather the bad and false to the great and good? and if this is true, does it not follow that despots are a necessity of the world's being?"

"Ah!" said his companion, "but that is not true—it is false, permit me to say, honestly, and with no desire to offend you—"

"Not at all—not at all: go on."

"I deny your maxim totally, sir—it is not true."

"Have not the records of the world proved it? Are they not darkened every where by deeds which prove the truth of the Bible, saying, that mankind are prone to deceit and desperately wicked?—have not the annals of all lands and governments shown conclusively, that truth and grandeur and purity have ever attracted to themselves envy and hatred, malice, and all uncharitableness? Come! let me hear you deny that men are radically hateful, false, unworthy of trust, as they are of respect: come, let me hear you deny that they are swine before whom it is the merest boyish folly to throw that brilliant pearl called liberty. You cannot deny the truth of this view:—men have always been radically false and unworthy."

"I do deny it, sir," said Waters, his brow flushing and his eyes suddenly growing brilliant with the fires of enthusiasm. "Never was any philosophy so weak, so wholly based on sand! It is a dreadful, an awful philosophy, that which scoffs at and seeks to overthrow all that is pure and worthy in our fellow-men—all that is brilliant and imposing for its truth and beauty in the annals of the race! I cannot believe that you speak seriously, for I have seen that in your eyes and your spoken words which is opposed to this terrible philosophy utterly. No, sir! men are not by nature destitute of truth and love, nobility and purity—the annals of the world show how untrue it is. Go back as far as you may, penetrate the gloom which wraps the overthrown columns of the Syrian desert, the Egyptian plains, and you will find in the midst of crime and falsehood the light of heaven; among those monsters whom God, for His own wise purposes, sent upon the earth, flowers of majesty and honor; in the moral desert those oases of verdure and pure limpid waters, which prove that beneath this burning sand the eternal springs exist, the germ remains. No; I do not deny that men have in all ages fallen and sinned—yes, they have hated and despised, blasphemed and cursed, dyed their right arms in blood, and revelled in the foul, the false, the unnatural. None can dispute it. I acknowledge it. But what is equally true is this—that every where the instincts of humanity, planted by God in it, have revolted against this abnormal state; love has effaced hatred, justice the spirit of wrong; heaven has opened and the abyss has closed!

"Go into this Golgotha of nations, this Jehosaphat of extinct generations, and question those dry bones which once supported living frames such as our own here now. They will make you but one reply—a reply which embraces the history of humanity—'I sinned, I repented; I was human, I endeavored to grow divine.' Look at Greece, Rome, Modern Europe—embrace at a glance the whole surface of three distinct civilizations, three diverse ages, from horizon to horizon, from their dawning in the East, fresh, rosy, and pure, to their sad and sorrowful decline—sorrowful and sad because the soul ever doubted—ever was afraid to hope for the new dawn! In Greece, art overthrowing rudeness, beauty driving away deformity—the good and beautiful passionately yearned for by all classes of men—eternally sought! The childlike and poetical nature filling the streams with naiads, the woods with dryads, the mountains with the oreads and the graces—every where the false, which is the deformed, overthrown to make way for the true, which is the beautiful. Arcadian temples glittering in the forests, altars of white marble crowning the blue mountains. Phidias and Apelles, famous in all countries for their incarnations of grace and beauty, rather than their incarnation of the Grecian idea! And not in sculpture and painting only did the true and beautiful conquer the false and deformed. In literature, Sophocles and Euripides purified the heart by pity and terror—Aristophanes lashed with his satire the unworthy and despicable—Homer embodied in his heroes grace and strength, as in Achilles—nobility and tenderness, as in Hector—in Ulysses, the dignity of suffering and misfortune. Socrates taught immortality — Plato penetrated the mists of prejudice and ignorance with that glance of lightning given him by God. Every where mind overcame matter, the moral conquered the brutal; and such was the force of their teachings, the vitality of their dogmas, that all the nations of the world turned their eyes to Greece as toward the dawn of civilization.

"The cry, 'Great Pan is dead!' was only heard when the Roman Colossus had strangled in his arms this nascent civilization, this pure ray of the dawn. Pan had taught men husbandry, and tranquil country happiness, and that wars should be no more. When he died, that cry told the nations that the glory of Greece had disappeared, and with it the only civilization which surpassed the ripe majesty of Rome. But that civilization was not altogether lost; Juvenal was greater than Aristophanes, as Cato and Cicero rose in moral height above the statesmen of Athens. You know well the history of that empire, stretching its vast roads through every land, and drawing to the great centre, the imperial city, towards which those vast highways converged the silks, and gold, and pearls of every land—the captives of all nations.

"I know that you would say that human depravity culminated in those emperors—and that they had fit subjects. Yes; God had given that race dominion, permitted it to conquer every land, and then cursed it with rottenness and decay. Men felt the divine curse, and shook their clenched hands at the gods in impotent wrath. See how every thing reveals the despair which fell upon the men of Rome; see how the race, blind, staggering, rioting in an eternal orgy, still knew their foulness, gnashing their teeth with rage at their own depravity; see how every thing became venal—

female honor, the arms of men, the suffrages of the legions. The commander who could glut the revelling multitude with the greatest shows was emperor—Messalina was queen. The race was staggering, despairing; they saw the night coming, and the lurid glare of burning cities lighting on their way to Rome those 'hammers of God,' Alaric and Genseric. They felt that the impending fate was the just punishment of the unspeakable corruption reigning in the land, and they sought to drown conscience in those moral stimulants which now horrify the world. They clamored for wild beast shows; they rolled on the seats of the Amphitheatre in convulsive laughter, when the slave was torn to pieces in the arena by the lion or tiger; they intoxicated themselves with blood to drown despair, and, drunk with horror, staggered and fell into the welcome grave dug for them by war, or pestilence, or famine.

"Then, on this worn-out world—this chaos of darkness and corruption, rose the sun of Christianity, blessing and healing. God took pity on the race, and would not overwhelm it with a new deluge; and men cast off their foulness, abjured their heathen gods, and and knelt like children at the foot of the cross.

"But I weary you, sir. Every where the annals of the world show the god-given instincts of the race, leading them to seek the true and beautiful—to embrace love in place of hatred. See how the northern nations worshipped their hero-souls, as the Anglo-Saxons almost did their brave King Arthur. They still yearn for them, and say they will return to bless the nations. The precursor of the returning god is still looked for in the northern solitudes by the rude islanders—and Arthur, the middle age believed, would come again, his sword excalibur turned to the shepherd's crook, and with him peace, love, and happiness. Look at all nations. In France, see how the convulsions of a thousand years have proved the yearnings of the race for something better, truer, nobler than their effete royalty, their nobility, exhausted by Duguesclin and Bayard. See England, grand and piteous spectacle!—heart of the modern world, as she was the torch, whose light glared on the crumbling props of old imperial Rome—the star of the new era. See England, groaning through all her history with the fatal incubus of a privileged class, sucking up all offices of profit or distinction; a king, whose person is sacred—who can do no wrong. . See her still seeking for the true, the pure, the just; see those men of England plunging into war and blood to find the jewel—beheading the king in the name of justice—embracing puritanism, because it clad itself in the robes of truth and purity—returning to their king, when puritanism became bigotry—love, hatred—justice, a scoff—and only to find in that son of the man they had beheaded a worse curse than any yet! For Charles II cursed the rising generation with corruption, unbelief, despair; no longer levying tonnage like his father—only destroying the honor of families; no longer holding down the nation with a rod of iron—only inaugurating that horrible comedy of the Restoration, which made all that is good contemptible—the honor of men, the fidelity of wives, the faith of humanity in God. The poor, struggling nation bargained for liberty and toleration—they received bigotry and licentiousness. Yes, yes, sir! this is the truth of that great revolution, and the English people therein embodied the history of humanity in all ages, every where. Yes, yes! if any thing is true, this is true—that men are not false and hateful, black from the cradle, foul from their first breath! On this conviction alone do I base my hopes for the future of the race—in Europe, America, every where. That this land we live in will prove mankind able to think, to act, to rule, above all, to love, I have a conviction which nothing can deprive me of. The old world totters; she is diseased, and though this disease may demand two hundred years to eat its way to the heart, yet it will finally attack the vital part, and all will crumble into dust. The new world lies bathed in the fresh light of the new age: here will the heart of man vindicate its purity; here the tiger will lie down, the serpent no longer hiss; here, I feel that God will accomplish the political regeneration of humanity, proving the eternal truth of these poor words I have uttered!"

The thinker paused, and leaning his brows on his hand, seemed to be buried in thought. The stranger was also silent, either from conviction or in order that he might marshal his thoughts for the struggle of intellects. But if this last were the reason of his silence, he was doomed to disappointment.

His companion rose and said:

"I fear I have wearied you, sir, and fear still more that you will think it discourteous in me to leave you, after thus taking up our whole interview in talking myself. But I have just recalled a business engagement at this hour—the clock has just struck."

"Well, well," said the man in the red cloak, who did not seem greatly put out by these words, "I cannot think hard of that. Your ideas, sir, have found in me an attentive listener, and if I led you to suppose that I believed nothing good could come out of human nature, I misconveyed my meaning. Let us part, then, for the present—we shall meet again, as my stay here will be prolonged for a week or two longer, and I count upon seeing you again. I do not fear a disappointment. We shall come together often in the future, I feel a conviction."

His companion bowed his head in token of willingness and assent, and looking at the door, said:

"Your room is No. 7, is it not?"

"Yes—that one opposite is occupied by a young gentleman from the neighborhood; and that one next to me by the young actress, Beatrice Hallam, I believe. Mr. Effingham seems to be her very good friend."

"Effingham!" exclaimed his companion.

"Yes, he has been an inmate of this tavern for two or three days—don't mistake and enter his room for mine."

Charles Waters could only bow his head: and turning away from the man in the red cloak, he went in silence down the stairs. The house seemed to stifle him; and when he reached the open air he seemed suddenly to revive, for his face was suffused with blood.

CHAPTER XXIV.

WARLIKE PROCLAMATION FROM THE SQUIRE.

Just as Charles Waters left the door of the inn, and while the stranger was still looking after him, with a curious expression upon his finely-moulded lips, the door of No. 7

opened, and Mr. Champ Effingham issued from it. The young gentleman, who had just been refreshing himself with a cup of chocolate, served to him in bed—was clad with his usual elegance and richness, and for a moment his eye dwelt on the coarsely-dressed stranger, who stood with the knob of the door in his hand, gazing, as we have said, after Charles Waters. The man in the red cloak surveyed him with great calmness, and some curiosity. An imaginative spectator might have fancied them the representatives of the old world and the new—the past and the future—the court and the backwoods. Mr. Effingham looked every inch the gentleman and courtier. The drop curls of his powdered peruke reposed ambrosially on his clear pale cheek, his lace ruffles at bosom and wrist were of spotless purity, his surcoat of cut velvet, with its chased gold buttons, just lifted up the point of his richly ornamented sword, and his waistcoat, silk stockings, cocked-hat, and jewelled hands, completed the vivid and perfect contrast between himself and the rude-looking, coarsely clad stranger. Plainly the court and the wilds, Europe and America—stood face to face.

The man in the red cloak having apparently satisfied his curiosity, made a slight and very awkward bow, which Mr. Effingham returned with negligent carelessness, and then re-entered his chamber, with a smile on his grim features. Mr. Effingham descended.

The reader will recollect that he had been at the tavern now for some days:—the manager had regularly enrolled him as a member of the "Virginia Company of Comedians," and availing himself of the privileges of his membership, Mr. Effingham had met Beatrice daily, in the theatre, in the tavern, every where. He was no longer a chance visitor, an occasional torment to be borne with, and endured patiently, in consideration of his going away soon; he was now her shadow, and in the young girl's own words, he "drove away all the sunshine from her life." At rehearsal she had seen daily his reckless and mocking smile, glittering and gloomy, follow her every movement—at the inn, when he condescended to appear at the common table, she had been transfixed by his burning glances—in all places and at all times he had obtruded himself with his ironical and yet sombre smile; a smile which seemed to say audibly, "You defied me, scorned me, thought yourself more than a match for me, and I have foiled you and conquered you, by superior will and reckless carelessness."

Whether Mr. Manager Hallam was conscious of Beatrice's unhappiness—of Mr. Effingham's treatment of his daughter—we are not able to say. At least, he took no notice of it, and was always ready to echo the young man's jests, and drink with him as long, and as deeply as he desired.

"At the Hall the storm was rising, and ere long it was destined to fall upon the devoted head of Mr. Effingham. Miss Alethea had deeply regretted her violence, and earnestly prayed for him, and that he might return to them again. She saw too late that her injudicious words had driven him away, and this she confessed to her father, with tears; but that bluff gentleman had pish'd and pshaw'd, and told her that she was too soft-hearted, and that she was not to blame —he would see to the matter! The rest of the household soon found out the dreadful fact that Mr. Champ Effingham had abandoned his home for the young actress, and the very negroes, following the wont of Africans in all years, discussed and commented on "Master Champ's" wild conduct. Will reflected upon the matter, with a dreadful feeling of alarm, and fear, and admiration, for the rebel—and Kate sorrowed in quiet, wiping her eyes frequently, as she bent over Carlo, and sometimes getting up from the table, and hurrying out, with no imaginable cause for going away, unless she had tears to hide. She loved Mr. Champ Effingham dearly—much more fondly, I am compelled to add, than my respected ancestor deserved—and wept for him, and every night and morning joined her hands together and asked God to bless him, wetting the pillow all the time with her tears. As I have said, this was by no means the spirit of the squire: he was indignant, he felt outraged, he knew now all about the matter, and felt excessive dissatisfaction at Mr. Effingham's conduct, as he called it. It never occurred to him that his own youthful career had been by no means immaculate, and without regard to Mr. Champ's peculiarities of mental organization, he determined to bring the rebel to subjection."

Thus far, the MS. from which these events were drawn; the extract may serve to explain the appearance of a mounted servant at the door of the Raleigh, where Mr. Effingham descended, after his meeting with the stranger. It was Tom, who, with many smiles, presented to his master a missive directed, in a large, firm hand:

"To Mr. Champ Effingham, at the Raleigh Tavern, Williamsburg."

Mr. Effingham frowned, tore open the letter, and read it, with a flush upon his brow, which froze the smiles of the shining African. Having gone through it, he crumpled it furiously in his hand, scowled upon the negro, hesitated, in evident doubt as to what course he should pursue, then, bidding the servant wait, hurried to his room.

The letter was in these words:

"*Effingham Hall, Thursday Forenoon.*

"MY DEAR CHAMP—I have heard of your conduct, sir, and have no intention of being made the laughing-stock of my neighbors, as the father of a fool. No, sir! I decline being advised and pitied, and talked about and to by the country on your account. I know why you have left the Hall, sir, and taken up your residence in town. Alethea has told me how you insulted her, and flouted her well-meant advice, and because she entreated you, as your sister, not to go near that young woman again, tossed from her, and fell into your present courses. I tell you again, sir, that I will not endure your conduct. I won't have the parson condoling, and shaking his head, and sighing, and, when he comes in the Litany to pray for deliverance from all inordinate and sinful affections—from all the deceits of the world, the flesh, and the devil—have him looking at the Hall pew, and groaning, until every body understands his meaning. No, sir! If you make yourself a fool about that common actress, you shall not drag us into it. And Clare Lee! have you no regard for her feelings? Damn my blood, sir! I am ashamed of you. Come away directly. If you are guilty of any thing unworthy toward that young woman, I will strike your name from the family Bible, and never look upon your face again. Remember, sir; and you won't be fool enough to marry her, I hope. Try it, sir, and see the consequence. Pah! a common actress for my daughter—the wife of the representative of the house of Effingham, after my death. 'Sdeah, sir! it is intolerable, abominable; and I command you to return at once, and never look upon that young woman again. For shame, sir. Am I, at my age, to be made a laughing-stock of, to be jeered at by the common people, at the county court, as the father of the young man that played the fool with the actress? No, sir. Leave that place, and come and do what you are expected to do, called on to do—take Clare Lee to the Governor's ball. I inclose your invitation. Leave that woman and her artful seductions. Reflect, sir, and do your duty to Clare, like a gentleman. If it is necessary, I repeat, sir, I command you to return, and never see that girl again.

"EFFINGHAM."

Mr. Champ Effingham read this letter with those manifestations of wrath and indignation which we have described, and as we have said, hurried to his apartment, bidding the servant wait.

Once by himself, he tore his unfortunate frill furiously, and shook his clenched fist at the representation of himself in the mirror.

"Dictation! I am a child!" he said. "I am to be whipped in, like a hound, because I choose to come and spend a few days in town here, and to be ordered about, as if I were a negro. I am, forsooth, to come back to the Hall, and humbly beg Alethea's pardon, for leaving her so abruptly, and hear the servants tittering behind me, and go, like a milk-and-water girl, to escort Miss Clare Lee to the Governor's ball! Curse me, if I will submit to be lashed into obedience, like a dog, and Miss Clare Lee may find some other escort. I will go to that ball with Beatrice Hallam, and I will act next week."

With which words, he sat down and wrote:

"I have received your letter, sir, and decline returning to Effingham Hall, or being dictated to. I have passed my majority, and am my own master. No one on earth shall make a slave of me. I have the honor to be,

"CHAMP EFFINGHAM."

Mr. Effingham read this note over, folded it, sealed it deliberately, stamping the wax with his coat of arms, and summoning a servant, ordered him to deliver it to the negro at the door. Then rising, with a mocking laugh, he went toward Beatrice's room.

CHAPTER XXV.

MR. EFFINGHAM REQUESTS THAT HE MAY HAVE THE PLEASURE OF ESCORTING MISS HALLAM TO THE BALL.

Mr. Effingham knocked at the door of the young girl's apartment, but being in doubt whether he heard her voice, was about to retire. He decided, however, after a moment's reflection, to enter, and opening the door, which yielded to his push, found himself in presence of Beatrice. She was sitting at the window, and leaned her head upon her hand, which lay upon the sill. She did not move when Mr. Effingham entered, and a second glance proved to him that she was asleep.

For a moment, Mr. Effingham gazed at the beautiful head bent down, the forehead moist with the dews of sleep, the small hand hanging down, from which the volume of Shakspeare, she had been reading, had fallen to the floor. None of these things escaped him, and for a moment he paused, silent, motionless, his eyes becoming softer, his brow less gloomy. Then the shadow returned; thought, like a hound, again struck the trail, for a moment lost, and the eye of the young man assumed its habitual fire, his lips their curl of scornful and gloomy listlessness.

Beatrice stirred in her sleep and awoke; it might have been supposed that the glittering eye fixed on her face, had not permitted the sleeper to continue insensible to the presence of the visitor. She opened her eyes and sat up, placing her hand, with an instinctive movement, on her disordered hair.

Mr. Effingham approached her. "I knocked," he said, negligently, "but was uncertain whether you answered or not, so I entered. How is Miss Beatrice to-day?"

"I am not well, sir," she said, resigning herself to her fate.

"Not well?"

"I am worn out, sir."

"Worn out?"

"Yes, sir; the exceedingly late hours I have kept lately, have injured me."

"All imaginary; you are accustomed to them."

Beatrice made no reply to these words, which Mr. Effingham uttered with careless indifference as he sat down.

"Have you been to the theatre, this morning?" he added.

"Yes, sir."

"Rehearsal?"

"Yes, sir."

"Well, that wore you out. That fellow, Pugsby, is enough to put any one to sleep, he's so somniferous."

"He did not come."

"And so after rehearsal, you came here?"

"Yes, sir."

"And went to sleep?"

"I tried to study, but could not."

"True; there is your Shakspeare on the floor."

Mr. Effingham picked the volume up with a yawn, and politely restored it to the young girl.

"By the by," he said, "when shall we appear together?"

"I don't know, sir."

"Come, now; wouldn't you prefer me as your vis-à-vis in acting to Pugsby?"

"It is perfectly indifferent to me whom I play with, sir."

"Amiable, at least! But we are going to play together soon."

"Are we, sir?"

"Yes, madam, the duchess! By heaven, you must have been born in a court, or you never could have caught the imperial air so perfectly! 'Are we, sir?'" continued Mr. Effingham, mimicking the frigid tones of the young girl's voice; "the devil! you carry acting into private life!"

"No, sir; I am not sufficiently fond of it."

"You hate it?"

"I do not like playing."

"You would prefer quiet domestic happiness, eh?"

"Yes, sir."

"Then, marry me," said Mr. Effingham, with perfect coolness, "I have half ruined myself for you."

Beatrice looked at him fixedly.

"Your great pleasure in life is to scoff at me, Mr. Effingham," she said, calmly.

"No, by heaven! There's my hand. Take it. I am just in the mood to-day to follow any whim which seizes me."

Beatrice was silent.

"You won't accept me, then?" said Mr. Effingham. "Well, that is wrong in you. Effingham Hall yonder comes to me, and you might indulge your dreams of rank and station to any extent, as we are of tolerably good family."

"I have no such dreams, sir."

"Well, then, your dreams of domestic happiness, but now discoursed of."

Beatrice was again silent; and Mr. Effingham burst into a harsh laugh.

"Ah, ah!" he said, "you don't reply, but I know very well what the expression of your ladyship's face signifies. You mean, Madam Beatrice, that you would have very little domestic happiness as the wife of reprobate Mr. Champ Effingham! Hey? Come, now, let us chat like tender friends, as we are. Is not that your thought?"

"I do not think we should be happy together, sir?"

"Why?"

"We are not congenial."

"Bah! we were cut out for each other."

"No, sir; indeed we were not."

"We were! Come, now, I'll prove it. We are both hypocritical——"

"Sir!"

"Both exceedingly worldly and unamiable——"

"Mr. Effingham!"

"And we love each other devotedly. Could better matches be found?"

"You are in a bitter humor this morning, sir," said Beatrice.

"I? Not in the least, as I believe I have replied to similar charges on previous occasions. I never was in more charming spirits. I have just had a little correspondence which raised my spirits amazingly. Just fancy my respected father writing me word that if I did not give you up, never see you again, the paternal malediction would descend. Think of it."

"Oh, sir!—did your father write that about me?" said Beatrice, suddenly losing her frigid indifference.

"Yes."

"Advising you to come away from this place?"

"Advising? not in the least!—commanding me."

"Oh, sir! then obey that command! Recollect he is your father! Remember that you will cause yourself to be talked about, and I shall be the cause of all this!—I shall be the means of distressing your father! Oh, sir, abandon me; leave the company which you have so rashly united yourself to; do not cause me the misery of standing between father and son! Be reconciled, sir! Oh, do not stay here, sir!"

Beatrice had risen, in the excess of her emotion, and stood before the young man now pleading for mercy—mercy for himself! Her eyes were full of earnestness and emotion, her words impassioned and tearful, her hands clasped before her in an attitude of what seemed irresistible entreaty.

Mr. Effingham leaned back, and looked at her with a mocking smile.

"You are really exceedingly handsome," he said, "and upon my word the gentlemen, and even the ladies of the colony, might show some cause for not liking you, and thinking it very naughty in me to come near you. Talk about me!—you think my infatuation for you *will* make me talked about! My dear Miss Beatrice, don't be hypocritical. You know well that I am at present the most interesting topic of conversation in the colony of Virginia. I fancy I can hear the tittering—the delightful gossip about my unworthy self, every where—here, in the upper country, south side, every where. Didn't you see how they stared at me, night after night, in the theatre? And some of the moral and irreproachable young ladies would no longer return my bows, if their respected parents would permit them to quarrel with so illustrious a nobleman as myself. Talked about? Bah! let us be easy, madam; we are both the scoff of Virginia!"

"But your family, sir," cried Beatrice, "much as you affect to despise general opinion—"

"My family will not care much for me—a little worry, and when the matter ends in some diabolical way, some annoyance: that is all! Come, don't talk of my family—or of any of these matters. Let us speak of acting."

"Oh, sir! I am sick. You have made me feel so badly by what you have said."

Mr. Effingham's laugh was the perfection of recklessness and scorn.

"Bah!" he said, "let us talk of business matters. I am going to act Benedick soon, and you shall play the part of your namesake. Can you act it?"

"Yes, sir—but I do not wish to again," said Beatrice, sitting down, overcome with emotion.

"You must not have a voice in the matter—it suits me, madam, and with all possible respect, I shall make my *debût* in 'Much Ado about Nothing.' What an exceedingly apposite piece to appear in! It will be a practical epigram upon public sentiment—the very title!"

"Will you really act, sir?"

"Yes: that will I! nothing can prevent me."

"Then I am the most unhappy of created beings," said Beatrice, tearfully. "Oh! to be the occasion of this altercation between father and son!"

"That is all arranged: and all will go on well now. We will have a delightful time at the ball."

"What ball, sir?"

"Have you not heard? Why, the Governor's. I am going to take you. You will then have an opportunity of seeing all the gentry of this noble colony."

Beatrice looked at the young man with astonished eyes.

"You would escort me, then, sir?" she asked coldly.

"Certainly."

"You must not, sir."

"I will."

"Oh, no, I will not go! I cannot go, sir—I am not invited, sir."

"Pshaw! I am, and of course I can bring any lady I fancy."

"Mr. Effingham!" said Beatrice, wildly, "I am not a lady! I will not accompany you, and be the occasion of a new and more distressing sorrow to your family. No, no, sir—I will not!" and the young girl's face flushed.

"Well—here's my respected friend and manager:—good morning, Hallam," he added carelessly, as that gentleman entered, smiling and rosy; "here, I have been talking to Madam Beatrice about the ball."

"At the Governor's, sir?"

"Yes."

"He wants me to go, father, and I must not," said Beatrice, covering her face.

Hallam stared; and his incredulous glance asked the young man if he really thought of such a thing. This meaning was so plain, that Mr. Effingham burst into laughter, and said:

"Yes, Hallam! I am going to escort Madam to the ball, and be her most devoted cavalier. Now talk to her about it, and remove her scruples—I must go and take a look at the streets of this great town."

And bowing, he went out.

The scene which ensued between the manager and his daughter is not one of those which we take pleasure in describing. Art cannot compass all things. Hallam saw the means of attaching the young man to Beatrice for ever by this ball, for his appearance there with her would be regarded as his public defiance of all the powers of society: and this social prejudice, he felt convinced, was all which prevented Mr. Effingham from marrying Beatrice. It was necessary thus to overcome her scruples, and he did overcome them. Beatrice, at the end of an hour of passionate pleading, fell back, weak, nerveless, overcome. She had consented to go to the ball.

CHAPTER XXVI.

IN WHICH A PISTOL FIGURES.

Mr. Effingham passed the whole of the day succeeding this interview in a state of mind more easily imagined than described. The reader will not have failed to perceive that his reckless, and scornful indifference, his mocking laughter, were but the mask which concealed a profound emotion of pain and depression. Proud, headstrong, and passionate, he had nevertheless experienced a sinking of the heart even in the midst of his violent passion, on reading the bluff gentleman's letter—and ill-advised as that letter undoubtedly was, he already bitterly regretted the tone of his reply. The consequence of these conflicting emotions was frightful:—he tossed about, gesticulated, astounded the members of the Virginia company of Comedians by replying to the simplest observations with insult, and betrayed every indication of a mind ill at ease, and charged with

> "that perilous stuff
> Which weighs upon the heart."

His brow was gloomy, his eye fiery, his walk hasty and by starts. So the day passed, and the morning of the next.

In the afternoon he went to his apartment, and sitting down, leaned his head gloomily on his hand. Where would all this end? That abyss he had imagined to be awaiting him, after the first interview he had passed through with the young woman, now seemed to open visibly before him. He had left his home—defied his friends—abandoned all that made life tranquil and happy—for what, for whom? For a woman who scorned him, and did not take the trouble to conceal that scorn; for a beautiful demon, who met all his advances with indifference or disdain, and, strong in her weakness, defied him with looks and words. If he had abandoned all that happy life for some angel of love and purity, whose heart was a treasure grand enough to console him for all the blasts of obloquy or the winds of scorn, there might have existed some reason which would have calmed him. But no! she hated him—scorned him—could not bear his presence!

He rose, and with clenched hands stood looking at his sneering and unhappy visage in the mirror over the fireplace. There he stood, young, handsome, graceful; clad in the costume appertaining to his rank of gentleman; the brow untanned by sun or wind, the hand white and jewelled, not brown, and hard and knotty with rude toil; every thing in the image reflected from the mirror betrayed the enviable position in the world which the young man sustained. The plain gold ring upon his finger was the gift of Clare years ago, when they were sweethearts; the beautiful cravat he wore, with its gold and silver flowers, was worked by the child at the Hall; the diamond pin in his bosom was a birthday present from his father—lastly, the snuff-box peeping from his waistcoat pocket had been given him by Lord Botetourt when he had admired it one day in England.

All this flashed through the young man's mind; and then, with a mental effort as rapid and comprehensive, he surveyed his future. What would that future be? Young, high born, wealthy, heir to the estate of Effingham and representative of that stately house, all honors and pleasures were open to him, did he but sit down and wait quietly. No exertion was necessary—the future was assured. Would that be his future? Would he go on in life surrounded by friends and tender relatives—gladdened by the smiles of true-souled companions, the tender love of gentle woman—and so passing his early youth, arrive at a middle age of influence and honor; his old age finally to come to him, bright with all that makes it fair and attractive—"as honor, love, obedience, troops of friends?" Would he keep up the honors of his ancient house—be a worthy representative of his honorable name; would he find in that gentle girl whom every one loved, the companion of his joys and sorrows, the light illuminating his existence to its close?

Was this his future, he asked himself, with a bitter curl of the distorted lip—could this be his destiny in life? No! that was not for him; he had made his election—thrown away the goblet of limpid and healthful water, to grasp the bowl foaming with its fiery and poisonous draught. The Circe had taken him captive—he was no longer human; no longer had any power over his will; felt that he would not, if he could, abandon the shore upon which he had cast himself away. No! that bright and happy future was not for him—he had forfeited it. Effingham Hall was closed to him—Clare despised or pitied him—friends had deserted him—he had stopped at the Siren isles, and never would sail forth again for ever. The name of Effingham would die if he had to uphold it—he would be stricken from the annals of his house—nothing remaining of his name and life but a sad and shameful recollection!

Again he gazed steadily at his sneering and unhappy image in the mirror—upon his pale cheeks, fallen away so quickly, upon his bloodshot eyes, his colorless, mocking lips, and the point to which his thoughts had carried him, was reflected in his visage so faithfully that a groan issued from his inmost heart. Then his eye fell upon a pistol, lying on the table, and he took it up and gazed gloomily at it:—a harsher, more mocking smile, wreathed his proud lip, and, cocking the weapon, he murmured the first words of the soliloquy in Hamlet.

"Yes," he said, "I know, now, what my lord Hamlet meant, when he asked that question of his soul:

> 'Whether 'tis nobler in the mind to suffer
> The stings and arrows of outrageous fortune,
> Or to take arms against a sea of troubles,
> And by opposing end them!'"

Then, looking with gloomy curiosity upon the murderous instrument, he said, with a sigh which resembled a groan: "Yes, now I understand those words:

> "*—To die! to sleep!*
> *No more!*—and by a sleep to say we end
> The heartache and the thousand natural shocks
> That flesh is heir to? 'Tis a consummation
> Devoutly to be wished!
> For who would bear the whips and scorns of time,
> The oppressor's wrong, the proud man's contumely,
> The pangs of despised love!'"

There he stopped, with an expression painfully affecting; and, sitting down, he covered his face with his hand, and was silent for a time. Then, the hand was taken away, and the head rose again—and on the lips the same mocking smile played with terrible meaning. He looked again at the pistol, and, with a sneer, placed the muzzle to his forehead.

"It is plain that I am a comedian," he said, bitterly; "I go for authority to plays! Well, now, if I were to play the tragedy to the end—imitate the Moor! Is it not easy? This little instrument ends all, at once!"—and his finger touched the trigger.

Suddenly a tap at the door startled him, and hastily uncocking the pistol, he thrust it into his bosom, and said, harshly and gloomily, "Come in!"

The door opened softly, a light step was heard, and little Kate Effingham entered the apartment. Kate, smiling and fond; her fair hair falling on her shoulders in long girlish curls; a tender, loving light in her mild, soft blue eyes; the little hands stretched out to greet him; her face, and form, and smile, and very dress redolent of home, and that happiness which the weary heart but now looked back upon, as the wrecked mariner clinging to the floating mast, about to be ingulfed in the dark waves, launches a last thought back to the sunshine and pure joy of his far inland home!

CHAPTER XXVII.

HOW MR. EFFINGHAM'S ROOM AT THE RALEIGH TAVERN WAS ILLUMINATED.

In a moment the child was in his arms, clasped to his heart. The fresh, bright-eyed little face—though now those eyes were bathed in dews of happiness—lay on his bosom, and two hot tears from the dry, weary eyes of the young man, rolled down, and fell upon the child's hand. For some minutes no word was uttered. Kate spoke first, and said, earnestly:

"Oh! I'm so glad to see you, cousin Champ—indeed, indeed, I am."

"And I am as glad to see you, Katy," he said, turning away; but no longer with that painful expression of mockery; "you came in like a sunbeam! I was so gloomy."

And again the poor, weary eyes were bathed in moisture, and the man's tears mingled with the child's.

"Come," he said, at length, "how is it possible you are here?"

And as he spoke, the young man caressed fondly the bright locks of the little head.

"Oh!" said Kate; "I just came by myself. I was *so* sorry, cousin Champ, when you went away, and have been crying about it often since—I couldn't help it. For you know you have always been so good to me. I couldn't help loving you dearly, and crying when you left us. Then papa got angry, and told cousin Alethea you had not done right; and then, when the parson came, he abused you, and papa quarrelled with him, and he's going away. Papa said no one should abuse you, and that you were not half as much to blame as they chose to say; and then went away to the library, and didn't come back to tea."

"But, Katy," said Mr. Effingham, turning away, "this does not explain how you—"

"Oh! I am coming to that at once, cousin Champ. You know I love you dearly—and I couldn't bear to think you were here all by yourself, and not happy. So as cousin

Alethea was coming to town in the chariot, me and Willie thought we'd come, too, and cousin Alethea said we might."

"Is Alethea in town?"

"Yes, cousin Champ; she's down at the store, buying a cake mould, and Willie was looking for a new whip. So I just slipped out and ran up here, and asked if you were here, of a gentleman—though I don't know if he is a real gentleman—wearing such a funny red cloak. He laughed, and was very good, and said you had just gone up to 'number 6,' and I came up, and saw the figure on your door, and tapped."

"Heaven sent you, Katy," said Mr. Effingham, pressing his tremulous lips to the child's forehead. "God knows what might have happened," he added, in a murmur.

"What did you say, cousin Champ?"

"Nothing, dear."

"What is this hard thing under your lace?" said the child, whose arm had struck against the concealed weapon.

"Nothing, nothing!" he said, hastily. And rising suddenly, he went to the open window, and hurled the pistol to the distance of fifty feet. Then returning, after seeing it fall into a pile of rubbish in the yard of the tavern, he took the child in his arms again, and leaned his weary head upon her shoulder.

"You don't seem to me well, cousin Champ," said Kate, tenderly, and endeavoring with the tact of a grown woman, to come to the subject which she wished to reach, without offending Mr. Effingham. "I don't think you are well, indeed I don't, and they can't take very good care of you in this place. I don't like it—it don't seem clean and nice. And then I'm sure you haven't got any body who can bathe your forehead as nicely as I can. Please come and go back with us, cousin," added the child, earnestly. "You can't think how happy it would make me, and all—indeed I would cry for joy."

"I can't make you cry, dear," said Mr. Effingham, with a fond look.

"Well, then, I'll laugh."

"I can't go now."

"But you are sick."

"No, no."

"Indeed—indeed, you're not well."

"Perfectly, dear Katy—but I am as glad to see you as if I wanted you to bathe my forehead."

"You don't seem to think that, cousin," said Kate, sighing, and looking wistfully at him, "or you would not leave us so long."

"Why, I have not been here a week."

"That's a long time—a long, long time indeed!"

Mr. Effingham softly smoothed the bright head.

"I was much longer away, when I went to England," he said, "and you did not write me a word to return, dear. You did send me enough of love, however."

"Yes, but I love you more now:—you didn't take much notice of me when I was a little chicken, running about the Hall—and then, and then, cousin—"

"What?"

"You know, you *had* to go England—"

"You mean—"

"Yes, dear cousin Champ," said Kate, with a tremulous but earnest voice, "I mean that you needn't have come here. Don't be angry with me, please."

"Angry with you!"

"For I love you so much. I don't think you ought to stay here now, indeed, you would be better at the Hall. Come now," she said, with an earnest pleading look, which made the little face inexpressibly lovely, "go back with me! won't you? Oh! I'll be so good if you'll go back; and so will Willie—for I will make him. Think how happy we would be, dear cousin Champ—indeed we can't be happy at all, while you are away. I can't."

And the little head drooped, the fair curls falling down, and veiling the child's cheeks. Mr. Effingham was silent, but he unconsciously clasped the small hand lying on his own more tightly, as if some invisible and hostile force were pulling him the other way, and in the child lay his only hope of resistance.

"You can't think how your being away has made me feel—indeed, you can't," continued the child, in a low voice, and glancing at his face with wistful, dewy eyes; "you know I never liked any body I loved to go away, and after papa, I love you better than any body in the world. Ever since you went, and papa got angry, I have felt as if I was going to fall sick—I was so sorry! Papa didn't look like he was well either, and sometimes I think I saw cousin Alethea looking sorry. When Tom was packing up your portmanteau, I thought you were going away, and put in it —"

"Did you put that Bible—"

"Yes, cousin Champ—for I knew you would like to read out of my little Bible."

Mr. Effingham rose, and going to his dressing-table, took the small volume from his portmanteau.

"Here Katy," he said, turning aside his head as he spoke, "I have not time to read it now."

"Oh, but keep it!"

"No--I don't wish to."

"Not when I ask you to, cousin Champ?"

"No—no—not now," said Mr. Effingham, with a shadow on his face.

Kate looked inexpressibly hurt, and two tears which she could not restrain, rolled down her cheeks. Mr. Effingham strode up and down the apartment—passed his hand wearily over his forehead, gazed wistfully at the child, and the book she held, and then away from her again. He stopped finally before the window, and looked out. Then he felt a little hand, warm and soft, take his own; and turning round, the child was again in his arms, pressed to his heart.

"Katy," he said, with a troubled voice, "I cannot keep your Bible now—I have not time to read it—and some one coming in here might take it."

Mr. Effingham's face clouded. The thought had occurred to him that some one of the rude, jeering actors might touch it—and at that moment he felt as if he would preserve it from such profanity at the hazard of his life.

"Keep it, dear," he added, tenderly, "I will read it if I ever—when, I mean, I come back to the Hall. Now, don't ask me to take it back any more, Katy—indeed, I cannot."

The child put the volume into the pocket of her frock, with an expression of quiet, uncomplaining sorrow, which was very touching.

"I'll promise to read it every day, when I get back, dear," said Mr. Effingham, "now don't feel badly."

"Oh! if you would only come back," she said, hiding her head in his bosom, and crying, "Oh! cousin Champ! if you would only come back! Oh, please do—please leave this place, and don't be angry with papa any more. They said you came—to see—to see—a—lady, cousin Champ. You know you've seen her now, and if she is good, and I know you would not like her if she was bad—if she is good she wouldn't have you to distress us to come and see her! Oh, where is she? I'll go and tell her myself, if you'll let me, how much we want you to come back to us, and I know you will not think I am presuming. Now, do let me go:—I'm sure she will not be angry with a little child like me—where is she, cousin Champ?"

Mr. Effingham held the child upon his lap, overcome with gloomy and yet hopeful thoughts. She looked into his face, and saw the troubled expression.

"Oh, come—come!" she said, in an earnest, pleading voice, "indeed you are not well. Oh, cousin Champ, you will not refuse me—your pet—please come—now cousin Champ—we'll all go back so nicely in the chariot—and—won't you?"

He looked at her for some minutes in silence, and said:

"Katy, do you believe in guardian angels?"

"I don't know—if you mean—"

"Then, do you believe in angels?"

"Yes! oh, yes!"

"And in heaven?"

"Yes: mamma is in heaven, and papa," she said.

"What do you think it is like?" he continued, gazing on the tender face, "a great city of pearls, and diamonds, and gold? Come, don't be surprised at my speaking so abruptly. Do you think there is really a heaven, and angels?"

"Oh, yes, cousin Champ—and I'm sure it is not made of gold and diamonds—I mean I don't think it is. I think it's a place where we all love each other more than we can on earth—and God, too."

"Can we love more than we do on earth?" he said, thoughtfully.

"Oh, yes—I believe we can—and then we will not have any thing in heaven to make us sorry. We won't be sick, and grieved, and all, but be happy, and love God for ever and ever."

Mr. Effingham made no reply; he only murmured to himself.

"Angels are good—like little children before they get bad," added Kate, earnestly; "there's a verse about 'the Kingdom of Heaven,' and it's being filled with good people, like little children. Must I show it to you?"

"No, no—I believe not," said Mr. Effingham, "I don't know that reading the Bible would do me any good. I believe what that verse says already, dear," he added, looking with moist eyes at the child, "and I meant that when I asked you about heaven; 'Suffer little children to come unto me and forbid them not—for of such is the kingdom of heaven.' Is not that the verse? I knew it was. Well, I wish I had died at your age."

"Oh!" said Kate, in a low voice, "I am not good enough—I'm very bad."

"You are heavenly in comparison with me."

"Oh, cousin Champ!"

"I am—well, well," he said, suddenly checking himself: and he murmured, "Why should I deprive myself of this child's heart."

"Indeed, indeed, you are not well," said Kate, gazing with a long, sad look, on the troubled and gloomy face, "and I think something has grieved you."

"No, no—"

"Let me read a little to you, please—I know you'll like—"

"No, no; I'm not fit to hear reading now, dear," he said, but more softly, and with less decision in his tone.

Kate noted this change, with that marvellous quickness of children, and said:

"Oh, yes; let me read you just a little about heaven. When I read it, I never feel sorry afterwards; and, if I am sick, it makes me feel almost well and happy. Sometimes I think about my being a little child, without any father or mother—any real father, I mean, though papa is my father—and I feel like crying; but I read a little in my Bible, and think that papa and mamma are in heaven, and that, if I am good, I'll go to heaven, too; and, then, I feel as if it wasn't much matter whether I felt sick and badly or not, so I kept myself good; for I will see them in heaven, if I obey God."

The weary and storm-tossed soul listened to these simple words, and felt a strange emotion at his heart, as if that heart had been frozen, and was slowly melting.

"For you know," Kate went on, earnestly, "this world is not a good place, and we can't be very happy here, though some things are very sweet and pleasant. We have to suffer a great deal here, and we must get mighty tired. But we ought not to complain when we have heaven to think of, where all will be happiness and joy. We feel wrong towards people very often, at least I do, and people behave badly to us, and make us suffer; but we ought to bear all this, when we think of living and loving dearly in heaven, for ever and for ever. Oh! let me read you where it says heaven is a place 'where the wicked cease from troubling, and the weary are at rest.'"

And, without waiting for a reply, the child opened her little Bible, and read, in a low, subdued, earnest voice, some verses, which the young man listened to in silence. Kate closed the book, and leaning her head on his shoulder, said:

"That sounds to me so sweet, that it makes me happy."

"Yes, yes," murmured Mr. Effingham, covering his eyes.

"Do you like to hear me read?" she asked, wistfully.

"Yes," he murmured again.

"Then," said Kate, with an expression of entreaty, which lit up her tender little face, like a light from heaven, and putting her arm round his neck as she spoke—"then come and go back! Oh, please come and go back, and I'll read to you whenever you want to hear me; and, oh! we'll be so happy, cousin Champ! I can't be happy while you are here, and I think that you are not well, may be, and haven't any body to do little things for you. Don't stay in this place, and be all by yourself. I'm sure cousin Alethea's sorry if she said any thing to make you angry; indeed, I know she is, for she said to papa that she ought not to have said something to you. Papa is dreadfully distressed at your going away, and, indeed—indeed—" (here the child's voice faltered) "I shall be so unhappy—so—so—Oh, cousin Champ, do come and go with me! Oh, please don't stay! You can't find any body to love you as much as we do, and till you come back the Hall will look dark to me."

The little arm around his neck drew him toward the door; the beseeching voice went to his heart, and melted all his pride, and hardness, and stubborn coldness; the half jest he had uttered about his guardian angel, seemed to become a heavenly reality—to be there in the person of that child, entreating him to go away with her.

"Oh, come!" cried Kate, clinging closer and closer to him, and turning her moist, tender eyes upon his own; "come with me, cousin Champ—come back with us—oh! you are coming. I knew you would. You wouldn't refuse me, I know."

And she placed one hand on the door to open it.

Before she could touch the knob the door opened, and a servant appeared on the threshold.

"A gentleman to see you, sir; ask him up, sir?" he said, bowing.

Mr. Effingham hesitated, and was silent. It might have been imagined that he feared to leave the child—to go beyond the reach of her voice, the brightness of her eyes.

"Well, well," he said, after a moment's silence, "whoever it is I will see him. Stay here, dear—wait till I come back—I will return directly. Say I will be down immediately," he added, to the servant.

Then stooping, and pressing his lips to the child's forehead, he said, tenderly and softly:

"Stay till I return, Katy; I will soon send this gentleman off, whoever he may be. I cannot lose you so soon, and I think, before you go—if I do not go with you—you may read me some more."

Kate looked inexpressibly delighted, and this expression of joy seemed to touch and please Mr. Effingham extremely. He threw a last fond glance on the child, and saying again that he would be back in a moment, went out and closed the door. Kate sat down overcome with joy and pride: her smile seemed to illuminate the whole apartment, dimming the very radiance of the sunlight.

Ten minutes passed thus, when suddenly a knock at the door made her heart throb; and rising quickly to her feet, she said, before she was aware of it, "Come in!"

CHAPTER XXVIII.

ENTER SHYLOCK, AND HIS SHADOW.

THE door opened, and two men made their appearance. We say *men:* it would be sacrificing too much to courtesy to call them gentlemen; for neither in their dress, features, nor expression, was there any thing whatsoever remotely entitling them to that distinction. He who came first was that worthy who had acted Shylock on the opening night, at the theatre near the capitol; and the reader may possibly recollect Mr. Manager Hallam's criticism of his performance, delivered in the presence of the worthy himself, on the next morning, at the Raleigh. His present state was not materially an improvement upon his condition that night, and having dined not very long before, his spirits were naturally in an elevated and generous condition. When Mr. Pugsby had emptied his pint of rum or his bottle of port—a delicacy which he did not usually indulge in, however—he felt at peace with all the world, and ready to embrace the whole of mankind. His companion was a lean, cadaverous gentleman, whose favorite characters were "Shallow," "Slender" the apothecary in "Romeo and Juliet,"—he had been assisting Mr. Pugsby in emptying his last bottle.

Kate beheld the entrance of these worthies with great alarm; though her womanly little air of dignity did not desert her. Perhaps it was rather distaste than alarm which she felt, child as she was, for certainly no contrast could have been imagined less to the advantage of the stage worthies. Kate, clad in her rich and tasteful little costume of silk and velvet—with her bright eyes and rosy face, looked like a flower, a picture, something beautiful, rich and rare, to be approached with reverence, and regarded with love and admiration:—she seemed out of place in the rough apartment, as some masterpiece of Titian, framed in gold, would look hung up in a wide garret, with a ceiling of dirty rafters. She had the beauty and tenderness of childhood: purity and gentleness enveloped her like a cloud. None of these things appertained to the worthies who now entered, inasmuch as they were extremely rough and common specimens of humanity, with bloated faces, and unsteady gait, and sleepy-looking eyes, which rolled, and winked, and leered, as authentic tradition relates of the ancient worthy Silenus.

Shylock hesitated for a moment on the threshold, and exhibited a species of inane surprise, at finding a child, instead of his brother-comedian, Mr. Effingham, in the apartment.

"Hum!" said Shylock, by way of signifying that he was about to speak. This expressive monosyllable was echoed by Shallow, who, to save himself the trouble of thinking, generally repeated or coincided in, the observations of his friend.

"Stand and unfold thyself," continued Shylock, striking an attitude, and facetiously pretending to consider Kate a ghost.

"Unfold—yes, unfold," echoed Shallow, stretching out his cadaverous hand as his friend did.

"Be thou a spirit of health or goblin damned? thou comest in such a questionable shape, I'll speak to thee!" continued Shylock, "hey? come, speak!"

Kate felt as if she should sink into the floor, and was so frightened that she could scarcely restrain her tears or command her voice.

"Come, come, pretty damsel!" exclaimed Shylock, with some impatience, and descending into prose, "come, why don't you answer? Who are you? Why are you here, instead of that jolly minion of the moon, that lad of metal, hight Childe Effingham?"

"Oh, sir!" said Kate, with a trembling voice, and retreating as the leering tragedian approached her, "Oh, sir, I am—Mr. Effingham—I mean, he is just gone, sir."

"That is no answer."

"No answer," echoed Shallow.

"A subterfuge."

"Perfect."

"And subterfuges are a deadly sin," said Shylock, whose words unconsciously flowed into a metrical shape.

"An awful sin," said Shallow.

"So now perpend, young damsel," continued Shylock, approaching the child, who shrank back, "either thou diest presently, or do'st relate to me the marvel strange, why thou art here—all armed in complete—no, thou hast no steel! Speak! what art thou? And if thou do'st conceal the least small thing—" Shylock drew out the knife which he was accustomed to whet upon his shoe, when Antonio was to be sacrificed, and flourished it with deadly meaning. Kate shrank further back and turned pale.

"Oh, sir, you frighten me!" she said.

"I'll eat thee whole ere the leviathan hath swum a league—"

Kate fell into a chair.

"Come," said Shylock, putting up his knife, "I'll be merciful, if I am a Hebrew vile, and thou, fair lass, a Christian."

"We'll be merciful," said Shallow.

"Therefore, unfold—unfold, I say!" continued Shylock, "art thou base, common, and popular; or, high and mighty, like Prince Hal?—discourse. Whence art thou?"

Kate murmured, with a throbbing heart: "From the Hall, sir."

"What is thy name?"

"Catherine, sir!"

"Well, Catherine, listen: thou shalt go below, and bid the tapster draw a measure of rum, which thou shalt bring to us. We are noble gentlemen, come hither to see Prince Hal, that noble bully. Do'st thou understand?"

"Oh, sir, I cannot! I don't know—"

"Do'st thou reply?"

"Oh, sir, don't come near me, I do not like you!"

"Not like me? Well, I will be calm! Go bid them draw the ale; do'st hear, thou varlet vile?"

Kate's indignation began to conquer her fear, and, child as she was, in the midst of such persons, her face flushed with anger, at the word *vile.* "I can't go, sir," she said.

"Cannot! sayest thou? Why, 'cannot'?"

"I do not know any body here, sir," she replied; "please let me pass out."

"Never! thou shalt pass over my dead body, rather."

"And mine," said Shallow.

"Oh, I must pass!" cried Kate, endeavoring to leave the room.

"Stand back! ill met by moonlight, proud Titania! But thou shalt not go hence."

"I must, sir!" said Kate, endeavoring to pass again, and nearly crying from fear and indignation.

"By heaven, thou diest!" And uttering these words, Shylock moved with unsteady gait to shut the door. But Kate was too quick for the worthy, and ran through, brushing against him as she passed. Shylock made a grasp at her, and caught the ribbon of her little hat, tearing the covering from her head. The next moment he would have reached her and brought her back by main force, but just as she was about to fall upon her knees, in despair, the door opposite opened, and a young woman, evidently attracted by the noise, appeared upon the threshold.

"What is this?" she said.

"Oh, ma'am! that man won't let me go!" cried Kate, "he has frightened me nearly to death. Oh, don't let him take me from you!" And clinging to the dress of Beatrice, she shrunk from the infuriated Shylock. Beatrice, with a single word and a look, closed the door in the face of that worthy, and she and the child were alone together.

CHAPTER XXIX.

KATE AND BEATRICE.

For a moment the young girl and the child were silent; Beatrice knew not what to think of the scene, and Kate was indulging in a hearty cry. At last she dried her eyes, and stopped sobbing by degrees, and looking at Beatrice, said: "Oh, ma'am, I'm so thankful that you saved me from that horrid man!"

"How did he come to annoy you, my child?" said Beatrice, looking affectionately at the sweet little face.

"Oh, he came in, and—and because I wouldn't go and get him something—for I couldn't, you know. Oh, he frightened me so!" and Kate began to sob again.

Beatrice wiped the child's eyes and got her a glass of water, all the time soothing her with kind words.

"Don't speak if it makes you cry," she said, softly.

"Oh, I am not frightened, now!"

"You are quite safe here."

"Am I quite?"

"Yes, that rude man will not presume to come into this room, and were he to do so, I would send him from it with a single word."

And Beatrice, with a disdainful motion of her hand, seemed to wish to dismiss so insignificant a subject. Kate looked at her attentively, for the first time, and said;

"Do you know him? I think you are too pretty and good to know that rude man."

Beatrice turned away.

"I am sorry that I am obliged to know him," she said in a low tone, "but how did you come to be pursued by him? It was disgraceful!" added Beatrice, with a generous flash of her proud, brilliant eye.

"I was waiting a minute for cousin, who had gone down to see a gentleman. He left me in his room, and I was so frightened when those rude men came in. I am not used to such people, you know;—papa don't have any visitors like them, and the gentlemen that come to the Hall are always kind to me. Oh, he drew out such an ugly sharp knife, and threatened to kill me!" added Kate, very nearly beginning to cry again. Beatrice looked at her attentively: some recollection seemed to be struggling in her mind.

"Strange!" she said, "I seem to have seen this child before—somewhere—where was it?"

And she pressed her forehead, and seemed to be buried in thought. Kate looked at her, and said, timidly:

"I am afraid ma'am, that you were busy when I came in."

"Yes, I was my child—but that is nothing."

"Were you sewing? what a pretty handkerchief!"

And remembering the scene she had just passed through, Kate used the embroidered handkerchief she had taken up to admire, for the purpose of drying a rebellious tear.

"I was not sewing," said Beatrice, with a look of weariness, "I was studying. But you have not told me, my child, how you came to be in the Raleigh."

"Oh, cousin Alethea, and Willie, and me, came to town. and—"

"Then you do not live here: but I forget—you spoke of the Hall, and there are no halls here."

"Oh, no: a hall is a house in the country."

"And you came to see your cousin—a gentleman who wears a red cloak—?"

"Oh, no! he's not my cousin—"

"Ah!" said Beatrice, her eyes suddenly dazzled with a rapid lightning-like thought, "your cousin—what is his name—the Hall—?"

"Cousin Champ is his name, and we all live at Effingham Hall. My name is Catherine Effingham—but papa is not my father."

Beatrice sat down, murmuring.

"Effingham!—Effingham—always Effingham! Yes—at the theatre!"

Kate misunderstood these half-audible words, and said:

"Did you ask if Effingham was our name, ma'am? Yes; and I know papa will be mighty thankful to you and cousin Champ too. He's a dear good fellow, and I love him dearly."

Beatrice remained silent, and turned away her face in order that the child might not see the painful and gloomy expression which dimmed the eyes, and took the tender smile from the lips.

"And you were in yon—in Mr. Effingham's room—were you, my child?" she murmured, at last.

"Yes; and cousin Champ had just gone down to see a gentleman. He told me to wait till he came back."

"Is he fond of you?" asked Beatrice, why she scarcely knew.

"I know he is!" exclaimed Kate, with a bright smile shining through her moist eyes.

"And you love him?"

"Oh, dearly! he is so kind and good!"

They were almost the very words which had escaped from the lips of Beatrice after her interview with Charles; and the recollection of that interview now came to efface the bitter expression which followed little Kate's words. The bitter smile only glanced, then flew away.

"Did your father bring you to town, my child?" she asked, pressing her hand upon her heart to still its throbbing.

"Oh, no!" said Kate, "papa is not pleased with cousin

Champ." Then regretting this speech, she added—"that is—I mean, ma'am—cousin Champ went away from the Hall, and hasn't been back."

Beatrice could not look at the child.

"And is he angry?" she said.

"Who?—papa?"

"Yes," murmured Beatrice.

"No, I don't think papa is much angry; but he don't like cousin Champ to be here."

"Why?" said Beatrice, in a low voice, and like a despairing soldier turning the weapon in the wound.

"He came to see some lady here, and papa and cousin Alethea do not like—"

"No, no—not a lady—"

There the young girl stopped, overcome, panting, avoiding the child's look, her head drooping, her forehead burning.

"I don't know who it is," said Kate, "but I think cousin Alethea said it was that young actress we saw act in the 'Merchant of Venice.'"

"Do you not recollect her?" murmured Beatrice.

"Who—Miss Hallam? Oh, yes! She wore a lovely fawn-colored silk, and was very pretty."

"I did not know I was so completely changed," said the young girl, turning away and smiling painfully. Then she said aloud:

"And so Mr. Effingham—your cousin—came to see the actress, and his family are displeased?"

"Yes, ma'am, we all want dear cousin Champ to come back. I don't think he ought to come here to see an actress. She is not good enough for him, and oughtn't to distress us."

"Oh, it is an unjust punishment!—it is unjust!" murmured Beatrice, with tears in her eyes: but Kate neither saw the tears nor heard these bitter words.

"I came to tell cousin Champ to-day he was too good for her—but I didn't like to," continued Kate, not observing the change in the countenance of Beatrice; "we read some in the Bible, though, and cousin Champ 'most promised to go back with me—"

"Did he!"

"Yes, ma'am."

"Oh, take him back!"

Kate was somewhat surprised at these vehement words, but said:

"I think he is going with us. I don't think he would leave us, all who love him so, for a common playing girl."

"Oh, it is unjust—it is unjust!" repeated Beatrice, in an inaudible voice. "I have not deserved it!"

"She's very pretty—for I believe it is Miss Hallam," continued Kate, "but she is not good enough to marry cousin Champ, you know."

Beatrice rose wildly, and said, with passionate tears in her eyes:

"She would not marry him!—she does not wish to! I am that actress! I am Beatrice Hallam! He has made my life miserable and wretched; he follows me, persecutes me, and will not leave me! Oh, I am not to blame—I am not! I do not deserve so much unjust blame—no, no! It is cruel in you to make me suffer so!—oh, it is cruel!"

And hiding her face in her hands, the young girl trembled and shook with passionate sobs. Kate was so much startled and alarmed by these passionate words that she stood for a moment motionless with surprise and astonishment. Then her tender little heart overcame every thing, and running up to the beautiful girl who had been so kind to her, she took her hand, and, sobbing, said:

"Don't cry!—please, don't cry!—I didn't mean to be so rude—indeed, I am ashamed and sorry—oh! please don't cry!"

And Kate herself cried, as if her heart would break. Beatrice suffered the little hand to imprison her own, and slowly raised her head again—her eyes full of tears.

"Pardon me, my child," she said, with noble dignity and calmness, "I did not mean to blame you—I could not help speaking abruptly and shedding some tears—for indeed I am not to blame. My lot is very unhappy, for I cannot even ask a little child like you to love me."

And her humid eyes dwelt with great softness and tenderness on Kate's fresh little countenance, over which large tears were chasing each other.

"I am glad I was near to save you from that rude man," continued Beatrice, rising, "and that is my only reward—my own feelings. I ask no other—"

Kate would have fallen into the tender arms, for very weakness and emotion.

"No," said Beatrice, gently repulsing her, "I am an actress. Come!"

And she went toward the door. At the same moment it opened violently, and Mr. Effingham stood before them.

CHAPTER XXX.

SHOWING TO WHAT USE A LOAF OF BREAD MAY BE PUT.

THE young man entered grasping his sword—which he had drawn half from the scabbard.

"Ah!" he said, with a deep sigh of relief: then turning upon Beatrice, he said: "I have to thank you, madam, for robbing me of my visitor!"

And his haughty eye flashed, as he put his arm round Kate, and drew her away. Beatrice made no reply—but Kate cried out.

"Oh! cousin Champ! Don't speak so to her! She was so good to me."

"Good to you, Kate! What do you mean?"

"Those horrid men! Oh, they frightened me so!"

Mr. Effingham looked from one to the other, to ask an explanation.

"What men?" he said.

"The men that came into your room."

"Men in my room! Who?"

"I don't know, indeed, cousin Champ, but they behaved very badly to me."

"Behaved badly to you!" said Mr. Effingham, his brow flushing with haughty fire.

"Oh, it was nothing," said the child, becoming alarmed at the storm she had aroused, "they only frightened me a little!"

Suddenly Mr. Effingham looked at the child's hair still disordered and rumpled—for the worthy Shylock, in pulling away her hat, had naturally dragged the well-brushed hair from its place. Mr. Effingham observed this at a glance, and said, with a flashing eye:

"Where is your hat, Kate?"

Beatrice rose.

"I can tell you what has taken place in a moment, sir,' she said, calmly; "it is nothing more than happens almost every day—only disgraceful, you know, sir. Mr. Pugsby annoyed your young relative, and the child came to my apartment for refuge. I gave it to her, that is all; and now, sir—"

Mr. Effingham did not wait to hear the end of the sentence. His eye burned fiercely, and hurrying out with the child, he said, hastily:

"Come, Katy, let us go to the carriage: I must put you in: I can't go to-day to the Hall. Ah, when you are once safe, we'll have a settlement—"

"But my hat, cousin Champ?" said Kate. Mr. Effingham's teeth ground audibly, but before he could make a reply, a voice behind him, loud and familiar, said:

"Here's your beauty's hat—where the devil are you going—"

It was Shylock, who came along the passage behind, and turning, Mr. Effingham saw the child's hat in his hand. A flash as of lightning blazed from the young man's eye, and to abandon Kate's hand, throw himself upon the leering worthy, clutch him by the throat, and hurl him headlong from the landing-place to the bottom of the stairs, was the agreeable employment of a single moment. But this did not satisfy Mr. Effingham's rage; and motioning the child to remain behind, he sprung down the steps, and arriving at the bottom just as Shylock, in a violent rage, rose up, he shouted wrathfully:

"Draw, you dog! draw! you wear a sword! Damn my blood, I'll have your heart's blood!"

And drawing his sword, the young man would have plunged it into Shylock's breast, had not the jolly host thrown himself between the combatants and received the thrust in a huge loaf of bread he was lugging into his larder. This incident so far delayed further employment of the weapon, which had completely passed through it to the hilt. The crowd then parted the infuriated combatants, and this consummation was one for which Shylock seemed devoutly grateful. Having only frightened the child for fun, as that worthy said, afterwards, Mr. Effingham's sudden attack upon him had taken him completely by surprise: and his blood had scarcely time to rise. So it was they were parted, and Shylock, muttering curses and threats of vengeance, retreated to his apartment. Mr. Effingham, with insulting disdain, called after him that he should have an opportunity to right his wrongs at the sword's point, though he might be excused from matching himself against such a cowardly villain; and so this little interlude ended.

Kate, sobbing and agitated, had put on her little hat, and now, with Mr. Effingham's hand in her own, left the inn. At the threshold they ran against Master Will, who, breathless, his face flushed, his mouth open, was running to ask if any one at the Raleigh had seen Kate.

"Here I am, Willie," said the child; "I'm not crying, you know—only laughing."

And Kate, after this abortive effort to show that nothing had happened, burst into a passion of tears. Mr. Effingham, with a short and curt greeting to Will, went on to the place where the carriage stood, and placed the child in it. Miss Alethea had felt much less anxiety about Kate than Will, and was still making her purchases. Will ran in to tell her that Kate was found.

Mr. Effingham was going away in silence, after pressing the child's hand, when, sobbing, she said:

"Oh, won't you kiss me? you are not angry with me, cousin Champ!"

And tears choked the tender, distressed voice—deep sighs shook the little frame of the child. Mr. Effingham bent over toward her, but, suddenly resuming his erect attitude, said, gloomily:

"No, no, Katy; I cannot kiss you. No; do not think of me in future; and never come near the Raleigh again. Have you your Bible?"

"I believe so," sobbed Kate.

"Good," he said, in the same quiet, gloomy voice; "I will love you dearly as long as I live, but I can see you no more. Good-bye," and, turning away, he muttered,

"The die is cast!"

CHAPTER XXXI.

WHAT MR. EFFINGHAM MEANT WHEN HE SAID THAT THE DIE WAS CAST.

LET us now endeavor to explain why Mr. Effingham acted so strangely toward the child, refusing to kiss her at parting, and exhibiting that singular solicitude about her Bible's safety, in the little pocket. The explanation of these matters will be found in that interview with the nameless gentleman, whom Mr. Effingham left Kate to go and see.

When the young man descended, he saw, seated in the ordinary, waiting for him, his friend, Jack Hamilton, the fox-hunter. A family tradition, supported by the family Bible, averred that this gentleman's name had originally been John, but this was not generally credited, so completely had the sobriquet by which he was almost universally addressed, come to be regarded as the name given to him by his sponsors in baptism. The face which Mr. Hamilton rejoiced in, was, perhaps, remotely responsible for this alteration in his patronymic; and it seemed almost impossible to feel that he should be addressed by any other name than a nickname. He was a hearty, laughing, honest-looking fellow, with frank, open eyes; a nose, which seemed to be everlastingly engaged in snuffing up the odors of broils and roasts, or critically testing wines; a voice, which greeted all, high and low, with nearly equal friendliness, cordiality, and heartiness. Mr. Hamilton was richly clad, but down his velvet pantaloons ran a long red stain, the blood of a fox he had followed to the death on the preceding day.

Mr. Effingham greeted him with unusual cordiality, and his languid, indifferent, *petit maître* manner seemed to have entirely disappeared—at least, this was the observation made by his friend.

"You were busy, were you not?" said Hamilton; "any friends?"

"No, no; I'm very glad to see you, my dear fellow."

"Well, that's understood, or, it would be understood," said honest Jack Hamilton, "if my visit was a mere dropping-in, as I passed by, to use the new slang which is becoming fashionable; but I came to say something to you, Champ. Come, let's take a stroll."

"I would—but—really—"

And Mr. Effingham thought of Kate.

"Oh, you need not fear being detained any time, scarcely. Come, we cannot talk here."

And, putting his arm through Mr. Effingham's, the fox-hunter led him away.

"Well, well," said the young man to himself, "Katy can amuse herself for a few minutes, until I return; and I must know what brings Hamilton to see me. He evidently has something on his mind."

They strolled out into the square, in the centre of the town, and found themselves thus insulated from the ears, if not from the eyes, of the community. Hamilton stopped, and said:

"I came to talk about this ball, Champ."

"What? at the Governor's?"

"Yes."

"Well, my dear fellow?"

"These actors, here, and the people at the tavern, are saying—"

"That I am going to it?"

"Yes."

"With Beatrice Hallam?"

"Yes."

"Well, they had the right to say so I announced my intention to do so," said Mr. Effingham, in a gloomy and hesitating voice.

"The people at the tavern have been talking through the town about it," continued Hamilton, "and so it got to the gentlemen in the neighborhood, and created quite a sensation."

"It seems that every thing I do creates something of that description," said Mr. Effingham, gloomily.

"But, really, you must confess that this—"

"Deserves to create a sensation, you would say: is it not so?"

"Well, Champ, I'll be honest with you, and say that I think it does."

Mr. Effingham passed his hand thoughtfully and wearily

across his brow. A struggle seemed to be going on in his mind. "If I fancy going with this young woman, I will go," he said, at length.

"You have not determined, then?" said Hamilton, displaying great satisfaction at these words.

Mr. Effingham mused. "I had determined," he replied, "but I do not know now if I shall go—I think not."

"Delighted to hear it! really now, Champ, you must permit me to say that you are too good a fellow to throw yourself away upon that young girl, though I grant you she is pretty. I suppose, though, you are running after her as we run a fox, for the glorious excitement of the chase. Up and away! ride all day and night! no matter if you break your neck, you gain the excitement and glory!"

Mr. Effingham's countenance displayed still the struggle going on in his mind. Then a bright light cleared away the gloom and doubt, and his features became serene and soft once more. He had thought of Kate, and now said: "Jack, I don't think I will go. No, I will not!"

"By George, I'm delighted to hear it!"

"You're a good friend!"

"I hope so; we have run many a fox together."

"Yes, yes!"

"Don't you remember the gray rascal we ran from Cote's to the ford? what a day we had—and Tom Lane has not got over his dislocated shoulder to this day."

"Those were fine times, fine times!" said Mr. Effingham, cheerily.

"And you remember, by George!" said Hamilton, laughing heartily, "I recollect it as if it was yesterday! You remember when we swept by the Hall like a parcel of wild devils, Tom Lane came near running over your little cousin—what was her name? I think it was Kate?"

"Yes, yes!" said Mr. Effingham, with a soft smile.

"A lovely little creature, and as good as she's pretty; I saw her at the Hall the other day, when I went to see my good friend, Miss Alethea—think of a bachelor, confirmed and obdurate like myself, having lady friends!—the child took my eye mightily, and I do believe she recollected the old times before you went to England!"

"Happy times, happy times!" said Mr. Effingham,

returning to his youth again, as the fox-hunter brought the past back to him with his familiar, honest voice, his frank eyes, and laughing reminiscences.

"Yes, they were happy enough," said Hamilton, "and you thought so then, I know, judging from the foolish things you were guilty of about Clare Lee. By George, she was a perfect little angel, and is yet!"

Mr. Effingham's head drooped.

"I remember when we all used to go to gather apples. I was a young man, then, but just as young as the youngest, and your favorite practice was to hold up the corners of her silk apron, until that black monkey, Joe, threw down enough to fill it—"

Mr. Effingham smiled.

"And as the little apron slowly got full, it weighed down more and more, and naturally you came closer to pretty Clare; and somehow your face struck against her own, the lower portions thereof! and—ah, Champ, my boy, you were a wild fellow then!" And Mr. Hamilton laughed heartily. His companion smiled, with dreamy eyes and tender lips, thinking of his boyhood and of Clare.

"After that, you took it into your head to go to England, and came back the perfect dandy you are," continued honest Jack Hamilton, with refreshing frankness.

"Yes, yes!" said Mr. Effingham, smiling.

"And snubbed us."

"No, no!"

"And swaggered about like a lord, and talked literature like a wit—what a wearisome thing literature is! And you altogether deteriorated! Come, now, deny it?"

"I'm afraid I cannot," said Mr. Effingham, thinking of Clare.

"Still our family—we are distant kin, you know—our family comes of too good a stock to degenerate, and I don't think your foreign journeyings, have hurt you much. The folks all about stand up for you, and have one eternal observation, which makes me yawn, about your 'sowing your wild oats.' They always shake their heads when my name is mentioned, and hint that my crop is always being put in, and never reaped and disposed of."

"You're better than I am, Jack," said his friend quietly.

"The devil! no compliments! If some folks heard that, they would dissent most emphatically!"

"Who?"

"All sorts of people, even down to that little chick we were talking of, Kate. By George, sir, you should have heard the eulogy she pronounced in your honor, on the visit I mentioned I made to the Hall!"

"What! little Kate praised—"

"Yes, I should think so: the private impression of any stranger who had heard her, would have been that her illustrious cousin united in his single person all the graces, attractions, and virtues of the greatest sages and heroes of modern and ancient times. Of course such extravagance couldn't deceive one who knew you as well as I did!"

Mr. Effingham found himself laughing delightedly, and murmuring, "Darling Kate!"

"Well, now, I'm glad to see that my well-meant advice is not needed," continued Hamilton. "You will not go to the ball with Beatrice Hallam?"

"No—no; I think I shall go back to the Hall to-day."

"Good! Take a seat in my turn-out! I'm glad you are not going there—for there would have come no good from it. Those fellows are very hotbrained."

"Who?"

"Oh, I was just thinking of what a party of fellows were saying of it," said Hamilton, not reflecting upon his words, or being at all conscious how injudicious they were. "They talked so that I thought I would come and see you."

"What did they say?" Mr. Effingham asked, with an imperceptible clouding of the brow.

"Oh, don't mind them. They got to talking, and said nothing but what was foolish—they said that your going with Miss Hallam was out of the question—and I agree with them."

"How out of the question?"

"Why, ridiculous."

"Ridiculous?"

"Come! my dear fellow, don't think of them."

"But what did they say?—who were they?" asked Mr. Effingham, feeling his anger rise at what he regarded as an impertinent piece of interference with his private affairs.

"I will not tell their names," said Hamilton.

"Well—their words, then."

"Their words?"

"Yes; what did they say of my going to the ball? Come, tell me, Hamilton."

"Well, as I came to tell you, I will," his friend replied, thoughtlessly; "they said it was wrong."

"Wrong!"

"Yes, and ridiculous."

"Is that all?" asked Mr. Effingham, with a curling lip.

"No!" said Hamilton; "they got to saying after the third bottle, that they would not permit it—by George! There it is out, fool that I am! But when did I ever fail to make a fool of myself!"

And conscious, too late, of his indiscretion, Mr. Jack Hamilton regarded his own conduct with profound contempt and indignation. He was not far wrong, if this were on the score of discretion: for his last words completely aroused the devil of pride and obstinate wilfulness, which had been put to sleep by those familiar reminiscences of youth and home, and Clare's tenderness—Kate's, too.

"Not permit *me* to attend the ball with Beatrice Hallam!" said Mr. Effingham, with disdainful pride. "By heaven! I will know who dared to say that!"

"I will not tell you," said Jack Hamilton, stoutly. Mr. Effingham's hand grasped the hilt of his sword.

"I have been insulted!" he said.

"None was meant."

"None meant!"

"I tell you, Champ; they had all been drinking, and did not know what they said."

"No man shall insult me, and say he was intoxicated! I will not take such a lame excuse, Hamilton."

"Come, now—challenge me," said his friend, coolly.

"No; I shall apply to the proper parties for redress."

"Of course, I am responsible, Champ. Come, run your short sword through me, and let out the foolish mind which has made me act so childishly!"

"Hamilton, you have acted as a real friend," said Mr. Effingham, with a frown. "I hold that no friend should hear another spoken of in such terms, without informing him of the assault upon his honor."

"What assault is there here, in the devil's name?"

"They said that my conduct was ridiculous—"

"A mere joke!"

"And they—the paladins of respectability and chivalry—they would not *permit* me to go to the Governor's ball—to escort Miss Hallam thither. By heaven! I'll make them repent it."

"Champ, you are as furious as a Spanish bull—you see red at a moment's warning! Come, moderate your anger."

"I am not angry!" said Mr. Effingham, furiously.

"Not angry!"

"No—I am indignant, though; and I will show these excellent gentlemen that my actions or intentions are not such as concern themselves. I shall find the paladins!"

"How will you?"

"Why, I will go to that ball with Miss Hallam, and if any gentleman in the room looks sideways at her or at me, I will call him to account for it. Your bottle critics will not fail to expose themselves!"

And Mr. Effingham's lip curled with anger and scorn.

"Presume to criticise my affairs thus!" he continued, indignantly, "I am then a child who is to ask permission of these worthy gentlemen—these potent, grave, and reverend signors—if I chance to feel a wish to escort a lady to a ball! Yes, a lady, Hamilton! for by heaven! I tell you, that Beatrice Hallam is as pure and high-souled as the noblest lady in the land! I know her well, and to my cost; and I tell you that she is the pearl of honor, delicacy, and truth. You may smile, and I know well what causes your mirth. You are thinking of my wild words, that day when I met you going out of town. Well, I was angry that day, because Miss Hallam had received my familiar addresses with proper coldness—had repulsed me. She was right—and I honor her for it. If she scorns me again, I may hate her, and taunt her; but at the bottom I respect and honor her. You look at me ironically! well, say I do love her—say I am infatuated about her—better men have made fools of themselves! whether that be true or not, one thing is certain, I shall allow no *man* to make a fool of *me!*"

And Mr. Effingham put his cocked hat on with a movement which betrayed his anger and indignation: he had taken it off during this speech to wipe his brow, moist with perspiration.

For a moment Hamilton said nothing.

"Well, Champ," he replied, at length, "I repeat that I was a great fool to tell you this, and I still hope you will regard these hasty words I have reported to you—I did it in the most friendly spirit—in the light they should be regarded—as the mere idle talk of young men. Come, dismiss your anger, and go back with me. Forget what I have said, and let the matter end."

Mr. Effingham shook his head, with a frown.

"It will end otherwise," he said

"You will not go to the ball?"

"Yes, I will."

"With Miss Hallam?"

"With Miss Hallam."

"It will be a dreadful thing for you:—you will be laughed at all over the colony."

"Let them laugh!" said Mr. Effingham, dsidainfully.

"You may even get a dozen duels on your hands."

"Oh, very well!—very well! I wish some little excitement. I have a good deal of time on my hands. I think it highly probable that some chevalier will espouse the cause of outraged society, and avenge its accumulated wrongs upon my insignificant person—if I do not give an account of the chivalrous gentleman myself!" added Mr. Effingham, with a scornful pride. Hamilton saw that he had raised a storm beyond his power to quell, and with mingled sorrow, and self-upbraiding, very unusual with him, led the way back to the tavern in silence.

"Well," he said, as they reached the door, "I have used my best efforts to persuade you to give this up, Champ: you are determined, I see, and I know it is useless to say any more. I have only to add, that as you are alone, and the enemy is numerous, I shall hold myself prepared to espouse your side in any thing which may arise of a hostile character. Good day."

And the honest fox-hunter, refusing to receive Mr. Effingham's assurances of regret, for any thing that he might have said, and declining to enter the tavern, parted from him, with a shake of the hand, full of cordiality and friendship. Mr. Effingham for a moment looked after him with friendly regard, then the old gloomy expression usurped its former place upon his visage, and he ascended to his chamber. Kate was not there, and he hurried out to look around for her. He heard voices in Beatrice's room—Kate's, he thought; "and hastening to the door, opened it just as they were issuing forth as we have seen. What ensued thereon, we have related.

CHAPTER XXXII.

IN WHICH PARSON TAG APPEARS AND DISAPPEARS.

"In former pages of this true history, I had occasion to set down a few reflections upon the feelings of my worthy ancestor, Mr. Effingham, when, having been repulsed by the young actress, he rode back to the hall. I come now to say a few brief words of Mr. Charles Waters, another of the characters whose mental development it is my duty to advert to. Charles Waters was, as the reader will have perceived, by nature a student and thinker. Unused from his very childhood to the amusements and employments of his associates, his character had assumed a peculiar mould. To strong feelings he united a cool and self-possessed intellect, and this intellect he had trained by hard study, and long and profound thought. Accustomed to live thus in the past and future, not in the present—or if at all in the present, only so far as to examine its bearing on that future—he had grown up without experiencing any of those sensations which men generally become acquainted with when they are thrown in contact with the fairer sex. In other words, he had passed his majority without experiencing what is universally known by the name of love. His character had thus become serious, and his countenance habitually wore an expression of thoughtful quiet. He seldom laughed, and scarcely ever joined in the rough, jovial converse of his father's guests—the boatman Townes and others—and though he was greatly beloved by this class of persons, and respected also, this personal popularity was rather to be attributed to his well-known goodness and nobility of character than his social traits. He had visited the theatre, as we have seen, on the opening night, in compliance with his father's request, not from any motion of his own. His father had imagined that his cheek was pale, his eye mournful, his health injured, by those incessant explorations into the ruins of systems and nations; the play, he thought, would be of service to him; and he had gone, and admired Beatrice Hallam, and felt some indignation when Mr. Effingham annoyed her—and nothing more. Then he had preserved that young woman's life, and there is much of significance in this fact. We experience warm regard toward those we have greatly served—a young girl is never afterwards wholly indifferent to the man who has preserved her life. He had felt the truth of this, and required no urging on his father's part to go and inquire how Miss Hallam had borne her accident. We were present at that interview, and were witnesses of the pleased surprise he betrayed at the exhibition by Beatrice of such fresh and virgin innocence and childlike enthusiasm. He came away, as we have seen, thinking of her, and thereafter for many days neglected his books, and felt at his heart the new and strange emotion I have spoken of. Then impelled by the desire to see again that enchanting face, hear again the fresh voice, so pure, and loving, and musical, he had gone to town persuading himself that business required his attention there, and at the office of the 'Gazette' encountered his friend, who, at the conclusion of their interview, had conveyed to him the intelligence that *number seven* was occupied by Mr. Effingham. We have seen how his face flushed and his breast labored as in a close atmosphere. He had intended to visit the young girl, but business called him away, and when he had dispatched it, the evening began to draw on, and he was obliged to return homeward. He returned, then, with that one thought in his brain—that one sensation in his heart. Persecuted—for this was plainly persecution on Mr. Effingham's part—loved and followed, for this, too, was as plain—Beatrice became more dear to him than ever. His breast heaved, his eye flashed, his haughty lip trembled, and he passed a sleepless night thinking of her. Then for the first time he started at his own feelings, and he felt his heart throb. He would be her protector from that man, who had, on the first evening of her appearance, annoyed and insulted her; he would watch over her, find if he really persecuted her—yes, and if necessary, avenge her! Then he stopped, like a horse at full speed suddenly checked by his rider. Where had his imagination borne him—what was he dreaming of? What interest had he in this young girl? say that he had preserved her life, would not any courageous man have done the same? She was grateful to him for that, there the matter ended; the service rendered, the thanks returned, what were they further but strangers? What was he to the young actress? The young actress! What could she be to him? She was a bird of passage with gorgeous wings, and magical singing, caressed, applauded, swaying all hearts—and he, what was he? An obscure man, without name, or wealth, or birth; his station repelled her, as her profession repelled him.

A thousand thoughts like these chased each other through his mind during the two or three days which followed his interview with the stranger; and then, drawn as by a magical influence—he sought Williamsburg again—he had an object, too, as will be seen.

Thus, the writer of the MS.: Charles Waters entered Williamsburg, and, thoughtful and absent, took his way along the main street toward the Raleigh. Suddenly, as he walked on rapidly, he found himself stopped by an obstruction. He raised his head, and found himself in the presence of the man in the red cloak. That gentleman was conversing with no less a personage than Parson Tag; and when Charles Waters joined them, the parson was about to pass on. He scowled upon the homely-clad man, bowed with patronizing condescension to the stranger, and with head borne magisterially erect, went down the street.

"There goes one of the lights of the age—one of the pillars of the church," said the stranger, with his habitual coolness, but smiling as he spoke, "the good Parson Tag! The worthy gentleman is indignant to-day, having, from his own account, just quarrelled with his wealthiest parishioner, Squire Effingham."

His companion raised his head at this name: and this movement did not escape the stranger's keen eye.

"Yes," he added, "there seems to have been some little private matter in the business. The squire has a son, my neighbor at the tavern—No. 7, you know—and this son, it appears, has been making himself the subject of discussion, for presuming to experience an honest friendship for the young actress, Miss Hallam."

The stranger did not fail to note the troubled and gloomy look of his listener, as they walked on toward the Raleigh.

"Well," he continued, "the parson took the liberty of condoling with the worthy squire on the reprobacy of his son, and, thereby, excited the rage of his parishioner. High words followed—the squire declared, indignantly, that he would permit no one to insult his son in his presence—that it was a mere youthful freak on his part—and that the Christian religion made it incumbent on all men, especially parsons, to exercise a little of the spirit of forgiveness, or affect the same, if they had it not. Tolerably plain, you observe, that intimation of his excellency, the squire. The interview ended by the parson's getting enraged, and declaring he would no longer live in a parish which was cursed with so unreasonable a member—and by the squire's replying, with a bow, that his holiness should be called elsewhere, as the parish had long desired. These are pretty nearly the facts of the interview, I suppose—sifted from the rubbish—and now, it seems to be understood that the good Parson Tag goes to the Piedmont region, and a Mr. Christian—an excellent name—takes his place. 'A mere milk-and-water family visitor,' says Parson Tag. Ah, these parsons, these parsons!"

And the stranger shook his head, in a way which signified that the representatives of the established church were far from occupying a distinguished place in his regards. Charles Waters had listened to this account with a troubled expression, which did not escape the stranger. The name of Effingham evidently excited some painful emotion—and he remained silent, until they reached the Raleigh. He inquired for Miss Hallam. She was not at the tavern, but would probably come in soon. He turned away.

He was diverted from his absorbing thought, by feeling the arm of the stranger in his own.

"Come," said his companion, "as I suppose you will wait, in view of the fact, that a lady is in the question—let us sit down here on the porch, the sun is warm and pleasant. Perhaps we may wile away a tedious moment. I leave this place to-day, and may not see you again for years."

Charles Waters sat down by the stranger.

"What a singular race these parsons are," said the man in the red cloak; "come, dismiss your meditations, companion, and listen to me. What do you think of them?"

"There are many worthy, not a few unworthy," said his companion, absently.

"True: but as they are an important element of our society, it seems to me that the proportion of the unworthy is too great."

"Yes, sir: they are a very influential class," said the other, endeavoring to banish his thoughts.

"And wealthy."

"Many I believe are."

"They love their tobacco salary—but after all we cannot complain of them. They are necessary, just as it is necessary to have a class that rules and a class which obeys."

"That is true in a very limited sense, sir."

"Why, we of the lower orders must look up to the gentlemen: fustian cannot rub against velvet. The wealthy gentleman and the poor laborer cannot associate with each other. One rolls in his chariot, the other digs in the field, and admires the grand machine rolling on with its liveried coachman, and glossy four-in-hand. The necessity of the thing is as plain as the fact, that we envy these lords of creation."

"We should not, sir."

"Pshaw!—whether we should or not, we always will envy and hate them. We are poor and obscure; they are distinguished and wealthy. Could a clearer case be made out?"

Charles Waters looked at his interlocutor with the same expression, as on a former occasion, when the stranger had said, "All men are false."

"To envy those fortunate possessors of wealth and ease, sir, is neither liberal nor true philosophy," he said. "True, there are classes, and must ever be, in some form; but the poor are not, and should not be the enemies of the rich—beyond all, they should not base such enmity upon the ground that the gifts of fortune are unequally divided. What a world we should have if that were so! We have here in Virginia all grades of wealth and rank, from that negro yonder rubbing down his horse, to Governor Fauquier in his palace. We have first, the rude ignorant servant indented for a term of years, and almost an appendage of the glebe—almost as much a slave as the negro. Then the coarse overseer, scarcely better. Then the small merchant, factor, and the yeoman, plain in manners, often very ignorant—but a step higher. Then the well-to-do farmer. Lastly, the great landed proprietors, with thousands of acres and negroes, wearing velvet and riding in chariots, as you say. Well, now sir, apply your philosophy! Let the well-to-do farmer hate the great wealthy gentleman—the common yeoman hate the farmer and the gentleman—the overseer hate all three—and the indented servant, following the example of his betters, hate all four of them, where would the clashing of these complex hatreds, these inimical and bitter envyings, have their termination? No, sir," said Charles Waters, raising his noble head, and speaking in that earnest and persuasive voice, which it was hard to resist being moved and convinced by—even by its very intonation—"No, sir: believe me—these harsh and bitter feelings retard the advance of our race, rather than forward its destiny. No sir—no! hatred is not the element of progress, as envy and uncharitableness are not the precursors of liberty!"

CHAPTER XXXIII.

HOW THE MAN IN THE RED CLOAK THREW HIS NET, AND WHAT HE CAUGHT.

The stranger was silent for some moments, then, drawing his old red cloak around him, he said:

"Liberty! Well, that is a great word; but, unfortunately, it is also one of those nobly-sounding terms which fill the ears only, never conveying to the brain much more than a vague and doubtful meaning. What is liberty? True, I ask you to answer a hard question; but you have drawn it upon yourself, companion, by your anomalous and contradictory statements."

"How contradictory, sir?" said his companion, losing his absent-mindedness, and looking earnestly at the stranger.

"Why," replied the man in the red cloak, coolly, "nothing could well be more paradoxical than your views. You agree that there are classes here, and elsewhere, separated by unreasonable distinctions, holding, as regards each other, unjust positions. You do not deny that we—we, the common people—are the mere hewers of wood and drawers of water for our masters, and, when I chance to say what is perfectly reasonable and natural, namely, that we must hate and envy these dons, why, you answer, 'No, no; envy and hatred are not the elements of progress, the forerunners of liberty.' I say, they rule us!—the wealthy gentlemen, the house of burgesses, the English parliament—why not hate and envy, and, if necessary, match ourselves force for force against them, and see if we cannot achieve this noble end you speak of—liberty!"

"Because force—the blind force of envy and hatred, striking in the dark, and without thought—is the mere movement of the brute, who closes his eyes, and tears, without seeing, whatever comes beneath his paws. No, sir! before we can overturn parliaments, and dictate laws, we must mould public opinion."

"Public opinion? What is that?"

"It is the great unseen power which governs the world."

"Oh yes; the opinion of kings and autocrats. Now I understand."

"No, not of kings and autocrats—of common men, the masses! The calm, just judgment, formed in silence, and without prejudice, of those men and things which figure on the great stage of life. Not the mere impulses of envy and hatred, any more than the jealousy of rank, but the cool, deliberate weighing of events and personages in the scales of eternal justice."

"Fine words. Well, then, you would not overthrow the present state of things; or, perhaps, you are well content with the social organization of this colony. We must not hate, we must not envy—all is for the best!"

"No, sir, all is not for the best; far from it."

"It seems to me that we are wandering in our ideas, and liable to misunderstand each other. Let us see, now—explain.

You are more or less dissatisfied with the present position of things; but you like the gentry, the Established Church, you admire the traditions of feudalism, and revere his gracious majesty King George. Eh? Come, let us know if you do not?"

"We must have misunderstood each other, indeed, sir. I would overthrow—or, at least, materially change—all that you have mentioned."

"What, the gentry—the church—the king? Treason!"

"That cry does not daunt me, sir."

"Beware; I shall inform on you, and his majesty will send for you to come and visit his handsome residence, called the Tower."

"Let me explain, briefly, what I mean, and meant," said his companion, too gloomy to relish these pleasantries of the stranger. "You have misunderstood me wholly—you would say that I am an advocate of the present, with all its injustice, its wrong, its oppression; and, that, because I am not willing to go and turn out proprietors of great landed estates, at the point of the bayonet; shatter those splendid mirrors, which reflect gold, and velvet, and embroidery, with a pistol's muzzle; organize the lower class, with bludgeons, hay-forks, cleavers, knives, and scythes, against the gentlemen, who roll in coaches, and eat from gold and silver plate—you would say, that, because these revolutionary proceedings, the offspring of envy and hatred, are not to my taste, I am an advocate of those oppressions, those bitter wrongs, inflicted on the commons by the gentry. No, sir! I am not an advocate of them; I know them too well. I have studied, as far as possible, with a calm mind, an unbiassed judgment, this vestige of feudalism which curses us, and I have found, every where, as in the old feudal system, wrong, oppression, a haughty and unchristian pride of rank, and birth, and wealth—"

"Good, good," said the stranger, no longer interrupting his companion.

"An unjustifiable pride! an unchristian arrogance, scorning charity, humility, all that Christ inculcated, as so much weakness!" continued the thinker, in his noble and earnest voice; "I find it here, as I find it in the history of England, of France, or Germany, of the whole feudal world;

among the gentry of to-day, as the nobles of the middle age! Go back to that middle age—see the great lord passing in his splendid armor, and surcoat of cloth of gold, on his glossy charger, followed by his squires, his men-at-arms, while the battlements of his great castle ring with trumpets, greeting his return: see the serf there in the shadow of the wall, with the ring around his neck, with his wooden shoes, his goatskin covering—swarthy, with his shaggy beard, his brow covered with perspiration, as becomes the villein, his cerebral conformation, as he takes off his greasy cap to lout low to his master, like the head of the wolf, the jackall, the hyena. That serf is no longer a man—he is a wild beast, with strong muscles and sinews like rope, who will fight well in the field, and be cut to pieces cheerfully, while his master reaps undying renown, covered by his proof armor of Milan—yes, he will fight and toil, and go home and kiss his children in their mud hovel—but he is not a man: his lord is a man—how can he be of the same race as that splendid and haughty chevalier, honored by kings and emperors for his deeds of chivalry, smiled on by fair ladies every where, like the noble dame who reigns in yonder castle with him. True, the serf has legs and arms, and his blood, strange to say, is much the color of the great seigneur's—but they do not belong to the same race of animals. They both feel it—are convinced of it. When my lord passes, see the back bent down; the eyes abased, as in the presence of the God of Day—the dog-like submission, when harsh words are uttered by the seigneur to his animal. The serf does not dream of there being any impropriety in all this—it is a part of the order of things that he should be a wild beast, his lord a splendid, noble chevalier, glittering with stars, and clad in soft silk and velvet. He always submits: he is a part of the glebe, the stock—like the horse, the hound, the hawk. Does the seigneur wish some amusement for his noble guests?—the boor comes, and with another of his class cudgels away in the court-yard, until he is covered with bruises, and falls or conquers: and the noble lords and ladies, glittering like stars in the balcony, throw *largesse* to the knaves, who lout humbly, and go down to their proper place—the kitchen. "There is the past, sir!—look at it!"

The stranger nodded.

"You don't like feudalism," he said.

"It makes me shudder, sir."

"How? why it's dead!"

"No:. it is alive."

"Alive, say you?"

"To this very day and hour."

"What? in full force?"

"No, sir—not in full force: far from it. But in a degree, at least, it exists."

"Hum! you are a metaphysician."

"No, sir, I am practical."

"You are a dreamer!"

Waters sighed.

"I thought you dreamed as I did," he said.

"Perhaps I do—who knows?"

Waters was silent.

"Define your idea," said the stranger. "I understand you to say—and we won't discuss the subject—that this thing we call feudalism—which has come in for so much abuse from you, still exists in a degree? Come! let us see how it looks in Virginia."

"We have but the shadow—thank God, the edifice has crumbled in part: but the flanking towers remain, and that shadow still lies like gloom upon the land. See how human thought is still warped and darkened by it—how rank and unwholesome weeds possess the earth!"

"Root out these weeds, then—begin! Hurl down these towers which shut out the sunlight,—your historical reading must have told you of the Jacquerie!"

"Yes, sir! and I have seen how that rising led to worse evils than before, for hatred was added to contempt. No, to attack this still vigorous remnant of feudalism, something besides hammers and pickaxes are necessary; gunpowder, even, will not blow it into atoms!"

"What, then?"

"The winds of Heaven! God will strike it; he has thrown down the donjon keep, where captives gnashed their teeth and cursed and blasphemed in darkness; he will also level with the ground what remains of the great blot upon the landscape!"

"Figures, figures!" said the stranger; "come, let us have ideas!"

"By the winds of Heaven—the breath of God—I mean those eternally progressive steps of mind, which go from doubt to certainty, from certainty to indignation, from indignation to revolution!"

"Very well; now we get on firm ground again. We meet and shake hands over that toast, 'Revolution!'"

"Understand me; revolution is not a slight thing. It levels many valuable things, as the hurricane and the tempest of rain sweeps away much more than the accumulated rubbish. Revolution, sir, is the last thing of all—the tornado which clears the poisonous atmosphere, cannot be loosed every day or year, for the land is strewed with ruins by it. The slow steps of public opinion must be hastened, the soil prepared for the seed, the distance made plain, the body armed—then, if it is necessary, the conflict."

"Ah, you come back to your ideas upon education, sir?"

"Yes; I would unfetter the mind."

"Enlighten it?"

"Yes, sir; I would teach the great mass of the people, that God made this world, not man; that wrong and oppression is not the normal state of human things; I would point out all the falseness, I would point to the lash-marks on the back; I would, if necessary, pour brine into those bleeding furrows!"

"Yes, and drive to madness—to what you deprecate, mad violence!"

"No! for minds would be enlightened, men would see—and seeing, they would wait. I would have them know when to strike; I would organize in their minds an opposition, quiet, stubborn, unbending, never-sleeping; a confidence in time, faith in the ultimate intervention of God using them as his instruments."

"You generalize too much," said the stranger; "let us come now to Virginia, at this day and hour. Let us see what are the great abuses. Speak!"

"First, an established church, which dictates religious opinion—forces itself upon all the community, armed with the terrors of the law."

"Yes, that is just; and I promise you something will be said soon about the twopenny-act. Well, the church! What else?"

"The offspring of that feudalism I have spoken of—aristocracy!"

"Yes, 'power of the best;' that is, the wealthiest. What next?"

"Laws, without representation!" said his companion, compressing in these short words the great popular grievance of the age.

"Ah!" said the stranger, with a grim smile, "there is something in that, too. What more?"

"What more? Is it not enough, sir, for the Established Church to wring from you, whether you conform or not, support for its ministers—to stuff itself and its tenets down your throat? is it not bad enough for the house of burgesses to legislate for the great landed proprietors alone, who form the body, ignoring the very existence of the common man, who has no vote? is any thing more needed to make us slaves, than laws passed in the English parliament, crushing our trade, our very lives, without representatives of us there in council?"

"I confess that seems to me quite enough," said the stranger; "and this great, oppressive, intolerant church—this haughty arrogance of rank—lastly, that English lawlessness, seem to me to constitute a case of mortification—gangrene—to be burnt out by the hot iron of revolution!"

"No! it has not gone far enough yet; let us advance step by step. At present we contemplate that great, intolerant, bigoted establishment with respect and awe; we bow to the grand chariot, doffing our caps; we search in our minds for what will justify that oppression of Parliament; we are not convinced that this great triple wrong *is* a wrong. We doubt; let us scan the matter calmly—dispassionately investigate the nature of things; let us educate our minds, we common people, and with the calm, unobscured eyes of truth, test the error. We will not say to the parsons, 'Off with you, you are the vermin of a rotten system, you shall not tyrannize over us!' No, let us, with the Bible in our hands, and God in our hearts, say, 'We come to try you, we come to know whether you are false and bigoted, or true and Christlike—'"

"Yes," said the stranger, "and those worthy gentlemen, who procured benefices by marrying the cast-off mistresses of lords, will, with one voice, for about the space of two hours, cry, 'Great is Diana of the Ephesians! We are holy, pure, and immaculate!' What, then?"

"Reason! the light of education still! flooding the whole system, lighting up every hidden crypt!"

"Good! And you would apply these fine ideas to the aristocracy, too?"

"Yes. I would have men scan that system also; not strike it blindly; I would have them come with the law of nature in their hands, the evangel of truth and justice, and say, 'Show us what you are. Show us if you are really our natural and rightful superiors. Show us whether those titles you derive from kings, are like the authority of those kings, derived, as they say, from God, and so, just and right. Show us if you are really superior beings, because you descend from the knights of the middle age—we inferior to you, your born slaves, because we draw our blood from the serf who tilled the glebe below your grandsire's castle walls. Show us if this mysterious sentiment of awe we feel in your presence, is direct from the Deity, planted thus in us to make us keep our places; or, whether it is the mere tradition of the past, the echo of injustice, the shadow of that monstrous oppression of the dark ages, yet lying on our souls?"

"Very well—and what then?" said the stranger. "Why, these worthy gentlemen would reply, 'Friends, the distinction of classes is absolutely necessary; some must rule, others obey; some wear fustian, others velvet; some must ride in coaches, and eat from gold plate, others jog along in the dust of the highway, eat their brown bread and swill their muddy ale. Order is heaven's first law. Come, now, and listen to this splendid passage from Shakspeare, about degrees in a state; it is there, in that volume with a gilt back in the gothic book-case—don't muddy the carpet with your dirty brogues, or stumble over that damask chair in reaching it. Very well. Now, listen! Can any thing be more just than these views? Some must be great, others small; one must vote, another be denied that privilege. We are gentlemen, you commoners. Can any thing be plainer, than that we should have the offices and honors, live easily, and sustain our proper rank, while you till the glebe, and leave your interests in our hands?' That is what they would say—what then?"

"Reason, again!" said his companion; "reason, turning away from the dazzling pageant, stopping the ears to shut out the rumbling of the coach and six, forgetting the past, and questioning that great evangel of right open in their hands—reason, which should weigh and test, and try the whole system by the rules of a stern, inexorable logic."

"I admire your logic! and you think that it would apply to English legislation on Virginia matters?"

"Yes; I would remonstrate, petition, debate with Parliament; I would exhaust every means of testing and overthrowing this cruel and bitter wrong; I would ask for light —ask nothing but that right should be made manifest—I would go to the foot of the throne, and say, 'Justice, justice, nothing but justice, as a British subject—as one laboring under wrong!'"

The stranger's lip curled.

"Well, your system is now tolerably plain," he said. "You would go and ask the parsons to tell you if they are, in truth, pure and immaculate—you would ask the gentry if they really are the distinguished gentlemen they pretend to be—you would fall at the feet of King George, and sue for leave to argue the matter of taxation with his gracious Majesty! Very well. Now, suppose—it is a very extravagant supposition, I know, and springs, no doubt, from my irreverent, incredulous, and obstinate prejudices—suppose, I say, that the worthy parsons thus adjured, as to their purity, were to tell you that they were the salt of the earth, and that your question was an impertinence; suppose—if you can suppose such an incredible thing—that the wealthy gentleman tells you that he is your born lord, and that he will commit you in his quality of justice of the peace, for misdemeanor, should you intrude upon him again with your wretched folly; suppose his gracious Majesty were to remove your humble petition with his royal foot, bidding you begone, and learn that when money was wanted to support his splendor, you were to sweat and pay it, and be silent on pain of being whipped in by armed soldiers; suppose these disagreeable incidents greeted your philanthropic exertions—what then?"

"Then, revolution! revolution, if that revolution waded in blood!" cried his companion, carried away by his fiery thoughts, and losing all his calmness and self-control; "revolution, with God for our judge! history for our vindication! If, after all their sufferings, all their wrongs, all the injustice of long years, of centuries, the prayers of humanity were thus answered—revolution! A conflict, bitter, desperate, unyielding, to the death! A conflict which should root out these foul and monstrous wrongs, or exterminate us! A revolution, which should attack and overwhelm for ever, or be itself overwhelmed! That is the hurricane I spoke of, sir! If God decrees it, let it come!"

CHAPTER XXXIV.

IN WHICH BEATRICE RETURNS.

WITH head erect, brows flushed, eyes clear and fiery, lips still agitated by the tumult of thought, the speaker was silent. His eyes then turned toward the stranger.

A singular alteration seemed to have taken place in his features, and the expression of grandeur and majesty which illuminated the rugged features, usually so cold, was startling.

The stranger's expression was so noble, his eye so bright and proud, his whole manner so completely changed, that his companion found himself gazing at him with an astonishment which he could not suppress.

"Pardon me, sir," said the man in the red cloak, in a voice of noble courtesy, strongly in contrast with his habitual roughness; "pardon me for the manner in which I have seemed to sift your opinions, and provoke a collision of your ideas with my own, in this and our former interviews. It is one of the bad habits which I acquired in a country store, and I find myself now its slave—since the temptation to open and study that grand volume, human nature, wherever I find it, has become irresistible. In your case, I have been instructed and interested; and though I say with a frankness which you may consider rude, that I have thought most of your thoughts before—still, sir, permit me to return you my thanks for an honor and a pleasure."

The haughtiest nobleman in the world would not have found in these words, uttered by the coarsely-clad stranger on the rude tavern porch, to a man of the people like himself, any thing to cater to his laughter or amusement; for the man in the red cloak seemed no longer to be coarsely dressed, his pronunciation no longer appeared vicious and incorrect; the very porch of the tavern seemed to be transformed by his magical voice and look into a palace portico.

"In all your views I concur," continued the stranger, "and your ideas are mine. God himself placed us in the condition we both find ourselves in, that mind might speak to mind, freely, sympathetically, with that frankness and plainness from which Truth springs, armed, ready for the conflict."

"Yes, sir," continued the stranger, with that high and proud look which his companion had observed once in a former interview. "Yes, sir! this Virginia of 1763 is in an unhappy state! Social organization to-day, with the influences that environ it, is one of those phenomena which occur but once in a century. On all sides murmurs, mutterings as of an approaching storm! Men doubtful of the ground they walk on—new ideas dazzling them—old institutions crumbling—the hand upon the wall tracing, in fiery letters, the mysterious future—that future crammed with storms—groaning like a womb which holds the destiny of humanity! The heavens are dark, the ways we tread devious and full of hidden snares. England, our tender mother, might say, who planted them? For England, from whose loins we sprung, has cursed us!—like a stepmother, she has struck, with a bitter and remorseless hatred, those who would be her children! She cursed us with this race of Africans who are eating us up and ruining us, and some day, in the blind convulsions of her rage, she will taunt us bitterly for asking what we do not grant ourselves—for demanding freedom, when our arms are holding down a race human as ourselves! Let her gnash her teeth in impotent and irrational complaint!—let her complain, we will not;

for God decreed that she herself, black with crime and injustice, should be the means of bringing hither this race, that in the future Christianity should dawn on that vast continent of Africa—that land where the very air seems tainted with paganism—where the very palms which wave their long plumes on the ocean breeze seem celebrating some horrible rite! No; this is not the head and front of the accusation which, in the name of justice and humanity, we bring against England. She has thrust upon us her despotic regulations. She has contracted suffrage. She has given to Lord Culpeper the whole territory from the mouth of the Rappahannock to the sources of the Potomac—enthroned him a prince and king over us! She has crushed our commerce by navigation laws which are so odious and unrighteous that the very instruments of her tyranny shrink from enforcing them! With a blind, remorseless hatred—a policy destitute of reason as it is foul with injustice and wrong—she has bound on this poor laboring brute, Virginia, burdens which crush her, under which she staggers, groaning, and tearing herself with rage, terror, and despair! She has made for herself a gospel whose commandments are—'Thou shalt steal'—'Thou shalt bear false witness against thy neighbor'—'Thou shalt have no other god but George III.' She has gone on from wrong to wrong, from injustice to injustice, until like those unhappy creatures whom the gods intend to strike, she has grown mad, lost her brain, her reason, braced herself to rush upon an obstacle which will hurl her back, as a wave of the ocean is hurled back from the cliff of eternal stone! Yes, sir, that empire rushes upon what will tame her! Already she speaks of an act decreeing that a stamp shall be placed upon every instrument written or printed of human affairs. Journals, deeds, conveyances—pleadings in law, bills of lading—on the marriage contract, and the bill for the headstone—nothing to be operative without that stamp! Well, sir, that act will make the cup filled with the bitter and poisonous draught run over—that law will make the infuriated animal, thrown on her knees, rise up, and then, sir, God alone knows where things will end! You wish to wait and let the old world pass away by virtue of its inherent decay, its immemorial rottenness—you would have the crumbling monument of wrong fall slowly, stone by stone, as the winds and rain descend upon it year after year! Such will not be the event, sir! The tornado you spoke of will bring down that godless monument, at one blow, with a crash that will startle nations! And do not think that this is not as legitimately God's act as the slow ruin you advocate. That Great Being unlooses the hurricane of revolution as easily as he sends the zephyr to cool the cheek, each in its place!—the hurricane here! You may even now scent the odor of the storm!"

And the stranger rose with such grandeur in his visage, such majesty in his attitude, such a clear fire in his proud eyes, which seemed to plunge into the mysterious future, and see with the vision of a prophet all which that future was to bring, that his companion felt himself overwhelmed, he knew not how, carried away in spite of himself.

"It is coming!" continued he, with indescribable grandeur in voice and countenance and attitude; "the storm which will topple down the edifice of fraud and lies, which has so long shamed the sunlight!—in that storm old things shall pass away, and behold! all things shall become new. The old world is decayed, she totters on the brink of the abyss prepared for her:—she rushes on, blindly, full of curses, and hatred—the gulf yawns—let her foot trip, she is swallowed up for ever!"

And the brilliant eye seemed to grow brighter still, the voice became more clear and strong. The rude visage of the speaker glowed as if the light of a great conflagration streamed upon it. His stature seemed almost to grow before his companion's eyes, and become gigantic, his two hands to be filled with thunderbolts!

"Yes, sir! yes!" he exclaimed, "the storm comes!—the tocsin of a revolution is already being sounded! Ere long the clash of arms will fall upon our ears, the sound of firearms and the roar of cannon. War and storm, tempest and hurricane, are waiting, like hounds held back by the leash, to burst upon this land. Let it come! let the storm roar, the lightning flash, the waves roll mountain high—God still directs that storm, and will fight for us! Let the bloody dogs of war be loosed, let them dye their sharp fangs in blood, they shall not daunt us. I repeat it, sir,—let it come!

I, for one, will grapple with the monster, and strangle or be strangled by him! Liberty or death!"

And the man in the red cloak, with a gesture of overwhelming grandeur, stood silent, motionless, his eyes on fire, his hands clenched as though the struggle depicted by his brilliant and fiery imagination were about to begin. Charles Waters, carried away by his tremendous passion could make no reply, and they both remained silent.

The stranger wiped his brow, and drew his cloak around him: then gazing on his companion with an expression of nobility and pride, which glowed in his eyes and filled them with light, said:

"And now, sir, we must part. I go hence to-day, having yesterday been retained in an important cause in Hanover county, brought by the Reverend Mr. Maury against the collector. I am for the defendant, and must prepare myself for a hard struggle. Permit me again to thank you, sir, for many hours of your company. I repeat, that you have done me a pleasure, and an honor: for I find in you a mind clear and strong, competent to test, to sift, to grasp, to wield those new ideas which will change the world. Do not dream that we will pass through the years, directly following this, without convulsions and a conflict, such as the world has never seen. Prepare yourself, put on your armor, get ready! For my part, I ask in that inevitable conflict, no better companion. These are no idle words, sir. I shall call upon you, and am well convinced, that my call will not be in vain!"

And bowing with lofty courtesy, the stranger entered the tavern. At the same moment the footfall of a horse attracted the attention of Charles Waters, and looking up, he saw Beatrice Hallam, who had stopped before the inn, mounted as usual on her tall white horse.

CHAPTER XXXV.

HOW BEATRICE PRAYED FOR STRENGTH TO RESIST HERSELF.

He rose and went toward the young girl, walking as in a dream. Those magical accents of the stranger's voice were still ringing in his ears—he almost thought he heard the roar of thunder, and the crashing of the sea—the air almost seemed alive with lightning flashes. For thunder, lightning, and a stormy ocean, seemed to be the elements of that grand, fiery oratory.

But he soon found this preoccupation put to rout by something more powerful than the grandest eloquence, the most overpowering oratory—a young girl's eyes. Slowly, his great thoughts fled away from his mind—the fate of Virginia was forgotten—mind beat an ignominious retreat, and the heart knew of but one object in the universe, a fresh, bright face that smiled upon him, a mild, tender pair of eyes, that filled with happy light when they fell upon him. He assisted the young girl to the ground quietly:—neither spoke, but their eyes were more eloquent than any words could have been. On their last meeting, Beatrice had hastened forward, exclaiming, "I am very glad to see you!" and now, when day after day, and night after night, she had thought of him with inexpressible tenderness, and come to feel, indeed, that her life was illuminated by a new, unimagined glory—now she did not assure him that she was glad to see him. The human heart in 1763 was much the same as at present, the reader will perceive.

So without speaking, she passed in and he followed her, with no need of invitation in words: her eyes said all—and they entered the little apartment which had witnessed so many memorable scenes. Then for the first time Beatrice, taking off her little hat, and throwing back her beautiful hair, which had become loose, said:

"Oh, you have been away so long! You promised to come often!"

How could he resist that earnest tender voice—how feel any more sorrow or disquiet—how prevent his heart from beating more rapidly, as these soft words sank into it.

"Indeed, I have not kept my promise," he said, with that gentleness and softness, which at times characterized his voice, "but fate has seemed to decree that we should not meet."

"That was very naughty in fate!" said Beatrice, with a winning little smile, "because we are good friends, you know."

And the soft voice trembled with its depth of meaning.

"Indeed, I can answer for myself," he said, sitting down.

"And I do not think I need say any thing for my part," answered Beatrice; "you saved my life."

And again, the tender eyes dwelt for a moment on his face, and were cast down.

"You have not forgotten that yet?"

"No—how could I?"

"Well, well, pray do not speak of it again. Has your wetting caused you any inconvenience? I hope not."

"Only a little cough—but I have not coughed a bit to-day."

With which, as if to improve the portion still remaining, the young girl began to cough, but with no violence.

"You see I began just because I boasted," she said, smiling. "Is Mr. Waters well?"

"Yes, very well."

"He was very kind to me," said Beatrice, gratefully, "please give him my best love."

And, without being conscious of any reason for it, she blushed, and turned away. It is probable that something similar to what was passing in her mind, passed in the heart of her companion also, for his countenance brightened, and grew very tender.

"My father sent you his best regards," he said, "and I came for the purpose of bringing them. I must confess, however, that I was somewhat selfish—"

"Selfish?"

"Yes; since I promised myself the pleasure of seeing you."

"Oh," said Beatrice, "please, don't let us make any polite speeches to each other."

"But, indeed, that is not mere courtesy; it is the truth," he replied. "I had such a quiet, friendly talk, when I was here before, that I wished to keep my promise, to visit you every day."

He had paused slightly before the word "friendly," and, conscious of the reason, avoided the frank, tender eyes.

"Why did you stay away so long, then?" she said; "indeed, I have longed to see you."

These words were uttered with great simplicity, and with that childlike frankness, which was one of the young girl's most striking traits of character. One would have said that she was so innocent and truthful, that she could not school herself with forms; and such, indeed, was the case. Beatrice was no longer the actress, in his society; she was the young, girlish being we have seen shouting after the sea-gulls, and said, "Indeed, I have longed to see you," without a thought of any impropriety.

"Fate would not let me come, as I said," he replied, smiling; "but, now I have conquered destiny, and bring you, not only my father's regards, and my own good wishes, but a trinket, which, I fancy, must belong to you. The initials upon it must be those of your mother."

Beatrice rose quickly, and ran up to him.

"Oh, have you got it?" she cried.

He smiled, and taking from his pocket a small locket of gold, attached to a narrow blue ribbon, handed it to her. Beatrice took it quickly, and with an eagerness which betrayed the importance she attached to it.

"Oh, I am so glad!" she said; "I am so glad you found it!"

"It is yours, then?"

"Yes, yes!"

"You must have dropped it, on the day of your sail."

"Yes, I must have."

"It was picked up, upon the river's bank, by my father, and, from the letters B. W. upon it, he fancied that it belonged to you."

"Yes, yes; I have worn it a long time, and I believe it was my mother's. But I don't know," added the young girl, with some sadness; "I never saw my mother, I believe."

"Did your father give you the locket?"

"No, I believe not. I do not remember. I think I wore it around my neck when I was a little child; at least, I have worn it as long as I could remember."

"I am glad to have been able to restore it; though the merit really belongs to my father."

"Please say I thank him very much," said Beatrice; "indeed, it is very dear to me. I had been to look for it."

"What! this morning?"

"Oh, yes; you know I am a great rider. So I thought I would just put on my skirt, and go to the river, where Mr. Townes lives—you know it was his boat we sailed in—and ask him if I had dropped it there, or in the boat."

"You had, then, been to the river?"

"Yes, indeed; and I had a delightful ride. Mr. Townes was very kind to me," she said, laughing, like a child, "and was good enough to praise my cheeks, and bless my eyes, and, I think he said he would drag the river, or something, for my locket. Oh, he praised you so!"

"Townes is an excellent and worthy man, and loves my father and myself very much, I believe."

"I will like him more than ever, hereafter; for you are my friends, you know," said Beatrice, with the most charming simplicity; "indeed, I like him very much already, for his kindness to me on the day we sailed."

"He really saved you," said her companion.

"No, no!" cried Beatrice; "indeed I owe my life to you."

He shook his head.

"I was very strong once," he said, "but have been of late devoured by a thirst for study—I was nearly exhausted when Townes came. But let us dismiss the subject. I am very glad your locket is safe."

And he gazed, with a look of great softness, upon her bright face.

"Yes, indeed, I value it highly," said Beatrice; "see how prettily 'tis chased."

He took and examined it.

"Here are the letters I observed," he said; "but they are nearly worn away. Still, as you see, they are distinct. There they are—'B. W.' The B. stands for—for—your first name, I suppose."

"My mother's name was Beatrice, I imagine. Strange," the young girl added, half to herself, "that father has never talked to me about mother."

And she sighed, and looked very thoughtful. He sat gazing on the tender, gentle face, the veiled eyes, and girlish lips; thinking he had never seen any one more beautiful—never, among those fair maidens who passed in their chariots like lovely princesses, enveloped in clouds of lace, with bright diamond-like eyes, and snowy hands hung out against the cushion of the door. The features of Beatrice were always striking for their purity and elegance, but the eloquent expression was the great charm of her face.

"I suppose it was my mother's," she added, "but I do not know what the 'W.' stands for. I'll ask father."

"Would it not be singular if it stood for Waters?" he said, smiling.

She started.

"Waters! Oh! how singular!"

"Beatrice Waters?" he added.

She did not reply.

"How strange!" she said, at length, buried in thought; "it is very strange!"

"What?" he said.

"The coincidence—Beatrice—Waters," she added, after a pause.

And her soft eyes met those of her companion, who looked at her with so much unconscious meaning, that she turned away, blushing.

"I am afraid we are not related," he said.

"I fear not," she murmured.

"Even if your mother's maiden name had been the same with my own, it would not follow that we were connected. There are many persons named Waters."

"Yes—I do not think, however, that the 'W.' stands for that."

"What then?"

"I do not know."

"It might."

"Yes," she said, with the same thoughtful look, "but I had a brother who died—he did not live with us—somewhere abroad—I never knew him—but his name was Wesley. I suppose that was my mother's name."

"Oh, you are determined that I shall not have the satisfaction of being your kinsman."

The tender face clouded.

"Would that be a satisfaction?" she said, softly.

"Ah, yes!" he muttered.

"I am an actress," said Beatrice, softly, and in a low tone, casting down her eyes as she spoke, "I had forgotten it."

And a moisture which she could not drive back made her eyes swim, and gathered on the long dusky lashes. Those swimming eyes went straight to his heart, an irrepressible gush of tenderness made his brow flush, and taking the little hand, he pressed it between his own, with a tenderness which made Beatrice burst into tears: for his meaning could not be misunderstood.

"Oh!" she sobbed, turning away and hiding her face with the other hand, "you are so good and noble! I felt it when you left me before, and more than ever now! It is so good in you to treat a poor young girl like me so kindly!—a poor actress, that other people look upon with contempt! Oh! how can I ever thank you! I can only—only bless you! and never forget you!—Oh I never—never will forget how kind you were!"

And bending lower still, the young girl sobbed and sighed; and then gently drawing away her hand, took from her pocket a handkerchief, with which she attempted to dry her eyes from which a flood of tears were gushing. That last word which she had uttered had jarred upon his heart strangely. "How kind you *were!*" Then she was soon to leave him—they were to be separated—this brief glimpse of happiness and joy was to disappear like a sift of blue between driving thunder clouds! "I will never forget how kind you *were!*" Then, she would be lost to him! she would pass on like a bird of the tropics, brilliant and beautiful, attracting all eyes and hearts, but sailing far away to other skies! He would see her no more! Her pure, tender face would never smile on him again! those large melting eyes would no more flood his heart with unspeakable happiness—that voice of marvellous sweetness and earnestness, so full of joy and softness and music, would no longer greet him—those small hands would no longer press his own, sending the warm blood to his heart, and filling his soul, his being, with a delicious tranquility, a pure delight! This enchanting form now before him, would, before many days—at most a few months—had elapsed, be to him but a memory, a picture for the eyes of the heart! She would leave him!—that one thought gathered into a burning focus all the scattered rays of tenderness in his heart, and that heart now throbbed passionately.

We have said that Charles Waters was a man of strong

passions, spite of his ordinary quietness—a quietness which sprung from self-control. Under that mild exterior he concealed a heart of powerful impulses, and he proved it on this occasion. Unable to bear the thoughts which the young girl's unconscious allusion to her departure had aroused, he yielded, giving himself up unresistingly to the flood of emotion.

"Oh!" he cried, seizing the young girl's hand and covering it with passionate kisses; "Oh, Beatrice! you wound me to the heart!—do not speak thus to me again! I cannot bear it! No, you are not a mere actress—no! you are the pearl of purity and honor! Never wound me again with such words, for they pierce my heart! But you will have no occasion, perhaps,—you are going to leave us! to leave me! No! I cannot endure the thought!—for I love you passionately, devotedly! I love you with my heart and soul, and would ask no greater satisfaction than to pour out my blood for you. You think I am cold because my face is calm: undeceive yourself: few men have so much fire in them—such a dangerous and fatal temperament when aroused. No, I am not cold, and I love you, Beatrice, with a love which has grown and increased in a short time to the height of a violent passion. Oh, no! you shall not go—you must be my wife—you *must* love me at last, because I almost worship you!"

No words can describe the brilliant expression which flushed the young girl's face, then left it pale. That flush was the evidence of an emotion of unspeakable happiness. The pallor was from the thought which darted through her brain like lightning. She saw all the future spread out before her like a sunny landscape, all the happiness within her grasp; she felt his arm approach her—and drew back with a start, a cry.

Her face was bathed in tears: her eyes swam; her lips trembled; all the nerves of the weak woman's form rebelled and shook—but the great heart remained.

"No," she said, with a passionate sob, which seemed to tear its way from her heart—"No! no! I cannot . . . ! It breaks my heart to say it—God pity me!—but no, no, I cannot! Oh, God will accept this agony I am suffering as an expiation for all sin I have committed!—no no! do not tempt me! my heart failed me for a moment, but is now strong—yet do not tempt me!"

And she covered her face, over which her hair fell down, and sobbed as if indeed her heart were about to break; scarcely hearing his entreaties, his prayers, his passionate assurances of love.

"I cannot be your wife," she said, at length, with more calmness; "God has not permitted me to be, and I submit! I am an actress,—do not interrupt me! for I have scarcely strength now to think or speak. I am a poor playing girl, with nothing in the wide world but my self-respect! I will not make your father blush for an unworthy daughter!—Oh let me go on!—I cannot take advantage of your noble devotion—I cannot weigh down and darken your life—for pity's sake, do not look at me so! do not! I cannot—oh, no! I cannot!—God has no pity on me—it is not my fault that I am such as I am—but I must suffer—Oh! it is a bitter suffering!"

She stopped for a moment, choked by her sobs; then went on:

"Your eye flashes! and I know well what you mean. Yes, you are noble and courageous—you would trample on this unjust prejudice—love me more for that; I know it, it is the bitterest of all—but—"

"Oh, I would die for you!—give my life, oh, how willingly, for—ah! let them dare!"

And his eye flashed, his breast heaved tumultuously.

"Why do you speak of that! Beatrice, I love you—love you so devotedly, so passionately, that I could ask no greater happiness than to dare the world's scorn for you—go down to death with you! But there is no scorn! What is there in our positions—I am poor and obscure, you are the admiration of all! They shall not deprive me of you! No, no! I cannot exist without you now—you are my soul, my life, my blood, my heart! I die without you!"

The young girl felt her heart yielding—her brain swam—overcome, exhausted, faint, she sobbed, and shook, and struggled with her rebellious heart. He saw the hesitation.

"Oh, be my own, Beatrice!" he cried, overwhelming her hand with kisses; "be my wife! the sunlight of my existence!—make my life happy—come, my Beatrice, my beautiful, noble girl!"

And opening his arms, he would have clasped her to his

heart. Overcome, powerless, another moment and his arm would have encircled her, her head lain on his bosom; but suddenly her hand fell on the locket, and she started back with a cry, and burst into an agony of tears.

"Oh, mother! give me strength, if you look down on me from heaven!" she cried, "give me strength against myself, against my own heart! Oh, I am so weak! I know what is right, and am tempted to do wrong! Mother! mother! give me strength! Oh," she continued, looking at him and sobbing violently, "do not tempt me—longer! Do not make me yield, and suffer remorse for ever while I live for this moment's weakness! I cannot be your wife! You tempt me in vain. I am—broken-hearted, but you cannot move me now! I am weak—exhausted—but—God has—heard me! I have—conquered myself!"

And falling into a chair, she fainted. Ten minutes afterwards she was stretched weak and exhausted on her couch, and Charles Waters was hurrying with a pale brow from the town.

Yes, she had conquered herself!—she had drawn back from those arms opened wide to receive her, clasp her like a poor dove beaten by storms to the true breast—her refuge. She had evercome that passionate yearning to fall upon his bosom, and—given up to love and tenderness—weep away all her unhappiness in those strong arms; she had closed her eyes to that seducing picture of such calm and lifelong happiness as his wife—she had resolutely bidden her heart lie still—she had by a sublime effort of devotion drawn back from that tranquil future to be passed with him;—but she was firm. Yes, the weak body had succumbed, the nerves given way—her strength had failed her, but not her soul.

The struggle, however, was not over. Stretched upon the little couch to which he had carried her in his arms, the conflict was renewed with her returning strength. Oh, how unhappy she was! What a poor, lonely, wretched thing she was! How heaven had cursed her when it made her destiny so miserable! How terrible that trial!—on one side love, with open arms and smiling lips, and eyes full of tenderness, saying to her, "Come, weary heart! come, poor unhappy child! here is a future of full, quiet happiness, a nature which your heart yearns for—both are yours—come!" and, on the other side, stern, inexorable duty, saying, with a frown, "Come away!—preserve your self-respect—close your eyes to this. Self-respect is all you have, retain your treasure!" Was it not bitter, she sobbed, was it not too much agony for one poor heart! and for a moment heaven seemed black to her—truth a mere lie—her moral sense was being deadened.

Suddenly her bare arm struck against something on the couch; she looked at this object and saw that it was a small Bible. She opened it and read on the fly leaf—"Catherine Effingham, from dear papa"—and would have closed it again, but her good angel held her hand.

"The child dropped it when she sat here, doubtless," she murmured, faintly.

And her eyes fell upon the open page, where she read, through tears:

"Come unto me all ye that labor and are heavy laden, and I will give you rest.

"Take my yoke upon you, and learn of me: for I am meek and lowly of heart: and ye shall find rest unto your souls.

"For my yoke is easy and my burden is light."

As she closed the book, her eyes expanded with wonder and solemn thought; her brow was overshadowed, then bright; then all this passed, and clasping the volume to her bosom, she sobbed, and prayed, and slowly grew more calm. A voice had spoken to her which she had not heard before.

CHAPTER XXXVI.

EFFINGHAM HALL—SLUMBERS.

While these events were occurring at Williamsburg—these various and conflicting passions, writhing, bubbling, boiling, and exploding—while the town began to thrill, and buzz, and rouse itself, and make preparation for the meeting of the burgesses, and the great opening day—all this while profound quiet reigned at Effingham Hall. Embowered in its lofty oaks, which only sighed and rustled mournfully in the sad autumn days, it seemed to sleep, looking, with its sunset illumined windows, like great eyes, on the broad woodlands and champaign, and the far river flowing solemnly to the great ocean. One might have fancied, without any violent effort of the imagination, that the great manor-house was a living thing, which mourned for something which had happened not long since. The casements rattled gloomily in the chill autumn evening, and the mourning winds, scattering the variegated leaves, sighed round the gables like an invisible host of mourners, then died away with sobs in the dim forest. The sun came up, but did not shine with cheerfulness and warmth—something seemed to have dimmed his light, and the rainy mist drooped long above the fields before his struggling beams could pierce and overthrow it. He went down in a pomp of golden clouds, indeed: but even they looked sad—for it was like a great monarch dying on his purple couch of state, and taking with him to the far undiscovered land beyond the immense horizon, all that blessed and cheered the hearts of nations. In the long nights, the breezes of the ocean sighed, and sobbed, and murmured to each other round the antique chimneys, and a sombre desolation, uncheered by any light but the great struggling blood-red moon's, appeared to brood over the broad domain of Effingham and the thoughtful, silent Hall.

Within, there was scarcely more cheerfulness than without. The servants moved about with quiet steps and subdued voices; for they felt that the echoes should not be aroused. The cloud on their master's brow awed them, and instinctively they spoke in whispers, and tipped in and out; and when a silver cup or salver chanced to fall, they started and held their breath, and looked round fearfully. Little was said by any member of the household; days, it seemed, passed sometimes without a word being uttered by any one. That gloom upon the old squire's brow repelled any advances—silenced any attempts at social intercourse. The meals passed in silence, with their array of almost motionless black servants, standing behind the chairs, and moving noiselessly in obedience to signs. All countenances were clouded, and, when the old gentleman had swallowed his chocolate, or eaten something with an obvious effort, he passsed in silence to the library, and was seen no more for hours.

Miss Alethea had grown unusually good-tempered; she did not scold, or rate the servants, or fill the house with clatter in her housekeeping, as her wont had been: she looked sad, and spoke little—passing her time in assiduous sewing on household articles—a dress for Kate, or else a frill for Willie, or maybe a neckcloth for her father. Orange was no longer in high favor, and would come and wag his tail, and look up wistfully, and whine, and then, finding that no notice was taken of him, would go and lie down on the rug, and, resting his chin upon his paws, gaze into the singing fire, hour after hour, in silence. Willie was, he knew not why, in low spirits; he often thought of Champ, now, and regretted all those hasty words he had uttered lately. His whip no longer waked the echoes of the old portrait-decorated hall; his halloos to the fox-hounds dragging their heavy blocks and baying hoarsely, were never heard now startling the silent lawn; the gallop of his poney never sounded on the gravelled road winding through the rich grounds up to the door. Little Kate had not had a ride behind him now for weeks—Willie had lost his relish for the amusement, and for all else, it seemed—he went slowly singing about the house, in a low, melancholy tone, and seemed to be looking for something which he could not find.

And what of little Kate? She was, perhaps, the saddest of them all. Her tender, sensitive heart had received a wound from that which had occasioned all this gloom in them. She loved him so dearly! as she had said, with her simple, childish truth—they had been so happy all those days and years before and since his return! How could she miss his presence and not grieve? They had such quiet, smiling talks together in the evenings, when stretched upon the sofa with his head upon her lap she had sung for him her little songs—"The Flowers of the Forest," "Birks of Invermay," or "Roslin Castle," in the clear sunny voice, instinct with so much marvellous sweetness, he had said, one day. They had walked together, hand in hand, far into the deep woods, and he had never complained of the pebbles hurting his feet through the frail Spanish leather slippers, as he had done in her hearing to grown ladies; they had looked upon the setting sun from the high hill westward from the Hall and then, turning round, seen the tall windows all in flame: he had taken such good care upon those rides that she should sit easily, and pressed the little hand clasped round his waist with such smiling goodness. She remembered so well his voice, and looks, and smiles—other people said they were affected or sarcastic smiles, but they were very bright when they shone on her; and now, when she no longer saw them, she missed their light, and sat down in her little corner, and wetted the silk of which Carlos was composed with silent tears. After one of these quiet, uncomplaining cries, she felt that she must see him, and she did, as we know, at the *Raleigh*. She came back from that interview with a greater weight than ever on her heart. She could not understand those gloomy words he uttered, but she heard him say, they could not meet again, and that he could not go back with her—and all the way back to the Hall, the child sobbed and shook, and hid her face, making no reply to Miss Alethea's questions. What could have changed him so at the tavern—so suddenly? She knew she had half persuaded him when he left her—and then the child shrunk and trembled, thinking of those scenes which followed. She sat down in her corner again, and mourned, and cried, and went on with her work, or said her lessons, with a dumb sorrow, which it was a cruel sight to see; at night, though, she was calmer—having read her Bible and prayed for him.

One day the parson came to see his parishioner and condole with him. He performed this parish duty by endeavoring to prove that the prodigal was not worthy to be his father's son, and that his "conduct" could not in any manner affect the squire: he wound up with a reiteration of his argument proving the young man's unworthiness, and then, to his horror, saw the squire rise, and flush to his brows with passion. High words followed—Champ should not be abused in his father's house, the squire said, by any person in Christendom! This was all the thanks he got, the parson said, with indignation: and proceeding thus from irritation on both sides, to rage, the interview had ended, as the parson had related to the stranger, Kate to her cousin. Parson Tag had drank his last glass of port at the Hall, and before many days had accepted a call from the Piedmont region, and so shaken the dust of the parish from his feet for ever.

Visitors talked about the weather, when they came to the Hall, and of the crops, the news from England, the approaching speech of his excellency, Governor Fauquier, at the opening of the House of Burgesses, and indeed of every thing but that one subject. Mr. Effingham's doings were, indeed, the talk of the colony, as he had said, with such disdainful indifference, but none of the colonists introduced the subject at the Hall. One day Mr. Lee and his family dined there, and Willie asked Clare, in the middle of a profound silence, if she was going to the governor's ball with brother Champ. Clare had colored, and her lip had trembled slightly, as she had answered that she did not think of going to the ball. Whereupon the squire had struck the table, and sworn that he would go and take her—and he had looked so mournful after his outburst, that Clare had said nothing. It was half understood that she and Henrietta would go—with the Effingham party, or accompanied by their cavaliers.

So the days passed, and Effingham Hall seemed to become more and more sad and still:—its inmates conversed less, and a deeper quiet seemed to reign. The winds that sobbed across the lonely autumn fields, and swayed backward and forward all the haughty oaks, seemed only to increase the stillness. So the Hall slept its sleep.

CHAPTER XXXVII.

WILLIAMSBURG: EXCESSIVE WAKEFULNESS.

While Effingham Hall was falling asleep more and more deeply, Williamsburg having passed through its night—that is to say, the period of time elapsing between the adjournment and the re-assemblage of the House of Burgesses, that galaxy of brilliant suns which periodically shone upon it—Williamsburg woke up from its long slumber, laughing, merry, full of activity and expectation. Already the grateful chinking of merry-faced pistoles were heard, as they rose and fell in jovial planters' pockets, while the owner pondered how to lay them out to the best advantage—already, though the meeting of the House was three days off, the town was filling fast; and on every hand jests and laughter, hearty greetings, the slamming of doors, the rattle of carriages, the clatter of hoofs, the jingle of spurs, and the neighs of horses, gave abundant proof that the joyous season had arrived. The taverns were filling rapidly, and mine host of the Raleigh was in full activity—running, that is to say toddling; bowing, that is to say ducking his fat head; laughing, that is to say shaking the windows, in honor of the jolly patrons of his establishment clapping him on the back, asking about his health facetiously, and calling for his rum, claret, and strong waters.

Whips cracked; the streets were full of sound; the men roared over their cups; the ladies filled the stores, running the clerks mad with orders; every thing said very plainly that the great gala day of the middle class had come: the class who visited the town but once a year with their wives and daughters, and were so determined to suck joy from every thing.

Through this laughing, jesting crowd some lordly equipage would pass from time to time, with its glossy four-in-hand, its liveried coachman and small footman on the board behind; and, through the window plainly seen, the lovely face of some young beauty, smiling in her silk and velvet, like the countrymen in their fustian; or else some fat, pursy squire, with puffy cheeks, and formal look, set off by his good wife in plain black silk and diamonds.

Young gallants, pranced by on their splendid horses; country carts toiled slowly on, laden with vegetables and drawn by diminutive, shaggy, solemn-looking animals; a thousand bright-faced, grinning negroes illuminating like black suns the buzzing, restless, laughing, jovial, hearty, shouting uproar—and behold! A drum comes from the distance, quickly rolling, trumpets blare aloud and split the ears, and mounted on his car of state—a cart fixed with a platform and pulled by three mules—the great Hallam rides in state above the tuneful throng. The drums deafen all; the trumpets shatter all tympana with a gush of sound, flowing from bearded lips, blowing for life; and high above the whole the noble Shylock rears a pine sapling with a placard beauteous.

That placard says, that at the old theatre, near the capitol, and by permission of his worship the mayor of Williamsburg, the company will that night enact the tragedy of Hamlet, written by Mr. William Shakespeare. Hamlet, the prince, by the great tragedian, Pugsby; Ophelia, by Miss Beatrice Hallam, the delight of the noble aristocracy and the wonder of the universal world. This information is conveyed in letters half a foot long, and with a profusion of exclamation points.

Such is the placard, gazed on wonderingly by those barbarous country people, who had never delighted their eyes with the sight of the great tragedian Mr. Pugsby, nor of Miss Hallam, the delight of the whole aristocracy and the wonder of the universal world; perhaps, indeed, had been so sunk in barbarism as never to have done aught but *read* the great drama written by the glorious Mr. William Shakespeare! But to-night they will go and have their ignorance of play-acting turned into grand illumination on the subject. Yes! they will go and see the play, the actors, and the noble aristocracy! Their pockets are well filled—five shillings nothing! And shouts sound louder, the great trumpet blares more shatteringly, the drum wakes the thunder, and the splendid pageant passes onward; Hallam and Shylock proud, and full of dignity and state. At the Raleigh—as on Gloucester-street and everywhere—life is jubilant, and men consider drinking, with every friend they recognize, a duty. And rum and claret, port and Rhenish, flow in streams, and doors bang, windows rattle, heavy shoes clump, merry lips laugh: Williamsburg scents the coming banquet of mind, spread by his excellency and the burghers—the boasted flow of reason and the soul—and, full of joyful anticipation, empties countless flagons at the Raleigh, kicks its chairs, plays cards upon its tables, and erects it into a great jolly temple—a temple where, at most reasonable charges, as mine host avers, they may worship Bacchus, Momus, and all the heathen gods.

CHAPTER XXXVIII.

IN WHICH THE TALK IS OF COSTUME.

Let us now descend from generalities to particular scenes, and in order to make this descent, ascend to Mr. Effingham's apartment in the "Raleigh." Aloof from all the bustle, confusion and laughter of the crowd, indifferent to it, or despising it, the young man sat thinking in silence, and glancing at times with a scornful smile on the merry groups, seen through the window, passing up and down the street. His lips wore that same bitter weary expression we have so often noted; his cheek was more sallow, his eyes more gloomy. He was clad as usual in the richest and most elegant manner, but the gayety of his toilette—the lace, the embroidery, the feather in his cocked hat, which lay beside him on the floor—was a mockery, contrasted thus with the moody and exhausted face.

The young man's lips moved, and he muttered, bitterly:

"Yes, now the die is really cast! While it rattled, I might have drawn back—now the throw has been made, it is but to raise the box, and the future is decided for the player—he is a beggar! Yes, I am mad; I feel that this infatuation amounts to madness!—this girl will ruin me! I love her, and hate her! She is an angel, and a devil! So pure and innocent in face, with such a bitter and scornful heart. By heaven, I'll conquer her—she shall be mine! And yet—and yet," he murmured, looking down, "why not draw back? There is time! And Kate! how I distressed the tender child, who loves me so much, more than I deserve—who, perhaps, saved me! I thought a ray of sunlight fell upon me when she came. She would have persuaded me; I feel it, I know it, I could not have resisted—dear child!" and the poor, weary eyes were softened, the mocking smile disappeared; "thank God, she loves me still. Why should I not go back now? But Beatrice! Aye, those chivalric gentlemen, who would display their courage at my expense. Ah!" he continued, smiling bitterly again, "they will not *permit* me to act as seems proper to me. By heaven, we shall see!"

And his reckless, dare-devil eyes flashed haughtily. At the same moment, the drums and trumpets of the cortège we have seen, attracted his attention, and he gazed through the window. There stood the noble Shylock, on the platform, moving slowly, holding in his hand the banner, on which was inscribed the words we have seen. The letters were enormous, and Mr. Effingham read, without difficuly, " Miss Beatrice Hallam, the delight of the noble aristocracy and the wonder of the universal world."

" Yes," he said, smiling grimly, as the procession passed slowly on; " yes, she is the delight of the noble aristocracy! I am one of that noble aristocracy, I believe, and she is my delight. Ah, Madam Beatrice! you go on now in pride and happiness, scorning me, and all who are not your abject slaves; but wait! You go to affect to-night, in the character of Ophelia, griefs you have never known, sufferings you can only imagine. Some day you will suffer really, and I shall be avenged."

He was not present at that interview with Charles Waters, and had not heard those prayers, and sobs, and despairing murmurs, or he would never have uttered that bitter taunt. For a long time he sat thinking of her, and would mutter curses and blessings in the same breath. He had estimated justly his passion—it was not so much love as infatuation. He did hate and love, respect and despise her; at one moment he thought her a devil, at the next he was convinced she was an angel. But, by degrees, these conflicting emotions settled down into a collected recklessness, so to speak—a careless, bitter, mocking unconcern, and he rose up, with a sneer.

At the same moment the door opened, and Mr. Manager Hallam made his appearance, jovial and smiling. Mr. Effingham sat down again.

" What the devil puts you in such a good humor, Hallam?" he said, with scornful carelessness.

" I am laughing at the people, sir."

" The people?"

" Yes, their folly."

" What folly?"

" At their surprise and wonder on seeing my placard."

" Yes; that was foolish enough."

"They absolutely looked all eyes, as the great Congreve was accustomed to say."

"Did they?"

"And the negroes!"

"What of them?"

"They looked like charcoal, with two lumps of fire in it."

"Eh? their eyes, you mean?"

"Yes."

"They are a facetious race."

"Oh, sir, they would make great comedians, I assure you. Now, there was one monkey-like boy, who went along, blowing the trumpet through his hands, beating two stones together for the drum, and at times sawing his left arm for the fiddle—really, now, in a way indicating lofty talent."

"In the low comedy?"

"Yes."

"The buffoon?"

"Well, low comedy requires something like that. How would a company of negro actors take here?"

"Take?"

"Yes, sir; would it attract?"

"Strongly—the attention of messieurs the justices. But come, let us estimate the receipts to-night."

"Impossible, sir."

"Come, think."

"Really can't say, sir."

"As much, think you, as on the night I perform?" said Mr. Effingham, with his usual disdainful coolness.

"Why, really—now—I should say not, sir. I calculate that you would draw a large crowd."

"There is but one obstacle to my acting."

"And that, sir?"

"Miss Beatrice Hallam."

"Beatrice!"

Mr. Effingham shrugged his shoulders.

"Yes," he said.

"How is it possible?" began Hallam, with some indignation.

"Come, no exploding," said Mr. Effingham, with cool disdain; "do not affect astonishment. You know she does not wish to appear with me."

"Not wish, sir!"

"Yes."

"Oh, you must be mistaken."

"No, I am not," said Mr. Effingham, gloomily.

"She is young, sir."

"Well, what does that mean?"

"And diffident."

"Bah!"

"She would prefer acting with her associates. But, throw any obstacles in the way—I would soon stop that, sir!"

"There is a virtuous father for you! You would command your child to do what she wishes not to do?"

"She is full of whims, sir."

"One of which whims is a contempt for the name of Effingham; is it not?" said the young man, with a curling lip.

"Oh, never, sir."

"Come, now, deny—"

"She honors, and looks up to you, sir."

"She has a queer way of showing it," he said, with gloomy scorn. "What makes her hate me so? I am really curious to know."

"On my word, sir, you astonish me, as the great Congreve used to say: Beatrice, I am sure—"

"Well, no more protests, and curse the great Congreve! Is the agreeable Shylock still determined to eat me for kicking him down stairs?"

"No—no. He is a reasonable fellow, and will take no more notice of the matter. I told him, sir, my opinion of his disgraceful conduct to your fair young relative, and he sincerely regrets it."

"Very well: I will take no further note of the knave. Only, on the next occasion, I shall pin him to the wall without warning, like an enormous beetle—my sword for the pin. He would be a striking object. Now, let us talk of my first appearance."

"Willingly—with pleasure, sir."

"The town is full?"

"Yes, sir."

"And more coming?"

"Yes: they are pouring in."

"Well, if it is now full, and they are pouring in, by the day of opening the House of Burgesses, that is in two days, they will be sleeping in the streets."

"Quite likely, sir."

"And hence it follows," continued Mr. Effingham, "that there is no danger of having a thin house to greet me."

"Oh, sir!"

"I understand you—"

"How could—"

"Yes! how could the fashionable Mr. Champ Effingham, of Effingham Hall, turning comedian, fail of a crowded house? You would say that?"

"Yes, sir: it is impossible."

"Well—perhaps you are right. But I choose to wait, and I have fixed upon the day after the opening of the House, for my débût. I shall appear in 'Much Ado about Nothing.'"

"As you say, sir. Well, we can easily get it up. The honor—"

"Bah: let us have no foolery! It's no honor to either party. Now for the dress—the costume: I have none that would suit the character."

"I think I can serve you, sir—though my best military dresses are still at Yorktown, in the sea trunks. I have not needed them yet."

"A military dress—rough soldier's costume, is indispensable: you know very well that *Benedick* is just from the wars."

"Indispensable, as you say, sir."

"Have you one here?"

"Let me see—"

And Mr. Manager Hallam, placing his fat finger upon his puffy brow, repeated:

"I think there is such a costume in my private trunk, in my room. Will you go see, sir?"

"Yes: I'll follow."

And the two worthies went out, and closing the door, bent their way to Mr. Manager Hallam's sleeping apartment, situated on the same floor.

CHAPTER XXXIX.

HOW MR. EFFINGHAM BECAME THE INSTRUMENT OF PROVIDENCF

The apartment occupied by Mr. Manager Hallam was an odd place, and we regret that, from its want of importance to the present narrative, we cannot give a description of it. It is sufficient to say, that the bed was covered with heterogeneous costumes, of all ages and nations—the table with prompt-books and rolls of paper containing "parts"—the floor with shoes, buskins, and sandals, which had trodden many stages in their day.

In one corner a large trunk, with heavy iron binding, and knobs, contained the manager's finer costumes. This trunk he approached, and unlocked with a key which he took from the breast-pocket of his doublet.

"Now, sir," he said, raising the lid, "I think I shall find what we want."

"Good," said Mr. Effingham, leaning over his shoulders.

The manager took out several parcels.

"Those are the fops," he said.

"Of course, they would not suit me," said Mr. Effingham, with his usual disdainful indifference.

"Oh, no, sir."

"Certainly not," said Mr. Effingham.

"These are the first class costumes—for the heroes," said the manager, unrolling another parcel.

"That would suit me as little," replied Mr. Effingham.

"Yes, sir—I mean—"

Luckily Mr. Manager Hallam was relieved from his lame apology. A servant entered, and said:

"There's a gentleman, sir—Mr. Joyce, sir—to see you—to get a private box at the theatre, sir."

Hallam rose quickly, which possibly might be owing to a slight love of money.

"Say I am coming," he replied to the servant: then turning to Mr. Effingham, he added, "just wait for me, sir—I'll be back in a minute. These business matters must be attended to."

And with these words he hurried out of the room, puffing and red in the face. Mr. Effingham had received this speech with extreme indifference, and gazed with great disdain on the half-emptied trunk: then he seemed to change his mind, and stooping down he turned over and tossed the costumes about, carelessly. Suddenly his eye fell upon one which seemed to suit perfectly his purpose. It was a dark military coat, with heavy embossed buttons, and an embroidered collar. He took it up, and said aloud:

"Well, here is what will answer my purpose, I suppose—a pretty heavy bundle! Come, let us try it on."

Had he done so, the whole course of this narrative, thereafter, would have been different—how different no one can tell. But he changed his mind before unrolling it, and added:

"Bah! I cannot judge!—let us go to Madam Beatrice, and ask her opinion. Doubtless she will afford me her valuable advice most willingly and sweetly. Of course she will."

And leaving the trunk open, he walked carelessly along the passage, and scarcely taking the trouble to knock, entered Beatrice's apartment.

The young girl was engaged as usual, in studying, and looked completely exhausted. Her eyes were heavy and red, her cheeks pale and thin; in her very attitude there was an indescribable air of weariness and sorrow which was painful to behold. The round shoulders drooped, the head inclined toward one side—seemed to be bent down by some ever-present grief: the bosom labored and heaved: she seemed to draw breath with difficulty. For a moment Mr. Effingham stood looking at this eloquent picture, returning her silent and cold gaze.

"Ah," he said, at length, "studying as usual, I see! Really, madam, you will injure your health, which, as you know, is very dear to me."

There was great bitterness in these words: but Beatrice made no reply.

"You do not answer," he said, still more bitterly; "perhaps I am not worth answering, madam."

Beatrice raised her cold, heavy eyes, and looked at him fixedly.

"Mr. Effingham, I am in no humor to converse this morning," she replied, coldly.

"With me: you never are, madam."

"With no one, sir."

"Are you sure, madam?"

"Yes, sir."

"Perhaps your dear friend is an exception."

"What friend, sir?"

"The Chevalier Waters," replied Mr. Effingham, with a sneer.

A flush of pain and wretchedness threw a lurid glow upon the young girl's brow, and she trembled.

"Come, now, madam, get angry if you please. That is your favorite amusement when I chance to address you."

She bent down and made no reply: and this seemed to irritate her visitor more than any words.

"Really your ladyship is in a charming mood to-day," he said, with a scornful curl of the lip; "you have chosen a new and brilliant means of insulting me."

"Mr. Effingham," said Beatrice, raising her head with cold solemnity, and speaking in a voice hoarse with sorrow, "I insult no one, sir. I have said that I was not disposed to converse to-day. I am not well, sir."

"You are always sick when I visit you," said the young man, pitilessly: his passion had changed his whole character: "you hate my very face, I believe. My presence is a discord. I have given up every thing for you, and you scorn me! Beware, Beatrice Hallam! God will punish you!"

Her lip quivered, and she looked strangely at him.

"Have you come to make me more unwell than I am, sir?" she said, pressing her hand upon her breast.

"No, madam," he said, with his former bitterness. "I came on business, strictly professional."

"What is that, sir?"

"To ask your most respectable opinion of my costume, in the character of Benedick. Having determined to ruin myself, I wish to do it handsomely—with the best bow I have and in the most appropriate costume!"

"Well, sir," said Beatrice, taking no notice of his terrible irony, "I listen."

And she closed her book.

"This, which I hold in my hand, madam, appears to me to be very suitable for the character of Benedick."

"I do not know, sir."

"He was a gentleman, you know, madam."

"Yes, sir."

"Ruined."

"I do not remember, sir."

"Yes, ruined in the wars—like myself, by this infatuation I have for you: wounded and scarred as I am by your scorn."

"Mr. Effingham, we waste time."

"Oh, pardon me, madam, my grief and agony are nothing to you—I had forgotten."

"My own occupy my whole thoughts, sir."

"Really! then *you* have griefs too."

"Yes, sir."

"Agony perhaps."

"Overpowering agony, sir," she said, hoarsely, and with a trembling lip. He looked at her in silence, and said, with some feeling,

"Then, you really suffer?"

"Yes, sir."

"Deeply?"

"Yes, sir."

"Then have some pity on my own," he said, in a voice of anguish, which was most affecting. "I love you, you scorn me! Do you know what that means? It means days and nights of agony—hours of despair, such as the bitterest foe would not inflict on his worst enemy—sleepless hours in the dim night, when the rain pours, and the winds groan, and your own groans reply. Have you no pity, Beatrice?"

He stopped, overcome with so many conflicting and terrible emotions, bending down his head and groaning.

"Did you only know what it is to love, and know that love can never solace your life!" he continued, passionately; "to see the paradise open and then close upon you! to love madly, and feel the cold hand of fate pushing you back inexorably!"

These broken words painted her own condition with such truth that Beatrice uttered a moan.

"I know it," she said, hoarsely.

"Then pity me!"

"I do, sir, from my heart!"

His face flushed.

"And nothing more?" he said, in a low tone.

"No, sir—no, no!" she said, shrinking back.

"Ah, you despise me—you hate me!"

"No, sir."

"I ruin myself for you, and you meet me with a contemptuous smile."

"I do not, sir."

"You will not love me."

"I cannot, sir!"

"You love another, perhaps, madam—already you have selected your future husband!" he said, becoming again bitter and scornful as before.

Beatrice turned pale.

"I shall never marry," she replied, in a low voice.

"I am not good enough for you, I make no doubt, madam!"

"You taunt me, sir."

"I do not—I offer you my hand!"

"I cannot accept it."

"Never?"

"Never!"

"Then we shall see," said Mr. Effingham, with that bitter and reckless laugh which at times issued from his lips, "force against force!"

Beatrice colored, and said, coldly:

"That is a defiance, sir."

"Yes—to the death."

"I despise it," she answered, with haughty coldness; then murmured, turning away, "God pardon me!"

"Ah, that is not singular; contempt for the person necessarily comprehends as much for all he can effect."

"Mr. Effingham, I am weary—I have my part to study."

"Well, madam, permit me to trespass upon your kind patience for a moment still. I came to ask of your great experience if this coat will suit my part."

"You may see at a glance, sir," she said, frigidly, "that it is moth-eaten, and unsuitable."

"Ah! I had not perceived that. Pray what shall I wear?"

"I do not know, sir."

"You act *Beatrice* in the comedy, I believe—or do some of those delightful characters your father has picked up here in the colony, and trained to murder dramas, take the part?"

"I know nothing of the matter, Mr. Effingham," she said, coldly.

"But *Beatrice* is young?"

"Yes, sir."

"Brilliant?"

"Yes, sir."

"And very scornful?"

"I believe so, sir."

"Then it will suit you admirably. Young, brilliant, and scornful! Could the description answer more perfectly! Shakespeare must have known you!"

"Mr. Effingham, your great pleasure in life seems to lie in insulting me."

"Insulting? Really you are very unreasonable, madam—"

"What, sir—is not—?"

"No, madam, let me say, even at the expense of politeness—for I know how ill-bred it is to interrupt you—no, it is not an insult, only the truth! It is very amusing, very laughable, but it is true—that you really *scorn* me. As to the *young* and *brilliant*, that is undeniable in your ladyship's presence."

"Mr. Effingham, I am exhausted—your voice agitates me—pray leave me, sir—"

Mr. Effingham listened to these coldly-uttered words of dismissal with an internal rage, which broke forth and displayed itself in a mocking and harsh laugh.

"Ah! you are very lofty, madam!" he said, with a sneer; "you bring your queenly airs from the stage for me! Nothing that I say, nothing that I do, provokes any thing but scorn and contempt from you! I have not sacrificed enough to you, perhaps! Do you know what trifling things—mere trifles, madam—I have left to follow your diabolical eyes! I have only forfeited the affection of my family, only lost my position in society, only struck cruelly a pure young girl's heart, who loves me! I have only left peace and happiness for agony and rage!—only abandoned love and tenderness for scorn and contempt—only given up loving faces and caressing hands for a woman who hates me and repulses me! These are mere trifles, madam!—they are nothing! What is the love of Clare Lee—that is her name—to me, compared to your overwhelming tenderness and affection? True, we have loved each other, I may say, I think, for years; true, we were bred together, and have always felt a tenderness toward each other deeper than words could utter or the eyes speak! True, her face filled with sunshine when she saw me, as my heart overflowed with joy at her innocent smiles! But what of that? You are all this to me and more! Your love is a treasure greater than her own; what matter if her heart is broken; what if she gazes from her father's window on the Hall which she once thought she would enter as my wife, and sobs and moans, and feels that henceforth life is dark to her—as I feel it is to me? *Your* tender heart, *your* loving nature, *your* mild, angelic soul, *your* overwhelming love for me will more than make me forget her. What matters it if the poor girl dies broken-hearted, are you not all my own?"

And overpowered by rage, and remorse, and agony, his brow wet with perspiration, his lips trembling, all his form shaking with the terrible war of emotions so profound and bitter, the unhappy young man, waiting for no reply, rushed from the room. Beatrice rose from her seat, trembling with excitement, and bursting into tears of agony, cried:

"Oh, is this really true! Is this a horrible dream, or not! God has cursed me! all that I approach is ruined. Oh, can I be the cause of this dreadful suffering, which I feel myself, in the heart of a pure, young girl? God pity me! But no, it shall not be!" she cried; "my life is lost and ruined—my very soul is giving way! But this stain shall not rest upon my memory—no, no! Oh, her name! I heard it—near his father's house—I will go there—tell her all—God give me strength!"

And hastening out, she ordered her horse, made her preparations quickly, and was soon upon her way to Riverhead, galloping feverishly.

So feverish had been her emotion, that she had not observed the presence of an object, which Mr. Effingham had dropped upon the floor of her apartment.

CHAPTER XL.

BEATRICE HALLAM AND CLARE LEE.

She reached Riverhead in an incredibly short space of time; and, dismounting at the gate, hastened to the door, and trembling, shuddering, followed the astonished servant into the reception-room, where she fell into a chair, exhausted, overcome, and shedding torrents of tears.

A light step startled her, and she rose, trembling, from her seat. The young girl she had asked for, stood before her.

"Did you ask for me—Clare?" said the young girl, wonderingly.

"Oh, yes! for you!" cried poor Beatrice, clasping her hands and sobbing: "I could not breathe until I saw you! I came to tell you that I am not the miserable creature that you think me! that I am not so abandoned as to wrong you so!"

Suddenly Clare recognized her rival, whose features had been hidden by the partial darkness of the room. She drew back with a sudden faintness.

"Yes! you shrink from me!" cried Beatrice, with inexpressible anguish in her voice; "and perhaps you are not wrong—you have heard so much falsehood of me! But you wrong me bitterly—my heart is bursting with this load of unjust scorn—I cannot bear it! It is cruel—oh, it is unjust!"

And she covered her face with her hands, and sobbed passionately. Clare felt as if she were about to faint; but indignation, and the bitterness of wounded love and pride sustained her. She looked at Beatrice with scorn, and shrunk from her as she approached.

"Do not—do not touch me!" she said, alternately flushing and turning pale.

"Oh, you are cruel!" cried Beatrice, wringing her hands; "you are cruel and unjust! He told me you were tender, and that every body loved you—and I find you with a heart harder than stone! You have no pity on me—you scorn me—my very presence is loathsome to you! Oh, madam, it is unjust!—it is a bitter and unmerited punishment! I never could have come had I really expected this—though what more had I the right to expect? But he told me you were so good—that your heart was so pure—that you were in such distress—how could I live with the thought that you despised and scorned me!"

Clare shrunk further back and trembled. Then she had been the topic of careless conversation between this unworthy creature and her lover! Her name, and her love for him, even, had been bandied in tavern purlieus with scoffs, and rude jests, perhaps! He had said she was "so good"—doubtless, deriding her soft, tender manner, so tame, compared with the fiery and brilliant carriage of this shameless creature!—her "heart so pure"—no doubt contrasting derisively her simple truth with the scoffing boldness of this woman! Then, to crown the whole, he had told this woman that she, Clare, was "distressed"—that she was pining for him!—that she envied, hated, would give life to hold the position of that rival in his affections! This last bitter thought put the finishing touch to Clare's agony, and she rose.

"I can listen to no more, madam!" she said, hoarsely, and with inexpressible anguish and indignation in her altered voice. "You are deceived—Mr. Effingham—if you refer to him—Mr. Effingham is nothing to me!"

And, shuddering from head to foot, she looked at Beatrice with an expression of sick and scornful aversion, which pierced the poor girl's heart like a dagger.

"Oh, no—no! do not look at me so!" she cried, clasping her hands, and sobbing as if her heart would break; "do not look at me so! I am not the unworthy creature you think me! I am innocent! He sought me—has persecuted me with attentions I abhor—he has made my life, dark enough, God knows, already, darker still by his eternal persecution. Oh! madam, you have no right to scorn me! You have no right—however much you may hate me! I am innocent before God of any thing done to give you pain—this rash young man has done all! Do you think I am his paramour, madam? I see your cheek flush and your eyes flash! Doubtless your maiden purity is shocked by the very word. But we, madam, we poor actresses have to look at and hear things coarsely, and call them by their names. God forgive you, if you thought that of me! I am a poor, unhappy girl, with no defence but my self-respect; but I am innocent—innocent as a child, in thought as in deed!"

And sobbing, moaning, shedding floods of tears, Beatrice stood before the young girl like an angel pleading for a word of love, of charity. Her fair hair had fallen, from the violence of her emotion, her snowy arms had let the cloak covering them fall down, her face was eloquent with a sorrow and despair which sublimated its tender beauty, and would have touched, indeed, any but a heart of stone.

Clare's was that heart; she only saw how lovely this young girl was; she only saw in her a triumphant rival, darkening her life, and taking from her him she loved. What did it concern her whether this woman was innocent or not? And the frigid, sick, and scornful look remained. She pointed to the door, and, unable to say more than—"this interview—must—end!" hoarsely and almost inaudibly.

"No, no! it shall not end," cried Beatrice, wringing her hands, and sobbing, and speaking with passionate grief; "it shall not end until you have heard me! I am innocent—Oh! I am innocent—before God! your distress is not upon my hands! He came and addressed me on the stage, the first night I appeared in this country—I drew back and endeavored to avoid him! He came to see me the next day. I tried to deny him any converse with me;—he staid,—he came again and again—he has made my life wretched! I shrink when I see his face, or hear his voice!—Ah, I am innocent of wounding you,—as God hears me, I am innocent!"

And falling on her knees, Beatrice hid her face in her hands, and shook with passionate weeping. She seemed so broken and overwhelmed by her sorrow, her accents were so profoundly miserable, she resembled so much some tender bird, wounded mortally and about to fall and die, that Clare, with all her pride and love, and hatred and indignation, melted. She struggled with herself, echoed the sobs of Beatrice, and then turning from her, murmured:

"Leave me—I cannot speak—I pardon you—God will—"

There she stopped, overcome by emotion. Beatrice raised her head.

"Oh, I have done nothing to ask pardon for!" she cried, in a voice of bitter anguish. "God is my witness, that I have acted as a loyal and pure woman! I saw your scorn of me was unjust, and it is—it is!—for I am innocent—I had no part in inflicting this wound upon you; you have reason to hate me—but you cannot—no! no! you cannot scorn me!"

"I do not," muttered poor Clare, sobbing and turning away.

"Oh, thank you! We poor girls are not like you ladies, protected and surrounded by every comfort, able to choose our associates," continued Beatrice, weeping, but betraying great feeling at these words from Clare. "God exposes us to every persecution and temptation! We are met with intoxicating applause upon the stage—a dangerous and fatal thing!—and there we fancy that we are really something more than human! Alas! we go out in the sunlight, and those hands, which applauded us, repulse us; those smiles are turned to frowns! The commonest woman that toils in the meanest employment, is more worthy. Contempt is our portion—for what are we but abandoned playing girls! Or, if not contempt, what is more dreadful—oh! so dreadful, madam, that you in your pure home here cannot imagine it. The temptation which a strong man offers to a defenceless girl, without a thought of that avenging God who looks down on this world!—I will not speak of it—I shudder to think of it!—my brain burns, and my temples throb!—God decreed that I should fill the position I do, and I know its terrors and its snares. Oh, do not undervalue them, madam! if a poor weak girl comes from that furnace of fire, still pure in all things, she is not fit for scorn!"

And the poor agitated breast labored and heaved, the cheeks were bathed in tears, the childlike hands trembled and could not arrange the hair, falling around the face so eloquent and pure.

And Clare felt her true woman's heart moved—with that high truth and worth which the reader will find she possessed from future pages of this narrative. She violently suppressed her sorrow and wounded love; she saw only a poor broken-spirited girl before her—a mere child she seemed;

praying and sobbing, and entreating mercy—or rather justice, but simple justice.

"I have listened—to you—and pity—you—and do not, cannot scorn you—or—hate you—" she said, in a broken and agitated voice, shedding tears as she spoke. "If I have been—unjust—to you, I pray for your pardon! We are all weak—and—poor;—God does not permit us to scorn each other!"

And covering her face with one hand, she felt as if earth was dark for ever for her from that day—heaven only left.

Beatrice heard these words with passionate delight, and burst into an agony of tears.

"Oh, you are too good!" she cried, seizing the hand of the young girl, which hung down, and covering it with kisses; "you are too good and noble, to speak so kindly to a poor, weak child like me! Oh, God will reward you! God sent me to you, to hear these blessed words from you—to know that my existence was not wholly cursed! God had pity on me, and inspired me with the thought! Oh, say again that you will not hate or scorn me;—forget that I am a common actress, one of a proscribed and branded class—one who has cruelly wronged you, however innocently;—forget that I am so much your inferior in goodness,—forget that my life has been thrown in contact with so much that is vile! See before you, at your feet, only a poor weak girl, who prays you not to scorn her!—See in me a feeble creature, like all mortals, weak and stumbling and sinful, like all the world, but with good impulses and pure feelings like the purest! Oh, bless me again with the sound of your kind voice—I am so helpless! so broken-hearted—so overborne by agony and suffering!" she continued, strangling a passionate sob at the thought of Charles; "so wretched—ah! so miserable!—Speak to me!—one more kind word, before I leave you—Oh, for pity's sake!"

And covering the hand she held with kisses, she half rose in an agony of weeping. And that hand she held was no more drawn away. The trembling forms approached each other with a last shudder, and the two women were in each other's arms: the bitter rivals, the wronged and she who had wronged her, the actress and the lady! Sobbing upon each other's shoulders, trembling like a single agitated form, they wept in silence.

A quarter of an hour afterwards Beatrice was on her way back to Williamsburg. God had spoken: her tears were happy tears.

CHAPTER XLI.

HOW MR. EFFINGHAM RODE FORTH, AND BEFORE MIDNIGHT REAPPEARED EN MILITAIRE.

After uttering that mad, passionate speech, so crammed with bitter and scornful irony, Mr. Effingham, as we have seen, flung from the young girl's room, in an access of rage, which tore him like a vulture's talons. He had passed through many of these fiery interviews lately, and had many such pale rages, which tore his heart for a time, then slowly subsided, like a storm muttering away into the distance. On this occasion he found himself, as usual, grow somewhat calmer, when her cold and inexorable face was removed from him; and soon his bitter, reckless smile returned, and mockery replaced anger.

He went back to the manager's room, and threw the costume disdainfully into the trunk; then, scarcely conscious of what he was doing, proceeded to restore the various bundles to their places. Fate still directed him, for who knows what would have occurred if that fit of absence had not seized him, and he had left those dresses where they lay—throwing down carelessly the one he had brought back upon them? He had just slammed down the lid of the trunk violently, when Mr. Manager Hallam returned.

"Ah, sir," he said, with a smile, "you are tired of the search; are you?"

"Yes."

"Well, I think there was little good in it. My military costumes are still at Yorktown."

"Are they?" said Mr. Effingham, coldly.

"Yes, sir, as I informed you."

"Did you?"

"Ha, ha! don't you recollect, sir?"

"How can I? I have just had such a charming interview with your amiable daughter."

"Ah! have you, sir?" said Mr. Manager Hallam, anxiously; for his matrimonial project never left his thoughts.

"Yes," returned Mr. Effingham, with scornful carelessness; "I think she is beginning to like me."

"I am sure of it, sir," said the delighted worthy.

"She seemed to brighten up, when I entered."

"Did she, indeed?"

"Of course she did! She seemed delighted to see me!"

"She is the most truthful and sincere girl in the world—a gold mine would not make her smile, if she did not choose to," said Hallam, with real fraternal pride.

"Quite true," replied Mr. Effingham; "she is perfectly sincere."

"Indeed she is, sir."

"And plain-spoken."

"Oh, remarkably!"

"And we spent half an hour delightfully."

"You are gaining on her, sir."

"You think she don't hate me, then?"

"Oh, sir!"

"Come, answer."

"Hate you, sir? Never, sir!"

"How then? Does she love me?"

This somewhat embarrassed Mr. Manager Hallam; for the young girl's demeanor to Mr. Effingham, when he had observed it lately, was exceedingly far from supporting an answer in the affirmative. But he replied, at once:

"I think she will in time, sir."

"In time!"

"Very soon, sir."

"Really?"

"Yes, sir; I have observed little things of late which prove to me that you are acquiring her affection; and she no longer—"

"You are right—I understand—she no longer scorns, and insults, and hates me—"

"Oh, sir!"

"She no longer tells me that she will never look at me

but with hatred and aversion. In our interviews now she smiles, and presses my hands tenderly, and seems to pity my pale cheeks, and languid eyes—my health is dear to her—or becoming dear—she is beginning to love me. Yes, as you very justly say, sir, I am 'beginning to acquire her affection'!"

And the young man laughed, with terrible irony—a laugh which jarred upon Manager Hallâm's ears, and dispelled, unpleasantly, the agreeable impression the words were calculated to produce.

"Bah!" continued Mr. Effingham; "let us leave love matters, and come to business. You have no Benedick costume here?"

"Really—I believe not, sir; but—"

"Have you at Yorktown?"

"Oh yes, sir."

"In trunks?"

"Yes, sir."

"Where are they?"

"Stored in the warehouse."

"Good; then you have a complete Benedick dress at Yorktown in trunks, stored in the warehouse?" said Mr Effingham, summing up with disdainful nonchalance.

"Yes, sir."

"Give me the key."

"The key, sir?"

"I am going to get the dress.

"You, sir!"

"Certainly; what the devil are you staring at?"

"Why—really, sir—"

"Give me the key!"

"Of course, sir; here it is," said the manager, taking a huge iron key from a drawer of the table.

"Is there but one trunk?"

"Three, sir."

"Well, the dress—"

"Is in the green one, bound with brass hoops."

"Very well. They know me there; and when I assure them further that I am a member of the company, there will be small difficulty. Order my horse," he added to a servant passing through the passage.

And the young man, without taking the trouble to say good-bye to Hallam, went out, and going along the passage, entered his own room, leaving the worthy manager in a state of stupor, staring after him.

"Well, really," said Manager Hallam, at length, "that young man is an extraordinary character. I don't know how to deal with him. He snubs me; I feel he is continually a-roasting me, and I don't know how to answer. He has such lordly airs—worse than the great Congreve. Well, he is going to act, and go to the ball with Beatrice; and then I'll have him. He is not good enough for her, I know, except that he is so rich. Effingham Hall comes to him, I understand; and that is enough."

With which Mr. Manager Hallam began to dream of the clover-enveloped life which he desired so ardently.

An hour or two afterwards Mr. Effingham issued forth, clad as before in his rich foppish costume—only that his slippers were replaced by elegant riding buskins reaching a little above the ankle and ornamented with rosettes: he seldom wore boots, then rapidly becoming the fashion among all classes. In his hand he carried an elegant gold-ornamented riding whip—and so he mounted, and, as the evening closed in stormily, set forth toward Yorktown.

Half an hour afterwards it began to rain heavily, and this circumstance distressed Mr. Manager Hallam exceedingly; without reason, however, for the theatre was crammed from pit to dome, and Beatrice had never been more completely overwhelmed with applause, or had acted with such overpowering splendor. They could not know what gave that supernatural power to the young girl's voice, that marvellous reality to the expression of her lips and eyes—but they saw the wonderful genius, and rose up with a shout that drowned the thunder rolling through the sky without.

Long before midnight the storm cleared away, and in the now silent streets the stroke of a horse's hoof was heard, and this horse stopped before the Raleigh. Mr. Effingham dismounted, and summoning the sleepy servant, gave his animal into his hands.

The horse was covered with sweat, and his mouth dropping foam.

Mr. Effingham was clad in a complete military suit—huge boots, curved heavy sword, broad belt, and Flanders hat. Mr. Manager Hallam had no such costume in his repertory, and indeed, Mr. Effingham had not visited the good town of York, at all.

CHAPTER XLII.

WHAT MR. EFFINGHAM HAD DROPPED.

Beatrice had reached Williamsburg just as the theatre was about to commence, and was compelled, without losing a moment, to hurry away to her painful duty. We may fancy that she felt little disposition to appear that evening: but one of the lessons of her hard life, was an unhesitating sacrifice of private feelings to her duty, and she repaired to the theatre, without even tasting a morsel. Indeed, she could not have eaten any thing—her heart was too much overcome by the thousand conflicting emotions she had experienced throughout the day; and she did not feel weak. Something sustained her, and she began her part with strange calmness. Never had she acted better, as we have seen—but those tumultuous plaudits fell upon unheeding ears: they were now painful to her—as that profession, which a cruel destiny forced her to pursue, was revolting and a cruel trial. She made her concluding bow with the same coldness which had characterized her, when, on her entrance, she had been greeted with thunders of applause; and then calmly returned to the Raleigh. She wished to be alone with her grief—to shed tears without being subjected to the wondering questions of any person:—she wished, after delighting the crowded audience, and sending them away thinking how rapturous her happiness and pride must be at such intoxicating praises—she wished to go and sob her heart into calmness, in the stillness of her chamber.

Bidding her father good night with a kiss at the door of her little room—from which another door led to her bedchamber—the young girl entered and lighted a taper. Then she observed for the first time, on the floor, that object which

Mr. Effingham had dropped, when he rushed from the room, and which in the tumult of her feelings she had lost sight completely of.

It was a little frock, such as were worn by very young children; and so slight was it, that Mr. Effingham had doubtless not observed that it had escaped from the bundle which he held in his hand. Beatrice picked it up, and examined it wonderingly, completely at a loss to understand how such a thing had gotten into her room. Why does she start so—why does her cheek flush, then grow pale again? On the collar of the little frock, is written in distinct though faded letters, "Beatrice Waters!"

Beatrice sat down, feeling too weak to stand: a sudden faintness invaded her heart, and her temples throbbed. "Beatrice Waters!—Beatrice Waters!" What did this mean? Whence could the frock have come—who brought it thither? Beatrice Waters? Had Charles then guessed correctly, and did the letters "B. W.," on the locket really mean this? She felt her mind whirl—her face flush and turn white again—some indefinable presentiment seemed to seize upon her, and the frock fell from her hand to the floor. For some minutes the young girl remained motionless—then she picked the dress up again. Suddenly she felt something in the pocket, and drew it out. It was a letter—faded and discolored, and worn at the edges. She tore it open and run her eyes eagerly over it—trembling—coloring—growing pale—breathing with difficulty. Then it fell from her hand, and pressing the other hand upon her heart, she leaned back overcome, as though she were about to faint.

The letter was in these words—words traced in faded yellow ink.

"A man about to die, calls on the only Englishman he knows in this place, to do a deed of charity. Hallam, we were friends—a long time since, in Kent, Old England, and to you I make this appeal, which you will read when I will be cold and stiff. You know we were rivals—Jane chose to marry me! I used no underhand acts, but fought it fairly and like an honest soldier—and won her. You know it, and are too honest a man to bear me any grudge now. I married her, and we went away to foreign countries, and I became a soldier of fortune—now here—now there:—it runs in the family, for my father was covered with wounds. She stuck to me—sharing all my trials—my suffering—as she shared my fortunate days. She was my only hope on earth—my blessing:—but one day God took her from me. She died, Hallam, but she left herself behind in a little daughter—I called her Beatrice, at the request of her mother. The locket around the child's neck, is her mother's gift to her: preserve it. Well: we travelled—I grew sick—I came to Malta, here—I am dying. Already I feel the cold mounting from my feet to my heart—my eyes are growing hazy, as my hand staggers along—my last battle's come, comrade! Take the child, and carry her to my brother John Waters, who lives in London somewhere—find where he is, and tell him, that Ralph Waters sends his baby to him to take care of:—she is yonder playing on the floor while I am dying. I ask you to do this, because you are an honest man, and because you loved Jane once. I have no money—all I had is gone for doctor's stuff and that:—he couldn't stand up against death! Keep my military coat to remember me by—it is all I have got. As you loved her who was my wife, now up in heaven, take care of the child of an English soldier; and God reward you.

"RALPH WATERS.

"*Malta, March,* 1743."

The last words were written hurriedly, and were exceedingly indistinct; as though the writer had been warned of his approaching death by a chill hand covering his eyes; but Beatrice ran over them like lightning, as by inspiration.

We may now understand why she leaned back faintly, dropping the letter from her nerveless hand. Here was the mystery illuminated suddenly by a flash, which made plain every recess, the most gloomy depths. All was as plain as light now! She was not Hallam's daughter!—that locket was the gift of her dying mother—that coat in Mr. Effingham's hand the soldier's—that little frock was the garment she had worn, a poor little baby, while her brave father, stretched upon his couch, was struggling with the cold hand of death, and dedicating his last moments to her own safety and restoration.

Her powerful and vivid imagination painted the scene with lifelike reality. The brave soldier dying—the poor apartment—the trembling hand contending with the dread angel—those dim eyes—herself a little child unconscious of all this—and the glazing eyes fixed on her as she laughed and prattled—and the last sigh of the stalwart breast a prayer for her! The scene was so real that she burst into a passion of tears, and sobbed until she was completely exhausted. Oh, that dear father dying there alone!—his brow covered with the sweat of the death agony, far away from friends and home, in a foreign land! That strong frame fighting with the destroyer—that face, which dawned on her memory now like a dim dream, convulsed with pain and dread for her after fate!

How could she bear to think of this and not feel her very soul overwhelmed with an agony like that which he had suffered? And she wept and sobbed, and shook with the tempest of her feelings; and then slowly grew more calm.

Why had she not been restored to her friends. Was not that old man, whose son had saved her, her uncle—Charles her cousin? And this thought dazzled her mind, for a moment darkened by that scene of death, plain through so many misty years. Yes, yes! she had heard the boatman Townes call him "Old John Waters." Thousands in the colony had come from England to retrieve their fortunes, and this must be her uncle!

Overwhelmed with this new weight of thought—bewildered by this new light streaming upon her mind, she felt her brain for a moment totter, and pressed it with her hand. The other hand was laid on her breast, through which shot an acute pain; that hand fell upon the locket—her mother's locket—and drawing it forth, she pressed it passionately to her lips, and again burst into a flood of tears.

Her mother! her poor mother, who had loved her dear father so much, and been his good angel until she died, away from her home and friends, as he did! This was her mother's, and she pressed it convulsively to her lips, and wept herself faint and quiet. The taper died away and flickered, but she heeded it not; for that whole scene again was passing through her mind, and she was far away in the bright south—that south which she had rightly dreamed she had been born in. Scenes now came to her which had been long buried in oblivion—ah! so long; kind faces, rude bivouacs, the implements of war—and orange groves! That far dim past enveloped her with its marvellous breath, and from it rose dear faces, tender smiles, rough, rude caresses of great bearded faces, and the sound of trumpets. Those trumpets echoed faintly through the air, and died away like an enchanting harmony—like the clear voices of gondoliers singing the wondrous lays of Tasso, under the starry skies of Italian nights. The far muttering of cannon then rose to her memory, and this, too, died away; and then rose beautiful rosy headlands, orange trees, and waves of gold rolling their molten fire to the great wide horizon in the sunset. Then her thoughts rushed backward to her after life—the English scenes, the theatres, the rough city life, the loud applause, the nights of study, the days of weariness and patient grief. Virginia rose on her last, and all she had suffered—Mr. Effingham's persecutions, the scorn and forgiveness of that young girl who loved him—lastly, the love and unhappiness of Charles. That thought made her cheek flush, she knew not why! Would not this change every thing—would she not leave the stage—would they not take her to their hearts, their long-lost child? Why had her father not obeyed that dying request of her real father? Was it because he could not find her uncle, or because self-interest was too strong for him—foreseeing her proficiency in his art? If the latter, was it not cruel in him? If the former, did she not owe him deepest love for his long years of tenderness and care?

Then these tumultuous thoughts disappeared, and that far dreamy land rose on her mind again—and with her eyes closed she saw it plainly—ah, how very plainly! She saw again those scenes which had but now come back to her with a reality more real than the outward world—a charm more marvellous and grand than she dreamed possible. Again, those strong bearded faces shone on her and uttered tender words—and one was far more tender than them all! Again, she heard those trumpets sounding like liquid gold, shattered and sprinkled in the deep blue air; again that faint and solemn murmur of the distant cannon rolled upon her, and spoke to her with its grand, eloquent voice, of a great conflict and the clash of arms! She heard them now distinctly—no longer dying away farther and farther into the dim past—but real, audible as reality, and instinct with a heavenly harmony which wrapped her heart in ecstasy and delight.

And then again she saw that wondrous southern land, where the blue skies drooped down upon a marvellous horizon—where the warm seas, covered with white-sailed ships, were ruffled by soft winds, laden with the rich perfume of orange trees and flowers—perfumes that set her dreaming, breezes that soothed her agitation and anxiety, like winds from heaven. Again, the vast wide sea rolled its great liquid gold, its billows crested with a fiery foam in the red sunset, gradually fading:—and above the whole, grand in its softness, beautiful for its light, rose the dear father's face—smiling upon his child!

The taper flickered and went out—she did not heed it, dreaming of the bright southern home and of his face. She leaned her head upon the window-sill, and dreamed and dreamed:—sleeping, those wondrous memories clung to her, and when the full sunlight streamed upon the tender, gentle face, waking her, she almost thought it was her father's kiss.

CHAPTER XLIII.

FROM THE MS.

"Let us pause here a moment," says the author of the MS., "and observe how events march onward obedient to the great Chief of heaven; how personages of all ages and conditions are but blind puppets in the hands of an all-seeing, all-wise Providence. Heaven decreed that this young woman should, in Virginia, be subjected to a persecution, more systematic than she had ever experienced in any other land before—and this persecution proceeded from one of that class which social feeling then separated from her own by barriers as striking and impassable as those existing between the peasant and the great lord. This persecution was to be a daily and systematic one, a trial of the temper and the heart—a test of the young girl's patience and her strength. It was to come to her at the theatre, in the street, in her apartment—every where. It was to insult, to worry, to irritate, to wound the subject of its enmity. It was to try the character of the young woman to the utmost, as the spur incessantly plunged into the quivering side tests the endurance of the noblest animal.

"Then, not satisfied with this systematic, chain-like train of wounds and insults, Providence one day sent a child of the same race as her arch-persecutor to her presence:—and from that child's lips came words which wounded, mortified, humiliated the already overburdened heart so cruelly, that the poor heart had cried out passionately against the injustice, and the bitter, cruel, terrible wrong.

"Then, having tried the young woman with such apparent harshness, that same Providence began to unroll the chain of circumstance—that chain formed of such a myriad of invisible links, links which by the short-sighted are called 'small events' and 'trifles,' but which hold the universe together. The instruments of all this persecution were to hasten the light upon its way to brighten Beatrice's life—and to do this, spite of themselves, not knowing what they did. All things were to work harmoniously to that end, nothing was to fall short, or occupy its wrong position. The trunks containing that much-coveted costume were at York—hence the two men were led to open that other one, wherein the secret of a life was shut up. The only obstacle to the revelation, was the man who knew it—he was called away. That this secret should dawn upon the proper person first, the coat is not unrolled—the young man goes to ask her advice. He becomes agitated, and in his agitation drops the child's garment—then he returns, and instead of throwing down the coat carelessly, replaces it with all the rest in the trunk: the time has not arrived for the manager to know that all is known. Thrown thus at her very feet, the young girl does not see the frock, until having made her peace with Clare, she returns to the stillness of her chamber. Then she knows the whole, and all is clear to her. But she has no harsh thoughts of the man she had called her father for so long—she does not cry out in bitterness against the cruel concealment which has made her so unhappy—which has placed her in that position which renders acceptance of the hand of Charles impossible. Why? Because the second chain of circumstance had been unrolled also. A child had been brought to the place by the presence there of him who had persecuted her:—a coarse ruffian had frightened her:—she had fled in her terror to the young girl's room:—there she had left her Bible—that Bible which was to affect the spirit of Beatrice, as the accident—the world would call it—of the child's frock affected her life. That Bible was to make her meek, to give her strength to bear the sneers and mockery and reproaches she was to be subjected to in that fiery interview. That Bible was to give her strength to hold fast to the victory she had won over herself, when Charles went from her in despair—the thought of which nearly bent her resolution, broke her remaining strength.

"Those two personages, man and child, whose words had wounded her more cruelly than all else, were thus fated to become the instruments of Providence—the one to reveal her far southern birth, the other to be the direct agent of her purification—spiritual birth. There was the chain—no link of it defective—bearing up the weight of a whole life; shaped link by link by Providence, and slowly, certainly unwound by hands which thought themselves at other work. Is there no overruling Providence?"

CHAPTER XLIV.

HOW THE GHOST OF MR. EFFINGHAM ARRIVED AT THE "RALEIGH," AND CALLED FOR SOME VINO D'ORO.

THE manuscript from which this veracious history is taken, contains many passages similar to that which we have just transcribed. The writer, indeed, seems very fond of tracing thus the secret steps of Providence—making plain the wondrous ways of that invisible Power which guides the universe in its onward course—directing men and events as it rolls the great globe through the realms of space, around the central sun of Eternal Law. The reader would, however, be apt to complain were we to transcribe many such pages; for this narrative is much more a development of events and characters than a bundle of essays. The words which men and women utter are far more powerful interpreters of what they think and feel than any mere comment on their thoughts and feelings by an indifferent person; and, acting upon this conviction, we shall proceed to deal again, directly, with the personages of the history.

We have seen how Mr. Effingham, with that blind and obstinate wilfulness, had clung to his determination to appear upon the stage, and how he had ridden forth to procure the necessary costume. We have also seen how he returned to the "Raleigh," a few hours afterwards, equipped in a complete military costume perfectly adapted to the character which he designed to represent. Busy with other and more important events, we could not follow him on his night ride; but we now proceed to show in what manner he became possessed of the costume—a costume which no less a personage than Mr. Manager Hallam himself had declared wonderfully appropriate, not without many exclamations and interrogatories, which were left unanswered.

Mr. Effingham, on the next morning, had just repaired to his room, after languidly conversing at the door of the "Raleigh" with half a dozen of the wild hangers-on of the dramatic company, to whose society he had learned to stoop in gracious condescension, when a singular circumstance attracted the attention of the worthies who surrounded the door. This circumstance was the arrival of a traveller, who, pushing his way through the crowd, halted at the door of the "Raleigh." This event, it is perfectly plain, was not in itself very remarkable, inasmuch as travellers were accustomed to come and go in Virginia at that period—to and from Williamsburg and the "Raleigh"—as at present. The observable circumstance about the foreign-looking gentleman, who now drew up and called in a loud, hearty voice for the ostler, was that, in his outward appearance, he presented a perfect counterpart of no less a person than Mr. Champ Effingham. His broad, muscular shoulders were clad in a rich velvet coat, which was stretched across them as tightly as the skin upon a drum; his waistcoat was of embroidered silk, and not more than three of the buttons had yielded and given way; his vigorous limbs were moulded on a scale entirely too large for the velvet knee-breeches and silk stockings, which fitted so tightly as to define every swelling muscle with the utmost distinctness. The rosettes had burst off from his shoes—his hands were saffron-colored, and you only found, upon close inspection, that he wore gloves fitting as closely as the cuticle—in one of these remarkable hands he carried a gold-handled riding whip. As he dismounted, the other hand arranged conveniently the hilt of a small, highly-decorated sword, and then raised from its owner's brows his feather-ornamented hat of the last London fashion.

The head thus bared was that of a man of about thirty or thirty-two, whose profession was evidently arms. The bright martial eye, black and full, could not be mistaken; the straight form, which indeed almost bent backward, so erect was it, plainly indicated the profession of the worthy. The face was an excellent one, not because it was very handsome, in the ordinary acceptation of the word, but for its frank and bold carelessness—its sunshine; in the open features mental and physical health fairly shone. The hair was dark and somewhat grizzled; the brow broad, and darkened by sun and wind; the eye, as we have said, black and brilliant; the nose prominent, the chin and under lip full of resolution and character. We say the chin and under lip, because the stranger wore a long and very heavy moustache, as black as jet, under which his white teeth sparkled when he laughed—very frequently, that is. For the traveller's face seemed to be made for laughing—it was so bold, so careless, he seemed to enjoy life so much that laughter more or less loud was a necessity to him, and he reminded the observer irresistibly of Hamlet's friend, Horatio. But a single glance was needed to perceive that this was

> "A man that fortune's buffets and rewards
> Had ta'en with equal thanks:"

a soldier who had been tossed upon the surges of war, until he had grown quite indifferent to storms, and, in the gloomiest weather, still saw the sunshine through the clouds; who, losing once, rattled the dice again; who took the world easily, and pushed his way, and laughed and drank, and slept and fought, contented, fearless, waiting without any apprehension for the fatal ball, taking the chances.

This is a brief and hurried sketch of the martial gentleman who, stopping at the "Raleigh" tavern that bright morning, delivered into the hands of the astounded ostler the bridle of his cob. Ned, the ostler, rubbed his eyes and gazed at the stranger precisely as the worthies on the portico were doing.

"Well, well, my friend," said the traveller, in a strong, hearty voice, "what detains you? my horse is weary."

"Yes, your honor—yes, sir—"

And Ned the ostler led away the animal, with his eyes still fixed upon the stranger, to the serious inconvenience of his neck, twisted until the blood covered his face.

The stranger entered the "Raleigh," politely giving the good-day to those gentlemen who, after staring at him with a curious look, made way for him.

Mine host stopped in the middle of a sentence, which he was addressing to one of his numerous patrons—a crowd of whom filled the ordinary—and the look which accompanied this sudden silence was more eloquent than any words. Then, suddenly recollecting himself, he bowed low, and said:

"Your honor is looking for me, the landlord?"

"Yes, *parbleu*," said the stranger; "my horse has gone to the stable, where they will, doubtless, take good care of him?"

"Oh yes, sir—the best ostlers, sir—"

"And now, mine host," continued the stranger, twirling his mustache, "now a stall for me."

"A stall! oh, your honor, sir—"

"Perpend, *mon ami*—a room, I mean."

"Oh yes, sir—I understand, sir. I have an excellent room, just given up by Farmer Williamson—number 3, sir—just up there, sir."

And mine host pointed to the stairs.

"*Bon*," replied his guest, "and send me a bottle of wine. I'm as thirsty as a fish."

"What will your honor have?" asked the landlord, still riveting his eyes upon the extraordinary counterpart of Mr. Effingham.

"*Val de Peñas*—my favorite vintage."

"I'm really afraid, sir—"

"Haven't the blood of Spain!" interrupted the stranger,

who exhibited some disappointment at mine host's apologetic grimace.

"We are just out, sir—exceedingly sorry, sir—but Mr. Williamson—"

"Well, well; give me a flask of *vino d'oro.* I must be satisfied.

Mine host made a second grimace, which was more eloquent than words.

"What! none of the *vino d'oro!*" cried the stranger, who seemed to understand perfectly well what the expressive features of the landlord indicated; "none of the bottled sunset, as one of my friends calls it! I really am afraid, mine host," continued the traveller, shaking his head, "that this hostelry of yours is not a place for an honest and Christian soldier to tarry in;—none of the wine of Lebanon?"

"Oh, sir!—the most unfortunate thing, I know—but really, now—my last bottle has just been sent up to Squire Wilton."

"I should like very much to engage in single combat against your Farmer Williamson and Squire Wilton! Most unjustifiable in them to be drinking up my favorite wines in this way!"

"We have some excellent claret, Madeira, and some Rhenish, sir, which I think your honor—"

"*Bon!* I choose the Rhenish. Send it to my room."

"Yes, sir; directly, sir. Would your honor give me your name to write in my book? I wish to keep that book, sir—for my family, sir—that they may know the distinguished gentlemen I have had the great pleasure to entertain, sir."

The stranger's mustache curled, and his white teeth shone under the black fringe.

"My name? Ah, very well," he said; "that is easy."

And raising up the hilt of his sword, the stranger carefully scanned some letters cut into the gold.

"My name is Effingham," he said. "*Parbleu,* I had forgotten it; as nothing is more troublesome to recollect than names."

And, leaving the landlord in a state of semi-stupefaction, the stranger pushed his way through the crowd, who drew back for him, and went up the stairs. The worthies who had witnessed his arrival, also, were present at the scene between the traveller and mine host; and now they crowded round the landlord, to give vent to their astonishment. We need not take the trouble to report their sage opinions. The general conviction was, that Mr. Effingham had a ghost, who, unlike himself, wore a mustache, and they waited for the reappearance of the spectre.

CHAPTER XLV.

BEATRICE REVEALS HER SECRET.

"It is not a trifling thing, when some soul, the noblest and purest ever sent by God to bless us, is torn from us by the hand of what seems a blind and pitiless destiny. This is, perhaps, the hardest trial of poor, feeble human patience, and, if the very soul succumbs, and the heart grows sour and bitter, is there any room for wonder? Under one of these overwhelming strokes, the head bows down and faints, as the knight of the middle age, struck by some gigantic battle-axe, lost his firm place upon the saddle, and was hurled to earth. All suddenly is gone—all that made life desirable—the sunshine and the blue skies—in place of them, darkness, despair.

"At such moments, poor humanity doubts its God; raises, perhaps, impiously-clenched hands to heaven, and, maddened by despair, blasphemes the being who has struck it to the heart. Its faith, and purity, and trust in God are gone; and the blood lingers in the veins, frozen, yet fiery; the eyes, by turns, glare and are glazed. Ere long this passes, however, and, if the mercy of God is not manifest, still the heart forces itself to believe—to trust in that mercy, and then, with the slowly-dragging hours, some of the bitterness passes; the day is not so dark; and if the sunshine cannot lie with such a glory on the earth again, at least we know and feel it is not wholly gone away for ever, but is there behind the lurid cloud, from which crashed the great thunderbolt which struck us.

"These trite sentences may indicate, in some measure,

the feelings of Charles Waters, when, leaving Beatrice after that interview, in which, overwhelmed by her agitation, she had fainted he left Williamsburgh pale and despairing."

Thus writes the author of the MS.

For days his soul was the prey of bitter and conflicting passions. For the first time he felt how completely she had grown to be a portion of himself. He never knew how much he loved her until he lost her. And now, when all the powers of his being were subdued to an unutterable tenderness for that bright, gentle creature—when he could not think, or read, or study, or see any thing around him, for her ever-present image—now, when he loved her passionately, with the full force of his affluent and large nature—now he felt an impassable barrier rise up between them—a huge wall, more durable than adamant—more lofty than the stars—a barrier which defied his utmost efforts, which must separate her eternally from him. He raved and tore his hair; he felt his heart growing sour—all those great and noble thoughts, which were wont to tenant the palace of his mind, like a troop of radiant angels, fled away; and if he again attempted to gather hope or tranquillity from the pure, veiled brows, they changed and gibbered at him like a troop of imps, and jeered and fled away with horrible mocking laughter!

So days passed—nights, almost sleepless: calm succeeded.

He began to feel the dignity of suffering:—he rose grander from his despair, and saw the sunlight through the clouds—the light of heaven. With his brow resting on his clasped hands, the strong man prayed, and went forth in the quiet evening, and was comforted. Nature looked on him with her soft, luminous eyes, and the bright river, and the autumn forest, spoke to him. He now saw what his duty was plainly. She was immovable; he knew, he felt, that she was lost to him: that she might passionately yearn to fall upon his bosom, but not yield. She might love him far more deeply than she had done—still, he felt well convinced that she would be equal to the struggle with herself. She could not turn his life into splendor,—be his dear wife: he had no claim upon her, would not ask to have any. But he could watch over her—protect her—if necessary, match his own heart and arm against that insulting annoyer.

Yes, all was lost to him—but she had gained, at least:—and so he returned to his labors in the field, and having finished his work, entered the house where his old father dreamed in the chimney corner, to prepare himself for another visit to the town. The old man and his son exchanged a tender greeting as he passed into his small apartment, and taking off his blanket coat, he donned his usual doublet of coarse drab. As he was putting on his hat, he heard voices in the next room, and going thither found himself in the presence of a servant whom he had seen frequently at the "Raleigh." The servant delivered to him a note, directed succinctly "to Mr. Charles Waters."

He opened it with a flush upon his brow, and read:

"Please come to me. BEATRICE."

A sudden paleness chased away the crimson flush, and the young man turned away and fell into a chair.

"Answer, sir?" said the negro boy. He made a movement of his head, and muttered:

"I will come—say to Miss Hallam that I shall come at once."

And again he read the simple words which had aroused such a tumult in his heart. Her hand had rested on this paper; she had traced those words——she was lost to him! Those were the thoughts which made him again breathe heavily and close his eyes.

Telling the old man that he would return very soon, he left the house, and took his way towards Williamsburg. Why had she sent for him? To rend his heart by the sight of that paradise for ever closed to him? To try herself, and show him that her life was not wholly dark? To say "you think that I am wretched, that I suffer pain because you suffer—see! I am calm?" No! none of these thoughts dwelt for a moment on his mind: his clouded brow plainly rejected all of them. Suddenly, a light like the flush of dawn broke over those gloomy eyes, and his face brightened like a midnight sky, illuminated by some great soaring conflagration. Could it be? Could she have sent for him to say "my strength has failed me—I cannot resist myself—I am too weak—my heart, my life, are yours!" Had she relented, banished that stern resolution, given herself up to what her heart called out for?—No! and the light changed to gloom again. He recollected too well that last faint cry of love and grief, of passion and despair, of weakness and strength. "You cannot move me now—I have conquered myself!" No, no!—that woman's resolution was adamant—he felt that all he loved her for was against him in the strife—her noble disinterested devotion, and strength of purpose to continue in the right!—could she have called upon him to protect her! had Mr. Effingham dared to persecute her in reality!—and with the thought his hand clenched, his breast heaved, his brows were curved into a haughty frown; his pace, already rapid, became the walk of a race-horse. He would soon know, for there was Williamsburg: he is in the streets: he passes through the noisy, laughing, bustling throng: he enters the inn: he knocks and goes into her room—she is there before him!

Beatrice rose, with such an expression of mingled anxiety and joy, that he remained for a moment without advancing, gazing at her in silence.

Beatrice broke that silence:

"Oh! this was very kind," she said, with that simplicity and tenderness, which at times made her voice pure music, "I could not have expected you so soon."

And her voice trembled slightly, as she placed her hand in his, with fond and confiding affection. A tremor passed over his frame as he took it.

"Do you need me—has any one annoyed you?" he said, coming with a bound to his absorbing thought.

"Oh no!" said Beatrice.

He breathed more freely, and sat down, passing his hand over his throbbing brow.

For a moment they both remained silent, scarcely daring to look at each other.

"You sent for me?" he murmured, with his face turned from her.

"Yes," said Beatrice, in the same low tone, "I was troubled, and unhappy—no, not unhappy—"

And her voice faltered.

"Unhappy?" he said, not feeling himself strong enough

to encounter her gaze: "what could have made you unhappy?"

The tone of these words plainly indicated that his meaning was, "*I* am the wretched and unhappy person—your suitor for a priceless boon denied to me—*I* have a right to feel miserable, you have not." Beatrice felt her heart throb, and her throat fill with tears.

"I have—much—to make me—unhappy!" she said, in a broken and faltering voice, "very much."

"Yes, yes, we all have—we are mortal," he replied, in a low voice, "I have had much myself."

"Oh, do not speak of that," cried Beatrice, bursting into tears, "I cannot speak if you do."

"I will not," he murmured, his large shadowy eyes turning to her own for a moment, then averting their gaze.

"I am so weak now, that I don't think I could endure another—such—" and the tears choked her.

He suppressed his emotion by a powerful effort, and taking her hand, said, sorrowfully:

"You shall not be agitated again by any thing I say; let us not touch upon that subject then. Tell me frankly, Beatrice, what you wished me to visit you for—you cannot have a more devoted—brother!"

Beatrice looked at him, with inexpressible affection, and murmured, "that might be nearly true."

"What?" he said.

She trembled.

"I do not think, father—Mr. Hallam—is my father," she said, greatly agitated.

"Not your father!" he exclaimed, raising his head quickly.

"It is so strange!" she murmured again, half to herself.

"Not your father!"

"I am certain that—heaven has—the wildest fiction could not"—

She stopped, overcome by agitation.

"Beatrice!" he exclaimed, rising erect, "something strange has happened: you tremble: you send for me: speak! What is this in my brain, my soul!—What is that so strangely familiar in your features!—my brain struggles—"

"Charles! I am Beatrice Waters—your Uncle Ralph's daughter! I feel it!—Oh, heaven has removed my doubts! —I do not need your assurance! You are my cousin!"

For an instant, the two hearts beat fast—the two frames felt a tremor run through them.

"Yes! heaven tells me, I am that little child!—the child of a father who died in that foreign land!—but speak! Had you not an uncle Ralph?"

"Yes," he murmured, looking at her as in a dream.

"Your father's name is John!"

"Yes!"

"You lived in Kent once!"

"Yes!"

"In London next!"

"Yes!"

"Your uncle died in—"

"In Malta, twenty years ago!" he said, scarcely conscious of what he was saying, scarcely able to speak from agitation—wonder—an overwhelming, undreamed of delight, which paralyzed his limbs, it seemed, arresting the very blood in his veins, making a lifeless statue of him.

Beatrice was almost as much agitated as her companion, and had uttered these hurried interrogatories with a trembling voice, a heaving bosom, a brow flushing and growing pale by turns. But when his last reply came—when he said, "In Malta, twenty years ago:" then her remaining doubt became a dazzling certainty; all mists swept away, and, covering her face with her hands, she murmured:

"I am his daughter!—God directed the orphan's steps! —I am his child!"

Her knees bent under her, and overcome, exhausted, she would in another second have fallen upon his bosom:—when suddenly the door was thrown open, and Mr. Effingham entered the apartment.

CHAPTER XLVI.

THE RIVALS AND THE GHOST.

THE rivals stood face to face, and surveyed each other, with glances which flashed and crossed like lightning.

They were both strong men: for one had the strength of passion, the other the strength of resolute courage, and great self-control.

How the singular interview would have commenced, it is impossible to say—for all at once, the wheezy voice of Mr. Manager Hallam was heard at the door, saying:

"Ah, Mr. Effingham! Mr. Effingham! I called after you, and you have made me lose my breath, puffing after you up the stairs. But here is metal more attractive, you would say, after the great Congreve—or, rather, the grand Shakspeare."

With which words, the voice took to itself the semblance of a puffy, red-faced gentleman, who entered smiling.

At sight of Charles Waters, however, the manager's face fell.

"Good morrow, sir," said Waters, calm and self-collected, spite of the various emotions he still experienced.

"Welcome, sir," said the manager, with some constraint. "We have a very fine day, sir—hum!"

And Mr. Manager Hallam cleared his throat.

"We do not see you so often as our friend Mr. Effingham," he added, for the sake of saying something.

"Which is probably attributable to the fact that I live here," replied Mr. Effingham, coldly.

There was a pause.

"You look agitated, Beatrice," continued the manager, turning to his daughter with a constraint which was very observable.

Beatrice turned away her head, and murmured,

"No, sir!"

"Are you sick?"

"Oh no, sir."

"Mr. Waters left his father well, I trust?" he continued, turning to the silent man.

"Perfectly, sir," was the calm reply.

"Commend me to him when you return—I feel as if we—had met before," the manager said, with some hesitation.

His constraint was so plain, that Charles Waters determined to remove it, by taking his departure. His presence evidently caused it; and it was not pleasant to behold. The strange and mysterious revelation made to him by Beatrice —a revelation which his mind still struggled in vain to realize—had moved him, as we need not say, profoundly; and the sight of the man who, beyond all doubt, knew and had been the chief actor in the hidden drama, then threw him into unwonted agitation. He wished for solitude and quiet to collect his scattered thoughts, and with a few commonplace words took his departure.

He had reached the top of the stairway, and was on the point of descending, when he felt a hand upon his shoulder.

He turned round; Mr. Effingham stood before him.

"A moment, sir!" said that gentleman, haughtily.

"Well, sir," said his opponent as coldly.

"Mr. Waters, I believe, who saved Miss Hallam's life?"

"My name is Waters, sir."

"And mine Effingham."

His opponent inclined his head coldly.

"Ah!" said Mr. Effingham, haughtily; "you will not understand; you are a marble statue. One would really say that my name had struck upon your ears for the first time."

"No, sir; I have heard it before."

"From Miss Hallam, doubtless?"

"Yes, sir."

"Coupled with a highly favorable opinion, I suppose?"

"No, sir."

"Ah! ah!—now we approach the point."

"What point, sir? It is impossible for me to understand your meaning."

These cold words seemed to irritate Mr. Effingham more and more.

"I mean, sir," he said, "that you and Miss Beatrice Hallam have been making me the subject of criticism—you have been indulging in abusive words relating to myself."

"You are mistaken, sir."

"Ah! indeed!"

"Yes, sir; but as you have thrust this conversation on me, I will add, that I have at different times spoken of yourself—not abusively—for that is a species of conversation which I do not indulge in—but critically; that, sir, I confess."

"Very well, sir. It only remains for you to repeat those critical observations."

"Mr. Effingham," said his opponent, "look at my face."

"Well, sir!"

"If you have ordinary acuteness, you must perceive that I adopt this tone of calmness by a violent effort."

"Well, sir; permit me to request that you will deign to look at me. If I spoke my true feelings plainly, they would cut as the edge of a sword cuts."

"A sword, sir?"

"Yes; have you one at home, sir?"

"No."

"Ah! I had forgotten—you do not wear this description of weapon."

His adversary's face flushed, and forgetting all his self-control, he said:

"If I do not wear, I use the sword, sir."

Mr. Effingham's eye flashed.

"Good! good!" he cried; "when shall we meet?"

"Meet, sir?"

"Yes!"

"Do you purpose defying me to mortal combat?"

"Precisely, sir."

"The reason?"

"I am not aware that a gentleman need give another any reason—I wish it. Is not that enough, sir?"

"I asked your reason, because it seemed to me, sir, that if this challenge should be given at all, it should proceed from me."

"From you!"

"Yes, sir."

"And, pray, why, sir," asked Mr. Effingham, haughtily.

"Because I am the aggrieved party."

"You!"

"Yes, sir."

"How, if it please you, sir?"

"I regret that 'tis not possible for me to explain—and this I should have reflected upon before speaking."

"Well, sir," said Mr. Effingham, coldly, but cold only by a violent effort, "it is a matter of little importance from which party the defiance comes. If from you, I accept; if you do not send it, I will. There, sir! Is that plain?"

"Perfectly, sir," said his opponent, turning pale with anger at the disdainful coldness of Mr. Effingham's tone, and losing, at last, all his self-control.

"Well, your answer? I waive all discussions of rank."

His adversary's brow flushed.

"Yes, yes, sir!" he said, "you are very courteous, and I trust your lesson in the sword exercise will be more worthy of attention than the present one you give me in politeness."

"Politeness, sir!"

"I mean, sir, that you adopt towards me a tone which is most insulting and unworthy."

"Sir!"

"Yes, most unworthy. You will waive all discussions of rank! By heaven, sir! I think the waiver should be on my side. Yes, sir, you have overcome my self-control—by pure force of continued insult driven me to anger. Well, sir, you shall hear my thoughts now. You have thrown to the winds all courtesy, you throw my station in society in my teeth, you think me a peasant—a mere boor—who should be whipped back to his place when he attempts to make his breast the barrier between a strong, passionate man, and a weak, feeble girl! For that is your real cause of quarrel, sir; you hate me because I stand between yourself and that young girl, yonder! Yes, sir, you hate me, and you imagine that I will yield to you—that your sword will pass through my heart, and that you will be left free to persecute that child, as you have done already, without hindrance. Undeceive yourself! I am no child! I promise you something more than a weak struggle—the struggle of a girl endeavoring to escape your approaches. Yes, sir! you shall have a fair field, and my heart's blood if you can take it! But guard well your own!"

Mr. Effingham was carried away by his rage—his eyes filled with blood—and, grinding his teeth, he drew his sword.

Furious, blind, mad with passion, no one knows what he might have done, when, suddenly, a loud "*Diable!*" was heard, and Mr. Effingham found his sword knocked up by the scabbard of another perfectly similar to it.

It was the ghost, who, coming out of his room, had heard the altercation, and arrived just in time.

CHAPTER XLVII.

THE GHOST EXPLAINS WHAT HAD TAKEN PLACE AT THE BACON ARMS.

Mr. Effingham turned abruptly, and saw his counterpart—the exact fac-simile of himself,—as far as dress went, be it understood.

"Ah, it is you, is it, sir?" he said, coldly, as he sheathed his sword.

"Yes, and *parbleu!* you are my friend of the *Bacon Arms!* Why, *bon jour, mon ami!*"

"Good day, sir; you came just in time. I was on the point of committing a very foolish and unworthy action, which, no doubt, would have displeased this gentleman."

"Morbleu! quite likely!" cried the stranger, twirling his moustache. "I do not consider the circumstance by any means extraordinary. Displease him? I believe you. It is calculated to displease a man to have a good short sword run through his midriff without even the satisfaction of making his own sword say click! against the invading weapon!"

And, without a moment's hesitation, the stranger turned to Charles Waters, and, bowing to him, drew the sword from the scabbard he held in his hand, took it by the point, and presented the hilt to the unarmed man.

"If we must have fighting—and I regard it as the natural state of human things—at least, let us have fair play, my friends," he said.

But Charles Waters drew back.

"Thanks, sir," he replied, "but we will settle our differences elsewhere."

"A duel?" said the stranger. "Well, I am not fond of duels—it is a villanous mode of settling the said differences. Hilf himmel! could any thing be more unreasonable than such a cold-blooded proceeding! Strike, strike, companion, while the blood is warm; strike, and so fall: or, if you stand, shake hands and go away with a quiet conscience! Drink, and be friends! I abominate your duels, though I have fought many."

"Well, sir," said Mr. Effingham, with his reckless smile, "come to-morrow and see another."

"Why, with pleasure!" returned the stranger; "are the arrangements made?"

"Not quite, the cause of strife having just arisen"

"Ah, ah! a pretty girl is in the affair! Morbleu, comrade, I'll see you in your sword exercise with pleasure, though you were going on contrary to the rules just now. A pretty girl, my life on it! Perhaps that charming little comedienne, Miss Hallam, whom I have seen in London, and who is here?"

"Yes, sir."

The stranger shook his head.

"Never fight about a woman," he said, sagely; "one always regrets it—always, comrade."

"Permit me to say that I consider nothing more appropriate."

"Appropriate! See how opinions differ. Perpend, *compagnon:* if you fight about the turn of a card, the rattle of a dice-box there is some philosophy in it—they are worth it—it is rational. But about a pair of eyes—a woman!—never!"

"Well, sir, I still hold to my opinion."

"And are going to fight?"

"Yes."

"Have you a friend?"

"Not yet."

"Let me act for you; and don't think I bear you any ill-will for the affair out yonder. We can easily cross swords on that, if necessary, afterwards," said the stranger, with the utmost calmness and good-humor.

"Thanks, sir," said Mr Effingham; "your offer relieves me from much trouble, and I accept it."

"Who is my principal? in other words, comrade, let me have your name—Effingham, is it not?"

"Yes."

"My own is—hum—well, I am called La Rivière—sometimes Captain La Rivière—not unfrequently the Chevalier La Rivière. Now for your opponent," added the stranger, looking keenly at Charles Waters.

"My name is Waters, sir," he said, "but I really do not see the necessity of—"

"Waters!" cried the stranger; "*tonnere!* is it possible!"

And dropping his hand to his sword hilt, he looked long and fixedly, with a strange expression, at the silent man.

"What surprises you, sir?" asked Waters.

The stranger made no reply; he seemed to have suddenly grown dumb; then he murmured,

"Waters!—Waters!—did you say Waters?"

"Yes, sir; Charles Waters."

The stranger, with his eyes still fixed with the same curious expression on the other, said to Mr. Effingham:

"I regret that I shall have to withdraw my offer to officiate as your second."

"Why, sir?" said Mr. Effingham, abruptly, and with some irritation.

"Come, come, comrade; because it pleases me. I can't give a reason at the sword's point," said the stranger, coolly.

"Pardon my abruptness, sir."

"Certainly, certainly," returned the stranger, with great good-nature; "and I will state that I think I was well acquainted with a relative of Mr. Waters, in the Seven Years' War."

"With my brother, sir!"

"Was he your brother, *mon ami?* A certain Captain Ralph; was that his name?"

"Yes, yes; did you—"

"Know him? Oh, perfectly well. Morbleu, we were inseparable! Excellent friends—devoted to each other—eating out of the same platter—drinking out of the same glass—loving the same damsels—marching together—sleeping together—defending each other—really inseparable, on the honor of a soldier!"

And the captain laughed, until his moustaches curled up to his eyes.

"I never can think of that man without laughing," he said; "he was such a ridiculous character—had been through so many odd adventures, which he was eternally relating—"

"Yes, yes; I recognize the portrait," said Charles Waters, hanging on the stranger's words.

"Faith, do you?" said the captain; "well, I should recognize him in the dark. You know, now, sir," he added, turning to Mr. Effingham, "why it is not proper that I should act as your second in a duel with the brother of my dearest friend."

"Well, sir, as you choose," said Mr. Effingham; "you are at liberty to act as pleases you, of course."

"Of course; and, therefore, I transfer my offer to Mr. Waters, here."

"Very well, sir."

"You are very kind, sir," said Charles Waters, calmly.

"Not at all, not at all; I owe that much to Ralph; but, *parbleu*, I can't go on the field a perfect counterpart of your opponent," said the stranger, laughing.

"I have been wondering, sir, at the perfect similarity."

The stranger laughed heartily.

"The plainest thing in the world," he said; "a real case of highway robbery at an inn, and to this moment I myself am as completely in the dark as to what it means."

"It means that I wanted your soldier's dress," said Mr. Effingham, coolly, "and took it."

"Leaving your own. Good! good!" laughed the stranger. "Don't think I am going to quarrel, or find fault. Nothing astonishes me in this world, and few things make me angry. Faith! I admired your strategy. Figure to yourself, as the French say," continued the stranger, turning to Charles Waters, and curling his black moustache; "imagine me stopping at the tavern called the 'Bacon Arms,' half way between this place and York, the port at which I landed. I am seated in the ordinary, amusing myself by tracing figures on the sanded floor, with my sword's point; I wait for the end of the storm and rain, knowing the value of a good hostelry, when, suddenly, my friend here enters, having outrun the wind, and desirous, like myself, of saving himself a wetting. He looks at me—he admires my costume, and faith! he had reason, for the great Frederic himself always regarded it with a smile of approbation. We drink—there I am never at a loss, morbleu—we converse—we abuse the storm—we become excellent friends. Now mark the sequel. At eleven at night the storm still rages; we agree to retire. Mine host has but one bed-room vacant, with two beds. We go to sleep—I wake up in the morning—and when I come to look for my proper habiliments, diable! they are gone. My good friend, too, has vanished, leaving, however, his own dress! What a comedy! Better than Closter Zeven! I take up the coat—I regard the breeches—I put them on, and turn myself in admiring them. But faith, they were too tight! My shoulders ached—my breast felt as if I was cased in armor—faith, it feels so now!"

And the soldier drew a long breath, which sent flying from the rich waistcoat the two remaining buttons; at which amusing circumstance he laughed again.

"And now, *mon ami*," he said, to Mr. Effingham, "take pity on a poor defeated comrade, who has got the worst of it, who came along groaning over his defeat, who, in conclusion, will cheerfully debate the right of property in the said costume, at the sword's point! Come now, be magnanimous; let us have a bout!"

"That is not necessary, sir," said Mr. Effingham, who had listened to the stranger with haughty indifference; "I have no need of the dress at present, as the occasion for which I took it in exchange for my own is deferred some days."

"Oh, you are welcome then, to it, comrade," replied the stranger, who, still looking abstractedly at Charles Waters, had not noticed the cold accent of Mr. Effingham's voice; "when you wish me to unshell myself, you have but to speak, and I will cheerfully do so. I will even place my whole travelling wardrobe, at York yonder, at your disposal."

"Thanks, sir: will you come now and resume your dress?"

"Yes, yes, at once—for these elegant velvets worry me."

"First, however, let me restore to you this bundle of Bank of England notes," said Mr. Effingham, taking from his purse the money, "I found them in the pocket of your coat—ten notes of ten pounds each."

"Good—good—I had forgotten them completely," said the soldier, thrusting them into his pocket without looking at them; "and now let us proceed to your apartment, *mon compagnon*. It is understood that this little affair takes place—"

"Day after to-morrow, if that is agreeable to Mr. Waters," said Mr. Effingham, with his disdainful coldness; "I have indispensable engagements."

"What say you, sir?" the soldier said to the other, "I act for you."

"When you please, sir," was the calm reply.

"Well, well now: that is arranged. We shall talk over matters in the course of the day."

And leaving Charles Waters, the two copies of each other entered Mr. Effingham's apartment—the one laughing, joyous, talking loudly; the other cold, silent, and with a weary, reckless look, which made the contrast perfect.

CHAPTER XLVIII.

HOW HIS EXCELLENCY, GOVERNOR FAUQUIER, GAVE A GREAT BALL, AND WHO WERE PRESENT.

The day for the meeting of the House of Burgesses had arrived:—indeed, the scene which we have just related took place on the afternoon preceding it.

We have already expended some words upon the appearance of the town for days before this important occasion, and can now only add, that the bustle was vastly greater, the laughter louder, the crowd larger, and the general excitement a thousand-fold increased on this, the long-expected morning. We have no space to enter into a full description of the appearance which the borough presented:—indeed, this narrative is not the proper place for such historic disquisitions, dealing as it does with the fortunes of a few personages, who pursued their various careers, and laughed and wept, and loved and hated, almost wholly without the "aid of government." It was scarcely very important to Beatrice, for instance, that his Excellency Governor Fauquier set out from the palace to the sound of cannon, and drawn slowly in his splendid chariot with its six glossy snow-white horses, and its body-guard of cavalry, went to the capitol, and so delivered there his gracious and vice-regal greeting to the Burgesses, listening in respectful, thoughtful silence. The crowd could not drive away the poor girl's various disquieting thoughts;—the smile which his Excellency threw towards the Raleigh, and its throng of lookers-on, scarcely shed any light upon her anxious and fearful heart:—she only felt that to-night the crowd at the theatre would be noisier, and more dense; her duty only more repulsive to her—finally, that all this bustle and confusion was to terminate in a ball, at which she was to pass through a fiery ordeal of frowns and comments; even through worse, perhaps—more dreadful trials. She had not dared, that morning, when her father told her he should expect her to *keep her promise*, and accompany the young man, after the theatre, to the ball—the poor girl had not dared to speak of her secret, or to resist. Then she had *promised*—that was the terrible truth; and so she had only entreated, and cried, and besought her father to have mercy on her: and these entreaties, prayers, and sobs, having had no effect, had yielded; and gone into her bed-chamber, and upon her knees, with Kate's little Bible open before her, asked the great heavenly Father to take care of her.

All this splendid pageant—all this roar of cannon, blare of trumpets, rumbling thunder of the incessant drums, could not make her heart any lighter; her face was still dark. And the spectacle had as little effect upon the other personages of the narrative. Mr. Effingham, seated in his room, smiled scornfully, as the music and the people's shouts came to him. He felt that all that noisy and joyous world was alien to him—cared nothing for him—was perfectly indifferent whether he suffered or was happy. He despised the empty fools in his heart, without reflecting that the jar and discord was not in the music and the voices—but in himself. And this was the audience he would have to see him play Benedick!—these plebeian voices would have liberty to applaud or hiss him!—the thought nearly opened his eyes to the true character of the step he was about to take. What was he about to do? that night he was going to the palace of the Governor with an actress leaning on his arm—there to defy the whole Colony of Virginia, in effect to say to them—"Look! you laugh at me—I show you that I scorn you!"—then in a day or two his name would be published in a placard, "The part of Benedick, by Champ Effingham, Esq."—to be made the subject of satirical and insulting comment by the very boors and overseers. These two things he was about to do, and he drew back for a moment—for an instant hesitated. But suddenly, the interview he had with Hamilton came back to him, and his lip was wreathed with his reckless sneer again. They would not permit him, forsooth!—his appearance at the ball with Miss Hallam, would be regarded as a general insult, and a dozen duels spring out of it!—he would do well to avoid the place!—to sneak, to skulk, to swallow all his fine promises and boasts!

"No!" he said, aloud, with his teeth clenched; "by heaven! I go there, and I act! I love her and I hate her more than ever, and, if necessary, will fight a hundred duels for her, with these chivalric gentlemen!"

So the day passed, and evening drew on slowly, and the night came. Let us leave the bustling crowd hurrying toward the theatre—leave the taverns overflowing with revellers—let us traverse Gloucester-street, and enter the grounds, through which a fine white gravelled walk leads to the palace. On each side of this walk a row of linden trees are ornamented with variegated lanterns, and ere long these lanterns light up lovely figures of fair dames and gallant gentlemen, walking daintily from the carriage portal to the palace. Let us enter. Before us have passed many guests, and the large apartments, with their globe lamps and chandeliers, and portraits of the king and queen, and Chelsea figures, and red damask chairs, and numerous card-tables, are already filling with the beauty and grace of that former brilliant and imposing society.

See this group of lovely young girls, with powdered hair brushed back from their tender temples, and snowy necks and shoulders glittering with diamond necklaces; see the queer patches on their chins close by the dimples; see their large falling sleeves, and yellow lace, and bodices with their silken network; see their gowns, looped back from the satin underskirt, ornamented with flowers in golden thread; their trains and fans, and high red-heeled shoes, and all their puffs and furbelows, and flounces; see, above all, their gracious smiles, as they flirt their fans and dart their fatal glances at the magnificently-clad gentlemen in huge ruffles and silk stockings, and long, broad-flapped waistcoats and embroidered coats, with sleeves turned back to the elbow and profusely laced; see how they ogle, and speak with dainty softness under their breath, and sigh and smile, and ever continue playing on the hapless cavaliers the dangerous artillery of their brilliant eyes.

Or, see this group of young country gentlemen, followers of the fox, with their ruddy faces and laughing voices; their queues secured by plain black ribbon; their strong hands, accustomed to heavy buckskin riding-gloves; their talk of hunting, crops, the breed of sheep and cattle, and the blood of horses.

Or, pause a moment near that group of dignified gentlemen, with dresses plain though rich; and lordly brows and clear bright eyes, strong enough to look upon the sun of royalty, and, undazzled, see the spots disfiguring it. Hear them converse calmly, simply, like giants knowing their strength; how slow and clear and courteous their tones; how plain their manners!

Lastly, see the motley throng of the humbler planters, some of the tradesmen, factors as they were called, mingled with the yeomen; see their wives and daughters, fair and attractive, but so wholly outshone by the little powdered damsels; last of all, though not least, see his bland Excellency Governor Fauquier gliding among the various groups, and smiling on every body.

Let us endeavor to catch some of the words uttered by these various personages, now so long withdrawn from us in the far past—that silent, stern, inexorable past, which swallows up so many noble forms, and golden voices, and high deeds; and which in turn will obliterate us and our little or great actions, as it has effaced—though Heaven be thanked, not wholly!—what illustrated and adorned those times which we are now trying to depict. And first let us listen to this group of quiet, calm-looking men—fame has spoken loudly of them all.

"Your reverend opponent really got the better of you, I think, sir," says a quiet, plain, simple gentleman, with a fine face and eye. "'The Twopenny-Act' made out too clear a case, in mere point of law, to need the after-clap."

"True, sir," his friend replies, smiling so pleasantly, that his very name seemed to indicate his character, "but I would willingly be unhorsed again by the Reverend Mr. Camm, in a cause so good. Every thing concerning Virginia, you know, is dear to me. I believe some of my friends consider me demented on the subject—or at least call me the 'Virginia Antiquary.'"

"I consider it a very worthy designation, sir; and in spite of my opinion, that 'The Colonel's Dismounted' is an appropriate title—I cannot be otherwise than frank ever—I am fully convinced that equity was with you. But here comes our noble Roman."

As he speaks, a tall, fine-looking gentleman approaches, with an eagle eye, a statuesque head, inclined forward as though listening courteously, a smile upon his lips, his right hand covered with a black bandage.

"What news from Westmoreland, pray, seigneur of Chantilly?" asks the opponent of the Reverend Mr. Camm. "Do they think of testing the Twopenny-Act by suits for damages?"

"No, sir," says the newcomer, very courteously; "I believe, however, that in Hanover county the Reverend Mr. Maury has brought suit against the collector."

"Ah, then we shall get some information from our friend from Caroline! See, here he is. Good day, sir!"

He who now approaches has the same calm, benignant expression as the rest—an expression, indeed, which seems to have dwelt always on those serene noble faces of that period, so full of stirring events and strong natures. The face was not unlike that which we fancy Joseph Addison's must have been—a quiet, serene smile, full of courtesy and sweetness, illuminated it, attracting people of all ages and conditions. When he speaks, it is in the *vox argentea* of Cicero, a gentle stream of sound, rippling in the sunlight.

"What from Caroline, pray?" asks the 'dismounted Colonel,' pressing the hand held out to him with great warmth. "Do the clergy speak of bringing suit to recover damages at once, for the acts of '55 and '58?"

"I believe not," the gentleman from Caroline replies, courteously, in his soft voice; "but have you not heard the news from Hanover?"

"No, sir; pray let us hear—"

"In the action brought by the Reverend Mr. Maury against the collector, a young man of that county has procured a triumphant verdict for the collector."

"For the collector?"

"Yes!"

"Against the clergy?"

"Yes!"

"You said a triumphant verdict?"

"One penny damages."

An expression of extreme delight diffuses itself over the face of the gentleman receiving this reply.

"And what is the name of the young man who has worked this wonder?"

"Mr. Patrick Henry."

"I have no acquaintance with him."

"I think you will have, however, sir. His speech is said to have been something wonderful; the people carried him on their shoulders, the parsons fled from the bench—I found the county, as I passed through, completely crazy with delight. But what is that small volume, peeping from your pocket, sir?" adds the speaker, with a smile at the abstracted and delighted expression of his interlocutor.

"An Anacreon, from Glasgow, sir," says the other, almost forgetting his delight at the issue of the parsons' cause, as he takes the book from his pocket and opens it. It is a small thin volume, with an embossed back, covered with odd gilt figures; and the Greek type is of great size, and very black and heavy.

"Greek?" says the gentleman from Caroline, smiling serenely. "Ah, I fear it is Hebrew to me! I may say, however, that from what I have heard, this young Mr. Henry is a fair match for a former orator of that language—Demosthenes!"

"Well, sir," says the Roman, "if he is Demosthenes, yonder is our valiant Alexander!"

"Who is he?"

"Is that fine face not familiar?"

"Ah, Col. Washington! I know him but slightly; yet, assuredly, his countenance gives promise of a noble nature; he has certainly already done great service to the government, and I wonder his Majesty has not promoted him. His promotion will, however, await further services, I fancy."

"Ah, gentlemen, you are welcome!" says a courteous voice; "Mr. Wythe, Colonel Bland, Mr. Lee, Mr. Pendleton, I rejoice to see you all: welcome, welcome!" And his Excellency Governor Fauquier, with courtly urbanity presses the hands of his guests.

" You will find card-tables in the next room, should you fancy joining in the fascinating amusements of tictac and spadille," he adds, blandly smiling as he passes on.

The next group which we approach is quite large, and all talk at once, with hearty laughter and rough frankness; and this talk concerns itself with plantation matters—the blood of horses, breeds of cattle, and the chase. Let us listen, even if, in the uproar, we can catch nothing very connected, and at the risk of finding ourselves puzzled by the jumble of questions and replies.

" The three field system, I think, sir, has the advantage over all others of—"

" Oh, excellent, sir! I never saw a finer leaf, and when we cut it—"

" Suddenly the blood rushed over his frill, and we found he had broken his collar bone!"

" The finest pack, I think, in all Prince George—"

" By George!—"

" He's a fine fellow, and has, I think, cause to congratulate himself on his luck. His wife is the loveliest girl I ever saw, and—"

" Trots like lightning!"

" Well, well, nothing astonishes me! The world must be coming to an end—"

" On Monday forenoon—"

" On the night before—"

" They say the races near Jamestown will be more crowded this year than ever. I announced—"

" The devil!—"

" Good evening, sir; I hope your mare will be in good condition for the race—"

" To destruction, sir—I tell you such a black act would ruin the ministry—even Granville—"

" Loves his pipe—"

" The races—"

" Hedges—"

" Distanced—"

" I know his pedigree; you are mistaken—by Sir Archy, dam—"

" The odds? I close with you. Indeed, I think I could afford—"

"Ah, gentlemen!" a courteous voice interposes, amid the uproar, "talking of races? Mr. Hamilton, Mr. Lane, welcome to my poor house! You will find card-tables in the adjoining room." And his bland Excellency passes on.

Space fails us or we might set down for the reader's amusement some of the quiet and pleasant talk of the well-to-do factors and humbler planters, and their beautiful wives and daughters. We must pass on; but let us pause a moment yet, to hear what this group of magnificently-dressed young dames, and their gay gallants, are saying.

"Really, Mr. Alston, your compliments surpass any which I have received for a very long time," says a fascinating little beauty, in a multiplicity of furbelows, and with a small snow storm on her head,—flirting her fan, all covered with Corydons and Chloes, as she speaks; "what verses did you allude to, when you said that 'Laura was the very image of myself?' I am dying with curiosity to know!"

"Those written by our new poet yonder: have you not heard them?"

"No, sir, upon my word! But the author is—"

"The Earl of Dorset, yonder."

"The Earl of Dorset!"

"Ah, charming Miss Laura! permit the muse to decorate herself with a coronet, and promenade, in powdered wig and ruffles, without questioning her pedigree."

A little laugh greets these petit maître words.

"Well, sir, the verses," says Laura, with a fatal glance.

The gallant bows low, and draws from his pocket a MS., secured with blue ribbon, and elegantly written in the round, honest-looking characters of the day.

"Here it is," he says.

And all the beautiful girls who have listened to the colloquy gather around the reader, to drink in the fascinating rhymes of the muse, in an earl's coronet and powder.

"First comes the prologue, as I may say," the reader commences; "it is an address to his pen:

> "Wilt thou, advent'rous pen, describe
> The gay, delightful silken tribe,
> That maddens all our city;
> Nor dread lest while you foolish claim
> A near approach to beauty's flame,
> Icarus' fate may hit ye!"

The speaker pauses, and a great fluttering of fans ensues, with many admiring comments on the magnificent simile of Icarus.

The reader continues, daintily arranging his snowy frill. "Mark the fate of the bard," he says, and reads:

> "With singéd pinions tumbling down,
> The scorn and laughter of the town,
> Thoul't rue thy daring flight.
> While every Miss, with cool contempt,
> Affronted by the bold attempt,
> Will, tittering, view thy plight."

"Tittering—observe the expressive phrase," says the reader.

They all cry out at this.

"Tittering!"

"Ladies do not titter!"

"Really!"

"Tittering!"

The serene reader raises his hand, and, adjusting his wig, says:

"Mere poetic license, ladies; merely imagination; not fact. True, very true! ladies never *titter*—an abominable imputation. But, listen."

And he continues:

> "Myrtilla's beauties who can paint,
> The well-turned form, the glowing teint,
> May deck a common creature;
> But who can make th' expressive soul,
> With lively sense inform the whole,
> And light up every feature?"

"A bad rhyme 'teint,' and a somewhat aristocratic allusion to 'common creatures,'" says the reader.

"Oh, it is beautiful!" says a pretty little damsel, enthusiastically.

"I am glad you like your portrait, my dear madam," says the gallant, "I assure you that Myrtilla was designed for you."

"Oh!" murmurs Myrtilla, covering her face with her fan.

The reader continues:

"See Laura, sprightly nymph, advance,
Through all the mazes of the dance,
With light fantastic toe;
See laughter sparkle in her eyes—
At her approach new joys arise,
New fires within us glow!

"Such sweetness in her look is seen,
Such brilliant elegance of mien,
So jauntie and so airy:
Her image in our fancy reigns,
All night she gallops through our veins,
Like little Mab the fairy!"

Laura covers her face to hide her delight, in the midst of universal applause.

The reader helps himself daintily to a pinch of snuff from a golden box, and continues:

"Shall sprightly Isadora yield
To Laura the distinguished field
Amidst the vernal throng;
Or shall Aspasia's frolic lays
From Leonella snatch the bays,
The tribute of the song?"

And as the gallant gentleman reads, he pauses at "Isadora," "Aspasia," and "Leonella," and, raising his head, reveals the hidden meaning of the verse by gazing at those beauties, who utter little cries of delight, and go into raptures.

He continues:

"Like hers I ween, the blushing rose
On Sylvia's polished cheek that glows;
And hers the velvet lip
To which the cherry yields its hue,
Its plumpness and ambrosial dew,
Which even gods might sip!"

Isadora and Sylvia cover their faces, and feel conscious of having made a host of enemies.

The reader reads on:

"What giddy raptures fill the brain,
When tripping o'er the verdant plain,
Florella joins the throng,
Her looks each throbbing pain beguiles,
Beneath her footsteps nature smiles,
And joins the poet's song."

Then there is a pause.

"Who is Florella?" they ask.

"Florella, ladies, I regret to say, is not present," the reader replies, embracing the brilliant and undulating throng with a glance.

"But who is it?"

"Are you really desirous of knowing?"

"Yes, yes.'

"I have been told that curiosity was not one of the foibles of the divine sex—"

"Come—come, Mr. Alston," says Laura, "on pain of my displeasure!"

"That is far too dreadful to endure," says the gallant, smoothing his frill with a jewelled hand, and bowing low, "Florella, ladies, is Miss Henrietta Lee."

"Exactly like her—excellent," comes from all sides.

Some more verses are read, and they are received with a variety of comment.

"Listen now, to the last," says the engaging reader.

"With pensive look and head reclined,
Sweet emblem of the purest mind,
Lo! where Cordelia sits!
On Dion's image dwells the fair—
Dion, the thunderbolt of war—
The prince of modern wits!

"At length fatigued with beauty's blaze,
The feeble muse no more essays,
Her picture to complete.
The promised charms of younger girls,
When nature the gay scene unfurls,
Some happier bard shall treat!"

There is a silence for some moments after these words—the MS. having passed from the gallant's hands to another group.

"Who is Cordelia? let me think," says Laura, knitting her brows, and raising to her lips a fairy hand covered with diamonds, absently.

"And Dion—who can he be?" says Isodora, twisting her satin sleeve between her fingers abstractedly.

"It is!—no, it is not!"

"I know, now!—but that don't suit!"

"Permit me to end your perplexity, ladies," says the

oracle, "Cordelia, is Miss Clare Lee, and Dion, is Mr. Champ Effingham!"

A general exclamation of surprise, from all the ladies. They say:

"It suits him, possibly, but—"

"He may be the prince of wits; still it does not follow—"

"Certainly not, that—"

"Clare is not such a little saint!"

"Let me defend her," says a gentleman, smiling; "I grant you that 'tis extravagant to call Mr. Effingham a thunderbolt—"

"Laughable."

"Amusing," say the gentlemen.

"Or the prince of modern wits," continues the counsel for the defence.

"Preposterous!"

"Unjust!" they add.

"But I must be permitted to say," goes on the chivalric defender of the absent, "that Miss Clare Lee fully deserves her character:—the comparison of that lovely girl, ladies, to Cordelia,—Cordelia, the sweetest of all Shakespeare's characters—seems to me nothing more than justice."

The gentlemen greet this with enthusiastic applause, for our little, long-lost sight of—heroine, had subdued all hearts.

"As regards Mr. Effingham," adds Clare's knight, "I shall be pardoned for not saying any thing, since he is not present."

"Then I will say something," here interposes a small gentleman, with a waistcoat reaching to his knees, and profusely laced, like all the rest of his clothes—indeed, the richness of his costume was distressing—"but I will say, sir, that Mr. Effingham's treatment of that divine creature, Miss Clare Lee, is shameful."

"How?" ask the ladies, agitating their fans, and scenting a delicious bit of scandal.

"Why," says the gentleman in the long waistcoat, squaring himself, so to speak, and greatly delighted at the sudden accession to his importance—the general opinion being that he was somewhat insignificant, "why, ladies, he has been running after that little jade, Miss Hallam!"

"Miss Hallam!" cry the ladies, in virtuous ignorance, though nothing was more notorious than the goings-on of our friend Mr. Effingham, "Miss Hallam!"

"Precisely, ladies."

"The actress?"

"Yes."

"A playing girl!" exclaims a lady, of say thirty, and covering her face as she spoke.

"Falling in love with her!"

"Possible?"

"Haven't you heard all about it?"

This home question causes a flutter and a silence.

"I'll tell you, then," continues the gentleman in the long waistcoat, "I'll tell you all about the doings of 'Dion, the thunderbolt of war, and prince of modern wits.' *He*, the thunderbolt of war?—preposterous! *He*, the prince of wits?—ludicrous! He may be the king of coxcombs, the coryphæus of dandies—but that is all."

The gentlemen standing around listen to these words, with some amusement and more disgust. It is plain that some secret spite actuates the gentleman in the long waistcoat.

"Well, let us hear Mr. Effingham's crimes," says Laura.

"By all means," adds Isadora.

"Of course," says Myrtilla.

"He has been making himself ridiculous about that actress," continues the chronicler, "and I have even heard, designs to marry her."

The ladies make a movement, to express surprise and indignation, but after a moment's reflection, suppress this somewhat ambiguous exhibition of their feelings.

"He's been at the 'Raleigh Tavern,' making love to her for a month," continues the narrator.

"At the tavern?"

"Yes, in town here."

"Did any one ever!" says the lady of uncertain age.

"Never! never!" chime in the virtuous little damsels, shaking their heads solemnly.

"He has left his family," the gentleman in the long waistcoat goes on, indignantly, "and they are dying of grief."

"Oh, can it be!"

"Certainly, madam. Why are they not here to-night?"

"Very true."

"Why is Clare Lee, the victim of his insincerity, away, pray tell me! They are not here—they are not coming, madam."

At the same moment, the usher announces the squire, Miss Alethea, and Miss Clare Lee—Master Willie and Kate being too small to be seen, which the squire had warned them of. The squire is as bluff as ever, and makes his salutation to his Excellency with great cordiality—Clare is pale and absent, presenting thus a singular contrast to Henrietta, who enters a moment afterwards, brilliant, imposing, and smiling, like a queen receiving the homage of the nobility around her throne. She sweeps on, leaning on the arm of honest Jack Hamilton, and the party are swallowed in the crowd.

Let us return to the group, whose conversation the new arrivals had interrupted.

"Well, I was mistaken," says the gentleman in the long waistcoat, "but any one may see that Clare Lee is dying slowly!"

At which affecting observation, the young ladies sigh and shake their heads.

"And just think what that man has thrown this divine creature away for," continues the censor morûm, "for a common actress!—an ordinary playing girl—tolerably pretty she may be, but vastly overrated—a mere thing of stage paint and pearl powder, strutting through her parts and ranting like an Amazon!"

"I think her quite pretty," says Laura, "but it is too bad."

"Dreadful!"

"Awful!"

"Horrible!"

"Shocking!"

These are some of the comments on Mr. Effingham's conduct, from the elegant little dames.

"He is ashamed to show himself any where," continues the gentleman in the long waistcoat, "and only yesterday met me on the street, and in passing, turned away his head, plainly afraid that I would not speak in return, had he addressed me!"

At which words the gentlemen are observed to smile—knowing as they do, something of Mr. Champ Effingham's personal character and habits.

"He actually was afraid to look at me," says the censor, "and I am told keeps his room all day, or passes his time in the society of that Circe, yes, that siren who is only too fond of him, I am afraid—and I predict will make him marry her at last."

The ladies sigh, and agitate their fans with diamond-sparkling hands. They feel themselves very far above this shameless creature attempting to catch—as we now say—Mr. Effingham: they pity her, for such a thing never has occurred to them—no gentleman has ever been attractive enough for them to have designs upon his heart. And so they pity and despise Beatrice, for wishing to run away with her admirer.

"He is heartily ashamed of his infatuation, and I saw him last night in the theatre, positively afraid to look at the audience—but staring all the time at her," continues the small gentleman.

"But that is easy to understand, as he is in love," says Myrtilla, with a strong inclination to take the part of the reprobate against his enemy.

"No, no, madam," exclaims the censor, "he was really ashamed to look at the people, and took not the least notice of their frowns: he does not visit any where:—he knows he would not be received—he is afraid to show his face."

It seemed that the gentleman in the long waistcoat was doomed to have all his prophecies falsified; for at that moment, the usher announced in a loud voice, which attracted the attention of the whole company:

"Mr. Effingham and Miss Hallam!"

CHAPTER XLIX.

HOW MR. EFFINGHAM AND BEATRICE DANCED A MINUET AT THE BALL.

Mr. Effingham entered under the full light of the central chandelier, with Beatrice on his arm. He carried his head proudly erect, his eye was clear and steady, his lip calm and only slightly sarcastic:—his whole carriage displayed perfect and unaffected self-possession. The thousand eyes bent on him vainly sought in his eyes, or lips, any thing going to show that he felt conscious of the dreadful, the awful social enormity, which he was committing.

Mr. Effingham was dressed with extraordinary richness. He was always elegant in his costume, on that night he was splendid. His coat of rich cut velvet, was covered with embroidery, and sparkled with a myriad of chased gold buttons; his lace ruffles at breast and wrist were point-de-venise, his fingers were brilliant with rings, and his powdered hair waved from his clear pale temples like a stream of silver dust. He looked like a courtier of the days of Louis XIV., dressed for a royal reception.

And how did Beatrice compare with this brilliant star of fashion—this thunderbolt of war, and prince of modern wits, as the muse in powdered hair and ruffles had characterized him. Poor Beatrice was quite eclipsed by her cavalier. Her simple, unassuming dress, of pearl color, looped back with plain ribbon, and without a single flower, or any ornament whatever, looked strangely out of place, thrown in contrast with the brilliant silks, and velvets, and gold buttons, and diamonds of her companion: her modest, tender face, and drooping head, with its unpretending coiffure, looked quite insignificant beside the bold, defiant countenance of Mr. Effingham, which returned look for look, and gaze for gaze, with an insulting nonchalance and easy hauteur. We know how reluctantly Beatrice had come thither—rather how bitter a trial it was to her, and we may understand why she looked pale and troubled, and—spite of the fact that she had just encountered the gaze of a curious and laughing audience, without any emotion—now felt her spirit die within her. It was not because she shrunk from comment, half so much, as from the fact that each moment she expected to see opposite to her the cold, pale face, and sick, reproachful eyes of Clare Lee—of Clare, who had thrown aside the prejudices of class, even forgot the jealousy of a wronged and wretched rival, to press in her arms the rival who had made all her woe, and that rival a common actress. It was the dread of her eye which made poor Beatrice tremble—this alone made her lip quiver and her brow droop.

His excellency Governor Fauquier came forward to welcome his guests, but started at the sight of Beatrice, and almost uttered an exclamation. For a moment he was staggered, and said nothing. This soon passed, however, and by the time Mr. Effingham had accomplished his easy bow, the governor was himself again, and like the elegant gentleman he was, made a low inclination before Beatrice. Then he made a pleasant allusion to the weather—that much abused subject, which has extricated so many perishing conversations—and so, smiling agreeably, passed on.

Mr. Effingham advanced through the opening, on each side of which extended a row of brilliant forms, sparkling with lace and jewels, without any apparent consciousness that he and his companion were the observed of all observers—without being conscious, one would have said, of those murmured comments which greeted, on every side, the strange and novel scene. His manner to Beatrice, as he bent down to speak to her, was full of respectful and chivalric feeling; his eye was soft, his lip smiling; the highest lady of the land might well have felt an emotion of pleasure in so elegant and noble an exhibition of regard. And this was not affected by Mr. Effingham. By no means. We have failed to convey a truthful impression of this young gentleman's character, if the reader has not, before this time, perceived that, with all his woful faults and failings, Mr. Champ Effingham had much in his character of the bold gentleman—the ancient knight. With those thousand satirical or scornful eyes bent on her, Beatrice was dearer to him than she had ever been before. Those elegant ladies and gallant gentlemen were saying, with disdain, "a common actress!" Well, he would espouse the cause of that girl they scorned against them all, and treat her like a queen!

Never had she had more complete possession of his heart—never had his heart thrilled so deliciously at the contact of her hand, resting upon his arm.

As we have said, all drew back from the new comers, and they entered through an open space, like a king leading in his queen. Mr. Effingham looked round, with a cool and easy smile, and led the young girl to a seat, near some elderly dowagers, in turbans and diamonds, who had enthroned themselves in state, to watch their daughters, and see that those inexperienced creatures did not give too much encouragement to ineligible personages. As Beatrice sank into one of the red damask chairs, the surrounding chairs suddenly retreated on their rollers, and the turbans agitated themselves indignantly. Mr. Effingham smiled, with his easy, mocking expression, and observing that one of the diamond-decorated dowagers had dropped her fan, picked it up, and presented it to her, with a bow. The indignant lady turned away her head, with a frown.

"Ah," said Mr. Effingham, politely, "I was mistaken."

And fanning himself for a moment negligently, he placed the richly feathered instrument in the hand of Beatrice.

"My fan, if you please, sir," said the owner, suddenly flushing with indignant fire.

"Your fan, madam?" asked Mr. Effingham, with polite surprise.

"Yes, sir! you picked it up, sir!"

"A thousand pardons!" returned the young gentleman, with a courteous smile; "did I?"

"Yes, sir! that is it, sir! In the hands of that—"

"Oh, I understand," returned Mr. Effingham; and with a low inclination to Beatrice, he said, holding out his hand, "Will you permit me?"

The fan was restored by the young girl, just as she had taken it—unconsciously; and the dowager received it with the tips of her fingers, as if it had been contaminated. At the same moment, the band struck up a minuet, and two couples began to dance.

"How graceful the costume of our young ladies is becoming," said Mr. Effingham, bending down courteously to Beatrice, on the back of whose chair he leaned.

Beatrice murmured, "Yes."

"Much prettier, I think, than that of fifty years ago," continued Mr. Effingham, smiling, and glancing respectfully at the elderly and indignant ladies, who were listening.

The fans waved furiously.

"There is a fitness about the fresh, new style," he continued, "and it suits youth. I do not quarrel, however, with the former costume—turbans, and all that—it is also suitable—for elderly ladies."

And Mr. Effingham, smiling meekly, seemed perfectly unconscious of the storm muttering around him. As he spoke, honest Jack Hamilton, who had left the Riverhead and Effingham party in the other room, approached, and with a movement of his head, asked to be presented to Beatrice.

The young girl could hardly return his bow; she felt such anxiety, that the power of movement seemed almost gone from her.

"Mr. Hamilton is one of my best friends, Miss Hallam," said the young man, who had rewarded honest Jack with a bright smile; "but I shall claim your hand for the first minuet."

"Oh no," murmured Beatrice; "I do not wish to dance. Oh, sir! do not ask me to dance!"

And she stopped, overcome by her emotion.

"Oh, I insist upon it!" said Mr. Effingham, smiling; "it seems to me that that minuet there is abominably performed, and the music is shockingly fast."

"Hallo, Brother Champ!" here said a voice, at his elbow; "ain't I glad to see you!"

And turning round, Mr. Effingham found himself in front of Master Will; but Master Will was so metamorphosed that he scarcely recognized him. Willie had carried out his threat to Kate, and had donned a complete cavalier's costume. His hair was powdered, and gallantly tied into a queue behind; his coat was embroidered and heavy cuffed; his waistcoat nearly down to his knees; his frill irreproachable; his stockings of most approved scarlet silk; and his shoes rosetted with ribbon, and with such high red heels, that the young gentleman walked as it were on tiptoe. Altogether, with his long queue, and quick-moving little feet, Will resembled a large rat, decked out with ribbons, and

—conscious of his frill and the good society he moved in,—on his best behavior.

"I'm delighted to see you," added Will, holding out his hand.

Mr. Effingham shook hands.

"'Say," whispered Will, "is that the girl you're in love with?"

Will started back before the tremendous frown of his brother; for Beatrice heard the words, and turned away her head. Mr. Effingham raised his finger, and was about to say something that would have annihilated the youthful cavalier, when suddenly he felt a soft, warm, little hand take his own, and turning round, he saw little Kate's bright, smiling face.

"Oh! I wanted to come before, but couldn't," she said, leaning her bright little head against his side; "I'm so glad to see you."

And she pressed the hand she held harder.

Mr. Effingham's cynical smile became soft, his head drooped toward the child; but suddenly Kate recognized Beatrice, who had been concealed from her by Jack Hamilton, motionless, coughing, trying to converse;—there was the lady of the tavern—the actress—the person who had caused them so much grief. She drew back sorrowfully, and her little face was covered with a shadow. Mr. Effingham saw it—divined the reason—and his face too was overshadowed. He was about to speak, when—the first dance having terminated some moments before—a second minuet was commenced by the band.

"Come!" said he to Beatrice; and taking her hand, he raised her, and led her forward.

"Not so fast," he said, with a gesture of his hand, to the musicians; "I cannot dance a minuet to a gavotte tune."

And he entered into the broad, open space with Beatrice the mark of a thousand eyes.

The group which we have paid some attention to already—that group which had expressed such delight at the verses of the accomplished (colonial) Earl of Dorset, and who had uttered such a variety of comment on Dion, Cordelia, and Beatrice—the group of which Myrtilla, Isadora, and the

Long waistcoat, were the shining stars—now gazed in horror at the presumption and effrontery of Mr. Effingham.

"Just look!" said Sylvia; "he is positively going to dance the second minuet!"

"With that actress!" said Isadora.

"The playing girl!" echoed Leonella, horrified.

"While we must wait!" added Myrtilla, with some show of reason.

"It is presumptuous!"

"It is shocking!"

"It is insulting!"

"It is outrageous!"

"I will not stand it!" here interposed the gentleman in the long waistcoat, boiling with indignation.

"Just look!" said Sylvia; "did anybody ever see such ridiculous respect and ceremony in a gentleman before?"

"You would think that she was a queen, and he a subject!"

"What a bow!"

"See how he takes her hand, bending to her waist!"

"Ridiculous!"

"But he is very graceful," hazarded Myrtilla, who, as we know, defended faintly Mr. Effingham's character, when it had been attacked by the censor.

"Well, suppose he does bow elegantly," said Isadora, spitefully, envying Beatrice her cavalier.

"True: we do not wish to have him for a partner," said Myrtilla, who was something of a wit.

"There, look at her!"

"Theatrical!"

"Affected!"

"Stiff!"

"Frightened!"

"She looks as if she was going to cry."

"Poor thing!" said Myrtilla; "I think she does not want to dance."

"Does not want to?"

"Pshaw!"

"She is too artful for that!"

"But look! her eyes are moist, as she curtseys, and they seem to beseech him for something," said Myrtilla.

"What odious artfulness!" cried Sylvia; "she pretends to look as if she was not dying for joy at being the partner of the fascinating Mr. Effingham."

"I suppose she would not ally herself with his family; they are too low," said Isadora, spitefully; "may be she has refused his hand."

"Quite probable!"

"Oh, of course!"

"Doubtless!"

And the pretty little damsels curled their handsome little lips ironically.

"She is an odious-looking creature," said Leonella; "did any one ever see such evidences of low birth?"

"Oh, I am sure you are wrong!" cried Myrtilla, too generous to keep silent; "I think she is very sweet."

"Well, she is not so bad, but—"

"Tolerable, but—"

"A pretty arm, but—"

"Fine eyes, still—"

"Graceful, yet—"

"I think she is an odious, artful, designing creature, but not at all too bad for her partner," here interposed the gentleman in the long waistcoat; and so the colloquy went on.

Almost every group in the room was uttering something similar to that which we have just listened to. The entrance of Mr. Effingham into the open space, to dance the second minuet of the evening, had caused an awful sensation. As he glided through the stately dance to the slow-rolling music, bowing profoundly, with his tender, lordly smile, touching the young girl's hand with chivalric respect, pressing his cocked hat to his heart at each inclination of his handsome and brilliant head, all eyes had been bent upon him, all tongues busy with him. And these eyes and tongues had taken equal note of Beatrice. The young girl moved through the old stately dance with that exquisite grace and ease with which she performed every evolution, and her tender, agitated face, as we have seen, tempered the wrath of many an indignant damsel. After the first burst of surprise and anger, the gentlemen, too, began to take the part—as Virginia gentlemen always have done, and always will do—of the lonely girl environed by so many hostile eyes and slighting comments. They forgot the prepossessions of rank, the prejudices of class—no longer remembered that the young actress occupied upon the floor a position to which she was not entitled;—they only saw a woman who had all the rest against her; and their sympathy was nearly powerful enough to make them lose sight of Mr. Effingham's defiance.

A murmur rose as the music stopped, and he led her to a seat; and then a species of undulation in the crowd, near the entrance into the next room, attracted attention. Mr. Effingham had his back turned, however, and did not observe this incident. He was talking to Beatrice in a low tone.

"You see," he said, with his calm, nonchalant voice—"you see, Beatrice, that this superb society, which you fancied you would find yourself so much out of place in, is not so very extraordinary after all. I think that I hazard nothing in saying that the second minuet was better than the first; you are, indeed, far more beautiful than that little dame, whose ancestors, I believe, came over with the conqueror—Captain Smith."

And his cynical smile grew soft, as he gazed on the tender, anxious face.

"It was not so dreadful an ordeal," he added, "though I must say we were the subject of much curiosity. I observed a group, criticising me, which pleased me. There was a fiery young gentleman in a long waistcoat, whom I offended by not returning his bow some months since—and I believe he was the orator of the occasion."

With which words, Mr. Effingham's lip curled.

"See! the very same group—every body, in fact, is gazing at us. Let them! you are lovelier than them all."

And Mr. Effingham raised his head proudly and looked around like an emperor. But Beatrice felt her heart die within her: that minuet had exhausted her strength; each moment she expected to see the pale cold face of Clare looking at her. Mr Effingham observed how faint she was, and leaning over, took a smelling-bottle from the hand of the old dowager, who had dropped the fan—bowing and smiling.

He presented it to Beatrice, but she put it away with the back of her hand: whereupon Mr. Effingham, with a second bow, restored it to the dowager, who, aghast at his impudence, beaten by his superior coolness, and overwhelmed with rage, took it without knowing what she did. Mr. Effingham thereupon turned, smiling, to Beatrice again:

"There seems to be something going on yonder," he said, leaning on her chair, and directing the young girl's attention to the flashing waves of the crowd, which moved to and fro like foaming billows, in the light of the brilliant chandeliers. Beatrice felt an indefinable and vague fear take possession of her heart. At the same moment, Master Willie came pushing and elbowing through the crowd.

"Cousin Clare is sick!" he said, "you'd better go and see her, brother Champ. She liked to fainted just now!"

Beatrice understood all.

"Oh, sir! let me go!" she cried, "go out with me! I shall die here!—oh, I cannot—that dance nearly killed me—and now!—Oh, sir, have pity, give me your arm!"

And rising with a hurried movement, she placed her hand on Mr. Effingham's arm. That gentleman smiled bitterly.

"Yes," he said, "this is the tragedy after the comedy! I understand this fainting."

"Oh, sir, have pity—I must go!" cried Beatrice, "I will go alone!"

Mr. Effingham held her back, and hesitated. At last he said:

"Well, madam—as you please—I have had a pleasant minuet—I will go."

And with the same cold, defiant ease, he led the young girl across the room, and issued forth into the open air.

Without speaking they traversed the walk, with its lindens and variegated lanterns, passed through the crowd of grooms and coachmen, who made way respectfully, and entered the carriage which had brought them. In ten minutes it stopped at the Raleigh, and Mr. Effingham, with a strange throbbing of the heart, handed the young girl out. At that moment he loved her so madly, so defiantly, that he would have given the universe to clasp her to his bosom.

He knew how such a proceeding would be received, however, and led her in silence to her room, where Mr. Manager Hallam was sitting by the fire, toasting his enormous feet.

Then with a bow he closed the door, and returned to the governor's palace.

CHAPTER L.

MR. EFFINGHAM RETURNS TO THE BALL AND DISCOURSES ON THE SUBJECT OF WAISTCOATS.

MR. EFFINGHAM made his re-entrance into the ball-room, with the same disdainful calmness which had characterized him at first. If as many eyes were not turned toward him, that was because he was no longer accompanied by the young actress—was a single cavalier.

Near the door he encountered that group, which we have twice listened to; and he approached with his satirical and careless smile.

"Ah, really, " he said, to Sylvia, "I am charmed to see you! Why, how adorably you are looking!"

And turning round before Miss Sylvia could reply, he added to Leonella,

"Your coiffure is charming!"

The expression upon the faces of Miss Sylvia and Leonella was so ludicrous, that Myrtilla burst out laughing.

"Ah!" said Mr. Effingham, in his most petit maître tones, "how could I have so long neglected to place my homage at the feet of the queen of beauty!"

Myrtilla laughed at this languid and elegant address to her.

"I cannot pardon myself," continued Mr. Effingham, arranging his drop curls; "if Phillis scorns her Corydon, and beats him with her crook, he cannot complain; his humbled eyes dare not rise higher than the ribbons fluttering on the bodice of his pastoral princess."

The fashion of the time, must plead Mr. Effingham's excuse for this extraordinary speech. Our lovely fore-mothers relished these rural allusions, and started with delight at the mention of Chloes, Phillises and crooks. And so Myrtilla made a laughing courtesey: and Mr. Effingham turned away. He found himself face to face with the small gentleman who had criticised him so pleasantly, and whose criticism his quick eye had seen reflected in his face, as the young man had danced opposite to Beatrice.

"Oh! really a great pleasure!" said he, now, to this gentleman, "are you here too?"

"Yes, sir," said the small gentleman, sullenly.

"And with as long a waistcoat as ever," continued Mr. Effingham, smiling.

"Sir!"

"Yes, a pleasant ball—but the society is somewhat mixed," said Mr. Effingham, with courteous smiles, "things are becoming changed. Is it not so, ladies? Gay, adorable shepherdesses, clad in the bloom and freshness of the spring—am I not right?"

"Yes, you are right, sir," said Sylvia, tossing her little head: a manœuver which Mr. Effingham rightly attributed to the fact that the damsel meant to allude to Beatrice.

"Why, nothing could be plainer," he continued.

"Nothing, sir!" here interposed the small gentleman, with a frown. Mr. Effingham slightly turned round, as much as to say "did you presume to reply to me, sir?" and went on superciliously

"Very mixed—shockingly," he said; "every body is beginning to mingle in society, and we now see all descriptions of costume. I do not complain of the simple dress of the lower class, yonder—I like it. What I allude to is different. I refer to those individuals who endeavor to make up by splendor what they lack in good-breeding, and who load their dress with all manner of remarkable and extraordinary ornament—"

Myrtilla began to laugh, mischievously glancing at the small gentleman, who winced.

"Shocking taste, and shows their condition," added Mr. Effingham; "they even persist in wearing those abominable waistcoats, as brilliant as the rainbow, and nearly as long—invariable indication of the parvenu."

And Mr. Effingham smiled amiably at the gentleman in the long waistcoat, who was furious—raised his hand with an air inexpressibly foppish, to the ladies, and moved on.

He encountered Jack Hamilton, who, in the midst of a group of foxhunters like himself, was laughing and talking at the top of his voice.

"Oh, here is Effingham!" said Hamilton, "where is Miss Hallam?"

Mr. Effingham replied, calmly:

"She got tired, and I returned with her. You see,

however, that I have made my appearance again—my friends, I fear, had not an opportunity to speak to me."

And his cold eye told Hamilton very plainly what he meant. Honest Jack laughed.

"By George! I believe they are all your very excellent friends by this time," he said; "they calculated without their Virginia blood, when they spoke of resenting Miss Hallam's appearance. They forgot that they were a dozen men matched against one woman."

"And a sword, Hamilton."

"Come, come," said Hamilton, "forget that, and don't let the fellows here, who are jolly boys, as you know, into our little secrets. They are waiting to be recognized by Monseigneur."

This was true; and when Mr. Effingham held out his hand to the party, who were all slightly acquainted with him, it was taken with hearty warmth, and not a few rough and sincere compliments paid to Beatrice, though they did not scruple to say as plainly that there "was no use in bringing her."

In consideration of their good feeling, our hero pardoned this: and then leaning on Hamilton's arm, passed on. Ten steps brought him in front of his Excellency—and that gentleman, no longer checkmated by the presence of Beatrice, turned away with great hauteur. Mr. Effingham only smiled, and passed on, leaving Jack Hamilton behind.

He went through the room with his cold, disdainful smile, seeking his adversaries:—strange to say, however, they seemed to be far from those ferocious personages described by Mr. Hamilton. He could find nothing to take umbrage at, and so he returned towards the door. The simple fact was, that, proud and disdainful as Mr. Effingham was, he feared to encounter the eye of his father, or of Henrietta, or Alethea, or Clare. He had understood the cause of the young girl's sudden faintness perfectly well. She had entered from the second room, and seen him dancing a minuet with that rival, whom she had so generously forgiven, and clasped to her pure, tender heart—and though Mr. Effingham was ignorant of the fact of the interview, he was at no loss to understand Clare's emotion.

This was the reason why he feared to meet her—and yet

with that dread was mingled a strange desire; as if he wished to stand before her and give her look for look, and break her heart and his own. Mr. Effingham began to feel a diseased craving for excitement—he had become accustomed to acute and painful emotions; he fed on them as his daily bread.

Fortunately this insane desire was doomed to disappointment. Clare had left the ball almost at the same moment with himself and Beatrice: had entered the Effingham chariot with the squire and his party just as his own carriage drove off.

Once, as Mr. Effingham drew near the door, he encountered the gaze of Henrietta, who had chosen to remain with Hamilton: and with rage in his heart he made her a low and exaggerated bow. Then passing by the gentleman in the long waistcoat, with a meaning look full of disdain and menace, he struck his hat upon his head, and rushed, almost, from the room.

His infatuation for Beatrice had never so closely approached madness as at that moment.

CHAPTER LI.

BEATRICE AND THE MANAGER.

HAVING thus briefly related the manner in which Mr. Effingham returned to the ball, and sought for adventures there like a second Don Quixote, though without the good fortune of the noble gentleman of La Mancha, we shall now go back to the moment when Beatrice re-entered her room, after the trying ordeal she had passed through.

As we have said, Mr. Manager Hallam was sitting placidly by the fire, which was far from uncomfortable at that advanced season of the autumn. Upon Beatrice's entrance he turned round, smiling. Beatrice was in tears, and sobbing.

"What in heaven's name is all this crying about?" asked the manager, who, having emptied his nightly two bottles, was in a most contented state of mind; "you are always crying, Beatrice!"

"Oh, father!" she said, and then stopped.

"Well, well," he said, impatiently, "speak."

"I am not well."

"How?"

"It was killing to me."

"Bah! every thing kills you, but you always continue alive, as I recollect hearing the great Congreve say, once on a time."

"I am really sick, sir."

"Was the ball brilliant?"

"Yes, sir."

"Was Mr. Effingham attentive?"

"Yes, sir."

"Did the set-up women treat you badly?"

"No, sir."

"You were treated politely?"

"Yes, sir."

"And danced?"

"Yes, sir."

"The governor bowed to you?"

"Very politely, sir."

"Then in the name of all the fiends what are you crying about, daughter? You are really a very extraordinary girl You go to a brilliant ball, with a handsome and attentive cavalier; you are not treated badly by the fine ladies, but very kindly; you danced among the best, the governor of Virginia made you a polite bow, and after all this, which would turn the head of any common girl with joy, you come back crying, instead of laughing, sorrowful instead of happy. Basta! as the great Congreve was wont to say, you are foolish!"

Beatrice sat down, wiping her eyes, and murmuring the words she had read in Kate's Bible, before going—"Oh, Lord, my strength and my Redeemer!"

"What is that you say?" asked Hallam, stretching his feet luxuriously on the fender, and looking with muddy eyes at the ceiling.

"Nothing, sir," said the young girl, trying to command her voice.

"Beatrice," said Hallam, "you are perfectly ridiculous; you are throwing away, by your folly and obstinacy, the most excellent offer—I say it without hesitation—which was ever made to an actress. One would really think that you were a duchess, with your rent-roll and estates, instead of the daughter of an actor, like myself."

Beatrice listened with a strange feeling to these words. Again that martial face rose for her from the far southern land; again she saw the soldier dying, and her tears flowed afresh.

"Instead of acting as you should do," continued Hallam, working himself into anger, "instead of being to this young man the brilliant and fascinating woman which you are—instead of managing him, and spurring him on, and attracting him—instead of giving him hope, and you know his intentions are perfectly honorable—instead of this, what are you doing? You are making your eyes and face thin with weeping, you are growing ugly from grief at having a splendid position in society thrust on you—you are defying my wishes, madam! You know I wish you to marry this young fellow. Answer; are you not disobedient?" and the manager pushed back his chair, angrily.

"Oh, father, father!" she cried, carried away by her feelings, "I do not wish to be disobedient. I will do all you wish me to do, but that! I will work day and night, and never complain—but do not, do not ask me to marry, or encourage this man! I do not like him, I shudder when he approaches; all my good traits of character—and, indeed, I have some—become changed to bad in his presence. He repels me; something tells me that he will be my curse yet! Oh, I cannot do as you command—I cannot smile and make myself attractive, and show him that I like him—for I do not! I should be the most miserable person living, were I his wife!"

"Really!" cried the manager. "Truly, madam, the countess is in her tantrums! You would be the most miserable creature alive, as his wife?"

"Oh, miserable, sir!"

"He repels your ladyship!"

"I tremble when he comes near me!" she cried, weeping.

"You would not marry him?"

"Oh, no; for it would break the heart of a pure girl, who loves him, and would have been his wife, if I had never seen him!"

"Really, you are very magnanimous! Pray, who is that girl?"

"Miss Lee, his cousin."

"What does her fate concern you, pray, madam?"

"She forgave me, and took me in her arms, and kissed me. Oh, God is my witness, that I would rather cut off my right hand than make her suffer again!"

"Where the devil did you enact that fine drama?" said the manager, frowning.

"I went to see her."

"You?"

"Yes, sir; at her home, near Mr. Effingham's."

"And, no doubt, told her how much you hated him; that you were not to blame if her lover was infatuated about you; that you had repulsed him, insulted him, asked him to leave you, exhausted every means to make him abandon his unworthy project, of marrying you—"

"Yes, sir—I did—"

"You did—'Yes, sir—I did!' sneered the manager; "you had the boldness to go and say that to a person, who will tell him every thing—"

"Oh, no, sir! for—"

"In future, madam," said Hallam, angrily, "you do not ride out without an escort. You might be guilty of worse things than this audacious proceeding."

At this unworthy insinuation, Beatrice felt the blood rush to her face, and her heart begin to throb with bitter and rebellious thoughts.

"Oh, father!" she cried, bursting into tears, "how can you be so cruel?"

"Well," he said, "I was wrong; but your conduct is bad enough, madam. I suppose this child was at the ball—his sweetheart?"

"Yes, sir. Miss Lee was present."

"How did he treat her?"

"He did not see her."

"Where is he now?"

"He went back, I believe."

"To see her!" cried the manager; "your prospects are ruined! Beatrice, from this moment—if it is not too late—you act just as I bid you! I will have none of your disobedience in future, madam! You shall not beard me with your cryings, and entreaties, and childish tears. You shall not ruin your own and my fortune in life. I command you, madam, to behave yourself in future, better. Take care!"

Beatrice felt her rebellious heart grow more bitter; she no longer thought of little Kate's Bible.

"I will have no nonsense, madam!" continued her father, in a rage. "I will not have a child like you, setting at naught all my wishes, and overturning all my plans in life, by your ridiculous folly. In future, you take no more rides to meet your lovers, or your lovers' sweethearts. Understand me—I will not be dictated to by my own child! As your father, I command you, in future, to give encouragement to this young man. Don't frown and look rebellious at me—I will not submit to any folly! If you choose to act as you have done, I choose to tell you the truth. You have ridden, Heaven knows where, to see, Heaven knows who. You have nearly ruined your prospects; he is now gone back, and if what you say about your interview with her is true, she will tell him all, and he will never look at you again! Madam!" cried the manager in a fury, "I shall not endure this! As your father, I command you to obey me! Take care—you have some silly religious feeling, and that feeling will tell you, that if you dare to disobey your father, God will take his account of you. I am that father—see that you obey me!"

The young girl's feelings were worked up to the avowal, her heart was agitated by rebellious and obstinate anger, but she could not throw off, all at once, her habit of affection and obedience. Still she could not remain silent, and she cried, with passionate tears: "Oh, you are not my father! God has revealed to me my real father. Mr. Effingham brought here this frock!" And with a quick movement, she drew from a drawer the child's garment. "That God, you speak of, revealed my birth to me!" she continued; "this letter has told me all. My father was Ralph Waters; my name is Beatrice Waters!" And overwhelmed with her emotion, the young girl sunk into a seat, almost fainting.

The manager snatched the frock and the letter from her in a violent rage. The truth all at once flashed on him—he had no one to blame but himself, and with a furious hand he tore his hair.

"Yes!" he cried, in a violent rage, "yes! you have dared to read that letter! you have dared to pry into what was my secret!"

"Oh, it was mine!" murmured Beatrice, bitterly.

"You have dared!"

And Mr. Manager Hallam again tore his hair.

"I could not help it, father!" cried Beatrice, calling on God to calm her wicked feeling of rebellion, as she spoke; "I felt compelled to read that letter! I did not mean—"

And she stopped, choked by her sobs. The manager sank into the chair from which he had risen in the excess of his rage.

"Oh, do not be angry with me, father!" cried Beatrice, burying her head in his bosom. "I did not mean to do wrong! I am your daughter still. Do not frown at me."

The manager slowly became calmer.

"I love you as much as ever," said Beatrice. "I felt wrong just now, when you spoke such harsh words—so unjust!—but now I am calm again!"

The manager began to cry—doubtless, like the great Congreve.

"Oh, father! I am so wretched!" exclaimed Beatrice. "I did not mean to make you suffer!"

"To be defied by one whom I have always loved!" ejaculated Hallam, half seriously, half from policy, giving way afresh to his emotion; "whom I raised from infancy, trying to find her family—defied by her!"

"Oh, I did not mean to defy you! indeed I did not!—forgive me, father! I am your daughter still!"

"I am a poor, childless old man!" muttered the manager, with his favorite choking cry.

"I will be your child!" cried Beatrice, weeping passionately. "I will love you as dearly as I always have done, you know, father—you have been so good to me! What matter if I am not your daughter in reality. What matter if I am the daughter of Ralph Waters—the brother of Charles's father." He started, but not with surprise; he had felt that John Waters must be Beatrice's uncle, for some days. "Why should I leave you, who have been so kind to me, because I was born in Malta, where my father died, and am not your daughter? You are my real father—God sent you! My real name is Beatrice Waters; but I will be Beatrice Hallam still. Oh, do not cry—you break my heart!"

She again buried her face in his bosom; but, hearing a noise, raised it again. Mr. Effingham stood before her, and had plainly heard the words she had just uttered.

The scene which followed was one of those which are best left to the reader's imagination. The pen can only describe passions, or trace utterances to a certain point—beyond that it yields the field to the painter, who alone can make the highest passions, the most conflicting emotions, eloquent. We may imagine the feelings of Mr. Effingham, on hearing from the gloomy and agitated manager, that his own act had revealed to Beatrice the secret of her birth; we may comprehend the rage of the young man on finding that, by his own agency, Beatrice had come to know that Charles Waters was her cousin, his uncle her father; we may further understand the despair of Hallam, the terrible agitation of Beatrice—we cannot describe them.

When Mr. Effingham went away to his room that night, he was a prey to one of his silent and sombre rages; he had raised this new barrier himself. The instrument of fate, and unknown to himself, his hand had opened that sealed book; and what the young girl had read had for ever separated her from him. That rival—bitterly hated before, now far more bitterly—would be her lawful protector; and whether in their duel he fell or conquered, nothing would be gained. A thousand tumultuous thoughts like these chased themselves through his mind—we cannot trace them—it is a repulsive subject, and we pass on.

CHAPTER LII.

TWO WATER-DOGS.

Mr. Effingham spent a sleepless night, and rose more agitated than ever. With a mind supernaturally active from feverous emotion, he embraced at a glance all his latter life. He followed the history of his infatuation for Beatrice from his first meeting with her in the forest, near Effingham Hall, through the scenes at the theatre, at her apartment, in the street, at the ball, to this last final denouement, which had come like the blast of the trumpet and the roar of the drum, to finish all before the curtain fell upon the drama.

He surveyed with a lightning-like glance his present position—the state of his mind and life. He felt more than ever that he must conquer that diabolical angel who had scorned him, or die. She must yield to him, or he would yield to her, and pass from the earth. He raved and tore his hair, and revolved in his gloomy and agitated mind a thousand plans. All were rejected after a moment's reflection, if that word could be applied to the operations of the young man's mind.

He rose in despair, and the room seemed too close to breathe in. He went out, gloomy, and breathing heavily. Suddenly, as he entered the passage, a loud, hearty voice made the windows jar, and, turning round, he found himself opposite to the stranger.

"Good day, comrade," cried the soldier. "What! gloomy on such a morning?"

"I am not well, sir," said Mr. Effingham, coldly.

"Come, drink a cup of this abominable Rhenish they vend at this hostelry," said the soldier, laughing. "You see me in excellent spirits. I am myself again!"

Indeed, the soldier was no longer cabined, cribbed, and confined in the tight, foppish suit he had originally worn, but was clad in the elegant military suit which we have seen Mr. Effingham return in, on the night he left Williamsburg for York. The costume seemed infinitely more appropriate for the stranger's vigorous and martial figure; the heavily-laced but dark uniform set of his person to great advantage, and his fine face, with its keen, dark eye and long black moustache, appeared to far more advantage beneath the rich Flanders hat. The stranger, in his present proper costume, was the model of a soldier.

To his merry observation, that he felt in excellent spirits, Mr. Effingham made no reply.

"Why, see now, you are moody, comrade! That is not

the philosophic state of a *bon soldat*, whether in the ranks, or in life, which, *parbleu!* seems to me as much a battle as Lissa, Glatz, or Minden. Come! hold your head up! I have good news for you!"

"What news, sir?" said Mr. Effingham, still cold and gloomy.

"Why, I am just about to go and arrange the details of our little affair:—that is to say, I am going to see Mr. Waters—brother of Ralph: an honest straightforward fellow was Ralph, though I say it, *parbleu!*"

"Well, sir!" said Mr. Effingham, already tired of his companion.

"*Arrange*, is not precisely the word, companion," continued the soldier, caressing the black fringe on his lip; "I believe the day after to-morrow is fixed upon—though the time, as all else, should have been left to us, the wheel-horses—the seconds. Your friend is Mr.——, you omitted to tell me, comrade, in the multitude of affairs we had to arrange:—you will recollect that you omitted it."

"Say at once, sir, that having a duel forced on me, I had not fixed every thing. Well, sir, I now say further, that I must defer the whole affair for a day or two longer. Circumstances," and Mr. Effingham's lip curled, "render me somewhat cooler in the quarrel."

The soldier looked keenly at the young man—but a single glance convinced him, that this delay did not spring from backwardness to match himself in combat against an adversary. There was the unmistakable fire in the eye; and fighting was a satisfaction to such a man, he felt.

"Perhaps you object to your antagonist," said the soldier, coolly.

"No, sir! I do not!"

"Come," said the stranger, "suppose we have a little bout here on the staircase. You really seem desirous of trying my ferrara, comrade."

"I have no such desire, sir," replied Mr. Effingham, coldly, "and if my tone is harsh, it is because I am in no humor to answer questions, or converse. I am not well, sir—arrange this matter as you choose. Mr. John Hamilton will act for me—but I repeat, that I will not meet Mr. Waters for three days or more."

"Well, well, companion, I can arrange that. By heaven! you must have something on your mind, but that is not my affair. I'll empty a cup of Jamaica—I'm done with the Rhenish—and get into my saddle. *Bon jour—au revoir.*"

And the soldier, curling his moustache, and humming a rude song, took his way down the staircase, his huge sword rattling against the banisters, and making with the jingle of his heavily-rowelled spurs, a martial sort of music eloquent of camps.

Mr. Effingham, gazing moodily after him, observed that he stopped suddenly at the foot of the stairs. A gentleman dressed in black had struck against him, owing to the fact that the said gentleman refused to yield one inch of the way. Then Mr. Effingham heard the important and pompously-uttered words:

"You should have more respect for the clergy, sir."

And no less a personage than Parson Tag came up, and with a cold bow passed into the apartment, next to his own —that one in which we have heard the man in the red cloak play his violin. The young man gazed after him moodily, and with a bitter smile; and hesitated whether he should return to his room, or descend. A glance at the bright sunshine of the clear cold autumn day decided him, and to escape its brilliance, he went into his apartment again, with a mocking and gloomy face painful to behold.

Then he sat down, as he had done on that day when little Kate had come to see him, and again embraced at a single glance, the sad and gloomy horizon of his life, where no sun shone, no birds sang. Again he went over the path which he had trodden—revived those bitter joys, those delicious agonies he had suffered. Full of gloomy wonder, he weighed all that had taken place in his acquaintance with Beatrice, and as before, that fatal, unavoidable question came to him, where would all this end? He had now defied society for her, and he was convinced that he stood lower in her regard than ever—he had given up all for her, she disdained him the more for his sacrifice. As his love increased, she grew colder—he was rushing toward the abyss! And that revelation which he had been the instrument of! Charles Waters was her cousin, and she loved him, perhaps! *He* had given that man the right to watch over her, to defend her. Thenceforward there was a new and more irritating obstacle.

"Woe to him, if he crosses my path before we stand face to face, sword in hand!" he muttered, with a sombre and threatening flash of his proud eyes.

As he spoke, a tap came at his door, and a servant entered.

"Well?" said the young man, raising his head with a movement which frightened the negro nearly out of his wits, "what now?"

"Two boatmen, Mas' Effnum—say they want to see you."

"To the devil with them!" he said: but suddenly he paused—a light shone from his eyes. Already his mind had conceived the outline of a strange, desperate, and audacious project.

"About my sail-boat? Yes; go and bring them here—go!"

And he motioned the negro feverishly toward the door. In two minutes the door opened again, and the rough-looking watermen entered, and with their caps in their hands, louted to the young man, standing respectfully on the threshold.

"Close the door and come in!" he said, gloomily: the door was shut, and obedient to a sign from Mr. Effingham, the watermen approached.

"About my sail-boat, I suppose?" he said, curtly.

"Yes, your honor," replied the water-dog, who seemed to be spokesman.

"Where is she?"

"Down at the landing, by Townes', your honor."

"You got up to-day?"

"Jest so, your honor—and she's as tight a little craft as ever walked the water—swifter'n a waterfowl."

Mr. Effingham looked strangely at the rough watermen, who turned their tarpaulins in their hands, and coughed respectfully behind them.

"Is she fully equipped?" he said.

"Out and out, your honor. I never see a jollier craft; and she carries sail enough for a merchantman. I was a sayin' to mate here only jest now, 'at I never hearn o' such a thing afore."

"And she is down there?"

"At Townes', your honor."

"All ready?"

"Ready as a squall, when the rags are taut."

Mr. Effingham looked at the water-dogs again with the same strange expression.

"Your name is Junks, is it not?" he said, motioning to the man to approach.

"Yes, your honor, and mate's name is Jackson."

"Very well—you are poor?"

"Poor as a lean cat, sir."

"Would you like to make fifty pistoles?"

The water-dogs opened their eyes.

"I'd sell myself to the devil for it," said the spokesman, laughing.

"No; I wish you to sell yourself to me," said Mr. Effingham, with haughty coldness. "Is this weather too cold for a night run down the river?"

"Your honor is jokin'—it ain't warm, but ta'int nothin' to the likes o' us."

"Whoever I brought, then, you are willing to shut your eyes?"

"Oh, your honor's got a frolic on hand? That suits me to a circumstance."

"And me, too, your honor," said mate, in a mumbling voice from behind his thick woollen comfort.

Mr. Effingham, looking keenly at these men, saw that they were such as could be bought for much less than fifty pistoles. Then he was silent. A struggle seemed to be going on in his mind—his brow flushed, then grew pale, and his cheeks were covered with a cold sweat. The water-dogs looked at him wonderingly, for his eyes were not a pleasant sight—they were like lurid lightning.

"Wait here," he said, suddenly, as he heard a door open and close without. "Don't stir until I return."

And hastily putting on his hat, he went out, closed the door, and crossing the passage, entered the room of Beatrice.

CHAPTER LIII

THE LAST INTERVIEW BETWEEN BEATRICE AND MR. EFFINGHAM.

BEATRICE had just come in, and was sitting in front of the fire, gazing sadly and thoughtfully into the blaze, when Mr. Effingham's entrance caused her to turn round. For a moment these two persons who sustained toward each other such strange and anomalous relations, maintained perfect silence.

At last Mr. Effingham, pale and gloomy, yet gazing at the young girl with passionate love, said abruptly, and in a low tone—

"We meet again; I trust you are well after the ball."

"Yes, sir," said Beatrice, in a tone of quiet, uncomplaining sorrow; "I do not think I feel worse than usual."

"You do not ask me how I am," he said, with painful earnestness.

"Pardon me, sir," she said, in the same low, sad tones. "I hope you are well."

"No; I am far from it—I feel as if my brain was bursting."

"I am sorry, sir—sincerely."

"You are so cold," he said, leaning on the mantelpiece, and gazing at her with fixed, stony eyes. "You have no pity on me."

"*I* pity *you*, Mr. Effingham!"

"Oh, you know what I mean," he said. "We know each other now. I mean that you meet all my love with coldness—a freezing coldness; or, if not, with cold indifference—with contempt! I mean that you do not cast your proud eyes down on the man who suffers, kneeling at your feet, because you despise him and his love. I mean that you have nothing but scorn for me, when I have nothing but passionate, devouring love for you. I mean that I love you—love you with all the power of my soul, with all my strength, with my whole being, and that you disdain to speak to me!"

"Indeed I do not, sir—oh, no! If I have been harsh or cruel, or unwomanly, I beg you to pardon it. I believe that I have spoken harsh words to you sometimes—I regret them. I have no right to scorn any human being, sir. God does not approve of such feelings. Pardon me!"

The earnest, low-toned voice went to his poor, bruised heart—her soft, sorrowful face took away all his anger.

"Oh, why will you not love me?" he said, with painful earnestness. "Why does your heart still remain closed to me? See me here at your feet, Beatrice, with my pride broken, my wilfulness all gone, seeing you only in the universe! You are to me the sole light which shines on the dark waters of my life—you know it, why so indifferent to me? Oh, I love you so passionately! so purely! I follow you with yearning eyes—I live in you and through you! Why still despise me?"

"I do not, sir—I must not feel so toward any human being."

"I have been criminally harsh—I have repented of it in the long hours of the gloomy night—repented bitterly."

"I have forgotten it, sir," said Beatrice.

"Then, for pity's sake, do not look at me so coldly!"

"I am not well to-day, sir."

He looked at her with inexpressible love, and said:

"Did you only know how much I suffer when you suffer!"

"I do not complain, sir.

"You must have had a trying ordeal last night."

"Yes; very trying."

"You were the queenliest of them all," he said, gazing on her with passionate love and pride. "Why should you not give me the right to lead you forth in the eyes of the world, as I did before that assembly?"

"Mr. Effingham, I cannot be your wife," she said. "We have said much upon this subject. It only distresses me."

"Why, Beatrice? Give me some reason for my wretchedness."

A deep flush covered the young girl's sad pale brow, as she thought of Charles Waters.

"We are not suited to each other," she said.

He saw the blush, and his own brow flushed. His supernaturally active mind discerned the hidden reason—left unexpressed—and a pang shot through his heart.

"That is not the real reason," he said, a shadow passing over his face.

"I can give no other," she said, with a deeper blush than before.

Anger began to invade the young man's heart like a bitter and poisonous vapor.

"The true reason is, that you love another," he said, with a cruel groan.

"Mr. Effingham!"

"Yes, yes; my rudeness is insulting—my plainness repulsive, I know it!" he said, bitterly. "But how can I feel my heart breaking, and not speak? You love that man!"

"Mr. Effingham, you must know"—she murmured, suffering painfully—"this is obtrusive, sir—I—"

"Oh, do not deny it, madam!" he said, giving way to his bitter and feverish emotion. "You scorn me and my love—you refuse my hand, because your heart could not go with it!"

"You agitate me, sir!" she said, "I am not well! These conversations can lead to nothing!"

"You mistake, madam!" he replied, with his old, gloomy bitterness, "they lead to despair, for I love you."

"I cannot prevent your suffering, sir—I cannot command you to leave me—if I could—"

"You would," he interposed, "you need not assure me of that, madam. You hate me—you scorn me—because you love that man who insulted me in your presence, here. Wo to him!"

And Mr. Effingham's brows grew darker, his eyes flashed with hatred.

"Remember he is my relative, sir," said Beatrice, flushing crimson.

"And your lover!"

"Mr. Effingham!"

"Oh, madam, do not cry out according to your wont. I have ruined myself for you, and naturally feel some objection to being robbed of you by a common boor."

"Sir!"

"Yes, I offend you!—make you hate me more bitterly: but for that same reason that I am lost from seeing your fatal beauty, and have defied all the powers of this society, I should be allowed to speak plainly, to throw aside the conventional rules which I have trampled on for your sake."

"I did not wish to go to that ball—it was a cruel trial," she said, coldly, and pressing her hand upon her heart as she spoke, "my father exacted it."

"You did not like your escort, I know," he replied, bitterly; "you were too good for him, as the vulgar expression goes."

"Mr. Effingham, this is unworthy!"

"Yes, madam! it is! I know it! But I cannot feel the poisoned arrow in my side, like St. Sebastian, and be silent—not cry out—not utter a groan! Oh, may you never know what it is to love, and that hopelessly!—to turn and toss on your sleepless couch through the long, weary hours of the gloomy night—to rave and curse and weep—to utter prayers and blessings, maledictions and blasphemies! may you never suffer this cruel agony, which leaves the heart torn, the cheek pale, the eyes heavy, the brain oppressed with a bitter and poisonous mist! may you never love, and feel that love is hopeless!"

And, overwhelmed with sour and gloomy emotion, he turned away. His words went to her heart, but it was almost her own situation which he painted, and this made her flush and tremble. But by a great effort she became calm again.

"You know not what you say," she murmured, "you know your own sufferings, not mine, sir."

"Yours! you have suffered this—"

"I have suffered much, sir."

"You have felt those pangs of despised love?"

"Mr. Effingham, you agitate me! you have no right to intrude upon my privacy thus: I am not well, sir—my sufferings do not concern yourself: pray leave me."

"Whom do they concern, then, madam?"

"Mr. Effingham!"

"Perhaps your chivalric cousin, Mr. Waters!"

"You make me unwell, sir!" said the young girl, flushing. The young man understood what this exhibition of emotion sprung from, and gnawed his lip until it bled.

"You might pardon that, if you had a little charity," he

said, bitterly; "I believe that I was the instrument in revealing your secret."

"Yes, sir—unconsciously."

"By which you mean, that no thanks are due me."

"I mean nothing, sir."

"Well, you are right, madam. I would have cut off my right hand before I would have had any agency in revealing that."

"You are truly very friendly."

"I do not pretend to be, where my love and despair are concerned," he said, gloomily; "I had some claim upon Beatrice Hallam, the actress—I have much less on Miss Waters."

"Mr. Effingham—I cannot bear this much longer!"

"You will leave the stage?" he went on, pitilessly.

"I do not know, sir."

"You hope to?"

"I do, sir."

"What a delightful time you will have with that noble gentleman, your cavalier!" he said, with sombre irony. "In future, I see that I shall not be allowed to kiss your hand, or approach you, even."

"Oh, leave me, sir!—"

"In future, my days must be without even your frowns and insults."

"Mr. Effingham, I am suffering!"

"*You* suffering!"

"Yes, sir."

"I thought, madam, that I monopolized the despair and agony of the whole world."

"You do not, sir."

"And because you suffer, you consider that you have the right to tear my heart. I am despised, because you suffer! I admire your logic, madam!"

"No, sir," she said, growing indignant at his insulting tone, "though much of that suffering has been caused by you."

"Because I have told you my love."

"No, sir—not that only."

"What have I done?"

"Every thing to persecute me: but I say again, that I

do not wish to remember that. I had forgotten it. Pray leave me—I am not well, and cannot bear any more agitation."

He gazed at her long and fixedly, with eyes burning yet stony, cold yet fiery.

"Beatrice," he said, in a gloomy and sombre voice, "this is the crisis of my life. This moment makes or mars me. I have given up all for you—left behind all that makes life happy to follow the ignis-fatuus of your love. If you cast me off, I am ruined—reflect."

"You make me suffer cruelly," said poor Beatrice, turning away, "but—oh, I cannot, will not marry you, sir! —I cannot!"

"For the last time!" he said, taking a step toward her, with clenched hands, and grinding his teeth; "you refuse?"

"Mr. Effingham, I—"

"You spurn my love—despise me and every thing connected with me—still scorn me? Reflect, madam!"

"I cannot marry you, sir. This interview is killing me. My breast is—"

"For the last time—yes or no?"

"No! then, sir: no!" cried Beatrice, rising, with her hand upon her heart; "I cannot, will not!"

With one hand he tore his breast, until his nails were stained with blood—the other opened and clenched, as though in his fury he was grasping some deadly weapon. He looked at her for a moment, with rage, despair, and menace, shook from head to foot, and muttering, "Breast to breast, then! force against force!" rushed wildly from the room, and passed into his own, the door of which closed with a crash. A quarter of an hour afterwards the boatmen came out and went away; and in ten minutes Mr. Effingham made his appearance, pale, and covered with perspiration.

He held in his moist and nervous hand a Bank of England note of large value; and muttering, "That, too, can be arranged!" went toward the room occupied by the parson.

CHAPTER LIV.

ÆGRI SOMNIA.

Events hurry on. As the passions and complicated movements of the drama develope themselves, the task of the chronicler becomes more and more difficult. We must proceed, however, to narrate, as clearly as possible, what followed the final outburst of the young man's fiery passion—rejected finally, as we have seen, by the object of his love.

Night drew on, cold and stormy. It was one of those evenings which succeed late autumn days, when the sun seems to set in blood, and the vast clouds reposing on the far horizon are tinged with that lurid light which resembles the glare of a great conflagration. The wind rose, and moaned, and died away, and came again, ever becoming chiller and more mournful. The moon rose like a great wheel of fire rolled up the sky, over which dark clouds drifted, driven by the wind; and the almost leafless forests seemed to be murmuring to themselves, and whispering some mysterious secret. The tall, gloomy pines waved like solemn giants, in the fitful moonlight, and the oaks ground their boughs together, or parted with their last rattling leaves, in the stormy gusts, which ever and anon swept over them, clattering their dry, hard branches.

In the town, every living thing soon housed itself from the chill wind and the gloomy, fitfully-illuminated night—and not the cold, cheerless air alone drove them to their firesides. Those were the times when men believed in witchcraft and every species of diablerie; and many persons in the town could make oath that they had seen horrible, uncouth figures, celebrating awful and mysterious rites on the wild, lonely common, near; where the pine bushes waved like deformed spectres, throwing long shadows over the dangerous ground. It was a night for fiends to be abroad in, holding their wild revels beneath the frosty light of the great solemn moon; and none cared to brave it, when a good fire and a cup of foaming ale awaited them. They looked round fearfully when the gust moaned by the gables; and told tales which dealt in terrible mysteries—in hidden treasure—in fiends, and black dogs guarding it—and how the witches, who had tormented honest Christians, had been burned, not long before, for an example to all evil doers. It was a night to believe in such things, and they trembled at every sound—at the very grating of the branches against the window.

All that day Beatrice had been in a state of agitation and nervous fear. The interview with her father on the night before, had succeeded the trying ordeal of the ball, and then the interview with Mr. Effingham had crowned all. That interview had affected her cruelly—never had she seen the young man so torn by passion, so completely overwhelmed with emotion—never had she known him to utter such despairing cries of agony and torture. It had made her suffer deeply, and shocked her nervous system dreadfully. In addition, she had not slept for more than forty-eight hours, and nothing so prostrates the nerves as this. We cannot wonder, therefore, that the young girl was exhausted in mind and body, by these various and complicated moral and physical trials—subject to a nervous trepidation, which made her start at every noise.

She went through the duties of the day, walking as in a dream, with fixed eyes, and heaving bosom; her agitation was so striking, that every body observed it, and questioned her about it. She made no reply to these questions—she seemed not to have heard them. Her mind was laboring with its burden of fear and agitation.

As the night drew on, she felt an indefinable dread. Seated in her room, alone, she started at every gust which sobbed around the inn, and trembled at every noise. The moonlight now streamed through the window like a flood of dark, fiery gold, then disappeared, swallowed up in the gloomy and threatening clouds, which swept over the sky toward the far, freezing ocean.

As the night passed on, and midnight approached, she fell into a sort of trance of thought. With a dreamy eye she ran over her whole life, since she had arrived in Virginia—she thought of those persecutions, of the adventure on the river, of her rescue, of that noble face, of those persecutions again, of the ball, of the strange revelation which had so changed her life.

As she thought of that strange conjunction of circumstances, her eye fell upon the volume of Shakespeare, open, from habit, on her lap. She read:

> "And pity, like a naked, new-born babe,
> Striding the blast, or heaven's cherubim, hors'd
> Upon the sightless couriers of the air,
> Shall blow the horrid deed in every eye,
> That tears shall drown the wind!"

The words seemed to apply strangely to her own case. Truly, that deed had been blown in every eye, by an accident which was plainly from heaven. With dreamy eyes, she read on, and came to the passage where the usurper sees the air-drawn dagger, and feels the cold sweat of horror bathe his brow, as he attempts to clutch it. She saw him, with his stealthy tread, gliding slowly, the murderous weapon in his hand, toward the apartment where the murder was to be committed—she heard his low breathing—saw his fiery eyes—almost thought that his awful invocation to the firm earth not to hear his stealthy steps, was really uttered—that she saw the tiger stealing toward his victim with deadly caution. The scene was so clear in her marvellously vivid imagination, that she trembled; and when a bird flew against the window, started up in an agony of fright.

She sat down again, endeavoring to calm herself; the fire was burning fitfully, and she tried to make it brighter. The last sticks, however, were burning out, and the trembling blue flame licked, and struggled, and clung to the whitening embers, and went out. She did not observe it, however; she was again buried in thought; and those thoughts fled to the far southern land, enveloped in such mysterious and dreamy interest. It seemed to her that the life she now embraced, with a drowsy and unsteady eye, must have been in another world—a strange, far world, which she could never go to any more forever!

Gradually her eyes closed, her head drooped on her breast, then she would start up, trembling at some noise; and then her head would droop again, the wild stormy gust would lull her, and the fitful weird light of the great, solemn moon, would envelope her gentle Madonna-like head in a flood of glory. At last, all her thoughts flowed into each other, merged their outlines, lost themselves in dreams, and overcome by exhaustion, the young girl slept; her head drooping on one shoulder, her long dusky lashes lying on her cheeks, her hair waving in profuse curls round the still agitated countenance.

She had a strange dream. She thought, as the second or third hour after midnight struck, or rather murmured through the silent inn—she thought that her window opened, and a man, enveloped in a cloak, stepped into the room through the opening. The dream was so real, that she thought she felt a gust of chill air blow on her. Then, this man approached her slowly, enveloped as before, in his long cloak and wide drooping hat; took her languid form in his strong arms, raising her without effort;—and passing through the window, bore her, she knew not how, to the ground. A horse stood waiting, and the man mounted, holding her still in his arms. Then they set off like the wind; and shaken by the quick movement, uttering a scream, as the chill air raised by the horse's gallop struck her person, she awoke, and found her dream a reality! What she had regarded as the mere conjuration of her excited fancy, was a terrible fact! what she had considered a mere freak of the imagination, was real, as the gloomy night through which the furious and neighing animal darted, obedient to the spur of his desperate rider! She was in the arms of a man, who wrapped her in his cloak with one hand, while he clasped her waist with the other—the bridle lying on the neck of his flying animal. In five minutes they had left the town and entered the gloomy forest.

CHAPTER LV.

THE FLIGHT AND PURSUIT.

Through the gloom as through the moonlight, under the drooping boughs of the dark pine forest, as across the lonely tracts of bare, waste ground—the furious animal, driven pitilessly by his rider's spur, fled on.

Clouds of foam flew from his reeking jaws, his glossy

coat became as wet as though he had just issued from a river; still he went on, his speed unabated.

The trees flew by—the moon came out and flooded the flying animal and his burden with its chill light, then swept beneath the clouds again; the cold wind moaned and sobbed, —still on!

The silent cavalier only drew his hat further over his eyes, clasped the young girl's waist more securely, wrapped more carefully in the thick cloak the tender body, which shuddered with cold in its thin dress.

That shudder passed over his own person, too, as if they were but one—had all feelings in common—but the horseman betrayed no other evidences of emotion, of life.

Once, his dark fiery eyes, glowing like coals, under his slouched hat, met her own; once his warm breath, almost his kiss, touched her cheek; but he did not kiss the cheek. It was only to see if her arm was rubbed against the pistols in his girdle, or the hilt of his sword.

Still on! The blast blew chiller, the wind seemed to sob, and moan, and laugh in cruel glee at her; the stars soaring out, looked at her with their pitiless and sorrowfully twinkling eyes, then were obscured again—still on!

She seemed still to be in a dream; the whole affair had occurred so suddenly, that the young girl could scarcely collect her senses. When she attempted to reason calmly, the dreadful position she occupied deadened her brain, and her mind wandered. Was this not all a mere dream still? Could it be real? Was it not the mere fancy of her excited and agitated mind? Could she not wake from such a horrible nightmare, and sit up?

As the thought passed through her mind, she felt the arm around her waist cling tighter, and suddenly the animal reared, made a desperate leap, fell upon his knees, sprung up again, trembling, and fled onward faster than before. She looked back, and saw a stream, with high banks; the current, of great width, glittered in the moon. It was a desperate leap, even for a phantom.

But she began now to collect her thoughts; and suddenly finding her voice, said, in trembling and agitated tones: "You frighten me! you hurt me! Is this a dream or a dreadful reality? You are killing me!"

The cavalier made no reply. Beatrice burst into tears, and struggled to release herself from his arms—those arms only held her tighter. She said, moaning, that her position hurt her; the cavalier dropped the bridle on his horse's neck, and with both arms raised her, laid her, so to speak, on his breast; and thus carrying her, like a child, again plunged his spurs into the quivering sides of the flying animal, and fled faster.

The ocean breeze grew colder, the odor of water began to fill the wild, wandering air; the night grew darker and more dismal.

Nothing was heard but the quick smiting of the horse's hoofs—the far, mournful cry of a whippoorwill, and the low sighing of the wind through the solemn pines, under whose boughs the animal passed, like some phantom steed of the German mythology.

She shrunk as the boughs bent down toward her—for they seemed to be gigantic hands of fiends, stretched out to grasp and carry her away; she sobbed, and wept, and entreated, but in vain—still on!

The flying animal issued from the forest, and entered upon a wild waste, from which the James River was visible in the distance, glittering like a silver mirror in the fitful moonlight.

As the young girl caught the flash of the far waters, she suddenly felt the animal arrested by an obstacle, which threw him to one side; a loud voice came to her ears—a voice which sent a thrill through her brain—the cavalier only wrapped her closer in his cloak, and with a muttered curse, fled on. The animal seemed to scent the water, to know that it was his bourne, and with incredible speed darted on, and disappeared in a hollow, thick with pines.

That obstacle which had arrested the animal, was the body of a man; and this man had grasped the bridle, been rolled on the ground by the chest of the flying horse, and then rising, seen the whole disappear like a phantom. It was Charles Waters, and spite of the cloak, the disguise, he had recognized Beatrice and Mr. Effingham.

For a moment the young man stood motionless in the moonlight, overwhelmed with horror; then clenching his hands, he fled after them with the rapidity of a race-horse.

He now felt the advantage of his country training—his days and nights spent in hunting; his speed was scarcely less than that of the flying horse.

As he fled onward, a thousand mad thoughts passed through his mind; curses were on his lips, fire was in his heart.

He blessed God for that strange feeling he had experienced all day, that Beatrice was in danger—a feeling which had accompanied him in sleep, had waked him while night still lay upon the earth: which had driven him forth toward the town—which had led him there to rescue her!

But could he? That animal was going faster than any mortal man could. He would be too late!

Whither were they flying?

That sail-boat he had seen coming up the river, on the day before!

He clenched his hands, and his eyes glared. Still he sped on.

Yes! that was the base scheme of that coward! Yes! he had kidknapped a defenceless girl! She was in his power!

A flame seemed to pass before his eyes; he felt his brain totter: no matter—on!

The river suddenly burst upon his view:—he ran on with staggering steps, heaving bosom:—he saw figures moving on the shore in the moonlight, heard the faint neigh of a horse. He felt the eyes filling with blood—his heart throbbed with the desperate exertion, like an engine—still on!

The moon shone suddenly on the white sails of a boat, as she veered round—the water danced in the moon, and against the silver mirror; he plainly saw the figures of three men, who carried by main force, some object in their arms toward the boat.

With fiery eyes, eyes which saw nothing clearly, but through a flame, it seemed, he still sped on. His strength was exhausted—he tottered as he ran:—he staggered, still on!

They reach the boat—they embark—she is gone! He tore his hair, and uttered a sob of rage and despair.

Suddenly a dark object interposed itself between the worn-out, exhausted, overwhelmed pursuer, and the bright water illuminated by the moon. This object was the hut of Townes the boatman, and a despairing hope flashed through his breast.

He staggered toward it—seeing flame—breathing fire, he thought. A light was burning in the window—a shadow passed to and fro.

He tottered, gasping, to the door—fell against it—burst it open—caught the boatman by the shoulder, and said, almost inarticulately:

"Come!—you must!—I must have!—look there!—they are carrying her off—Miss Hallam, who sailed in your boat!—she is my cousin!—mercy!"

And staggering he would have fallen, had not the boatman caught him in his arms.

CHAPTER LVI.

ON THE RIVER.

The boatman Townes was one of those men who understand perfectly at a single word, and act quickly. The broken exclamations of Charles Waters, told him plainly all that had occurred—he understood in an instant.

"Blast my eyes!" he cried, cramming his tarpaulin on his head, "I knowed somethin' was a-goin' on! But I didn't dream o' this! I heard them horse's hoofs, but the devil himself couldn't a' dreamed this! I'll have the craft ready in a minute! Stay here, and catch your breath, Charley, and we'll live or die together!"

With which words the boatman grasped a heavy stick, threw down another before Waters, who was nearly fainting, and rushed from the hut.

With two bounds he was at his boat, and slung off the chain which held the bark to the shore. Then with a rapid and experienced hand he caught, and tore open the sail—tied it to the gunwale, and seized his oars. Charles Waters was at his side panting, his eyes on fire, his looks fixed upon the other boat.

Obedient to oar and sail, the "Nancy" darted from the

shore, and plunged her cutwater into the silver expanse raising clouds of cold spray.

The other boat was much of the same description :—her size was greater—she was more ornate—that was all.

On fire with his terrible emotion, his eyes burning, his body trembling, Charles Waters bent to his oar like a giant : it was as much as the boatman could do to keep the craft from whirling round, so tremendous were these strokes. The boat flew.

"Look!" cried the boatman, "I can see him! It is young Mr. Effingham!"

"Yes!—don't stop!"

"Him!" cried the boatman, wonderingly.

"Yes! 'you would live and die with me!' row!"

"That will I!"

And plunging his oar into the water, the powerful boatman sent the craft twenty feet.

The men in the other boat, plainly saw that they were pursued, and bent to their oars.

The bark groaned with its enormous mass of sail, and careened dangerously. Standing in the bow, with one arm around Beatrice, Mr. Effingham looked on gloomily. He knew very well that a deadly encounter was imminent—this encounter he both desired and dreaded :—dreaded because Charles Waters was her cousin.

The young girl tried to shrink from him.

"Oh, for pity's sake, do not carry me away!" she cried.

He only gazed bitterly at her.

"Oh, it is cruel!" she cried.

"You were cruel to me!" he muttered, hoarsely.

"They are pursuing us—they will rescue me!"

"Yes, when I am dead."

"Oh, it is Charles!" she cried.

"Yes, your excellent cousin: we shall meet soon—I see they are gaining on us!"

And Mr. Effingham drew a pistol.

"Oh, for mercy's sake!—mercy! do not fire!" exclaimed Beatrice, clinging to his arm.

"Be easy, madam," said Mr. Effingham, gloomily, "I only meant to try the lock: the sword will settle it. Row, there, row!"

And seizing an oar himself, he bent to his task with desperate energy. He dreaded the encounter more than he would acknowledge.

Beatrice kneeling and watching the boat which was pursuing them, could only pray.

That boat fled toward them like a seagull. It seemed to dart rather than move. Every stroke of the large oars whirled it onward through the foamy surges, and the mast groaned.

" We are gaining !' cried the boatman, " look ! "

And he raised his hand, to indicate the position of the two vessels.

" Row ! row ! " cried Waters, hoarsely.

The boatman bent to his oar again. The little bark flew over the water, leaving a long track of foam, which glittered in the moonlight. Her triangular sail bent in the wind—her mast groaned—she bore on like a living thing.

The excitement of Charles Waters was terrible. His brain was on fire, his heart felt as if ice were pressed to it. That woman whom he loved more than all the world, was being torn from him by his insolent rival—who had plainly compassed her abduction by some skilful trick!—she was being borne away before his eyes! And uttering a groan of rage, he threw in a strength in his oar-strokes which seemed almost supernatural.

The boats neared—but the greater surface of sail on the foremost still made escape probable. The strength of the rowers must soon wear out at the rate they were going—then the foremost boat would leave her pursuers behind. She was already flying before the wind, and, as we have said, careening perilously.

" Oh, they will escape!—I am wearing out!" cried Waters, with a despairing groan.

" Cheerly, cheerly !" answered the boatman, " we'll give 'em a whack yet."

And he rowed more powerfully.

" I will throw myself into the water and die there, but I will overtake them ! "

" Look ! " shouted the boatman, " her mast's snapped ! hurrah ! "

It was true—the boat could not carry the press of sail,

and too well built to capsize easily, the frail mast had broken under the press, and fallen over the side with all its mass of canvas.

The craft was no longer any thing but a wreck :—like a wounded sea-bird, whose wing has been broken by the huntsman, she paused in her course, veered round and threatened to go down with every wave.

The pursuers darted toward her like lightning—they were now not ten yards off.

Again the foiled and infuriated young man drew his pistol, and this time it seemed with deadly intentions.

The barrel glittered in the moonlight as he levelled it. Then again he replaced it with a curse, and with one arm round Beatrice, as though he would die with her, awaited the approach of his pursuers.

They were but two men—yet he knew they were desperate.

The boat darted toward him—the sides of the small vessels crushed together : Charles Waters and the boatman, armed with their heavy clubs, threw themselves from their own into Mr. Effingham's craft.

"You come to your death !" cried the furious young man, rushing toward Charles Waters, "woe to you !"

His foot caught in the sail which cumbered the gunwale, and he half fell.

Beatrice rushed toward her cousin, and he caught her in his arms. At the same moment Townes levelled the foremost waterman with his club : the other grappled with him, and endeavored to plunge a knife into his side.

Mr. Effingham rose overwhelmed with fury. His blood boiled with rage—he was in one of his madnesses of passion.

He saw only that one sight before him—Beatrice clasped in the arms of his hated, abhorred rival. He only understood that that rival had defeated him, despised him.

The blood rushed to his head—he staggered, and drawing his pistol, levelled it at Charles Waters' breast, and fired.

A sudden careening of the boat deranged his aim, and the ball, drawing blood from Beatrice's shoulder, struck the waterman Junks, just as he had nearly strangled Townes, and had lifted his knife to stab him.

That sudden careening of the boat, saved the life of Charles Waters and his friend.

"Oh! you've got it! blast you!" cried Townes, as his adversary fell.

Mr. Effingham saw all: he saw his two companions disabled—he saw himself left alone to contend against his enemies—he saw that all was lost.

One thing remained—revenge! And as Charles Waters, seeing him rise sword in hand, raised his arm, protecting Beatrice with the other, the infuriated young man plunged the weapon into his breast.

Waters fell backward, dragging down Beatrice who had fainted. The sword snapped off in his body within six inches of the hilt—only the hilt and the stump remained in Mr. Effingham's hand.

With a wild cry the boatman, Townes, threw himself on his knees beside his friend, and, crying like a child, sought to stanch the blood.

"No—do not—mind me!" said Charles Waters, faintly, and turning deadly pale as he spoke, "attend to —— Beatrice!"

And drawing the blade from his breast with a desperate effort he fell back.

The boatman tore his hair with both hands, and wept until he was worn out. Suddenly he started up—woe! to that man! He was alone on the boat, with the wounded and dying.

A hundred yards from the boat, he saw the young man swimming desperately toward the shore. Exhausted, overwhelmed with horror, the boatman sunk back and fell, his head striking heavily against the side of the boat.

CHAPTER LVII.

THE FATHER AND SON.

Mr. Effingham, uttering a wild curse, had thrown himself into the water as Charles Waters fell, and still holding the stump of the bloody sword, had struck out toward the shore.

At one moment he determined to make no effort to reach the shore, to let the dark waves ingulf him—but nature prevailed. Still grasping madly the weapon, he swam toward the bank, and issued from the water near the point from which he had started.

His horse was grazing where he had left him, and came whinnying to him.

He mounted, and plunging the broken sword into the scabbard, looked over his shoulder.

There was the bark upon which the mortal encounter had just taken place—a dark object upon the silvery expanse.

He turned from it gloomily.

Where should he go?

He looked around him from side to side, and shook his head. That was a hard question. But one thing he knew—that he would not stay there to be devoured with rage and despair.

Motion! motion! and striking his spur into the animal's side so cruelly, that it neighed with pain, he set forward furiously, his hair streaming in the wind—his lips writhing—his eyes glaring with despair.

All was thenceforth lost to him—he was lost!—his infatuation for that diabolical angel had ended, as he predicted, in a terrible crash, which shook the props of his whole life! But at least he had no longer that rival.

Every noise startled him—he trembled at the moaning of the wind—shook at the fitful shadows:—the moon seemed to grow pale, the stars to fade. Still the wild animal fled on—the bridle on his neck—his sides reeking with sweat.

The young man knew nothing of the road he was taking:—he did not see that the animal, with a strange instinct, had followed the road to the hall, avoiding the town.

Still on! more desperately, still he urged the flying horse with his spur—he tried to outrun his thoughts in vain. They pursued him like ferocious bloodhounds, and caught him with their sharp teeth, and tore him!

The sobbing, panting animal bounded onward wildly—passed mile after mile, and entered the forest stretching around the hall, just as the first streak of dawn reddened in the east.

The young man raised his head and looked around.

"This place is familiar to me," he muttered, "it is home!"

And he groaned.

The poor moaning animal halted in front of the great portico; and, panting, covered with sweat, foaming at the mouth, stood still. Mr. Effingham dismounted and passed his hand over his neck—the affection of that animal was grateful.

Suddenly a voice startled him and he turned round. It was a negro just risen, and his face expressed the greatest delight at seeing his master back. Mr. Effingham gave him his hand—ordered him to attend to his horse—and then, scarcely knowing what he did, entered the hall, sombre, and moving slowly.

He sat down in the library, where a fire had just been kindled, for the squire was accustomed to rise very early: and looking round, took note of all the familiar household objects, which he had not seen for so long—years, it seemed to him.

There was the squire's writing-table covered with papers, and ears of corn, and specimen apples, and large heads of wheat. There was the plain leather-bottomed chair with the marks of powder on the carved back, where the old gentleman's head had rested. There was the book-case half open—the "Gazette" lay on a chair—Willie's new whip was on the floor. There was his mother's portrait over the fire-place:—he turned from it with a groan. There was little Kate's embroidery now finished, and converted into a screen:—he looked away from that too. And the shadow on his brow grew deeper:—his pale lips writhed.

A step behind him, startled him, and he rose. The squire stood before him.

The old gentleman's pride was all broken in his heart, by the sight of his long lost son; and he would have grasped his hand hard: but Mr. Effingham drew back.

"No sir," he said, hoarsely, "do not touch that hand: there is blood on it!"

"Blood!" echoed the horrified squire, with wide distended eyes.

"Blood!—the blood of a man: perhaps that of a woman too."

And the shadow in the dark eyes grew deeper.

The squire fell into a chair overwhelmed with this announcement: he could not speak at first. At last he regained his voice, and said, with a gasp:

"Blood? whose blood?"

"A rival's."

"Who?"

"Mr. Charles Waters."

The old man groaned.

"That woman!—that woman!" he said, in a low voice, which trembled piteously.

"Yes, sir, that woman!" replied his son, with eyes which resembled nothing human, "you were right in warning me against her. She has ruined me—I am lost!"

The squire could not reply:

"I have committed a murder, sir," continued Mr. Effingham,—"see, my sword is still bloody, I believe—"

And drawing from the scabbard the stump of the weapon, on which some drops of clotted blood still hung, he threw it on the floor before the old man.

"A murder?" cried the squire, turning deadly pale.

"Well, sir—no: not an assassination, for his arm was raised to strike me, and he was not alone—"

"Thank God!—I am spared that!" groaned the old man.

"But it is scarcely better," said the young man, in the same tone of gloomy calmness, "I carried off a woman, sir: that woman, whom you rightly dreaded so:—yes, she has been my evil genius—my fate! I loved and hated her—I was mad! But this is from the purpose. I carried her off—was pursued—first on land—then on the water—we were attacked—my associates in the diabolical affair were both disabled, one of them by myself, one by his adversary—then I plunged my sword into my enemy's heart, having first tried to kill him with my pistol, thinking, from a stumble I made, that he would strike me unprepared. That is it, sir."

And looking at the squire with lurid eyes, the young man paused.

"I believe the ball wounded the woman," he added, hoarsely.

"But thank God, you did not kill in cold blood!" cried

his father, "it was while your blood was hot, and in a struggle. My poor son! how fatally this has ended!"

And the squire covered his face.

"Yes, sir—ruin has been the end for me:—henceforth, I am lost. As I shall probably be wanted by the officers of the law some time to-day, I think that we had better decide upon something."

"Yes—yes!" cried the squire, starting up, "you are right! The officers of the law arrest you!—my son!"

And the old man, with some of his youthful heat, flushed to the temples.

"The middle age is past," said Mr. Effingham, with the same sombre calmness; "we cannot drop the portcullis, and from our castle bid defiance to all foes."

The squire fell into his seat again.

"There is one way which ends all, and well ends it," continued the young man, with the calmness of incipient madness; "I have another pistol—if the water has not wetted the powder."

And he drew it from his belt. The squire wrested it, with a groan, from his hand.

"Well, sir—you are right. I feel that this is the act of a coward. I have no intention of committing suicide:—what remains?"

"To the continent!—Oh, you can go to Europe."

"I'm tired of it, sir."

"But Virginia—you cannot remain in Virginia."

"True."

"The paper, there!—see what vessel sails, and when. Perhaps one goes from York, or Norfolk, this very week."

And the squire seized the paper: the first words he read, were:

"On Saturday, the 21st, will sail from the port of York, for Amsterdam, *via* Liverpool, the bark CHARMING SALLY, Capt. Fellowes—"

"That is to-morrow! Oh, go in this vessel!" cried the agitated squire, losing all his pride, and melting at the sight of the pale and disfigured features of his son.

"Well, sir—that will suit me as well as any thing else."

"I will send off a servant to engage your passage in the

ship, instantly—Cato will understand :—he is as secret as night : instantly ! "

And the squire hastened out.

Mr. Effingham sat down again with the same stony calmness :—that calmness would not have pleased a physician. He was in that state of despair which deadens the nerves.

Suddenly a light step came down the stairs—Kate entered—saw him—ran to him, and with a face radiant with joy, threw her arms round his neck, and pressed her cheek to his own. Then, as a sequel to all this, she burst out crying, from pure delight.

Mr. Effingham removed the arms, and rose :—she shrunk back, frightened at his expression—it was terrible.

" Oh, cousin, Champ ! " she cried, " you won't drive me from you ! "

He was silent.

" Oh ! you are not angry at me, for ——, oh ! you make me feel so badly ! "

And she sobbed.

" I cannot talk to you now—I cannot kiss you—I am not angry with you—" he said.

And muttering to himself, he went his way to the chamber, which he had occupied before leaving the hall, and disappeared at the turn of the great staircase from Kate's eyes. The child sat down, and wept piteously.

The day drew on, and still the young man remained in his chamber. Miss Alethea passed in and out, making preparations for him, and her face was observed to be bathed in tears. The squire shut himself up in his library, and only once came out to ascend to Mr. Effingham's chamber.

About noon a visitor in a military dress, and with a countenance convulsed with passion, came to the Hall, and was closeted for an hour with the old man in the library, from which were heard high voices, "parbleus ! " and exclamations. Finally the voices moderated, and the visitor, still much moved, but more calm, came out and rode away.

The squire went to the young man's room, and told him that the brother of Charles Waters—Captain Ralph Waters, had just come and informed him, that his brother was not dead—though he was despaired of—and the young woman scarcely at all injured. A flush greeted this information then a sombre frown.

"Was there no challenge left for me," he asked.

"By Captain Waters?"

"Yes, sir."

"None"

And the squire, to avoid further embarrassing questions, went out. The Captain had come to take Mr. Effingham's life in return for his brother's—simply and purely—and he would have "left a challenge," had the squire not made him change his mind. How this was effected must remain a mystery.

The night drew on cold and gloomy, and Mr. Effingham was to set out for York soon after midnight. He and the squire sat up talking, for neither could sleep. No persons were present but themselves, and we know nothing of that conversation.

About two o'clock, when a chill wind had arisen and moaned round the gables, Cato came and reported the horses ready, and took his master's baggage.

Mr. Effingham then wrapped himself in his cloak; buckled on a new sword, calmly, and went out.

As he entered the passage he was approached by a small figure clad in white. This was Kate, who was in her night-clothes, and who pressed with her bare feet the chill polished oak of the floor.

"Oh, cousin Champ!" she sobbed, "please don't go without kissing me! They made me go to bed, but I couldn't sleep, for you were going. Oh, don't go away feeling angry with me. Please kiss me!"

The hard heart was overcome: he stooped down and took the child in his arms, and pressing her to his breast, two large bitter tears rolled down his pale thin cheeks. Then hastily kissing her, he again wrapped his cloak around him and passed on.

In fifteen minutes he was in the saddle.

The wild wandering wind sobbed mournfully around the lofty gables and through the pines.

This was the sound which greeted Mr. Effingham as he turned his back upon the Hall, and rode forth into the cold, gloomy night.

CHAPTER LVIII.

THE AUTHOR OF THE MS. SPEAKS.

"Here let us pause," says the author of the manuscript from which these scenes are taken, "and looking back on the current of events which we have seen flow on through light and shadow, endeavor to extract briefly their significance.

"In the history of my respected ancestor, Champ Effingham, Esq., I think I discern something which reminds me of an Eastern fable I have met with. The enemy of Humanity, the tale relates, came and found the first man sleeping calmly under the palms of paradise: and gazing long at him, endeavoured to find some weak point of attack. But the lordly face of the sleeper made him groan with rage and disappointment. He saw the brows made to conceive pure and noble thoughts—the chiselled lips shaped to express those thoughts, and utter prayer. He saw the strong arm, with its iron muscles, moulded wondrously to strike and overthrow wrong, should wrong trench upon the fair fields it cultivated:—all repelled the enemy. At last he observed the movement of the sleeper's heart, and kneeling down, tapped upon it with his finger. It sounded hollow, and the enemy smiled, as only fiends smile.

"'Here is a cavity!' he muttered; 'I will fill it with passions!'

"And, leaving the sleeper writhing in his slumbers, the enemy of souls disappeared.

"My worthy ancestor, Mr. Effingham, seems to have afforded proof that this fable is not wholly fanciful. His passions were so strong that he was led by them to the commission of actions which he often regarded with wondering disgust in after years:—that infatuated young man whose acts he recollected, scarcely seemed to be himself. His mad passion for the young girl had changed his whole character. Chivalrous and noble, it made him persecute a woman, and exhaust the depths of bitterness and weakness. Sweet-tempered and affectionate, under all his languid and satirical indifference, if the phrase may be used, his character was changed by that infatuation into one of sour and bitter scoffing and mocking sarcasm. Careless of the prejudices of rank, and disposed to treat all men with cordiality and kindness, it made him taunt with low birth the rival who supplanted him. Venerating his father, it led him to write to that father a letter of cold defiance—and lastly, it made him commit an action which madness alone excuses—the forcible abduction of an unoffending girl:—and his wild, turbulent, mad career, was wound up by an attempt to take the life of a man whose only crime was love for that woman who had driven him mad.

"Mr. Effingham was a true descendant of the man tempted by the fiend, and filled with passion.

"But then we may observe in this career equal proof of what Mr. Charles Waters had said to the man in the red cloak—that the human heart is not radically false and hateful, but suffers for the crimes it is led by passion to commit, cruelly; and ever strives to disentangle itself from the meshes of that fiery net which is bound around it by fate.

"In the midst of all his delinquency—when he was persecuting the young woman—defying society and his family, uttering unworthy and insulting words to his rival—carrying off Beatrice—striking at the heart of her defender:—all this time, remorse and sombre rage with himself burned in his agitated heart like fire. We have traced some of the scenes in his lonely chamber, in which these stormy emotions were bared to his own consciousness, even in words—and we have seen on one occasion, that the fury of his suffering and remorse nearly led him to self-destruction. We have seen how on that occasion he caught the child to his heart, and called her his guardian angel and blessed her:—at that moment his good impulses were strong, and had not the words of his friend revived the slumbering passion in his heart, many of the events herein narrated would never have occurred.

"Even in the midst of his most furious rages—when he tried to persuade himself that he was the victim of cruel injustice and unjustifiable scorn, his heart still whispered to him that he was the wrong-doer; and in that night and day after the river-fight, his remorse grew to a climax. We have seen how he was touched by the affection of an animal, how he mingled his tears with those of the child when she bade him farewell. Those tears were not unmanly ones, and are pleasanter to think of now, to me at least, than all his fearless acts, his scornful defiances cast in the teeth of the universe.

"I have not space to speak further of those other personages who were grouped around my ancestor, the central figure of them all, and attracting to his splendid and fiery graces, his wild passions, every eye: Beatrice—pure and lovely creature! whose portrait I have vainly striven to delineate, must be passed by: and Charles Waters, too; the pure thinker. In after pages of this history I shall endeavour to develop further those feelings which, so much more than mere events, enter into the lives of my personages."

CHAPTER LIX.

TWO SCENES ON A WINTER NIGHT.

The writer, after these moral reflections, which we have transcribed for the benefit of our readers, goes on to narrate how, after the fight upon the river, the two watermen leaped into the "Nancy," and without exchanging compliments, excuses, or regrets, ran off with that craft; even Junks with a bad wound in his arm, rowing as if the officers of the law were already on his track:—further, he goes on to tell how Charles Waters, by his own request, was borne to his father's: —how Beatrice, stanching her bleeding arm, would not leave him:—how the old man wept and sobbed as he met his dying son:—how the Chevalier La Rivière, otherwise Captain Ralph Waters, uttered furious "morbleus!" and threats, and tore his moustache:—and how, day by day, nursed by the tender hand of Beatrice, the young man's wound in the shoulder-blade grew gradually better, and his deadly pallor changed more and more to the hue of health: —all this is related by the worthy writer of the MS., at considerable length.

It is not necessary to dwell upon these scenes: the reader, no doubt, will be able to understand all that is necessary without the aid of the chronicler. Let us pass over a month, and on a winter night enter the plain and simple, but cheerful and comfortable mansion of the old fisherman, and see what the inmates are engaged in.

The apartment is the one which we have already entered several times, and a cheerful fire is burning in the wide, rude fireplace. Two stones serve the purpose of andirons, and a hook stands out prominently from the great cross-beam. The light of the fire fills the room, bathing in its full rich flood of warmth and brightness the nets, the fishing rods, the brown rafters overhead with their strings of onions and bacon flitches; and these humble objects take a glory from the brilliant light, and seem to laugh and move about as the flame rises and falls, in a sort of ecstasy.

In one corner of the great chimney sits old John Waters with his venerable gray head bent down, his face bright with its habitual smile of simple good-nature and kindliness. The old man occupies the chair of state, which is woven into a species of basket-work and softly cushioned—the work of Charles. He wears his ordinary dress of fustian; his stockings are of woollen, and his huge shoes are decorated with huge buckles. His gray hair is tied in a queue behind, and in his hard, bony hand the old man holds a corn-cob pipe, which he replenishes from time to time by inserting his fingers into the ample pocket of his long waistcoat, and then thrusting the bowl into the ashes, from which it reappears crowned with a burning coal, and sending up clouds of fragrant smoke.

Opposite, and crouching on his stool, sits Lanky, the cart-boy, who seems to be eternally protesting against something, for he shakes his head from north-east to south-west incessantly, and gazes into the fire with a profundity which would have delighted Newton. Lanky is clad in a pair of ornamental woollen stockings, and has enormous feet, which occasionally are stretched out toward the blaze, then withdrawn, as the warmth penetrates too feelingly into his shins:—his short clothes are of leather, and are much soiled—his waistcoat is tattered and torn, and the pockets are stuffed with whip-lashes, nails, and iron rings, apparently the debris of some defunct harness;—his coat has lost a portion of the skirt. Lanky has been working all day—has been with the cart of fish and vegetables to Williamsburg; and now, like an honest fellow with an excellent conscience, takes his ease on his stool, and munches when the hunger fit seizes him, his bread and bacon, and, as we have said, carries on that silent protest against something or somebody, with his head, which closely resembles a pine knot.

Immediately in front of the cheerful fire, and seated close to the rude pine table, Townes, the boatman, and the Chevalier La Rivière—or, dropping this nom-de-guerre, Captain Ralph Waters—occupying themselves with a sheet of paper, lying on the rough board, on which the Captain has traced a diagram, the lines of which are something less than an inch in breadth. Townes is clad in his usual dress, half sailor, half farmer, whole boatman. The Captain is resplendent in the fine military suit which we have seen Mr. Effingham dressed in, and his long sword lies by him on a settee. His moustaches are longer and blacker than ever; his eye more laughing, his voice louder, his "parbleus!" more emphatic, as he explains the diagram of the battle of Rosbach to the boatman.

"Faith! there it is!" says the Captain, twirling his moustache, and making a dig at the paper with his broad-nibbed goosequill, "there is the river Saal—these dots here represent Marshal Soubise's forces, opposite the head-quarters of the great Frederic; and here, at this line, Prince Hildbourghausen had posted himself."

"Hill—who?" asks Townes, scratching his head, "talk it out plainer, Captain."

"Hildbourghausen!" says the soldier, laughing; "faith! that is nothing to some of the jaw-breakers I have been compelled, for my sins, to pronounce, *mon ami!*"

"Hell—bug—housen," says the boatman, in a low, meditative tone, "now I've got it!"

"Well, here was the river—we crossed on the 5th of November, all colors flying—a glorious day, and a glorious set of devils to fight it out—though I say it. I can't go over the battle—but fifty thousand mounseers bit the dust, or were taken:—see, here was my share."

And opening his coat, the soldier showed a deep scar on his breast.

"A bayonet did it—but I ran the fellow through for it,

and the great Frederic made me a captain. What a beast he was !—And morbleu ! what a leader ! "

" Well, now, seems to me," says Townes, " them things don't pay. Is scars all you get in the wars, Captain Ralph ? "

" No, I'm indifferent rich."

" Really, now."

" Yes."

" How did you get the pistoles together ? "

" They were not pistoles, *mon ami*—they were florins and guilders," says the Captain, with a strange, wistful smile, which is a pleasant sight to look upon.

" Guilders ?—I have seen some of that coin," says old John Waters, cheerfully, " come tell us, my son, something more of your doin's than you have done."

The Captain pauses for a moment, and passes his hand over his eyes dreamily: then he raises his fine head, and says, manfully :

" Very well, *bon père:* ten words, more or less, will do that. You know that when I was eighteen, and had an indifferent smooth face, I ran away—half with your knowledge, half without—"

" You were not a bad son," says the old man, pleasantly.

" No, I believe not. Well, I got to Europe, found that I must starve or enlist, and having a natural turn for eating heartily, and an intense aversion to starving, at once accepted his gracious and serene majesty's shilling. We were shipped at once to the Continent, and under the Great Frederic, the Protestant champion, as we called him, fought like a parcel of honest English dogs, every time we could meet with the mounseers, who were equally the enemies of Prussia and England.

" Very well, I knocked about—got a wound at Rosbach, also my Captaincy—had a public compliment paid me after Lissa—a devil of a fight, comrade !—and at Glatz had the misfortune to be taken prisoner, as I was about to run my hanger through a fellow all bedizened with lace—a Colonel, at the very least. I mention the great pitched battles—the skirmishes, countermarches, night-encounters, here, there, every where, are understood. Well, I was taken after Glatz —Glatz was in '59, mark you—to a little town in the interior, where a fort was held by the troops of his Gracious Majesty, the King of France—in the Rhine-land. There I became no longer a bachelor."

With which words, the wistful expression again passed over the soldier's face.

"She was a soft, bright-eyed girl—I don't know how I ever came to love her," he murmured; "she was a good wife to me, and having sold my commission at her earnest request, I lived in that little town for two whole years—or thereabouts. She was a tender heart—my poor Katrina."

And the Captain frowns, to conceal his emotion.

"Married, my son—you ain't a-tellin' me you were married?" says the old man.

"Yes, yes," says the soldier, raising his martial face with a sigh. "I married and lost my wife—all within two short years."

There is a silence.

"Poor thing: she loved me devotedly, and left her whole fortune to me. What did I want with it, when she was gone?—well, well, the money amounted to some fifteen or twenty thousand pounds English coin, and that is what I have."

"Twenty thousand pounds!" ejaculates Townes, with astonishment.

"Yes, yes," adds the soldier, "but in spite of the fine fortune—a great fortune for a poor soldier, her death nearly unmanned me! She was a good girl!"

And with dreamy eyes the Captain twirls his moustache, and sighs. His auditors are silent.

"After that," he continues, "I found myself no longer fit for peace—the void in my heart, friends, called for war. How could I live there, looking on all those objects she had looked at with me? No, no! I could not, and I buckled on my sword again. Ah, *mon ami!* ah, *bon père! vous ne savez*—bah! English is the best! Well, well! I went back again to the camp, did my duty, they said—got some more wounds—and slowly my good spirits came back to me!—She was a good wife!—she is in heaven!—"

"And you came away when the war ended, Captain?" says Townes, "for I hearn tell somethin' 'bout the peace o' Fontybull!"

"Fontainbleau, *mon ami*—yes, I threw up my commission then—turned my back on camps, and as my heart began to grow strong again, it turned toward old Virginia here. I got into the first ship, leaving my gold in London there—and came over. The sea voyage set me up again—that, with the fighting, and here I am as fresh and hearty as a lion."

With which words the Captain looks with great affection at old Waters, and seeing that Lanky is nodding. stirs that gentleman up with his foot. Lanky starts and looks around in utter and profound astonishment—at which comical expression the boatman laughs, and Captain Ralph goes on with his adventures.

Let us now pass through the door directly in the rear of the astonished Lanky, and look around us. The apartment is wholly different from the one which we have just left: it is smaller and neater. The fireplace is surmounted by a tall mantel-piece, upon which are ranged a number of old volumes, and in the recess to the right, some neatly-constructed shelves are covered with more books, and a great number of papers—chiefly old copies of the "Virginia Gazette." Immediately beneath this bookcase, if we may call it such, stands a small table covered with sheets of paper, some of which have been written upon, while others contain geometrical diagrams. A little window, with very small panes of thick, bluish glass, opens on the river, sleeping in the chill winter moon. In one corner of the room, a low narrow bed is seen—in the corner opposite, a partition juts out, indicating that a narrow staircase leads from without, to the two small rooms above.

Before the fire, which sings and murmurs cheerfully, are seated Charles Waters, and on another, but lower chair, Beatrice. He is very pale, and his cheeks are thinner than their wont; but his clear eye is as full as ever of frank truth; his sad smile as sweet.

Beatrice is radiant with that tender and childlike beauty which characterizes her; and as she sews and talks in a low tone, when he is not reading to her, she raises her large melting eyes to his face, with a look exquisitely soft and loving. Both are clad very simply.

There is for a time silence in the small cheerful room, which, with its homespun carpet, and rude shelves and ruder rafters, is yet extremely neat and cheerful, and home-like. The voices of the interlocutors in the next room come to them indistinctly.

The words, " She was a good wife ! " however, are heard plainly: and Beatrice raises her tender eyes.

He smiles faintly.

" Ralph is telling some of his adventures," he says, " but they cannot be more singular than those which we have passed through."

And his eye dwells with great tenderness on the gentle, girlish face.

" Oh ! how strange—yes, how very strange ! "—she murmurs, gazing into the fire : " it seems to me almost like a dream."

" It is a bright reality, which has restored you to us," he replies, taking the little hand.

" Yes—yes."

And her head droops, quietly. The round rosy neck is half illuminated, half shadowed, by the fitful firelight; and the curls seem to nestle closer : the face is plain, and a dewy glance trembles from the eyes.

" After so many wanderings, so many singular experiences, such rude contact with the world, and all sorts of people—ah ! to see you here at last, it is strange indeed."

" Yes—yes—but he was very kind to me : " she murmurs.

" He was a kind-hearted man, and loved you, Beatrice : I do not know whether he made any exertion or not to find us and restore you—and I do not attach very great blame to him. Ah ! had I found you, I should have hesitated long before parting with you."

And the thin hand plays gently with her own.

" He was very kind to me," she repeats, in a low tone, " and that last interview with him in this room was very trying. You remember, Charles, how bitterly he complained, at first, that I would not return to Europe with him—"

" You could not."

" No, I could not ! and yet I felt very deeply the separation: I told him so, you know, and thanked him for all his fondness and kindness, to poor Beatrice Hallam, his daughter for so long:—and so you know he relented, and shed some tears, and took me in his arms, and said he did not blame me—that I was right—that blood was the strongest, after all:—and so he blessed me and kissed me, and now he is far away on the sea, sailing for the old world."

With which words Beatrice droops lower, her hair covers her face, she weeps in silence.

He looks at her with inexpressible affection, and caresses with his pale hand the tender head. She raises her face, and he sees the tears.

"Weeping, dear!" he says.

"I cannot help crying a little, thinking of him," she murmurs.

"But, they are not bitter tears."

"Oh, no!"

"You do not regret your determination?"

"Oh, no—no!"

And she looks at him with so much love, that his heart throbs, and his pale cheek is for a moment reddened, as if the flush of some golden autumn sunset bathed it.

"You do not complain of having to leave all that brilliant life?" he says.

"I thank God, that I was permitted to abandon it."

"For our poor house, here—ah, it is very poor."

"But I have you—and uncle—and— "

The weak voice gives way.

"And we have you—" he murmurs, holding out his arms with an expression of pride and joy, which illuminates his countenance like a glory.

In a moment she is in his arms—pressed to his breast, sobbing and weeping, and nestling close to his bosom. She will be his dear wife, she says—she has promised that she will forget all for him in future—never grieve—she is not grieving now, her tears are tears of joy, she feels that God has been very good to her, and she is happy.

And the red firelight lingers lovingly upon them, heart to heart, cheek pressed to cheek: the moonlight struggles to come in and share their joy:—the room is still and holy. And from the adjoining room, come cheerful voices soon, and merry laughter, and the loud camp-expletives of Captain Ralph. Then the voices moderate, the soldier's tone is lower, he has gone back to his happy days: and as they listen, the gentle head resting confidingly on his bosom, those low words are heard again, and echo in their hearts:

"Yes, comrade—a good wife!"

END OF VOL. I.

THE VIRGINIA COMEDIANS.

BOOK II.

CHAPTER I.

HOW CAPTAIN WATERS THREATENED LANKY WITH THE BASTINADO IF HE SIGHED.

SINCE the events we have related, more than a year has passed.

March, 1765, has come.

We cannot pause here to narrate those important political events, which marked the period between the winter of 1763 and the spring of 1765: but in the course of our history, the results of those events will unfold themselves and rise to view, as the coral reef long growing beneath the ocean and unseen, raises at last its dangerous wall above the waves—events which made more noise than breakers: upon which lordlier ships were shattered, than ever strewed the fatal coasts of Madagascar.

In place of regaling the reader with an historical disquisition, we shall proceed to relate the adventures which befell the personages of our narrative, after the violent denouement in which, as in a huge vortex, so many of the dramatis personæ were swallowed up.

March has come again into the world, as that merry month promises to come in all future times·—with wind, and rainy gusts, and chill moonshiny nights, and flowers peeping from the sod looking for April, and their close-friend the gentle May. The earth smiles again, and begins to forget the snow and ice :—the days are growing warm again, but fires are still far from uncomfortable. So at least thought a military gentleman, who warmed his hands listlessly by a cheerful blaze, on the day at which we have now arrived.

Captain Ralph Waters sits in that room, of the old fisher man's mansion, which listened in the winter of '63, to the narrative of his adventures. The room is very little changed —the Captain scarcely more. He is as handsome and martial-looking as ever—his moustache is as long and as black —his face as open and careless—his sword clatters as gayly, and his spurs jingle as serenely as before. Perhaps it is not exactly correct in us to say, that his face is as careless as ever :—for, though there is no absolute *care* upon the martial countenance, there is a decided expression of ennui.

The worthy soldier stretches out his legs, draws a long breath from the bottom of his stalwart chest—and yawns portentously: he then twirls his moustache, endeavoring to give it the warlike and gallant curl toward the eye, but the moustache rebels, as if it were weary, like its master, and persists in curling in the opposite direction.

The Captain, after several attempts to coerce the rebellious ornament, submits and yawns again.

"The fact is," he says, addressing his hat and cloak which—hanging on a nail,—bear no bad resemblance to an exceedingly thin gentleman, walking on the air,—"the fact is," says the Captain sighing, "I am going to pieces here, like a ship cast upon the shore and falling away, timber after timber. My good spirits are leaving me, parbleu! —I am dying of ennui."

And having made this communication to the hat and cloak, he relapses into silence for a moment.

"I really think that I will set out, and go and find *mon bon père*, and Charley, and Beatrice, in their mountain home. I have not seen them, hilf himmel! since last fall: —they talk about something they call 'Springs,' up there, and its benefiting Beatrice's cold! All nonsense! I assert that there is nothing in them, for they did me no good, whatsoever!"

And having thus floored his imaginary opponent in debate, and proved that the medicinal baths were folly, the soldier again paused.

"I wonder where that farcical fellow Lanky is," continues the Captain, again attacking his moustache, "he makes me die a-laughing, with his opinions upon love and all that. I fancy, however, that Miss Smith has not been enlightened on her admirer's real sentiments yet."

And the Captain smiles.

"Heigho!" he adds, again yawning, "what the devil is come to me! I am expiring of ennui—I am becoming fat, I really believe—I have no longer any muscles!"

And to test the reality of his fears, the Captain draws his hanger, and makes half a dozen furious lunges at the cloak, which suffers considerably.

"I'm as strong as ever," he adds, with a sigh, "I must go and find somebody to quarrel with, or *ventre du pape!* I shall die."

At the same moment Lanky Lugg enters—clad nearly as we had the pleasure of seeing him on a former occasion, and wiping his face with an exceedingly dirty sleeve. Lanky's feet are perhaps larger than ever, his hands more like reaping hooks, his head more like a pine knot, than ever it has been at any previous time. But there are some changes observable in the gentleman. His stockings are more ornamental than before, his clothes less ragged, his gait more proud and impressive. When he bows his head from northeast to south-west, he presents the appearance of a mandarin figure fillipped by the finger of a child.

As Lanky enters, the Captain makes a terrific lunge at him, the sword's point only stopping within an inch of his breast:—at which horrible circumstance, Lanky starts back in profound terror, and looks at his master with astonished eyes.

The Captain bursts into a laugh.

"Don't be afraid, *mon garçon!*" he says, "I am only taking a little exercise."

But the explanation does not satisfy Lanky, who keeps at a safe and respectful distance, scratching his head.

"Lanky," says the Captain, "I am dying of weariness."

Lanky is unimpressed.

"Come, give me a little advice, you rascal! Oh! you are afraid of my toasting iron, are you? Well, here it goes."

And the Captain throws away the sword, which falls with a tremendous clatter upon the table. This reassures his companion, and obedient to his master's sign, he sits down in the chimney corner.

"I am getting tired of life, Lanky," resumes the Captain, "existence, parbleu! seems to me not worth having, so to speak. Come, give me your views. What do you think?"

"I never thinks about nothin', Cap'n," says Lanky; "leastways—"

"Never think!"

"I does sometimes—yes, I does," adds Lanky, correcting himself.

"What do you think of? Of Donsy Smith, I'll wager."

Lanky draws himself up like an emperor.

"I ain't seen that young 'ooman lately, Cap'n," he says.

"Have you quarrelled?"

"No, Cap'n."

"How then?"

"Parted."

And Lanky groans.

"Lanky, you are getting into bad spirits," says the Captain, "I shall not permit that, *Diable!* if we are both down, what will become of us?"

Lanky nods his head, with a sigh.

"Don't sigh, you rascal—I will not allow it: no retainer of mine shall sigh on pain of the bastinado."

Lanky apparently does not understand this rhetorical paraphrase.

"Take a slice of bacon, and a mug of beer, and get your spirits again," continues the Captain.

Lanky assents to this, and is soon munching and drinking.

"Now advise me, animal!" says the Captain, "egad! I am perfectly ennuyé," and the soldier yawns.

"S'pose you fall in love, Cap'n," says Lanky, with his mouth full.

The Captain greets this suggestion with a laugh.

"I cannot," he replies.

"You ain't tried."

"Have you?"

"Yes, sur."

"And successfully?"

"Yes, Cap'n."

"Miss Smith, eh?"

"Miss Smith and me, is 'most quit—" says Lanky, wofully.

"But she was the object of your affections?"

Lanky nods, wofully.

"I think then, I shall follow your advice," says his master, "and as you are a man of taste, I will adopt your own sweetheart."

Lanky starts.

"Rather a pretty girl, too," says the Captain, caressing the midnight fringe upon his upper lip.

"Oh, Cap'n!" Lanky observes, overcome with horror.

The soldier bursts into laughter.

"Well, well!" he says, "don't fear: we shall not probably be rivals—but don't be too well assured. Let us now dismiss the subject, and on this fine March morning, lay out some plan for amusement."

Lanky reflects.

"There's the races sir, near Jeamston," he says soon.

"But they're a month or so off. Now in a month I shall die, at the present rate. Something else, *parbleu! mon ami!*"

"S'pose you take a ride, Cap'n: I never see a day better for't."

The Captain yawns.

"Well," he says, "I believe I shall follow your advice; go and get the Arab."

Lanky rises obediently.

"No: the roan," says the Captain.

"He's cast a shoe, and that's a fact, Cap'n."

"Diable! then the Arabian—Selim, as the heathen dog I bought him of calls him."

Lanky goes out, and the Captain yawns uninterruptedly until he returns.

"Ready, sir," says Mr. Lugg.

The Captain then buckles on his sword, issues forth and mounts the slim-legged animal, who whinnies at his approach. He throws the bridle on his neck, and trusts to Providence to direct him. Lanky meanwhile resumes his meat and beer, and saws imaginary obstacles with the stereotyped north-east and south-west movement of his visage.

Before following the soldier on his morning ride, let us return for a moment to those personages who no longer light up the rude mansion with their pleasant faces as of old—and whose whereabouts we have heard Captain Waters very briefly allude to in his muttered soliloquy.

We have seen how Hallam and his "Company of Virginia Comedians," had, like birds of passage, disappeared from Virginia, after gathering in those "sweet fields"—to carry out the simile—as much golden grain as could be found therein: and the whispered words of Beatrice, as she sobbed and poured out her tender regrets to Charles Waters, have put the reader in possession of the particulars of that last interview between herself and her pseudo father.

We may understand readily how the young girl's reluctant and half-formed desperate resolution to remain with Hallam, had melted before the tender caresses of the kind old man, her uncle—the more than tender looks and words of him whom she had loved so dearly, and yet given up with a bursting heart, at the call of inexorable duty. Thus she had remained—and soon after the scene upon the river, the company had taken their departure, and were no more seen in those borders—not any more, for ever.

Hallam, Shylock, Shallow, Mr. Effingham—all these had passed from Beatrice's horizon, leaving it bright and calm: and in the fresh sunshine now she saw alone the figures of her kind uncle, and her tender Charles, and jovial honest Captain Ralph, and Townes, and Lanky—all smiling on her, full of love for her. Thus the poor dove, beaten so long by storms, and tossed about from land to land; exposed every where to persecutions, similar to those under which we have seen her labor; thus Beatrice found her life all at once changed: her heart suddenly filled with light and joy. God had heard the prayers she had uttered, and the harbor was now reached: henceforth she was safe from storms.

Her objections were now all removed, and Charles Waters become her husband: and to him, too, life opened and grew brilliant with an untold splendor: all his sadness passed—his face was bright and joyous—she was beside him, loved so long, denied to him so long, now all his own.

The spring following the autumn and winter, whose events we have related, passed away, and nothing clouded the unalloyed happiness of the household, but a slight cough which Beatrice had caught, she said, far back as her first arrival in Virginia, that day when she fell into the water from the "Nancy."

With the quick apprehension of a lover, Charles Waters magnified this slight indisposition, and determined to go and take up his residence for a time near one of the newly discovered mineral springs, beyond the mountains. Beatrice resisted this proposal at first, and laughed at his apprehensions—and indeed her cough was the least possible, and gave her no pain at all. She saw, however, that if she persisted in her opposition he would be pained, and so she assented; and ere long Charles and herself, and old John Waters, who would not leave her, his new-found daughter and little pet, all went away and took up their sojourn in the far mountain land, leaving the unfortunate Captain Ralph to amuse himself with Lanky in the paternal mansion.

Captain Ralph had, upon reflection, determined to remain; having become accustomed to jovial society, he said, those backwoods would kill him—spite of having the *bon père*, Charley, and that "Marguerite des Marguerites"—Beatrice, to narrate his adventures to. Mr. Jack Hamilton and himself had become great friends, and this had for a time diverted the active soldier's ennui; but Hamilton could not fill up all his time; and the Captain was beginning to spend many weary hours, such as we have seen him yawning through, when our story again opened.

About once a month the lazy and leisurely post brought him letters from the far mountains; and carried back huge epistles from the Captain in return. In these epistles the soldier narrated many things, not even disdaining to detail the progress of Lanky Lugg's love affair, which we shall see something of in the course of our narrative. Beatrice and the rest always laughed heartily at these accounts; and their letters to the soldier were full of mirth, and tenderness, and joy; especially those of the young girl, who experienced a species of wistful sadness, whenever she wrote the name of her dead father, "Ralph Waters."

We shall now leave them, happy, joyous, in their far mountain home, and proceed to the history of other personages of the drama.

CHAPTER II.

AN ADVENTURE.

Let us follow the Captain.

Mounted on his beautiful steed, he set forward, utterly careless whither his steps tended—leaving philosophically to the intelligent animal this portion of the matter. The horse took the road toward the mountains, as if he knew where his master's heart was.

"Very well," said the Captain, "that suits me, Monsieur Selim, perfectly well. If you put forth that speed of yours, you will reach them in a day, or less!—Strange," continued the soldier, "how that girl has won upon me! By heaven, she's an angel—but faith! I can't go so far to-day—I am intensely lazy. What a day to be lazy in, too! It's extravagant."

And the soldier looked admiringly at the trees just putting forth their tender leaves, the grass just beginning to peep up and lie a verdant background, for a thousand flowers; the little streams dancing along joyously in the gay sunlight. He listened, with pleasure, to the small birds which chirruped gayly, and plumed their wings in the fresh bracing wind of March, and went rising and falling on the air billows, predicting summer and warmth. All pleased him. On the day before there had been quite a heavy fall of rain, and all the streams were swollen, and overflowed their banks. The Captain had more than one of these to cross in his path, but seemed to attach very little importance to them. He allowed the water to splash his boots with great indifference, and rode on carelessly, humming a merry song all about Marshal Soubise and the great Frederic. The soldier's voice was excellent, and he gave the "Tra la! tra la!" with great force and spirit—completely to his own satisfaction, indeed.

He came thus, singing merrily, and looking around him, with the roving and curious eye of the partisan, to one of those hollows in the hills, such as are found frequently in all portions of Virginia. The road which had for a mile or two traversed a species of wooded upland, now descended abruptly into the gorge, and mounted the thickly firred declivity beyond. Through the gorge ran a deep stream, which, swollen by the rain, had overflowed its banks, and now rushed on under swaying pine boughs, with a merry brawl, which sounded far from unpleasantly. The sunshine gilded the rushing stream, the bold hill beyond, the thick firs, and rude masses of rock: and so picturesque was the scene, that Captain Ralph paused a moment, and looked at it admiringly.

His fit of admiration soon subsided, however, and touching his horse lightly, he passed down the steep road, having resumed his song with new spirit. Selim hesitated a moment, as he was about to place his delicate hoof in the water.

"Tra la! tra la!" came from the soldier's lungs lustily, and apparently satisfied that this signified "go on!" the beautiful animal plunged into the water. In an instant his back was covered, and Captain Ralph Waters experienced a disagreeable sensation about the lower part of his person.

"Morbleu! we are in for it!" he cried, drawing up his knees, despairingly.

Selim snorted, and began to swim.

"Right!" cried the soldier; "Go on, comrade! What is a trifling wetting!"

And in defiance of the obstacle, the Captain began again, more lustily than before, to troll his ditty. Selim swam vigorously; dashed the water from his glowing chest, and by the time his master had arrived at the chorus of his song, reached the opposite bank.

He emerged from the water like a statue of glittering ebony, and the soldier, with a careless shake of his clothes, was about to proceed onward, when suddenly his attention was attracted to the opposite declivity, which, as we have said, was singularly steep and rugged.

Down this road there now came, at full speed, a chariot drawn by four spirited horses, who had plainly run away, for the coachman in vain endeavored to check them, by vigorously tightening the reins, and uttering violent cries.

The animals, with their rosetted heads fixed obstinately sidewise, took no notice of these signs, and swept onward at a gallop down the declivity toward the stream, dragging the huge chariot like a mere nutshell, rudely over the stones. At every bound the framework cracked, at every stone the unwieldly vehicle rumbled and groaned.

"Parbleu! here will be a smash!" cried the Captain, as the animals rushed towards him; "in an instant they will be buried in that stream!"

At the same moment, the head of a gentleman emerged from the door, and over his shoulders were seen the affrighted faces of two young girls.

"Women, *morbleu!*" cried the soldier; "to the rescue!"

And as the furious animals rushed headlong toward the stream, he caught, with a powerful hand, the bridle of the leader next to him, and exerting all his strength, made him swerve.

Selim reared and fell upon his haunches, as the hot mouth of the animal struck his neck, and the Captain, clinging like a vice to the rein he had grasped, was drawn half from his saddle. The other leader, checked thus suddenly, reared, and his hoof struck the Captain's arm heavily.

In another instant he would have been hurled, in spite of his great strength and activity, beneath the feet of the animals, when the gentleman whose head he had seen, and the coachman, both came to his assistance, and the coach-horses, still struggling, panting, and furious, were subdued.

The Captain rose erect in his saddle again, and seeing the terrified faces of the ladies at the window of the chariot, took off his hat with his left hand, and made an elegant bow.

"Excuse my rudeness, Mesdemoiselles," he said, "that devil of an animal has nearly broken my right arm, parbleu!"

And the soldier made a wry face, as he tried to move it.

"I owe you a great many thanks, sir," said the gentleman, who had now abandoned the horses to the coachman; "we should have run great risk here—indeed, I may say that you saved our lives."

"Not at all, not all—no thanks," said the Captain; "but faith you would have got a wetting, sir; and I very much fear those charming young ladies would have had their silks and velvets utterly demolished. Upon reflection, I am convinced that so far they owe me thanks."

"Pray let us know then, whom to return them to," said the gentleman, with a courteous smile.

"To Captain Ralph Waters—sometimes called the Chevalier Waters, and the Chevalier La Rivière, by the rascally French, who translate every thing, parbleu!" said the soldier.

"Then, Captain, myself and my daughters are deeply in your debt. My name is Lee, and I insist upon your going with us to my house at Riverhead, to have your bruise dressed."

"My bruise? Oh yes! I had forgotten it: but, excellent sir, I do not attach importance to these trifles. A bruise, more or less? Basta! tis nothing. Still I will gladly go with you, for I am dying of ennui."

"Thanks, sir—now let us see to the means of returning."

The coachman soon reassured Mr. Lee upon this point. The horses were now quiet, he said, and would go along easily. They could not cross Duck creek, as it was too deep, but the horses could be turned, and they could take the cross-road to Riverhead. So the horses were turned, and Mr. Lee, entering the carriage, the huge vehicle rolled up the hill which it had descended so rapidly, and took the direction of Riverhead; Captain Ralph Waters following composedly by the window, and when not exchanging compliments with the ladies, continuing to hum in a low voice, his "Tra la! tra la!"

CHAPTER III.

HOW CAPTAIN RALPH INFORMED MISS HENRIETTA LEE THAT WAR WAS THE NATURAL RELATION OF THE SEXES.

An hour's ride brought thom to Riverhead, and the chariot rolled around thc gravelled circle, and stopped before the large portico.

The old mansion looked much the same as it did on that day, when in company with Mr. Champ Effingham, we first entered its wide hall; and the soft leaves of spring began to rustle around the gables, and throw their delicate and restless shadows on the ancient walls. On that day, when Beatrice, full of grief and mortification, had entered the house, it looked silent and dismal, and the winds of autumn sobbed around it mournfully:—now, times and personages were changed. In place of a sad, weary-looking mansion, there was a pleasant, cheerful one:—in place of a poor wounded heart, a frail trembling form at the door, there entered under that broad portal, a martial merry stranger, with huge moustache, and jingling spurs and sword, and serene brows and lips, save when the brow was elevated by its appreciation of some odd humor, the lips moved by laughter.

Autumn was gone—merry and laughing spring had come.

They entered. Henrietta and Clare retired to make their toilettes for dinner, and Mr. Lee explained briefly how he had been to visit a neighbor, where he had spent the night—was returning—how the horses took fright at something: how they had been unable to check their fury, or leap out. He wound up with a second expression of grateful thanks.

The Captain refused to receive them, and declared that he was delighted to have met with something to arouse his blood. Then Mr. Lee offered him a dressing-room. No, he did not need it: and in the middle of the conversation the young girls made their re-entrance.

Then came thanks again, which the Captain received as before—and Clare, with a delightful look of kind courtesy in her sad little face, held out her hand. The Captain pressed it with martial and chivalric respect to his lips.

He thought that this ceremony would be repeated immediately with the lily hand of Henrietta: but he wás mistaken. Henrietta's thanks were returned with much more coolness and stateliness than Clare's; and she made no movement indicating an intention to surrender her hand to the soldier. She was clad as usual, with the utmost elegance and richness, and looked like a queen—except that her mischievously sparkling eyes somewhat belied her royal air.

The Captain submitted to this refusal with great good-humor, and looked admiringly at the brilliant countenance. Henrietta gave him back his gaze, and declared afterwards, that she had never met with such an impudent person in all her life before. Perhaps Captain Ralph was conscious of what was passing through the young girl's mind, for he turned away in a moment smiling.

Ten minutes afterwards a servant announced that dinner was ready, and Henrietta hastily grasped her father's arm. The Captain smiled again, as he offered his own to Clare, and said to himself, "Why, she don't like me, parbleu!" And so they entered, and took their places, the Captain making grimaces.

Clare saw the expression of his countenance, and said, suddenly:

"Oh, sir! you gave me the arm which the horse bruised—I am very sorry!"

"Nothing—a mere trifle!" said the Captain, sitting down; "do not give yourself a moment's uneasiness about it, madam. We soldiers are accustomed to these incidents."

"You have seen some service then, sir," said Mr. Lee, as dinner proceeded; "though I might have known that from your appearance simply."

"Yes, yes," said the soldier; "not a little, excellent sir. I was seized with a roving fit when I was a beardless youth, and left home and the bon père—old John Waters, the fisherman down there is my father, and an excellent father, morbleu! See what bad habits I have caught!"

Mr. Lee smiled.

"Is it not shocking, madam," continued the soldier, addressing Henrietta, "that even in the presence of such charming persons as yourself and mademoiselle, here, I should not be able to drop my little peculiarities ? "

" I suppose it is the result of your profession, sir," returned Henrietta, coldly. She had not forgotten the stare yet.

" Certainly, certainly " said the Captain, " undoubtedly ! We poor soldiers cannot be expected to be very polished. We find ourselves whipping out our ' morbleus ' and ' egads,' parbleu !—see there, again ! Really, it is deplorable ! "

And the Captain seemed so much vexed with himself, that Clare could not help smiling.

" Ah, *you* appreciate the soldier's disadvantage, madam," said Captain Ralph, returning Clare's smile.

" Humph ! " said Henrietta, to herself—" that means, I suppose, that I am very unreasonable, and do not."

" Madam—your elder sister, I presume—she looks much older—does not appreciate the said disadvantages, I fear," continued the Captain, " and that is, I think, unreasonable."

Henrietta frowned, and seemed to relish very slightly this verification of her thoughts.

" Nothing could be more natural, Captain Waters," she said, somewhat piqued, " than that you should retain some of the ways of camps. It would be unreasonable, as you have said, to look for any thing else in—"

" A rude soldier. Well, I finish your thoughts, and you are right. We had hard times under his gracious Majesty, the great Frederic of Prussia. *Diable!* blows came as thick as hail, and there was little polish except that on steel caps and halberds, madam ! Do not, however, understand me as complaining. No, we had a glorious time—fighting like devils, drinking, bivouacking, taking towns, chasing the French ; ah ! it was a glorious life—believe me, madam, a thing to stir the blood, and make one happy ! "

With which words, the Captain raised his arm enthusiastically, and in consequence uttered a distinct and unmistakable

" Diable ! "

" Your recollections seem exceedingly vivid, sir," said Henrietta, with a satirical curl of her lip, " take care of your arm ! "

" Excellent advice ! " cried the Captain, laughing, " admirable ! "

"Will you not let me get you something, to dress the bruise, sir?" said Clare, softly, "it is very little to do for you, after exposing yourself to so much danger for us."

"No, no! a thousand thanks, however, my dear Miss Lee," said the soldier, "you really make me regret that I did not break both arms!"

And having uttered this witticism, Captain Waters emptied a huge glass of wine to Clare's health.

"It would be hard for you to suffer such a calamity now, after passing through so many wars," said Mr. Lee, with a smile, as the young ladies rose to leave the table.

"Yes, yes," said the Captain, throwing a last smiling glance upon Henrietta, "yes, Mr. Lee—after so many blood-and-thunder battles, cannonading, charges, and assaults on towns and ports, and every thing of that description—you are right: it would be a *bêtise* to have my arm broken by a horse, *parbleu!*"

"You were about to speak of your campaigns just now, when we were drawn off by a discussion, in regard to camp-manners," Mr. Lee said, smiling.

"My campaigns? Ah! I cannot draw the diagram, as well as I can handle my halberd in the ranks, sir."

"You fought at Rosbach?"

"Yes, excellent sir."

"Were you with the Duke of Cumberland?"

"No, Heaven be thanked. Being nonplussed is bad—but by Marshal D'Etrées!"

And the soldier's moustache curled.

"Lissa, perhaps, was another of your battles," said Mr. Lee, who seemed to be curious on the subject of the Seven Years' War:

The Captain nodded.

"Not Glatz, I hope."

"Yes," said the soldier.

"Really you must have seen a great deal of service, Captain Waters," said the old gentleman. "If it is not too much trouble, would you be good enough to explain the position of the forces at Lissa—the numbers of combatants and other matters. The subject interests me deeply, and you were an eye-witness?"

"Yes, my dear sir—yes: Will I explain, say you? Why certainly."

Mr. Lee bent over, much interested. The Captain poured some drops of wine on the table, and elongated them into the lines of a diagram, with his finger.

"Mark you—our force was only 30,000, that of the enemy close upon 100,000," commenced the Captain; "it was fought on the 5th of December, and this was the position of the battalions: the great Frederic here—there Prince Charles of Lorraine, and General Nadasti. Do you understand?"

"Yes, yes," said Mr. Lee, bending over.

"Well, parbleu! now for the battle."

And the soldier began.

We regret that we cannot follow him, in his stirring and excited narrative—a narrative in which men and actions rose visibly before the auditor, colored by the brilliant and vigorous mind of the soldier. The battle of Lissa, in which the great Frederic surpassed Rosbach, has unfortunately nothing at all to do with our history, and we are compelled to omit the Captain's account of it—an account which Mr. Lee listened to with rapt attention.

"That was it, *parbleu!*" cried the soldier. "Frederic never surpassed it in all his wonderful campaigns—the old Satyr! Imagine a wild boar cool and laughing—there is the man, at Lissa. Well, after that last charge—a perfect hell of guns and troopers, rushing on like a lake of fire suddenly let loose, all was said! The enemy were nothing but a parcel of sheep. We took nearly 30,000 prisoners on the field, and 40,000 more, to say nothing of guns and wagons, at Breslau. *Tonnere!* it was a day which a man remembers all his life, and I hear the drums rolling over Breslau now—as I hear plainly the tumult of that great tremendous battle, roaring, crashing, rising and falling;—I almost smell the blood!"

And the soldier's eyes were illuminated with a brilliant and martial fire, which riveted the gaze of his deeply-interested auditor.

"Ah, sir," said Mr. Lee, "I envy you those experiences—you are very fortunate: how grandly you must have felt after that fight."

"For a time—yes, friend. But it was not the most agreeable sort of life. True, we have wild and splendid adventures, passion, excitement, and delight. But there is some suffering, believe me—yet let us not speak of that. I could relate some of my experiences of that suffering phase—but it is not necessary. Parbleu! I don't regret any thing."

And the two men rose, and betook themselves to the drawing-room.

After an hour's conversation, in which Henrietta preserved the same expression of coldness and pique, the soldier rose to take his leave.

Mr. Lee held out his hand courteously, and said:

"I should esteem it a favor, Captain Waters, if you would occasionally call and see me here. I am an old man, and do not visit much myself: do not stand upon ceremony."

"Ah, mon ami," said the soldier, "you would have some more battles—is it not so?"

"Yes—you have guessed my hobby," replied the old gentleman, smiling: "but I fear you will become weary."

"Not at all. I am fond of going over my adventures, and you know we can always defer the subject, until the fair ladies, here, retire. While they are present, we will discuss the last fashions and *modes de Paris*."

With which the Captain twirls his moustache, and directs an engaging smile toward Henrietta.

"Indeed, sir!" says the queenly young girl, "you must have a very low opinion of our sex."

"How! my dear madam?"

Henrietta feels some resentment, at this easy mode of address, and becomes more indignant than ever, at the Captain's impudence. But she replies:

"The injustice lies in your imagining that we think of nothing but dress, and cannot understand battles."

"Ah, you do *me* injustice, now," says the Captain. "I am so far from thinking your charming sex averse to battles, that I am convinced that war is the normal state of their lives."

"War, sir?"

"To be sure! nothing plainer. Ah, my dear mademoiselle, you cannot deny it! You make war, for ever, on the unfortunate rude sex. Is it not so?"

"I do not, sir."

"Possibly: then you are an exception—I can understand that *you* do not care for us—but nevertheless, madam, war is your sex's natural state. See, the artillery of your eyes—how fatal is it! What fatal, death-dealing glances, you throw. By heaven, it is worse than gunpowder, and many a tall fellow has succumbed. Well, well, I see I am wearying you. I shall now respectfully bid you farewell."

"I hope your arm does not pain you, sir," says Clare, softly.

"Not now, madam—scarcely at all:—'tis a mere trifle—not like the cut I got at Glatz."

"Remember, Captain, that Glatz is promised me," says Mr. Lee, "and I shall give you but a day or so to rest, after fighting Lissa over for me. When shall we expect you?"

"Morbleu! very soon! I assure you that I am dying of weariness down there—the bon père, Charley, and all, are gone—behold me all alone, a sole cavalier, fault of better."

"Why does he not speak in French at once," said Henrietta to herself, satirically.

"Do you speak French, madam?" asked the Captain.

"No, sir," said Henrietta, more piqued than ever, at having her countenance read so easily, "why do you ask?"

"Faith! I saw you smiling at my unfortunately un-English way of talking."

Henrietta made no reply.

"Nothing is more natural, than that you should have acquired the habit, in the Seven Years' War, Captain," said Mr. Lee, "and I promise you that I will listen to your account of Glatz, if it is given entirely in French."

"Well, sir—prepare yourself very soon. As I said, time hangs on my hands, down yonder. Lanky, he is my servant, amuses me sometimes, but I find much time on my hands."

"Your visit will be a pleasure, and an honor, sir; and permit me, again, to thank you for your service rendered to us to-day."

"Oh, it was nothing, as you know: and now, sir, I must go—as I perceive that Mademoiselle Henriette—have I mistaken your name, madam?—No? Well, I am afraid you tire of me—and I take my leave."

With which words the Captain bowed to Henrietta cavalierly, to Clare profoundly, and again shaking hands with the old gentleman, issued forth and mounted his horse.

"A splendid girl!" he said to himself, as he got into the saddle, "what if I seriously thought of marrying? I am sure she would have me—we would suit each other perfectly."

And laughing quietly to himself, the Captain returned homeward, humming his "Tra la! tra la!"

CHAPTER IV.

AN ENCOUNTER ON THE HIGHWAY.

Two days after the scene which we have just related, Henrietta and Clare were sitting in the drawing-room at Riverhead, waiting for their father, who was making his toilette, to accompany them out to dinner. The chariot stood at the door, with its four glossy horses, and liveried coachman and footman.

Henrietta was amusing herself with a new book, at which she laughed from time to time merrily. Clare was sitting quietly engaged upon some small ornamental work, and her sweet tender little face, wore its usual expression of quiet sadness, as with her long dusky lashes resting on her cheek, she pursued her occupation.

At last Henrietta threw down the volume, petulantly.

"I cannot have any peace of my life!" she exclaimed.

Clare raised her head.

"How, sister?" she said.

'For thinking of that rude man's impudence!"

"Who—Captain Waters?"

"Yes."

"Did he offend you?"

"My goodness, Clarry! how unobservant you are! Did you not hear his impertinent speeches to us?"

"No, sister."

"Well, I heard them! and I think he is odious!"

"Odious?"

"Hateful!"

"Oh, you ought not to place too much stress upon his roughness, sister," said Clare, "he has not been bred in courts—he has been fighting, you know."

"Is that any reason why he should insult a lady?"

"Insult you, sister!"

"Yes, Clarry—you know he did. 'Ladies could not understand any thing but fashions,' indeed! He would wait until we had retired, to narrate his heroic achievements!"

Clare smiled faintly.

"I don't think he meant to offend you, or me, sister," she said.

"Well, I choose to be offended, Clarry, whether you do or not! Really! 'The artillery of my eyes—war the natural relation of the sexes!' Was any thing ever more impudent!"

"It was a very harmless jest, I think," replied Clare.

"I think it very impudent."

"Oh, no, sister."

"There you are, Clarry, with your excessive good-nature! You see nothing improper, in the free and easy address of this rude man—who—"

"Who did us a very great service, sister," added Clare, softly.

"Well, suppose he did: any gentleman would have done as much. Do not understand me to say, however, that I think him a gentleman."

"Papa says that he is a very worthy gentleman."

"Humph!" ejaculated Henrietta.

"He says," continued Clare, "that from his own account he must have fought very bravely,—'like a lion,' papa says—"

"Yes—his boasting!"

"No, no—papa says that he never mentioned himself, unless he was questioned."

"Mock modesty!"

Clare smiled again, with the same faint, quiet expression.

"You are determined, I see, to dislike Captain Waters," she said, "and I cannot convince you, that he meant no offence when he was here."

"No, Clarry, you cannot."

"Your prejudices are very strong, sister."

"Yes, they are, and I confess that I think this gentleman is odious, hateful, impertinent; and I will never see him again."

As she spoke, a loud, hearty voice, was heard to say in the passage, "Parbleu! you need not announce me, friend!" and Captain Ralph entered, smiling and cheerful

"*Bon jour, mesdames!*" he said, bowing, "or if you do not like French, permit me to inquire about your health in good English."

"Thank you, I am well, sir," said Clare, with a courteous little inclination of her smiling face.

"And Miss Henrietta?" said the Captain, "I am sure, if outward appearances are to be relied on, she is distressingly well, in awfully good spirits."

"I am very well, sir," said Henrietta, coldly.

"Any more adventures, madam?" asked the Captain, with great interest, "no horses running away again, eh?"

"No, sir."

"Then, you have not missed me?"

"No, sir!" said Henrietta, with great emphasis.

The Captain smiled.

"Well, then, you are in my debt somewhat," he said.

"How, pray sir?" asked Henrietta, with cold surprise, and a look which was intended to transfix and render speechless the audacious visitor.

"The plainest thing in the world, morbleu!" said the Captain, "I am a bachelor."

"Sir?"

"I live all alone down there, in my cabin on the river—where the *bon père* used to live, you know."

"No, I do not know, sir."

"Ah, well! that does not alter the fact," said the Captain, with a cheerful smile, "it is the paternal mansion—my father, my dear madam, is that excellent old fisherman, John Waters. But he is now away with Charley—in the mountains; and thus I am alone by myself—as lonely, parbleu! as an unfortunate bear, forced to suck his paws for amusement."

"Well, sir?" said Henrietta, as coldly as ever.

"Well," continued the Captain, smiling, "it naturally

follows that I am in want of company. When I see others surrounded with it, I break the tenth commandment—though not the clause relating to my neighbor's wife. When I left you two days since, my unfortunate mansion seemed more lonely than ever. *Voila tout!* That is why I missed you."

And the Captain curled his moustache toward the eye, with a fascinating smile. It was Henrietta's *lip* that curled.

"I would counsel you to marry then, sir," she said, satirically, "a companion would cheer your loneliness."

"See! now, what a remarkable coincidence of thought!" cried the soldier, laughing. "*Parole d'honneur*, Madam Henrietta, you have hit upon just what occurred to myself!"

"Indeed, sir!"

"Yes, indeed—verily, as the English chaplain of our regiment used to say, with a dreadful drawl, however, through his nose. Yes, indeed—upon my word of honor as a soldier! That has struck me—yes, I want a wife. For you know I cannot be all the time with Jack Hamilton, and those stupid members of the ruder sex."

"Mr. Hamilton is one of my friends, sir," said Henrietta, more and more piqued.

"Ah? Well, he is a good fellow—an excellent fellow! Parbleu! a delightful companion, and we have emptied many a jovial cup together:—a good comrade—*Seigneur Mort-Reynard*, as I call him. Guess, now, his name for me!"

"I have very little turn for guessing, sir."

"Shall I reveal it then?"

"If you fancy, sir."

"Certainly, I fancy. He calls me—the *farceur!*—his name for me is *Don Moustachio!* What a deplorable attempt at a jest."

"It is at least characteristic, sir," said Henrietta, with a satirical smile.

"Why, yes," replied the Captain, "there is some justice in designating me by my moustache."

And the Captain caressed that ornament affectionately; his white teeth glittering under the ebon fringe like huge pearls.

"A good companion is Hamilton," he added, "and I

have many excellent friends of the same description. But after all ma'm'selle, there is nothing like the divine sex."

"Thank you, sir!"

"Oh, you think me insincere!"

"No, sir!"

"You think I flatter you."

"Was any portion of your observation intended for me, sir? Really you are very kind!"

"Any portion for yourself! Why the whole of it was for you."

"A thousand thanks, sir," said Henrietta, with the same satirical expression.

"You deserved it, morbleu!" added the Captain, "and lest I may be considered ungallant by Miss Clare, I will say that she deserved even more."

Clare smiled politely.

"You are very gallant, I think, Captain Waters," she said.

"I gallant!—oh, no! ma'm'selle: I am only a rude soldier. I handle the pike and halberd, sword and pistol, carbine and musket, much better than the implements of peace—smiling words, polite speeches, and all that. Frankness, madam, is my only virtue—but that I claim to have in excess."

"It is a quality I very much admire, Captain Waters," here interposed the voice of Mr. Lee, who had entered behind the soldier; "give you good day, sir."

And the old gentleman shook the soldier cordially by the hand.

"You are going to ride, sir," said the Captain; "I believe another of my shining merits is, that I always happen to arrive *malapropos.*"

"No—our ride is of no importance: to-morrow will do as well. You came to dine with us, doubtless, and so I will send the chariot back."

Henrietta could not restrain a little sigh of dissatisfaction: to be disappointed in their ride!—to be obliged to entertain the soldier all day long! It was too vexatious."

The Captain heard the sigh, and catching the expression of the young girl's face, smiled. He had her at his mercy, and for a moment paused maliciously.

At last he said, laughing:

"No, no, sir! I could not think of forcing you to defer your excursion: I perceive that mesdames here are bent upon it."

"We were only going over to Effingham Hall, sir—a matter of no urgency:—merely a friendly call," said Mr. Lee. "You shake your head. Ah, well sir—go with us. What say you?"

"I have not the pleasure of Effingham Hall's acquaintance," said the Captain, coldly, "though I remember going there one day, to challenge Mr. Effingham, Jr."

"A challenge, sir!" said Henrietta.

"Yes, my dear madam. Mr. Effingham, Jr., aforesaid, ran his toasting iron through my brother's shoulder, and as there was a little affair already nearly hatched between them, I thought it my duty to take Charley's place."

"But you did not fight!" exclaimed poor Clare, "you know—"

There she stopped, with her face overshadowed.

"No, Ma'm'selle Claire, *vous avez raison.* No! we did not, and that for one circumstance which would not interest you. The young gentleman went away, doubtless ignorant of the fact that I had called."

Poor Clare's head drooped, as the Captain uttered these words, and she murmured, "Yes, he went the same evening." She alone knew all.

"Therefore," continued the Captain, "I decline going to Effingham Hall: but that does not prevent my riding by the chariot, mesdames, for a mile or two. I am desperately tired of that Lanky's society."

And, smiling, the Captain issued forth with the company.

"Ah, your beautiful horse again," said Mr. Lee, "an Arabian, sir?"

"Yes, I took a fancy to him in Constantinople, and bought him for a handful of piastres. A beautiful horse is the next thing to a beautiful woman!"

"Thanks for the comparison, sir," said Henrietta, disdainfully.

"Is it not just?"

"Sir?"

"Come, is not Selim handsome? Answer, ma'mselle."

"Yes, sir—well?"

"That satisfies me: and faith! I am so well pleased with getting the better of you in the argument, that if you want him, I will present you with Selim."

Henrietta looked at the soldier.

"You would suit each other: he's a charming horse," said the Captain, laughing.

Henrietta was completely overcome, by these audacious compliments: and could only say, coldly:

"Thank you, sir—I have a riding horse."

"Will you ride on horseback, or with us?" interposed Mr. Lee.

"On horseback, sir—parbleu, on horseback. I am more at home in the saddle—and Selim understands me."

And passing to the carriage door, the Captain gallantly assisted the young girls to enter the huge vehicle, laughing all the while, at the successful generalship which forced Henrietta to give her hand to him.

The chariot then rolled off toward Effingham Hall, and the Captain, mounting Selim, who stood ready, rode toward it, humming his eternal "tra la! tra la!" which he occasionally changed, for the sake of variety, to "Tirra lirra! tirra lirra!"

He rode for some miles by the carriage window, and managed to materially deepen the impression of his impertinence upon Henrietta, by declining to understand her satirical repartees, and applauding them as so many evidences of sprightliness, with which he was delighted. When the chariot arrived at the road which led from the highway to Effingham Hall, the Captain drew up.

"You will not go with us, then?" said Mr. Lee, "I hope you have no quarrel with the squire, sir?"

"None—none: I may even say, I think that we are good friends, since I recollect some very polite speeches he made on our former meeting. But I must go to Williamsburg this morning. I had quite forgotten that this is the day of the arrival of the mountain post."

"Ah, yes—your father—"

"Precisely, my dear sir—father, brother, sister: how could I neglect that, morbleu!"

"Well, sir: then we must hope to see you at Riverhead soon again."

"With pleasure! with pleasure! *Mesdames, bon jour!*"

And the Captain bowed elegantly, taking off, and lowering to his saddle-bow, his hat with its dark feather. The carriage rolled on, and Captain Ralph continued his way, alternately humming his song, laughing to himself, and addressing himself to the woods, in a half audible tone.

He had nearly reached the town, when the sound of a horse's hoofs attracted his attention, and raising his head, which had been for some time hanging down listlessly, the soldier saw within ten rods of him, a gentleman who was riding toward him, mounted on a splendid sorrel.

Something in the air of the traveller, struck him as strangely familiar; and his keen eye plunged beneath the drooping hat, which, black like the stranger's clothes, covered his brow.

The traveller drew nearer—raised his head quickly: and the two men at the same moment recognized each other.

The new comer was Mr. Champ Effingham.

CHAPTER V

TWO ENEMIES.

THE two men looked at each other for some moments, in perfect silence.

Mr. Effingham was much changed:—his face was thinner, and had more character in it; his costume was more subdued and in much better taste, though it was as rich as ever; and his whole air and carriage was much more calm and collected, than it had ever been before. But still the old weary listless shadow in the eyes remained: and one might have seen on a closer examination, that those eyes were not so brilliant and youthful looking as before—that this man must have lived long in a very short time, and—perforce of cramming passion, so to speak, into his life—grown prematurely old. The eye was clear, it is true—but it was not happy: the lips were as handsome as ever, but two diverging lines betrayed suffering and thought:—the pale brow was not so smooth as it had been. Mr. Effingham looked like a man who had exhausted all stormy emotions and become calm again:—not so much the calmness of satisfied desires, as the slumber of discordant emotions.

The reader may imagine from these few words of hasty description, that this man, a portion of whose wild career we have attempted to delineate, had lost that conspicuous grace and fire, which formerly drew all eyes toward him:—that he had grown old, as a young man does, by wild courses and extraordinary dissipation:—that Mr. Effingham had no longer any marked characteristic, at least pleasant characteristic. This was only partially true. He was plainly a man of far more character than ever—a finer cavalier, every way stronger, so to speak, than before. The slight stoop in his shoulders, which betrayed the intense thinker, gave to his figure a singular nobleness of outline; his sword was worn with a grace very unlike his old petit maître habit; his broad brow, no longer disfigured with a wig, rose above the thoughtful eyes like a tower: his costume, as we have said, was rich but simple; and to sum up all in one word, Mr. Effingham looked like a man who had suffered and grown harder, and as a consequence of that suffering and new strength, left behind many of his youthful follies:—and so, achieved, if not happiness, at least calmness.

The Captain, with his keen, rapid glance, took in all these details at once, and then, with a haughty inclination of his head, was about to pass on.

Mr. Effingham raised his hand, and with great calmness—though a slight flush rose to his cheek, as he spoke—said:

"Would you be good enough to give me a moment of your time, Captain Waters? I have something to say to you."

The soldier tightened his rein, and waited in silence for his companion to speak.

"This is a meeting which I have long desired, sir," continued Mr. Effingham, stroking the mane of his horse.

The soldier inclined his head coldly, without speaking.

"I can easily understand that my face is not agreeable to you, sir," continued Mr. Effingham, in the same courteous and placid tones which had characterized the first words addressed to the soldier. "I do not complain of that: I have no right to. It were singular if we met as good friends after the scenes which we have passed through—or, more properly speaking, those between Mr. Charles Waters and myself. I do not expect you to give me your hand—I do not ask that. But I have misunderstood your character, if, after the few words I have to say, your mind and heart remain bitter—if you are still my enemy."

"We are not enemies, sir," said the Captain, coldly; "matters are all ended—accounts closed—we are indifferent to each other."

"Pardon me, sir: but that cannot be. In this world persons who have sustained the singular relationship toward each other which we have, can never afterwards be wholly indifferent."

"You had something to say, I believe, sir?"

"Yes, sir; and I shall proceed to say it, resolutely refusing to adopt the tone toward yourself, which you adopt toward me."

There was so much courtesy and dignity in these words, that Captain Waters felt that his haughty and freezing manner was unreasonable.

"I have no desire to insult you, Mr. Effingham," he said; "we are nothing to each other, and, morbleu! have I not already declared that I do not regard you as an enemy."

"Well, sir, for that I thank you," said Mr. Effingham, as calmly and courteously as before; "and now, sir, let me say what I have desired to utter, in the hearing of your family, for a long time. Let me briefly tell you—for you perhaps do not know all—let me tell you the nature of those events, whose disastrous or nearly disastrous climax you arrived in time, and just in time to witness. I am not fond of the particle 'I,' and beg that you will permit me to adopt another form.

"Well, sir, there lived a year or two ago, near this place where we now meet, a young man of strong passions and violent impulses. He inherited the traits of his family—strong feelings under an indifferent and easy exterior. One day that young man met with a girl—it was in that very forest, sir, which you have just emerged from—a young girl of rare and dazzling beauty, a beauty which still blinds me when I gaze upon it, though I have passed through much to distract the mind since that luminous face shone on me. Well, sir," continued Mr. Effingham, whose voice for a moment had changed singularly—"Well, sir, it was the old tale: he loved her—devotedly, passionately, madly: so madly that he even now doubts whether it was not a species of madness, that strange, wild infatuation!

"He approached her, and told her rudely and carelessly, as a 'gentleman' so called speaks to an actress, that he loved her. He thought her an ordinary comedienne, such as he had known in London—she was not such: she was a noble girl, as pure as an angel, and as good as she was beautiful. Without a moment's hesitation, she told him that there could be nothing in common between them—that she did not desire him to pay her attentions—that she did not wish him to approach her. Well, he raved and tore his hair, and suffered dreadfully when he heard these words—for he loved her passionately. He left his family and became a member of the company of Comedians, and offered her his hand—not once, but a score of times. She still refused to smile upon him."

Mr. Effingham paused for a moment: again stroked the mane of his horse, and went on calmly.

"One day this young man saw a rival in her presence, and read in her blushes, in the tones of her voice, in her eyes, that this rival was the favored one. That drove him mad, and he felt that thenceforth all was lost to him: spite of his love, spite of his abandoning all for her, spite of his devotion, she was not even indifferent to him he saw. She trembled at his approach—as the dove does when the hawk appears:—she shrunk from him with aversion. You may imagine, sir, that this added to his infatuation a thousandfold: it rose to such a height, his passion and consequent suffering was so dreadful, that one day he placed the muzzle of a pistol to his brain and might have killed himself, had not God ordained that he should live. God interposed, and for a moment, a single moment, he was calm,—for a moment only, however."

Again the young man paused, and the Captain saw his eyes wander. He continued:

"God had ordained further, sir, that his own act should

reveal the secret of the young girl's birth, a strange history! and by so doing he gave his rival a new and stronger hold upon her. He was thenceforward her blood relation—legally and morally bound to protect her.

"You may understand now how that unfortunate man's passions were worked up to the point of desperation. He loved a woman with a species of infatuation; he had given up every thing for her: she was about to be torn from him by a successful rival. Is not that a powerful combination of unfortunate circumstances, sir? Well, this combination was what assailed that man in a weak moment. By one of those accidents which seem to be produced by the direct agency of the Devil, the tools of a mad scheme appeared upon the *tapis.* Two boatmen—desperate characters, and ready for any mischief—came to say that the young man's new sail-boat was waiting in the river—at that moment his design was conceived:—Yet he determined to give the young girl a last opportunity to save herself and him."

Captain Ralph saw a shadow cross his companion's brow, and pitied his suffering: that suffering was very plain.

"He went to her and threw away his bitterness," continued Mr. Effingham, calmly, "his scoffs, his taunts. He opened his poor afflicted heart to her and said, 'I love you —I suffer cruelly—I must always love you—I shall die unless you consent to become my wife!' She felt sincere pity—she was suffering herself—she no longer looked at me coldly. The young man—I do not like these 'I's,' sir—for a moment hoped. Vain hope!—she ended with a passionate refusal:—stung by his taunts she declared that nothing would induce her to wed a man like him—she could not, would not marry him! He tore his bosom with desperate hands—it was not the first time—and rushed from the room.

"In half an hour his scheme was all arranged. The boatmen were directed to be ready:—a venal parson was near, who for a bribe of two hundred guineas promised to wed the parties without asking any questions, at a spot down the river fixed on.

"The forcible abduction of the young girl, was all that remained to be compassed. He raised her while she slept in her chair, bore her to the ground, and carried her off!

"He was pursued—his rival was the pursuer—they came together on the river: the young man's confederates were overcome: he was left alone, foiled, beaten, laughed at. His rival raised his hand to strike—the young man's sword pierced his breast, God be thanked, not wounding him mortally."

The Captain nodded in approbation of this sentiment.

"After that the victim of infatuation—of madness, I may nearly say," Mr. Effingham went on, calmly, "left the country, and went into foreign lands, with blood upon his hands, he thought. He repented bitterly—he spent days and months of that suffering which surpasses all the rest—remorse. At length he found in time and thought some alleviation, and his peace was restored completely—can you believe it, sir?—by a letter saying that his rival had recovered from his wound.

"That is all, sir:—except that the unfortunate man who enacted this tragic drama, has returned to the scene of those unhappy events with a calmer heart, a brain no longer obscured by the mists of passion and pride. That man now says to the brother of his rival—the man he has injured—'I have repented bitterly of all this—I have no pride for you, none that will make me refuse this reparation of words, all which I have to offer—I acknowledge my fault—I deplore the suffering which I occasioned.'

"This is what I had to say, Captain Waters," added Mr. Effingham, calmly and courteously, as before, "I have said it, and am content that you shall fold your arms in your cloak, and refuse to touch my hand. My duty is done."

"Refuse your hand?" said the honest soldier, "morbleu! I do nothing of the sort! There is mine! I hated you mortally until this moment: now I assent, and will maintain, that you are a worthy gentleman!"

And Captain Waters forgetting completely all his enmity, shook Mr. Effingham's hand cordially.

"You afford me a pleasure, which I have not experienced often in my life," said Mr. Effingham, with noble simplicity.

"No polite speeches!" said the soldier, "we understand each other. A quarter of an hour ago, I would cheerfully have run you through with my hanger, for your treatment of

Beatrice and Charley:—I thought it was all mock generosity, when they said this very thing you have told me, that you seemed to be laboring under a sort of infatuation. Parbleu! they have both forgiven you long ago: why should not I?"

"I am sure you no longer regard me in the light of an enemy. I have offered you an explanation which—"

"Is perfectly satisfactory and convincing," said the Captain, with his frank, jovial voice.

"Where are they now?" asked Mr. Effingham, with a slight shadow upon his brow.

"Who, Charley and Beatrice?"

"Yes, Captain."

"Up in the mountains."

"I trust they are quite happy."

And his eyes seemed to be fixed upon that past, which had gone from him like a wild dream. He could scarcely realize that those fiery passions had burned in his bosom.

"I hope, Captain Waters, that we shall meet frequently," said Mr. Effingham, at length; "I must leave you now, as I have just arrived in Virginia. Give you good day, sir."

And bowing with the same calm air as before, Mr. Effingham continued his way toward the Hall, while Captain Ralph went in the opposite direction.

CHAPTER VI.

OLD FRIENDS.

THE Riverhead chariot rolled lazily up to Effingham Hall, an event which caused the sleepy-looking pointer basking in the sun upon the portico, to rise and wag his tail, in sign of indolent satisfaction, and well-bred welcome.

The Hall has no longer that still, slumberous, melancholy air about it, we have observed upon a former occasion:—indeed, the very reverse is the fact. Effingham Hall has waked up with the spring—and that joyous season, continuing, as in Shakespeare's time, to "put a spirit of youth in everything," has touched with its merry and joyous hand the trees, the grass, the very gables of the old manor-house, and all is bright and cheerful.

The tall old trees, with their tender budding leaves, are rustling in the merry winds of March:—the sunshine lies like a glory on the great portico; and the lawn, growing already green and soft, is dotted with a thousand flowers which raise their bright heads and smile, or cheerily shake the dew diamonds from their gay petals when the breeze agitates them.

From tree to tree dart the early songsters of spring, making the air vocal with their chirping:—and it is very plain that more than one courtship is going on in the tall elm yonder, from which a concert by delighted blue birds' artists, incessantly fills the air. They are no longer "prophesying spring," as our poet says: their prophecy is fulfilled, and they are rejoicing like so many able editors, who have foretold events and seen them come to pass. The oriole carols too, above them all, from his high spray, which, swaying backward, forward, sideways, in the wind—rocks his bright gurgling throat and ruffled feathers gaily. A thousand little swamp sparrows flit about: and bear up twigs from the margin of the sparkling stream: and dart after each other in excess of glee; and almost tumble over each other in the blue mid air, from pure merriment.

Dozens of negroes—ranging from little ebon balls, clad in unmentionable costumes, to the stately white-haired Catos and Dinahs—pass about from out-house to out-house:—horses are led in long rows from the huge stable on the hill, toward the field:—dogs roll and bark and meditate with staring eyes upon the lawn:—and in the midst of all a flock of dignified geese ambulate like great seigneurs with their wives, and startle with their cackle all the stately, serene peacocks, who with brilliant plumage and restless movement of their burnished necks sail slowly onward—bright-crested swans upon an emerald sea.

And pleasanter than all—more excellent to hear and look upon, are the sights and sounds from the Hall itself.

From the open window comes the merry murmur of the harpsichord and a child's voice full of tender grace; adding a splendor to the time—the perfect merriment which nothing ever affords but music. And then the music stops, and there appears upon the portico the burly figure of our old acquaintance, the squire, who finds his skirts suddenly grasped by laughing hands, and two merry eyes, as azure as the heavens, laugh like the lips.

The squire is in exuberant health, and is clad just as we have seen him before. His broad plain hat, which has lost its loops and is rolled up shovel fashion, covers a face reddened and embrowned by exercise and exposure:—his huge coat brushes against his strong thick silk stockings, which disappear in heavy half-boots:—and his long waistcoat is nearly covered by his frill, soiled now like his wide cuffs and stockings, with the dust of his fields. The squire has just returned from his morning ride over the plantation, and has been listening to Miss Kate Effingham performing upon the harpsichord, and singing one of his favorite airs. She now holds him back by the skirts, begging him to wait for her.

This young lady may possibly still dwell in the reader's recollection. She has scarcely changed at all since we saw her last, and is positively not a bit larger. She is the same bright little creature with sparkling eyes, and rosy cheeks, and crimping laughing lips which are the color of cherries, and reveal when their owner laughs, a row of small teeth, much whiter than pearls, if not so rounded and regular. Kate is dressed almost exactly as we have seen her formerly. Her hair is still unpowdered, and falls in curls upon her neck, around which extends a foam of snowy lace. Her half-frock half-coat, with its embroidered velvet under-vest still abbreviates itself—after the fashion of the time—in close proximity to the knee: and the same scarlet silk stockings, plunge themselves into the identical rosetted, red-heeled shoes. Kate is perhaps merrier than we ever saw her, and when she demands that the squire shall wait for her before proceeding to assist the visitors from the carriage, there is a violent contention between laughter and the faculty of articulation, which results in a rush and jumble of the two, which puts the merriment of the blue birds to such shame that they are silent.

"Good morrow, neighbor," says the squire, assisting Henrietta and Clare to the ground, with the elegance of a perfect courtier; "and you, my little mice, how are your small selves?"

With which the squire squeezes Henrietta's hand, until she screams.

"Thanks, sir," says the laughing girl; "I was much better before I saw you!"

And she shakes her hand, upon which the old gentleman's fingers have left distinct white marks.

"You are not fond of having your hands pressed?" laughs the squire.

"No, sir."

"By an old fellow like me, I mean—and I take your reply as given to the whole question. Well, well, I believe you are right. I am rather an ancient cavalier, but the sight of you young folks, all roses, pleases me."

"That is my failing, I believe," says Henrietta, laughing, "but not Clare's."

"No," says the squire, "and I am sorry to see your cheeks so much like lilies, Clare."

Clare smiles.

"You know that is my style, sir," she replies, "I never had a bright color, but I am quite well."

"And as good as ever, I do not doubt," says the squire, as they enter the mansion pleasantly.

"And me, sir—does that apply to me?" says Henrietta, laughing.

"No, madam."

"I am 'as *bad* as ever,' I suppose."

"I hope not!" says the old gentleman, delighted at his witticism.

"Thanks, sir," Henrietta replies, with exquisite demureness, "thanks for an excellent character. And now I am going to leave you and papa to discuss your deeply interesting plantation affairs, and take off my hood."

"By all means. I cannot see your pretty face now:—and Clare is as bad, see! I believe she cannot kiss Kate, for her huge coiffure."

And the squire, laughing gayly, leads the way into the library, followed by Mr. Lee—leaving the young ladies in the hands of Miss Alethea, who has just emerged from the kitchen.

Miss Alethea looks more placid and good-humored than when we knew her formerly, though her stateliness has not in the least changed:—and she comes forward and kisses, in Virginia fashion, both the girls. Then they are led away to the sanctum up stairs to remove their wrapping, and make their toilettes for dinner.

Seated in the library, the old gentlemen discuss matters in general, over a decanter of sherry: and dispute with the utmost vehemence, on the most trifling matters, in the good old way. Both are fortified in their opinions as a matter of course, and they deplore each the other's prejudices and unreasonableness. But let no one suppose that these word-quarrels were not the most friendly contentions imaginable. There were no better friends in the world, and they were only pursuing the immemorial habit of Virginians to discuss, contradict, and argue on all occasions.

Some of these contradictions are amusing, and rather vague.

"The fact is, my dear sir," says Mr. Lee, philosophically smoothing down his waistcoat, "the fact is that after all we have said, and after all that can be said on this point, things are—"

"I deny it!" says the squire, vehemently, "they are not!"

"But listen now," continues Mr. Lee, with a persuasive and earnest voice, "you are too quick. I was going to say, and I think you will coincide with me—you ought to, if you do not:—I was going to say that the present state of this country is such that these men will—"

"No! I join issue with you there," interposes the squire, argumentatively, "they will do no such thing, and I am surprised to hear you say it!"

"I have not said it yet!"

"You have."

"What have I said?"

"You said, that considering the present state of England—"

"No! of this country."

"You said England!"

"Positively I did not."

And so the argument goes on, thick set with contradictions and dogmatical assertions.

At last—the worthies having glided gradually from the

rude highway of politics, into the pleasant paths of neighborhood gossip—the conversation grows quite friendly and placid again, and there are no more contradictions:—those weapons being made use of exclusively in polemics. They talk of the races to be held soon at the course between Williamsburg and Jamestown:—of the probable entries:—of the amount of subscription, and the chances of Sir Archy's overcoming Fair Anna or Dare Devil. From this they pass to county court matters, and the demoralizing effect of the absence of game-laws. This leads the squire to descant at length, and in a tone of indignant reprehension, upon the course of the defendant in a certain chancery suit, by the style of "Effingham et al. *vs.* Jonas Jackson, sheriff of York county, and as such, administrator de bonis non, with the will annexed, of John Jones, dec'd." This affords the squire an opportunity to express his opinion of the high court of chancery, which he does at some length, and with refreshing frankness and directness.

So completely absorbed is the worthy gentleman in this interesting subject, that he quite loses sight of a piece of information which he has been on the point of giving his visitor, for some moments. Let us leave him vituperating the whole system of equity, and enter the adjoining apartment—the drawing-room—from which the merry music of the harpsichord is heard. Perhaps we shall be able to find out from others the nature of this intelligence.

Clare sits at the harpsichord playing, and little Kate, perched upon a cricket at her side, is turning over the leaves of the music—while Miss Alethea and Henrietta exchange neighborhood gossip, near the opposite window.

Clare finishes the piece she is playing, and turning her quiet, good-natured face toward Kate, says, smoothing back the child's locks as she speaks:

"Is that the piece you wished me to play, Katy?"

"Oh yes," says Kate, her eyes sparkling, "and now you mustn't play any more—for I have a great piece of news to tell you!"

And the child's eyes fairly dance, as she draws a letter from beneath her girdle.

"A great piece of news?" asks Clare, with a smile, "what is it, pray?"

"Guess!" says Kate, covering the letter with her hand.

"I am afraid I am a poor hand at guessing, dear," replies Clare.

"Can't you think?" persists Kate, with a joyous rush of laughter in her voice:—for if Rubini had tears in his voice, it may be said that Kate had laughter in hers: "can't you think now, cousin Clare—just try, now."

"Well," says Clare, smiling at the brilliant face of the child, "has Will written you a love letter, and asked your hand?"

"No, indeed," Kate replies, pouting like a duchess, "he asks me to marry him twenty times a day."

"Indeed!"

"Yes, indeed: he's a dreadful plague. But come, now, cousin Clare, guess again."

"Let me see: you have a letter, that is plain."

"Yes."

"And this letter contains the news?"

"Yes, yes, cousin Clare."

"Good news?"

"Oh yes, indeed!"

"Of what sort?"

"Oh! now that would be telling you, you know. But I'll see if you can guess it then. Somebody's coming!"

And Kate's eyes dance again: while a shadow suddenly passes over the tender face of her companion.

"Somebody coming?" murmurs Clare; "I think I can guess now—"

"I knew you could!"

"Mr. Effingham is coming back?"

"Oh yes! cousin Champ! See, here is his letter from London. Look, what a funny mark upon it:—he says he will be here early in April, and this, you know, is the first week of March."

And Kate clasps her hands.

"Shall I read it?" she says.

Clare shakes her head sadly.

"Then you may yourself, cousin," says Kate, offering the opened letter; "I know cousin Champ wouldn't care for *your* seeing it."

But Clare puts the offered letter aside with her hand.

"Well, if you don't like to read it, you can listen just to this. He says he may be here even sooner than April. Just think! We'll have the dear old fellow back so soon, and he'll have so much to tell me," adds Kate, with a queenly little air; "you know how much we love each other."

Suddenly the letter is removed from Kate's hand, and the voice of a youthful gentleman, who has entered unperceived, says petulantly:

"There you are, praising brother Champ again. It is really vexatious, Kate."

And Mr. Willie Effingham looks mortified and indignant. This young gentleman has scarcely changed more than Kate, and is clad at present in a handsome little pearl-colored cocked hat, rosetted shoes, a coat with a rounded skirt, and a bright scarlet waistcoat. His right hand grasps a riding whip, and on the floor at his feet lies a school-book, which he has dropped to take possession of the letter.

"It is really too bad," says Will, allowing Kate to repossess herself of the letter, without much struggling; "I believe you're in love with brother Champ."

"I am so," says Kate, "and you're jealous, Willie!"

With which words the young lady laughs, to the great annoyance of her cavalier.

"Jealous, am I?" says Will; "that's all the thanks I get for giving up the game of Prisoner's base after school, and coming home to see you. Never mind!"

And Will shakes his head.

"Did you, now?" asks Kate, touched by this piece of devotion.

"Yes, I did."

"Well, let's make up, Willie."

"Then give me a kiss."

"Indeed I wont!" cries Kate; and she struggles to avoid the proffered embrace.

"Heyday!" says the voice of the squire at the door, as that gentleman enters with Mr. Lee; "fighting! Is it possible, Will?"

Will ceases to struggle: but abstains from any explanation.

"We were not fighting, papa; but he wanted to kiss me,

and you know it is not proper for young ladies of my age to kiss gentlemen—is it?"

And Kate throws a fatal glance from her brilliant eyes towards Willie, who, seeing the prize snatched from his grasp, utters a sigh.

The squire laughs, and asks the child "What letter that is?"

"Cousin Champ's, you know, papa."

"Yes, yes: I was just telling neighbor Lee," the squire says to Clare, "that Champ was coming back soon."

The hoofstrokes of a horse sound on the gravel walk, but they do not hear them.

"He writes," adds the squire, addressing himself equally to Clare and Henrietta, "that we may expect him early in April—sooner, perhaps."

A spur sounds on the portico, but the harpsichord, which Clare touches softly and absently with her finger, drowns the noise.

"Kate, here, has taken possession of the letter as her rightful property," continues the squire, "and offers to exhibit it, I believe, to every body—the little minx. They were great friends."

The shadow of a man falls upon the passage.

"Well, I'll be glad to see the boy; and God grant him a safe passage to the old Hall again."

As the squire speaks, Kate utters a delighted scream and in a moment rushes to the arms of a gentleman who stands upon the threshold.

"God has already granted that, sir," says Mr. Effingham.

And amid a burst of exclamations, he enters the apartment.

We need not describe the scene which followed the entrance of Mr. Effingham:—how the squire did little more than press his hand, and gaze delighted on his face:—how Clare tried in vain to still her agitated and throbbing heart:—how the rest of the group overwhelmed the young man with a thousand congratulations. The reader may fancy all this with less trouble than we could describe it. We must leave to fancy, too, the crowd of bright-faced Africans, who jostled each other at the door:—the uproarious chanting of

"Oho—oho—oho—oho!
Mas' Champ come home agin!"

which rose from the lawn, after the fashion of the time and place.

Yes, Mr. Champ, after all his weary wanderings, had returned to his good old home.

CHAPTER VII.

HOW CAPTAIN RALPH LAID HIS COMMANDS ON MR. LUGG.

"LANKY!"

"Sur?"

"You're a villain."

"Oh, Cap'n!"

"A most unconscionable villain!"

"Oh no I ain't, Cap'n."

"You are, you rascal! Don't contradict me!"

"I didn't, Cap'n."

"You did."

"I didn't, Cap'n."

"There is a pretty proof of it: you are contradicting me now, you villain! I'll cut off your ears!"

"Oh, Cap'n!"

And Lanky raises his hand affectionately toward his auricular appendages, with a dreadful conviction that their size and prominence would render them an easy prey to the enemy.

Captain Ralph addressed the above emphatic words to Mr. Lugg two or three days after the scenes which we have just described. The worthy soldier was sitting after breakfast, with a meerschaum between his lips, with his feet in close proximity to the hook fixed in the beam above the great fireplace of his mansion. From time to time, clouds of snowy smoke would issue from beneath his huge moustache, and rise in circles to the rafters overhead, upon which the red beams of the morning sun reposed, turning the dusty timbers into bars of gold.

Lanky sat as usual, in his chimney corner, and from time

to time touched furtively the strings of an old battered violin, which lay upon his knees :—gazing all the while into the blaze, which drove away the cool river mist with its crackling laughter.

The Captain looked at his retainer for some moments in silence, after the outburst we have faithfully chronicled above ; then added :

" Play that reel again—"

And the Captain, stopping to smoke a moment, Lanky raised his violin with alacrity to obey his master's bidding.

—" If you dare, you rascal ! " finished the Captain, whose sentence had been broken off in the middle. Lanky's arm subsided immediately, and the fiddle fell back to its former position on his knees.

" Raly, Cap'n," said Lanky, scratching his head, " nobody can't please you. Now you know you told me, bein' as you gin me a holiday to-day, to bring out my fiddle and scrape for you. And now," added Lanky, with an injured air, " you're a tellin' me that I dasn't play no more. Oh, Cap'n ! "

And after this stereotyped protest, Lanky remained silent.

" I told you to play, because I wanted to hear music, parbleu ! " said the Captain, " but that was a quarter of an hour ago. I have changed my mind. I don't believe you are much of an artist, with all your distinguished reputation in the neighborhood. You scrape horribly, and your in strument is an awful one."

Lanky, though deeply hurt and indignant at this double attack on his violin and his reputation, did not answer. " Oh, Cap'n ! " was all that his muttering lips enunciated.

At the end of ten minutes, Captain Ralph laid aside his meerschaum, and stretched his legs.

" Lanky," he began.

" Sur ? "

The Captain paused for some moments, yawning.

" When did you see Donsy Smith ? " he asked, at length.

Lanky started.

" Oh, Cap'n," he said, " I ain't seen that ere young 'ooman for a month o' Sundays."

" Have you quarrelled ? "

"No, sir."

"A rival?"

Lanky groaned.

"What horrible sound was that which issued from your diaphragm, you villain?" asked the Captain.

"I never said nothin', sur."

"You sighed."

"Did I, Cap'n?"

"Yes, and do you know what these 'heighos' mean?"

"He'o's, sur?"

"These sighs, you rascal?"

"No, sur."

"They signify that one is deeply smitten by some angelic fair one. Eh? do you understand?"

"I think I does, sur."

"When I said 'have you a rival?' you sighed, or rather groaned. Now I understand from that, that you are far gone."

"Oh, Cap'n."

"Come, now, you have a rival?"

"I b'lieve I has," said Lanky, piteously, but beginning to saw his head from north-east to south-west, according to his habit.

The Captain observed this favorite manœuvre, and began to laugh.

"You have a rival, eh?" he said; "a successful one?"

"I dun'no, sur."

And Lanky groaned again, and sawed his head worse than ever. The Captain twirled his moustache with a delighted look.

"Listen to me now, Lanky," he said, bursting into laughter; "listen to my advice, *mon ami*. Here you are groaning and sighing, and declaring in your delicious patois that you have not seen your dulcinea for ages:—you are plainly in high dudgeon, and have abandoned the field. Now, sir, hear what I have to say. No retainer of mine shall disgrace me by succumbing to a woman—laying down his arms because the bastion frowns with guns, instead of being wreathed with flowers. *Tonnere!* you villain, it is a personal slight upon myself, and I won't have you give up in this way to your little Donsy, who is only coquetting with you! Do you hear, sir?"

"What kin I do, Cap'n? I can't do nothin," sighed Lanky.

"There it is. again—with your eternal groaning! Be a man, you rascal, or, parbleu! I'll hang you by the legs to the rafters!"

Lanky started at this terrible threat, and took a bird's-eye view of matters, coming to the irresistible conclusion that the posture suggested by his master would not only be disagreeable, but would have the effect of adding a new and undesired charm to the landscape.

"Oh, sur!" he ejaculated.

"Now listen," said the Captain, "and do not sit there moaning and groaning, sighing and crying, when as a brave man you should buckle on your sword—figuratively speaking—and advance upon the enemy. What is that enemy? That, morbleu! is the first question with every courageous and rational soldier. In the present instance a woman—a young woman, or as you say in your barbarous dialect—'young 'ooman.' Now, sir, I commence by laying down the proposition that every member of the fair sex may be overcome by well-directed and courageous generalship. They, of course, despise a mere sighing, lachrymose lover, with his heart in his hand, and a propensity for moonlight and soliloquy:—basta! I am throwing away my philosophy on your thick head! What do you know about soliloquies and moonlight!"

And the Captain paused.

"I don't know nothin' 'bout slil'kees," observed Lanky, "but I hunts 'coons by moonlight, sometimes."

"You unsentimental villain!" said the soldier, "are you not ashamed of yourself, to mix up the divine sentiment with 'coons—as you barbarously term it:—to mingle *tendresse* with the consideration of furs!"

"You was goin' to give me some advice, Cap'n," said Lanky, desirous of averting the Captain's indignation.

"Well, you villain: in place of advice, I give you commands! I command you to resume offensive operations immediately, and yield not one point."

Lanky looked dubious: these generalities were plainly distasteful to him, since he did not very clearly comprehend their meaning.

"Oh, Cap'n! I dun'no what that means," he said.

"It means this, you villain! When Donsy or any other young lady endeavors to turn you around her thumb, to make you do just as she desires, to wheedle, and coax, and bring you over—resist, morbleu! Yield not a single point, as I said before!—never yield a point to one of the fair sex; for observe, you pine knot! the ambitious desire to rule in these enchanting creatures, closely resembles a body of water pent in by a dam. Give it but one little point to issue through, and *diable!* it rushes on, and carries all before it. Never yield to women—it is a bad precedent: respect them, love them, fight for them, die for them,—but never yield to them, you unreasonable villain! *En avant!* with a brave heart, and without thought of surrender:—ask no terms, yield in nothing: refuse to see brilliant eyes, to listen to coaxing words; close your heart obdurately, and victory is yours! Bah!" continues the Captain, "here am I advising you as to your course, when the first advice should be to show your nose to your sweetheart: how can she respect such a lover. As your master, sir, I command you to go and make yourself agreeable to your sweetheart, and not disgrace me by giving up the battle in this way."

Lanky touched the violin absently.

"But how kin it be done, Cap'n?" he said. "I ain't giv' up: I never intends to giv' up! But oh, Cap'n, when a feller feels all sorts o' ways, how can he make hisself agreeable?"

The Captain laughed heartily. Lanky took courage at this, and continued, sawing his head:

"I ain't a goin' to giv' up! No I ain't! He's too young for her, and 'sides, he ain't as good lookin' as I am."

"Who—your rival?"

"Yes, sur."

"Who is he?"

"Will Efn'um."

The Captain burst into a tremendous laugh.

"What, that little fellow, Lanky?" he said.

"Yes, sur."

"Morbleu! you astonish me."

"You know Donsy goes to school to the parson, sur, and so does Will Efn'um.'

"There near town?"

"Yes, sur."

"Well, now, I command you to enter the field at once, and prosecute hostilities," said the Captain. "Go, you rascal! I give you a holiday."

Lanky rose, with his fiddle under his arm.

"Won't your honor want your horse?" he said, scratching his head.

"Yes—morbleu! I forgot. I must go and fight Glatz for *mon ami* over there. Saddle Selim."

"Yes, sur."

And Lanky went out. In a quarter of an hour Captain Ralph was riding towards Riverhead, singing merrily one of his numerous repertory of camp ditties; and Lanky, having first smoothed his hair, by means of a coarse comb, and a triangular bit of looking-glass, was proceeding, with his violin under his arm, toward the town of Williamsburg.

CHAPTER VIII.

ICHABOD: A HEBREW WORD SIGNIFYING THE GLORY HAS DEPARTED!

WE shall follow Lanky.

He threaded the paths of the forest, traversed the tracts of waste land, and hit the points where the brooks were crossed by logs, stretched for the convenience of pedestrians from bank to bank, with unerring precision. No doubt those moonlight—but not sentimental—excursions discoursed of to the Captain, had made him familiar with all the devious ways of the country ride; and so ere long he drew toward the school-house, which was situated in an open glade of the forest between Williamsburg and Effingham Hall.

The "old field school," as these establishments have been called from time immemorial, was a plain edifice of logs of some size, and roofed with boards held in their places by long poles pinned to the eaves by huge pegs. The windows were small, and secured by shutters of oak, heavy and creaking on their hinges. A log served for a step before the half open door, and from the chimney, which was of stone, and built up outside of the edifice, a slight curling smoke rose. To these schools, as at the present day, children of all ages and classes, and of both sexes, resorted—for education, their parents thought, for amusement, the youngsters were convinced.

But Lanky—sawing his head, and picking absently on the strings of his violin—did not look at the school-house, as he approached. His eyes were fixed upon the groups of scholars of both sexes scattered through the glade in merry play—and particularly upon one group, in the centre of which stood, with laughing eyes and ruddy cheeks, half covered by the owner's sun-bonnet, a young girl of some sixteen summers. Lanky's sudden accession of rapidity in the sawing operation, plainly betrayed his secret. That was the lady of his heart, and his admiring eyes surveyed with true lover minuteness, her neat plain dress, her careless locks of glossy black, and the firm little foot in its plain strong shoe.

Miss Smith was, as we have said, the centre of a group of maidens—and these maidens were gazing with delight upon a parcel of youngsters, who, ranged in a long row with their faces towards Lanky, listened to the oracular observations of their chieftain, whose back was thus turned toward our friend. The youngsters were clad in semi-military costume, with paper hats, girdles of fluttering ribbon; and each one carried martially erect upon his shoulder, something to represent a gun—whether that something chanced to be a hickory stick, a portion of a fence rail, or a cornstalk. The corn-stalks, however, predominated, and seemed to be the favorite weapon.

The young chieftain was clad with something more of pretension: he wore epaulettes, at his side hung a tin sword gracefully, and on his head was perched a conical hat made of the paper which had once enveloped a loaf of sugar—now decorated with ribbons, and sacred to Mars.

The chieftain held his head erect, and addressed his observations to the company, with great importance, though many of the troop were his elders. As we have said, the young maidens stood looking up, and encouraging the soldiers with their smiles;—upon the conviction, it would seem, that being handsome, chivalric, and brave, they deserved the approbation of the fair.

This was the state of things, as nearly as we can describe it, when Lanky sauntered up, with his violin under his arm. No sooner had the young maidens caught sight of the well known pine knot head, the ornamental stockings, the huge shoes, above all, of the battered violin, than they abandoned the youthful disciples of the god of war, and ran precipitately towards Lanky, crying out as they ran, for a tune and a dance.

"Oh yes! now, Lanky!"

"Play us a tune!"

"A reel!"

"Let us have a dance."

"Not a reel!"

"A May dance!"

"Both!"

And Lanky suddenly found himself assailed by a dozen maidens, and ordered to strike up immediately. In proportion to Lanky's popularity, and satisfaction therefrom, was the neglect and excessive dissatisfaction of the youthful soldiers. The smiles of ladies fair, are proverbially valuable to gentlemen of the military profession; and the reader may imagine the feelings of the cornstalk regiment, and their proud commander, at finding themselves thus abruptly deserted, with all their shining graces, for a common country bumpkin, with a caricature head, a battered violin, and a pair of feet which were beyond the power of pen or pencil to exaggerate.

The youthful chieftain, whom we now beg leave to introduce, as Captain William Effingham, "of the Cornstalk Company of Virginia Volunteers," his enemies added—Mr. Willie Effingham was perhaps the most indignant of all. He had just commenced a splendid and stirring oration, which dealt in tremendous denunciation of the acts of Parliament and King George, in relation to the colony of Virginia, and finding himself the centre of a circle of admiring auditors, had branched out with a vigor and splendor of rhetoric, which was calculated to procure his arrest as a dangerous and inflammatory rebel, when the untoward event which we have just related, happened. To add to his mortification, his own sweetheart, as he called Miss Donsy Smith, had joined the deserters; she had been listening to his oration with admiring attention, he thought: he was doing the heroic in presence of his ladylove—and now, for all this, to be abandoned without hesitation, for the aforesaid country bumpkin. It was horrible!

Lanky resisted the entreaties of his maiden friends, and sawed his head more vigorously than ever at Donsy.

"Now, Lanky!" said that young lady, with an expression of coquettish entreaty, "I know you won't refuse me!"

"Hum!" said Lanky.

"Now, Lanky!"

"Miss Donsy, you ain't treated me well, and you know it!" he said, touching the strings of his instrument.

"*I* not treated you well? My goodness!"

"You know you haven't."

"How, Lanky?"

"Never mind!"

"Oh, it's too bad in you," said the young lady, "to refuse me—and I liking you so much."

With which Donsy darted a killing glance at poor Lanky, who felt his heart melt.

"*Now*, Lanky!" she added.

But our friend remained obdurate in spite of the hundred solicitations, the cries and exclamations echoing on all sides.

"Here comes Will Effin'um," he said, "he'll play for you!"

And Lanky smiled with the superiority of a great artist in presence of a mere tyro. Master Will approached, followed by his regiment, who had been hastily disbanded.

"What did you all run away for?" asked Will, gloomily.

"To have a dance!" cried Donsy.

"A dance?"

"Yes, Lanky's goin' to play for us."

Lanky sawed his head.

"You are always coming to spoil fun, Lanky," said Will, surveying his rival, "and I won't stand it."

Lanky fired up.

"Come now, Will!" cried Donsy, "you shan't ruin our sport. Play on, Lanky!"

Lanky remembered the Captain's advice, and refused.

"Oh!" said Donsy, in a hurt and mortified tone.

Lanky closed his ears, and directed defiant glances toward Will.

"You will not refuse Donsy!" continued the little maiden, and in a whisper, "*your* Donsy!"

Lanky's heart began to succumb: his resolution was oozing out at the ends of his fingers.

"You can't, after seeing how I hurt my hand with the slate Sally Jones was drawing an ugly picture of you on!" continued the maiden, holding out a small hand upon the back of which a red mark was visible.

Lanky's resolution began to flow away; it no longer oozed.

"Look how red it is!" continued the maiden, with a sly glance at her admirer, and placing the hand in his own as she spoke.

Lanky's knees shook as he took it in his own.

"Really now!" he said, in a murmur.

"Yes, indeed—and it's not the first time I've taken your part—for you know how much I like you, Lanky!" said the little maiden, throwing a deadly glance upon her beau, and pressing his hand in her own.

Lanky forgot the Captain completely, and with a hesitating movement tuned a string.

"Please now, dear Lanky," said Donsy, tenderly, "a nice May dance."

Lanky's fiddle went to his shoulder.

"He shan't play!" cried Will, indignant at the tenderness bestowed upon his rival, "stop!"

Lanky with a scowl struck his violin with a vigorous hand, and making his bow fly backward and forward like lightning, struck up an animated tune, to which the delighted girls, and alas! the Cornstalk Regiment also, commenced dancing, circling hand in hand around the pole on the summit of which floated the regimental banner.

Will, we are compelled to say, did not really care a copper for Donsy, and he bore no real ill will to Lanky: but when he found himself thus ignominously abandoned, his authority despised, his rival preferred, he fell into a passion and looked around him for some means of venting his wrath.

The means were not visible:—alas! his brave soldiers

were flying madly around the pole, hand in hand with the merry school girls, who with bonnets thrown upon the ground, and floating hair, and merry twinkling feet, to say nothing of bright eyes, and ruddy cheeks, and laughing lips, were no longer conscious of any thing upon earth, but a sensation of excessive delight as the landscape revolved, and danced like themselves; and the violin continued to fill the air with its roaring, crashing, jubilant, rejoiceful laughter.

Will drew his sword and threw his cap upon the ground:—Lanky continued to flash his bow across the strings regardless. Willie in a rage rushed toward him:—Lanky only raised his chin toward the sky, and shaking his head and foot, rapturously roared on.

Will was about to charge the enemy, to vent at one fell blow all his wrongs and hatred, when suddenly a bell rang in the school-house, the door opened, and Lanky, with an elegant bow, placed his violin under his arm and took off his hat.

The master appeared upon the threshold, silent, in awful state, and that master was no less a personage than our old friend, Parson Tag; Parson Tag, who disgusted at the slenderness and poverty of his Piedmont parish, had resigned;—Parson Tag, who had abandoned the surplice for the coat of formal cut; the prayer book for the classic; the shovel hat and the staff for the profane cocked hat and ferrule. The church might have got tired of him:—he forestalled any disagreeable circumstances which might have attended that event, by getting tired of the church:—the clergy might have insisted on his leaving their ranks:—he avoided that by leaving them himself. And now, like a great and good man, the ci-devant parson bent his powerful mind to teaching the young ideas of an old field school the art of shooting.

The appearance of the pompous and austere gentleman, at once silenced the fiddle, paralyzed the dance.

"What profane sound was that I heard?" asked the parson, looking round with an air of importance and reproof.

"This here fiddle, sir," replied Lanky, with great politeness.

"Begone you son of Belial," said the parson, "and you

boys and girls, come into school. The period allotted to exercise and recreation has expired."

With which words the worthy gentleman retired into the school-house. The scholars trooped in—Will and Donsy coming last.

"Now," said Donsy, "you shall not fight: ain't you ashamed of yourself, Lanky, to refuse so long to play and we not have half a dance!"

And the country beauty smiled on her admirer, until he forgot the import of her words.

"You were wrong too, Will, and you know it," said Donsy, "to try and break up our dance! It was too bad!"

And she gave her hand to Will, with a smile—threw a kiss with the points of her fingers to the violinist; whispered, "Come and see me soon, dear Lanky;" and entered the school-house.

Lanky remained staring at the door, through which the dazzling vision had disappeared, in utter disregard of Captain Ralph's philosophy and advice. The reason was, that Lanky was in love.

CHAPTER IX.

INTRODUCES A GENTLEMAN ONCE VERY POPULAR IN VIRGINIA.

Lanky stood for some moments gazing, as we have said, at the door through which his lady had vanished, and during this time his mind seemed to be engaged on some problem which he could not solve. Not until a humming noise from the school-house, and some merry faces at the window attracted his attention, did he become conscious of the singularity of his posture: and seeing that he was undergoing that disagreeable ceremony, being laughed at, he slowly departed. As he turned away, his thoughts took words unto themselves, and shaking his head, he murmured the profound sentiment:

"These women kind are mighty hard to understand!"

The expression of his opinion on this subject seemed to quiet Lanky somewhat, and he took up a line of march toward home, without perceiving that he was followed by a youthful individual, who had been a delighted auditor of his fiddle playing.

The word 'individual,' is perhaps the best to apply to the person in question, as it leaves no distinct impression :—any single word attempting to describe him, would miserably fail. It was a something in the shape of a human being about three feet high, with a large woolly head, a laughing phiz, resembling in color and texture charcoal, a glittering set of teeth, and a roll in its walk which seemed to indicate the peculiarity known as bandy legs. This figure wore a man's coat, all tattered and torn, and in consequence of the wearer's smallness, the waist of the old coat was at his knees, and the skirts dragged the ground. We refrain from describing the rest of his attire, from a reasonable regard for our reputation as a veracious chronicler. We can only say that the garment called a tunic by the ancient Romans had here reached its last degree of dilapidation : and that the Gallic vesture was of that description that it cannot possibly be described.

We have expended thus much description upon the figure now following Lanky, because—more fortunate than brave men who lived before Agamemnon—he has secured a poet and an immortality.

The grotesque little goblin, who as we have said had witnessed the exhibition of Lanky's skill with extreme delight, now followed in his footsteps; sawing his left arm with his right, in imitation of the motion of the bow arm; rolling his head, chin erect, from side to side; and executing a species of dance something between the waddle of a goose and the antics of a monkey.

Lanky was not aware of the honor paid to his performance, and went on thinking of Donsy and his prospects.

"The fact is," said Lanky to himself, "I never ken say any thing when Donsy's lookin' at me. I lose my wits directly she begins to smile and talk sweet to me, and look at me so! *I* couldn't do what the Captain said I ought to —hold my head up and talk bold and free! I can't say nothing—I feel so curious. What a unfortunate young man I am!"

And Lanky sighed; and went on still thinking of Donsy, and wholly unconscious of his 'following.'

"Now there's no use talking," he continued after a pause. "I never *ken* tell her how much I love her—I needn't try. I don't know any way to do, but to write a letter and tell her all about it, though she knows it well enough now. But what good would that do? I never would have the courage to put it in the office in town, and run the chance of that old fellow Smith laughin' at me. Oh me! that would be dreadful! I could write it well enough, for Mr. Charles showed me how to make my letters:—but how afterwards? *I* couldn't have courage to hand it to her. 'What's that?' she would say! And then I'd feel like I wanted to creep through a hole. Who could I get to send it by?"

Lanky heard a subdued whistle, and turning his head saw the boy following him, and sawing away with an accuracy of imitation which was worthy of the most elevated praise.

"What are you doin', Crow?" said Lanky, "and how did you get here?"

"I git here jest so, Mas' Lanky," replied Crow, making ready to jump out of the way of a blow, but sawing away as enthusiastically as ever, "I been listen to you playin'."

"Idle as usual, you little monkey," said Lanky, "where are you goin'?"

"I ain't gwyne nowheres."

"Why ain't you workin'?"

"Is'e free; *I* is," said Crow, executing a pas seul.

"An idea struck Lanky all at once, that Mr. Crow might act as his messenger and postman, that young gentleman being a privileged character whose presence would excite no more remark than that of a shadow.

Just as this idea occurred to him, they reached the highway, on the opposite side of which was visible the path leading toward the abode of Captain Ralph. Lanky raised his hand to his hat to salute a gentleman who was riding by: and this ceremony was closely imitated by Mr. Crow, who added the further honor of a complete 'turn about,' in the process of executing which, we are sorry to say, his long skirts got in his way, and he made a considerable hole in the sandy road with his head.

It may be readily understood, that Crow agreed to place himself completely at the commands of Lanky for a very slight gratuity:—we need not follow them. Let us rather accompany the cavalier who had passed; and as this will lead us into company a step higher, commence another chapter.

CHAPTER X.

HOW MR. JACK HAMILTON, FOXHUNTER, AND BACHELOR, ASPIRED TO THE HONORS OF A WIG, A SUIT OF BLACK, AND A GOLD-HEADED CANE.

THE gentleman was our old acquaintance, honest Jack Hamilton:—for by this honorable prefix was the worthy fellow now almost universally known.

Mr. Hamilton had changed very little—not at all we might venture to say. He had reached that middle ground of human life, extending from thirty-five to forty, when the mental and physical organization of man seems to stand still, neither increasing nor decreasing in strength, bloom, or grace: —when nature seems to pause upon the summit of those piled up years, before descending slowly into the vale of age. When a man has arrived at this point in his pilgrimage toward the other world, his eye embraces a more ample horizon, than at any former or later period. On one side lies the brilliant land of youth and childhood, with its murmuring streams filling the fields with music, its myriads of delicious flowers, burdening the faint pure air with perfume;—and by these streams so bright and sparkling, among these flowers whose odor haunts the memory, glide forms which filled with joy, and freshness, and a tender bloom, the whole happy period of youth. What joy, what freshness, in the bright eye and lip of the boy's sweetheart!—what a tender bloom upon the cheek, which blushed with delight when the loved one approached! And farther still into that past, the man's eye plunges and finds again the all-embracing mother's love, the father's tenderness—those things which words fail to utter, leaving the heart to speak!

And on the other side the now mature man sees stretching the cool and shady path of age, evironed with a thousand quiet joys, which, if they have not all the light illusion and romance of youth, to gild them, still are quite as genuine as the rapturous pleasures of that brilliant golden youth—the sunset almost shames the dawn! And if at the end of that quiet path, there stands a white stone—and if to reach that bourne the foot must sometimes tread on thorns, still upon the marble there is carved a symbol, and a suffering head, which makes the weary heart forget those thorns, because they are sanctified for ever, by encircling the brows carved there.

Embracing at a glance the whole horizon, extending thus from childhood to old age, the man of true heart, standing on the summit of manhood, does not shrink. For if the bright fields he looks back upon were filled with strange delights, the path he has yet to tread is not sombre, does not want for consolations—if the light of dawn was fresh and golden, a light streams from the Cross, cut in stone, and rising o'er the champaign, which is far more pure. For it murmurs to the spirit "Peace!"

And now, if the reader is disposed to find fault with this philosophic and meditative digression, we can only say that we regret it, requesting him to pass over any future digressions of the same description. Let us then return to Mr. Jack Hamilton, whose middle-aged appearance, and two or three gray hairs, led us away.

Mr. Hamilton rode on composedly, and soon reached Effingham Hall, which was not very far, as we know, from "The Trap," where the forlorn and unhappy bachelor pined in single blessedness, and uproarious mirth. Mr. Effingham was standing before the fire-place in the dining-room, amusing himself by gazing through the window, at the cloud shadows.

Hamilton grasped him cordially by the hand, and this exhibition of friendly regard was returned with as great heartiness.

"I'm glad to see your familiar face, Hamilton," said Mr. Effingham, "and I do not think you have changed in the least."

"Not a bit, I believe," returned the fox-hunter· "but, by George! you have."

Mr. Effingham looked out of the window.

"Are all the boys well?" he asked at length.

"Yes."

"And fox-hunt as much as ever?"

"More!"

"What an easy, careless time you must have, with that passion for the chase, Hamilton."

"Well, I don't know. It has its drawbacks," replied his friend. "but suits a disreputable bachelor like myself."

"It is a great thing for the blood; I used to hunt—and I can understand what you mean, by saying that it has its drawbacks; a broken arm, collar bone, or leg, for instance."

"I did not mean that, Champ, my boy. A good rider can always avoid that—but the ladies don't like it."

"The ladies?" asked Mr. Effingham, with his habitual faint smile lighting up his calm, weary face, at the mortified tones of his friend.

"Yes, yes," said Hamilton.

"Explain yourself!"

"Why, Miss Alethea here, for instance."

"Alethea?"

"Yes."

"Does she lecture you?"

"By George! I should say she did. She never allows me any rest. I never introduce the subject of fox-hunting, but I am immediately informed that a gentleman of my standing in the community should turn his attention to other and more important matters; for instance, the improvement of the parsonage of the new and popular Mr. Christian, parson of the parish, or getting together a fund for supplying the unfortunate little Indians over there on the river with *braccæ*, as the Latin term is—*vulgo* trowsers. Yes, sir! that is what makes me complain of the disadvantages of my unfortunate bachelor and fox-hunter condition. But enough; where are they all to-day?"

"Alethea and my father have gone over to Mr. Lee's."

"Then you are all alone."

"Yes—little Kate is here somewhere, I think."

"A nice little creature,—and did you have a pleasant passage?"

"Tolerably."

"From London?"

"Yes."

There was a pause for some moments, at the end of which time Mr. Hamilton went into a fit of laughter, and cried out:

"By George, Champ!—or if that oath is getting disreputable, owing to his gracious Majesty's saying and doing—by Jove! here am I dying to know all about your travels; and according to the good old English custom, followed by friends immemorially, we are dealing in the most ridiculous commonplaces. Come, speak!"

And rising, Mr. Jack Hamilton assumed, what we believe is known as the "Virginia position," before the fire—that is to say, a contented and indolent attitude, with the shoulders bent forward, the coat skirts under the arms, the right leg extended at an angle of ten or twenty degrees in front.

"I have nothing to tell about my travels," said Mr. Effingham, wearily, and gazing as before at the cloud shadows floating over the fields. "I went, knocked about, and came back—that is all. What news of any consequence is there in the neighborhood?"

"None."

"There is to be a race soon, down near Jamestown?"

"Yes."

"I think I shall go, though I take little interest in these matters. Much politics talked about in the neighborhood?"

"Politics? there is nothing but politics talked. That infernal Stamp Act is looked for every day, and the colony is getting red hot.

"They are right," said Effingham, with a slight çolor in his wan cheek, "it is an infamous measure—and I saw the whole affair in London; it will be passed."

"Let 'em take care!" said Hamilton.

"Yes," replied his friend, growing calm again; "you rightly judge that it is an extreme test. But do not let us talk politics, I have no spirits for it."

Hamilton looked at his friend curiously.

"Were your travels very dull?" he asked. "It seems to me that you have returned not much improved in vivacity, Champ."

Mr. Effingham raised his eyes, making no reply. Hamilton returned his gaze, in perfect silence also, and for some moments the friends looked thus at each other. Suddenly Mr. Effingham held out his hand, and said:

"Well, Hamilton, if we must touch upon that subject—if I speak of it—I know of no man better than yourself. Come! you think I am dull—spiritless—with less vivacity than ever?"

"Yes," replied Hamilton, cordially pressing the hand of his friend, "your cheeks are thinner and paler, your forehead has the mark of thought upon it, your mouth does not smile in a wholesome way. I repeat that you are less vivacious."

"I was never very bright," said Mr. Effingham; "but can you not understand that there is in my case, to be estimated and allowed for, a great force, an enormous motor?"

"A great force?"

"That of reaction!" said Mr. Effingham, calmly.

Hamilton had never been quick of apprehension, and it must be confessed, did not understand the profound meaning of these words.

"Well?" he said, however.

Mr. Effingham paused for some moments, looking calmly through the window.

"Those clouds are very fine," he said, "and the shadows are beautiful."

Then he added:

"But I was going to speak of myself. You wish to know something of my travels, of my feelings, and all?"

"Yes."

"Well, Hamilton," continued Mr. Effingham, as calmly as before, "you are a good friend, and I need not play the reserved with you, though I assure you I feel no disposition to dissect my own heart. It is not a pleasant task, but it can do no harm."

And after a pause of several minutes Mr. Effingham continued:

"You will no doubt recollect the affair which created so much agreeable comment in this neighborhood, a year or two ago:—an affair which, commencing like a comedy, came near ending a tragedy for all the actors, among whom I held, I believe, a distinguished rank. It is not necessary for me to go over that matter for your entertainment, for I think you know very nearly as much about it as I do myself: how I loved with a wild and passionate infatuation a splendid and fiery woman, who, from the first moment we encountered each other, became my fate. You knew all that, and no doubt understood the sequel: the tragedy (to return to my theatrical metaphor) requires no prologue for you."

"But in relation to that young girl who exerted so powerful an influence upon my life," continued Mr. Effingham, "let me say two or three words. On our first meeting, in the tall forest yonder, she said, in reply to my questions, that she 'was not a lady,' and in this characteristic speech lies the whole explanation of what followed. Had I loved her as a lady—or rather, to correct myself, had I approached her as gentlemen are in the habit of approaching ladies, much which afterwards occurred would never have taken place. I chanced to do what under any circumstances I think I should not have done. I went to the theatre, and there I saw that her criticism of herself was, as far as the mere letter went, strictly true. She was not a lady in the ordinary acceptation of the word; and, blinded by my pride, my love—infatuation if you will—I continued to regard her as an actress, from that moment to the last scenes of the affair. Do not, however, imagine that my love was any thing but the purest, after the acquaintance that I made with the rare and wonderful texture of this woman's nature. No! I loved her madly, but with profound purity—for I am not naturally an impure man, and never adopted the revolting habitudes of the soi-distant noble society of England I have never regarded women in the humbler ranks as the natural purveyors for the amusement of gentlemen. I loved this girl madly, but not, for that reason, coarsely: and I think, that in the course of the intensely dramatic scenes we had together, I must have offered her my hand more than a score of times. You see how it was; I scoffed at and taunted her, railed at her coldness, and sneered at her 'prudish airs' as I called them: but I also honored and respected her at the bottom of my heart, for her purity and nobility of nature. That brings me back to the few words I wished to say of this young girl."

And, after a pause, Mr. Effingham continued, with perfect calmness,—

"She was one of those rare and extraordinary natures, who unite the most opposing and incompatible traits of character in one harmonious whole. You read this characteristic in her very eyes, which melted or fired, were brilliant or dim, flashed gloriously with imperious disdain, or swam in the dews of tenderness and childlike innocent emotions. Upon the stage she was the character she personated—nothing more nor less, for she completely lost her individuality, and forgot the world of reality, entering free and untrammelled into the brighter world of art—the splendid domain of imagination. I have seen her, Hamilton, pass from emotion to emotion with such a marvellous ease and strength that I almost feared to approach her afterwards; I felt, as you may imagine a man would feel, were some queen or empress to converse familiarly with him in disguise; then, throwing off the cloak which covered her imperial robes, reveal herself in all the haughty and dazzling beauty of rank and power. This young girl at home was a mere child, affectionate to her coarse old father, unaffected, simple; you would have thought her rather dull at times. In her character she was the queen of art, and what art was made to interpret, beauty and passion.

"You follow me, do you not? I mean that this girl was in intellect above all the women I have ever known; in resolution more than a match for thousands of men: and with all this she had the heart of a child,—the innocence and purity of a young girl who has never left her mother's side. You may now understand how passionate my infatuation must have been, for I have always experienced a powerful attraction towards truth and nobility, and, of course, a cordial respect for strong character. I loved her, and finding my advances met with indifference and cold aversion, which afterwards changed to passionate aversion and no little dread at times, you may imagine that the fire was blown into a whirlwind of flame.

"I was carried away with passion—I found myself openly defied—I executed that exceedingly unworthy scheme of abduction."

Mr. Effingham looked out of the window at the cloud shadows again, and paused for some time.

"Well," he continued, at length, "after that denouement I went away, you know, and you now ask me to give you some account of my travels. I cannot recall any thing which makes them very interesting. It was the old tale, which we sometimes read in romances; where the despairing lover who has committed some wild act which drives him from his native country, seeks distraction in travel, and endeavors, by changing his residence incessantly, to escape the thoughts which follow him as the shadow follows the body moving on. I ran all over Europe—went to Constantinople, Egypt, Syria; smoked abominable tobacco in Smyrna, and eat disgusting macaroni in Naples. Rome was rather interesting, and I think the happiest portion of my time was spent among the Bernese Alps, in the cottage of a herdsman, with an artist from Florence, who was an excellent companion, and aroused me whenever I fell into one of my fits of rage and despondency.

"I had many such fits, and suffered no little remorse; for I was uncertain whether my rival was dead or not. I had no desire to kill him, strange to say, and was extremely pleased to hear of his recovery by a letter received while I was in Florence. You may understand from this, that by force of travel and incessant novelty, my infatuation for that young girl was slowly being worn down and smoothed away, as the tire of a wheel is worn by the leagues it passes over, and the obstacles in the track. I understood for the first time then, that my madness had spent itself perforce of its own violence, as a storm does, and was gone. I did not grind my teeth and curse that rival, and, if the intelligence of his recovery and marriage was not agreeable, that feeling soon wore away. But my cheerfulness (vivacity, to use your own word) did not return with the disappearance of the afflicting emotions which had tortured me so long. No, I now began to comprehend the truth of the dogma, that the mental system closely resembles, in its modes of operation, the physical. You know that when the human—I mean the physical—system is put under the effect of an excessive stimulant, whether that stimulant be the grape, or opium, or some poison, taken in a quantity not sufficient to produce death—there is, for a time, an unnatural exaltation, a tremendous accession of velocity in all the wheels of life.

The blood rushes like a flood of fire through the veins—the senses become a thousand times more acute. I will give you an instance, and then finish my idea.

"At Smyrna I went one day into one of those shops where opium is provided for the true believers, and mats for them to smoke upon, and lie extended on when the divine exaltation overcomes them. I was always curious to investigate the *causas rerum*, and I wished to experience the effects of the drug which was said to possess such extraordinary properties. Well, the old animal handed me a sort of chibouque, and in a few moments I was smoking like the faithful around me, some of whom were already beginning to totter. As I smoked the opium, the objects in the apartment began to fade, a sort of mist waved before my eyes—then all disappeared, and I entered, it seemed to me, another world—a world so brilliant and beautiful, that any description would only mar it. It is enough to say that life seemed to have passed away with all its suffering, and boundless happiness in another sphere of being opened on me. My blood seemed to roll on like a golden river; I could hear the murmur of the waves; my feet trod upon clouds, not earth—I felt as you may imagine felt the Persian Peri, in the fable when she entered Paradise.

"Well, I woke up with a suicidal sensation:—a desire to leave the world where a man had to support the bundle of nerves which were driving me to agony, with their jarring and aching. A physical exaltation, you observe, had been succeeded by a physical reaction just in proportion—as the balance descends upon one hand, because the other side rises above the natural level, the normal condition. Perhaps I never suffered greater physical torture, and so you have the illustration, a very lame one, of my trite dogma.

"I had reached the period of my travels where the post brought me that letter containing the intelligence of my rival's recovery: and I was about to say that in spite of this weight raised from my breast, I did not become cheerful again—and that, because the stormy emotions I had experienced began to react as the physical organism feels the reaction of hashish or other stimulant. I was completely flat, if I may use the word, and I am so now, in spite of my sight seeing; spite of all the bright eyes in Italy,

France, England, which have shone on me—and I assure you that I was regarded as a very grand seigneur on the continent, owing to the reasonable plumpness of my purse, especially by the Italian damsels. They wearied me—as art, literature, plays, society of all descriptions wearied me. I felt through all this that the proverb of the Preacher shone like a fire—that all was vanity—the very vanity of vanities. I grew quite calm, and am so now, as I said.

"But stay: there was an incident in London which may possibly add another touch to this picture of myself undergoing the distracting effects of a European tour:—it goes to show that my feelings were not quite deadened by the countries, scenes, personages, I had seen—the time which had elapsed.

"In London, one day, I chanced to raise my eyes to the door of a theatre, and I saw the names of the members of the 'Virginia Company of Comedians'—the worthy gentlemen were to play that evening. You see they had by that time returned from Virginia to England, and were figuring in the humbler characters they were suited to. I know not what feeling seized me, and I determined to go and see them play that evening. I went, and found these men just the same easy, jovial, and coarse characters which I had known them to be formerly:—for you know I had the honor to be an accredited member of the 'Virginia Company of Comedians,' and was favored with the society of these worthies. There they were now, just the same:—Hallam strutted in his pompous good-humored way; Shylock, as one of these fellows was called, still exhibited an admirable burlesque of tragedy:—the Virginia Company had become a London Company, that was all.

"The effect produced upon me by the sight of these men was singular. I seemed to go back in actual reality to that former time so filled with fiery passion, with love, disdain, hatred, despair. The very atmosphere seemed to envelope me again—that atmosphere again filled my veins with fierce heat, and so powerful were these emotions, that, carried away by my old fury, I drew my short sword, and would have struck a gentleman who stood by me, had it not been wrested from my hand. He was enraged—I could not explain, or rather he would not hear my vague excuse—we fought on the next morning. But nothing came of it;—he was a lame hand, and I disarmed him, and allowed him to depart. I do not think I recovered from the effect of that performance for a whole month :—but it was the last muttering of the storm—the tempest after that died away completely, and I now feel convinced that nothing can again arouse in me those tempestuous memories. Soon after the incident I have mentioned, I left London, tired, completely wearied of every thing European, and experiencing a singular sentiment of home-sickness, which I had read of in Virgil, and many poets after him; but had never believed in before. I actually began to feel some return of warmth in my frozen breast, thinking of Virginia here—the Hall—my father—the children, and the servants. I cannot say that any of my yearning—the rhetorical word, I believe—was directed toward the ladies of the neighborhood: no, I have done with women, Hamilton, and shall in future avoid them, as the helmsman avoids the sunken rock, the whirlpool, or the muttering storm: well, this is by the way. I was about to tell you how I found that my heart was no longer subject to these stormy memories; and I proved that satisfactorily to myself on my arrival—after a tolerably pleasant passage of two months—in Virginia.

"Do you remember—but you must—my sojourn in the old days at the Raleigh tavern? Yes? Well, I also remember it very distinctly! Let me tell you how I tried myself, and found that my heart was thenceforth as cold as ice, and equal to any test.

"I had occupied, in those former days I have alluded to, an apartment in the tavern known as number six; and she—you understand—had two rooms just opposite. Having arrived in the town from York, at which port I disembarked, late in the evening, I resolved to spend the night there, and I ordered the apartments formerly occupied by the young girl to be prepared for me, with the direct intention to try myself That this trial should be final and definite, I arranged the apartments just as they had been in the past:—the first, I mean, for of the second, her bedroom, I knew nothing, having never entered it. A bureau had been removed to a different position: I changed it to its former place: the slight couch was out of place: I restored it. An eight-day clock ticked on the high narrow mantlepiece—I removed it, and substituted the oblong mirror which had once graced it—leaning forward from the wall. I ordered a single wax-light then to be placed upon the table in the corner, and went and procured a straw hat, such as she wore, with red ribbon, for I remembered all perfectly; and this I threw down upon the couch.

"I wandered about for an hour near the theatre, the Governor's palace—along Gloucester street—reviving her image in my mind: then as night drew on, I went to the apartment—paused at the door and knocked, opened the door and entered. The dim wax-light threw long shadows through the room, and the illusion was complete. I could almost fancy that she had just passed into the adjoining chamber, having thrown down her hat upon the sofa.

"Well, I sat down, smiling, and with my hand upon my brow, summoned all that past, so full of brilliant and passionate figures, and more fiery and passionate emotions, back to me. I commanded those days to rise and defile before me in a long glittering line; and I went over every scene, every sensation, every emotion, whether of suffering or delight, happiness or anguish. I mean that I recalled them, by an effort of memory, not that I really felt them. No: I did not flush, and grow pale, and tear my breast, and rave, as was my wont formerly:—I smiled. I saw that splendid passionate beauty again, but she no longer filled my heart with delirious love, mad anguish: she *interested* me merely. I felt, as you may imagine a man feels, when he is listening to some fine effort of an improvisatore;—where the passions, feelings, incidents, all, interest without moving you very deeply, however tragic. The drama of my life was merely a drama to me now: and I smiled at my old infatuation. To make the drama complete, I raised the window—summoned perforce of my imagination the instruments of that wild and unworthy scheme; and then, with a stealthy tread, approached the chair which she had lain sleeping in. I saw again her enchanting face, with its tender languid beauty as she slept:—the profuse curls upon her snowy neck, the undulations of her figure, as half reclining in the chair, she drew long breaths, worn out with watching, and slumbering heavily. I saw it all, and would have smiled again at the comedy I was playing, had not my conscience reproached me bitterly for that act:—that stratagem which was so unworthy of me, as it is unworthy of a man to cheat a child. I sat down again, and thought of her in her far mountain home, the happy wife of my rival—I left out no particular, I tested my heart to the very bottom—and what was the result? Why, indifference, Hamilton! My infatuation was dead, and I slept as soundly that night in the apartment she had moved about in like a bright sunbeam, as ever I did worn out with travel in the inns of Switzerland.

"Well, here I am now, and I am happily over all that—the play is played, the curtain has fallen on the whole, and it is forgotten. Let it go: I went and took my part in it of my own accord, and cannot complain that the fiery passions of the drama have worn me out. I *am* completely worn out, and there you see, I have returned precisely to what I commenced with."

Hamilton had listened to this narrative in almost perfect silence; and he now remained silent for some time longer. At length, looking curiously at Mr. Effingham, who, stretched languidly in his chair, was gazing listlessly through the window, the honest fellow said suddenly, with some embarrassment:

"Champ, have you seen Clare Lee yet?"

Mr. Effingham looked intently at his friend for an instant, and then turning away his eyes again, said, indifferently:

"Yes."

Hamilton found himself at a loss how to proceed. Mr. Effingham came to his relief.

"I know what you mean," he said, calmly; "and I will answer the question which you have not asked—but you have looked it. You mean, Hamilton, that perhaps my indifference to every thing, my deadness, if you like the word, springs from the fact that I have not yet seen the girl whose presence used to have such an effect on me. You are mistaken: I have seen her, and I was perfectly calm. On the day I arrived at the Hall, she chanced to be here on a visit, and when I made my appearance she was standing directly in front of me, leaning on the harpsichord. Let me confess that I did experience something like a distinct emotion upon seeing her, but, my dear fellow, it did not last. My heart is too much like a sullen lake, deep and black :—it is not moved by so slight a breeze—and I was quite calm again in a moment, and bowed low, and turned round and conversed with a placidity wholly unaffected. I do not say that the sight of Clare," continued Mr. Effingham, in a slightly altered tone, "did not afford me a certain degree of pleasure and pain. I loved her once, and my affection was of that simple, tender description, which outlasts a thousand bursts of passion: for it makes up in depth what it lacks in fire. But I was not deeply stirred—and I think I felt greater pleasure at seeing all here, than at meeting her. Ah! I think she has almost forgotten my wild vagaries—a good girl!"

And Mr. Effingham, for a moment, looked less weary. Hamilton was thinking of the narrative he had just listened to, and endeavoring by an exertion of his not very powerful mind, to arrive at the psychological significance of it. Mr. Effingham came to his assistance.

"You are puzzling yourself," he said, with a languid smile, "to make out what I am, Hamilton. What is the sum total of all these various emotions, conflicting passions? I will tell you. It is weariness, indifference, and content, if I may be allowed thus to couple what seem to be incompatible things. I assure you that I care for nothing in the world. I love the family, I am fond of the Hall here; but these feelings are not very strong. As to my convictions opinions, I believe in nothing, Hamilton, I care for nothing. I get angry sometimes, thinking of his gracious Majesty's legislation on Virginia matters; but after all the thought comes 'What is the use? Why should I trouble myself about his Majesty? He wearies me.' As to any ambition, any social or political aspiration, I have none; it wearies me, just as every thing wearied me in Europe. I played whole days and nights, in Paris, and got up and kicked aside the pile of cards around my ankles, with perfect indifference; I was neither elevated nor depressed by good or bad fortune, and gave a check on my banker, if I lost, or stuffed the gold I won into my pocket, without emotion, good or bad. I went and listened to innumerable tragedies, incessant operas in France and Italy; they wearied me. I believe I fought three or four times, with men I had no intention to insult—I left the ground after these events, with my scratches, when I got any, as I came; indifferently. I have no gallant experiences to add to this—I got enough of women here, and made a resolution to avoid them, to which resolution I have religiously adhered. Well. you see I am worn out—I believe in nothing—I take interest in nothing—I do not complain—I shall probably vegetate here, and become a fat, honest squire, presiding, possibly, at county courts, and talking knowingly of tobacco, and the prices of cattle and of blood, and so, at the appointed time, go the way of all humanity. There it is."

And Mr. Effingham gazed at the fire as calmly as he had spoken. Hamilton looked at him closely for some time, and then said:

"Champ, you want a physician!"

"A physician?" asked his friend.

"Yes."

"I am not sick!"

"Yes you are.'

"I?"

"Yes, you."

"Sick?"

"Very sick."

Mr. Effingham nodded.

"Oh! I understand you now;" he said, "my mind you fancy, is not healthy."

"I don't imagine any thing about it. By George! I know it."

"Well?"

"Let me be your doctor?"

"You?"

"Yes."

"Very well," said Mr. Effingham.

"Will you follow my directions—take my prescriptions?"

"That depends wholly upon their flavor."

"Come now—you retreat at once."

"No."

"If I ask nothing unreasonable?"

"Will I put myself under the direction of Doctor Hamilton?" said Mr. Effingham, smiling faintly at the honest fellow's earnestness; "is that what you meant to say?"

"Yes."

"Well, I promise that much very cheerfully."

"Good!" cried honest Jack; "I'll cure you, by George! and make you a jolly companion again, or I'll eat my head."

"You would have an awful indigestion," replied Mr. Effingham; "but let me hear your scheme."

"No, that does not concern you; I take the responsibility of the drugs. No cure, no pay."

"And what will be your pay, provided you succeed?"

"The satisfaction of hearing you laugh loud enough to shake the windows, and seeing you become the jolly boy of former times again."

"Jack, you are the best friend I have, upon my honor, I think," said Mr. Effingham. "I wish you were as excellent a physician."

"Never mind! by Jove! we'll make the trial. And as you say you do not believe in any thing, I do not ask you to believe in my proficiency in the art, until you feel it. I am going now to see Tom Lane. Goodbye."

"Do not go yet; come, you are fashionable."

"No, I must go," said Hamilton, shaking hands with his friend, and putting on his hat. "My horse is there—I told them not to take him. By Jove! look at him! he's a splendid fellow. Did you ever see such a sweep of the loin? Remember now—I commence next week!"

And whistling merrily, Mr. Hamilton departed.

"There goes a happy man, and an honest fellow," said Mr. Effingham, going languidly into the library; "an intelligent mind too. There is only one delusion under which he labors—he thinks he can cure me."

Mr. Effingham took his hat and cane, and strolled out on the lawn.

"Very pretty, and very wearisome!" he said, looking at the landscape. And he turned away.

CHAPTER XI.

THE OTHER PHYSICIAN.

JUST as Mr. Effingham turned to enter the Hall again, weary already of the lovely afternoon, spite of its azure skies, and singing birds, and pleasant breezes rustling the leaves, and the small brilliant flowers scattered over the lawn, he heard a merry child's voice calling him, from the banks of the little stream which gurgled over its mossy rocks, at the foot of the hill.

He looked round, and saw Kate, who was running towards him, making signs to him.

"Oh, Cousin Champ! come and look at Snowdrop!" she cried, enthusiastically, as she grasped his hand and turned her bright little face with its sparkling eyes and laughing lips up to him; "just come and see how pretty I have made Snowdrop, please!"

Mr. Effingham smiled, and allowed himself to be led down the hill toward the stream. On the grassy margin stood a young heifer, as white as snow, munching with indifferent pleasure, grass, moss, and the early flowers. Snowdrop, as Kate had dubbed the heifer, exhibited a most extraordinary appearance, which fact was attributable to her mistress, it was very plain. The animal was decked out with a multiplicity of red and blue ribbons tied in fluttering bows; and altogether presented an extraordinarily picturesque spectacle, as she quietly, and with the air of a conscious favorite, munched the flowery grass.

"Just look! isn't she pretty!" cried Kate, in a paroxysm of delight. "Did you ever see any thing prettier in all your life, now, Cousin Champ? So! Snowdrop, so—so!" and Kate caressed the white neck of the heifer, who raised her intelligent head, and licked the hand of her young mistress.

"Are those the ribbons I gave you," asked Mr. Effingham, smiling, "brought all the way, with the rest of your presents, in my trunk from London?"

"Oh no!" cried Kate, "I wouldn't set Snowdrop up

so! No, indeed! I'm going to make something nice with them, something for you."

"What, pray, Katy?"

"Why a knot for your sword hilt, or a lovely bow for your coat, to wear at the party."

Mr. Effingham smiled again.

"I have done with all those vanities," he said, "and I shall be very plain at the party, which it seems they are bent on."

"Oh yes! it will be so nice; but you mustn't dress in black, Cousin Champ."

"What then—white and ribbons, like Snowdrop?"

"Oh no, in blue and gold—your pretty suit you know."

"Do you think Snowdrop would be handsome if she was blue, and you decorated her with gold-colored ribbon?"

Kate burst into a shout of laughter.

"Oh, wouldn't that be funny?" she cried, shaking with merriment. "What do *you* think, Miss Snowdrop—tell me now?"

Snowdrop remained mute.

"You must teach her to converse," said Mr. Effingham.

"I believe I could!" cried Kate, "she is so smart, and good, and likes me so much. Don't you, Snowdrop?"

And Kate paused for a reply. Instead of replying, however, the heifer, having exhausted the spot she stood upon, moved away indifferently from her mistress, and vouchsafed no further exhibition of regard. She began to graze quietly on the flowery margin, at some distance.

"The horrid thing!" cried the child, "to be so ungrateful! Well, she may go along."

Mr. Effingham smiled again.

"Tell her goodbye, and let us go in, and look at the new book of engravings," he said.

"No," Kate replied, laughing, "I won't take any more notice of her. Listen how the bluebirds are singing! and look at Tray, yonder, rolling on the grass!"

They approached and entered the Hall, and Mr. Effingham took from the book-case in the library, the book of pictures. The man and the child amused themselves over it for some time, Kate sitting in his lap, as was habitual with her. At last the volume was gone through with, and laid aside.

Kate laid her head on Mr. Effingham's shoulder, and sang in a low tone, thoughtfully. Mr. Effingham gazed for some moments quietly into the little face, and said:

"What is that you're singing, Kate?"

"'It's hame, and its hame,'" replied the child, "I didn't know I was singing."

"It is very sweet:—commence now and sing it through, for me. I like to hear you."

"Do you really?" said Kate, smoothing back her hair.

"Yes, indeed."

"I'll always sing when you ask me, then; but you know I'll do any thing you want me to."

And Kate sang, in her small child's voice, and with great sweetness:

"It's hame, and it's hame, and it's hame I fain wad be,
O hame, hame, hame, to my ain countrie;
There's an e'e that ever weeps, and a fair face will be fain
As I pass through Annan water wi' my bonny band again;
When the flower is i' the bud, and the leaf upon the tree,
The lark shall sing me hame in my ain countrie!

"Hame, hame, hame,—hame I fain wad be,
O hame, hame, hame, to my ain countrie;
The green leaf o' loyalty's beginning for to fa',
The bonny white rose it is witherin' an' a';
But I'll water't wi' the blude of usurping tyrannie,
And green it will grow in my ain countrie!

"Hame, hame, hame,—hame I fain wad be,
O hame, hame, hame, to my ain countrie;
There's nought now frae ruin my countrie can save,
But the keys of kind Heaven to open the grave
That a' the noble martyrs wha died for loyaltie,
May rise again and fight for their ain countrie.

"Hame, hame, hame,—hame I fain wad be,
O hame, hame, hame, to my ain countrie;
The great now are gane, a' wha ventured to save,
The new grass is growing aboon their bloody grave;
But the sun through the mirk blinks blythe in my e'e,
'I'll shine on ye yet in your ain countrie.'"

The tender little voice ended its sweet carol, and for some time Mr. Effingham was quite silent, caressing, absently, the child's small hand, which lay in his own.

"That is a very pretty song, Kate," he said at length; and in an abstracted voice he repeated:

'When the flower is in the bud and the leaf upon the tree,
The lark shall sing me home in my own countrie.'

"That might apply to me," he added, smiling, "you know that I have come back just as the larks are beginning to sing."

"Oh, yes!" cried Kate, "and I am very much obliged to the larks for singing you home."

"Then, you are really glad to see me back?"

"How can you ask me that?" Kate said, reproachfully.

"Why are you glad? Come, tell me," he asked smiling.

"Because I love you," said the child, simply.

"And why do you love me?"

"Because you love me," said Kate, laughing, "isn't that the best reason in the world?"

"Indeed it is a very good reason, and is very true: but come, tell me what you think of me, Kate—I am anxious to know."

"I can't answer that: how could I?"

"Am I good, or bad?"

"Oh, you're good!"

"Not very—I do not think I shall ever die of excessive goodness. But go on—what else am I?"

"You are kind," continued Kate, with a bright affectionate look in her small face.

"Am I?"

"Yes, indeed: to me especially."

"That's because you are such a poor little creature, not much higher than my thumb," said Mr. Effingham, forgetting his weariness, and smiling.

"Indeed I am not," said Kate, "I'm nearly an inch taller than I was last year. Oh! you're jesting," she added, with a laugh.

"Well, go on now, and tell me something more about myself. I am anxious to know. Am I very agreeable—witty, amusing, entertaining? do you ever laugh heartily when I talk to you?"

"No, I don't think I do: but you know you have not come back very well."

"Who, I?" said Mr. Effingham, "why I am the picture of health."

"No, indeed you are not, cousin Champ: your cheeks are thinner and paler than I like to see them."

"My face pale—thin?"

"Yes—and it grieves me: indeed it does."

"Are you ever grieved at any thing, Kate? I thought that you were always so bright, and merry, and laughing; playing with Willie, and decking out Snowdrop, and running about like a sunbeam incessantly, that you never stopped to think a moment, much less to grieve."

"Indeed, you are mistaken: I think a great deal," said Kate, "I think when I am playing, and sewing, and even when I am singing."

"What do you think of?"

"Of any thing—of you, or papa, or myself, or mamma."

"Of your mother?"

"Yes, cousin Champ," said Kate, quite simply, "you know mamma is in heaven."

Mr. Effingham made no reply.

"But what do you grieve about?" he asked at length. "You said you grieved, Katy."

"Yes, I grieve, but not often. I grieve about you sometimes."

"Since my return?"

"Yes, cousin Champ, and while you were away too. I didn't like you to be away—for you know you were my playmate."

"Yes," said Mr. Effingham.

"I had other playmates—Willie and Tommy Alston, and Sue Ashton, but I liked you the best: and then you know I thought you couldn't be so happy across the sea as here."

"I don't think I was."

"I used to want you to come back mightily: and I've prayed often for you, too."

Mr. Effingham smoothed the bright little head in silence.

"You don't know how delighted I was, when your letter came," continued Kate, laying her cheek on Mr. Effingham's shoulder.

"Were you?" he said, smiling.

"Yes, but I thought you would come back looking better—how did you grow so pale?"

And the child looked affectionately at the white brow, and thin cheek.

"Am I pale?" he said, "well, I must get rosy again, and not make my little pet grieve."

"Indeed, I wish you would look merry and well again—I don't like to see you looking so tired, and as if you did not care much for any thing."

These words were so perfect an echo to what Mr. Effingham had said of himself a little while before, that he was struck.

"But, suppose I do not care for any thing?" he said. "Listen now, Katy: suppose I considered life, this world you know, a place where people dressed up and went through their parts, as a matter of course, because other people were looking at them; and suppose I thought that all their merry faces, and laughing, and going on, was affected—and often hid a feeling of disquiet, I mean painful feeling. Suppose I did not take any interest in any thing, because the world was not bright, and disagreeable things were always putting me out of temper:—suppose I really did not care any thing for the world, or the people in it?"

"But that would be wrong," said Kate, simply.

"How?"

"Because the world is not so bad and disagreeable."

"Isn't it?"

"Oh, no."

"But if I thought so?"

"Well, cousin Champ, I think you still ought to do your duty."

"My duty?"

"Yes: you know there is a great deal of good to be done in the world, and nobody has the right to leave it undone. Don't be offended with me:—I wouldn't say it, you know, if it wasn't right; or, I mean, if I didn't think it was right: and I don't mean you."

Mr. Effingham was silent.

"I read a good deal in my Bible," said Kate, "and oh! did I ever tell you what a strange thing happened? I missed it one day—my little old Bible, that papa gave me, you know—and I couldn't think where in the world it was. Well, about a month afterwards it was brought to the Hall, by somebody, without any message, and wrapped up so nicely."

For a moment a cloud passed over Mr. Effingham's face, as he recalled those past scenes, which the child with the thoughtlessness of youth had apparently forgotten. This cloud soon passed away however, and he said:

"You dropped it somewhere, and some honest person found it. Do you read much in it, Kate?"

"Oh yes, every night; and I ought to, you know, because God has been so good to me, and he commands us to."

"Yes."

"We ought not to forget God," said Kate, "at least, I ought not to, for he sent papa to take me, when I hadn't any father or mother."

Mr. Effingham passed his hand over her hair, softly.

"That was our duty," he said, "you are our blood, and besides," he added, smiling, "you are not so poor, Katy: you are quite a little heiress."

"I know papa says, I am not poor," Kate said simply, "but money you know couldn't buy love."

"Indeed,—no."

"And every body loves me," said Kate. "It makes me happy to think of that, and I try to be good."

The child's face wore such a simple, tender look, at the moment, that Mr. Effingham turned his eyes from it, to a portrait over the fire-place, which wore an expression strikingly similiar.

"You are very much like my mother, Katy," he said, softly, "you know your father and mine married cousins."

"Did they? I am very glad—they are in heaven together, you know, cousin Champ" she said, simply.

Mr. Effingham looked at the child again, and felt his heart much softened.

"You are a good little creature, Kate," he said, "and I think it does not hurt me to talk to you. Now come, let us take a little walk. The evening is very fresh and pretty and I think you will enjoy it."

'Oh yes!" cried Kate, springing up, "I'll get my hat in a moment."

And she ran up stairs, and returned almost immediately, with a small wide-rimmed straw hat decked with ribbon, and a light velvet pelisse, which she threw around her shoulders, rather to feel that she had some wrapping on, than because the pleasant afternoon required it.

Then hand in hand the man and the child issued forth, and took their way along the white, winding road, toward the gate, visible at some distance through the wood.

CHAPTER XII.

A LANDSCAPE WITH FIGURES.

Kate and Mr. Effingham reached and passed through the old gate, and determined to extend their walk to a knoll, two or three hundred yards beyond the little stream which crossed the road. The stream was rendered passable by means of a narrow footway, constructed of two large logs, above which extended a slender sapling fixed to a tree upon either side, and meant to answer the purpose of a balustrade.

Kate entered upon the narrow path over the brawling little stream, with fear and trembling and laughter. The swaying banister, so to speak, was very insecure, and one might have supposed that Miss Kate Effingham was taking lessons in the noble art of rope-dancing, so carefully, with her right arm extended, did she balance herself upon the insecure footway.

"Oh, me! I'll fall in! I'm sure I shall!" she cried, "oh, cousin Champ!"

Mr. Effingham smiled, and said:

"Well, madam, you chose to precede me. It is your own fault."

"Oh!" continued Kate, making the most extraordinary gyrations with her right arm, "oh! the tree is giving way!"

In fact, the sapling began to bend more than ever.

"I shall fall in! I know I shall!" cried Kate, laughing, and trying to steady herself. "Oh! cousin!"

Two strong arms raised the child, and bore her across.

"Thank you!" she cried, "I never should have got over, I think."

And they proceeded toward the hill, which they soon reached. From the summit, there was a fine view of the Hall, which raised its princely walls above the embowering foliage in the sunset. The windows seemed to be on fire with the crimson light of evening, and the rich rays died away across the broad champaign in roseate splendor—fainting, failing, dying. It was one of those lovely scenes which are so common in Virginia, when the sun seems to linger, loth to leave the fair fields and tall forests.

"Look, Katy," said Mr. Effingham, "that is as pretty a sight as you could find if you were to travel a thousand miles."

"It's lovely!" cried Kate, leaning her head against his shoulder, and gazing at the landscape with her large bright eyes; "and look at the clouds!"

"Yes: all gold. There is nothing as fine as this in Italy—though I have seen something like it from a hill near Florence. Ah! they have painters there—there are no painters, no artists in Virginia: the time has not come—but it will come."

"Look!" cried Kate, "there is the carriage."

And she pointed to the left, where the winding road plunged into the woodland. There, indeed, was the Hall chariot rolling on slowly toward them, the four glossy horses lit up by the last rays of the sun.

"Somebody's with them," continued Kate; "see what a fine-looking-man, and what a beautiful horse. I never saw any thing as pretty."

"As the man—or the horse?" asked Mr. Effingham, with a faint smile.

"Oh, the horse! look what slender, pretty legs he has, and what a fine head and mane."

"The man?"

"Oh, no! you are laughing at me: the horse: who can it be?"

"It is Captain Ralph Waters," said Mr. Effingham, calmly, "let us go and meet them."

Kate gave a delighted assent to this proposition; and descending the hill again, they reached the stream just as the carriage drove to the bank.

"Ah! there's my excellent cousin!" cried the voice of Miss Henrietta Lee, from the chariot: and the brilliant head of that young lady projected itself from the window.

Mr. Effingham bowed: and then turning to Captain Ralph, said in his calm, courteous voice:

"I am glad to see you again, sir: give you good evening."

"Why, good evening, companion," replied the Captain, "delighted to see you, though I did not anticipate that pleasure."

"I have been taking a short walk—myself and my little cousin."

The Captain made Kate a very courteous little bow, which that young lady was much pleased with.

"A short walk, eh?" continued the Captain; "how is that?"

"There is the Hall, sir—it is not far."

"The Hall?" said the Captain, drawing rein, "ah! the Hall!"

And a cloud passed over the worthy soldier's brow.

"I believe I must return," he added, approaching the window of the carriage, and bowing to Henrietta, Alethea, and the squire.

"I trust, Captain Waters, that you will not be so unfriendly as to leave us at the door of my house," said the old gentleman, with frank courtesy: and he added, in a lower tone, "I understand, sir, that your last visit was on a disagreeable occasion, and did not tempt you to repeat your call: but let the past sleep; you will do me an honor and a pleasure."

The Captain twisted in his seat, twirled his moustache, and made no reply.

"Do not afflict me, sir," said the squire, in the same low tone, and with as much cordial courtesy as before, "by causing me to recollect events which should be forgotten. Come, sir—I ask you to do me a personal favor."

The Captain half yielded, muttering to himself.

"The ladies must be tired of me," he said; "I am only a rude soldier, sir: come now, Madam Henrietta, say! are you not tired of me?"

This was one of those decisive questions which can only be answered by a lady in the negative; as she could not say yes, therefore, Henrietta said nothing.

"I am sure that I shall be glad if you go, sir," said Miss Alethea, "and I am quite as sure that Henrietta will."

No reply from Henrietta.

"Ah, well," said the Captain, seeming to conquer his repugnance at last, "many thanks. I will weary you a little longer. But is this young lady going to walk?" continued the soldier, pointing to Kate. "Take my horse, he is perfectly gentle, *ma petite Mademoiselle;* will you not? I will fix the stirrup for you."

"I'm afraid, sir," Kate replied, laughing; "I don't mind walking, if I was over the run."

"Basta! then permit me to transport your small ladyship," said the soldier, laughing.

And he rode up to the fallen tree, upon which Kate was standing. The child was quite delighted with this proposition, and first interrogating the old gentleman by a glance, was soon perched behind the Captain, who bore her across in an instant behind the carriage.

"Do you like your seat, Ma'mselle?" asked the Captain.

"Did you speak to me, sir?"

"Yes, yes: Ma'm'selle is the outlandish for *miss.*"

"Yes, sir—I like to ride on such a pretty horse."

"Then I'll carry you all the way, *ma foi!*"

"I don't want to leave cousin Champ," said Kate.

Mr. Effingham, who had crossed the brook, smiled, and opening the door of the chariot, entered it.

"Now, Katy, you may be at rest," he said, "I am very well here, and you shall have your ride."

The chariot then rolled on and soon drew up before the Hall, as did Captain Ralph, behind whom Kate was sitting with delighted countenance. Will, who had just returned from school, came forth and assisted the ladies from the carriage with dignified courtesy, and the whole party entered the old mansion, Willie lingering behind to ask Kate who that man with the moustache was?

CHAPTER XIII.

IN WHICH THE COMEDY PROCEEDS.

"I do not know how you can say so, sir."

"Is it not true, Madam Henrietta? Come now, say, is it not?"

"No, sir; why should 'ladies in general prefer a fop to any other species of admirer?' You perceive, sir, that I repeat your own words."

"Yes; and I maintain that they are dooms correct. I set up my rest upon that proposition, and defend it as becomes a soldier, and one long cognizant of the humors and peculiarities of the divine sex," continued the Captain, gently caressing his long black moustache, and bending forward with great earnestness in his chair.

While the Captain and Henrietta converse upon one side of the room, Mr. Effingham sits languidly looking out of the window near Miss Alethea upon the other: Kate and Will are holding an animated dialogue by the harpsichord; and the squire is in the distance exchanging compliments with the parson of the parish, who made his appearance at the Hall soon after the entrance of the party. Mr. Christian is a quiet, benevolent-looking gentleman of about forty, with an open, pleasant eye, a mild manner: and he wears the clerical suit of black, and white neckcloth. Dark colored leggings reach to his knees, and in his hand he carries the shovel hat worn by the clergy.

And now that the reader has these different groups before him, in the old portrait-decorated, carved-wainscoted drawing-room, let us return for a brief space to Miss Henrietta Lee and her admirer:—for by this time Captain Ralph has come to assume that position, having fought the battle of Glatz for her own and Mrs. Lee's amusement, and having found in Miss Henrietta—whether from interest or a disposition to redeem the character of her sex—an attentive and silent listener. This circumstance has pleased the Captain, and sure of his auditor, he now branches forth into a discussion of the interesting peculiarities of her sex.

"Nothing could be truer than the proposition I have had

the honor to lay down, my dear Ma'm'selle Henrietta," he continues, "let me hear you deny that the adorable sex—the French term, that—is not better pleased with the gay fops who adorn this wicked world, than with the more unpretending individuals of the masculine gender. There is no earthly doubt of the fact, and I feel convinced that a lady of your discrimination, upon a calm view of the facts of the matter, will not venture to deny the truth of the aforesaid proposition."

"I do deny it," says Henrietta, with a toss of her brilliant head, which diffused a light cloud of perfumed powder through the air; "I deny it wholly, sir!"

"For the sake of argument, doubtless," replies the Captain coolly, and exhibiting very little emotion at the lady's manner.

"I never argue, sir!" said Henrietta.

"Yes, yes: logic is not the failing of your admirable sex, madam."

"Indeed, sir!"

"Verily, as our chaplain used to say. But come, let me say a word on this subject: you know how much we masculine animals love to hear ourselves talk—morbleu! almost as much as the ladies: though not quite."

Henrietta preserves a disdainful silence:—but her manner is not so cold. She begins to regard Captain Waters as an amusing as well as audacious gentleman.

"Instead of combating the proposition, I will explain the reason thereof," says the soldier, laughing. "And pray what is a fop? Why a gentleman that wears drop curls, carries a muff of leopard skin, pardy! and ambles elegantly on his high-heeled shoes through the minuet, or other agreeable divertisement. His hands are as soft as a woman's, and are covered with rings: his cheeks are delicately vermilioned with the new French thing called rouge, which being translated is, as you are probably aware, *red*;—his lace is redolent of perfume, and his sword is an inch or something of that sort in length, and covered with knots of ribbon. He takes snuff: he minces his words: he is exquisite:—behold the picture of an elegant gentleman—called by some a fop, by others a dandy."

"Hum!" says Henrietta.

"Now what comparison can there be, my dearest Miss Lee, between one of these noble seigneurs all glittering with embroidery and covered with perfume, and an ordinary fellow —a man of the law, a planter, or a soldier? Their hands are respectably large:—their garments are plain—their swords very lengthy and fit for honest blows—they are guiltless of perfume, and never mince their words or amble. They are much more apt to whip you out a pardy! or morbleu! and their manner of walking is decidedly of the *stride* description. Behold all. See here the difference! at my French idiom again you perceive."

"Yes, sir."

"Well now, can any thing be more natural, more reasonable than the preference your sex have for the former class, madam? The elegant gentleman fascinates you with his drop curls and lovely red cheeks: his muff is ready for your little hands, and should they encounter his own there, they are soft and white:—you admire his grace in the ambling minuet: you are fond of perfumes such as he uses, and his nice little ribbon-decorated sword does not frighten your feminine hearts. How could you ever look at a brown face, a stalwart hand, a plain cavalier, after this enchanting picture? Impossible!"

And the Captain twirls his moustache with a delicious expression of self-appreciation.

"I suppose you mean," says Henrietta, satirically, "that ladies judge wholly by the exterior, and do not like you, sir."

"Me? not like me? No, no, I am an exception!"

"An exception, sir?"

"Yes indeed!"

"Pray, how?"

"I unite, my dear madam, in my own person, the graces of both classes."

"Sir!" says Henrietta, completely astonished at this climax of audacious conceit.

"I know it is in bad taste to say it," replies the Captain, liberally and gracefully; "but I am anxious to disabuse your mind of the impression that in this matter I am actuated by any feeling beyond a philosophical interest in the question, calmly considered. No, no, I have never had the misfortune to be defeated in a fair fight by any man living."

"Then the ladies every where have admired you, am I to understand, sir?" says Henrietta, with her satirical curl of the lip.

"Well now—really—you embarrass me extremely!" replies her cavalier, affecting an innocent and confused expression. "Morbleu! I have no right to reply to that question."

And the Captain looks mysterious.

Really the vainest creature I have ever met with—odiously vain!—is Henrietta's inward comment.

"Ah, you think me very vain!" says the Captain.

Henrietta starts: this acuteness of the soldier is beginning to surprise and annoy her.

The Captain observes the movement she makes.

"Come now: confess I am insupportably vain!" he says; "and quarrel with me for answering your own question. By heaven! I feel as if I *had* been guilty of something horrible—the bare idea of which causes my hair to stand on end!"

And the Captain assumes an expression of such terror, that Henrietta's sense of the comic overcomes her, and she laughs in spite of herself. Conscious however that this will flatter the soldier, she assumes again her habitual expression of satirical indifference, and says:

"Well, sir, having proved, to your own satisfaction at least, that our sex prefer fops to rational men; pray now proceed to inform me why I especially prefer them. You observe, sir, that I use your own words again."

The Captain sees that he has advanced one step: he is called upon to speak.

"Why *you* prefer them?" he asked, desirous of gaining time.

"Yes, sir."

'You wish to know, my dear madam, why I ventured to say that you were likely to appreciate this class very highly—the reason—"

"Yes, sir: I believe I speak plainly."

"Very plainly, morbleu! and with the most charming voice!"

This evasion of the point piques Henrietta's curiosity, and annoys her at the same time.

"You seem to wish to dismiss the subject, sir," she says.

"Dismiss the subject?"

"Yes, sir!" replies the young girl, with a satirical flash of her proud brilliant eye, "you are not fond of logic, it seems, though your sex, you say, monopolize it to the exclusion of my own."

An idea strikes the Captain, and his face beams; all at once he finds himself extricated from his dilemma.

"I do not reply to your insinuation, my dear Miss Lee," he says, "it would take up time. I proceed to tell you why I think *you*, of all others, would prefer these soft, amiable, delightfully tranquil, word-mincing gentlemen; and I think that if you would cast your eye upon that mirror yonder, you would require nothing more."

"How, sir?" says Henrietta, gazing at her brilliant image in the mirror.

"Why, it would show you a pair of bright flashing eyes, lips full of animation and brilliancy,—in a word, you would see a young lady full of fire and spirit. See here, morbleu! the whole matter in a nutshell."

Henrietta's lip curls.

"Really you must aspire to rival the Sphinx, sir," she says.

"I, madam? Oh, no! I have no desire to match myself against that wonder of antiquity; and I think my point quite plain."

"How plain, sir?"

"You see brilliant eyes there; at least bright eyes: do you not?"

"Well, sir?"

"Animated lips?"

"Proceed, sir."

"Life, quickness, animation?"

"Well, what next?"

"Nothing, my dear madam, all is explained. You prefer the aforesaid quiet, amiable, unoffending fops, because they are so completely contrasted with yourself. Like seeks unlike—you know the proverb."

"Then, sir, I am not 'quiet'—"

The Captain finds that his anxiety to escape from one dilemma has plunged him into another, and he utters a sonorous 'hum!'

"Nor amiable—?"

"Really, madam—"

"Nor unoffending?"

"What an unfortunate man I am," says the Captain, with well-counterfeited contrition. "I do not understand the English tongue, owing to my long sojourn in foreign lands. I foresee, Ma'm'selle, that we shall not get on in English. High Dutch, Prussian or the French, for heaven's sake, or I am ruined, totally, completely—*ayez pitie!*"

Henrietta again feels a violent desire to laugh, so profound is the Captain's chagrin—or rather the affectation of chagrin. Feeling unwilling to encourage him, however, she plays with a diamond necklace round her neck, and tugs at it indifferently.

"Take care!" says the Captain, "I observe a portion of your necklace loose, and—"

The caution comes too late: the unfortunate necklace parts asunder and drops upon the carpet.

The Captain picks it up gallantly.

"There, now!" says Henrietta, with an expression of annoyance, "you have made me break my necklace, sir!"

"*I*, my dear madam?"

"Yes, sir: if I had not—"

But finding the explanation likely to turn out somewhat embarrassing, she pauses.

"Your explanation is perfectly satisfactory," says the soldier, laughing.

"What explanation, sir?" says Henrietta, more piqued than she cares to show.

"Why, the explanation you gave of my agency in the destruction of the unfortunate necklace.'

Henrietta tosses her head.

"I gave none, sir," she said.

"Really, madam—"

"Well, sir?"

"Permit me to observe, that you undoubtedly did explain."

"I was not conscious of it, sir."

"Perhaps not: but I heard it; and I am so profoundly convinced of my criminality by the aforesaid explanation, that I hold myself the real author of this unhappy circumstance."

"Well, sir, as you please."

But this does not satisfy the Captain, who with the art of a consummate soldier has already graven out the plan of his campaign."

"Am I not guilty?" he persists.

"If you choose, sir."

"Yes, or no?"

"Yes, then, sir."

The Captain exhibits great delight at this avowal, and with his white teeth shining merrily under his black moustache, returns the broken necklace to its owner, and continues conversing with the utmost sang-froid and good humor; as if indeed he had just rendered a service, instead of causing an annoying accident.

Let us now turn to the other groups, which are as busily engaged in conversing as the Captain and his friend—or enemy—Miss Henrietta.

"It may surprise you, sir," says Mr. Christian to the squire, in his mild quiet voice, "but I do not consider the present Church system so perfect as you seem to, though I am a member of that system. I think that there are many and great abuses in it; and I can understand how these abuses have attracted so much attention from the new reformers of the age."

"We have too many reformers, parson," says the bluff squire; "they'll reform and reform, until no form is left in any thing."

"I thought, sir, that the legislation of parliament upon matters connected with this colony found in you a determined enemy. I am, as you know, a stranger here, but still—"

"They do, sir!" interrupted the squire, "I am opposed to the death to the whole policy of the present ministry—meddling with our affairs here, and presuming to speak of a stamp duty! It is abominable! But that does not blind me so far as to make me hate the good old established Church."

"I would be much grieved to hear that you hated it, sir," says Mr. Christian mildly, "but we may cherish a system and yet not be blind to its abuses."

"What abuses under heaven are there in our Church, sir?—the good old system under which my forefathers lived and died? It is a queer question to ask you, sir—but you have thrown down the gauntlet!"

Mr. Christian smiles.

"It is not customary for persons of my profession, Mr. Effingham, to throw down defiances. Believe me, such was not my intention: I meant only to express, in a Christian and moderate spirit, my fears of the operation of our present system. You ask what are the abuses in it: I think I can reply in very few words. The presentation to parishes, in the first place, is very unjust in its operation—that privilege being often granted to noblemen and gentlemen who do not care how parishes are governed. I have known instances, sir, where persons were named for this sacred duty—and who were called to it, in truth too, sir—persons, I say, whose lives had been more scandalous than I can describe, and who carried the vices of this world into the bosom of the holy Church."

"Well, sir—there is something in that, and I have heard that the worthy who preceded you, parson, was no better than he should be. I'm glad we are rid of him, and I send Will to his school from pure charity."

"I did not wish to make allusion to any one, sir—God forbid: that is not my place."

"A good exchange! I'll say that much, parson," says the honest squire, "but the other abuses?"

"I will mention but one, sir: and perhaps what I say may surprise you. I think the union of Church and State impolitic."

"The union of Church and State impolitic!—impolitic!"

"Wrong, then, sir," Mr. Christian replies mildly to these impassioned words, "I think it a great injustice."

"How, in heaven's name?"

"Thus, sir. The sentiment of religion is so high and pure, depends so completely upon the untrammelled operation of the human heart, that any legislation which tends to circumscribe and reduce it to rule must eternally fail, and operate wofully for the great interest of mankind. This sentiment, sir, must be permitted to be a law unto itself; nothing can direct it; nothing should interfere with it. Especially and terribly unjust are those laws which say to the follower of Christ, 'you shall not worship at any shrine but one, and that shrine you must support.' You perceive, sir, that I am as far advanced in my reform ideas as the most zealous *new light*, as I believe those who dissent from our Church call themselves. I cannot help myself, I cannot say what I do not think, and, after much prayer to God to enlighten me, and give me just and true understanding, I am compelled to say that I believe religious toleration the first and most important duty of a state."

Mr. Christian ceases speaking, and gazes thoughtfully and earnestly into the lawn. The squire clears his throat, marshals his logic, and with a preparatory "hem!" commences his refutation of the parson's views. Let us, however, leave the worthy gentlemen, and pass on to the harpsichord, not pausing to hear Miss Alethea inform Mr. Effingham that Clare had a headache, and could not come, or to listen to her companion's weary and languid discourse. Let us pass on, and hear what Will and Kate are saying to each other.

Comedy goes out of its proper field when it deals with fiery passions, or grand personages or events; but, if it cannot usurp the function of tragedy, it has this to recommend it, that it may safely deal with every species of character, of every class and every age; and when in this pursuit it finds a peculiarity, it may paint it and vindicate itself, however humble and apparently insignificant the personage or the trait may be. The reader must have been convinced, before this, that the second portion of our history is destined to deal with comedy more than the former portion, though that boasted a company of comedians,—and in this he has not been mistaken.

Will and Kate are persons of the comedy, and we must not neglect them now or at any future time.

They are holding an animated conversation, as we have said, by the harpsichord, and Will seems to be in possession of something which Kate desires to see very much.—She leans forward on the cricket she occupies, and with her bright eyes fixed upon Master Will, is plainly desirous that he shall unroll something which he holds in his hand. This something is in the shape of a roll of parchment, and Will hesitates, and hesitating, rubs the side of his nose with the scroll.

"Now Willie," says Kate, "I think you might show it to me."

Will rubs the other side of his nose.

"What is it?" continues Kate; "you say it is nice, and pretty, and will make me happy—my goodness! what is it?"

Will assumes a meditative attitude, and smooths that portion of his face upon which he hopes hereafter to have whiskers.

"Guess, Kate."

"I can't."

"Well, try."

"Is it poetry?"

"No."

"A picture?"

Will hesitates, and then says:

"No: not exactly."

"Let's see," says Kate, "what can it be? You said it was 'nice' and 'pretty,' and I would like it—didn't you?"

Will, finding his description cast in his teeth, and apparently dubious whether it is wholly correct, satisfies himself with a doubtful nod.

"Is it a nosegay?—but I see it isn't," says Kate, in despair.

"No, it is not," Will replies.

"What is it? O, my goodness gracious! what can it be?" says Kate, laughing and perplexed.

Willie looks a little sheepish.

"I don't think I can show it to you," he says, stuffing the roll in his breast.

"And not tell me?"

"I think not.

"Now, Willie!"

Will is obdurate.

"O, Willie, what is it?"

"Really, Kate, you are very curious."

"Women always are, you know—always. Now Will!"

And Kate laughs merrily, and attempts to gain possession of the scroll.

"What will you give me to show it to you?"

"Any thing."

"Hold up your mouth!"

And Will, with the gravity of a judge, fixes his lips for a kiss.

"I won't," says Kate.

"Not kiss me!" cries Will, in despair: and shaking his head he adds, mournfully, "then I needn't have got Sam Baskerville to write this."

"Oh, it's writing," says Kate, clapping her hands, "now I know."

Willie remains silent.

"It's a love letter, please let me see it," adds his lady love.

"You will not so much as give me one kiss," says Willie, showing a strong disposition to put his knuckle in his eye, and prize out a tear.

"Ladies of my age must preserve the dignity of their position," Kate says, with delightful gravity.

"Not kiss me!" repeats Willie, with a look to which his former piteous glance was jolly merriment; "then I needn't have got Bill Lane and Ellen Fellows to make the Roman letters, and paint the wreath of flowers, and hearts, and arrow."

And Will looks the picture of patience on a monument smiling at grief, or another deeply chagrined figure, which the reader may imagine.

Kate bursts out laughing:

"Oh there's a wreath of flowers, and a heart—two hearts you said—and an arrow, may be two arrows—"

"Only one," murmurs Will, in a heart-broken tone, and gazing piteously through the window, "wouldn't give me a kiss—me!"

"Well, may be—who knows—but I won't promise."—Kate says,—"let me see it first."

Will, with averted head and nerveless grip, resigns the parchment, and Kate, seizing it, unrolls it quickly. At the top of the page is painted a wreath of flowers, in the middle of which two deeply crimson hearts are pierced by an intensely silver arrow. Above flutters a bow of ribbon, and beneath, in the most ornamental letters possible, Kate reads, half aloud, the following:

"THIS INDENTURE, made in the month of March, of the year of grace one thousand seven hundred and ninety-five, in the Colony of Virginia, Continent of North America,—"

"Sam Baskerville's father was Sheriff, and he knows all about it," says Willie, regarding the parchment with forlorn interest.

"—between William Effingham, Esq.," continues Kate, "of Effingham Hall, and Miss Kate Effingham, of ditto, spinster,—"

"Me!" cries Kate.

"There! that's the way it is," says Will, with forlorn resignation.

"— Witnesseth," continues Kate, mastered by her curiosity and reading without stopping, "that for and in consideration of his, the said William Effingham, Esq's., profound affection and unutterable love, and liking for her the said Kate Effingham, spinster as aforesaid, he the said William Effingham, Esq., doth hereby endow the said Kate Effingham, spinster as aforesaid, with all that property, lying and being in the county of Gloucester, and known as *the Cove*, with all and several, each and every, singular and plural, the fields, tenements, messuages, hereditaments, tenures, and remainder, to say nothing of the reversion and contingent remainder, neither to mention the executory devise thereof—and all this property, he the said William Effingham, Esq., gives to the said Kate Effingham, spinster, because his father gave it to him last Christmas Only provided, and on the condition specified, well understood and no mistake, that she the said Kate Effingham, spinster, who is one of the nicest girls in the Colony—"

"I gave him that part!" murmurs Will.

Kate continues shaking with laughter, and curiosity.

"— shall on the execution hereof according to the style and meaning, intent and signification of it, the said indenture—that she the aforesaid spinster, shall agree to espouse in the bonds of wedlock, for richer, for poorer, in sickness and in health, him the aforesaid William Effingham, Esquire."

"Oh!" cries Kate; but goes on.

"—And to the better understanding of this indenture. it is hereby stated that he the said William Effingham, Esquire, has not at this time, nor ever hath had during any previous time, whereof the memory of man runneth not to the contrary, any affection, love, or desire to enter into matrimonial engagements with Donsy Smith, spinster, who is a nice girl, but not equal to the aforesaid Kate Effingham, spinster. And to the end that all shall be done in the premises the commonwealth's writ of subpœna shall issue, summoning the parties to this indenture, to affix their names to the same: and your petitioner will ever pray.

"Given under our hands and seals, the day and year aforesaid.

"William Effingham, Esq., [Seal.]
[Seal."

Kate finishes the paper and drops it, laughing loud.

"What are you laughing at, Kate?" says Will, mournfully.

"It nearly took my breath away!" cries Kate. "Oh, goodness!"

"Won't you sign it?" pleads Willie, "say, dearest Kate?"

The young lady observes for the first time the profoundly mournful tone of her admirer, and feels the tender sentiment of pity invading her heart. She sighs. Will hears this sigh, and seizes her hand with impassioned expectation.

"No—I don't think—" says Kate, bending her head, with the air of a lady overwhelmed by confusion.

"*Now*, Kate—do sign! We'll have such a delightful time playing down at the Cove—!"

Kate sees the splendid vision, but endeavors to resist. She loves Will devotedly; why not make him happy, when a flirt of the pen can compass that end?

Will throws upon her an affectionate glance, and endeavors to put a pencil in her hand. As he bends down, a little pincushion falls from his waistcoat pocket.

"What is that?" says Kate.

Willie looks the picture of guilt.

"A pincushion!" he murmurs.

"The one I gave you, Willie?"

"N—o," says Will.

"Who gave you this?"

Will looks desperate.

"Donsy!" he murmurs, in an expiring voice.

"And where is mine, pray sir!" says Kate.

Will turns pale, but answers like a man—though a very much frightened man:

"I gave it to Donsy, for this!"

"Then I won't marry you, Willie!" cries Kate, putting her handkerchief to her eyes, "no! that I won't, sir!"

"Oh, Kate! I didn't mean—"

"I won't hear any excuses, sir—I don't want them. To give my pincushion away! Oh! Willie!"

And putting down the true-love indenture, Kate turns from her desperate admirer and pouts beautifully.

"Ah! *petite Mademoiselle*, you are annoyed," says the Captain, "I am sure that gallant little *Monsieur* has not done it."

Kate's face clears up, and a smile like a sunbeam drives away her mortification.

"Yes, sir," says Willie, "I am guilty."

And having made this manly confession, he hastily rolls up the true-love indenture, and stuffs it in his pocket. Then he links arms with the not unwilling Kate, whose ill-humor has nearly vanished, and they run out on the lawn to catch the last rays of twilight, and in child phrase, "make up."

We need not return to the groups whose conversation we have listened to. Our history does not require that we should listen to more:—and as far as one party went, this was even rendered impossible. Captain Ralph rose to take his departure. The squire of course pressed him to remain and sup, but this the worthy soldier declined. He must be at home before the night had set in. Would he then honor them by coming on Thursday next to dinner? If possible.

And so with a consolatory assurance to Miss Henrietta, that he would visit her soon again, the Captain went away.

On the portico he met and bade farewell to the "little Ma'mselle and Monsieur;" and then the twilight swallowed Selim and his rider.

CHAPTER XIV.

AT THE TRAP, AND ELSEWHERE.

One morning, a few days after the scenes we have just related, Mr. Effingham received a note couched in the following terms:

"My Dear Champ:

"Come over to 'the Trap,' and dine and sleep with me. Be sure to be in trim to ride through a cane-brake, that is, in buff and leather: and ride Tom—the large piebald: he's a glorious animal, by George!

"I count on you to obey this, which comes from your
Friend till death,
Jack Hamilton."

"'The Trap,'—on a splendid morning."

For a moment Mr. Effingham was determined not to go, and ordered the servant who brought the note to be directed to wait. The servant from the Trap had departed however, and Mr. Effingham finally determined to embrace his friend's invitation.

"Why annoy the honest fellow?" he said, "he is one of my very best friends, and I cannot afford to throw away such—I have not enough. Now what can he want? Here I am languidly speculating, and cannot, to save me, come to any conclusion. It is too late in the season to hunt—and yet he says I must come in buff and leather. I am to ride Tom, and sleep there. Decidedly I will give it up."

And Mr. Effingham dismissed the subject from his mind, returning it seemed to some vague train of thought that had possession of his mind. Sitting before the slight fire of crackling twigs, with his feet upon the old grotesque andirons, he gazed into the coals:—then upon the old portrait high upon the carved wainscot—then through the window on the breezy lawn, covered with flowers which bowed their heads as the wind passed over them. The blustering wind of March rang merrily round the gables, and whistled through the keyhole, and rose and fell, and died away. Only the ticking of the huge clock in the hall was heard in these pauses, and footsteps of Miss Alethea, or Kate, or some servant—in the apartments overhead.

The thinker gazed long at the portraits.

"I believe in blood," said Mr. Effingham, musingly. "The blood of men is quick or sluggish, generous or mean, just as that of animals is. The race-horse has an ancestry of race-horses—the common drudge, an ancestry of drudges; the offspring of tigers are fierce, as the lamb follows its dam in meekness—very trite and very true; every thing true is trite. And man, the supreme animal, is not an exception. There now is old Harry Effingham, in his armor—he fought at Agincourt, they say, and did good service with his stout arm. And there is the Chevalier Huon, of Effenghame, as they call him, the *princeps* of all, who married a damsel of the accursed race of Mahound, the family chronicle says, in the Crusades—a wild fellow, I do not doubt, and perhaps I have now, in this good year of grace, 1765, something of Sir Huon in me. Possibly; I came very near wedding one who —well, well; I will not rake in those cold ashes. What boots it? The fire is burnt out, it is true; but why soil my fingers? I think I have suffered enough. If not pleasure, give me the next thing, apathy, which I think I have."

A servant entered, to replenish the fire.

"Ned, have the piebald, Tom, saddled, and brought round," said Mr. Effingham.

"Yes, sir."

The servant retired, and Mr. Effingham fell into another fit of thought, from which he was roused by the intelligence that his horse was ready.

"I suppose I may be allowed to disregard the caution about dress," he said to himself. "Bring my boots and spurs," he added, to the servant.

He was soon on his way, and before long, reached the Trap. This abode of Mr. Jack Hamilton was a very handsome specimen of the old hipped roof mansions which crown so many hills in Virginia, and one might have seen at a glance that none but a bachelor resided there. The front door was permanently open, one hinge having given way, and the few abortive efforts to open and close it, having resulted in nothing more than a semi-circular mark upon the floor. The door had been in this condition just one year, and remained unchanged until—but we anticipate. Upon the small porch half-a-dozen dogs were dozing, and snapping at the flies; and in the yard a score of hounds bayed, gambolled, basked in the sun, or dragged their blocks.

An old white-haired negro came, with the well-bred courtesy of the Virginia family servant, to take Mr. Effingham's horse, and he entered.

Jack Hamilton came forth to greet him, and then they entered the dining-room, or rather the apartment used for that purpose when Mr. Hamilton was alone, which was very seldom. Here Mr. Effingham found half-a-dozen gentlemen from the neighborhood, all his acquaintances. They received him with the cordial frankness of boon companions, and after a few questions about his travels, commenced again conversing, at the top of their voices, on hunting, plantation matters, politics—especially upon politics. Did half-a-dozen Virginians ever remain together half an hour, without talking politics? We have never been present on such an occasion.

Dinner, and copious libations—perhaps we might say copious libations and dinner also—succeeded. Afterwards a cloud of smoke, from as many tobacco pipes as there were men, Mr. Effingham excepted, and then politics more ferociously than ever. Navigation laws—yes, sir, infamous, unconstitutional—dare to pass that stamp act they talk of—try it—the continent will be in a blaze—pshaw!—yes sir! in a blaze—puff! puff!—I tell you, sir—no, sir—yes, sir—I like the governor—he don't suit the times—here Oscar! Is this Black's pup, Jack? But we refrain even from reporting stenographically this chaos of voices, the new Babel of confused tongues.

The afternoon passed, and night came, and then a substantial supper, preceded by a walk out to look at the horses, the dogs, the tobacco, the stock, every thing. Then all go to the door to greet a stalwart gentleman, approaching on a fine roan; and Captain Ralph greets his friends with a multiplicity of *morbleus!* and they all sit down to supper.

After supper, cards, and wine, and tobacco smoke. Spadille reigns supreme, and the Captain loses a pile of gold, spite of his most desperate efforts, a circumstance which causes him to explode a whole magazine of gunpowder-like *morbleus!* and curse the stars, which are made responsible for the ills that happen upon earth, much too often.

Mr. Effingham has long since heard that the object of the gathering is nothing less than a real *bona fide* fox-hunt, spite of the lateness of the season, and the smile which has greeted this transparent device of the worthy Jack Hamilton, has yielded to apathy again. Mr. Effingham will ride after the hounds—it is not worse than idleness.

Cards and dice lose their charm at last, pipes emit only acrid-smoke, claret, and the best Jamaica, only make the head muddier, even politics has died a natural death, and the revellers sleep.

But before the day has reddened in the east, they are flying after the hounds, who have struck a warm trail, and the far distance swallows them, the yelping of the dogs dies away, the Trap has caught silence, and holds it tight.

Mr. Effingham rides more madly than them all. He begins to think that Mr. Hamilton is not so contemptible a physician as he thought him, for his cheek is full of blood, which was before so pale; his eyes are brilliant; his breast feels no longer as though some heavy load oppressed it—he is conscious of the effect which the body exerts upon the mind. Mr. Effingham's habit was to sleep late in the morning; here he was scouring the cold, fresh, shivering, dewy fields, before sunrise, following the music of the dogs, and whirling over fences, ditches, and hollows. One or two of the hunters stumbled, and once a rider was rolled in a ditch. Mr. Effingham positively found himself laughing.

They rode all the morning; they had started one of those old gray foxes, who take pleasure in running all day, and sleep all the sounder after their hen-roost supper, for the exercise. By noon Reynard had disappeared—sunk into the earth—vanished; the dogs were at fault, and after two hours search for the provoking animal's traces, the hunt was abandoned.

Mr. Effingham, Captain Ralph, and Jack Hamilton, took their way back together; calculating the distance they had ridden between twenty and thirty miles, perhaps more. Mr. Effingham was not at all weary, and said he never felt better.

They passed Mr. Lee's about noon, and the old gentleman insisted on their going in to dinner. To this, Mr. Hamilton and the Captain consented at once, but Mr. Effingham at first demurred.

"You will offend Mr. Lee, Champ, my boy," said Hamilton, in a low tone.

Mr. Effingham gave his friend a strange look, sighed languidly, and entered with them.

How it was, Mr. Effingham did not know, but Jack Hamilton persuaded him to stay, and return with him, and whenever he intimated to his friend a desire to go, the intimation was received with a look which seemed to say, "Don't hurry, my dear fellow; just let me finish this anecdote to Miss Clare, and I'm with you;" or, "Let us hear Miss Henrietta finish that rattling song which the Captain has worried her into singing;" or, "Just let me refute these ideas of Mr. Lee, on the mode of curing tobacco." And so evening drew on, and Mr. Effingham, to his own astonishment, did not feel very unhappy.

They were all gathered now around the harpsichord, whereat sat Henrietta, dazzlingly beautiful, and striking indifferently all her visitors, with her satirical speeches, and proud, laughing eyes.

The Captain listened with delight, or an excellent affectation, to

"In the golden days of good Queen Bess,"

and declared that he had never heard any thing more beautiful, except the songs of the French soldiers on the night preceding the battle of Mindon. This observation caused Miss Henrietta to say, that perhaps Captain Waters preferred male to female voices. To which satirical observation, the Captain, with great candor, and cordial frankness, replied that he did. Miss Henrietta thereupon requested a song from some gentleman present, but failing in her desire, retired to the opposite side of the room, where Captain Ralph permitted her to remain, very cheerfully.

Finding this position somewhat dull, Miss Henrietta returned by degrees, from the window to the sofa, from the sofa to the centre-table, from the table to the harpsichord again, with a volume in her hand. She said that nothing was more stupid than these accounts of battles—holding the history of the late war, open, as she spoke. The Captain roused himself, and replied, politely, yes, it was a very fine evening. Miss Henrietta thereupon tossed her head; the Captain said that the perfume of the hair-powder she used was delightful. Thereupon Miss Henrietta, in great ill-humor, turned her back upon him, and began to talk with Mr. Effingham; and not to be exceeded in civility, the Captain turned his back too, and began to converse, very cheerfully, with Clare and Mr. Hamilton.

Clare, as we may imagine, supported with difficulty this long interview with Mr. Effingham. He had not addressed more than half a dozen words to her, and these had been characterized by a calm reserve; but once or twice their eyes furtively met, and they saw plainly that each was watching the other. Clare seemed uneasy at his presence. Mr. Effingham felt his heart stir, in the young girl's presence—a nameless charm seemed to envelope her—but he kept his resolution to avoid engaging in any conversation which could bring on any allusion to former times and events. This was not difficult, for Mr. Hamilton engrossed much of Clare's attention, and she seemed to seek in his society a refuge from that of Mr. Effingham. He commented inwardly on her evident partiality for his friend, trying to say calmly to himself that he would make her an excellent husband. Perhaps the gloom upon his brow grew somewhat deeper, when the innocent girl smiled upon Hamilton so kindly and sweetly, but he controlled his feelings.

She sat down, at the request of Mr. Hamilton, and unaffectedly commenced singing. The song was "Logan Water," and she sang it with great feeling and sweetness. The sound of her voice affected him strangely, and sitting down, he drank in the clear, tender carol, his dreamy eyes fixed on her face.

That song revived all the past for him. She had sung it often for him, and perhaps this was what led her to refuse Mr. Hamilton's request for that particular song at first. As she sang, all those bright, happy days of youth, returned to him :—the days in the woods—the evening playing games—the mornings, when, with her fair hair unbound, she ran hand in hand with him, over emerald meadows, by rippling, laughing streams. Again the birds carolled over head, as they carolled in the past, and a flood of memories flowed in upon his apathetic heart, and made its dull tide leap again. As the last notes died away, he felt as though he were leaving some fairy isle of warmth and verdure, and a million flowers, to breast the cold, stormy seas of real life ; and with the last plaintive notes, the volume of his memory closed again, and his heart sank.

As she rose, they exchanged a long look ; and Mr. Effingham turned away.

Her look had said : " Do not avoid me thus, because we have both been unhappy and unfortunate ; because our relations are changed, forget, as I do."

His own said as plainly : " I have tried your heart cruelly, I know it ; I suffer without complaining, or expecting the past to return ; you can never love me again ; I do not complain. I deserve all ; but will bear my suffering in silence."

Had the lips but said it !—had those glances spoken plainly !

Mr. Effingham, when he departed, merely bowed. He looked at her again, with his old dreamy gaze, and went away with his companions.

As he went to his chamber that night, he murmured : " Well, I was mistaken ; some of the old feeling, for a wonder, still remains, surviving the storm. Let me beware of it."

And his head sank as he spoke

CHAPTER XV.

AT THE HALL.

Our narrative does not require a lengthy description of the great dinner and ball at the mansion of the squire. When we have said that the noble mansion blazed from top to bottom with a thousand lights, that chariots constantly rolled up, and deposited beautiful dames and gallant cavaliers, that they dined in state, and danced and feasted and made merry, we have said all that is necessary. As to describing with a mere pen one of these old festivals, which still occasionally fill with laughter and high revelry some old houses, the thing is simply impossible. Some great artist, uniting a genius for the humorous and the noble, the rude and the elegant, the grotesque and the beautiful, might possibly delineate one of these old jubilees, and the singular old race who delighted in them; we cannot, yet we may, before passing on to the real events of this narrative, pause a moment to jot down some of the salient points of the brilliant gathering.

In addition to the chariots with their rumbling wheels, neighing horses, and cracking whips, there came great numbers of brave cavaliers upon good steeds, in parties, laughing and jesting, or singly. Sometimes these gentlemen accompanied the chariots, as in the case of Mr. Hamilton, who rode dutifully by the Riverhead coach, the said coach containing Mr. Lee, Henrietta, and Clare, who had consented to attend the ball, only after repeated requests from her father, who had observed and regretted her inexplicable dislike to visiting at the Hall for some weeks past.

The dinner was a splendid affair, and there was much marshalling of the guests in their places—his Excellency, Francis Fauquier, Governor of the Colony, sitting on the squire's right hand. The dinner proceeded as those pleasant pompous old affairs were wont to, and in due time the gentlemen were left to their politics and wine. There was not much political discourse, however, in deference to his Excellency. It was not polite to denounce his gracious Majesty, his ministry, and their darling money-project, the stamp act; and to speak favorably of any one of these, was more than any guest's courtesy could compass. So they discussed the weather and the crops, and the seven years' war, last passed, and, above all, the approaching races near Jamestown, from which they glided into erudite disquisitions on the pedigree of racers.

As night closed in—they dined early, even on state occasions, in those honest days—the cavaliers betook themselves to the drawing-room, and there insinuated themselves into the glittering throng of lovely dames, all powdered and furbelowed and flounced, and then arose that buzz which, in our time, by force of progressive increase, has grown into a stunning uproar, in which every one endeavors, by raising his or her voice, to drown the voice of every one else.

The smiling cavaliers, in powder, ruffles, embroidery, long waistcoats, and silk stockings, betook themselves to paying devoted court to the fascinating dames in lace, diamonds, satin robes with trains, and shoes portentously high in the heels; and so, with flirting fans, and winning smiles, and low bows and little graceful curtsies, the time passed. Then the well-instructed musicians, led by Mr. William Booker, colored gentleman, violinist and appendage to the glebe of Effingham, struck up a minuet, and the furbelows and silk stockings bowed and curtsied with ambling swaying movement, with cocked hats pressed upon the heart, and fans expanded, and then closed again, and many an unguarded heart was taken captive, and many silk stockings accompanied as many furbelows through the dance of life thereafter, fascinated with each other in that dance of pleasure.

His Excellency danced with Miss Alethea, though this is not one of those matches which we have foretold. Clare danced with Mr. Hamilton, while Mr. Effingham looked on and sighed; lastly, Kate danced with the noble Earl of Dorset, whose brilliant verses we have listened to upon a similar occasion, at the metropolitan city of Williamsburg, and the fresh, frank face of the child pleased all, and made all love her. As for the sensations experienced by Master Willie Effingham, and Master Tommy Alston who was dying for love of Kate, we prefer not to venture upon such a tragical subject. The noble Earl, on that occasion, made two mortal enemies for life.

So the stately minuets glided onward to the lofty music, rejoicing, one would say, with a low, melodious, well-bred laughter in its undertones at all this pompous ceremony, and graceful reverential bowing, and low curtsying. Then came supper, in due time, where healths were drank many fathoms deep, and where the ladies took scarcely more nourishment than they do at present. Then the gay, glancing, merry hours fled on with music once again, and finally, when midnight had long sounded, the ball drew to an end with that merry and enlivening divertisement, a Virginia reel.

If the music for the minuet was glad and merry, under all its stately and prim cadences, the music of the reel was more than unaffected merriment:—the merriment was mad, desperate, exuberant, headlong and uproarious. The right arm of the noble minstrels darted furiously up and down—the violins and hautboys nearly cracked with the immense flood of harmony; and if the lovely damsels smiled befoie, they laughed out loudly now: and flashed like shooting stars from end to end of the great room:—and scattered perfumed powder in a cloud:—and then, as the mad music stopped with a long scrape, stood still with laughing lips and panting bosoms, and red cheeks and dancing eyes, fanning themselves and uttering little rapturous exclamations, and assuming die away airs: and so the reel too was dead:—it ended all.

Perhaps the most picturesque portion of the whole festival was the breaking up. In those times, they drank deep, and a gentleman imbibed his two bottles as he wore his sword —as a matter of course. The consequence was—heads being much the same then as they are at present—that more than one of the gallants present on the occasion found themselves elated to the pitch of noisy merriment, and the Effingham woods echoed back their shouts and songs for leagues.

The chariots resumed their burdens:—though many staid at the ball all night—the gubernatorial coach, with those six glossy white horses which have become history, bore off his noble Excellency: and amid a tremendous clatter of negroes' voices, cracking whips, rumbling wheels, and merry exclamations, the festival, like all bright things, went onward to the future.

Mr. Effingham assisted Clare to enter the Riverhead chariot, with grave softness and courtesy: pressing Hamilton's hand with friendly warmth; and so the carriage rolled away, and Mr. Effingham's heart went with it.

As he entered his chamber, he murmured as before, "The storm has passed, but all of the old feeling is not dead:—beware!" and, sleeping with his pale face illumined by the broad full moon, he dreamed of her, and saw her glide before him with veiled brows and tender eyes and open arms. And when he tried to clasp her to his heart she vanished.

A shadow crossed the sleeper's forehead, and his hand stole to his brow. Then his face grew serene again—the brow clear and soft. He heard her singing.

CHAPTER XVI.

SKETCHES THE COURT TO WHICH THE HON. MR. CROW WAS ACCREDITED AS AMBASSADOR.

Absorbed in what has been going on at the Hall, at Riverhead, at the bachelor Trap of Mr. Hamilton, which has never caught a wife yet for that worthy gentleman, we have treated with undeserved neglect and improper silence the affairs of Lanky and his sweetheart—Donsy Smith, daughter of Mr. A. Z. Smith, the rosy little factor at Williamsburg. But the historian cannot give his attention at the same time to the Lords and Commons: while the Lords prose in their lofty elevation. the Commons debate furiously in the lower house:—and so the entertaining prosiness and fiery debate cannot be reported at one and the same time. For fear, however, that our lame metaphor will break down if we push it farther, and betray its want of application to the characters of this history, we shall proceed to narrate simply what followed the resolution taken on that bright spring morning by our friend Lanky, and how Mr. Crow—or "Jeames," as he was wont to call himself with noble simplicity—acquitted himself in the arduous and responsible character of Envoy Extraordinary and Minister Plenipotentiary near the Court of Parson Tag, King of the Oldfield School, and Emperor of the Ferule.

Perhaps the shortest and most satisfactory means of putting the reader in possession of the events which attended the embassy of the Honorable Mr. Crow will be to present those events in a direct and dramatic form. Then shall we see how umbrage was taken by Emperor Tag, at the person and intent of the ambassador, as well as at his unambassadorial costume:—how the right of the Minister Plenipotentiary to appear in his every day citizen's dress was harshly questioned; even his right to appear at all; and how in the hour of danger that costume afforded him no protection, and led by its deficiencies to a speedy resignation of his high and responsible duties. Let us not, however, anticipate: every event in its place.

Willie arrived at school some time after the proper hour, mounted as usual on his small pony, and he entered with some fear of a reproof. But in this he was mistaken. Parson Tag was mildly courteous, and most pleasantly good-humored. To explain this singular and unwonted circumstance—for the parson usually administered justice like Dionysius, the tyrant—we have only to inform the reader that the worthy gentleman had been present at the Hall on the previous evening, and had delighted his inward man with sundry viands and vintages of the most savory description. He had been treated with great courtesy by the well-bred host, also:—and thus he was in a highly amiable state of mind—especially toward Willie. If the reader is surprised at the fact of the parson's attending the festival at the Hall, after his quarrel with the squire, we can only say that our sketch of this worthy's character must have been defective. He was not the man to despise an excellent supper and delicious wines, because he hated and had quarrelled with the host.

The school was busy as usual, and a long row of girls and boys stood in the middle of the floor conning their lessons, and preparing for the fiery ordeal. On the benches ranged round the apartment sat many more, leaning their slates, or copy-books, or grammars, on the long desk which extended equally with the benches from end to end; and these hard little students were engaged apparently in the most intense toil.

Some grasped their hair furiously at sums in arithmetic, which persisted in turning out wrong:—for how could the remainder be greater than the figures from which the others were subtracted? Some went on voyages of half an hour around the world, taking in spices of Sumatra, Ceylon and the Sunda isles; fighting their way into inhospitable Japan; taking a census of the population of the exclusive cities of Pekin and Shanghai and other Chinese places: some fought their way into the noble English grammar, others bent down over copy-books, endeavoring painfully to enunciate in legible letters the propositions that "Honesty is the best policy," and that "Evil communications corrupt good manners:" and when a spatter fell upon the page, the hearts of the urchins were fillèd with dreadful visions of descending ferules, and aching blistered hands.

The little maidens were busy, too, in all these branches; and with atlases before them, heard the nightingales singing in the valley of Cashmere;—and sailed along the Tigris in a splendid barge to visit the great Caliph Haroun at his Bagdad palace;—and swam to the sound of melodious guitars in gondolas on broad canals in Venice:—and looked carefully for the mountain by the royal city of Grenada, whereon pausing wofully, the handsome Moslem uttered the "last sigh of the Moor." Others were busy with arithmetic, and copying just as the boys were; and the only difference was that they did not anticipate chastisement for delinquency. The parson had lived in his adopted country—Virginia, that is to say—long enough to find that it was not customary for one of the ruder sex, however lofty his station, to lay his hand "even in the way of kindness" upon one of the opposite sex, however humble, and so the little maidens only dreaded "demerits," and these they struggled to avoid.

What we have thus briefly described, was the exoteric and external appearance of things:—which would have struck a stranger, and caused him to believe that of all the scholars that ever gladdened with their industry and application the pedagogic heart, those of the pedagogue in question were the most prudent and exemplary. A somewhat closer view, however, would have revealed what we must borrow another scientific word to characterize—the esoteric phase of the Oldfield school. From time to time the maidens and urchins exchanged laughing and mysterious glances over their slates or atlases:—the lips of the damsels would move with exaggerated expressiveness, to the end that from the movement of those cherry-like appendages, their cavaliers might divine what they meant to express. Then when the cavaliers remained obstinately dull and would not understand, the little maidens made signs upon their fingers, after the well known manner of the dumb; and when the still obtuse urchins shook their heads, little scraps of paper were hastily covered with stealthy pencil marks, and rolled up and tossed invisibly across, while the maidens seemed to be deeply immersed in study. And the urchins read, "Just look at Sally Jones and Tom Lackland!"—or, "You promised me an apple!"—or, "Have you done that horrid sum?"—or, "Robert Dawson don't know his lesson again, and the parson'll whip him. Ain't it shameful?"

Another esoteric phase was going on *sub rosâ*, that is, under the desk: small hands of little maidens were squeezed there in the most gallant and impassioned manner by chevaliers who coveted an opportunity to expire nobly in defence of their ladyloves:—and fruit, cakes, tarts, biscuits, were smuggled, as lasting proofs of devoted and disinterested affection:—and while the hands were being pressed under the little aprons, the noble cavaliers assumed an innocent and abstracted expression which would have done them credit in the eyes of indifferent observers:—and then at the master's dreadful glance the beaus retreated from their sweethearts precipitately, and betook themselves to study:—that is, to studying the manner of passing "playtime" to the best advantage, turning over the leaves of their spelling-books with well-executed art, and deeply immersed in the study—which we have mentioned.

No event of any importance disturbed the even tenor of the noble academy that morning. True, some half a dozen unfortunate dunces were feruled for being destitute of brains; true, a youthful gentleman, with a genius for caricature, was caught just as he had put the finishing touch to a splendid design of the parson on his slate—which design represented the worthy gentleman arrayed in a shovel hat some leagues in width, with a body formed of a tobacco hogshead, from beneath which issued an enormous pair of feet crushing to death a squealing tythe pig:—true, the wailing of the dunces and the unappreciated artist filled the room and struck terror into cavalier and lady, boy and girl alike:—but these little occurrences were not uncommon, and things went on very pleasantly until "playtime:"—when all rushed forth free as air, and wild as little colts turned loose in a green pasture, with liberty to roll, and run, and turn somersets, and gambol to their hearts' content.

The noble monarch of the school remained within, enthroned in state upon his rostrum, from which he surveyed the unfortunates, who, having neglected their tasks, now had the excruciating and tantalizing pleasure of hearing their companions shouting at their play out under the blue sky. The noble parson embraced the opportunity to comfort his inner man with sandwiches and Jamaica rum, gazing, as he partook of these humble condiments and liquids, upon the sketch of himself we have already described.

Let us leave him there, enthroned in state, and go and breathe that fresh air which is driving the little maids and urchins mad with full delight. It is more wholesome.

CHAPTER XVII.

CROW MAKES A SPEECH ON THE STAMP ACT AND SUFFERS THE FATE OF POPULARITY SEEKERS.

Look!

Perhaps the two things most similar and at the same time dissimilar, are a play-ground and that work-ground which we call the world. In both these are aspirations and passions; loves and hatreds; sad and merry faces; toilings after objects not worth the pursuit; and neglected pleasures, which far outweigh those which humanity run after with such ardor and enthusiasm. The child is father of the man; and his offspring follows the bent of its parent:—pursues, and loves, and suffers and rejoices, and runs the wild, laughing or despondent race; and then the bell of fate summons the weary player to the shades within, where no sun shines, no blue sky arches overhead—save in the eye of faith and hope.

But with all this similarity, we know that the real difference is very striking. How gaily, thoughtlessly, the boy plays, and laughs and rolls upon the grass, and climbs for birds' nests, and is pleased with trifles—not dreaming of the time when all his hopes, his illusions, his romance, his thoughtless lightheartedness will change, and he will have to go and buckle on his armor for the struggle with that strong enemy—human life. How the little maidens run and play and gambol with their boy sweethearts:—their hair flowing unconfined, their eyes dancing for pure merriment, their hearts free as yonder bird's who cuts the blue air on his joyous wings towards the rosy east:—they know not, will not, cannot believe that the time will come when that hair must be primly bound up; then turn gray: when those eyes will be dimmed with care and suffering: when those hearts, so wild with pleasure now, will be made to suffer cruelly by some of the little urchins with whom they play now laughingly. Let us thank heaven for childhood's lightness, however. The spring should not be tried until it is tempered.

The reign of marbles had come in: and those who have reflected philosophically upon these matters, will recall the fact that schoolboys like men are subject to furores. The games which balls figure in are everlasting—always popular: but marbles, prisoner's base, and "fox and a warner" are subject to the laws of change:—that is to say, they are at one moment neglected, then placed high upon the throne of popularity.

Marbles reigned then:—nothing was heard for a time on the joyous playground but those cabalistic words, "vence"—"things"—"leave lag"—"come to taw"—"stop pokin'"—let's plump"—"play for havin's"—"got my ownses"—"fat!"—"knuckle down"—"turnin's"—etc., etc. We have more than once endeavored to arrive at the origin and philosophic significance of these terms, but always vainly. "Vence" still remains in our minds destitute of any imaginable root in Hebrew, Sanscrit, Greek or Scandinavian: and the origin of "lag" like that of the popular German beer, is doubtful.

So they played: and many large proprietors were "broke:"—and others acquired large fortunes, which they stowed in their capacious pockets. The girls for the most part played at skipping rope, puss in the corner, and hunt the slipper—the soft grass affording a very agreeable emerald carpet for the purpose:—or they partook of the contents of their little baskets with great gusto, giving a portion to their non-marble-playing cavaliers, who had finished their own commissary stores some time before. A biscuit from a maiden was considered proof of incipient affection—an apple, of tenderness—but a tart, a real cherry tart, with crimson blood, and yellow, crisp delicious crust!—that was an evidence of passionate and eternal love.

Having exhausted marbles, the young gentlemen betook themselves to leap-frog, many of them rolling on the grass thereat. The artist of Parson Tag took a forlorn sketch of the scene as he gazed at it mournfully through the window—the reader will understand that this young gentleman, in addition to his flagellation, had been kept in—and having been obliged with a view of this sketch, which has remained in existence to the present day, we have taken the liberty of using it for the benefit of our readers. It represents the youths in their cutaway coats, and short clothes, and woollen stockings, flying over the heads of others, who stoop with their hands upon their knees; and under a tall oak a group of girls are watching the vaulters, and laughing at those who roll upon the ground, victims to the immoral practice in the steeds, of raising the shoulders as the frogs leap. Among the maidens we recognize Donsy perfectly—older than the rest, and laughing louder as Will rolls upon the ground.

Will breaks up the game, and suggests an undress parade of the Cornstalk regiment, which proposition is hailed with pleasure. Captain Effingham thereupon marshals his soldiers, using a piece of fence rail for a sword; and, mounted on a stump, makes them a patriotic address—this time uninterrupted—wherein he repeats his father's views upon the Stamp Act, which he believes to be a measure whereby the heads of everybody in the Colony of Virginia are to be chopped off. He denounces it, therefore, and calls on his companions to organize an opposition to the tyrant; and concludes with the observation that there is for himself but one alternative—either victory or death!

This speech is much admired, and a small storm of cheers crackle through the air; filling the orator's bosom with grateful emotion; his soldiers, however, decline hearing any more, as Donsy is heard to scream terribly: and they rush towards her to ascertain the origin of her emotion.

It was very simple. Just as Master Will had arrived at the grand burst, in which, as we have said, he declared his sentiments on the subject of death and victory, Donsy Smith, who had been listening admiringly, heard a low whistle behind her shoulder, and, turning her head, her cherry lips had nearly impressed a salute upon those of Mr. Crow, who sat squat behind her, grinning and goggle-eyed—resembling, indeed, a small goblin of Ethiopian extraction.

Mr. Crow, finding himself the observed of all observers, marched forth into the open space, the thumb of one hand in his mouth, the other hand holding up the skirts of his lengthy coat. He seemed to feel that he was well worth seeing, and to court observation; his costume was, if possible, more diplomatic than ever, and his eyes brighter. His appearance was hailed with a great shout,—immediately a dozen hands seized him, and he was hoisted to the stump, and ordered to make a speech at once, on pain of dreadful punishment.

Mr. Crow does not display extraordinary confusion at this honour,—does not press his hand upon his waistcoat, or the portion of the frame usually covered with that garment; does not bow or simper. He looks around with an expression of modest confidence and amiable good nature, sucking his thumb.

"A speech!" they cry.

"A speech from Crow!"

"Hurrah!"

Mr. Crow takes his thumb from his mouth, and finding himself in a difficulty, draws upon Mr. William Effingham's ideas, which he has listened to with great attention.

"Well, gemblem," he says, with modesty, "I'se oppose, myself. to dis stump ac."

"Hurrah!" cry the scholars, "speak out, Crow."

"I'se gwine to 'pose it!" continues Crow, extending his right arm, with an electric gesture. The crowd shout and hurrah.

"I'se gwine myself to 'pose choppin' off my head!—'Two'nt do noways, gemblem! Just think how a feller 'd feel!"

This sentiment produces loud applause, which Mr. Crow acknowledges by waving the hand holding his coat tail, and, consequently, that portion of his vestment also.

"I'se gwine to go agin it to death!" continues Crow, with an heroic gesture, "I wants my head! how could I eat! how gwine to drink! how gwine to do nothin'! 'thout a head. Them's my senimers, gemblem—I say victry or deth."

And Crow brandishes both arms tremendously, and fights imaginary foes. His speech is received with tremendous applause, and a popular ovation is organized in an instant. Mounted on a rail, which is borne on the shoulders of half a dozen of the scholars, who split their sides laughing, the orator makes the circuit of the play-ground triumphantly. To be sure, the ovation, like all such things, has its disadvantages, and Crow makes more than one appeal to be permitted to sink into obscurity again. But these entreaties are disregarded, and he only has leave to change his horseback position from time to time, by leaning forward on his hands.

He says it hurts! they reply that it can't possibly.—"Oh yes, it do!" says Crow, writhing. "Stuff your coat tails under you," say the urchins. Crow resigns himself, with the air of a great man in misfortune,—when suddenly the bell rings, and the rail—and, consequently, Crow—drops to the ground.

Crow lies there until Donsy passes, rubbing his knees.

The master appears at the door: Crow's back being turned he does not see him.

Donsy draws near, laughing. Crow makes mysterious signals to her, which, at last, attract her attention.

Crow shows a letter, pushing it at her: Donsy bends down her laughing face, and asks what in the world he means. Crow makes mysterious signs of silence and precaution. Donsy stretches out her hand to take the letter, upon the back of which she reads her own name, written in large, sprawling characters. Crow winks—Donsy smiles—when, suddenly, the letter is grasped by a rough hand—Crow starts up, under the application of a switch, and Parson Tag, pursuing him, with infuriated visage, calls upon him by the designations of "rascal," "villain," and "wretch," to stop.

Crow runs for life—the parson pursues for the gratification of revenge—his skirts flying, his puffy breast heaving with the exertion and his wrath.

CHAPTER XVIII.

HOW THE AMBASSADOR WAS UNHORSED AND THEN HORSED.

The muse is proverbially jealous and capricious—else would we endeavor to describe the greater than Olympic race which then ensued:—the windings, the turnings, the desperate efforts of the great orator and ambassador to escape the impending fate. Still thundered on behind him like an avenging Nemesis the irate parson, and Crow saw the shadow of his outstretched arm grasping at his coat tails.

New rapidity is added to his headlong speed:—he runs like a deer, and bounds like an antelope:—when, most disastrous event!—event ever to be deplored by Crow and all his posterity!—his feet trod on his coat-skirts, and, rolling on the ground, he became the prey of the enemy.

They had circled back to the school-house; and the parson had not far to bear his captive, whom he grasped by the waistband of his unmentionables and indescribables.

He enters in awful state—with gloomy brow, portentous frown. The assembled company are terror-struck, and regard Crow with horror and trembling, but with interest too:—as in old days the populace of Rome looked on the ox going to the altar to be immolated.

The parson looks round for a moment in silence:—he regards Donsy with an awful frown.

"What is this letter, brought by that villain?" he says to her.

Donsy blushes and murmurs:

"Indeed I don't know, sir."

"You do not know?"

"Indeed, I don't know, sir."

"Donsy Smith, you are telling me a falsehood!" says the worthy, with a deeper frown.

Donsy flushes to the roots of her hair, and looks indignant.

"I never did—tell—a falsehood—in my life!" she says, sobbing.

"Very well, madam!" replies the parson, "we shall see! I have a notion that this letter will clear up matters, and as your preceptor and spiritual guide, I shall open it. William Lane," continues the worthy, addressing the author of the sketch of himself, " take care that that rascal who brought this does not escape. Hold him tight, sir."

William Lane holds Crow tightly by the collar, and surveys him with forlorn interest, thinking he would make a good sketch.

The parson without further preface tears open the letter and reads the following words, written in large uneven characters, with the end of a stick apparently.

" Oh my dear Miss Donsy !

" How ken I express myself writin' to you. I feel all over a-tremblin' and skeered, and I'm 'fraid the pen 'ill drop from my hand 'fore I get thru. I couldent tell you how much—there it is, comin' right out. Oh my dear Donsy, if I may call you my dear Donsy, which I'm 'fraid you'll git mad. Nobody in the whole wide world ken love you like I do. 'Deed they can't—I've been a-lovin' you now for one year and you don't know it, or perhaps you do, if so i'm mistaken' I told the cap'n that I couldn't say nothin' when you was lookin' at me, and he told me to go and talk to you and look up bold and not giv' up : I tried to, but I couldent, and you know how you twisted me over yo thum, i don't complain—i don't—but I think you ought to like me sum, cause I've been faithful to you, and never would have anything to do with Sally Jones, who is a pretty girl too, you know.

" And now my dear Miss Donsy—or if you'll let me call you so, my dearest Donsy, take pity on poor Lanky ; I love you a heap, and I think you ought to like me sum , i can't play on my fiddle or work for thinkin' of you, and I never can forget you—no I can't. I thought I'd write it down, as I couldn't say it, and Crow will carry it : the black boy from town, you know.

" O ! Donsy, I love you so much, indeed I do. So no more from your friend, till death, and loving,

" LANKY."

" Poscrip'. Don't show this to any body, and don't let the girls or boys see it, they would laugh at me. O ! if I could only do somethin' for you—kill somebody, or do somethin' of that sort, you know.

"Your lover till death,

"LANKY."

"Poscrip' agin. To-morrow's Saturday, and the cap'n says I may have honda'. I'm comin' to see you, and we can go a fishin', you know. You've caught my heart, O! my dear Miss Donsy, or rather, dearest Donsy.

"Your devoted lover till death,

"LANKY."

The parson reads this epistle with a countenance working with rage.

"And you dared to bring this, did you!" he says to the unfortunate Crow, who rubs his coat cuff in his eyes despondingly, "you are the black boy from town the letter speaks of, are you! You are the villain that dared to come and hold surreptitious intercourse with my female scholars, bearing amatory missives, like this barbarous production!—you are the messenger, are you!"

Crow does not understand the meaning of "amatory missive," and "barbarous production," but he feels a dreadful consciousness that he is guilty of committing those two crimes, which he regards with horror, and fears a terrible punishment for. He is not suffered to remain long in doubt. The parson, rolling up his cuffs, and grasping a long and pliant birch, cries:

"Horse the villain! You, sir! you William Lane! immediately, sir."

And Crow, spite of his desperate struggles, is placed upon the back of Mr. William Lane. The parson looks at him for a moment, with gloomy and irate interest: Crow, with his head turned sideways, regards the dreadful birch, and calculates the impending ruin. His hands are held tightly by the "horse:"—his coat skirts are arranged gracefully upon each side: his legs kick the air:—the hour was come.

"Now, you rascal!" says the parson, "I have caught you!"

And the birch descends upon the unfortunate Crow, who writhes with anguish.

"Now, you've caught it!" cries the parson, whistling his birch through the air, and bringing it down upon the repentant ambassador again.

"Oh, mas' parson! oh, mas' parson!" cries Crow.

The blows fall thicker—the ambassador cries out more loudly—the parson pants with the exertion—the unfortunate Crow writhes.

"Try that again, sir?" says the parson, striking quicker.

Crow protests with overwhelming earnestness, that he has repented—will reform. Debarred from using persuasive gestures with his arms, he kicks his legs, following unconsciously the great precept of Demosthenes.

Donsy looks on with indignation, and she does not care to conceal it. The parson sees this expression, and says, in a pause of his exertions:

"Very well, my lady! you are presuming to frown when I am punishing this wretch!"

"It is unjust!" cries Donsy.

"Take care, madam!"

"It is!" sobs Donsy, "and you had no right to snatch my letter and read it:—that you hadn't, sir!"

And she sheds a torrent of mortified tears—the parson regarding her with a mixture of surprise, scorn, and anger.

"You presume, then, to lecture me, madam!" he says.

Donsy repeats obstinately:

"You had no right to read my letter!—no, you hadn't!"

The parson takes a step toward the girl.

"Don't provoke me, you little hussy!" he says, "or I'll whip *you* too."

"Me!" cries Donsy, overwhelmed with indignation, and dread of the disgraceful punishment.

"Yes, you! I'll whip you, within an inch of your life!"

"No, you won't!" cries Will Effingham, starting up, "just try it!"

But before the parson can turn round, this champion is sunk into the shade immediately: the door bursts open with a loud noise—a stool is turned over, and Donsy has a second and more irate champion.

CHAPTER XIX.

IN WHICH A CHARIOT AND FOUR HORSES COMES TO THE RESCUE.

THE new champion is no other than our friend Lanky—but so disguised that we should scarcely have known him by twilight. He wears an old cocked hat of the Captain's, a pair of his cast-off boots, and around his waist is buckled an old sword, which clatters against his boots:—all which decorations he has assumed by the advice of the soldier, to make an impression on the heart of his ladylove.

Lanky had followed his messenger, seen the capture of his letter, the pursuit of Crow, and the capture of that gentleman:—he had gone to the door when it was closed;—seen the parson reading disdainfully, the splendid epistle which it had taken him a week to concoct;—and then witnessed the sacrifice of Mr. Crow:—all this with anger and indignation which gradually grew hotter, and began to boil within him. Then he had seen Donsy remonstrate, had heard the parson threaten her—lastly had seen him advance toward that empress of his heart, with an upraised rod to inflict upon *his* Donsy a disgraceful punishment. Then he boiled over, rage carried him away—he burst open the door, and rushed in, regardless of consequences.

The parson turns, with a tremendous frown upon his visage.

"Try it! yes, try it!" cries Lanky, drawing his sword and boiling over, as we have observed, with indignation, "just touch Donsy! let me see you!"

The scholars gaze at the champion, and tremble.

"Yes, it's shameful to be a threatenin' a girl! you know it is!" continues Lanky, trembling with excitement, and stamping upon the floor with his great feet; "a man who would hurt a girl don't deserve any sort o' respect!"

The parson, for a moment paralyzed by the audacity of the intruder, and doubting whether he is not some grand seigneur—makes no reply: but suddenly recognizes Lanky: Lanky the country bumpkin: Lanky the barbarous heathen, ignorant even of the existence of syntax and prosody: Lanky the scum of the earth. He starts forward to attack him.

But Donsy interposes to protect her cavalier—she seizes the uplifted rod. The parson utters a cry of rage, and endeavors to release his arm, and strike the girl.

Lanky rushes at him thereupon, and grapples with him furiously—Donsy screams—Crow rolls—the parson struggles with his enemy, and with one of the quick movements of his elbow, strikes Donsy, who falls into the arms of Will Effingham, rushing to her rescue.

Lanky, driven to fury, clenches his teeth, throws his whole weight upon his antagonist's breast, and they both fall, Lanky's sword striking against the benches with an awful clatter.

"Murder!" cries the parson.

"Oh Lanky!" says Donsy.

"Go it!" says Will.

But Lanky cannot strike a prostrate foe: had he been a knight of the middle age, his martial sword no doubt would have entered the breast of his enemy. But Lanky is a simple country young gentleman of the eighteenth century, and he rises.

The parson starts to his feet again, furious, raging:—he seizes the tongs: he launches those useful instruments at Lanky, and knocks down the unfortunate Crow, who disappears like a ball of charcoal through the open door, and is no more seen.

Lanky thereupon draws his sword:—the parson seizes a stick of wood: Lanky brandishes the deadly weapon—the parson grasps his billet;—the bitter enemies prepare for the final and decisive charge, the great struggle which shall decide all.

This is the position of affairs, when there appears at the door a martial and stalwart looking gentleman, with a long black moustache and laughing face, who cries in loud, strident tones,

"*Morbleu! Diable! Sacre!* Why it's Lanky!"

And overcome by the ludicrous figure of the parson and the intensely warlike attitude of Lanky, Captain Ralph bursts into a loud laugh. Lanky turns at this noise, recognizes his master, and dutifully lowers his sword.

"*Que le diable!*" cries the Captain, laughing again. "Was the like ever seen? What! fighting the clergy, you villain? I'm ashamed of you!"

Lanky restores his weapon to its place, and hangs his head.

"He wanted to whip Donsy," says Lanky.

"Whip a girl?"

"Yes, Cap'n."

"Bah! is that possible, reverend sir? It cannot be that you would have struck a child, and that child a girl?"

The parson draws himself up haughtily, and drops the stick of wood.

"Permit me, if you please, sir," he says, looking sidewise at his interlocutor, "to act as seems proper to me in my own school!"

"Basta! I shall permit no such thing! Ah! your reverence, you are greatly mistaken if you think the State of Virginia is like the frontier of Germany. You will recollect."

The parson looks gloomily at the Captain, striving to recognize him.

"Who are you, sir?" he says.

"*Ma foi!* Waters is my name, and you will recollect that we had the pleasure of carrying a halberd, side by side, somewhere about the year '55. Eh? Well, sir, I repeat that your reverence can no longer carry the high hand, and make the women and girls scream, as you once used to, when you drove them in crowds from their quarters in the villages. Bah! you disgust me, you great gobemouche, and I think that Lanky must decidedly have been in the right."

Strange and tremendous to relate, the parson no longer looks bold, or retains his proud, haughty attitude; he cowers before the disdainful words of the soldier; he permits Lanky to make his report without interruption. The Captain exonerates Lanky, but observes that, as a general rule, it is improper to attack the clergy with carnal weapons, and then makes a sign to Donsy, who approaches, sobbing.

"Ah, my dear Miss Donsy," he says, gallantly, "I assure you I understand perfectly Lanky's infatuation now! But believe me, if you have a pretty face, Lanky has a warm and excellent heart—*bon garçon!* and as true as steel, with that pine knot head of his. Now see! I am sure the parson will treat you well in future, for my sake."

The parson feels himself in his enemy's power: he is growing humbler and humbler.

"Come, don't cry," says the worthy Captain, "that is bad."

"I'm not well, sir. I have been sick lately. I'm not crying, sir."

With which Donsy sobs.

"Morbleu! I never could bear tears. Egad! I'll take you home. Where do you live?"

"In town, sir."

"Too far to walk if you are unwell; faith! you shall go with me."

Donsy looks at the parson dutifully, who nods a sullen assent, and says to the Captain:

"I'm afraid your horse will not carry us both, sir."

"My horse? I have none."

"Sir?" says Donsy.

"I can offer you better than a horse, Miss Donsy," says the Captain, and he leads her out, Lanky following.

Not far from the door stands a splendid chariot, with four fine pawing horses, reined in by a plethoric coachman. Behind on the shining footboard stands another servant, and the whole equipage is in the richest and finest taste. Lanky's eyes expand to the dimensions of saucers; the Captain laughs.

"My new coach, pardy!" he says. "Permit me to introduce it to you, Mr. Lanky; just arrived, and my jewels with it."

"Your coach, sir?" says Lanky, in an attitude of wonder.

"Yes, indeed."

"Your jewels, sir?"

"Pardy!"

"Oh, Cap'n!"

And after this supreme exhibition of surprise, Lanky remains in a trance of wonder and admiration.

"I heard that infernal racket you were raising in there," says the Captain, as he leads Donsy towards the chariot, "and felt a presentiment that you and your new ornaments had something to do with it. I jumped out—entered! Voila toute!"

And the Captain assists Donsy in, and motions Lanky to follow.

"Oh, Cap'n!" says Lanky.

And this is all he can say. The Captain enters last, the door is closed, and, wheeling round, the coach takes the road toward Williamsburg, which it has just left. Lanky preserves the silence of admiration and triumph. His stalwart arm has rescued his lady love; a fairy chariot rolls up to bear her and him away from the enemy's clutches; he rides in state, on velvet cushions, his head reposing, like a proud, gigantic pine knot, on the silken lining of the vehicle. He looks at Donsy, who sobs in one corner, and he can make no reply to his master's raillery.

The small shop of Mr. A. Z. Smith, factor, is thrown into a tremendous excitement by the coach stopping before the door, and Mr. A. Z. Smith issues forth, hat in hand. He is anxious to know the wishes of his Honor, who, without replying, hands out Donsy, to his profound astonishment. Lanky greets Mr. A. Z. Smith with dignified courtesy, and offers his arm to lead Donsy in, with his nose in the air.

The Captain now explains all, with a profusion of morbleus and laughter. Mr. A. Z. Smith vituperates the parson with his wheezy little voice, and when Captain Ralph empties a cup of rum with him, Lanky's prospects have taken a great stride. That young gentleman makes the appointment to go on a fishing ramble in the morning, being Saturday, and then he re-enters the coach with the air of a nobleman, his hand upon his hip, his hat cocked over one eye, his boots clattering, his sword making a martial clangor, as it bangs against the door. Captain Ralph regards these things with a smile, and says, "to the Raleigh."

They stop before the tavern. Lanky does not stir.

"Get out, you villain!" says the Captain; and Lanky flies out like a rocket.

"Oh, Cap'n!" he observes.

"I have determined not to make my visit," says the Captain. "I shall return home on Selim; you need not wait, Lanky, as you will walk."

And the Captain twirls his mustaches, with a laugh, and enters the tavern. As for Lanky, he gazes after him for a moment, sighs, pulls his hat over his eyes, and sets out for home, with the philosophic reflection that one cannot always ride in chariots.

CHAPTER XX.

THE AUTHOR OF THE MS. EXPLAINS SUNDRY THINGS PERTINENT TO THIS HISTORY.

"I HAVE endeavored in portions of the preceding pages," says the author of the MS., "to trace the changes of feeling in two different persons, whose fortunes enter largely into this narrative. In the first place, I have tried to show how Miss Henrietta Lee—proud, high-spirited, aristocratic, and full of well-bred contempt for every one not unmistakably a gentleman in blood—on their first interviews, regarded Captain Ralph Waters, the honest and high-minded soldier, with great disdain. I have shown how she addressed him, when she condescended to do so, with frigid coldness; resented his easy sang froid in her presence, as a deliberate offence; summoned all her pride of blood and rank to suppress her audacious admirer's ease, and reduce him to his proper place. We have seen her in repeated interviews, preserve this coldness less and less; then complain of him, having lost her silent disdain; then launch forth into an obstinate, hand-to-hand encounter of wit with the soldier; finally, begin to be amused at his unaffected nonchalance, his martial and brilliant narratives of the campaigns he had fought almost from his boyhood to the present hour; and feel some anxiety to rescue her character from the imputation of preferring the exact antipode of himself—the fop!

"Miss Henrietta Lee was, of course, not conscious of this gradual change of feeling towards the soldier. For not one person in ten thousand ever becomes aware of his or her feelings until some great crisis reveals them in their strength and power. It is a common adage, that we do not know how much we love certain persons until we have lost them; and this is but one instance, taken from a thousand, of the truth of the observation I have made.

"But if Miss Henrietta Lee was not aware of her change of feeling toward Captain Ralph Waters, she must have felt that he was not wholly the same to her as formerly; she must have perceived that she no longer looked upon him with cold disdain, lordly contempt; that was no longer possible.

'She had prepared herself to encounter the rude and offensive manners of a mere camp-soldier; a rough man, who had won her father's friendship by relating the incidents of the war in Europe. She had expected to find simply a disagreeable, vulgar individual, who knew nothing of the rules of good society, who would stumble over the chairs, commit eternal gaucheries, make himself a nuisance and an eye-sore. All this she had expected, and she was deceived. She found a man who was quite cognizant of the rules of good breeding, who bowed with the utmost grace, and with the exception of his French expletives, was quite irreproachable.

"She did not come to this conclusion without a struggle with herself; and she tried to say disdainfully, that all this was affected, that he was a mere adventurer, that he was ashamed of his origin, and wished to rise from the class in which he was born. But the disdainful smile disappeared, her scorn she felt was unjust; and Henrietta Lee, with her proud, wealthy nature, never committed a deliberate injustice. She was above that, and this sincerity of character now made her confess to herself that in imagining Captain Waters a mere adventurer, ashamed of his origin, and seeking to conceal it, she was mistaken. The Captain had a score of times taken occasion to say that he was the son of a fisherman, with the most unaffected calmness; that he was proud of his father and his brother; and it was very plain that this pride and affection was not put on for the nonce, or it would never have been spoken of so often. No; Captain Waters was not ashamed of his lineage; he had not been bred up in the midst of the singularly graded society of the colony; he felt no inferiority in the presence of any one, that was plain. The commander over him in battle was his superior—not the citizen who wore finer clothes, and had a finer ancestry. What Charles Waters arrived at by logic, the Captain came to by pure instinct, and the instinct had been stronger than the logic. No; Captain Waters was not desirous to hide his low birth; he did not apologize for it, he did not regret it; he regarded it as a circumstance in his life of small importance, as long as he was the fearless soldier, the honest heart. All this was plain to Henrietta.

"Now, when a proud nature finds that it has done injustice, the first result is a strong reaction in opposition to the former sentiment. The proud, brilliant mind of Henrietta Lee had never stooped to any petty meanness, and those who suffered from her wit and liked her least, confessed that she had never been guilty of narrow and illiberal things, even. Her aristocratic feeling was a portion of her blood—uncontrollable; and this she did not regard as wrong at all. So when she found that she had done Captain Waters injustice she began to like him, and to laugh in private over his amusing stories; and with the natural feeling of her sex, to admire those martial traits of the soldier which she had quarrelled with.

"We need not proceed at present to trace the change of sentiment farther; in future pages of this history the reader will perceive what further attended this young lady's revulsion of feeling toward her admirer. I shall proceed now to speak of my respected ancestor Champ Effingham, Esq., and *his* feelings briefly.

"I need not repeat the description of his own feelings given by himself to his friend Mr. Hamilton, and had one not listened to that monologue, I suppose none could fail to have conceived a very accurate idea of this gentleman's character from the former portion of the history. Let me then pass at once to the first interview between himself and Miss Clare Lee, the tender and sincere woman, whom I have given so little space to in this narrative. His heart had experienced a deeper emotion in that interview than he chose to confess; he was not perfectly calm, though his long apathy had given him the habit of suppressing every emotion with a rod of iron. No; her soft, tender face, so full of former happiness, and eloquent of his far golden youth, shone on him like a bright harvest moon—full of peace, and joy, and love. His dull blood had leaped, his stagnant heart had throbbed; once more he experienced a sensation of that pure, delicate, tender joy, which is never found in fiery, devouring passions. He felt that his mad infatuation had scarcely diminished that sentiment shrined far back in the recesses of his heart; that the flame had not reached those depths; the MS. recording his bright youth had not been burned; all then was still the same: as clear as ever.

"Still he determined to avoid Clare sedulously, and for a double reason :—first shame, and then fear. Not that my worthy ancestor was really ashamed of his infatuation—ashamed in the ordinary meaning of the term. I am afraid that his headstrong nature seldom felt the sentiment. But he experienced a rational doubt of his reception at River-head by the young girl whose heart he had so cruelly tried; whose pure, tender love, he had slighted for a wild passion. He did not fancy playing the repentant—striking his breast and crying *mea culpâ!* pity! This was quite out of the question in the present instance with Mr. Effingham, and to avoid all disagreeable scenes, he resolved to continue in Virginia the resolution he had adopted on the Continent; here as there, he would avoid all women.

"I have said that my respected ancestor's second sentiment was fear—that is fear of himself. After that volcano-like explosion, he dreaded his own passions; he was perfectly well convinced that when aroused, these passions were as fetterless as the wind; and he indulged, what seems to me looking back now on his character, a rational fear of his feelings.

"But Mr. Hamilton had by a word on the day of the fox-hunt, persuaded him to conquer both these sentiments, and enter. Then he felt that his resolution was not very strong; that the very strength of feeling which caused him to make those precautionary resolutions, now led him to break them at a single word.

"He spent the day; and all that day the feeling that he loved her still was gaining ground: he dwelt on her tender face with pensive, drooping eyes, the faint weary smile growing brighter as he went over the soft past; he experienced a strange emotion of purity and gentleness in her presence; she seemed to make the world bright for him again, throwing a new light on the landscape of his life, like dawn after the dim moonlight, or the white glare of snow.

"That song which he had heard her sing so often in the past—the happy golden past, when he was young and loved her so tenderly—came finally to complete his change of feeling, and he knew that he loved her more than ever —far more; more profoundly, truly, tenderly. Then, at the same moment, he saw her giving kind glances to his friend, and all of these glances pierced his soul; but his face did not move, only the shadow returned. He went as quietly as he came, speaking with his eyes only, and those eyes asked nothing. When he lost sight of her his head drooped.

"The evening at the hall was a great trial; it was plain that she and Hamilton were little less than lovers—she was so kind—he so devotedly attentive. He spoke to her but once or twice, and then calmly and quietly; and, as we have seen, pressed Mr. Hamilton's hand with a warmth which indicated something more than regret at parting. Thus he laid no claim to her heart—he felt it was gone from him. But he could dream of her; and how he dreamt I have related.

"These few words of comment will enable the reader to comprehend more easily the events which follow. Though preferring to write down what the characters of my history said to each other, from the conviction that their traits are most easily developed by themselves, I have thought fit to pause here, to speak thus briefly in my own person of Captain Waters, and my respected ancestor. I now proceed."

CHAPTER XXI.

HOW THE WHOLE COLONY OF VIRGINIA WENT TO THE JAMESTOWN RACES, AND WHAT ENSUED.

The races!

That word always produces a strong effect upon men in the South; and when the day fixed upon for the Jamestown races comes, the country is alive for miles around with persons of all classes and descriptions.

As the hour of noon approaches, the ground swarms with every species of the genus homo; Williamsburg and the seafaring village of Jamestown turn out *en masse*, and leave all occupations for the exciting turf.

As the day draws on the crowd becomes more dense. The splendid chariots of the gentry roll up to the stand, and group themselves around it, in a position to overlook the race-course, and through the wide windows are seen the sparkling eyes and powdered locks, and diamonds and gay silk and velvet dresses of those fair dames who lent such richness and picturesque beauty to the old days dead now so long ago in the far past. The fine-looking old planters too are decked in their holiday suits, their powdered hair is tied into queues behind with neat black ribbon, and they descend and mingle with their neighbors, and discuss the coming festival.

Gay youths, in rich brilliant dresses, caracole up to the carriages on fiery steeds, to display their horsemanship, and exchange compliments with their friends, and make pretty speeches, which are received by the bright-eyed damsels with little ogles, and flirts of their variegated fans, and rapturous delight.

Meanwhile the crowd grows each moment, as the flood pours in from the north, the south, the east, the west—from every point of the compass, and in every species of vehicle. There are gay parties of the yeomen and their wives and daughters, in carryalls and wagons filled with straw, upon which chairs are placed: there are rollicking fast men—if we may use the word becoming customary in our own day—who whirl in, in their curricles: there are barouches and chairs, spring wagons and carts, all full, approaching in every way from a sober walk to a furious headlong dash, all "going to the races." There are horsemen who lean forward, horsemen who lean back; furious, excited horsemen, urging their steeds with whip and spur; cool, quiet horsemen, who ride erect and slowly: there are, besides, pedestrians of every class and appearance, old and young, male and female, black and white—all going to the races.

These latter gather around the booths erected by the stand and discuss the various mixtures of Jamaica there displayed in tempting array; and near by, all varieties of edibles are set out, and attacked. Ale foams; healths (and individuals) are drunk; bets are made.

The vulgar blacklegs, if we may speak so disrespectfully of that large and influential class, congregate temporarily around the tables where a dozen games of chance are exhibited; and here they amuse themselves while awaiting the great supreme gambling of the race.

The crowd is all in a buzz, which at times rises to a shout; it undulates like a stormy sea; it rolls and murmurs, and rumbles and laughs—in a word, it has come to see the races.

The hour at last arrives, and a horn sounding from the judges' stand, the horses are led out in their blankets and head coverings, and walked up and down before the crowd by their trainers, who are for the most part old gray-headed negroes, born and raised, to the best of their recollection, on the turf. The riders are noble scions of the same ancient stock, and average three feet and a half in height, and twenty pounds in weight. They are clad in ornamental garments; wear little close-fitting caps, and while they are waiting, sit huddled up in the grass, sucking their thumbs, and talking confidentially about "them there hosses."

Let us look at the objects of their attention; they are well worth it.

Mr. Howard enters the bay horse *Sir Archy*, out of Flying Dick, by Roderick.

Mr. James enters *Fair Anna*, a white mare, dam Virginia, sire Belgrave.

Captain Waters enters the Arabian horse *Selim*, descended in a direct line, he is informed, from Al-borak, who carried the prophet Mahomet up to heaven—though this pedigree is not vouched for. The said pedigree is open to the inspection of all comers. NOTE—That it is written in Arabic.

There are other entries, but not much attention is paid to them. The race will be between Sir Archy and Fair Anna, and perhaps the outlandish horse will not be "distanced."

The horses are stripped, and the excited spectators gather round them and commence betting. Two to one is offered on Sir Archy; he takes every eye; he is a noble animal. His training has been excessive, and the sinews web his limbs like cords of steel woven into network; he strides like a giant, his eyes blaze, he bites at his groom.

Fair Anna is a beautiful little creature, as slender and graceful as a deer, with a coat of milky whiteness; and she steps daintily, like a kitten. She is known, however, and those who have seen her run, know that she has extraordinary speed and bottom.

The Arabian horse is unknown, and offers few indications of either speed or strength. The ladies say he is lovely, however, and the old jockeys scan the animal attentively, and discover some unusual points.

But the ladies, for the most part, admire the white mare above all; and the young damsels and gentlemen of youthful years request their parents to furnish them with some guineas to bet upon the lovely animal. The old planters, having for the most part staked large sums on Sir Archy, decline this request with petulance. Among these juveniles, seized with the gambling mania, are Master Willie Effingham and Mr. Tommy Alston, who espouse different sides. Tommy admires fair Anna, Will, Sir Archy. Having no money beyond a crown or so, they content themselves with staking that, and Kate is called upon to hold the stakes, which she does with great good nature.

"Ah! you are betting, I think, petite ma'mselle!" says a sonorous and good-humoured voice.

Kate raises her eyes, and recognizes Captain Ralph, who rides his roan. She smiles, for the kindly honest voice of the soldier pleases her, and says:

"Oh no, sir! I was just holding stakes for Willie and Mr. Alston."

"Mr. Alston? Oh—*pardonnez:* I understand."

And the Captain laughs, and asks how the betting goes.

"Two to one on Sir Archy," says Kate quite easily.

"And on Selim?"

"I'm sure he's the prettiest, and I know he'll win, sir," says Kate, "but the bet is on Sir Archy and Fair Anna."

The Captain laughs, and rides on: he draws up by Mr. Lee's chariot.

"Ah good-day, my dear mesdames," he says, "how is the betting, pray?"

"I have bet largely against Selim, sir," says Henrietta, "I know he'll be beaten."

"Beaten, say you, my dear madam?"

"Yes."

"By what—rods?"

"No, sir, by Sir Archy."

"Ah, you think so?" says the Captain, pleasantly. "Well, I do not agree with you, morbleu!"

"He's found his match," says Henrietta, with a mischievous sparkle of her brilliant eye.

"So have I," replies the Captain, with a look which makes Miss Henrietta blush.

She endeavors to rally.

"What will you bet, sir?"

"I? I will bet you a thousand pounds to a penny, that Selim wins the race. See how infatuated I am! What say you, morbleu! madam?"

Henrietta smiles satirically.

"Suppose we wager something more valuable, sir" she says, "something rare!"

"What shall it be?"

"This ringlet against one of your *morbleus!*"

The Captain relishes this pleasantry and laughs.

"Ah, madam!" he says, "the stakes are not even: suppose I stake the contents of this box, against the said ringlet."

And the soldier draws a morocco case from his bosom.

"What is it?" says Henrietta.

"I deny your right to ask," laughs the soldier.

"Unjust!" says Henrietta.

"Why, 'faith?"

"Because, sir, you know what my stake is—while I do not know yours."

"How do I know what it is you offer to bet, madam?"

"Why it is this ringlet, sir."

And Henrietta twines around her beautiful jewelled hand a glossy curl which reposes on her cheek.

Captain Ralph laughs, and replies:

"Ma foi! I know it is: but I maintain that I am not enlightened yet:—the said ringlet may be a wig, my dear madam."

Henrietta pouts: Clare smiles.

"I assure you, sir, that I never wear wigs," says the lady.

"Well, madam, then I will, for the sake of argument—no, for the sake of betting, admit the reality of that exquisite curl; and yet I must be permitted to make a request."

"What is that, sir?"

"That you will let Miss Clare hold my stake, and promise not to open it, or seek to find what it is."

Henrietta takes the morocco case, and looks at it curiously, hesitating.

"Well," says the Captain, laughing, "I see our wager is at an end, pardy! You refuse my conditions."

"No, sir, I accept."

And Henrietta hands the case to Clare.

"I suppose I may retain the curl until it is won—if that ever happens, monsieur?" she says, satirically.

"*Oui! oui!*" responds the soldier, laughing, "assuredly, and now what is our bet, pray? I see the judges about to give the signal to prepare the horses."

"I bet," said Henrietta, "that Sir Archy or Fair Anna will beat Selim."

"The first heat?"

"As you choose, sir."

"Well," says Captain Ralph, "I close. Remember Ma'mselle Clare," he adds to her companion, "that Madam Henriette and myself have laid a wager of that morocco case and its contents, against a curl of her hair, that Sir Archy beats my Arabian the first heat. Do not forget!"

"The first heat, sir?" asks Clare, in her mild voice.

"Yes," replies the Captain, "there will be three I am informed—three of two miles each. The horse which wins two out of these three heats, of course beats the field."

Clare nods.

"Prepare the horses!" comes from the judges' stand opposite.

Captain Ralph leaves the ladies with a gallant bow, and pushes his way through the swaying and excited crowd, toward the spot where the animals are being saddled.

A tremendous hurly-burly reigns there; men of all classes, boys, negroes, gentlemen, indented servants—all are betting with intense excitement. The dignified grooms endeavor to keep back the crowd:—the owners of the horses give their orders to the microscopic monkeys who are to ride. Mr. Howard, a fine-looking, somewhat supercilious gentleman, says to his rider:

"Jake, trail on a tight rein the first mile, press gradually on the second, and win the heat by half a length: if you are an inch before that, I'll murder you, you villain."

"Yes, massa," replies Jake, with a satisfied smile, and great cheerfulness. "I gwine to do dat very ting, *I* is."

Mr. James is a solemn-looking Napoleon of the turf, and impresses upon his rider a whole volume of instructions, with gravity, and a serious and affecting earnestness.

"Feel Sir Archy from the word proceed," he says, "and if it appears from a calm review of all the circumstances, that the mare has got the heels of him, come in half a head before him. If the mare fails to get her speed in the first brush, refrain from pushing her:—it is a matter of no importance to win this the first heat—but be sure to come to me before the second."

"Yes, my massa."

Captain Ralph says to his rider:

"Give me your whip:—good! now take off those spurs. Very well: now remember to keep silent—do not speak to your horse, do not tug at his rein: simply keep him in the track, and aim to keep the inside. Do not trouble yourself to win the heat—the rest I think is safe. Remember to lean far forward, and if there is danger of being distanced, I permit you to whistle in the horse's ears. Again, do not push to win this heat. Go!"

The riders are raised by one leg into the saddles: they gather up the reins: the drum taps: they are off like lightning.

The course is a mile in circumference, and they go round it before the excited crowd can look at them a dozen times. They whirl past the stand, and push on again.

Sir Archy leads: Fair Anna trails on a hard rein: the Arabian is two lengths behind: but he is not running.

They thunder up the quarter stretch: Sir Archy is bounding, like some diabolical monster, far before his companions, spite of his owner's cries: the Arabian has come up and locks the mare: they run neck and neck. Sir Archy whirls past the stand, and wins the heat by a hundred yards. The immense crowd utters a shout which shakes the surrounding forest.

The owner of Sir Archy looks with ominous meaning at Jake:—that youth begins to tremble, and says that he couldn't hold him. Mr. Howard turns to the horse. Sir Archy's eyes glare—he does not sweat at all: his coat is covered with a dry dusty oil, and he pants dreadfully: he is over-trained.

Fair Anna is as wet as if she had just swam a river: the moisture streams from her: she looks like an ivory statue in a fountain. The grooms rake the sweat off in foamy floods: she breathes regularly.

The Arabian's coat is merely glossier: an imperceptible moisture bathes it, and he is quite still: he does not pant: his breathing is calm.

The horses are again enveloped in their hoods and blankets. Captain Ralph returns to the Riverhead carriage.

"Parbleu! you've won, my dear madam!" he says, "behold, here I am very unhappy!"

Henrietta does not quarrel this time with his French, but laughs triumphantly.

"A favor?" continues the unfortunate Captain, with a melancholy air.

"Oh, certainly!" cries Henrietta.

"I ask that you will not open the morocco case which—*miserable!*—I have lost, until you return home. Is it very hard?"

"Oh no, sir; and I promise without hesitation. Give it to me, Clare."

And she takes the case, puts it in her muff, and smiles.

"Any more betting, sir?" she says, satirically.

"Who, I?'

"Yes, sir."

"Assuredly!" says the Captain;" do not think, *chere ma'm'selle*, that I am very much cast down. I am so far from that, I assure you, that I am ready to take the field again."

"Well, sir."

"Then you will bet again, madam?"

"Yes, indeed."

"*Bien!* I now stake all that is left me in the world—though not quite. I stake my horse, Selim, against the curl and the pair of gloves you wear, with the knot of ribbons at your girdle thrown in—all upon the final issue."

Henrietta blushes; for, however common such gallant proposals were at that day, she cannot misunderstand the meaning of the soldier's glance, and reddens beneath it.

"That would be unfair, sir," she says.

"Not so, my dear madam; for are you not sure to lose?"

"To lose?"

"Yes, indeed."

"No, sir; I am sure to win."

"Bah! you ladies have such a delicious little confidence in the things you patronize, that it is really astonishing. You think Sir Archy will beat Selim? Pshaw! you know nothing about it."

This piques madam Henrietta, and she smiles satirically again as she says:

"Well, sir, I do not want your pretty horse—but if you insist, why, I cannot retreat. I shall, at least, have the pleasure of returning him to his master."

The Captain shakes his head.

"A bet upon such terms, is no bet at all, my dearest madam," he says, "for, I assure you, if I win, you will return home curl-less, glove-less, and ribbon-less. All is fair in war—and love."

With which words, Captain Ralph darts a martial ogle at his companion. This piques her more than ever.

"Well, sir," she replies, "if you are determined, have your desire."

"Good!" cries the captain, "we are just in time. There is the horse. Remember now, Ma'm'selle Clare, that we have lain a wager on the final issue. I bet Selim against a curl, a pair of gloves, and a piece of ribbon, that the Arabian beats the field. Miss Henrietta, that he will not. *Voici*, I do not ask you to hold my stakes," adds the Captain with a laugh as he bows, "for I think that will be as much as his rider will be able to do!"

And, with another gallant bow, the Captain rides away toward the horses.

The boys are again instructed much after the same fashion: the signal is given in the midst of breathless suspense, and the horses dart from their places.

They dart around, Sir Archy again leading: but this position he does not hold throughout the first mile: he gradually falls behind and when they pass the winning-post he is fifty yards in the rear. His owner tears his hair, but the crowd do not see him—they flush and shout.

The second mile is between Fair Anna and the Arabian, and they lock in the middle of it: but the Arabian gradually takes the lead, and when they flash up to the stand he is ten yards ahead. Sir Archy is distanced and withdrawn.

It would be impossible to describe the excitement of the crowd:—the tremendous effect produced upon them by this reversal of all their hopes and expectations. They roll about like waves, they shout, they curse, they rumble and groan like a stormy sea.

The horses are the objects of every one's attention. Their condition will go far to indicate the final result—and Sir Archy being led away and withdrawn, the race now will be between Fair Anna and the Arabian.

Mr. James looks more solemn than ever, and all eyes are turned upon him. Captain Waters is not visible—he is yonder, conversing with the ladies.

But the horses! Fair Anna pants and breathes heavily. her coat is drenched more completely than before with perspiration; her mouth foams: she tosses her head: when the rake is applied to her back a shower falls.

The Arabian is wet all over too: but he breathes regularly: his eye is bright and his head calm. He has commenced running. The first intention of Mr. James is to give up the race, but his pride will not let him. He utters an oath, and gives renewed instructions to his rider. These instructions are to whip and spur—to take the lead and keep it, from the start.

The moment for the final struggle arrives, and Captain Ralph merely says, "Rein free!"

The boys mount—the crowd opens; the drum taps and the animals are off like lightning.

Fair Anna feels that all her previous reputation is at stake, and flies like a deer. She passes around the first mile like a flash of white light: but the Arabian is beside her. For a quarter of a mile thereafter they run neck and neck—the rider of Fair Anna lashes and spurs desperately.

They come up to the quarter-stretch in the last mile at supernatural speed:—the spectators rise on their toes and shout:—two shadows pass them like the shadows of darting hawks :—the mare barely saves her distance and the Arabian has triumphed.

If we could not describe the excitement after the second heat, what possibility is there that we could convey an idea of the raging and surging pandemonium which the crowd now came to resemble? Furious cries—shouts—curses—applause—laughter—and the rattle of coin leaving unwilling hands are some of the sounds. But here we must give up :—as no mere pen can describe the raging of a great mass of water lashed by an angry wind into foam and whistling spray and muttering waves, which rise and fall and crash incessantly, so we cannot trace the outline of the wildly-excited crowd.

The Captain wipes Selim's neck with his white handkerchief, and the panting animal raises his head and whinnies.

"See, gentlemen!" says the soldier laughing, while Mr. Howard scowls proudly at him, "Morbleu! my horse is merely a little warm—just come to his speed! Why did I not stake my whole fortune on him!"

And uttering this preposterous jest, the soldier caresses Selim, who manifests much pleasure thereat; and sending him back to the stable, mounts his horse and goes and claims his wager from the mortified Henrietta. She takes off the gloves and hands them to him, with the ribbon knot, which she detached from her girdle with a jerk betraying no slight ill-humor.

"There, sir! at least I am honest, and pay my just debts!" she says: "but please leave my curl."

The Captain folds up the gloves, wraps them in the ribbon, and places the whole in the pocket of his surtout.

"Leave the curl?" he says, laughing, "Oh, of course! But I assure you, my dear Ma'm'selle Henrietta, that my liberality is only for the moment. I shall claim it some day or other. All is fair in war—and love!"

With which words the Captain laughs louder than he was ever known to laugh before.

CHAPTER XXII.

SHADOWS OF THE PAST: SOMEWHAT GROTESQUE

THE reader must have perceived from the foregoing sketch, that "the races" in Virginia in the year 1765, did not materially differ from those at the present day:—but we have not quite finished our brief and hasty sketch, and he must suspend his opinion.

Still we cannot enter into any thing like a full description of the ceremonies which took up the remainder of the day:—just as we have been unable to draw a full length portrait of the fox-hunt—the festival at the hall—and further back, the grand opening day of the house of Burgesses. As we have said in former pages, this narrative is rather an account of the fortunes of a certain set of personages, and the events which directly affected them:—so the reader must be content with a very brief and imperfect sketch of the amusements which followed the triumph of Selim.

The race was gotten up by a number of subscribers, and though a purse was not suspended from a pole for the victorious jockey to take down, every other ceremony was observed.

These ceremonies were characteristic of the times, and an outline of them may amuse the reader.

First, a number of stalwart countrymen entered the ring—the races between the remaining horses having been run be it understood—and these hardy gentlemen are armed with stout cudgels, which they brandish around their heads in furious style, much after the manner of those gentlemen who followed, and flourished the quarter-staff in honor of that noble outlaw, Robin Hood.

The victor in the awful game is to have a hat worth twenty shillings, and this hat, of the cocked species, with a handsome feather, is suspended from a pliant pole above their heads.

The signal is given, and the brave combatants close and rain down a shower of blows, which rattle like hail, and cause the crowd of spectators to utter shouts of delight. The victor is no other than our old friend Townes, who says as he perches the fine hat on his bushy locks:

"Well, I dusted 'em! Their jackets won't want a brushin' soon agin!"

And he marches off amid great applause.

Next comes a wrestling match, and the prize of the victor here is a pair of velvet buckles, which are exhibited to all. The contestants enter the ring and tug and whirl, and roll and fall. Is the gentleman who is declared victor, and who bears away the buckles in triumph, called by the euphonious name of Junks, or not? We cannot know certainly, as his name is not announced: at least, he is an undeniable water-dog, and will drink up his silver ornaments, we may be sure.

Then comes a running match, the prize for which is a pair of handsome shoes, with rosettes of ribbon; and running being an amusement which may be indulged in without fear of a cudgel blow or a fall, many enter the lists—among the rest, Mr. Bill Lane, the artist. He has practised the amusement when parson Tythetobacco was on his track, rod in hand, and to such perfection that he now distances all competitors, and bears off the shoes in triumph.

Another running match immediately. It is between "twelve youths, twelve years old, to run one hundred and twelve yards, for a hat worth twelve shillings." The requisite number of young gentlemen enter the lists and start off. Sam Barkerville is declared victor, his powers of running having been cultivated by humorous fleeing from his father, the sheriff, who, by poetic license, has been the imaginary holder of the legal writ of *ca. sa.* against Barkerville, jr.; and the hat worth twelve shillings is handed to the young gentleman, who cocks it over one eye, and marches off amid applause.

Next the herald holds up a handsomely bound volume, fluttering with ribbons and glowing with gilt, and proclaims that the best singer among the divine sex will take the prize, the said volume being a quire of ballads of the most approved description, with the accompanying musical notes.

A dozen blushing maidens advance and alternately sing such ballads as they fancy, in little fluttering voices, and with downcast eyes. The last who performs upon the occasion sings "The lass of Richmond hill," and her song is received with tumultuous applause. She is unanimously declared victor, and the beautiful volume is duly presented to Miss Donsy Smith, who receives it blushing, and retires into the throng, who greet her with two distinct rounds of applause, her bright, cheerful face having gained this young lady a host of friends.

Then comes the great and paramount contest of fiddlers, —many more in number than those who shared with "his glass and his lass" the liking of "old King Cole, that jolly old soul." In other words, the fiddlers are more in number, and they use instruments which range from those of back-woods construction—emitting awful and terrible discord, like veritable bulls of Bashan roaring, and pigs from the coast of Guinea squeaking—to excellent ones, worn and discolored by incessant use, and full of melodious power. The prize for the best performer is a fine new instrument, direct from London, and, in addition to this, the victor is to have the privilege of presenting a pair of silk stockings to the "prettiest country maiden on the ground."

The fiddlers stand "all in a row," and tune their instruments. Then, at a given signal, they play, one after the other, such pieces as they fancy, and exert their best powers to win the fine instrument. They roar, they crash, they storm, they pour a whirlwind of rapid, glittering notes upon the air, deafening the ears and setting the crowd to dancing almost; or else they link the sweetness and draw it out long and slow, like golden ribbon, or a stream of moonlight—sighing, crying, sobbing, laughing;—all this the violins do, with extraordinary movement in the heads and arms of the noble musicians. The air is filled with harmony, the crowd applauds, the happy artists hold out their hands. Nineteen hands are withdrawn abruptly; the twentieth receives the prize, over which are hung the silk stockings.

Lanky is the victor. Lanky no longer in boots and sword and cocked hat, it is true; but, at least, far more like an elegant cavalier than usual. For a moment, Lanky blushes,—scratches his head; then he twitches the string of the violin, and starts with joy at its excellence. This gives him courage: he places the silk stockings on the end of his fiddle bow; they hang there with a truth of outline which raises a shout in the crowd. Lanky steps forward, makes a dive at a portion of the crowd, throwing his head at them, —so to speak;—and lo! the silk stockings are seen to leave the end of the bow, and elegantly repose in a straddling posture around the neck of Miss Donsy Smith.

The crowd shout; the violins commence again; Jamaica rum,—"to wet their windpipes," says the chronicle,—is handed round, and immediately the twenty fiddlers all in a row begin to play furiously with the ardor of despair, such a different tune! Pandemonium is broke loose—a shudder runs through the crowd—they fly with their hands in their ears, with shouts of laughter.

So far, we have followed the veracious chronicle, invention having almost nothing to do with the scene we have sketched; but there is one gentleman whose performances on the occasion of the races we nowhere find any allusions made to. We consider this unjust, and proceed briefly to speak of him.

He is a colored gentleman; perhaps as much as three feet and a half high. He wears a long coat, whose skirts drag the ground; he sucks his thumb occasionally; he rejoices in and is proud of the name of Crow, but prefers the more modest and friendly appellation, "Jeames." He has suffered unmerited misfortunes lately, but, like a great man, is not cast down, and has come to the races with the noble intent to struggle against the effect of those misfortunes. He has not betted largely, but no one has taken more interest in the horses. He has criticised them; admired them; openly and candidly extolled them,—acknowledged their good points with simple frankness. He has lost his all—three half-pence—upon Sir Archy, but is not cast down thereat. He rises above his bad fortune, and preserves a noble equanimity.

He provides himself with a dilapidated cornstalk, and looks on while the cudgellers play. He flourishes the cornstalk around his head gracefully, and when it hits one of the dignified grooms, Mr. Crow does not disdain to take to flight —averse as he is, from principle, to contention. When the wrestlers commence, he takes his cornstalk in his arms and struggles violently with it, and finally trips it up, and falls triumphantly on it. When the running begins he drops his cornstalk foe, and, tying his long skirts before him, takes to running also, uttering enthusiastic "hooras!" He wins, in his own opinion, and takes off his ragged straw hat, without a rim, worn only on extraordinary occasions, and politely presents it to himself, and places it proudly on his head again—having fairly won it. When the maidens sing, he assumes a modest and bashful air: but with the advent of the fiddlers, his real representative powers begin to show themselves. He resumes his cornstalk: he breaks it in two; he grasps the shorter piece, and with his left hand inserts it under his chin. He then screws up the broken end to tune it, flourishes in his right hand the lengthier portion, and strikes the trembling lyre. As the fiddlers proceed, he proceeds also—fast or slow, enthusiastically with jerking head, shaking body, patting foot: or sentimentally, with his chin up, his eyes fixed upon the blue sky, with a die-away expression, his bow drawn slowly and rapturously over its counterpart. He finishes with the grand outburst of the twenty performers, and goes into ecstasies: his rapture passes all bounds: he sways, he shakes, he bows, he bends, he executes leaps, he turns somersets—still playing. But comes the cruel fate—he is not appreciated: he suffers from the effect of an uncultivated musical taste in the million. Mr. Crow in his ecstasy rolls upon a projecting boot—the boot rises up—Mr. Crow is hoisted—he disappears like a black snowball swallowed up in nothingness. He is gone—vanished—all the fiddles stop.

The day is wound up with a profuse banquet, at which the subscribers, their wives and daughters, refresh themselves with excellent roast beef and turkey, and a variety of wines. Perhaps a picture of the graceful and imposing scene would be worth drawing, but space fails us:—the eloquent discord of the twenty violins still drives our senses mad. We leave the dinner, therefore, to the reader's imagination: we leave him to fancy the merry talk, the allusions to the races, the congratulations offered Captain Waters, the praises of the fresh little country beauty Donsy Smith, the toasting of Captain John Smith, of old days, who landed yonder on the river when he came here—that immortal soldier to whom a monument should be erected, all declare—in whose honor a "Jamestown Society" should be instituted, to meet yearly in the month of May; and eat good dinners, fish and flesh and fowl, in grand appreciation of his noble deeds. We leave all this to the reader's imagination, and can only say that the banquet, *sub Jove*, was a very merry and happy affair, and that the birds were of the same opinion that evening, when the brilliant party, having fled away, they picked up crumbs, and twittered gayly.

And so the brilliant party fled away, as all bright things fly far from us into the west, and dead days of the past. Where are they now, those stalwart cavaliers and lovely dames who filled that former time with so much light, and merriment, and joyous laughter? Where are those good coursers, Selim, Fair Anna and Sir Archy; where are black and white, old and young, all the sporting men and women of the swaying crowd? What do we care for them to-day? What do we care if the laces are moth-eaten—the cocked hats hung up in the halls of Lethe—the silk stockings laid away in the drawer of oblivion? What does it concern us that the lips no longer smile, the eyes no longer flash, the hands no longer move, the faces no longer laugh? What do we care for all those happy maiden faces—gallant inclinations—graceful courtesies—every thing connected with the cavaliers and dames of that old, brilliant, pompous, honest, worthy race?

They have gone away to the other world; their lips are dumb; their heads have bowed and their backs long bent, and they have carried away their loads and themselves to the happy or the miserable isles. We care so little for them, that the poor chronicler who tries to make them speak again to-day is scarcely heard: but still it is his province, he must speak in spite of all.

CHAPTER XXIII.

IL SEGRETO PER ESSER FELICE.

Mr. Effingham had not gone to the races for the same reason which had prevented Mr. Ralph Waters from attending the party at the Hall. The Captain felt an unconquerable repugnance to break bread under the roof of one who had stood in such a relation to his brother and his cousin formerly; practising, unconsciously, the Arabic custom which he had met with in his travels in the East. In like manner, Mr. Effingham could not go and smile, and caracole, and laugh at the joyous festival; it was too diametrically opposed to his feelings.

We shall perceive more clearly what those feelings were by entering the Hall on the evening succeeding the races, ascending the broad pine stairs, and going into Mr. Effingham's room.

The sun was just setting, and a stream of bright rosy light streamed through the tall windows on the opposite wall, and on the occupant of the room, who was seated in a tall carved chair, such as our ancestors much affected, with that singular taste for the stately, the grotesque, every thing but the comfortable, which they possessed—at least in regard to furniture. Mr. Effingham looked even paler than usual, and his eyelids drooped, the dusky lashes reposing on his wan cheek. His hair, free from powder, and hanging down upon his shoulders, was brilliantly illuminated by the rosy ray, and the single diamond upon his white hand glittered. That hand hung listlessly, the arm reposing upon the red damask cushion, and the other hand supported his cheek.

As he mused, gazing at the bright flood of sunlight, a faint smile, like the reflection of the moon in water, dwelt upon his pale lips and in his weary eyes. Then a sigh escaped from the lips, and the breast heaved.

"Surely I have suffered much in my life," he said, in a low voice, with another weary sigh. "The fates seem to pursue me; they will not permit me to pass any day, unless it is more or less clouded. What a career mine has been—how forlorn, how full of sad and unhappy events leaving so many painful recollections. My boyhood was pure and happy, and I laughed at care as the child heart laughs at every thing; incredulous, obstinately hopeful, I saw before me a long life of merriment, and I was never weary of the joy which flowed into my heart from the bright world. All things were *couleur de rose*. I had an open hand; a generous, loving nature—I could have taken in my arms the whole world from pure love and joy. I wandered through these forests singing; I ran gayly over the breezy hills;

I rode and hunted and lived an existence full of fresh and vigorous emotions: life to me was one long carnival. And what a carnival! What lovely masks—what picturesque and beautiful dresses—how many thousands of flambeaux seemed to flood the air with their bright flashing light! I heard wondrous music in every thing,—the trees, the streams, the very sky was vocal with those vôices which are ever calling, in their clear, soft tones on youth, and telling it to enjoy! enjoy! enjoy! I loved a pure heart then—I thought she loved me."

Another sigh more profound escaped from the pale lips; the faint sad smile again lit up the face with its twilight.

"Oh yes! she loved me then," he continued in a murmur; "that is my pride and happiness, my quiet joy now in these weary days, when life seems wholly exhausted for me—happiness gone past never to come back. What golden hours we passed! Ah! men may talk of the love of children slightingly, and stroke their beards and say they cannot feel the sentiment in its full force. It is a fallacy. There is nothing in after life so wholly pure and strong and grand as the first love of a boy—as his devotion, tenderness, and sincerity. In this after-life, our passions come to be matters of calculation; we look to settlements—we estimate eligibility—of rank, or wealth, or age. Youth, with its grand blindness, looks to none of them. It sees but one object in the world—wants not the money or the station, asks but the heart!"

He paused: and then went on sadly.

"Yes, those were golden hours—very happy hours. How beautiful she was! I think there never was such pure and tender beauty in a human face! I remember, as though it were yesterday, the child's face beaming on me, while the birds were chirping in the trees and the brook laughing. I thought the birds were envious of her singing when she carolled clearly in the bright fresh morning. She wore a wreath of roses in her hair, and carried on her arm a basket full of flowers; how clearly I see all again—well! well!"

And the head drooped pensively again in the waning sunset.

"Then, in the after days, when I came back from Europe," he continued, sadly, "I loved her just as before—

but did not find her fill so completely my whole heavens. Still, it is true she rose for me like a pure, lovely star; but the hours had drawn on slowly, and other stars had risen which distracted my attention. Especially that fiery planet which whirled through its brief orbit and so narrowly escaped being quenched in blood!"

He looked gloomy for a moment: but very soon the old sad, weary smile came back as his eyes were raised to a bookcase in the corner. On this bookcase stood two statues: and by these statues lay some withered flowers. He rose, took down the withered nosegay, and sat down again in the same listless way. He looked at them sadly, and placed them against his cheek with a forlorn smile.

"She gave them to me one afternoon when we were walking hand in hand in the old garden," he murmured, wistfully, "and I told her they were not half so fresh and bright and purely beautiful as her face. I see her soft, tender blush—I feel her hand tremble: at that moment life-long happiness was in my grasp—the brilliant pearl, a pure loving heart—well: I threw it away! It is gone: another has enshrined it in his heart.

"Well, this is but one more hope gone—one more memory to make my days and nights weary, to multiply these weary sighs. I cannot, do not complain—yet I loved her! loved her dearly: well, well, it is passed. She will be very happy: he is a worthy gentleman, a kind heart. She will not think of me often; I am not what I was. Poor sword!" he continued, sadly, looking at his weapon lying on the table, "you and your master have lost edge: you rust wofully. That master is no longer the gay and laughing cavalier whispering to ladies, and met every where with smiles—the proud heir of Effingham, living his life with nothing any where but those welcome smiles:—like these poor flowers he has withered; his freshness is gone."

A low voice singing came from the next room, and Mr. Effingham recognized Kate's accents. By a singular coincidence, she was singing, "The flowers of the forest," that sweet and plaintive air, which seems to resemble the sighing of the wind, the murmur of the flowers, the low trembling of an Æolian harp in a calm evening when the airs are almost dead.

"Yes, they are gone," said Mr. Effingham, his head drooping: "yes! yes! love, youth, every thing rosy, hopeful, brilliant is gone and withered away: and life has drawn near no longer any thing but a stern, hard reality. Yes, the flowers of the forest went away with the autumn—they withered like these I hold. Withered! that is a strange word—can it apply to a human heart?"

The tender voice of the child came from the adjoining room, and the fresh, pure accents pleased and quieted him: he smiled faintly.

"No, I believe my heart is not wholly withered," he murmured, "like my hopes."

And reclining in the tall carved chair, his sad eyes wandered to the sunset, waning slowly over the great forest with a pomp of golden clouds. His face was bathed in the rich rosy light, and his calm eye gazed steadily upon the blood-red orb. It was one of those real pictures which surpass the masterpieces of the greatest painters, and the flood of light poured upon it like a crimson stream. Strikingly handsome, pale, thoughtful, with chiselled lips, and long, waving hair, and rich, elegant costume—the mere externals would have rejoiced an artist: but no artist could have caught the sad smile upon the lips; the calm, uncomplaining sorrow in the eye; the posture so full of calm, almost languid repose.

As he gazed on the sunset, the shadow in his eyes disappeared in a degree: his brow cleared up partially; he sighed, but no longer so wearily with such painful languor.

"Well, well," he murmured, "there is the sun going down after running his course honestly, and giving light to all; warming the earth and quickening the germ within its bosom. The seed has started beneath this warmth; the leaves begun to bud; the birds have rejoiced in it, and the whole universe grown stronger, brighter, fresher since he rose this morning. And now he sets, quite calmly, having done his duty—ah! that is Kate's word! Duty? that is surely something, and it seems that the sun has not stopped shining ever because clouds interposed and dimmed him! Why should a man grow faint and murmur then, and fold his arms and be idle, because the world is not a fairy land of roses and perfumes—where a sweet do-nothing reigns? That *dolce far niente* cannot be the secret of happiness: I feel that it is not—and I have always laughed at those Arcadian dreams of shepherdesses and shepherds with their crooks, making languid love, and sighing and dreaming the long days away in beautiful woodlands by the murmuring streams of fancy.

"No, life is not a bower to dally in, to be happy, careless, in; where all is sunshine. I feel it in my heart, and trample on that Epcurean philosophy which teaches such a doctrine. All things work—nature nowhere rests in these unhappy delights which lap the heart in down and tell us that the cold wind cannot reach us—that it should not. That wind—even though it be a storm-wind—is healthy, fresh, invigorating, like the breeze which stirs the leaves yonder in the sunset. The sun is going—slowly, gradually—he has done his duty, and will rise to-morrow to commence again! Have not men a duty?"

He paused with dreamy eyes gazing upon the sunset.

"I have suffered—I have enjoyed—I have tasted life—drained some delicious draughts, and been driven delirious by them," he continued. "Come, let me see if there is no way open yet for me to imitate the sun, and do some good in the world. Poor brain! I fear it is dulled now, and the heart no longer warm: but I will put away my flowers at least, and not sigh over the old days."

He replaced the nosegay on the book-case, and as he did so, he heard Kate come tripping along the broad passage singing. But this time it was a merrier song—one of those laughing ditties which have rung through so many houses, filling them with the contagious laughter of the singer. Mr. Effingham smiled, and was pleased to hear the fresh, merry voice.

"The little chirper," he said, "merry as usual!"

Kate came running on her tip-toes, and carolling that old ditty, in which the singer asserts that her lover, who is gone to the fair, has promised to buy her "a bunch of blue ribbon;" and if there had been a multiplicity of bunches of ribbon of all imaginary colors promised to Kate, she could not have carolled her little ditty with more contagious merriment.

She stopped at the door, and tapped. Mr. Effingham,

leaning his arm on the mantelpiece, said, "Come in, Kate!" and his voice was much less sad.

Kate entered bright and sparkling, tripping, and running on her tiptoes, with her curls flying, and her eyes dancing.

"Oh my goodness! here you are all by yourself," she said. "You mustn't be moping, now you know, cousin. I won't allow that."

"Pray, what right have you, madam, to command me?" was the smiling answer.

"I? Why you belong to me, you know. Gracious!" continued Kate laughing, "did any body ever?"

And the child put her arm round his waist, and drew him toward the door.

"Come now, cousin, and take a walk with me," she said.

"I'm rather dull, Katy."

"You mustn't be."

"Suppose I cannot help it."

"But you shall."

There was no resisting her entreaties, and Mr. Effingham soon prepared himself for the walk. As they went forth in the clear, still evening of the month of flowers, the birds sang overhead, the streams ran merrily, the whole earth seemed lapped in soft repose. The bleat of sheep came from the hills, the cattle bells were tinkling as the long line came slowly back from the pasture, and the wagoners returning from their work, were singing their rude African songs, and jesting with each other gayly. Flocks of gay birds were circling through the sky, and filling the wide air with joyous carollings. The thousand tranquil noises of a country evening, gave a light and music to the time which cities never feel. And then the songs died away through the forest like a merry laugh; the sheep no longer bleated, but with lazy lips; the cattle drew near home; and the low tinkle of their bells was hushed. The birds, too, folded up their wings, and only chirped occasionally as they went to sleep. The night had come.

The tranquil hour, and all these quiet sounds, calmed the sad heart, and made it lighter; and he looked fondly on the little, bright-eyed face at his side. And Kate burst out joyfully singing:—

"When the flow'r is i' the bud, and the leaf upon the tree,
The lark shall sing me home in my ain countrie."

Mr. Effingham gazed at the child smiling, and said:

"I know who is my lark, and I'm glad I am home in my own country to hear the songs she sings."

So they returned home through the quiet evening to the old hall, whose chimneys still glowed in the sunset, and sent up a golden flood of curling smoke. The dogs rose up and came to have a romp with Kate. The squire's face was smiling as he looked up from his newspaper; the house smiled not less brightly; and his face was sad no longer.

The healthful voice of nature had spoken to his heart, and he was calm.

CHAPTER XXIV.

HOW THE SEIGNEUR MORT-REYNARD PREACHED AND PRACTISED.

THAT merry fox-hunter and incorrigible bachelor, Mr. Jack Hamilton, or as Captain Waters called him, Seigneur Mort-Reynard, was holding a confidential conversation with Miss Alethea in the library—when we say confidential, we mean personal—inasmuch, as the colloquy in question busied itself with the moral delinquencies of the identical seigneur, and especially referred to his reynard-hunting propensities.

When Mr. Effingham entered, he found that his friend was engaged in that forlorn and desperate undertaking—arguing with one of the opposite sex. Mr. Jack Hamilton was accustomed to plume himself upon his knowledge of the female character; to mention with pride and satisfaction the fact that he had always seen through them, as he expressed it, and been enabled by his splendid sagacity to detect and escape their wiles; in a word, he would often inform his Nimrod associates over their claret, after a jovial hunt, that he knew women perfectly, and that he was so old a fox that the swiftest of them could not run him down. And yet, with all this boasted knowledge of the sex, with all this profound insight into their peculiarities of organization, the unfortunate man was absolutely arguing a proposition with a lady. The poor fellow had really not learned the first and most commonplace rules of the science which he boasted. And how he did boast when he got Tom Lane, and Charley Cotes, and the rest, snugly seated at a jovial supper at the Trap!

"My dear fellow," this keen student of (female) human nature would say, with one arm resting on the table, the right hand holding to his lips a glass of claret, "you are not as old as I am, and will not take my advice, and leave the girls alone. Avoid them, sir!—this world would get on gloriously were it not for these women—with their sighings, and oglings, and flirting fans, and rustling flounces. All the trouble in the universe—more or less—is caused by them, and many a tall fellow—in the Shakespearian sense, I was reading him yesterday; a good writer!—many a fine fellow, brave, and holding up his head, has bit the dust before 'em!

"Just look! Here is a jolly companion, ready to run a fox to the death, to hunt deer on the coldest night that ever a fryingpan shone in, what I call a boy of metal, ready for fun, and joyous as the day! ready to clash glasses, to laugh at matrimony, to break through every thing which bothers him, and as brave as Julius Cæsar. Well, sir—the bottle stays with you!—just look now how the thing works! He goes to some ball or other, makes the acquaintance of a pair of blue eyes, lips to match—to say nothing of the rest. He looks—the infatuated fellow will not cut and run as a brave man may, when he knows the enemy can beat him easily—he dances with her—goes bowing and ambling, and mincing his steps and smiling through a minuet or a quadrille: he squeezes her hand—the poor, infatuated boy! Never squeeze a woman's hand, sir! by Jove, it is too ridiculous. Well, the unhappy victim of the eyes, does this more and more: he returns her ogles, he thinks her courtesies, as she holds out her silken skirt, the very sublimity of grace, by George! he feels a something creeping over him, that makes him feel like a thousand pins were sticking in him, and as if the black rascals, who are scraping away on their fiddles, are playing rainbow music, on moonlight violins, with bows made of flowers, by Jove! The reel finishes him, sir!—he dances it with her—her face flushes up, her eyes sparkle, her satins rustle, she shoots him down, by Jove! with her eyes, and takes his heart, which he is holding in his hand, and puts it in her pocket—if ladies have pockets, which I doubt.

"Now, mark me, sir—not bad claret, this!—from that minute, he is gone! He leaves hunting—he passes over to the other side, when he meets us jolly fellows on the road; he frowns when we refuse to acknowledge that all the sense, all the virtue, all the brilliancy of the world, is found in women; and let any one dare to assert that his particular paragon is not the pearl of all—the top froth—the moonlight and flowers—the head and front of all. Try it! a cock-sparrow is nothing to him. He whips out his hanger, by Jove! his eyes blaze up, he makes a pass at you, and runs you through the gizzard, causing a large and affectionate circle to mourn your loss.

"All this, sir, is caused by women—from their passion for matrimony. Men, sir, are to them, what the fox is to us—they take pleasure in running them down and slaughtering them. No, I am wrong—they are not so easy as that: they are like cats, sir, when a mouse falls into their clutches. They tie the infatuated poor fellow to their apron-string—they watch, and smile, and simper, and die away: but try to escape, sir, under the impression that the enemy is lulled to sleep. By Jove! sir, the claw comes out from the velvet paw, and you are gone! You are married, sir!—you are led like a sheep to the slaughter, and you may bleat as much as you choose, by George! You are thenceforth a married man, and your bachelor joys are all gone. Try a fox hunt if you dare—madam will make you rue it: speak to your bachelor friends—she'll scratch you, sir. From that moment you are a joyless, married man, and your whole life is to be spent in working like a drudge for a set of little dirty-faced darlings, who make you get up fifty times in the night, and won't let you read your newspaper for crawling over you.

"That's it, sir: you are an unfortunate married man. You dare not ask your friends to dinner, or if you feel that it is a shame not to, you say in a mild and sheepish voice, 'Really, now, my dear Tom (or Jack, as the case may be), I am delighted to see you; your face reminds me of old times (poor fellow, so it does!) come and—I hope you can make it convenient—you are sure you have no engagement—I should be happy—Do you know—my—wife?' And, by George! sir, he hangs his head, and looks like he had been caught stealing a sheep; for he knows that madam will sit up like a lump of ice, and make personal observations unpleasantly alluding to his past life with us jolly fellows, and when she has him, sir, alone, will make the watches of the night miserable with a lecture behind the curtains, in which she will prove, to his own, and her own, satisfaction, that he is falling back into his old abominable courses, when he used to commit the deadly sin of sitting up a-nights, and rattling the dice, and eating suppers, and chasing reynard with us jolly boys, by George! He knows she'll lay it all out to him, with that eloquence which she possesses in such a high degree; and no wonder that the poor fellow blushes, and hesitates, and hems! when he ventures to suggest that his old friends should visit him—the reprobates, as madam calls them. I, for one, would not go and dine with him—I should shake my head, and go on my way, in pity, not anger, and I would empty six bottles, and run down fifty foxes to get his face out of my mind. Yes, sir, that is the short and the long of it—your fate will be to find yourself henpecked! Avoid them in time, by Jove! never put yourself in their power, or you are gone—you are, indeed! Never laugh and talk with them—never visit them—above all, sir, never argue with them, for you are sure to get the worst of it. Lay this down as a general rule, that a woman will always have the last word; and, secondly, that no woman ever yet understood how a demonstration followed a fixed set of premises;—logic is not their weakness, sir, they don't understand it; but what they do understand, is jumping to their own conclusions, and sticking to 'em like grim death. One of their conclusions is, that all men of right ought to be caught, if eligible. Now, sir, you needn't resist—they will convince you: the only way is to do as I do—never go near them, and cultivate a bachelor life."

And after these diabolical sentiments, Mr. Jack Hamilton would empty his claret, pour out a second glass, and begin singing, "Oh, a jolly life for me-e-e! A jolly life for me!"

Let us return from this digression to the Hall, which we have left, to listen to Mr. Hamilton's advice given to his bachelor friends at the Trap. But it is not our intention to report the words uttered by Mr. Hamilton and Miss Alethea. It is enough to say that the Seigneur Mort-Reynard proved his own philosophy to be perfectly correct, and was quietly unhorsed by Miss Alethea in every charge—that lady managing the weapons with her habitual air of prim and stately grace.

"Ah, here's Champ coming to the rescue!" cried the delighted seigneur. "I am in a bad way here, friend Effingham. Miss Alethea has been proving satisfactorily that I am a most hardened sinner."

Miss Alethea smiled, with a wintry look, but said nothing.

"I am glad to see you, Jack," replied Mr. Effingham, suppressing by an effort the painful emotion caused by the sight of his rival; "how did I miss seeing you when you rode up?"

"Oh, I slipped through the lane by the stable; I wanted to get the nearest road to Riverhead."

"Ah!" said Mr. Effingham, coldly; but immediately suppressing this exhibition of feeling, he added, calmly, "present my best respects to the family."

"Including Clare?" said Mr. Hamilton, easily.

"Yes, sir," said Mr. Effingham, austerely: and he picked up a book to conceal his emotion. Then conscious that this tone was a great injustice to his friend, he said, "I am rather unwell to-day—I hope you are as hearty as ever, Hamilton."

"I?" said the Seigneur Mort-Reynard, laughing; "why I never felt better in my life. We had a glorious—"

Suddenly the seigneur paused: he saw the eye of Miss Alethea fixed on him, and suppressed the remainder of his sentence with a sheepish look.

"I am going over to carry Miss Clare these gloves," he added. "She commissioned me to procure them in town for her."

"You know the size of her hand, then?" asked Mr. Effingham, not to have his painful silence observed.

"Her hand? I think so! The sweetest little hand. She laid it in my own buckskin one, and by Jove!—a thousand pardons, Miss Alethea!—and I measured it by laying my fore and middle fingers upon it. They were just the width of her hand, and her thumb was the size of my little finger."

"Ah!" said Mr. Effingham.

"Yes, indeed! Now if the ladies only wore some species of covering on the lips!"

Mr. Hamilton paused with a laugh.

"On the lips, sir?" asked Miss Alethea, who was not quick at a jest.

"And I measured with my own, as I measured the hand!" said the seigneur, laughing.

Miss Alethea drew herself up: Mr. Effingham's face flushed. His friend did not perceive it, apparently, and went on.

"I really think I am becoming a lady's man," he said. "Here I am running about buying gloves, and flirting fans, and making myself useful in a variety of ways. I really should not be surprised if I ended by attaching myself to some fair lady for life!"

"A good resolution," said Mr. Effingham, looking away. "As for myself, I am growing more and more careless in these matters."

"That reminds me, Champ," said Miss Alethea, "that we are all invited to Mr. Lee's to-morrow."

"I shall not go."

"Why?"

Mr. Effingham looked at his sister, but suppressed his irritated feeling.

"I am not very well," he added, "please say as much."

"Now, Champ," said Mr. Hamilton, "permit me to observe that you do wrong in neglecting the ladies over there. They are really charming—and though I confess what I probably should conceal, that for certain reasons I am not an unbiassed judge between Miss Henrietta and Miss Clare, yet I assure you I think the former a most beautiful and lovely girl."

This speech was so plain that Mr. Effingham felt a pang shoot through his breast: he said nothing.

"They were talking about your neighborly behavior," continued his friend, coolly, "and Clare—Miss Clare, I mean—said that you had scarcely been near them since your return from Europe. That is not friendly, and they think you are driven away by that Don Moustachio, Captain Waters, whom you do not like ! "

We regret to say that this was a fib : the fox-hunter had no reason to suppose that the Riverhead family had any such thoughts.

Mr. Effingham replied :

" I do not dislike Captain Waters—we are good friends."

" Why then stay away ? "

Mr. Effingham replied by the same look which had greeted a similar question from Miss Alethea. And the same suppression of his irritability ensued.

" I stay away because I visit nowhere," he said.

" Ah, you fear the bright eyes of Henrietta ! " said Mr. Hamilton.

This quiet assumption that Clare could not be the source of fear from her peculiar relations towards himself—Mr. Hamilton—produced a painful effect upon Mr. Effingham. He began to feel some rising indignation, too, at these banterings from a man who had asked him with a twinkle in his eye, in a former interview, " if he had seen Clare ?"—upon his return, the reader will remember. Therefore to Mr. Hamilton's bantering charge, that he feared Henrietta's eyes, he replied, coldly :

" I think you might have added Miss Clare Lee to the number of those I do not visit at Riverhead, from a sentiment of fear."

" Clare ? " said Mr. Hamilton, with some surprise, " but, my dear fellow ! she is wholly out of the question."

" How, sir ? "

" Hum ! " said Mr. Hamilton, looking mysterious, " perhaps I am not at liberty to speak : there are certain things which should not be alluded to, I believe."

Mr. Effingham turned his head aside, and his breast heaved :—his cheek grew paler. Then he conquered this emotion, so painful and trying : and turning to his friend, said, as he offered his hand :

" You are right, Hamilton, I will go to-morrow ! "

And his head sank. Ten minutes afterwards the Seigneur Mort-Reynard rose and departed.

CHAPTER XXV.

GENERALSHIP OF DON MOUSTACHIO.

When the Hall chariot drove up to the residence of Mr. Lee on the succeeding day, it contained—in addition to the squire, Miss Alethea and Kate—Mr. Effingham. He was perfectly calm, though a little paler than usual, and greeted the ladies with calm and proud courtesy. Mr. Lee was delighted to see them,—exhibiting much more satisfaction, indeed, than might have been expected from one merely discharging the stereotyped duties of a host: and soon the squire and himself were engaged in an obstinate political dispute, which was carried on with various brandishings of the arms, contortions of the visage and flirting of the coat-skirts. But let not the reader imagine that because we have made the squire and Mr. Lee, whenever this narrative has brought them together, dispute vehemently, this disputing is a radical peculiarity of the country gentleman always,—no: he sometimes converses, and does not argue. But those were troublous times, and men's minds were agitated; and whenever the Virginia mind is agitated it brandishes the weapons of oratory, before donning the instruments of national warfare.

But there was another reason, at least in the case of Mr. Lee, for this propensity to talk. Captain Waters had not made his appearance since some days before the races, and the old gentleman missed the loud-voiced soldier. The "Virginia Gazette" and the talk of the girls was a bad substitute, and Mr. Lee now opposed every thing the squire said for the pure sake of talking. For it is well known that people who dispute talk the most and the loudest.

In the middle, however, of a lengthy and involved sentence, which was trampling disdainfully on Lindley Murray, Mr. Lee found himself greeted by a martial and courteous voice, which said:

"A charming day, sir!"

And Captain Ralph entered, caressing his moustache and distributing smiles. Behind him came Willie, who had begged off from the parson and followed Kate with devoted love.

There was a general shaking of hands, and after some desultory conversation, dinner succeeded. After the meal, the various members of the party began conversing. Mr. Lee and the squire sat in the porch smoking their pipes and brandishing their arms, starting up and removing their legs from the balustrade when the fire of the pipes fell on them in the heat of debate, and from time to time replenishing, and lighting the cob pipes with a coal, brought by an *ingenui vultus puer ingenuique pudoris* of the African race, on a two-pronged fork. When the pipes were refilled, these politicians commenced puffing and arguing with new zest.

Mr. Effingham and Clare had walked out into the garden: the Captain, before issuing forth also with Miss Alethea and Henrietta, passed a few moments conversing with Kate, who sat by him on the sofa, the object of Willie's devoted regards.

" Ah, Monsieur Willie," he said, " I am pleased to see you: and you, *petite mam'selle*," he added with a laugh to Kate, " or signorina, or signoretta as the Italians say when they wish to address a very pretty, bright-faced little lady: are you well—*bien aise?*"

" *Merci, monsieur! parfaitement!* " cried Kate, laughing, and to Willie's profound consternation.

" *Ah! possible?* you speak French ? " said the delighted Captain.

" No, no, sir," said Kate, smiling merrily, " that is all I know: please don't speak to me in any thing but English."

The Captain liked the fresh child's face, and said:

" I will not, then: but indeed, little miss, I ought to be allowed to use French to describe to you the little Alsatian girls—charming little creatures—whom you resemble: especially in costume."

Kate assumed a delightful little womanly air, and replied primly:

" Oh, sir, that about the costume spoils all. Do they dress like me—in Alsatia? Where is that, sir? "

" On the Rhine, petite mam'selle, and the costume is like yours. Handsome colored dress, laced in front and ornamented with ribbons—fluttering, morbleu! like flags! skirt,

I believe they call it, looped back just so, like your own, and this skirt very short like your own again ; hair, lastly, unpowdered and parted in the middle."

"Oh, my next dresses are going to be made long," said Kate, "and papa says I shall have my hair powdered."

"Ah! that will spoil the likeness! You should see your counterparts, Mam'selle Kate, with their water-jars on their heads, coming from the fountains singing."

"They must be very pretty," said Kate, and then she added quickly, laughing and covering her mouth, "indeed I didn't mean that! you know I did not, sir!"

The Captain laughed heartily, and saying, "parbleu! I think it very true, they *are* like you and are very pretty little creatures!" turned to the elder ladies.

Willie cast gloomy and jealous looks at Kate, and made signs to the effect that he did not admire Captain Waters, and would like to engage in single combat with that gentleman.

"Aint you ashamed!" said Kate, "to be doing so!"

"Who is this individual?" said Willie, with a grand air.

"Captain Waters, sir. You know that very well."

"Hum!" said Willie.

"You are jealous!"

"I aint."

"To be quarrelling with every body who speaks to me. You ought to be ashamed of yourself, and I like Captain Waters a thousand times better than you. He laughs with me, and you do nothing but quarrel."

Willie looked so much hurt and mortified at these harsh words, that Kate relented, and said :

"Now Willie—don't be angry—you know how much I like you."

Willie refused to be comforted.

"I didn't mean I liked him better than you."

Willie shook his head.

"For you know you are my sweetheart," added Kate with a fatal glance of her bright eyes.

Willie brightened.

"Am I?" he said.

"Yes indeed."

Willie put his hand into his bosom, drew out the true love indenture, and unrolling it, said solemnly :

"Sign it ?"

Kate burst out laughing, and cried, "Oh no ! no ! I am not of age, sir ! See they are looking at us and laughing. Oh Willie ! and there's Mr. Hamilton."

Willie rolled up the contract with a deep sigh, and then followed Kate out into the grove.

Mr. Hamilton entered just as the colloquy ended, smiling, good-humored, shaking every body by the hand. The moment he made his appearance, Captain Waters, with consummate generalship, offered his arm to Henrietta, bore her off with a triumphant smile, and disappeared.

But two observations had passed between the gentlemen.

"*Bon jour, Seigneur Mort-Reynard !*"

"Why, good day, *Don Moustachio !*"

The former was uttered by the Captain, with malicious courtesy and a low bow ; the latter observation was characterized by a defeated and humbled look, which we suspect was somewhat affected by Mr. Jack Hamilton. The explanation of all this was, that Mr. Hamilton had mentioned Miss Alethea among the list of ladies who were the enemies and lecturers of bachelors, in the Captain's hearing, a few days before ; and now the Captain, by his rapid and consummate strategy, left him to make himself agreeable to the lecturing lady, while he, the soldier, with his head erect, his breast shaking with laughter, bore off Henrietta.

CHAPTER XXVI.

HOW HENRIETTA RETURNED THE DIAMOND NECKLACE.

THEY descended to the lawn.

"I am glad you came, sir," said Henrietta to the Captain.

That gentleman assumed a delighted expression of countenance, and replied :

"Really, my dear Madam Henriette, you flatter me extremely."

"Flatter you, sir ?"

"Yes, morbleu!"

"How, sir?"

"Why, when a lady says in a soft, charming voice, and with a tender glance, to one of the ruder sex, 'Ah! I am glad you came!' what can it be but an exhibition of extraordinary regard, and how can the rude individual aforesaid prevent himself from experiencing a sentiment of pleasure at such a flattering observation?"

Henrietta listened to this reply, and said, satirically, when the Captain had finished:

"You are slightly mistaken, sir—in two things."

"What are they?" asked the Captain, with great anxiety.

"First, sir, I did not speak in a 'soft, charming voice'—

"Ah, madam," commenced the gallant Captain.

"Let me proceed, sir: nor with a 'tender glance'—tender, indeed!"

And Miss Henrietta pouted.

"See now," said the Captain, "there is another illustration of a fact which I have always asserted."

"Pray, what fact, sir?"

"That we do not ourselves know the tone in which we speak—are wholly ignorant of the expression of our eyes, morbleu!"

And after this audacious bit of philosophy, the soldier looked around him, with a delighted and self-satisfied air, at the grass, the trees, the various pleasant objects visible on the well-kept lawn they were traversing.

Henrietta felt a strong disposition to take her hand from the arm of her companion; but this feeling of pique soon passed: she had almost learned to bear the soldier's banter by this time.

"I did not doubt, sir, when I denied having flattered you," she said, with a somewhat satirical expression, "that you would, with your extreme fertility of invention, find some proof of the assertion you made; but jesting aside, Captain Waters, I wished to see you; and that is the simple truth."

"There again!"

The young girl took no notice of this triumphant exclamation, and drew from her reticule the oblong morocco case, which we have seen her win upon the day of the race.

"About this, sir," she said.

The Captain perused the clouds.

"Yes," he replied; "nothing could be truer!—a charming afternoon."

And he looked around with great satisfaction.

"The necklace, sir—"

"I agree with you."

"Is entirely too—"

"Yes, they are equal to nightingales. As you observed, the song of the oriole is as clear and musical as a silver trumpet!"

"I observed no such thing, sir," said Henrietta, piqued at the wanderings of her companion.

"Ah!" said the Captain, readily, "but you might have said it; for nothing could be more just. I have heard the Bendermere nightingales—the birds who love the roses so, you are aware, my dear Mademoiselle Henrietta, in Gulistan, which signifies, if I am not mistaken, 'Land of Roses.' Well, I give you my *parole d'honneur* I don't think they are much finer than that oriole."

"Captain Waters!"

"Yes, he's a glorious fellow—looks as if he was singing himself away into smoke. I expect to see him rise to the clouds in a moment, like the curl rising up from those graceful pipes yonder."

This beautiful illustration did not satisfy Henrietta, who was more and more piqued.

"Captain Waters, will you or will you not listen to me?" she said, pouting.

"Listen to you? How could you ask such a question?" said the Captain, gallantly.

"Well, sir, as it is so pleasant to hear my voice—"

"It is pure music!"

"Be good enough, sir—"

"Ah, I am very bad!"

"To listen while I speak ten consecutive words."

"Fifteen, fifteen," said the Captain, generously.

"Very well, sir—a little of your attention also. I trust ten words will be enough."

"I will give you twenty-five—thirty," said the Captain,

with a noble and enlarged liberality; "I will even listen if you honor me by conversing throughout the ensuing night."

Henrietta uttered a little sigh, which meant plainly, "Was there ever such a provoking man to talk to!"

"I am dreadfully disagreeable, I know," said the Captain, translating his companion's sighs into words as usual, "but you are going to weary me to death about that miserable necklace. You are going to make me send it back to the port of New York to have it altered, re-set, something."

"No, sir."

"What then?"

"I wish you to send it back to be retained, or present it to some one else."

"How so?"

"I cannot accept it, sir."

"Accept!"

"Yes, sir."

"Why, you won it fairly; it is the spoils of a fair battle—of your bow and spear: you won it."

"No, I did not, Captain Waters. I laid a very ridiculous wager—of a trifle against a trifle, I thought. My stake—I believe that is the word—was this curl—"

"Which reminds me that I won it on the final result!" cried the Captain. "Come, pay your debts, morbleu! my dear Madam Henriette."

"For heaven's sake, sir, let me go on."

"You have finished the thirty words," said the Captain, with ready logic. "My curl! my curl!"

Henrietta, in a paroxysm of impatience, pulled down and bit the curl in two, and threw it in the direction of her companion. The Captain extended his hand and received it as it fell.

"Parbleu, 'tis far more valuable than I expected!" he cried; "as far more valuable as a row of pearls are than a pair of miserable and unhappy scissors!"

Henrietta could not retain a smile at this grotesque and ridiculous speech; which, like all the Captain's observations, seemed to be intended solely to defer the subject he wished to avoid.

"I am pleased to hear that my teeth are pearls," she

said; "I did not know it before, sir. And now—but for heaven's sake what are you doing, sir?"

The Captain, in fact, was holding his sword up before him, point down. He made no reply, but touching a little spring, opened the hilt, and deposited the curl in the cavity. After performing this remarkable operation, he lowered the weapon again, and twirled his moustache.

"That is my receptacle for title deeds, curls, and other valuables, *ma foi!*" he said; "that is to say, it will be if I ever get any title deeds. But I have made a good beginning!"

And he burst into laughter, significantly. Henrietta chose not to understand this laugh—perhaps did not—and said:

"When you interrupted me, sir, I was about to say that I laid a wager with you, and staked what I considered a trifle—"

"No, no!" interposed the Captain.

"Against what I thought was equally unimportant," continued Henrietta.

"The curl was much the more costly," said the Captain, "and morbleu! I will not now exchange."

"You exacted a promise from me," continued Henrietta, not heeding these interruptions, "that I would not open the case until I returned home. I did not, thinking it some trifle. Instead of a trifle it is a magnificent diamond necklace."

And opening the case, she drew out the necklace, which was of extraordinary beauty and value. The diamonds were very large, and set in the most tasteful manner. The bauble must have been worth at least a thousand guineas.

"Take it, Captain Waters," said Henrietta, "I cannot keep it."

"How vexatious," said the Captain very seriously; "what in the world am I to do with it? Besides, I am not entitled to it—you know very well I am not, madam."

"I do not consider the wager binding, sir; I cannot accept it."

"Answer, now, did you not confess the other day at Effingham Hall," continued the Captain, readily, "that I had caused you to break your own necklace?"

"Yes, sir."

The Captain looked triumphant.

"But, sir," said Henrietta, "that was in one of those piques which I am afraid I have indulged in very frequently in your presence."

"Yes, I am a terrible annoyer!"

"I meant to blame myself, sir," said the young girl; "I am somewhat quick, and I now embrace the opportunity to say that I trust you will pardon any harsh words I have been led to utter."

"Harsh! it is impossible that you could!" cried the soldier, delighted at getting away from the subject of the necklace.

"Very well, sir; I am glad you think so well of me. Now take the necklace."

And she held it out. The Captain became again despairing.

"Why you have a double claim to it," he said; "first, I broke your own; secondly, and lastly, you have fairly won this."

"My hand is almost tired, sir."

"What am I to do?" cried the Captain, disconsolately; "if I take that back to my house it will lie about—be thrown here and there; Lanky will perhaps take possession, and Donsy Smith will be the ultimate possessor!"

With which words the Captain groaned.

"Lanky?—Donsy Smith? Who in the world are they?"

"The first is my servant, the second his sweetheart," said the Captain, ready to weep.

Henrietta burst into a laugh.

"Do you really mean that you would permit your servant to take such a beautiful necklace?" she said, admiring the glittering jewels.

"What could I do with them?" asked the forlorn soldier; "besides, I think they would become my honest retainer's sweetheart—Donsy. She is a charming little creature!"

"How? Do you know her?"

"Yes, indeed—very intimately. She had a pleasant ride with me the other day."

Miss Henrietta imagined a picture of Captain Waters in

the saddle, with the arms of a "charming little creature" round his waist as she rode behind, and was not much pleased with the effort of her fancy.

"Donsy is a fine, bright faced girl,—very lady-like and pleasing; they would suit her," said the Captain, with a thoughtful sigh. "Yes, yes, she's a sweet creature, and I nearly threw Lanky into a fever some weeks since, by announcing my intention to enter the lists as his rival."

"You, sir?" said Henrietta.

This exclamation did not displease the Captain.

"Yes, yes, my dear madam, even me. She would make me a capital wife, and I assure you I am becoming tired of single blessedness. In one word, I want a wife."

Henrietta made no reply.

"Stop!" continued the Captain, "you must have seen Donsy, down there at the races!"

"I, sir?" said Henrietta, coldly.

"Why, yes! Do you not recollect a lovely little creature, of seventeen or thereabouts, who won the finely-bound volumes of ballads in the singing match after the race?"

"I believe I saw her," said Henrietta, with the freezing air of a duchess.

"Well, that was Donsy," said the Captain, apparently absorbed in the bright memory, and fixing his eyes thoughtfully on the clouds.

"And you would marry this little—"

Henrietta stopped; she could not find a word.

"Fairy?" suggested the Captain, cheerfully; "why I do not see any objection beyond the affection Lanky bears her. You know, my dear Mam'selle Henrietta, that I am not of very excellent family—as opinions go, for, frankly speaking, I think I am. My father is an old fishmonger,—the name applied derisively, you will recollect, by my Lord Hamlet, to the counsellor Polonius. Charley's a small farmer; Beatrice was an actress. Charley's my brother; Beatrice my sister. We are all poor, but honest," continued the Captain, laughing, "and I think the *bon pere*—health to him!—is the most honest of all!"

With which words the Captain looked cheerfully, and with a fine light on his martial features, toward the west.

Henrietta, for a moment, made no reply, the hand holding the necklace hanging at her side. Then, looking at the martial face, which, with its high and proud look, and its warlike appendages, towered above her, flooded with the red sunset, brow, and eyes and cheeks,—the brow and cheeks browned by sun and wind,—the clear eyes, giving back the golden flush of evening, she said in a low voice:

"Captain Waters, why do you so incessantly allude to this subject of birth? Do you fancy for a moment, sir, that I do not consider you as true a gentleman as the noblest in the land? That I am blind to the fact that you are a brave soldier and a refined man, worthy of all respect? You cannot think that I consider you ashamed of your birth! Why, then, say this so often?"

"Ashamed of my birth? True, I am not, my dear Mam'selle Henriette," said the Captain. "The *bon père* is a nobleman; Charley's a seigneur—chevalier of the middle ages; and Beatrice,—parbleu! Beatrice is a born duchess!"

And the Captain burst into laughter.

"We are all sovereigns—for we're honest!" he continued, with a quick change in his expression to an aspect of noble pride. "My father, mam'selle, is brave and honest, and with a great heart—morbleu! a noble, kindly, generous heart; I am indifferent ready with my hand, to open it, or close it on a sword hilt,—that is my profession; Beatrice is a wealthy, golden nature, as true as she is beautiful, as good and pure as she is lovely; and Charley—tonnere! my dear madam, my brother Charley is one of those natures which are very seldom met with. I have seen dukes and generals, lords and ministers; I have heard all talk; I have seen all speak with those noble lips, the eyes: well, madam, I have never met a more powerful soul than Charley's. He has the strength of calmness;—but I am wearying you. Enough—no! you are right, my dear madam,—I, perhaps, have even too high an opinion of my family!"

And, after this outburst, which, every word of it, was spoken with a proud sincerity which lit up the martial features, like the sunset, Captain Ralph was silent.

Henrietta replied, in a low voice:

"This was not necessary, sir."

And she held up the necklace for him to take.

"Oh, heaven preserve me! I thought we had dropped that subject!" said the soldier, resuming his tone of vexation and humor.

"I cannot accept such a valuable present, sir," said the young girl, with some embarrassment.

"Then oblige me by keeping it for me," said the soldier. "I really have no receptacle for it."

Henrietta hesitated.

"You need not wear it, my dear mam'selle," he said.

Henrietta hesitated still.

"Well," said the Captain, "I suppose Donsy must have it;—morbleu! 'tis vexatious, for here your name is engraved upon it beneath here—at least, your initials, my dear Miss Henriette; and I must send back the bauble to have them erased. See!"

And pointing to a small gold plate, he showed her the letters H. L.; but these letters were so engraved that space was left upon the plate for another letter.

She understood; a deep blush suffused her face; her head drooped.

"Will you not keep it?" said the Captain.

"Yes," she said, in a lower tone than she had yet spoken.

A brilliant light illuminated the martial features of the soldier, and they walked on in silence.

CHAPTER XXVII.

THE TWO TREES.

Clare and Mr. Effingham, as we have said, had gone into the garden.

He had quietly taken her hand in his with a calm and mild look in his shadowy eyes, placed the hand on his arm and led her into the old garden, where they both had played in childhood, and talked merrily in the old days, whose every flower bed, and row of trim box, and towering tree, was old and familiar and dear. And she had followed him with some slight agitation, but a soft look of maiden diffidence, which made her more beautiful than he had ever seen her look before.

It was one of those evenings which seem to unite all the freshness of the spring, all the gorgeous wealth of summer, all the melancholy softness of the misty autumn, and the golden Indian summer, into one perfect whole. The perfumed breezes, laden with the odors of a million early flowers, came softly from the far south ; the oriole hung on the poplar spray, and sung his soul away for joy ; the leaves, and buds, and flowers, had all the tender velvety softness of the early spring ; and over all the great sun poured the fresh crimson light of morning.

Mr. Effingham walked on for some time in silence. Then, pausing in a grassy nook, he pointed, with a mild glance at the young girl, to two trees which grew side by side.

"How long ago it seems!" he said, with a pensive accent, which was quite calm and unaffected.

"Yes," said Clare, in a low voice, "we were children."

"And now we are grown-up people," said Mr. Effingham. "We have almost wholly forgotten those old happy days when we planted those trees,—when, taking your hand in mine, I said, "Clarry, we will come here every day we live, and see how we are growing. Do you not remember?"

"Yes," she murmured.

"I at least have not kept that resolution ; have you?"

"I have come very often," she said, in the same low tone.

He looked at her for a moment : and not a trait of the soft, tender face, the mild, dewy eyes, the innocent, artless lips, escaped him. She stood before him the loving ideal of his dreams ; the memory he had summoned in that evening musing ; the child-enchantress of his youth, who ever stood before his mind's eye, holding out her arms to him, her brow wreathed round with flowers, her eyes and lips murmuring, "Come!" He felt what he was losing, a contraction of his pale brow proved it, and the hand he laid upon his heart. But these exhibitions of emotion soon passed away, and his face regained the calm sadness which habitually characterized it.

"When I asked," he said mildly, "if you had kept that

child resolution to come and look at these trees every day, I did not mean a reproach. Ah no! That is assuredly not possible from me to you. I came to speak to you quite calmly, as those who have been happy children together may speak to each other; and to open my heart to you. This is due to myself. It will make me happier, and I cannot lose the occasion to make my lot somewhat brighter."

He paused for a moment, and continued in the same low, mild voice.

"What I have to say is a confession, Clare—there is no harm in my calling you by that name now—a brief confession, which will explain much in my career, which I doubt not has made you look unhappy when my name ever was mentioned in your presence. And let me speak first of those days which we passed here. Now, it seems, long centuries ago. I loved you dearly as a child: you were my saint, my ideal—nay! Why blush, Clare? You must have known it from my eyes; yes, my heart spoke to you much more plainly than my lips could speak. I say again you were my ideal, all my world was full of you. I dreamed, and sang, and thought of you alone. The old romances took a glory from your smile, and I understood for the first time what the 'love of ladies' meant, and how the old chevaliers willingly perilled life for their idols. You gilded my existence with a new, undreamed of light; the future expanded before me like a boundless horizon where all the glory of the sun, all the perfume of the breezes, all the fairy melodies of whispering pines and flowers were mingled into one harmonious and perfect ideal of warmth, and joy, and beauty. I saw only you in the wide universe—you were the star that guided me upon my way—you kept me pure—and your eyes seemed ever on me; still and calm and innocent eyes that blessed me. I recall you now so perfectly, that my frozen heart beats again and again. I am a child. I recall all those happy days; you were a merry, bright-eyed child, full of tenderness and joy! and the breath from that far past comes to me again—faint, like the odor of those spring flowers yonder in the grass, but strong as fate. I see you as I saw you then—an incarnation of pure grace, and tender joy, a fairy from the far land of dreams—my love—my blessing.

"Well, well: you will tire of all this prosing: let me

pass on. I loved you. I asked nothing better than to live and die with you; for I thought I could not breathe without you. I grew older, and I loved you still with the same pure feeling, and the child's heart was grafted into the wild boy's breast; and in all his wild pranks and dissipations you were in his heart, softening and blessing him, and making him more pure. I changed for the worse, somewhat—you, if you changed at all, for the better; your childlike innocence was all the more striking in the girl; your face assumed the tender seriousness of incipient womanhood. I could not love you more than when we were child-lovers; but I loved you with more strength and calmness. I thought that feeling would remain unchanged through all shocks and changes. Well!"

He paused again, and looked at the two trees thoughtfully: his brow was slightly overshadowed.

"Well," he continued, mildly still, "I went to Europe, that changed my life, and made me lose sight of my innocent star. No longer near you, I was a worse, a less pure man. I plunged into every species of dissipation; I felt developed in me that fiery character which I inherit from my race. Aroused, you know, we pass all bounds. Draw the curtain over that mad time, when, nominally at Oxford, I lived in London; that may be omitted.

"I returned to Virginia, here, with the heart of a worn-out gamester. Nothing interested me. I was, as far as my capacity to enjoy simple things, completely exhausted. Every thing wearied me; life was a lame and tedious comedy which I played without caring for the hisses or the applause. I passed my days in idle lounging; I slept long, and passed my whole time in a terrible mental indolence, the most dreadful of all. I had lost sight of you—you were no longer in my eyes; but I now feel and know you were in my heart.

"I came and brought to you my weary air and exhausted feelings. You did not draw back on finding the man so different from the boy; you held out your hands to me with the old, frank, childish kindness and affection, and my heart was touched. The past came back to me, and I was not so gloomy. That was the crisis of my life—the turning point; every thing was balanced; a hair in either scale would have turned it.

"Fate decreed that your innocent face should not shine on me; a rude hand struck the balance, and all was over. That strange young girl came to Virginia, and I became infatuated. You know the unhappy history of that delirium; the family blood again. I do not hold down my head and blush, and say forgive me—no! I say that my actions were those of a madman; that I was infatuated; that I now regard that whole drama as some wild dream. I say further, that I have cruelly suffered, that I have bitterly expiated my offence; that the pang that tore my bosom more cruelly than all, was the thought of you; for I have lost you. Well! After that mad, wild dream, I went to Europe again, and had my despair and suffering in due season, and then came home again as you see me, almost apathetic. I have done with feeling, I shall never love again."

He stopped; his bosom heaved: he went on.

"My tedious talk, no doubt, has wearied you; but it was my duty, Clare, to come and tell you by the trees which we planted in our happy childhood, why I had not remained faithful to that vow we made. I have shown you how cruelly I was tortured by a mad infatuation; how my headstrong passions drove me to commit actions which I regard now with horror; how through all my unfortunate career, that golden childhood I have spoken of, was shrined in my heart of hearts. There was no impropriety in my telling you this, for I know all. He is my friend, and has a noble heart. Well! well! I will try not to suffer too greatly; and here under the shade of these trees we planted, amid the scenes of all our childhood joys, I ask God to bless you, Clare, and thank you for the small share of purity I have left, and say to you, 'I will love and cherish your memory always, as that of the tenderest soul, the warmest, purest heart that ever was in human bosom.' No! do not speak—enough; here comes little Kate, who resembles you, for she is good and pure. I have spoken with difficulty; it is not easy to be calm when all one's hopes are gone for ever; it is better that you should not speak."

And placing her hand upon his arm, he led the trembling, blushing, weeping girl away, and to the house. He was outwardly calm, and all the way back to the Hall he remained quiet and silent. It was the silence of despair; that scene had overcome him, and his heart was faint.

CHAPTER XXVIII.

IN WHICH THE HISTORY DESCENDS TO THE LOVES OF CORYDONS AND PHILLISES IN ARCADY.

"Lucy!"

"Did you address a observation to me, Cap'n?"

"Yes, sir; on a former occasion I stated that you were a villain and a wretch; I now add, that you are a poltroon!"

"Oh, Cap'n! Cap'n!" cried Lanky, who being wholly ignorant of the meaning of the word *poltroon*, naturally considered it something infinitely worse than *wretch* and *villain.*

"Yes, a poltroon!" continued the Captain, "and I will wager a hundred pounds that your benighted ignorance is such, that you do not know what it means."

Lanky scratched his head.

"Come! say now, you rascal."

"A poltroon?" said Lanky, studying the table; "is it an individual who is broke into a hen-roost, and wringed the necks of the cock-a-doodle-doo's, Cap'n?"

"No, you villain: you will never guess, at that rate."

"Oh!" cried Lanky, "it's a feller who plays upon the fiddle and don't know how!"

"No, sir."

"Then I give it up, Cap'n: but I ain't a poltroon—*I* ain't—that is, if it's any thing bad, leastways very bad."

And Lanky was silent.

This conversation took place three or four days after the scenes we have just related, in the mansion of the Captain. The sun was declining—it was a pleasant afternoon, and the waves of the James were lapping with a long swell upon the shore beneath the cottage. The Captain occupied his habitual seat, formerly used by old John Waters, and smoked his meerschaum; Lanky sat doubled up upon his cricket, his hands clasped around his knees, his fine new fiddle lying near; his pine-knot head, and enormous feet, and striped stockings and brilliant fustian waistcoat, all illuminated by the joy shining from his eyes. Something had evidently occurred very pleasing to Lanky, and his thoughts were plainly agreeable thoughts.

After his reply to the Captain, Lanky would have continued his meditations, but this his master was by no means willing to permit.

"You say," continued the soldier, pouring forth a cloud of snowy smoke, "that my charge against you, you scaramouch, cannot be any thing bad,—'leastways very bad,' as your elegant dialect has it. Now, sir, I will let you know that 'poltroon' is *not* a flattering expression. It means a coward, sir!"

"Oh me! a coward, Cap'n!"

"Yes."

"Me a coward?"

"Yes; I understand, sir, you are pluming yourself upon overcoming one of the clergy the other day. Are you not ashamed, you villain, to attack a holy man in the conscientious discharge of his dignified and ennobling duty of training up the youthful intellect in the paths of virtue and exalted purity?"

And having addressed this stern reproach to Lanky, the Captain smoked faster than ever. Lanky's face assumed an expression of consternation.

"Why, Cap'n," he said, "you called him a *gobmoush*, yourself!"

The Captain frowned.

"I am not you, sir," he said, "and I am surprised that you place yourself on a level with me. The parson was an old fellow-soldier, and we can interchange these small compliments; but you, sir, are bound to regard him as a noble spiritual guide."

Lanky scratched his head.

"I say you are a poltroon, you rascal," continued his master, "in spite of your ferocious attack upon a man only armed with a stick of wood, while you had a sword."

"Oh! Cap'n, he was a-presumin' to threaten Donsy."

"There—that is where you are a coward."

"Oh, sir!"

"Donsy is the word."

"Cap'n?"

"Ah! you don't understand. Well, sir, I say that you are a coward because you have not attacked and reduced to submission that citadel."

" *Me*, Cap'n ? " said Lanky, with a self-satisfied smile, like the sunshine on a pine knot.

" Yes, sir, and that in spite of every thing I have done for you."

Lanky smiled again.

" I gave you a seat in my coach by your sweetheart,—I drank some execrable rum for your sake at that Mr. A. Z. Smith's, the villain; I have done my best, opened the trenches, fixed the scaling ladders, and when the word to advance upon the fortress is passed to you, morbleu! you hang fire, and lie down in despair like a sleepy dog.'

Lanky burst out:

" Oh, I ain't done it!"

" What do you mean ? "

" I fit it out," observed Lanky, triumphantly

" Speak, you scaramouch! how have you done—have you really charged the enemy ? "

" Yes, sir—leastways, I been a-courting Donsy," said Lanky, with simplicity.

The Captain burst into laughter.

" Have you really ? " he said.

" Yes I is, Cap'n."

" Tell me how it was, and if I find that you have acquitted yourself bravely, I'll retract that unjust aspersion on your courage."

Lanky seemed nowise averse to complying with this request, and said:

" You know, Cap'n, Donsy and me had a nice Saturday together, after the things 'at took place at the Oldfield school."

" Do I know it? not a whit of it, master scaramouch. Speak."

" Well, sir," said Lanky, with an expression of modest pride at his own generalship, " we had a nice fish that day, and we had a walk, yestiddy, down in the woods."

" You unconscionable rascal—not content with water scenery, you must explore the woodland, too."

" Yes, Cap'n: that's just what we did; we 'splored the woodlan'. On the previous 'casion we had a good time; but oh, Cap'n, that wa'nt nothin' to the other."

" You had a pleasant fishing frolic, did you ? "

"Yes, sur; 'fore we went away in the fine coach, Donsy and me made a bargain to go on the next day a-fishin' together. Well, Cap'n, we went thar—and I 'tacked the enemy all the time. I remembered what you told me, sur, and I kept my chin up and my eyes straight—for, you see, havin' reskied Donsy from the parson, I was proud."

"Very well, sir."

"Donsy did'nt laugh at me much, I tell you; but she was quite still, an' good, an' we fished all day; and when we come back, she giv' me both her hands, and said, in her nice little voice, 'Come again, soon, Lanky.' I feel like a villain talkin' 'bout it," continued Lanky, "but you ain't hard to talk to, Cap'n."

The Captain appreciated this compliment and smoked on.

"Then come the races," continued Lanky, "and you know, sur, me and Donsy both got a prize; she got the quire of ballads, an' I got the fiddle."

"Well, sir."

"I got the stockin's, too, said Lanky, proudly, "and they was to be giv' up to the han'somest girl upon the ground. 'Course, sir, I giv' 'em to Donsy, *I* did."

"Of course; I'd have liked to have seen you presume to give them to any one else."

"Well, sur," continued Lanky, embracing his knees and not heeding this interruption, "Donsy liked that, and I think it made a impression on her, Cap'n. 'Tai'nt every day that girls get silk stockin's, I tell you, and they like 'em accordin'."

"A profound remark, sir," said the Captain, "and quite true. I admire the moral and philosophic sentiments with which you adorn your discourse, Lanky; you are a man of sense."

Lanky received this compliment with a modest expression, as who should say, "Well, I believe I am," and so continued:—

"Them stockin's walked into her 'fections, Cap'n."

"You mean, sir, that she donned the said stockings and walked into yours, eh?" said the Captain.

"Oh, sur, she done that long before I giv' her the stockin's."

"Well, proceed."

"She smiled so sweet on me that day, sur," continued Lanky, proudly, "that I thought I'd make a 'pintment with her, and put the question 'mediately."

"Quite right, Lanky."

"I thought I heard somethin' a sayin' to me, 'Go in, Lanky—go in an' win;' I'm—"

"Exactly what every great man would tell you—not excepting the grand Frederic."

Lanky was proud of this comparison, and proceeded:

"So I tol' Donsy I was comin' next Saturday—bein' last Saturday, sur—to walk with her in the woods and play my fiddle."

"Ah, you rascal! not content with personating Mars, the god of war—you are ambitious to excel Apollo, the god of music."

Lanky felt prouder still at this nobler compliment than the first.

"Well, sur," said Lanky, "she said she would—and promised to bring her quire o' ballads; it's mighty purty, sur, an's got a picture in the front that beats the world—all of lovely ladies an' han'some gentlemanses a playin' in the woods."

"Ah—really?"

"Yes, sur; and they've got long waistses, and carry things with a crook at the top, and ribbons are flutterin' every where, and they are a smilin' an' simperin' an'—makin' love," added Lanky, after hesitating a moment.

"Making love! that's why you like the Corydons and Phillises so much! Go on, sir."

"Well, Cap'n," continued Lanky, clasping his hands round his knees, twirling his thumbs one over the other delightedly, and gazing at his feet, "well, sur, me an' Donsy went—and oh! we had such a time. Would you b'lieve me, she had brought a whole bundle of red ribbons; and when we got to where we was to eat the snack—"

"Snack! you horrible and atrocious wretch! Did you mix up snack with love? Lanky, you are a dreadful fellow!"

"Oh, sur, you know we was hungry; but Donsy didn't eat much—nuther did I: and she only nibbled off a little piece o' biscuit, like a pretty mouse, you know, Cap'n."

"Rascal! to compare your sweetheart to a mouse!"

"A *pretty* mouse, Cap'n," said Lanky, correcting his master; "but, howsomdever, I'll go on. I broke a cake in two, and says I, 'Donsy, that's my heart, if you won't love me.' She laughed, and took a cake and eat it like a heart. 'This is mine, Lanky,' says she, blushin.' 'May I have it?' says I; and she didn't take away her hand,—only she started up, droppin' the cake into my hand."

"And what did you do with it, sir?"

"I eat it, sur," said Lanky, with great simplicity.

"Go on!" said the Captain, shaking with laughter.

"Donsy started up first an' told me she would sing, and I must then play. Oh! what a voice she's got, sur! It makes me feel like honey was a droppin' down from the sky, and a feller had his mouth open!"

"A fine sentiment," said the Captain, generously.

"Well, sur, then I played my fiddle, and you may be sure I made it say, 'Donsy, I'm a dyin' for you.' I didn't play any but the mournful chunes, an' I made 'em talk to her, and she understood, for she sort o' blushed, sur. Well, I got through, an' then Donsy, laughin', took up the ribbon, an' pointin' to the picture in the book, said I must have ribbon knots tied all over me, sur. I didn't keer, an' she tied 'em—on my coat, my breast, my elbows, my hair: and then she did herself so too. Oh, sur, how she looked! I felt a sort o' tremblin' when I saw her beautiful hair all flutterin' with ribbons; the body of her dress covered; her shoes with big rosettes in 'em; and, if a feller might be allowed to say it, the silk stockin's I giv' her, on. Oh! she looked so bright an' red an' laughin'; and when she give me a sort o' crooked thing, and took one herself, she looked like the lady in the picture. She stopped a little then, an' I see her blush. 'You shall be my shepherd, Lanky,' she said, in her melojus voice—and I answered quick as lightnin', 'Then you must be my shepherdess, my dear Miss Donsy,' and she blushed agin! I knew the time had come, sur," cried Lanky; "I recollected your advice, an' I put the question right to her!—and made her a speech!—and it's all arranged!—and she's agreed to marry me!—and she's the sweetest creatur in the world!—and I love her to distraction !—and I feel like a villain, and a rascal, and a hen-roost thief for tellin' 'bout it !—and—"

Lanky burst into tears, and swayed about, and laughed, and cried. The recollection of his happiness had brought on an access of joyful tears in the honest fellow: and the Captain laughed no longer at him.

"Lanky," said he, "if the Corydons and Phillises of antiquity were as honest lads and lasses as you and Donsy, the old Arcadian days were truly happy!"

And Lanky only said:

"Oh, Cap'n!"

CHAPTER XXIX.

VISITORS.

Captain Ralph did not laugh at Lanky again, for he respected the sincerity and truth of his rude, boorish retainers, highly. He knew that Lanky, at that moment, loved Donsy as purely and delicately as the highest gentleman in the land—and one of Captain Ralph's rules was, never to deride sincere emotion.

"Well now, Lanky," he said, "you tell me that Donsy has consented to marry you?"

"Yes, sur," said Lanky, in an inarticulate tone.

"Are you fixed to marry?"

"I'm 'fraid not, sur."

"Hum!"

"But Donsy says she'll wait a thousand years for me, sur."

"That would be too long," said his master.

"I know she'd do it, sur."

"No doubt: but then she would be a thousand and seventeen years old; much too antique to enter into matrimony. She is seventeen, eh?"

"Nearly eighteen, sur."

"And you?"

"I was nineteen last month, sur."

"All right, morbleu! and now, what would you say if I set you up in the world?"

"Oh, Cap'n!" cried Lanky—literally *cried.*

"That would be an expressive observation," said the soldier, looking kindly at his retainer; "but I mean how would you like to farm?"

"Oh, sur!"

"You mean you would like it very well?"

"Oh, Cap'n! me an' Donsy would—"

And then the honest fellow stopped, unable to proceed: the splendid vision overcame him.

"Suppose I were to give you a lease of the cottage here, with all appurtenances—carts and every thing—the fifty acres, and the boats: the rent to be paid out of the proceeds at your leisure?"

"Oh, sur!"

The Captain smiled.

"Do you think, however, that Smith will consent?"

"I dn'no, Cap'n."

"Have you asked him?"

"For Donsy? no, sur."

The Captain shook his head.

"I'm as good as he is, sur," said Lanky, proudly; "an' my mother was a real lady, sur—old farmer Brock's daughter. I never could git to talk right—but I loved her, sur, mor'n any thing. That's what Donsy said, sur—says she, 'Lanky, I like you because you loved your mother so:' that's what she said, sur."

And Lanky cried.

"Well, well," said the Captain, "listen now. I will try and get friend Smith to consent. Don't be cast down, *mon ami*—there is no reason. *Diable!* many an honest fellow has had harder times than that to get his sweetheart. I repeat that I'll try and make Donsy's *bon père* give his assent. And now, I return to the cottage."

"Oh, sur!"

"I want some splendid palace to live in. *Diable!* what is life worth if one is not an emperor?"

Lanky nods affirmatively.

"I must have an empire!"

Lanky nods again, quite sure that if his master really wants it, the empire—which is an ambiguous thing to him—will assuredly come.

"Having bought a chariot and horses, I naturally want some place to put them in," continued his master, smoking.

"Oh yes, Cap'n."

"Perhaps, like you," continued the soldier, "I may, some day, get a wife: I am wearying of this bachelor existence—and who knows what may happen?"

"Who knows?" echoed Lanky, philosophically.

"Therefore, I may give up the cottage for the time: the bon père and Charley are with Beatrice up there, and when they wrote spoke highly of the land, and wished to remain: strange they have not written lately," added the soldier, his clear eye looking toward the west.

"The mail ain't safe, sur."

"Yes: that accounts for it. Well, all this goes to explain, Lanky, that I shall probably become an emperor—and then, I promise you this place as long as you want it, at a nominal rent, to pay when you can—to the *bon père*. Should he wish to return here, you must pack up and go, bag and baggage: but don't fear, I will provide for you."

"Oh, Cap'n, you are mighty good to me!" said Lanky, gratefully.

"Good to you? *parbleu!* no retainer of mine shall ever suffer."

"Donsy 'll be delighted, sur."

"Parbleu! I almost envy you your bride!" laughed the Captain; "she is a charming little creature."

"Then she's so good, Cap'n."

"Yes, I don't doubt it."

"Are *you* goin' to get married, sur?"

The Captain laughed.

"Doubtful!" he said.

"The lady 'll git the kindest sort o' husban," said Lanky, with grateful sincerity.

"Now, sir, you flatter me!"

"Oh no, sur."

"You say the *lady*."

"Yes, sur!" said Lanky; "the finest lady in the land needn't be 'shamed to marry you, sur!"

"Why, dear Lanky, perpend! You are as good as I am."

"Oh, Cap'n!"

"All honest men are worthy; and, *morbleu!* I think Donsy will have in you a better husband than she would find in me. I am a roving soldier, clattering along, always ready for the field, *morbleu!* and impatient of control: while you—you are a most respectable looking citizen, with that splendid pine-knot head, and see-saw movement. *Basta!* you will become a squire;—but who comes here? two horse-men at the door! *Diable!*—see to them!"

And Captain Ralph rose. In fact, two gentlemen had reined in at his door: they now dismounted, and Lanky holding their horses, with many bows, came toward the cottage door.

The Captain met them on the threshold.

CHAPTER XXX.

UTOPIAN DREAMS.

He who came first, was a man of about thirty, but looking much older. In his keen eye could easily be discovered the strong and excitable character of his intellect: across his high forehead extended the lines of incessant, brooding, anxious thought: around his grim mouth, were two semi-circular furrows, which gave a rigid and iron-like expression to the whole lower portion of his face. Captain Ralph needed but a glance at this man, who was clad in a suit of plum-color, with silk stockings, and who wrapped himself in an old red cloak, to perceive that he was in the presence of one of those born leaders, who burn up, with the fires of their genius, all that opposes itself to them.

His companion was taller, and carried himself with elegant simplicity. His eye was mild and benevolent—the features comely, and full of character—his head covered with a curling flaxen wig, and his dress plain, but rich.

The man in the red cloak came forward, and made a curt ducking movement with his head, and extended his hand. The captain grasped it hospitably, and then, in the same manner, shook hands with his smiling companion, whose greeting was very plain and courteous.

"Can Mr. Charles Waters have gone elsewhere to live?" said the man in the red cloak, sitting down, and speaking in a strong, rough voice of sincerity and open plainness, "I came to visit him, sir."

"My brother—my name is Ralph Waters, sir, a captain in his Majesty's Prussian corps, formerly," explained the soldier; "my brother is now residing in the mountains, and will regret not seeing you."

"Yes," said the man in the red cloak, "we are old friends."

The other visitor had, meanwhile, taken his seat in a corner, and with a courteous, "Will you permit me, sir?" to Captain Ralph, in his clear, silvery voice, had betaken himself to perusing a legal record. "I trust the urgency of my business will excuse this seeming discourtesy, sir," he added, "I am much pressed for time in a very important case."

And soon his smiling face was buried in his record.

The Captain turned again to the man in the red cloak.

"I think we have had the pleasure of meeting at the Raleigh tavern, formerly, *mon ami!*" he said, "pray were you not there in the autumn of '63?"

"Yes," said his visitor, "and I now recollect you."

"Charley has spoken of you frequently; and even has used some very extravagant terms in praise of your acute and vigorous intellect."

The stranger smiled grimly: the circles around his mouth growing deeper.

"Did he?" he said.

"*Morbleu!* yes! he was quite extravagant—though observe, companion, I do not say that he was too much so."

"You are complimentary."

"I never compliment."

"Well, sir, I will then return you my own opinion of Mr. Waters. I found him one of those clear, vigorous minds, which carry all before them—in debate, in thought, in battle, whether that battle be of words, or of swords. He will harden into an intellectual giant. I tested him."

"Ah, you have a keen eye!" said Captain Ralph, twirling his moustache, "you are, peradventure, some sorcerer, who can read men's minds by merely looking at them."

"In a degree, sir."

"And when you hear them talk," continued the Captain, laughing, "what then?"

"I have found out as much of them as I need."

"*Diable!* 'tis a great talent. Say, now, what do you find in me, sir?—for you have both seen me, and hear me talking now."

"I do not pretend to sorcery, Captain Waters," said the stranger, in his strong, rough voice, "but I think I can divine your character, without much difficulty."

"Ah, well! speak then, sir: I assure you, you interest me greatly."

"You are frank, sir."

"Ah, *morbleu!* I believe I am."

"Perfectly sincere."

"Thanks, thanks!"

"And you would strike in a good cause with that sword upon the table, until it fell from your hand."

"*Ma foi!* so I would."

"Well, sir, I read that very clearly in your face—in your eye—in your lip; for they are all full of martial fire and frankness. Beyond this, I cannot speak: but I saw more in your brother, for I knew him longer."

"Ah! well, speak now of him!"

"Willingly; it gives me pleasure: for I found in that young man, sir, the mind I had been looking for to help me in the work which I see before me. I gauged him from the first, and my object from that moment was, to dive into the depths of his soul, to study line by line, joint by joint, articulation after articulation, the character of his genius. We went to the root of government—he taught me: I commenced by laughing—I ended by feeling the flood in my eyes as he spoke. I studied that young man, and I think I understood him."

"Why he is as open and transparent as the day: your study was thrown away, it seems to me, *mon ami!*"

"No, sir: and the proof is that I wished to talk farther with him, for which reason I came by with my friend from Caroline. No, sir, you are mistaken; that young man is not transparent, or, if so, 'tis the transparency of the tropical seas, where the eye pierces hundreds of feet, to the far depths which seem very calm, till the wind lashes them to fury. There is the man in that illustration, sir," said the stranger, drawing his old red cloak about him, and appearing to take a peculiar delight in speaking of Charles Waters, "very calm, very pure, very simple and limpid, so to speak: but once roused, I fancy he would be more dangerous than the most furious—as the calm sea, lashed by the wind, becomes more fatal than the noisiest brook. His weakness, however, in one point, was great—in his heart. That is too soft and easy: it will interfere with him in the struggle, I foresee. But the intellect, the reason, ah! sir, that is so powerful in its humility, so strong in its weakness, that I predict it will grow up gigantic, if God spares him for twenty years. At present—excuse me, sir, but I find a strange pleasure in speaking of that man—at present, his mind is in the transition state: he is too full of love for humanity, not to say it profanely;—he wants hardness: his ideas are too grand, he cannot bend them down to common things wholly—he cannot mount step by step upon that ladder which reaches to the sky—he would soar. As a proof of this I have but to mention his political theory: will you listen, sir?"

"Parbleu! I am delighted to hear you talk," cried the Captain, "and yours is a face, mon ami, which promises ideas."

The stranger smiled grimly.

"I am only a poor member of the House of Burgesses," he said, "but let me tell you one of Charles Waters's grand ideas; those grand ideas, as I said, are his weakness. He commences by saying that the present bond with England cannot last—"

"The devil!" are you sure of that, companion?"

"Perfectly sir, but to continue. Next, Mr. Waters uses the word Republic."

"A grand word, but—"

And the Captain shook his head.

"Next, while I listen attentively, he begins to speak of that republic, and his scheme is, that the free white people who have reached their majority, should wield all power."

"I doubt the feasibility of that," said the Captain.

"Next," continued the stranger, "he explains the republic which he imagines. Follow me now, sir—that is his idea. The people shall elect the sheriffs, the clerks of courts, the justices, the burgesses, even the governor of the State."

The Captain again shook his head doubtfully.

"That is not all," said the stranger, "he has gone further. Virginia, he assumes, will not be the only colony which will cast off the chains. All the rest will follow—all as far north as Massachusetts, which will arm its very slaves against England. Then, sir—for with his grand confidence, he assumes our success in the struggle—then he has arranged what he styles the federation of the colonies, in the shape of a league offensive and defensive, to be known as one nation, as the 'Federated Colonies,' or the 'United States,' or by some other name which shall denote the terms of the compact. And now mark the conclusion of his scheme. Having made all offices and dignities spring from the people in this colony of Virginia, he says that the officers of this federated government should also be elected by votes. He would have a great supreme justice of the peace, to be called a protector or president; a great senate, and a lower house, also elected by the people; a great national court, also elected by the people; one grand national organization, partaking of the character of an empire, and a league of sovereign countries. His Utopia is complete, perfect, not a rod or a wheel wanting in the machine, not a flaw in the work; it is only a pity that 'tis but a Utopia, for of course such a monstrosity can never exist."

The stranger paused a moment, then added:

"This is one of the grand weaknesses of Mr. Waters which I mentioned, sir; those splendid Utopian ideas which will disappear as his intellect matures, leaving it all steel. But I have even respect for his fallacies, for they spring from a man of trained intellect, and impassioned, political genius. Yes, sir, from a brain of rare fertility, and power, and strength, for it is humble; from a soul that goes up to the upper air, and looks down calmly above the mist and rain. The hours spent with him impressed me so profoundly, that I have come hither to say to him, 'Now is the time, sir—this is the crisis—you promised to assist me—keep that promise.'"

"To what do you refer?" said the Captain, "to politics?"

"Assuredly."

"The stamp act?"

"Yes."

"You believe it will pass?"

"I know it."

"And you count on Charles to render you assistance of some description?"

"Yes, sir, a great assistanee."

The Captain shook his head; the stranger's glance interrogated him.

"I very much fear you have forgotten the old maxim, that where love enters, every thing else disappears," said the soldier.

"Love, sir?"

"Charley's married."

The stranger reflected for a moment, and replied—

"Well, sir, marriage makes a man stronger. One is not a perfect citizen until he has given to society those hostages of fortune, which Lord Bacon speaks of."

"I doubt much whether his mind is as full of political ideas as formerly, *mon ami*," said the Captain, "he has never lived, he writes, until now."

The stranger reflected.

"He is in the grand mountains yonder, with a wife who, morbleu! has never had her equal; he says the country is a paradise, and that the world is dead to him."

The stranger shook his head.

"In one word, he is happy and contented, sir," said the Captain.

The stranger uttered a sigh, which seemed to say, "all is over then."

"I will send him any message, companion," said the Captain, "or if you want a good arm for any active service, why, for Charley's sake, my own is yours."

The stranger rose, shaking his head.

"I trust 'tis no disparagement to say, sir, that you cannot supply his place," he said. "When the time comes I know you will be at your post, Captain Waters; but your brother is different. You may think all this very strange, but I repeat that I need all the lights to guide me on the dark path I shall soon tread; and this torch I came to seek cannot have its place supplied by another. I fear that 'tis gone from me—that I must go alone. I see many noble lights around me," continued the stranger, with his high, calm look, and glancing at the gentleman seated in the corner poring over his brief, "but I do not think they will guide me as far as I wish to go; again sir, let me say that the impression made upon me by Mr. Waters, must be my excuse for this strange conversation."

"Not at all! not all!" said the Captain. "I am most happy to hear Charley praised; and he will, I am sure, be glad to hear of your visit."

"Well, sir," said the stranger, "when you write again, say that I remembered his words, 'If God decrees revolution let it come!' Say to him, that this decree of God has gone forth; that he is needed."

And bowing with his old, awkward bow, the man in the red cloak, refusing to stay and sup, took his leave, followed by his companion, who exchanged a cordial and smiling farewell with the Captain.

In ten minutes they had disappeared in the direction of Williamsburg.

CHAPTER XXXI.

HOW THE PARSON CURSED THE CAPTAIN BOTH IN LATIN AND FRENCH.

Captain Ralph Waters was one of those men who have too high a regard for themselves, not to keep their word in the amplest and most perfect manner. Having promised Lanky to arrange his matrimonial affairs if possible, he mounted Selim on the morning after the visit of the strange man in the red cloak, and set out for Williamsburg, *viâ* the Old Field School.

It was one of those days in May which drive away, by simple force of their own brightness, every care and annoyance. The sky was blue; the streams ran merrily, sparkling in the sun; the woodland rustled gayly in the warm spring breeze; and far up in the clouds the lark made himself an invisible song, which filled the air with music.

All nature seemed to be laughing and singing—not the streams, and skies, and birds alone—the very flowers which gemmed the glades and sunny hillocks, turned smiling faces to the merry sun, and plainly knew that May—the month of flowers—had come.

The soldier was not behindhand; his mood did not clash with the joyous season. Naturally, life was bright and joyous; to him, with his strong, hearty senses, that drank in brilliant colors rapturously, and took delight in pleasant odors, and felt the world was happier for the singing birds. And not to neglect his own duty, he added his own joyous "tirra-lirra!" to the concert; in so loud and hearty a voice, that the oriole who was shaking his trills down on the blue air from a lofty pine, paused with a pleased surprise, and listened.

Thus the Captain drew near the school-house and slowly approached the door.

"Ah! not a palace of education like the European Academies," he said, "and even not quite equal to 'William and Mary' in the town yonder. But morbleu! 'tis not on that account to be despised. It seems to me that there is a large amount of excellent information to be acquired in these log houses, even though the source of the stream be muddy as it is here. I have a notion that the Colony of Virginia will some day turn out a number of distinguished men,—at least it is probable; and then the Old Field School will be rendered honorable, as the forest lyceum where the young patriots drank in their first ideas. A man gets a better knowledge of life in these places, ma foi! with the birds singing, the trees rustling, the sun dancing along them:—they look *free!* In the old world all is battered up between hot brick walls, in crowded thoroughfares. The only misfortune is that *I* got neither one or the other."

And as if in defiance of the agency of fate in this particular, Captain Ralph began singing lustily his song again, and ended with a loud "tra la! tra la!" that shook the forest.

This song attracted to the open window of the school-house a number of faces, among the rest that of Miss Donsy Smith. Without dismounting the Captain approached and touched his hat gallantly.

"Ah, Miss Donsy! delighted to see you," he said, "do you know me?"

"Yes, sir," said Donsy, blushing, for the Captain's laughing eye very plainly said, "I know all."

"Well, Miss Donsy," said the soldier, lowering his voice as he leaned down to Donsy, who bent her head through the window, "Lanky has been making a clean breast of it!"

And he laughed. Donsy blushed crimson and was silent.

"'Tis a *bon garçon*," continued the Captain, restraining his hilarity, "and he will make an excellent husband. I have promised him to go and see your respected father, mam'selle, and I thought I would call by and gather strength for the attack from your bright eyes. Ah! I think Lanky is very fortunate, parbleu!"

"Oh, sir!" said Donsy, with tears in her eyes, "he is so good you know—I am not good enough for him."

The Captain admired the fresh, sincere face, the earnest voice, and said, laughing:

"*Diable!* I think then that all is arranged, if you have such a mutual liking. As for Lanky, he is dying for you, Mam'selle Donsy; and I really begin to think that I should acquiesce in the old saying, 'love conquers all things,' and leave you and Lanky to fight it out, morbleu!"

And the Captain again burst into laughter. Donsy only blushed more deeply still, and gave him a look which said "Please see my father and ask him to consent; I never could speak of it to him."

"Well, well," said the Captain, twirling his moustache, "I will go on then in my course and do my best: but really I think the shortest way will be to whisk you through this window, carry you off to my robber strong-hold, capture the parson, your pedagogue, and force him to tie the nuptial knot at a word. How would the venerable man look, think you, seated behind me, jolted up and down as I galloped? Faith! he would make a picture!"

And, enamored of his own fancy, Captain Waters burst into a roar of laughter.

"Who are you talking with there, Donsy Smith!" cried a pompous and severe voice suddenly from the interior.

The Captain put his head through the window.

"With me, parbleu!" he said.

The parson, who was seated in state upon his rostrum, hearing a class recite and occasionally ferruling the delinquents, started back as the martial head, with its long black moustache, sparkling eyes and brilliant smile, appeared. Behind this warlike visage, surmounted by its Flanders hat with its dark feather, was seen the fine spirited head and flowing mane of the Arabian. The appearance of this vision nearly took the parson's breath away, and he murmured:

" *Vade retro sathanas!* "

" Ah, your reverence!—*bon jour!* " cried the Captain laughing.

" Good day, sir," muttered the unwilling parson.

" I trust your reverence is well to-day; charming weather—and a charming sight to see you sitting there teaching the young idea, instead of, as you formerly were in the habit of doing, following the tuck of the drum, behind some warlike captain."

" *Anathema!* " observed the parson, who, afraid to vituperate in English, selected the Latin language for that purpose.

" Ah? " inquired the Captain politely.

" Nothing, sir."

" I am going to town, your eminence, any commands? "

" No, sir."

" I trust your reverence has not had an indigestion; you look badly—sour, if I may say so."

" I am reasonably well, sir."

" Delighted to hear it; you would be a loss to the parish."

And the Captain turned again to Donsy, whose fresh face was not many inches from his own.

" Well," he said, " I am going."

" Thank'ee, sir," murmured Donsy.

" I will do my best, morbleu! "

" I am sure you will," said Donsy, in the same low, grateful voice.

" I have promised Lanky the cottage we live in."

" Oh, sir! " said Donsy, looking at the soldier gratefully, " you are very kind."

" Not in the least."

" Indeed you are, sir."

" No—I expect to be paid."

"Paid, sir?"

"Do you think I intend to neglect my business to go gadding for you and Lanky, ma'mselle, to say nothing of giving up my mansion to you, without any reward?"

"Your reward, sir?" murmured Donsy.

"Yes: do you refuse it?"

"What can it be, sir?"

"Answer—do you refuse?"

"No, sir."

"Very well, then, I will exact payment in advance!" said the Captain, with his joyous and loud laughter.

And bending down he brushed the girl's cheek with his huge moustache, which caused that portion of Donsy's face to turn the color of her lips—which were crimson.

The parson saw all, and rose up, brandishing his ferrule and muttering an unmistakable "*Sacre!*"

"Take care, your eminence, I understand French!" cried the Captain, "objurgate me in Latin, not in the *Français!*"

And before the parson could reply, the head exchanged a confidential look with Donsy, and disappeared. In five minutes the forest again resounded with the "tirra lirra!" which slowly died away in the direction of the town of Williamsburg.

CHAPTER XXXII.

HOW THE CAPTAIN PROVED THAT LANKY WAS A GREAT NOBLEMAN IN DISGUISE.

THE Captain continued his way, quickly forgetting this little incident, and soon reached the town and the shop of Mr. A. Z. Smith.

In this history, which aims at presenting in a brief and rapid manner, some view, however slight, of the various classes of individuals who formed that Virginia of 1765, it would be unjust to wholly omit, after touching upon the peculiarities of the Crows and Lankys, all mention of the *factors* as they were then called. These men were the agents of English merchants, and their business was to arrange the shipping of tobacco from the various wharves; to negotiate for its purchase in London or Liverpool; and to receive and transmit to the planters the price received for the great staple. They willingly undertook, also, to attend to any commissions for goods from England: and the planter had only to deposit with his factor the measure of his person, the size of his extremities, and the style of garments he wanted, to ensure a suit from London direct, by the best maker. The factor did all this, and more, for a very small percentage.

The factors were of the opinion, for the most part, that life was an agreeable institution, the chief end of which was to make money throughout the week, and on Saturday finish the week with a carouse around a bowl of punch or lamb's wool: they practised this habit at least; and one of the most zealous advocates of this mode of life was Mr. A. Z. Smith, who, as we have seen, kept a small shop on Gloucester-street, not far from the "Raleigh."

Without further digression—for this worthy will scarcely reappear in our history—we shall proceed to follow the Captain.

He drew up before the door of the shop, and Mr. A. Z. Smith made his appearance, smiling and rosy as usual. The attrition of the lamb's wool seemed to have made his countenance red; and its owner at the same time very good-humored. Smith took the Captain's outstretched hand with the air of a man who feels himself greatly honored.

"Ah, Captain, you do me a great pleasure—really now," he said, with that polite air he had caught from the noble aristocracy.

"Basta!" said the Captain, hitching his horse to a rack before the door; "don't make me talk until I have tasted your Jamaica. I'm as thirsty as a leviathan, *seigneur bourgeoise.*"

The factor smiled, as a man smiles when rosy visions rise in his mind.

"Come in, come in, Captain," he said.

And they entered the shop.

It was very small, and the goods for sale were of the simplest description. Onions hung in strings from the rafters—flitches of bacon kept them in countenance—buckets and tin pans and whips were suspended in graceful and artistic relief. On the small counter stood open boxes of tobacco, and a number of household utensils; and beside these smirked the round face of a single shopman. Behind the shop was a small private room—and this was the real counting-house—where Mr. A. Z. Smith received his noble visitors, and where a huge safe and pile of ledgers testified to his usefulness in the community, and his well-to-do condition in life.

To this private room he led the Captain, smiling; and from a secret receptacle under his desk drew out a flat black flask, which contained his favorite Jamaica, which was excellent. He placed this before the Captain, with some glasses; gave his visitor the seat of honor, and without solicitation drank to his excellent good health.

If the factor was rosy and cheerful, Captain Ralph was moody and dispirited. He shook his head, after the first sip of rum, and almost groaned.

"You are not unwell, Captain?" said Mr. A. Z. Smith.

"Yes, yes," murmured the soldier.

"You are sick?"

"Mentally so, my dear fellow—I feel a sentiment of great remorse."

"Remorse, Captain?"

"Yes, my dear companion, real remorse, and you have something to do with it."

"I, Captain?"

"Yes, indeed; your rum has caused it."

"My rum?"

"Yes, yes; do you not remember my visit the other day?"

"In your splendid new chariot, Captain? Oh, yes! It would not be easy to forget it; it is one of the finest in the colony."

"Delighted that you are pleased. Well, on that occasion I drank some of this Jamaica."

"Yes, Captain."

"Well, companion, now listen to the enormity I have been guilty of. I went home, sir, after drinking some of this nectar—yes, this liquid ambrosia, and like an ill-humored fellow called it—what do you imagine?"

"Not *bad*, Captain?" said Mr. A. Z. Smith, turning pale; "not *bad?*"

"I called it *execrable*, a much worse word than 'bad,' mon ami."

And the soldier groaned.

"Never mind, sir," said Mr. A. Z. Smith, affected profoundly by the Captain's painful feeling of remorse; "never mind, sir, you have changed your opinion; have you not?"

The Captain swallowed a mouthful, and looked rapturously at the ceiling. That was enough—no reply was needed—that look said more than words.

"Let us speak upon more cheerful subjects," said the Captain, sighing; "I have just had the pleasure of seeing your daughter Donsy, *mon ami.*"

"Donsy, Captain?"

"Yes, yes, at the Old Field School yonder. A charming little creature, *ma foi!*"

"She's a good girl," said Mr. A. Z. Smith, with a cheerful look; "the light of the house."

"And that made me hesitate, comrade," said the Captain, "before visiting you to-day."

"Hesitate?"

"Yes, indeed; you would be loth to part with her, I know."

"To part with her?"

"Yes."

"With Donsy?"

"Yes, yes, companion."

"I do not understand you, Captain," said his host, smiling.

"I had some idea lately of asking Miss Donsy's hand."

"Oh, captain—a great honor!"

"Honor? Bah! I say, sir, that the man who gets Ma'mselle Donsy will be fortunate."

"Indeed he will, sir; I have not been twenty years at work without laying by a plum."

"There you are, with your eternal commercial ideas."

"Oh, sir," said Mr. A. Z. Smith, afraid that he had committed something in bad taste—than which nothing horrified him more.

"You think I mean 'fortunate' in a pecuniary sense. You cannot understand the divine sentiment, morbleu!—really, friend Smith, I am ashamed of you!"

Mr. A. Z. Smith looked contrite, and murmured an apology.

"I thought of applying for Ma'mselle Donsy's hand myself," replied the Captain, "but I am not at present in a condition to marry—her; and besides, I am now aware of the fact that ma'mselle's affections are engaged."

"Engaged, Captain?"

"Yes, sir, she loves devotedly one of my best friends—morbleu! a noble fellow."

"Oh Captain."

"A heart of gold—a glorious boy—you know him, or I am mistaken."

"Who can it be, Captain?"

"My friend Mr. Lugg."

The factor whistled. "What! Lanky!"

"Yes, sir."

The factor repeated that astounded noise with his lips and said:

"He a friend of yours?"

"Yes, sir."

"He a noble fellow?"

"Nothing less, sir."

"He a heart of gold—a gentleman—your friend?"

"Yes, he is all that."

"Why, Captain, he's a mere country bumpkin; Donsy shall never marry him—by George, sir, she shall not speak to him again."

"Friend Smith," said the Captain.

"Sir."

"You're a booby; permit me to make that observation to you in a friendly and appreciative spirit, and to tell you that, considering the length of time you have been in this wicked and woful world, you are no better than a child, morbleu!"

Mr. A. Z. Smith, instead of getting angry at this plain and unmistakable charge, held down his head.

"Donsy shall not marry so much beneath her," he said; "that I am resolved on."

"Beneath her?"

"Yes, Captain."

"How is Lanky beneath Donsy?"

"Why, he's as poor as a rat."

"He is no such thing."

"Why sir, he is a common farm-worker—was with Mr. Waters, your relation, I suppose."

"Who, the bon père? Certainly, he is my relation," said the Captain, with great good sense.

"Well, sir, how can you say Lanky is not poor? He's an honest fellow, I don't mind saying that, but I know that he is as poor as a church mouse."

"I don't believe church mice are poor," observed the Captain philosophically, "and if they were, I deny the application to Lanky."

"He not poor, sir?—Oh!—"

"Listen, *mon ami:* I am rich. As rich as Crœsus and all the monarchs of antiquity put together, from Sardanapalus, king of some land or other, down to the present time. I roll in wealth—I don't know how to spend it. I can't find an outlet for it—I am painfully overburdened with gold and land."

"Oh, my dear sir!" cried Mr. A. Z. Smith, looking respectfully at this gigantic proprietor.

"Now, observe: Lanky is my friend—and I have taken up the idea that he will be improved by marriage. I questioned him—he replied that he was exceedingly willing—having secured the affection of your daughter, Ma'mselle Donsy."

"He!" cried Mr. A. Z. Smith.

"Yes, indeed—Donsy is passionately in love with him—he with her—I have determined to see them married."

"Never, Captain!"

"Because he's poor, eh?"

"He is not only that, but his family is not good," said Mr. A. Z. Smith, with a self-satisfied air.

"His family!"

"Yes, sir."

"Why, he came over to Virginia—his ancestors, I mean—with your noble forefather Captain John Smith, the Chevalier."

The factor reddened with delight: his highest ambition was to be considered the descendant of the great soldier—and in fact half of his liking for Captain Waters, sprung from the fact, that that gentleman bore no bad resemblance, with his long black moustache, to the picture of Captain Smith, hanging up in his counting-room. So that when his visitor said that Lanky's family came over with the conqueror—that is to say, Captain Iohn Smythe—the factor replied in a much calmer voice:

"Really, did they now, sir?"

"Yes, indeed, *mon ami*," said his visitor; "Lanky's father was the shield and mace-bearer of the Captain, and always held his lance and helmet. He buckled the arms on his charger—the Captain allowing no one else to do it—when the worthy Smith ran a tilt with Sir Powhatan down there upon the tournay ground near York."

Mr. A. Z. Smith looked dubious.

"Do you doubt it, sir?" said the Captain; "here is the herald's coat of arms of the Lugg family. Here you will see that they spring from the great family of the Lugdunenses who formerly owned all London, for which reason that place was called originally Lugdunum, Sir Ernanton Lugdunensius was the founder of the house, and the Chevalier Villiers de Lugge was the one who came over with your ancestor, companion—he was first cousin to George Villiers, Duke of Buckingham."

Mr. A. Z. Smith then saw the Captain unroll a parchment, and hold it before his dazzled eyes.

"What is that, sir?" he murmured, overcome by the prospect of having such a son-in-law.

"Why, the genealogical tree."

"Lanky's?"

"To be sure."

"I can't read it, sir."

"No wonder, as it is written in Arabic—done when Captain Smith and Sir Villiers were together in Bessarabia fighting the Turks. It is further continued by another hand —and you will observe that Lanky's immediate ancestor was Selim Lugg, Esq."

Mr. A. Z. Smith, as was quite natural, failed to comprehend the pedigree of the Arabian, and the Captain soon rolled it up again.

"Now I have disposed of that," said the soldier; "the

family is superior, or at least equal, to your own: and now sir, to speak of the money part."

"Oh, Captain Waters!" said the little factor, with a remonstrating gesture.

"Let me go on," continued the Captain.

"Well, sir."

"I have—or I will—put Lanky in possession of the cottage on the river yonder."

"A very good house, sir, and some few improvements would make it elegant."

"Yes: and the land—fifty acres— is not bad."

"Excellent, sir!"

"Lanky shall have all at his own terms—and by heaven, if he wants a thousand pounds he shall have it."

"You are very liberal, Captain."

"Do you be, also."

"Hum!"

"Give him Donsy, comrade."

"Oh—I don't think we can spare her, Captain."

"Bah, you will not be separated, the cottage is a mere step, companion."

Mr. A. Z. Smith was evidently struggling between two opposing forces.

"Do you say he shall be set up in the cottage?" at last he said.

"Yes, *morbleu!*"

"And he loves Donsy?"

"Passionately, *ma foi!*"

"And Donsy him?"

"Donsy will have no one else in this world, companion. The house of Smith will be extinct—for she'll be an old maid."

"It's hard to lose her!" sighed the factor, who really loved his daughter exceedingly.

"She will not be the same happy sort of sunbeam, companion," said the Captain; "give your consent and make her happy. Come, now, and pledge your consent in a cup of this delightful Jamaica, and your brave ancestor up there shall witness the compact—and if he could, I am sure he would twirl his moustaches in the excess of his satifaction.

This double attack finished Mr. A. Z. Smith:—his pride

in his Jamaica, his pride of family, and in addition his love for his daughter had been brought in play, and he succumbed.

"Well, he shall have her," he said; "Lanky's a good boy, and though Donsy might a' looked higher, he'll make her a good husband."

And the factor sighed.

"That's well," said the Captain, rising; "and I knew you would place more stress on that honesty of Lanky, friend Smith, than on this question of lineage, about which I have been telling you the most unconscionable amount of lies. *Diable!* sir, I honor you! and I promise that you shall have the commissions of my whole family and estate, when I have the former—now, *bon jour*, companion: I'll go see Lanky, parbleu!"

And the Captain set down his empty glass of Jamaica, and went out humming his old song.

In half an hour he had conquered his enemy.

CHAPTER XXXIII.

GRAND MUSTER OF THE CORNSTALK REGIMENT.

INSTEAD of returning homeward, the soldier determined to proceed to the office of the "Virginia Gazette," and purchase a number of that journal: and also stop a moment at the Raleigh, and look to the condition of his horses there.

He rode into the yard and to the door of the huge stable, which was much more capacious than that one at Beanksome, where "a hundred steeds fed free in stall." The stable of the Raleigh would have accommodated more still: and at present it was quite full, the honorable the members of the House of Burgesses beginning to arrive in attendance on the opening of the House. Captain Ralph surveyed the bustling throng of stable-boys and grooms with much pleasure—bent his neck into the stable and saw his four glossy horses, delighting their souls with an abundant supply of oats—delivered a pistole into the hands of the hostler, with the promise of another, if the appearance of the animals pleased him when he came again, and the promise further that he would spit the said hostler with his sword if their condition betrayed neglect:—and after these agreeable and cheerful ceremonies, bent his way to the Gazette office.

He rode up to the door and received his paper from an urchin of inky hue, placed there to sell the journal at sixpence per copy, and then, turning Selim's head toward home again, dropped the bridle on his neck, and went along, perusing the paper.

"'Arrival of the *Lucy*,'" he read; "'parliament—stamp act introduced—speech of Colonel Barri opposing it; ministers—Townshend—Grenville; sums raised to be expended in America; post roads—hum! hum!—public sentiment in the colonies exaggerated—no real opposition—hum! hum!" Thus the Captain continued glancing over his journal, when suddenly he heard a loud, shrill squeak, a rattling drum; and raising his eyes found himself opposite the "Raleigh" and in the midst of a popular gathering. This gathering was of every conceivable description of individuals—but these individuals were for the most part juvenile, and the negroes had decidedly the preponderance. To describe the costumes of these latter would require much more genius than we possess. Hogarth, in a golden mood, might have succeeded; but what pen can adequately portray an under tunic fluttering *en arrière*, after the manner of a flag;—what mere description can paint a pair of unmentionables held up by one suspender, made of leather, and worn at the knees in a manner painful and shocking to behold?

It was a crowd of this description in the midst of which Captain Ralph now found himself; and which Selim pushed his way through with the unimpressed air of a child of the desert whom nothing astonishes.

But the cause of the crowd? Ah! that is worth seeing. It is nothing less than a muster of the entire "Cornstalk Regiment of Virginia Volunteers," Captain William Effingham commanding.

The regiment are as picturesque as ever in costume and equipment:—they hold their heads up proudly, and shoulder their guns, or the substitutes for guns, described formerly —with an air which says, "We are proud of ourselves, our cause, and our commander;" they march on, in single file, to the sound of a drum and fife, the former uttering an incessant rattle—the latter a deafening scream.

Captain William Effingham precedes the whole—even precedes the music; and his head is bent backwards, with proud satisfaction, as, sword in hand, and sugar-loaf cap on head, he marshals and directs his brave companions.

In front struggles a youthful gentleman,—it is Mr. Barkerville, the artist,—under the weight of a tall pine sapling, from which floats a silken banner, which utters a joyful flapping noise when the wind strikes it, and causes the great artist to reel and gasp. Upon this banner, which has been presented to the Cornstalk regiment by Miss Kate Effingham, of Effingham Hall, the work of whose fair hands it is—upon the banner is inscribed in letters of golden silk the thrilling motto:

NO STAMP ACT

FOREVER!

LIBERTY OR DEATH!!!

and whenever the youthful soldiers gaze upon it, they shout tremendously, and utter wild hurrahs, and waver about in the excess of their hot patriotism.

We have dismissed the bold musicians too briefly: let us look at them. Is not the fifer an old acquaintance? His coat is much too large and long for him; he wears a straw hat innocent of rim, and much dilapidated; he has bandy legs, protruding lips, a woolly head; he no longer possesses any thing but the remnant of a shirt. It is Mr. Crow—Crow in his glory; Crow rejoicing; Crow patriotic, and full of grand ideas, hostile to tyranny,—especially to the Stamp Act. This hostility causes him to surpass himself; his fife utters cries of rage and triumph which are fatal to surrounding ears; his eyes dance like meteors; his cheeks are puffed up to the size of squashes; his rugged sleeves are agitated; and his gait is the mixture of a jump, a dance, a hop, and a run, which we have once described. Mr. Crow is at the summit of human felicity, and when he pauses in his fifing, and, with a noble gesture, silences the drum which one of his relations has been promoted to at his solicitation, he takes off his ragged hat, and waving it, utters a " hoora ! " drowning all the rest.

Captain Ralph, pausing at the door of the "Raleigh," saw the grand procession, with its following of ragged black urchins, and vagrants of every description, sweep on. As he was about to go onward again, laughing, toward home, he heard a grave and strong voice beside him say :

" Give you good day, Captain Waters ; we are well met ! "

He turned, and saw the man in the red cloak, whose face still wore the grim smile with which he had been gazing at the Cornstalk soldiers.

" Ah ! *bon compagnon !* " cried the hearty soldier, holding out his hand ; " good morrow ! delighted to see you again."

" We meet, sir," said the stranger, whose face had resumed its rigid expression, " on an occasion which recalls the topic of our conversation yesterday. Did you read that banner ? "

" Yes, faith ! 'No Stamp Act for ever,'—meaning, I suppose, eternal opposition to that measure ; then 'Liberty or Death'—*ma foi !* that, at least, does not admit of a supposition. It is grandly unmistakable."

" You are right, sir," said the stranger, whose eyes again seemed to grow full of his eternal predominant idea, and to blaze—so to speak—with that idea ; " 'tis a grand sentiment, and I assure you, sir, that this banner, boyish as it seems, speaks the sentiment of the whole colony."

" Parbleu ! perhaps," said the soldier, dubiously.

" Who gave them their ideas, sir ? " continued the stranger. " Urchins do not read parliamentary debates and boil over politically without some instigation. Their fathers, sir ! Their fathers have spoken of that infamous measure—and see the indication of men's opinions in the actions of boys."

The soldier nodded his head in sign of acquiescence.

" Those boys will be men soon," continued the stranger, " and will wield vigorous swords ; that fife and drum will yet sound on grander occasions, I predict."

Then, breaking off suddenly, the stranger said :

" Any news of Mr. Charles Waters, sir ? "

" No," said the Captain, " and—egad ! I think the mails are no better than they should be. Bad, this, very bad."

"I see the 'Gazette' in your hand," said the stranger, drawing his old cloak around him and smiling grimly; "have you not read how the proceeds of the Stamp Act are to be applied to the improvement of the post roads? But, sir," he continued, "I detain you. When you write to Mr. Waters, place at the bottom of your letter the words: 'Come! come! you are wanted!' Now, sir, I must go to pay a visit which I have promised to a young friend of mine, named Jefferson, at the college—a young man of much promise, with a strong political genius. I want these sort of men; I wish to see their faces round me when I rouse the storm; I wish, above all, to have men like your brother near me. Good day, sir."

And wrapping his old cloak around him closer still, spite of the mild May morning, the stranger made his awkward bow and disappeared in the crowd. The Captain looked after him a moment, muttering, "an odd fish, that!" and then touched the Arabian with his heel. Selim went on down Gloucester-street, and was soon out of the town.

Half a mile from the place, Captain Ralph discerned two figures approaching across the fields; they were a young man and a girl, and, as they drew nearer, he recognized Lanky and the mistress of his heart. The soldier smiled as they came up, bowing to him.

Lanky hung upon his countenance; taking hope or despair as the Captain smiled, or looked gloomy. We are sorry to say the soldier amused himself with Lanky's anxiety in this manner for some time, and he refused, for some moments, to reply to Donsy's appealing glances.

At last he burst into a laugh, and cried:

"Morbleu! 'tis easy to see that you foolish children are in love. Basta! was there ever such a folly as you have committed. You, Lanky, you villain, going and falling up to your ears in love with a pair of blue eyes; and you, Miss Donsy, with a pine-knot, surmounting a pair of striped stockings. It is alarming! But, not to keep you longer in suspense, monsieur and ma'mselle,—I have encountered the enemy—the parent of Phillis consents to an alliance between his daughter and her Corydon; in a single word, my dear Miss Donsy, your father consents to your marriage."

And, before the enraptured Lanky could impress a kiss

upon his sweetheart's cheek, Captain Ralph bent down and relieved him of that trouble, after which, he rode on, laughing and singing, toward home.

"Parbleu!" muttered the Captain, as he rode along, with his arms hanging down, "a good day's work for those silly folks there, standing under the tree, still,—by Jove! she's in his arms! Well, well; if I am so good a strategist in another's cause, should I not make some headway in my own?"

CHAPTER XXXIV

HOW MR. CROW WAS TRIED FOR UNOFFICER-LIKE CONDUCT, WITH OTHER INCIDENTS OF A FOREST PICNIC.

"This is a wicked world," says the author of the MS., "and, in his pilgrimage toward a better, man must meet with many things to shock and anger him. But there are many pleasant things to look upon as well. I think one of the pleasantest sights in the world is the innocent joy of children. It is not necessary that a man should grow old before he can experience this feeling of happiness, at seeing young persons enjoy themselves; it is not necessary that the head should grow white, the heart calm and philosophical, the senses dulled to those delights which strong and excitable youth takes such delight in. No; this feeling need not await the annihilation of the fiercer passions, the dulling of the heart,—to come then merely as a forerunner of old age, which takes children on the knee and sighs over them, and, at the same instant, over that bright childhood which, in them, rises up again before the grandsire's eyes. I hold that man made of coarse and rude stuff, who does not feel his heart stir with pleasure at the innocent laughter of a child,—who does not see in the child character some of that primal light which streamed on Paradise, from the blue heaven, yet undimmed by any cloud. Mr. William Shakespeare has said, in his matchless writings, that the man who has no music in his soul should not be trusted; and far less would I trust the man who did not find, in the gay prattle of children, a music sweeter than the harp of Æolus."

Thus does the worthy author of the manuscript, from which we take these veracious events, discourse upon his love for children, which, as the reader may have observed, has elsewhere appeared in this history. The sentiments of the worthy gentleman are very well in their way, but we may be permitted to doubt the propriety of prefacing with such grave reflections, an excursion of the Cornstalk regiment into the Effingham woods, for the purpose of holding therein a picnic. Still, we have preserved this little paragraph of our respected chief, and, having accurately transcribed it from the discolored manuscript, will proceed to speak briefly of the festival.

Sure never morn dawned clearer than that Saturday! The very skies seemed rejoicing, and the birds were positively delirious with delight. The streams sang too, and rattled the diamonds in their beds with ceaseless glee, and jumped up to the boughs which drooped down toward them, and ran laughing by. In the fields the colts gambolled for joy, the sheep tossed their heads, the cattle bells were tinkling, tinkling, tinkling, and playing without musical notes to guide them,—from mere improvisation—merrier melodies than any in Don Juan or the Barber of Seville. The merry May was laughing everywhere, and, not to be outdone, the members of the Cornstalk regiment, stretched under the lofty trees in a glade of the forest, laughed louder still.

They had been marshalled before the portico of Effingham Hall, by that noble commander, Captain William Effingham, who made them a speech, as usual. In the midst of this speech, he had found the attention of his auditors grow distracted: and then Captain Effingham had perceived, at a glance, the cause of this movement. There issued from the broad portal, a bevy of fair ladies—very youthful—and at the head of them Miss Kate Effingham, whose face was brighter than all the rest together. Miss Kate was clad in a charming little dress of green, and on her glossy curls was perched a snow-white gipsey hat, with fluttering ribbons: her companions, rosy-cheeked like herself, were quite as happy looking, and all brightened at their approach, for the noble Cornstalk regiment was gallant and chivalric to the echo. There was one gentleman who displayed a joy far more extravagant than all the rest: Crow was his name, of noble lineage and ancient ancestry; of undeserved misfortunes, yet a noble soul: in a word, one of that great class of poor gentlemen, of which Virginia has been proud always. The joy of Mr. Crow may require explanation, for however great his gallantry, that sentiment could not prompt the enthusiastic somersets which he turned as the young maidens issued forth. Behold the cause! Behind them came a young African, bearing upon his shoulders a huge hamper—a hamper which said plainly, "I am full of cakes, and pies, and apples, and a thousand cates"—which positively groaned for very fulness—which weighed the bearer down for very joy. This made Mr. Crow rejoice: this filled him with sublime anticipation—this caused him to utter the shrill scream upon his fife, which made the little maidens stop up their ears, and shout with laughter.

And so they have reached the glade in the forest, and played by the stream, and laughed and ran, and gathered flowers, and held the yellow butter-cups beneath their chins, and blown away the thistle-down with puffed up cheeks, and chased the striped ground-squirrels to their rocky nests; and played, and laughed, and danced, and sang, until the very forests echoed with their joyous shouts, their merry carol, their exuberant, overflowing, wild, delirious, childlike, merry, gay and joyous mirth, delight, and ringing jubilant laughter.

Tommy Alston is there, and many other Toms, and Roberts, Williams, Johns and Jacks; and numberless Fannys, Susans, Carrys, Ellens, Phœbes, Marys, and a Cynthia to add her morn-like softness to the May. Mr. Alston and Willie have forgotten their league offensive and defensive against our poetical friend, the noble Earl of Dorset: they are rivals: and they struggle for the privilege of waiting upon Kate, and hunger for her smiles more than for any hamper-smiles; and gather flowers for her, and pick out apple seed for her to name, and when the candy with its poetical mottoes is produced, contend who shall bestow upon the little beauty the verses most indicative of burning love, and everlasting, fond devotion.

For now the hour of noon has come, and they are stretched upon a sunny bank, beneath a noble oak, whose leaves but half shut out the sunlight; and the jolly hamper sits upon a mossy rock, the centre of all eyes. They rifle it with joyous laughter—taking out first a noble pie of birds and fowl. They plunder this of its jellied contents, and without solicitation the young maidens eat away, very unlike the heroines of romance. This does not lower them however in the opinion of their Corydons, who also bid adieu, for the moment, to romance, and plunge their pie-crusts into willing mouths, and talk inarticulately for that reason. Then they pass on to the sweet things, and the pie is generously abandoned to Mr. Crow, and his relative who beats the drum—which useful instrument is hanging on a tree above them. Mr. Crow's mode of eating is not so elegant as we might expect in a gentleman of such high birth, and with such grand and noble political ideas. He takes the brown crock, which contains the picturesque debris of the rifled pie, and carrying it to some distance, deposits it upon the ground, and then sits down, extending his lower members upon each side of it. Thus fixed, he can look down rapturously into the recesses of the crock, and plunge his fingers in without difficulty. He does this, and the rich savor causes his eyes to roll like stars, his mouth to grin, his body to shake with laughter. He sees approach, crawling, the disconsolate young drummer, whose flag—but we refrain: he perceives a hand held out: he hears a beseeching voice—but all these things are unregarded. His rapturous eyes fixed on the trees above, he does not deign to see. The drummer crawls up to the pie with cautious movement; he extends his hand—he grasps the finest morsel—ho! the hand of Mr. Crow darts between—the eyes of Mr. Crow flash terrible lightning—the face of Mr. Crow is charged with fury, and a gloomy rage: the unfortunate drummer must wait until there is no longer any thing left but a morsel of crust and a little gravy. This much is generously abandoned by Crow, who, having finished his first course, arrives at the laughing group stretched near, by a series of somersets. He reaches the group just as Kate, who is laughing rapturously, is about to put a small lump of French candy into her mouth. Here was the opening for genius: he squats behind her; he extends his hand; the candy disappears, and Mr. Crow's eyes roll with delight, and his cheek protrudes like that of a monkey who has stolen a hickory nut, and endeavored to conceal it in his mouth.

This feat of Mr. Crow is considered audacious by the

indignant gallants: they lay violent hands on that gentleman: but they call a drum-head court-martial, at the request of the delinquent.

The criminal is arraigned according to the the rules of war: he is called upon for his defence by the uproarious group.

This call is not unanswered: Crow mounts upon a fallen tree: he looks around him with the air of a great orator: he scrutinizes the features of the Court of Inquiry and calculates the chances of an acquittal: the chances are of an azure hue.

Kate is called upon to testify, which she does laughing, and to the effect that the prisoner is guilty. Crow endeavors in vain to exclude the testimony, on the ground of incompetency in the witness: his point is overruled by the court.

Other witnesses testify: the case is made out: he is declared guilty, and then called upon to say why the sentence and punishment should not follow.

Crow brightens at this: there is a last chance: and his ideas are quickened to astonishing vigor by the sight of the executioner trimming a grape vine.

He stretches out his hand persuasively: assumes a grave and lofty attitude, and commences his defence. He bases it upon three points:

I. He wanted the candy.

II. He liked the taste of it.

III. He did not take it.

He elaborates these points; makes a tremendous speech; and winds up with a burst of eloquence which he fondly hopes may avert the impending fate. In vain; popular prejudice has warped the members of the court; he is declared guilty of unofficer-like conduct; he is unanimously sentenced to receive the bastinado.

Crow writhes, struggles, beseeches; in vain: he is tied to a sapling with handkerchiefs, all the time uttering piercing cries of anguish. He repents, he says: he do; he calls upon Miss Kate Eff'nam to intercede for him, but that young lady's prayers are unavailing; the grape-vine is raised; Crow makes himself as small as possible; the instrument of torture is about to descend; the crowd laugh; the punishment for unofficer-like conduct is about to begin, when suddenly Mr. Crow utters a loud exclamation, to the effect that: "Ef there ain't Johnny Booker wid his old banjo!"

All eyes are suddenly turned to the spot indicated by Crow's outstretched hand, and there, indeed, is seen Mr. Booker passing, with his banjo beneath is arm. Crow reaps the reward of his presence of mind, for the crowd immediately rush towards Mr. Booker, and take him prisoner. Mr Booker is a relative of the fiddler at the Hall, and lives at the Bowling Green. He is as great a master on the banjo, as his relative is upon the violin. His face is the color of ebony; his eyes roll; his lips protrude; a huge shirt collar saws his ears.

He is good natured, and willingly consents to "rattle on his banjo" in consideration of a portion of the feast. He partakes of the remains of the hamper, assisted by Crow, who has untied the handkerchiefs, and escaped; between them they dispose of all that is left; then Mr. Booker tunes his banjo and commences.

The party join hands and fly to the hilarious music around the oak; the forest is full of laughter; the banjo player rolls his eyes, sways about, pats his foot; the air is wild with the uproarious rumble, as the flying fingers dart across the strings. By and by Mr. Booker becomes wild with delight at his own performance; he executes a pirouette over Crow, who lying on the ground is rapturously imitating him with the assistance of a piece of fence rail; he commences singing the song which has brought his name and his dwelling-place down to modern times, encircled by a halo of glory; he plays so fast that the furious dance runs over itself, mingles its performances in inextricable confusion, and finally stops from pure inability to proceed.

The young ladies, half reclining on the ground, pant and laugh, and declare that they never before had such a dance. Mr. Booker bows in appreciation of this compliment, places his banjo under his arm, seizes a chicken's leg, and goes on his way rejoicing.

As they are still laughing and panting, they see a stalwart gentleman riding upon a beautiful horse; and this gentleman, who is singing and further amusing himself with twirling his moustache, makes a most gallant salute with his hand. Kate cries that it is Captain Waters, her friend and admirer, and runs to shake hands with him, an infliction which the laughing Captain submits to with great equanimity, after which he disappears, singing.

Kate comes back and finds Willie furious; she quarrels with him. Will repents, and solicits the favor of a reconciliation, which is granted as soon as asked. Will, emboldened by this, draws out his true love indenture, and requests the favor of her signature. Kate laughs, and says Willie is a goose; and as Jemmy Alston at the same moment requests a song from her, she strikes up merrily:

"I'm ower young to marry yet!"

and all are delighted with her arch eyes and laughing voice, even down to Crow, who turns somersets for joy, and makes the forest echo with his stunning laughter, and his wild "hooras!"

Here let us leave the party as we found them—laughing; and if the present history returns no more to that great regiment with patriotic souls, and splendid banner, and immortal fife-player more than all the rest, the reader must not think that we have been guilty of neglect. Considering the number of personages whose fortunes we must finish narrating, the great regiment has occupied space sufficient. In some future history, we hope to chronicle its warlike achievements, and heroic deeds; especially the campaigns of Mr. Crow, that great leader and fife-player of the Revolution.

At present, we must bid the Cornstalk regiment, even Mr. Crow, a long farewell.

CHAPTER XXXV

THE SEIGNEUR MORT-REYNARD TAKES HIS REVENGE UPON DON MOUSTACHIO.

We shall follow Captain Ralph.

He was received by Mr. Lee with open arms, that gentleman not having had for some days an opportunity to exchange ideas with any one upon the various exciting political topics which were beginning to agitate profoundly the minds of all men in the colony of Virginia. The soldier was an excellent outlet for the flood of communication which had been dammed up for some time, and the old gentleman took exclusive possession of him the moment he appeared; they then talked uninterruptedly until dinner, when the Captain had an opportunity for the first time to address a few observations to the young ladies, and to Mr. Jack Hamilton, who had "just dropped in," as he expressed it, in passing. This breathing space, however, did not last very long, and when the stamp act, the navigation laws, and the meeting and probable action of the House of Burgesses had been exhausted, Captain Ralph was called on to discuss the various events of the seven years' war, and to illustrate those events by diagrams drawn as before, upon the table with a drop of wine.

The Captain escaped finally to the ladies in the parlor, whither Mr. Jack Hamilton followed him, and he tried to converse with Henrietta. But he found it for some reason very difficult; he could not extract from Miss Henrietta much more than blushes and "yes's," and "no's," and he finally gave up in despair, and took his leave with a decidedly gloomy feeling. Looking as we do calmly upon the scene, we may very easily discern the cause of Miss Henrietta's blushes and constraint,—of the soldier's consequent gloom. For the first time, he had grown blind.

Mr. Jack Hamilton followed the soldier, and they rode on together. The Captain endeavored to return to his habitual good-humor, and after a time succeeded in producing something resembling a laugh.

"Ah, *mon cher* Seigneur Mort-Reynard!" he said, "it seems to me, that you are practising finely all those beautiful precepts which you enunciated in my hearing some days since?"

"What precepts, my dear Don?" replied Mr. Hamilton.

"Why, your woman-avoiding doctrines."

"Hum!" said Mr. Hamilton.

"It is really laughable," continued the soldier, "to observe how great the difference is between the preaching and practising of human beings in this wicked and sinful world. Now here are you, my dear Mort-Reynard, uttering the grandest and most philosophical sentiments—sentiments which cause your friends to regard you with a mixture of respect and admiration, and basta! no sooner are our backs turned than you go, morbleu! and practise just the reverse."

"Hum: you think so?" observed Mr. Jack Hamilton, "you are very keen-eyed, Don Moustachio. Come, how have I erred?"

"How!"

"Yes, indeed."

"Are you not making desperate love to Miss Clare, par bleu—are you not going to change your bachelor condition?"

"Hum!"

"Answer!"

"Well, if I did."

"Well, if you did, indeed! Egad! you will turn your coat. Never have I heard such an enthusiastic tirade as you uttered the other day. Oh, by heaven! *you* would not fall into the snare! *you* would not be caught by a woman, a pair of blue eyes, I think you said. We young and inexperienced fellows might fall victims to the *belle passion*, but *you*? Not the Seigneur Mort-Reynard, whose days were to be sacred to the pursuit of foxes, and to the disappointment of all individuals of the divine sex who laid traps for the Seigneur Jean Reynard Hamilton! Ah, *mon ami*, you are one more victim—you are an unfortunate specimen of the trapped—the bamboozled—the defeated—the circumvented! You will ever be to those who know you, parbleu! a shining instance of the fallacy of all human calculations, of the overwhelming powers of the sex—of the truth of your own declaration that when a woman has once determined to marry a man he need not resist—that there is no hope—that he might as well go to the altar, like a lamb to the slaughter!"

And the Captain twirled his moustaches and laughed triumphantly. He did not see the twinkle of mischief in the Seigneur Mort-Reynard's eye;—he did not see the joyous look, which indicated the power of revenging himself upon his reviler.

"Well, well, my dear Don," said Mr. Hamilton, "I confess there is something in what you say."

"You acknowledge it?'

"Yes, yes."

"Poor fellow!"

"True, I am very unfortunate, but how could I resist such a pair of eyes?" said Mr. Jack Hamilton, plaintively.

"Quite right," replied the Captain, "they are much too blue and bright."

"Yes, yes."

"Your favorite color."

"Precisely."

And Mr. Hamilton sighed.

"Don't take it too much to heart, *mon cher*," said the Captain, still laughing, "many a stalwart fellow has suffered the same misfortune."

"I know it, Captain."

"No one can resist."

"No one," said Mr. Jack Hamilton, disconsolately; "and even such a strong-hearted cavalier as yourself must not think to entirely escape; you have not, I think."

"I?"

"Yes, indeed."

"You think I am trapped?"

"I do, indeed."

"Madam Henrietta, you mean, perhaps!"

"Yes, my dear friend."

"Hum, hum!" said the Captain, in his turn.

"Do not understand me as blaming you for falling a victim to her brilliant eyes," said Mr. Hamilton, "it is quite natural."

"It would be, I confess," said the Captain, cautiously.

"Come, don't deny it."

"Deny what, *mon cher?*"

"That you are over head and ears in love, my poor friend."

The Captain uttered a sonorous "hem!" and said:

"Really, you are, I think, mistaken."

"No, indeed."

"I in love!"

"Yes, Don—desperately—profoundly; and there is only one thing in your condition which makes me sorry for it, as your friend. Her affections are engaged."

"Engaged!" cried the Captain, betraying by his downcast countenance the secret he would conceal.

"Yes, indeed!"

She engaged?"

"Her affections I said."

"Her affections!"

"Why Don," said Mr. Hamilton, "you must be blind. Have you not observed Mr. Effingham's attentions?"

"Mr. Effingham!"

"And the manner in which she receives them?"

"No," said the Captain, moodily; and too much cast down to observe the twinkle of triumphant mischief in his companion's eye.

"Why then you must be high gravel blind."

"*Diable!*" cried the Captain, to Mr. Hamilton's great delight.

"You see therefore your chances are not so good as you thought."

"Hum!" said the Captain, measuring himself in thought against his rival.

"Effingham is her cousin, and you know cousins are proverbially dangerous."

The Captain made no reply, preserving a gloomy silence.

"I thought I'd mention it," said his companion, in a friendly and commiserating tone; "for we have taken so many foxhunts together, that I naturally feel an interest in all that concerns you."

"Effingham!" muttered the Captain, buried in thought.

"Yes, yes; I say again you really must be blind—you cannot see."

"This troubles me, Hamilton," said the Captain; "and I don't mind telling you that I do admire Miss Henrietta."

"Right! perfectly right!" replied Mr. Hamilton, shaking with triumphant laughter; for one of the greatest delights this worthy gentleman could experience was in the perpetration of what is called a practical joke.

"You are quite sure of what you say?" continued the Captain, gloomily twirling his moustache.

"Sure? can you ask!"

"Morbleu! 'tis too bad," said the soldier; "I thought Effingham was remarkable for staying away from the house."

"Ah! a mistake, my friend; you are not there every day."

"True," replied the Captain, with the same gloomy look.

"Now, do not attribute," said Hamilton "to any bad

feeling at your own bantering, this little piece of information. Of course I never deal in jokes of a practical nature —oh no, my dear Don Moustachio—utterly impossible with my frank and unsophisticated nature."

And Mr. Jack Hamilton smiled with irony and triumph.

The Captain continued to think gloomily over what his companion had just said, and they rode on in silence.

Hamilton could scarcely contain his laughter; and once or twice was on the point of betraying himself. He felt some remorse, too, and this also was near causing him to inform the Captain that all this story was a mere effort of the imagination. But suddenly he remembered more than one joke of a practical and horse-play nature which Don Moustachio had played at his expense, and his heart was again hardened. He determined to leave his companion in ignorance for two or three days at least; then have a party at the Trap; relate the Captain's jokes at himself, and then detail his revenge.

They reached in silence the opening of the road which led from the main highway into Effingham Hall. Hamilton drew rein.

"I must go in here, my dear Don," he said; "come and see your rival."

"Thanks, sir," said the soldier, gloomily, "but no, I prefer proceeding on my way."

Hamilton smiled.

"Ah, you are gravelled," he said.

"Not at all," said the Captain, frowning.

"You are angry."

"Morbleu, not at all!" said Captain Ralph, looking daggers.

"Well, that is right!" said his friend, ready to explode with pent-up laughter; "don't suffer these little trifles to disturb your equanimity. You are a bold cavalier, my dear Don, and I should feel a dreadful amount of trepidation were you my rival—had you selected in place of Miss Henrietta—well, well, we will not speak of that. Do not think that I bear you any grudge, and have been jesting; of course I have not; we are boon companions, jolly hearts, lads of metal, sworn friends;—bear up! Perhaps you stand some slight chance yet, and a powerful exertion of your warlike strategy might possibly end in defeating the enemy, who, however, I should tell you as a friend, is a very dangerous antagonist. He is her cousin—he is pale and interesting—he is a man whom a woman may both admire and pity; and you know very well, my dear Don, when a woman experiences a sentiment of pity for a man what it proverbially leads to! Don't be cast down, however. Let me see you in a day or two."

And shaking with laughter Mr. Jack Hamilton bowed to his companion, who rode on moodily, and took his way toward the Hall. When he had lost sight of the Captain, he uttered a shout of laughter which made the wood echo again. He had taken his revenge at a single blow; and we shall see what came of it."

CHAPTER XXXVI.

THE SEIGNEUR MORT-REYNARD CATCHES A TARTAR.

The triumphant Mr. Hamilton went on laughing, as we have described, toward Effingham Hall. He soon reached the mansion, and tying his horse, walked in, whistling merrily; he seemed to be at peace with himself and all the world—to be revelling in the quiet pleasure of a man who has an excellent conscience, and has just overcome by pure force of genius all opposed to him.

He found the front door open, and without ceremony entered, and proceeded to the library, where he did not doubt he should find some one of the family. He was not mistaken; seated languidly by the window he saw Mr. Effingham.

Mr. Effingham was looking out of the window, and so profound was his gloomy reverie, that he was not aware of the entrance of his visitor. His brow was even paler than usual—his lips were more weary—his head drooped, and his eyes were half closed and full of shadow. His posture, too, was very indicative of his mood; it betrayed languor, indifference, utter prostration of spirits.

Mr. Effingham was not aroused from his gloomy and

absorbing thought until the fox-hunter laid his hand upon his shoulder.

"Why Champ," he cried, "thinking eternally? Really you will get your blood in such a state with this keeping in the house, that even running a fox won't set it going."

Mr. Effingham shrunk from the hand, and replied coldly:

"I am not very well."

"Not well!" cried Hamilton; "that's because you don't ride out."

"No, it is not," said Mr. Effingham.

"I tell you it is," said Hamilton, who honestly believed what he said.

"Well," replied Mr. Effingham, in the same cold and calm voice, full of constraint, "have it as you will."

Hamilton was not quick at observing moods, and engaged in contemplating a picture of the winning horse at the last Derby races, which the squire had just received from England, did not pay much attention to his companion's accent.

"Ah, well!" he said at length, "perhaps not—perhaps you are really unwell, but what a splendid second thigh that fellow's got, by George!"

Mr. Effingham made no reply, gazing out of the window again. Mr. Hamilton looked at him.

"Why, Champ, you really don't seem well to-day," he said.

"I am not."

"You are brooding over something. By Jove! your eyes are as deep and gloomy as Bob Ashell's after his losses at the Jamestown races, where that consumed little horse of Waters' beat Sir Archy. Bob had bet heavily on Sir Archy, and he cursed Captain Waters' racer from Dan to Beersheba."

"Ah?" said Mr, Effingham.

"Yes, indeed! and Howard said no less. They couldn't deny that the Captain had complied with all the rules—given them a full trial of his horse before the races—shown Selim's pedigree, and all that; but it seems the Arabian didn't begin running until the second heat on the race-day; and then you ought to have seen hin. By George! sir, he fairly picked up the miles and tossed 'em behind him, and Waters might have got a thousand pounds for him after the third heat."

"Indeed?" said Mr. Effingham, with the same cold and constrained air.

"Yes, indeed," continued Hamilton, carried away by his mental contemplation of Selim, "but the Captain absolutely declined—where the devil does he get all his money?—and prefers riding him. By Jove! just think of a man's riding a horse worth a thousand pounds every day!"

And Mr. Hamilton groaned at the Captain's extravagance.

"I have just left him," he continued, "and I ran a good joke on him, which I'll tell you another time—by George! it will make you die a-laughing."

And Mr. Hamilton burst into a roar of laughter, which did not relax Mr. Effingham's face, however, in the remotest degree.

"The villain has been overcoming me lately on a variety of occasions," Hamilton went on. "The last was the other day, but I had better not mention that: the explanation would be awkward."

And Mr. Hamilton laughed again.

"We have been over to Mr. Lee's," he continued, "and you never did hear such an infernal clatter as those two men kept up, with their wearisome political discussions."

"Indeed?" repeated Mr. Effingham, like an icicle.

"Yes, sir, by George! they nearly drove me crazy. Nothing but the Stamp Act this, sir! the Stamp Act that, sir! the Stamp Act the other, sir! the Stamp Act, here, there, every where: in the middle, all around, on both sides! In the same way it was the Navigation Laws this, that, and the other! The opening of the House, and the Governor's speech! The seven years' war, which I was in hopes had all been fought and forgotten! Then it was this nightmare of the Stamp Act again! By Jove! when the time comes, I shall be ready to fight if need be, but where is the use of this eternal wearisome discussion? Don't it weary you?"

"I am not fond of politics," said Mr. Effingham, more and more coldly: he was about to add a "sir" to his sentence, but refrained.

"By George!" said Hamilton, "I believe you are fond of nothing on earth."

"You are mistaken."

"Of what are you fond?"

"Of quiet," said Mr. Effingham, in a freezing tone.

Hamilton did not observe it.

"Ah, that means you do not like to engage in these eternal discussions. Well, we sympathize then."

Mr. Effingham inclined his head coldly, making no reply.

"It don't follow, however, that you need engage in them when you visit Mr. Lee," continued his visitor; "a man is always at liberty to escape to the ladies."

Mr. Effingham was silent.

"There is Henrietta always ready to discuss fashions, travel, books, every thing but politics."

Mr. Effingham continued still silent, but his breast heaved.

"Of course Clare would not amuse you," Hamilton went on, "absorbed as she naturally is in our approaching—hem! see what a fellow I am!"

And Mr. Hamilton seemed to wish his tongue in Guinea, Jericho, or other remote place, where it would not easily be got at. Mr. Effingham turned away his head, and his brow darkened.

"Clare is a woman out of a thousand," continued his visitor, "just the girl for a jolly fellow, not too soft and lackadaisical, but quite soft enough to smooth down those bachelor asperities which interfere with a fellow's standing in society. She is a finer girl than any within fifty leagues, though I say it.

He did not observe Mr. Effingham's frown.

"You would be benefited now," continued Mr. Hamilton, "if you would go over there oftener, and not persist in shutting yourself up here so secluded and lonely. By George! you'll expire of weariness."

No reply: but the brow grew darker.

"Come, tell me how this ridiculous habit has grown on you?—why don't you go and see Henrietta?"

Mr. Effingham's eye flashed.

"She's a splendid girl."

No reply.

"Of course I don't speak of Clare: by the bye, you used to pay her some attention—"

He did not observe the flush rising in the cheek.

"You were even sweethearts in childhood. How things change in this world: women don't continue to like a man because they were fond of him when he was a boy."

Mr. Hamilton was treading upon dangerous ground: Mr. Effingham was losing his self-control rapidly, as his heaving breast, and eyes filling slowly with a lurid fire, plainly indicated.

"Strange! isn't it?" continued Hamilton, "that after having at her feet so many elegant fellows, Clare should—well, well, where am I rushing? I can't keep any thing secret. But the more I study these women, the more I am puzzled. I can understand you, now, and 'most any man—but a woman? By George! that's beyond me—they're too deep. Now, I should have thought Clara would have liked—some people, better than, well, say, *other people:* that's non-committal. By George! you are pale, Effingham! How this staying in the house is hurting you! You are growing a perfect girl."

Mr. Effingham was indeed pale, but this pallor sprung from rage: every word that Hamilton uttered was another dagger plunged into his heart, and these were poisoned daggers—poisoned with contemptuous coolness.

Hamilton assumed a commiserating air, and said with a cool and easy smile,

"Why do you stay from Riverhead? Clare's present relation toward a nameless individual should not keep you from the house. Come, tell me why!"

The measure was full.

Mr. Effingham rose to his feet, and said haughtily, and with flashing eyes,

"Mr. Hamilton, be good enough to shape your discourse in such a manner, that I may not be compelled to insult you in my own house!"

"Insult me!" cried Hamilton.

"Yes, sir! your air of astonishment does not deceive me—I am not the dupe of your good-humored surprise at my address. You know well, sir, that I have cause to insult you. Not content with making me wretched and miserable beyond conception, by depriving me of the heart of the only woman I have ever really loved, you choose to come here, and, under the protection of this roof, utter your insulting and ironical speeches in my very teeth! By heaven, sir, I will not endure it! I am not sudden in quarrel, sir, and have no desire to engage in any altercation; but, beware, sir! Woe to the man who strikes me, as you have done, through the heart!—let him not count upon a very lengthy forbearance! You affect to feel surprise, sir—you look shocked! Very well, you are at liberty to assume any expression of countenance you fancy! I have endeavored to prevent my feelings from mastering me, sir—I have more than once curbed my rage, and my despair—yes, in my despair, it is humiliating to say it, but I wish to be frank—I have more than once concealed the emotions produced in me by your unfeeling and unworthy allusions; but I now say to you, sir, that my patience is exhausted. I shall not always put a rein upon my anger—I will not attempt it. Go, sir! and laugh at me with that lady who has chosen you in my place, as she had the right to do. Go, sir! and mock, deride, sprinkle your ambiguous voices, and despise me to your heart's desire. But beware, sir, how you come hither to taunt and jest at me—to make me the butt of your wit and humor—to insist that I too shall join in the laugh at myself, and wait until you have gone, before I tear my breast and curse you!"

It was impossible to describe the passionate emotion with which these words were uttered; Mr. Effingham looked dangerous; his eyes flashed; his lip writhed; his haughty brow was covered with perspiration; and his teeth were clenched. As he uttered the last words, he surveyed Hamilton with one of those haughty glances, which seem like flashes of fire, and for a moment hesitated whether he should add any thing to what he had uttered. The struggle was brief; he restrained himself, and bowing with cold dignity, he left the room.

Hamilton for a moment continued gazing after him completely dumbfoundered, and in no little anger. Then as he disappeared, the fox-hunter rose, hesitated a moment, grasped his hat and whip furiously, and hastily left the house.

"By Jove!" who would have thought it?" he said. "I thought, however, it was wrong. This joking will ruin me!"

And uttering a prolonged whistle, indicative of anger and dissatisfaction, he mounted his horse and rode away.

CHAPTER XXXVII.

A COUNTRY CHURCH IN 1765.

If the reader will deign to cast his eyes back, he will see that the events we have just related, occurred on days immediately succeeding each other. Captain Ralph had finished Lanky's business on Friday morning; the picnic in the woods had taken place upon Saturday forenoon, that day being holiday for the Cornstalk regiment; then this same Saturday had seen the soldier on his way to Riverhead, and had witnessed his defeat by the fox-hunter. Lastly, the scene we have this moment related, occurred in the afternoon, at the Hall, as the reader knows.

We now beg leave to continue our history, with the events of the next day—Sunday; and for the purpose of connecting the narrative by links so plain that they will need no commentary at our hands, shall accompany the Effingham Hall carriage to church.

The chariot drove up to the old edifice, which was gilded by the fresh light of the pure May morning, and deposited its freight at one of the doors, at which stood a group of young men, whose self-imposed duty was to assist the ladies from their chariots when they arrived. The chariot contained the whole family from the Hall, who looked very calm and happy, with the exception of Mr. Effingham, whose face was unusually pale, and all entered the old church and devoutly knelt. Perhaps a word of description would not be inappropriate here; for these old houses of the Lord differed, we need not say, materially from those of the present day and generation. Christ Church was an old building of discolored stone, and above it waved the boughs of a great elm; the windows and doors were surmounted by little roofs, so to speak, supported by iron rods; a stone slab lay before each door. Within, the feet trod upon flag stones, and the pews were enormously high, and with perfectly straight backs. In these, the audience were almost buried. On the walls of the chancel were inscribed the ten commandments—gilt letters on an azure ground; and below the reading desk and pulpit, stood the box and bench of the "clark," whose duty was to make the responses. The pulpit was very lofty, and in the shape of a tub; it was reached by two circular flights of steps, and above it was stretched a canopy, on the nether side of which a golden star irradiated, while upon the summit, a dove expanded its wings, symbolizing the spirit of the Holy Ghost.

The old edifice, as we have said, was overshadowed by the boughs of a great elm, and beneath this elm were a number of monuments, which told the virtues of those who slept beneath. Some of the tombstones were adorned with coats of arms, and flourishing panegyrics, which make the dead more noble and perfect than the great father of Manrique; —many an *armiger* was made matchless and superior to Bayard the reproachless knight; many a noble lady had her charities narrated in that grand eulogistic rhetoric of the past, and still lived in the eyes of all, through the veiled head carved on the stone, with clasped hands. But then there were other memorials which more deeply impressed the beholder—plain stones, indicating the resting-place of some child, with those simple inscriptions which affect men so strangely as they wander through these resting-places of the dead; for all that is sublime is simple. Great feeling does not rant; and these small white headstones seemed to have more of the other world about them, so to speak, than the fine monuments which, though the feeling of those who erected them were doubtless quite as pure, yet seemed to cling still to the pomps and vanities, dead now to those who slept.

The tombstones, white, against the green velvety grass, made the churchyard pure and happy, not gloomy. They looked calm and peaceful; and the good Mr. Christian's flock listened more attentively, as they murmured the responses more devoutly, for having before their eyes those memorials of rest and peace. · And children played about them: men came and read the inscriptions, and mused, thinking of the holy dead; and even the birds singing above the old edifice seemed better pleased to have the marble headstones there. So the old mansion rested quietly beneath its whispering elm, among the graves. It looked calm and hopeful, giving promise of another world.

Mr. Christian's sermon was upon humility, and the danger of pride and vaingloriousness—of those moods of mind when the heart and brain fancy themselves equal to every thing, and so spurn all humble thoughts. He spoke of that sublime humility of our Saviour, when he washed his disciples' feet; and the low, eloquent voice was full of soothing, tender emotion. He then presented the evils arising from a haughty and overbearing spirit, and denounced them with impassioned vigor: he branded the proud and self-willed man until the picture grew hateful and repulsive; he then depicted the strength and greatness of humility, even in a worldly sense: the overwhelming power of conscious weakness. Finally; he enforced his doctrines by the Saviour's command to men, to grow like little children in hnmility if they would enter into the kingdom of heaven. All this the worthy pastor enforced with a mild strength which produced a strong impression upon his hearers. When he raised his hands to bless his flock before dismissing them, all hearts felt purer for his teachings, and charity and humility were in every face.

Then succeeded that lengthy shaking of hands and interchange of neighborly gossip which characterizes, we believe, all country churches. And so while Miss Alethea was inquiring about a variety of interesting matters within, with her lady friends, the squire laughed without, strutting about in his fine Sunday suit, and not imagining for a single moment that he wanted humility:—the preacher's sermon was meant for other people.

Mr. Effingham leaned against the trunk of the great elm, pale, haughty, and only half returning the bows made to him. Once, however, he did rise suddenly erect and make a proud and ceremonious inclination of his head:—Mr. Hamilton had bowed to him in passing. Beyond this, he showed scarcely any consciousness of where he was. Absorbed in his gloomy reverie, he paid as little attention to the brilliant groups of fair ladies, who looked with no slight admiration on his pale, handsome face, as he had done to the sermon. That sermon had not produced the least impression on him—he had not heard it even; for near him sat Clare, and all his gloom had returned at sight of her.

He loved her now a thousand fold more than ever: she was dearer to him than all the world beside: the sight of her brought back to him every happy day he had spent in the past—the knowledge of the fact that she was lost to him renewed his most passionate anguish. It was a singular spectacle which he presented, standing thus in the middle of the gay, laughing crowd, as perfectly isolated as if that crowd did not exist, and nothing were around him but the calm white tombstones. His brow, as we have said, was pale, his eyes were shadowy, his lips compressed; he might have been taken for one of those characters of romance who throw their fiery passions and wild natures into the tranquil stream of ordinary life, and lash it into foam. And, in Mr. Effingham's case, this, as we know, was not very far from the fact;—he had defied society for a woman, carried that woman off, and done many other things which much better suited heroes of poetry or opera grandees, than a plain Virginia citizen;—and now we see in his face the ravages of that wild, passionate character, so dangerous when aroused.

The congregation slowly dispersed, and the Riverhead carriage and that of the squire drew up together. Mr. Effingham saw a form that made him tremble pass before him. His hand for a moment sustained the white arm, covered only with a diaphanous lace, as he assisted her into the chariot, he knew not how. A shadowy mist seemed to envelope all from which a pair of soft blue eyes, and a young girl's blushing cheeks emerged—and then the four horses were whipped up, he heard distinctly the crack of the lash, and the vision disappeared. He saw two cavaliers, one riding upon each side—the one was smiling the other gloomy. The smiling one was Mr. Hamilton, who was talking through the window to Clare, and looking back occasionally at Mr. Effingham, who ground his teeth. The gloomy cavalier was Captain Ralph, who had caught a smile directed by Henrietta towards Mr. Effingham, and totally unseen by that gentleman.

We may hazard here the observation that lovers are

wholly destitute of conscience, magnanimity, common sense, and ordinary courtesy. Mr. Hamilton was laughing at his friend, the Captain was quarrelling with a smile of simple courtesy.

Mr. Effingham entered the Effingham chariot with the squire, Miss Alethea, and Kate, and Will mounted his pony. The old sexton locked the church, and, putting his spectacles away, tottered homeward. Church was over.

CHAPTER XXXVIII.

THE CHILD AND THE PORTRAIT.

THE great clock at the Hall has just struck ten; and those echoes, which seem to wake as mortals go to sleep, answer it through the shadowy apartments.

Mr. Effingham and Kate are seated in the library reading; a few twigs in the great fireplace crackle and sing as they crumble into white ashes; the burning embers slowly donning those snowy hoods which shroud them when they are about to die. A faint blue smoke occasionally curls upward, and the old grotesque brass handirons cast shadows.

For a time, nothing is heard but the singing of the fire, which has not yet mastered one or two sappy twigs.

At last Mr. Effingham lays down his book, and utters a sigh which attracts Kate's attention.

The child raises her head from the Sunday-school volume she has been reading.

Their eyes meet: she gazes at him wistfully—at the pale brow, the sad lips, the weary eyes: his head droops.

The child closes her book, softly approaches him, and lays her hand upon his shoulder. Mr. Effingham smiles sadly, and passes his hand slowly over the bright locks of the child.

"What is the matter, cousin?" asked Kate, "I don't like to hear you sighing so."

"Nothing," he says.

"I am afraid you are not happy," Kate says, wistfully, "and I cannot feel happy if you are not."

Mr. Effingham only presses the little form more closely with his encircling arm.

Kate continues, laying her cheek on his shoulder, and looking up softly into his shadowy eyes:

"I don't think you are well, dear cousin, and it grieves me. Indeed, indeed it does."

"I am not sick—no, not sick," he murmurs, "but—"

And his hand unconsciously seeks his heart and rests there.

The child understands at once, with the marvellous instinct of affection.

"That is the worst kind of sickness," she says, in a low, tender voice, "heart-sickness."

"Do you think my heart is sick?" he says with a wistful smile, his head drooping more and more.

"I don't know," the child answers, turning aside her face.

"I should be very unhappy were that so," he continued.

"Yes," murmurs Kate.

"And still more unhappy, if you, dear, ever felt what—"

He does not finish—the form of the child is agitated slightly.

"Men can bear having their hopes all disappointed,—their affections chilled,—their lives rendered dark and gloomy by those afflicting trials, which they must pass through in existence," he goes on thoughtfully, "but children should not feel them;—were you to be distressed, Katy, I think I should find it harder to bear than all."

The child's face turns away still.

"I pray you may never feel the afflictions I have gone through—formerly," he says.

The head nestles closer and the tender form shakes.

"What is the matter, dear?" he asks, observing this.

Kate makes no reply.

"Have I made you feel badly? See how thoughtless I am! Why, Kate—crying?"

She leans upon his shoulder, sobbing; her eyes are full of tears.

"I can't help it, cousin," she murmurs; "I know it is very foolish; I am only a child—don't mind me."

"Only a child, Katy? Ah! if I could go back to the

time when I was only a child. I am a man now—but don't cry, dear?"

"I won't," says Kate, sobbing and wiping her eyes; "it is not right to cry, but you know I can't bear to see you distressed."

"I have got over it—if I was so," he replies, caressing the child's hair; "come, now, Kate—don't cry."

"I will not," says the child, and she dries her tears, and slowly becomes calm again.

"I am very foolish," she murmurs, "but I won't give way any more. It is not right for us to give way to all our feelings, and I didn't think I should. But I was thinking of what you had suffered, and I couldn't help it. I'm done now, and don't mind me, cousin Champ. It is all over."

The low words die away in the quiet room, and there is a silence, the man's hand still thoughtfully caressing the child's hair.

"Kate," he says at last, "I think I would like to hear you read a little from your Bible; I did not listen in church to-day."

"Oh! yes," says Kate, "I will get it presently."

And in a moment she has returned, and is seated in his lap, with the book open.

"Will you hear this?" she says, with a soft look of her dewy eyes, and pointing as she speaks to a passage on the page.

"Any thing, Kate," he says.

And the child, leaning her head on his breast, commences reading in a low, earnest voice, slowly and feelingly:

"'But he was wounded for our transgressions; he was bruised for our iniquities: the chastisement of our peace was upon him, and with his stripes we are healed.

"'All we like sheep have gone astray; we have turned every one to his own way; and the Lord hath laid on him the iniquity of us all.

"'He was oppressed and he was afflicted, yet he opened not his mouth: he is brought as a lamb to the slaughter; and as a sheep before her shearers is dumb, so he opened not his mouth.

"'He was taken from prison and from judgment: and

who shall declare his generation? for he was cut off out of the land of the living: for the transgression of my people was he stricken.'"

The soft low voice paused, and the child seems to be absorbed in thought: her eyes go back, and she reads lowly:

"'He is despised and rejected of men; a man of sorrows and acquainted with grief; and we hid, as it were, our faces from him: he was despised, and we esteemed him not.

"'Surely he hath borne our griefs and carried our sorrows; yet we did esteem him stricken, smitten of God, and afflicted.

"'He was wounded for our transgressions; he was bruised for our iniquities;'" repeated the child, closing the book and fixing her eyes thoughtfully upon the fire; "'bruised for our iniquities.'"

The low, earnest voice dies away into a whisper, and she is silent.

He looks at the thoughtful little face for some moments, and says:

"Katy, I wish you could make me good."

"I? I, cousin Champ?" she says.

"Yes, indeed; like yourself."

Kate shakes her head sadly.

"I am not good," she replies.

"If you are bad, what am I? The idea is not agreeable," he murmurs.

"What did you say, cousin?"

"That is just what I wished to hear you read," he says, sighing; "and now, Kate, remember what I asked you once upon a time!"

"What, cousin?" says the child, thoughtfully.

"I asked you to tell me what heaven was—what you thought it was."

"Did you?—but I don't know."

"What do you think?"

"I think it is a place where every body loves God."

"Yes," he says.

"And that's why I think it must be happier than this world, where we don't love him enough. Oh! cousin Champ," she goes on, thoughtfully, "what a happy place heaven must be. I think of it in this way. I think of the people and things I love best in the world, and of all the happiest things we have. And then, when I feel so calm and grateful, I say to myself: 'all this is nothing to heaven!' For in heaven, you know, nothing can ever hurt us: here we have to suffer, and sometimes the people we love do not love us, you know, and we are afflicted and distressed; or they change, you know, from loving us, and don't care for us any more: or they grow sick and die; and all this interferes with our happiness. It is not so in heaven, the Bible says. There we love God, and you know God does not change if we obey and love him: he will always love us dearly if we love and fear him. There is no sickness in heaven, and no affliction—and then, again, think of eternity! Eternity! I don't know how to think about it, but the thought of eternal happiness seems very plain to me. In this world, we can't live very long, you know, and no matter how happy we are, we must soon die and give all up. In heaven, we won't die ever, you know, and we will not suffer, but be happy and love every body for ever and ever."

Kate is silent; she is thinking.

"I try to be good," she continues, thoughtfully, "and I pray mamma to look down on me and keep me good if she can; but I'm afraid I'm very bad. I don't think about God enough and the Saviour, and I am too thoughtless, as we were in the woods yesterday, you know—when we had our picnic. But I can't help laughing when I feel like it easily; but I mustn't be too thoughtless. I try and think about heaven, and how happy mamma and papa are, you know; and how good Jesus was to us, to be 'bruised for our iniquities.' Oh! think," repeats the calm, low voice, "he was *bruised*, cousin Champ—'bruised for our iniquities.'"

And the child is silent again.

He looks at the tender, thoughtful face, and from it to the portrait over the fireplace.

"Strikingly alike!" he murmurs, and then adds aloud:

"Yes, dear, we are very bad to forget it—as I do always: well, well, you have made me feel much happier, and now you had better go to bed."

Kate raises her head, kisses him according to the Virginia custom, and after leaning her face affectionately on his shoulder for a moment, slowly retires.

He looks after her for some minutes: raises his eyes again to the portrait: looks at the little Bible: hesitates, buried in thought. Then he rises suddenly, goes to the table, opens his portfolio, and taking a pen and a sheet of paper, writes:

"My dear Hamilton:

"I regret the harshness and passion of my address to you yesterday. I trust you will not permit it to remain in your recollection. I have no calmness on that subject, and for this reason must ask you never again to allude to it. I am afraid of myself. For God's sake! don't arouse the devil in me when I am trying to lull it, at the risk of breaking my heart in the attempt.

"I have nothing more to add.

"Your friend,
C. Effingham."

"*The Hall, Sunday night.*"

Then folding up this note, he directed it to Mr. Hamilton, placed it on the mantel-piece, and with a long, gloomy, sorrowful look, regarded the portrait of his mother. That portrait seemed to smile on him—the mild eyes to bless him: those eyes seemed living once again, and the lips almost moved.

A profound sigh shook his bosom, and his head drooped: but when he retired his heart was not so heavy, and that sombre bitterness of mood had passed away. The old, sad look came back again, and the moon lit up the pale countenance with its light, and smiled.

The weary heart slept tranquilly.

CHAPTER XXXIX.

HOW CAPTAIN WATERS WAS CHALLENGED TO MORTAL COMBAT.

"The manner in which Captain Ralph vituperated Lanky, upon that occasion, was positively shocking. In the first place it was uncalled for; in the second place it was ungenerous, considering Lanky's inoffensive character; in the third place, it was too great an expenditure of genius upon an humble personage, and an ordinary occasion.

"The Captain swore philologically, and with an eye to ethnology. He proceeded geographically, first exhausting that department of Spanish and Portuguese, after which he went on to France, and swore that oath-loving land quite through, from Gascony and Provençe to Normandy. He did not neglect Germany and Prussia, and paid due honor to Italy, where the science has perhaps arrived at its climax. And in all this flood there was no mixture of the deeply impure. The Captain's expletives were of that pleasant and humorous description, which are not inconsistent with a very charitable nature, and we may in a single word describe the handling of this great master, by saying that he swore poetically and from the imagination, not coarsely and from envy and hatred.

"Having exhausted Syria and Persia, the Captain modestly paused: he had not travelled further, and great as was his ill-humor, he would not trespass on his fancy. Instead of doing so, he seized his sword, and placing himself in position, called on Lanky to defend himself. Lanky replied by mentioning his master's military title, with an 'Oh!' before it; and this not being satisfactory, the Captain lunged furiously at him, and several times grazed the unfortunate Lanky, who uttered cries of despair and terror, as he shrunk and curled himself up to avoid the imminent sword point, flashing like a fiery serpent's head before his breast."

Thus far the author of the MS.

It is scarcely necessary for us, in explanation of Captain Ralph's ill-humor, to do more than refer to the scene between himself and Mr. Hamilton, narrated in former pages of this history. The present outburst occurred on the Monday immediately following; and in it the Captain poured out all the wrath which had been slowly gathering, like a storm, for forty-eight hours.

When he had nearly terrified Lanky out of his wits, he calmly restored his sword to its scabbard, and sat down.

"Oh, Cap'n," said Lanky, "did anybody ever see—"

"Basta! you villain, don't appeal to me!"

"Oh, Cap'n!"

"Off with you!—I'm in a man-eating humor. Stay if you dare, you rascal, and I'll fry you!"

"Fry me?"

"Yes, morbleu!"

Lanky meditated for a moment, and thought how he would feel if this terrible threat was carried into effect. The idea was disagreeable in the highest degree, and he made a step towards the door.

"Stay!" thundered the Captain, "the sight of that pine knot head, you Scaramouch, keeps me from having a fit of the blue devils."

"The blue devils, Cap'n?" asked Lanky, pausing.

"Yes, sir."

"Are you subjic to 'em?"

"No, you rascal: but I am threatened with them. One thing consoles me, however: threatened men live long."

Lanky inclined his head, in token of acquiescence.

"Sim Trabbles said he was goin' to cut me up into sossige once," said Lanky, "an' I aint cut up yit."

"Well, sir, what do you fancy I care for you and Mr. Trabbles? Sink Trabbles! you rascal!"

"Oh, Cap'n!"

"Dance, there!"

"Me dance, Cap'n?"

"Yes, this moment."

Lanky looked around, groaning.

"They aint no music. Oh, Cap'n," he added, "what's the matter with you?"

"I'm in an ill-humor, you Scaramouch—terribly angry."

"Cap'n," observed Lanky.

"Sir?"

"What is a Skarrymush?"

The Captain regarded his retainer for a moment with contemptuous pity.

"Look in that mirror," he said.

Lanky obeyed.

"Well, sir?" said Lanky.

"You have all the reply I deign to give you! Now take yourself elsewhere, you gobemouche."

"Gobmush!" cried Lanky.

The Captain aimed at him with a volume that was lying

on the table, and Lanky took to his heels, and disappeared, deeply wounded at being called those two dreadful names, ending with "mouche."

Left alone, the Captain twirled his moustaches, and relapsed into gloom again. It was a splendid day of May, but the Captain did not see the sunlight; the birds sang among the forest boughs—the Captain did not hear them: the river lapped upon the shore, the white-capped waves laughing for joy: the Captain did not heed them. For the worthy fellow was troubled; he had, for the first time, found opposed to him a dangerous rival; he was doubtful what course to pursue, for, perhaps, the first time in his life—that life so filled with shocks, and blaring trumpets, and quick blows.

He remained silent and motionless for half an hour: then his eye suddenly lighted up, and rising he opened a drawer, took out pen, ink and paper, and dipping the goose-quill into the inkstand, began to write, in large, heavy letters, and with great rapidity.

Let us look over his shoulder: these words appear beneath his flying pen:

"My dear Companion:

This is an unhappy world, and devious are the ways thereof. Man—especially a rude fellow, morbleu!—knows not what to do often; he is puzzled; he hesitates and stands still. Do you ask me what I mean by this small moral discourse? Parbleu! I mean that I am the rude fellow and the puzzled man.

"If you were an ordinary rival, basta! there would be few words. I would solicit the honor of being allowed an opportunity to pink you; and there 'twould end. I'd go on in my course or fall: and so finish. But I can't well run you through. *Diable!* I should say not. You are her cousin, you are a *bon compagnon*, you smile when we meet. See the difficulty.

"Ah! were you only not unfortunately so placed—for how can I act? I put it to you as a man of sense and reason, is there any opening? Indicate it, my dear companion—zounds! the sword shall not touch my hand unless I am compelled.

"See, now, I am a rude soldier, a mere war animal, a

fighting hack, or if not a hack a military personage—I think I can venture on that general description. Well, now, what can I do? I beg you, *mon ami*, to give me your ideas:—what say you to a bargain that we shall see the charming mademoiselle only on alternate days? to avoid collisions, you observe. These little matters are disagreeable, and often end in an appeal to the toasting iron, morbleu!

"For me, I don't conceal the fact that I shall prosecute the war with vigor. I have advanced to the trenches, and the next movement will be to hoist the ladders: then, the trumpet and the assault. I know nothing beyond this—I'm a mere baby—*tonnere*! I am as innocent as a child. Therefore, my good companion, come to my assistance. We are rivals—basta! don't let us have any ambiguities, or concealments. I would conquer, I would see you defeated; *Voila tout!* But I would do so without placing myself in position—you understand—I am tired of fighting every thing out: I am becoming decidedly a man of peace, a quiet and moral citizen—I wish, even, as you may understand, to become a respectable married man.

"I thought the chances were tolerable, but *diable!* I find I have a rival whom I cannot despise if I would. You are a good-looking, gallant fellow, morbleu! and just the man to interest a woman, as a friend of mine observed lately. I honestly confess that I'm afraid of you. Observe again! You are her cousin; parlous adds companion: yet I do not despair.

"I write this—which I send by Lanky, simply that it may not resemble an invitation to the duello—I write, I was going on to say, to ask you, *bon ami*, *bon compagnon*, how we are to arrange the matter. I'm weary of cut! thrust! and then blood.

"Send back your answer by the Scaramouch who brings you this. *Toute à vous.*

"Ralph Waters."

Having read this letter over hurriedly, and finding it express his ideas with tolerable distinctness, the Captain summoned Lanky, who made his appearance with an air of dreadful apprehension, for the vision of himself frying had produced a more and more disagreeable impression, the more he thought upon the subject. He was much relieved to find that he was only wanted to officiate in the character of a messenger—not at an *auto da fe.*

"Take this to Effingham Hall, and deliver it to Mr. Effingham," he said. "See here upon the back 'Mr. Effingham, Effingham Hall.' Then wait for an answer, you villain."

Lanky placed the letter in his pouch, put on his hat, and mounting the cart-horse, set off.

The Captain sat down again, listless, and venting morbleus: and very doubtful whether his letter would answer the desired object.

"But what could I do!" he said, "parbleu! I am checkmated. I don't want to fight Effingham—I don't want to have any further altercation with one related to Ma'mselle Henrietta; ah! but I wish still less to be beaten. Morbleu! was there ever such an unfortunate event!"

And the Captain relapsed into silence and thought.

He was aroused by the sound of hoofs, and looking out saw Lanky dismounting. Hours had passed without his being conscious of the fact.

"Well, well, the answer!" he cried impatiently.

"Here it is, sur," said Lanky; and drawing forth a billet he politely presented it to the soldier. Captain Ralph tore it open and read:

"Sir,—

Your letter is offensive—I will not make any derogatory agreement with you, sir. I would rather end all at once, and I hereby call on you to meet me, sir, this very day, at the Banks' Cross-roads. At five o'clock this evening, I shall await you.

"I have the honor to be, sir,

"Effingham."

The Captain stood aghast—read the letter over, then crushing it in his hand, fell into a rage, which caused Lanky the most dreadful trepidation.

"Morbleu!" cried the Captain, "fighting is his forte, is it!—he would end the matter so, would he! Very well, we shall see."

And seizing his sword he buckled it on, and ordered

Lanky, in a voice of thunder, to saddle his horse. Lanky obeyed, trembling, and in a quarter of an hour Captain Ralph was on his way to Hamilton's, where he expected to find some second, in case Mr. Hamilton was engaged to act for Mr. Effingham.

CHAPTER XL

ON THE GROUND.

THE fox-hunter displayed the most unaffected astonishment at the Captain's communication, and would at once have revealed the trick he had played; but a sight of the letter stopped him.

After reading it over twice, he shook his head mournfully, and said it was a most unhappy affair—but really, he did not see any other mode of settling it. Then he hastily left the room, and a roar of laughter succeeded; immediately after which Mr. Hamilton's voice was heard reprimanding the servant, who had no doubt uttered this disrespectful sound —in a tone of dignified astonishment.

Soon afterwards, dinner was announced, and Hamilton advised his friend not to drink much, as it would unsteady his hand in the coming encounter.

"I will not conceal from you, Captain," he said, "that I think it will be a mortal duel. Effingham is a bitterly passionate man, and hates you profoundly. Come now, my dear fellow, set down that glass of claret."

The Captain drank it off.

"Basta! I've tried all sorts of fighting," he said, "and there's some reason in what you say. But a glass of claret? Morbleu! I believe you are laughing."

"I would not be guilty of laughing, at such a crisis," said Hamilton, "when one, or perhaps two, of my friends are about to fall."

"Well, well," said the Captain, "we shall see."

And he remained quite composed until the hour of half-past four had arrived. Having the duel thus forced on him, the worthy fellow's mind was quite at ease.

Hamilton had the horses brought, and the two men mounted.

"Banks' Cross-roads is a good place for a duel," said Hamilton, sighing.

"Ah?" said the Captain, twirling his moustache.

"Yes, my dear fellow—yes," replied Hamilton, "it is a most eligible position to fall upon—gracefully, you know."

"I hope to stand up," said the Captain.

"Well well, it is possible you may not be killed," continued his companion, with great commiseration in his voice. "Effingham is probably out of practice, and you stand some chance."

"Some chance? I?" said the Captain, "why, Hamilton, just as sure as you sit in that saddle, I shall kill or disarm him. Basta! he has forced it on me."

"I am glad you are so confident," said Hamilton, "but I think it my duty to say that Effingham was considered one of the best swordsmen in London."

"Was he?"

"Yes."

"I'm glad;" replied the Captain, "all the more satisfactory. Let us get on, comrade!"

And putting spurs to his horse, the Captain galloped onward followed by Hamilton, who looked at him—when their eyes met—with pitying regard.

They reached the cross-roads just as the Captain's repeater indicated the hour of five.

Mr. William Effingham, with his friend Thomas Alston, Esq., was standing on a grassy hillock at the point where the ways meet.

"Well, my little man," said the Captain, goodnaturedly, "did your brother send you to announce his coming?"

"Did you address me, sir?" asked Mr. William Effingham, arranging his diminutive frill.

"Morbleu!—I certainly did, *petit monsieur*."

"Be good enough to allow our respective seconds to arrange the preliminaries of the combat," observed Mr. Effingham, with an important air.

"Our seconds!—the combat!—the preliminaries!" cried the Captain. "Where is Mr. Effingham?"

"I am he, sir."

"You!"

"Yes, sir."

"You wrote me that answer?"

"Yes, sir."

The Captain laid back on his horse and shook with laughter. Hamilton echoed it. Master Will looked hostile and indignant.

"*You* received my letter!" cried the Captain.

"I did, sir."

"*You* answered it?"

"I have replied to that question already, sir!"

"Why, it was directed to your brother, *monsieur.*"

"It was directed to 'Mr. Effingham,' and that is my name, sir."

"Lanky gave it to you, then?" said the Captain, rolling about with laughter.

"He sent it in by a servant, sir, and I returned my reply through the same channel."

The Captain remained silent for a moment, then bursting into a roar of laughter, louder than any previous roar, cried:

"Well! mine has been a wild life, full of odd adventures, but it was left for this day to bring the most splendid comedy to light I ever acted in! Basta! Did any one ever—"

"Never!" cried Hamilton.

"And you were ready to fight me with that huge sword!" cried the Captain to Mr. William Effingham, who indeed had buckled around his waist his brother's largest rapier.

"I was, sir," he said.

"And on what quarrel?"

"We are rivals, sir," said Will, "you confess it in your letter."

"Rivals!"

"Yes, sir."

'How, in heaven's name?"

"I am not ignorant, sir," replied Mr. William Effingham, with lofty dignity, "of the advances you have made to my cousin, Miss Catherine Effingham. I have not been blind, sir, to the fact, either at the Hall on a former occasion, when she rode behind you, or at Riverhead, the residence of Mr. Lee, when you were pleased to compliment her costume, nor last Saturday, sir, when she hastened to you as you passed upon horseback, near our party, and gave her hand to you. You seem to be about to deny this, sir: it is useless: the death of one of us will end all. Mr. Alston will arrange the terms of the combat with Mr. Hamilton."

And Mr. William Effingham drew himself up and assumed an air of noble dignity.

The Captain and his friend had nearly expired with pent-up laughter during this discourse. But the soldier suppressed his agitation: when his opponent had finished, he replied with a low bow, and in a voice of respectful solemnity:

"I beg to assure you, Mr. Effingham, that your suspicion that I designed, or now design, paying my addresses to your beautiful cousin, Miss Effingham, is wholly a mistake. Much as I admire that fair and lovely lady, I should never place myself in your way."

"Hum!" said his enemy.

"I therefore repeat, and here declare in the presence of yourself, of Mr. Hamilton, and of your friend, Mr. Alston, to whom I beg leave to present the assurance of my highest regard, and most distinguished consideration—I repeat, I say, in the presence of all here assembled, that I renounce all pretensions to the hand of Miss Effingham from this time forth. If any paper is necessary to be signed, I will sign it: I will, "*parole d'honneur! morbleu!*"

And Captain Ralph bowed again, stuffing his frill into his mouth.

"That is perfectly satisfactory, Captain Waters, and I offer you my friendship," said Will, brightening up.

"I accept it with delight," said the Captain: and bending down, the mortal opponents shook hands.

"And now I think my hoax has proceeded far enough," said Hamilton, laughing.

"Your hoax?" said his friend.

"All I said the other day, returning from Riverhead, was a pure invention," said honest Jack, laughing triumphantly, "and now, my dear Don Moustachio, it seems to me that I have paid you for all your practical jokes upon myself, at a blow."

With which words honest Jack Hamilton laid back and shook triumphantly.

For a moment the Captain looked indignant: then his face brightened: then he burst into a loud laugh, and cried, holding out his hand:

"Was ever such a villainous plot so perfectly successful! *Morbleu!* Hamilton, I acknowledge you are my master! Any feeling of spite, *mon compagnon*, is lost, *parbleu!* in admiration of your strategy!"

The Captain stopped to return, with great respect, the bows of Mr. Effingham and Mr. Alston, who, mounting their horses, rode off with graceful dignity.

The Captain looked after them—waited until they had disappeared, and then burst into a perfect roar of morbleus,—laughter, and delighted appreciation of the whole joke.

"Tonnere! Hamilton, you are a great genius!" he cried, "would any body have suspected from your face, on that ride, that you were tricking me! *Morbleu, mon ami!* I consider it equal to any thing in ancient or modern history."

Mr. Hamilton assumed a modest and deprecatory expression.

"No—no," he replied, mildly.

"There you are!" cried the Captain, "your face is like a woman's, when she says, 'I will consider your proposal, sir—la.' *Diable!* let us start equal again: after this, war to the death!"

And the Captain rode onward with his companion, toward the Trap.

"To-morrow—well, we shall see!" he muttered, as he rode home that evening, "the scaling ladders are ready!"

CHAPTER XLI.

WHICH THE READER SHOULD BY NO MEANS OMIT READING.

"The reader will, no doubt, be able to comprehend without difficulty, what Captain Ralph meant when he informed himself confidentially that the scaling ladders were ready.

The malicious communication of the Seigneur Mort-Reynard had made him feel very doubtful whether he could plant the instruments of assault securely: he looked through the Seigneur's spectacles and saw a dangerous enemy upon the citadel, ready to pour down on his devoted head, fire and boiling oil, and all deadly implements of warfare.

"But now all this had been cleared away—the enemy had turned out no enemy at all: and that was the explanation of the Captain's speech.

"On the next day, he donned his most dangerous weapons, and cased himself in his most war-proof armor; then with trumpets sounding, and banners flying, advanced to the assault."

Thus does the author of the manuscript, in that practical style of which he is so fond, chronicle the fact that Captain Ralph Waters set out for Riverhead with the intention of making a matrimonial demonstration. We suspect that the "dangerous weapons and war-proof armor," were only smiles and (hair) powder, and moustaches gallantly curled: that the "trumpets sounding," were simply the soldier's habitual ditty, ending in "ta, la! ta, la!"—lastly, that the "banners flying," were a pure figment of the author's imagination.

It is not now necessary to chronicle the details of the interview: we shall more directly arrive at its result by looking over the Captain's shoulder as he writes—having returned in the afternoon from Riverhead, with an expression of countenance far from downcast.

Seated at the rude table of the cottage, and making a tremendous scratching with his pen, which he handles much after the fashion of a sword, the soldier writes these words: while Lanky, seated in a corner, his day's work finished, looks on admiringly.

"DEAR SIR, FRIEND AND COMPANION:—

"Not simply 'sir,' because you are what I have written—friend, companion. Let me out with what I would write at once—and in the best manner I can write it, being but a rude soldier, unused to handling the pen.

"With great respect, dear sir, and companion, I would

ask permission to pay my addresses to your charming daughter, Henrietta.

"This may surprise you, and"—the Captain earsed a '*morbleu*' here—"and I confess you have some reason: but I have not fought all those battles, Glatz and Lissa and the rest, with you, and found no enemy myself, but a courteous host. Alas, *mon ami!*—I am defeated wholly: can't hold up my head, and come to you and say I am conquered.

"Let me speak of myself first—that, it seems to me, is necessary, being almost a stranger in the land. You know my family—an honest one, I think, at least I am accustomed to regard it such. I am not ashamed, rather proud of it—thus much in justice to myself.

"I was quite young when, led by the spirit of adventure which God plants in the bosoms of the youthful, I left Virginia, to which land, through all my wanderings, my heart turned with filial devotion. I went to Europe. I entered his Majesty's service, in which I continued until the peace of Fontainbleau, with an intermission of two years—two years which now live in my memory as the brightest period of a rude, wandering life, crammed with a thousand vicissitudes, a host of emotions, for the most part emotions of glad triumph and success.

"Those two years saw me married to a good wife, a tender heart,—one of those natures which God sends upon this earth to bless the lives of us rude soldiers and soften them. I had the unhappiness to lose my wife; the hand of Providence took her from me, and, to my great regret, I had no children to remind me of that so long-loved companion. Well, well, let me pass on: that wound has healed—or nearly.

"I plunged into war again.—I exhausted its delights, and they are not slight, sir, with all the blood and wounds, and suffering. I returned hither to Virginia, led by the never-dying sentiment of love of country. I only sojourned in Europe; this was my home. All that I retained of those years of battles and marches, and countermarches, was the title by which I am usually addressed. I was discharged. I left his Majesty's service, which I heartily rejoice and thank heaven for, the great Frederic not being a commander to my taste.

"Upon her death-bed, my wife,—whom God bless and

make eternally happy, as she made me happy in this life, often pillowing my rude head, when I was wounded, on her bosom —my wife charged me to marry again, saying, that marriage made me better, curbing my natural propensity to wander, and making a quiet citizen of me,—which is true Ah ! sir, she was a good wife and I am a better man, for that brief dream of happiness. Enough !

" In relation to my worldly goods, let me adopt the European custom and omit nothing. I am not poor, thanks to some guilders gathered in my profession and what my wife *left to me.*

" I, therefore, ask that my addresses may receive your sanction ; I am convinced your daughter does not regard me with indifference, and this I had abundant proof of on this very day. Enough of that ; but this I add, that before addressing myself to you, I would receive no avowal from Mademoiselle Henrietta, binding her. I trust 'tis what every honorable man would do.

" You have it all, friend and companion ; you know me for what I am,—a rude soldier, but a loyal man. Speak.

" Always your friend,

" RALPH WATERS."

The Captain wrote this letter without thought, as he would have spoken : and sealed it without reading it.

He then summoned Lanky, and placing it in his hands, bade that unfortunate messenger deliver it to none but Mr. Lee himself, waiting an answer.

Lanky returned in three hours.

" Well ? "

" Answer to-morrow, sir."

" Good ! "

And Captain Ralph sat down composedly, and leaning his head upon his hand, seemed to be thinking of some old days,—upon the Rhine it seemed, and of a woman ; for his lips murmured : " a good wife—God take her to himself ! "

Early on the next day a servant brought a letter, which the Captain tore open at once. It contained these words simply :

" I accede to the request of Captain Waters. I know

him for a brave soldier, and a most honorable man. I ask nothing more. The rest lies with my daughter.

WINSTONE LEE."

The Captain raised his head, and Lanky started back at the radiant expression of his countenance.

"Oh! Cap'n!" he murmured.

"Lanky, my dear fellow," said the Captain, "I think your chances for the cottage are bad—very bad."

"Oh! Cap'n! why?"

"I am going to be married myself," said the soldier, "go and saddle my horse!"

And Captain Ralph twirled his moustaches with a look of such triumph and happiness that Lanky was consoled.

His master's joy was his own.

CHAPTER XLII.

HOW CAPTAIN RALPH AND HENRIETTA TOOK A DRIVE TOGETHER, AND WHAT FOLLOWED.

As we did not consider it necessary to relate the particulars of the Captain's last interview with Miss Henrietta Lee, so we shall for the same reason omit any description of the final and decisive assault, to adopt the phrase of the author of the manuscript from which these events are taken.

We can only say that when the soldier issued forth from the mansion of Riverhead his countenance was more radiant than ever, and that he twirled his moustaches toward the eye with an obstinate vigor which caused them to yield in spite of themselves and assume the killing air in absolute perfection.

On the very next day the gallant Captain might have been seen again before the door of Mr. Lee's mansion, this time seated in a handsome curricle drawn by his handsome roan. It was a beautiful morning, and the white gravelled walk glittered in the sun, the firm heel of the soldier clashing on it, as with jingling spurs—his old habit could not yield to change—he entered the wide portal.

In half an hour he emerged again, and this time with

Miss Henrietta on his arm. That young lady was as radiant as the morning:—her eyes shone brilliantly, and her rich dress was dimmed by the bright color of her cheeks.

The Captain assisted her into the vehicle, followed, and, gathering up the reins, set forward towards the cottage.

For some time they rode in silence: nothing was said: but at last Captain Ralph shook his head and sighed.

"It is not agreeable," he said; "no, it is repugnant."

"What?" she asked in a low tone, looking inquiringly at his disconsolate face.

"This thing of taking you from the abode of wealth and comfort—morbleu! from the bower of ease and elegance, my dear Miss Henrietta, to the humble cottage which I—unhappy that I am!—inhabit."

And the soldier groaned.

"I thought we had dismissed that subject," she said in the same low tone.

"Yes," said Captain Ralph, sighing again, "I understand. You, my dear wife to be, are one of those noble natures who can adapt themselves to any thing. Yes, I fully believed you when you said yesterday with that charming sincerity which, parbleu! is the most graceful and delightful trait of your charming and admirable character, *ma chère*, when you said you would not marry for mere wealth: and if the man of your choice had it not, that you would forget all and follow him—to the world's end, you said: alas!"

And Captain Ralph uttered a groan which seemed to indicate an overburdened heart.

"Yes," he continued, "I understand how it is that having cast a favorable regard upon the poor soldier, and seen that he is honest and loyal, and likely to be faithful for ever and the day after, my dear Henrietta—I can understand that you with your grand abnegation of self, weighed his worldly position as nothing: which, morbleu! is oftener done by our honest Virginia girls than people can be brought to admit. I can comprehend all that: but the fact of my abject poverty none the less wounds and mortifies me."

With which words the lady's companion twirled his moustache forlornly.

"You make me feel badly by speaking thus," said Henrietta, turning aside her head.

"Badly?"

"Indeed you do," she murmured.

"I am sorry," he said, crying; "but it is proper for me to say a few words more, *ma chère!* Do you see that horse?"

"Yes," she said, in a low voice.

"Does he look human?" continued the Captain, disconlately.

"Human?"

"Like a man," explained the soldier.

The lady looked at him in astonishment.

"Ah, I see," said the Captain, "you don't understand. That horse, *ma chère*, is a man."

"A man!"

"Yes, and his name is Von der Dank," said the Captain, gravely.

"Oh!" said Henrietta.

"Nothing but the truth. Does he not belong to that respectable merchant of Rotterdam, and am I not in fact driving the worthy Von der Dank in harness? 'Tis positively unchristian."

And nettled at his own bad feeling, the Captain laid the lash across the representative of Mynheer Von der Dank, who tossed his head and flew along gallantly.

"Then not content with driving Von der Dank," continued the soldier, "I must commit the further impropriety of running the pasha Omer at the races. Selim, my dear Henrietta, is an Arabian whom I stole in the Orient from the pasha—it is humiliating to confess it: but there should be no secrets between us."

Henrietta looked at her companion with wide eyes.

"True, every word true," said the Captain, sighing; "and to drive Von der Dank in harness, and run the pasha Omer for the amusement of a crowd of Christian dogs—as they call us—seems to me nothing less than sheep stealing, or what my servant Lanky fancies the highest disgrace—henroost robbing."

The Captain's head drooped.

"You are jesting," murmured Henrietta; "surely—oh! how foolish I am to mind you."

"Jesting? I wish I was: 'tis too sad a subject however. And that is not all."

"Not all?"

"Do you see that necklace around your neck? But of course you do."

"Yes," said Henrietta, scarcely knowing what to say.

"Well, my soul! that necklace represents Simpkins & Co., of the port of New York. You are wearing Simpkins around your neck—his arms encircle you. Just think of it!"

And the Captain groaned with jealousy and mortifi cation.

"Don't answer me," he continued, "my feelings are poignant enough already. Let us get on to my hovel which you see in the distance yonder. Von der Dank, proceed my friend!" and he lashed the worthy merchant; "the pasha awaits you in the stable, and you carry, in addition to your master and his bride, the firm of Simpkins—that I should be alive to say it!"

The roan seemed to be very well content with his enormous load, and the bright curricle flashed on under the green boughs and through the sunlight: and ere long stopped before the door of the cottage.

Lanky stood there, louting low, his cap in his hand.

The Captain assisted Henrietta out, and pointing to Lanky, who was holding the animal, said:

"That, my dear Henrietta, is the gentleman who made my fortune."

"Then you have a fortune after all," laughed the young girl, good-humoredly.

"No, no, I mean that Lanky was the means of my winning you—my pearl, what do I say! my rose, my diamond!"

"Pray how?"

"He is the lover of Donsy."

"Donsy?"

"Donsy Smith."

"Indeed!"

"Yes, yes," said the Captain, "and but for him I should have laid my heart—perhaps, who knows?—at that charming young lady's feet."

"Indeed!" said Henrietta, with something like a pout.

"Yes, verily and in truth—*en verite*, as they have it over yonder. But his affections having been engaged by the said Donsy, you may fancy that I was far too honorable to interfere. Honor is all I have left now," the Captain groaned.

And he led the young girl into the rude house.

"Look around," he said.

Henrietta obeyed.

"Is it not humiliating?"

"No," she said.

"Look at that table."

"Yes."

"Contemplate those chairs."

"Well," repeated Henrietta, in the same good-humored voice.

"Deign to survey those rafters, from which—heaven preserve us!—dangle strings of onions, and material, unpoetical bacon flitches."

"They look very nice," said Henrietta, laughing.

The Captain groaned.

"And to take you from your wealthy and elegant abode to such a hut," he said.

"I suppose I am content," she said, cheerfully.

"A lady eat onions!" cried the Captain.

"I did not promise that," she laughed.

"A lady partake of bacon!"

"I believe a great many ladies do daily."

"A lady sit upon chairs like those at such a table as that!"

"They are very nice to rest in, and my wrapping is very well here," said Henrietta, sitting down, and laying her silk pelisse upon the rude pine table.

The Captain shook his head, sighing piteously.

"That is all affectation, *ma chère*," he said, forlornly.

"Indeed 'tis not."

"Yes, yes."

"I am perfectly contented."

"With your future abode?"

"Yes," she said simply.

The Captain uttered a sigh.

"It wounds me," he said, "to the very heart thus to drag down the star of my life. But how can I help it?"

"I am glad I am a star," said Henrietta, smiling, "but I do not feel as if I were dragged down."

"All devotion—grandeur: it springs from your woman's nature. Just look around—just look at that pine knot at the door."

"Pine knot?"

"Yes, yes; at my scaramouch—at Lanky."

She laughed.

"This is your future mistress, Lanky," said the Captain.

The pine knot louted low.

"I am very glad to see you, Lanky, and to make your acquaintance," said Henrietta, holding out her hand, with a charming smile.

Lanky colored, and did not dare to take the hand.

"Won't you shake hands?" said Henrietta, smiling.

Lanky trembled and approached.

"Oh, ma'am!" he said.

And he found his huge paw inclosed in a soft white hand, like velvet, which pressed it kindly.

Lanky disappeared, staggering with delight.

"Look at him!" sighed the Captain; "see the difference between that ridiculous country bumpkin, in his striped stockings and fustian waistcoat, and the well-fed butler you are accustomed to see, Henrietta."

"I like Lanky the best," she said, smiling; "he seems very honest."

"Yes, yes, a *bon garçon*, and would die for me."

"Then," said Henrietta, simply, "I shall like him more than ever."

The Captain's martial face was illuminated with a look of pride and happiness which changed it instantly, and made it radiant.

"*Morbleu!* Henrietta," he cried, "you are the pearl of your sex, the queen of the heart, as you are the queen of beauty! And can you consent to leave your father's house, with all its elegance, its comfort, its quiet pleasure and soft repose, to become the inmate of this cabin, the wife of the rude soldier who stands before you? Can you bid adieu to every brilliant scene, to all your past life, spent in the midst of so much ease, even splendor, to light up my poor hut with your smiles—my life with your fair and beautiful eyes?

Can you consent to take a poor soldier, a rough adventurer, a common fellow, with nothing but a loyal heart?"

She murmured, "Yes."

"You cannot leave that position without a struggle, however," he continued. "Does it not rend your heart to descend so low—to leave Riverhead for this cottage—to become the mistress of a hovel? Can you look with equanimity upon a future where no sun shines, where you must contend with common, coarse, material obstacles—with vulgar want, and struggle on without casting a single longing look back on your past?"

"Yes," she said, putting her hand in his, "I have you."

"Shall I put the roan up, sir?" said Lanky, appearing at the door.

"No," sighed the Captain, relapsing into gloom; "we will return."

And offering his arm to Henrietta, he passed through the door, and slowly assisted her into the vehicle again, sighing.

"Suppose we take a short drive before returning," he said.

She nodded good-humoredly.

The Captain only groaned in reply, and lashed his horse, who set off like lightning upon the smooth road leading up the river.

"Your gloom distresses me," said Henrietta, in a low voice; "for heaven's sake forget these mere worldly circumstances; they do not affect me for a moment. I would not have given my hand to the richest gentleman in the land for his riches only. Why should I estimate what I do not value so highly? Look at the sunlight, and hear the birds singing. We enjoy them as much as though we were a king and queen; and I think the river singing down upon the shore is happiness enough!"

And she looked as perfectly happy and contented as it is possible to conceive.

The Captain only sighed, and shook his head, murmuring:

"You are a noble heart."

"Indeed I'm not," she replied, cheerfully, "but I am far

more than contented. And, besides, father will not let us want any thing—you forget that."

"Oh!" groaned the Captain, "that is too humiliating! A strong-armed soldier like me marrying for money! Do not speak of it, Henrietta—it is dreadful. I did not seek your money—if you have any of that disagreeable commodity—the Shakespearian word, I believe. I hate and despise what is vulgarly called cash!"

And in the excess of his wrath at finding that his future wife would probably have a large fortune on her marriage, the Captain lashed the roan until that unfortunate animal fairly flew.

"Let us not speak further on this subject," he added; "let us enjoy the landscape. See the river—see those noble mansions crowning the fine hills. *Parbleu!* the goods of this wicked world—particularly of that wickedest portion, Virginia—are not equally divided. Now it seems to me that I ought to have one of those fine houses. Society owes me a house and plantation. I will establish a school of politics with that cardinal principle. I will become agrarian. I want land."

Henrietta smiled.

"We can do very well without it," she said.

"Contemplate the fine old houses," continued the Captain, sighing; "look at the smiling fields—I covet those fields, I break the tenth commandment horribly, morbleu!"

"The whole?" asked Henrietta, smiling.

"Yes, yes."

"Do you covet your neighbor's wife?" she laughed.

The Captain smiled sadly.

"No, no; I believe you have me there," he said; "I don't want any wife but the one who will soon be mine legally, and I may add, equitably—in fee-simple."

And having made this great display of legal knowledge, the Captain stopped sighing.

"See what a fine house across the river," he added.

"Yes; but I think Mr. Wilt's, here, is far prettier."

"No, no."

"Indeed, I think it is."

"Well, I have a moment's business with that gentleman. Will you go in?"

"Oh yes."

A quarter of a mile was passed over, and the vehicle stopped at the door of one of those fine old mansions we have heard the Captain covet. It fairly smiled in the bright May sunlight, with its gables, dormer windows, and old trees.

An aged negro came to the door, and held the horse respectfully for the soldier. He assisted Henrietta out, and they entered.

"Why, they have new furniture," she said: "I know all about 'Flodden,' and it looks very much changed."

"Ah!"

"Yes indeed! how strange! but how handsome it is."

They went into the parlor, and the well-fed butler stood bowing.

"James," said Henrietta; but stopping, she added, "why, it is not James?"

"My name is Thomas, madam," said the courteous black gentleman, not seeing the Captain's signals of wrath.

"Thomas! why where is old James?"

"He went away, they tell me, ma'am, with Squire Wilts."

"Went away!"

"The squire done moved to his t'other house up the river, ma'am, and master there done bought the place—'Floding' I b'lieve they calls it."

Suddenly Thomas started and shook: he saw the wrathful eyes of the soldier on him.

Henrietta could say nothing; the whole flashed on her; she only looked in silence at the Captain.

"Yes, my dearest Henrietta," said that gentleman, "I understand what you would say. You mean that I have deceived you—and, morbleu! you are perfectly right. But ah! I could not deny myself that scene at the cottage—I could not omit such pleasure. It was not to try you. Oh no! parole d'honneur! I felt that useless. But in this world we cannot get too much happiness, and in your devotion to your rude soldier, there was such happiness as he has seldom experienced in this wicked world.

"Yes," continued the Captain, "'Flodden' is my home now, the squire having disposed of it privately to me, taking in exchange for it some twelve thousand pounds I had lying idle. Let me embrace the opportunity further to assure you *ma chère*, that Van der Dank, the pasha, and the New-York firm, are all honestly paid—the animals are mine, the bracelet yours. We have enough, thank Heaven, to live quietly upon, and you will not be compelled, my dearest Henriette, to descend as low as onions."

With which words the Captain, laughing, full of pride and delight, smoothed softly the head that lay upon his shoulder.

"Now we shall return in a different manner," he said; and he gave an order to the butler.

That gentleman bowed low and vanished.

A quarter of an hour afterwards, a magnificent chariot drove up to the door, drawn by four horses, whose bright coats and rosetted heads shone in the merry sunlight.

The Captain led the young girl forth, and assisted her into the coach: then followed. The courteous black butler bowed—the old superannuated hostler smiled; for he liked the frank face of the soldier;—and the vehicle set off at a gallop. Captain Ralph was partial to rapid motion.

They did not speak for some moments; then the soldier said:

"But how are you pleased with your house, ma chère?"

"Very much," she said, smiling; "but I like the cottage and Lanky best, I think!"

Which caused the Captain to burst into laughter. In two hours they reached 'Riverhead.'

CHAPTER XLIII.

IN WHICH MR. EFFINGHAM STARTS WITH ASTONISHMENT.

"My goodness!" said Kate.

Will looked dignified.

"Did you really now?" continued the mistress of his heart.

"Yes,madam," replied Will.

"Who would have thought of such a thing but you! Gracious! it almost takes my breath away to think of it!"

And Kate placed her hand upon her breast and gasped,

and panted in a manner which was delightful to behold; her eyes dancing all the while, her utterance struggling with pent-up laughter.

Miss Kate Effingham, and Mr., otherwise Captain William Effingham, patriotic leader of the Cornstalk regiment of Virginia Volunteers, exchanged these observations on the day after the scene at the Cross Roads. Kate was sitting at the harpsichord whereon she had been playing; Master Willie was perched upon the table, from which he dangled his dignified legs, clad in their silk stockings and pumps, which latter were ornamented with huge rosettes and silver buckles.

Kate's hair flowed on her shoulders, which were bare, and from time to time she removed it from her rosy cheeks, and placed it behind her ears; her white arms were bare to the shoulder nearly: she was clad in intense pink, and wore golden clocks. She had been singing a song of which the following is a specimen, as nearly accurate as possible:

> "'Tis in the field the farmer goes,
> And there his seed the farmer sows,
> But you nor I nor nobody knows
> How oats, peas, beans, or barley grows:"

and during this pleasant ditty, Master Will had been kicking his heels to keep the time.

He had then startled Kate, by relating his abortive attempt to murder his rival, and thus the exclamation, "My goodness!" and the further observation, "gracious!" had been produced. After this accurate and detailed description of the circumstances of the interview, we may proceed to hear what the devoted lovers are saying.

"I'm sorry it takes your breath away to think of it," said Will, with dignity; "but that's the way you always treat me. I never can please you:—here I am running my life into danger for you, and you only laugh at me."

"Goodness gracious!" cried Kate, "I didn't."

"You did."

"Very well, sir, Tommy Alston never contradicts me."

"There, you are going to drive me distracted with that gawky Alston."

"Gawky! hum!"

And Kate pouted.

"You know he is!"

"He is'nt a bit."

"Now you are contradicting me," observed Will, with great good sense

"Well, you deserve it: you know you do. Tommy was a great deal more attentive to me at the picnic than you: and you would have let Jim Crow take my candy—but *he* wouldn't."

Will felt that this charge was unjust, and, not being able to contradict Kate, determined to go and challenge Mr. Alston immediately. He rose for that purpose.

"Where are you going?" said Kate.

"I am going to make your Mr. Alston give me satisfaction."

"Satisfaction! Oh me!"

"Yes, madam."

"To fight?"

"Immediately."

And Will made a motion to go.

"Oh Willie!" cried Kate, holding him back.

"Before night one of us shall sleep in death!" cried Willie, looking concentrated daggers.

Kate uttered a scream.

"Willie, you frighten me to death!" she cried, "I was only joking. You were very good to me at the picnic; and I didn't mind that foolish little fellow, Jim. Didn't he turn funny summersets? My gracious! just to think of him makes me die o' laughing."

And Kate burst into such a ringing peal of laughter that Willie's hostile ideas disappeared like mist before the sun.

"What a fine time we had!" said Kate, struggling not to laugh all her words into stammerings; "only think of the drummer, too! and Johnny Booker, from the Bowling Green, and the way Jim Crow ate that pie!"

"It was splendid!" said Will, whose spirits were restored completely.

"And it wasn't far from where you were going to fight that ridiculous duel," observed Kate.

Will's face clouded.

"Ridiculous?"

"Yes: did any body ever hear the like? Of course, I'm flattered, and all for your doing it for me; but to think Captain Waters was courting me. It was too funny."

"Funny!" said Will, with dignity; "Mr. Waters did not think so, madam. He formally renounced all claims to your hand."

"He was laughing at you."

"Laughing! laughing! laughing!" cried Will, with increased indignation, "he shall explain!"

And he would have rushed forth.

"Oh, Willie! Willie!" cried Kate in despair, and holding him tight; "you will kill me: I am very nervous and sensitive."

"Laughing!"

And Willie struggled.

"Oh no! he couldn't have laughed at you," said Kate, "for he is a very good-humored gentleman, and he must have felt that you were doing a brave action, Willie. Come now, let us make friends."

Will shook his head.

"Oh Willie!" pleaded Kate, "to refuse me who—who—love you so much!"

And Kate slew him with her eyes.

Will still hesitated.

"You say you love me?"

"Yes, indeed! so much!"

"How will you prove it?"

"By any thing you ask."

Will looked triumphant, and drew from his breast the true-love indenture, which he unrolled. At sight of it, Kate drew back, laughing.

"You said you'd do any thing," said Will.

"Oh! not that!"

"There is a pen on the table; now, Kate, keep your promise."

"Oh! I cannot!" Kate cried, laughing, and wringing her hands, and assuming an air as of one about to cry.

Will moved toward the door.

"Oh! you are going to fight a duel," said Kate; "it is my duty to prevent bloodshed!"

And, seizing the pen, she affixed the words "Kate Effingham" to the flower-and heart-ornamented love indenture.

"There!" she said, throwing down the pen, "will that satisfy you?"

"That is sufficient!" said Will; "now for one kiss!"

"One kiss, sir?"

"It is habitual," said Will, with dignity; "engaged people always kiss."

And he opened his arms to clasp his mistress to his heart. The fair Chloe fled, however, from the outstretched arms, and they closed on air.

In running out, Kate struck against Mr. Hamilton, who was coming in; whereupon Willie assumed an expression of dignity, and rolling up his indenture, was content.

Kate, however, distrusted this dignified deportment, and, bidding Mr. Hamilton a laughing good-morning, continued her flight some way upon the lawn, her hair streaming, her feet tripping merrily.

She paused finally under an oak, and looked back; Will was not pursuing; and, satisfied upon this point, she began singing, and so wandered on until she reached a sort of summer-house in the dell, a favorite resort of Mr. Effingham.

She found him there now, reading, his brow resting on his hand, the flowering vines falling around him as he half reclined upon the trellis work.

Kate stole behind him, and before he knew it leaned her head upon his shoulder, and uttered a little, quiet laugh.

The pale face was raised from the volume, and, leaning his head upon that of the child, his old pensive smile came to his lips.

"What are you reading, cousin?" asked Kate

"The writings of Steele," he said; "and now I suppose you are quite as much in the dark as ever."

"Oh no! I read once a very pretty piece he wrote."

"What was it?"

"I don't know, but it is in the other volume: where he tells how he cried when his father, I believe it was, died, and had a battledore; and his mother was crying, too, I think. Poor fellow!"

Mr. Effingham smiled.

"I believe these children criticise better than we men

do," he murmured; "but, Kate," he continued, "don't you like his merry pieces better?"

"I think I do; but you know I don't know any thing about London, or any cities."

"I am glad you do not; you shall grow up a pretty little flower of the woods."

"Thankee; I'm not a weed, I'd have you to know, cousin Champ."

"The lily of the valley and the violet are not weeds," he said, musing, as he looked at the bright face.

"Oh please, come, gather some violets with me?" said Kate.

"Oh certainly," he said, smiling, and the man and the child were soon bending down over the grassy banks of the stream for all sorts of flowers. They spent half an hour in this occupation, and then slowly returned to the Hall, which was hidden from the summer-house by a clump of trees.

Kate ran in, crying out, and admiring her nosegay. Mr. Effingham followed.

He did not see a horse tied near the gate: he did not observe a hat in the hall of the mansion.

He opened the door of the library, and witnessed a spectacle which made him start. It is necessary that even the chronicle should pause before proceeding to describe the enormity. Let us commence a new chapter.

CHAPTER XLIV.

DIAGNOSIS AND TREATMENT OF DR. MORT-REYNARD.

Mr. Effingham beheld the Seigneur Mort-Reynard, otherwise Mr. John Hamilton, that incorrigible bachelor, fox-hunter, and rival, in the act of impressing a chaste salute upon the lips of Miss Alethea!

So far from betraying any astonishment or indignation at this outrageous proceeding, the stately Miss Alethea, serene and shining in black silk, appeared to regard it as a matter of course, and submitted to it with an equanimity which was refreshing to behold. She betrayed some embarrassment upon Mr. Effingham's sudden entrance, and a slight color came to her cheeks; but that was all.

Not so Mr. Jack Hamilton. That gentleman presented the painful spectacle of a man caught in the act of filching a sheep from its rightful owner: he avoided Mr. Effingham's eye: he drew back from Miss Alethea: he considered the feasibility of disappearing up the chimney, or through the window at a bound.

At last he seemed suddenly to recover his powers of locomotion: he stammered some hasty words, and bursting into a roar of laughter, thrust a letter into Miss Alethea's hands, and took to flight. In ten minutes he was seen galloping away like a deserter.

Mr. Effingham, with flushed face, and haughty looks, stood silently gazing at Miss Alethea.

"You needn't show such great astonishment, Champ," said Miss Alethea, calmly smoothing her hair, which, we regret to say, was somewhat disordered, "Mr. Hamilton and myself have been engaged for half a year. I suppose there is something for you in this letter: it is directed to you. How foolish in Mr. Hamilton to be running away so: he is incorrigible. Well, there is the letter: I must go now and attend to my housekeeping."

With which words Miss Alethea sailed slowly out, her black silk rustling: Mr. Effingham standing perfectly motionless in the middle of the floor—the letter lying on the table.

"Engaged for half a year!" he said, as in a dream, "engaged! Alethea! Hamilton!"

His eye fell on the letter, and he tore it open and read it like lightning—his brow flushing, now with anger, then pleasure, then this latter expression chased away the former, and his face was radiant. He dropped the letter and uttered a sigh, which seemed to remove instantly a mountain from his breast.

The letter was in these words:

"My Dear Champ:

"I know what I have done is disgraceful, and horrible, and awful, and all that—but it was meant well, and I don't care what you may say; it has succeeded. The time to acknowledge the trick is come, and here goes. It went this way:

"I saw you come back from Europe completely knocked up—worried out, as you said, and you will remember that I announced my intention to become physician in ordinary to you, the very first time I saw you. You thought the fox-hunt was all—I know you did, and you are one more added to the list of those people, by George! who give Jack Hamilton credit for only about as much sense as a man could put into the left eye of a sparrow. No, sir! I'm deep, and I set to work at once, as I am going to tell you in this letter. I would rather not have a scene and a *vivâ voce* explanation after your blood and thunder address to me the other day, which made me as mad as blazes—an improper and vulgar expression, but it conveys the idea strongly.

"This was it. I say I saw you come home knocked up, and I hadn't been living so long in the world without understanding that you wanted to have some pursuit—some object. I'm thirty large odd, sir, nearly forty, in fact—don't mention it among the ladies—and in that time I had gathered some ideas. I know what I am going to say will make you mad, by Jove! but what do I care? I am a triumphant M. D., and if the patient runs the physician through the gizzard for cauterizing and curing him, society will frown upon the act: if any thing, the doctor's reputation will increase!

"I determined from that very interview that you should go back to your passion for Clare: it was only sleeping—I resolved to wake it. Being engaged to Miss Alethea, who promises to make a respectable and moral man of me—and I only hope she may not be disappointed—I had a natural disinclination to having a brother-in-law who would go about all the time looking like a thunder cloud, and as pale as those spirits called ghouls, who feed on human flesh, as I have read somewhere in Shakespeare, or the Dictionary—which fact makes them disagreeable associates, as a man never can feel sure that they are not anxious to eat him. I resolved, therefore to twist you round my thumb, and I've done it—triumphantly! I dare you to deny it! You are at this moment desperately in love with Clare Lee—your boyish adoration was not a shadow to it: you very nearly cut me to pieces the other day for asking what kept you from visiting her! Deny it if you dare—and ah! my dear boy, here is the agreeable part, what will make your vanity unbearable, here is the triumph of my tactics: she loves you! she does, upon my soul!

"But let me proceed, step by step, by George! I know human nature, and especially woman nature, sir—I am master of that: they can't trap me—not they; but my knowledge of the masculine temperament is equally profound. I have always observed that men and women, like hounds, run after what flies from them. I doubt whether even my dog Tinkle would grab a fox, if the fox came and sat down quietly by him and said, 'I would rather be grabbed than not—grab me, old fellow.' I know Tinkle, sir, and Tinkle would reply, 'Off with you, you are a disreputable hen-roost thief: I won't have you near me!' But let the fox run, and look! Tinkle will run him until his tongue hangs out of his mouth like a red ribbon. It's just so with men—and you are no exception. I tell you, sir, that you began to fall back in love with Clare the moment you found, or rather thought, she was running from you into my arms. That roused you; you cursed me from Dan to Beersheba and back again for a false friend; but you fell a victim to my artifice! If I had not played that nice little trick, what would have been the consequence? Why you would have found that Clare loved you as much as ever, in spite of your goings on, because she has forgiven you: and you would have dawdled over there once a week or so, and come back as dull as ever, and drawled 'yes, yes, a nice girl, very agreeable, fond of me—but I'm done with women!' Nothing, sir, would have come of it. But, now! what did I do? Why, I sacrificed myself on the altar of friendship, like a hero: I bore your murderous looks—I declined to see your fireball eyes, I took no notice of your tones of voice. I practised on you, sir, and I twisted you over my thumb—I made you jealous—I told, on a moderate calculation, one thousand lies about myself and Clare, which lies, as an honorable man, you are bound to take upon yourself—they having been told in your service. I then took up a large portion of my valuable time in praising you at Riverhead. The lies I told you were nothing to what I told Clare: I revelled in the imaginary, sir—I made you out the greatest hero of modern times—I said you were a saint, for which heaven forgive me: I did what every man is conscientiously bound to do for his friend—in vulgar and deplorably coarse phrase, I *plastered* you, sir.

"I made Clare believe that you were dying of love for Henrietta—this was to put her on her guard; after that, as she was a woman, I defied her to do more than speak to you. Her pride kept her from showing that she cared for you; I tricked her admirably.

"Having worked my diabolical and disgraceful scheme up thus, I carried it on—I revelled in it—you had a spice of that the other day when you boiled over; and that really made me angry; by Jove! I could have cut your throat then, and afterwards overwhelmed you, and mortified you, with telling you all I had done for you. I persist in saying that my triumph is complete. By George! I admire myself.

"And now, presume to quarrel if you dare, with all this; it was well meant, and you know it has turned out as I say. Pardon your old friend Jack, my boy, and acknowledge the elevation of his moral character. Go and tell Clare you love her, and don't fear that, when you have explained all, she will discard you. She loves you, by Jove! in a way that makes me desirous of standing in your shoes: that is to say, that the sentiment I have inspired Alethea with is much more moderate and dignified.

"The game's afoot, my boy; go it!

"JACK HAMILTON."

Mr. Effingham uttered a second long-drawn sigh, and rose like Columbus when the New World dawned upon him.

And in an hour they stood together by those two trees planted in their childhood, now so far away, but shrined as a jewel in their heart of hearts. And again he pointed to the trees, and spoke of that bright childhood, and his sufferings since then, and all the misconception which had cleared away as a cloud passes from the sun, and leaves all bright again, and full of warmth, and hope, and joy.

And, overhead, the oriole's song sprang upon the air, but could not match the music of her voice; as none of those bright beautiful red buds of spring beneath their feet could hold comparison with the bright rosy cheek which lay upon his bosom. The soft blue eyes were turned up to his own; thenceforth, his heaven was clear.

CHAPTER XLV.

ON A MAY EVENING.

The voice was like a fairy's; all the old Hall rang with it, and the bright-winged birds without laughed gayly for pure, honest, artist-joy at hearing it. Kate almost excelled herself; but yet it was plainly without thought she sang, coming along from the staircase, tripping toward the portico in the mild, tender evening.

Upon that portico—the portico of Effingham Hall—sat several of the personages who have illustrated this history—contributing their gay utterances and honest countenances to the narrative.

The Captain sat there, merrily laughing with Miss Henrietta, who, ever and anon, tossed her bright laughing head, scattering the snowy powder through the sun-flushed atmosphere, as her admirer—nay, her lord to be—uttered some of his jovial and heretical sentiments on the subject of the fair sex. As for the Captain, he was plainly in a very joyous mood, and vented more *morbleus* than ever graced that ditty of the youthful poet, chronicling the journey to Mos cow.

Near them sat—*mirabile dictu*—Lanky and his mistress. This was a freak of the Captain, who, passing by the Oldfield school in his fine chariot, had discovered Lanky holding a confidential interview with Donsy after school under an elm; and so, addressing the astonished Corydon by the name of "villain," brought him—nothing loth—and Donsy with him, to the Hall; it being understood that the chariot would have to return by nightfall round by Williamsburg. Lanky looked amazed when he was spoken to, and shook his pine knot head unconsciously, and regarded his huge feet and striped stockings with the air of a bewildered scaramouch, as the Captain afterwards confidentially informed him. As for Donsy, she was a very quiet, well-bred little lady, and answered everybody with soft courtesy and simplicity. She was clad simply but very neatly, and seemed to wish to be away with Lanky laughing and talking.

Behind all sat Mr. Effingham and Clare—silent; gazing upon the fair spring sunset. It was not plain at first where the soft little hand of Clare had betaken itself; but this mystery upon a nearer scrutiny was soon explained. It rested in his own.

Lastly, the squire read his brown, heavy-typed "Gazette," and grumbled at his Excellency; and from time to time rolled back his wristbands and looked out upon the fields, and spoke to Miss Alethea near.

So they sat, when Kate, singing like a bird, came to them; and behind her, Will—Will, with devoted love; Will, with perfect abnegation of his personal identity; Will, devoured by his tender and everlasting devotion, which caused him to blush, and cast beseeching glances, and extend his arms, and only grasp the air. The rustle of a document shrined in his bosom—so to speak—however, consoled him. And drawing forth the true love indenture, he threw his eyes upon that fascinating document, and seeing the signature, was comforted.

Kate put her arms round Mr. Effingham's neck, covered his eyes with her fingers, and his face was wrinkled into a smile. He guesses very soon who it is; and she entreats him and cousin Clare to come and see her fine new book, given her by Willie.

They go into the library and admire the book: and Kate, admiring it more, and clasping it to her breast, runs to show it to Captain Waters and cousin Henrietta; still singing, ever singing.

The light of the dying sun streams through the tall, old windows on them, and the hand still nestles in his own.

They stand before the fireplace and gaze into each other's faces, and unspeakable happiness lights up the tender lips of Clare, the pale brow of her lover.

Again she speaks, in her low, tender voice, of all that past which now is but a dream to them—almost a marvel. Again, she tells him how she had thought of him through all; and even when her rebellious woman's nature filled her heart with bitterness toward him, and with resolutions never to look upon him more, how still the old childhood had risen up again, and how her feelings had all changed, and bitterness gave way to pity for the wan face she had heard of, pity finally to a love more deep than ever—what she speaks of now.

And so the sunset dies away in rosy splendor, laughing through the woods: flaming on windows, gilding every brook; and streaming on the gothic bookcases, and old carven chairs, and on them as they stand before the fireplace, and the portrait.

And gazing upon that portrait, the man's heart is melted in his breast, and tears come to his eyes; and his heart is full of holy love, and on his lips trembles a word which is addressed to one far from him, past the sunset—"mother."

He draws her head down on his bosom, and then pointing to the picture, tells how he had thought to die when she died; his dear mother, now an angel up in heaven; but that God had let him live to cry for her like a little child, and pray to be united to her once again; and now to have a bosom on which even such tears as these might be wept trustingly, without fear, ever.

And so the sunset streams upon them, going far away; and as the red light dies, he draws her closer to him; and his hand smooths her hair; and pressing on the pure white forehead a long, tranquil kiss, he murmurs "Clare!"

CHAPTER XLVI.

THE HURRICANE COMMENCES.

Our comedy is almost finished. Having conducted Captain Ralph and Lanky, Mr. Effingham and his friend Hamilton, to say nothing of Henrietta, Clare, Miss Alethea and Donsy, even Will and Kate, very nearly to the hymeneal altar, the history pauses, like a wind which, rising in a whisper, swells and ever grows, and then dies away in silent murmurs in the distance.

But there are necessary to the narrative one or two more scenes, which we must briefly speak of.

All Williamsburg is in terrific commotion ; a moral storm is raging there, and men look about them, measuring each other with doubtful eyes. At the office of the "Virginia Gazette," an enormous crowd is collected, and within, are heard the presses rolling rapidly, and vainly striving to strike off sufficient copies of the journal, to supply the eager hands held out to take them.

The street is full of people passing to and fro; the crowd undulates; a murmur rises which at times swells into a great shout.

Suddenly the multitude raises its startled head. A bell begins to toll—slowly, solemnly, with a melancholy expression, which seems to echo the feeling of the crowd.

The explanation of the gathering, of the demand for copies of the journal, of the tolling bell, is simple. The vessel lying yonder at the port of York, and just from London has brought the intelligence of the passage of the STAMP ACT.

For this reason the crowd murmurs, and stretches out its Briarean hands towards the printing office, where an additional number has been hastily composed, containing the provisions of the act.

As they receive the papers unfolded, they hastily glue their eyes to them, and with dozens of persons looking over their shoulders, scan the ominous words. Upon a barrel, at some distance, is mounted a man who reads to that portion of the crowd next him, the contents of his paper.

The population of the town flow backward and forward, as the blood flows in the veins and arteries. But the office of the journal is the heart, to which all the streams return, from which the flood pours, ever making way for others.

The crowd is for the most part composed of men who seem to be of humble rank, such as are not accustomed to criticise very strongly any acts of government; but among these rude forms are seen great numbers of the richly clad members of the House of Burgesses, whose powdered heads and embroidered doublets present a strong contrast to the coarse fustian of the commoners.

The faces of the burghers are troubled—doubtful ; they

are to act, not merely murmur, as the popular voice murmurs; and the crisis is enough to try the soul. On one side, England with her tremendous strength, her overwhelming power by land and sea, and her immemorial prestige of sovereignty; upon the other, a few weak colonies, scattered over a wild continent, and scarcely knowing each other—or whether if one rises in opposition, the rest will not march to put her down. On one side an act of Parliament armed with all the weight of a solemn resolution of that great government; upon the other, a mere popular sentiment, which only stammers "Liberty—the liberty of free born Englishmen!"

And this very day the trial comes:—for Governor Fauquier will open the House of Burgesses, and officially communicate to that body the intelligence of the passage of the act:—and they must at once make submission or throw down the gauntlet of defiance.

The crowd, as they respectfully make way for them, follow them with their eyes:—they seek to read in the faces of the burghers what reply they deign to make to his serene Excellency.

Those men whom we have seen at the Governor's ball formerly, pass through the crowd—with animated faces, eagle eyes. That stately Roman head stooping forward upon the shoulders to which a hand in a black bandage is raised from time to time, towers above the press, and with clear strong eyes, surveys the excited throng with philosophic interest.

The bland lover of Anacreon reads hastily his journal.

The benevolent looking gentleman whose silvery voice we have alluded to, whom we have seen lately at the mansion of the soldier Captain Waters, raises his serene face above the crowd, and one hand placed upon his heart seems to be saying to that heart, "Be calm—rashness is worst, not best—wait for the hour—be still—be moderate—exhaust the means of protest—until all is trampled on do not strike!"

And there beside him is the man who has uttered many words in this history: who eternally brooding with fiery soul over one grand idea, now revels in the rising storm, and feels his heart bound at the muttering tempest. He wraps his old red cloak around him; elbows his way with scant courtesy from group to group; listens to every word; gauges the height of the flood as it rises and begins to foam, and estimates the strength which it will finally possess, when, striking the great dyke which opposes it, the water shall break loose. He smiles grimly from time to time, and utters detached sentences in his vigorous, somewhat affected patois, which very plainly is meant only to open his way to the rude natures gathering around him.

His words—even his chance words—burn: for they have fire in them. He condenses volumes into a sentence, and utters bitter taunts.

"Strip your shoulders, strip!" he says, "the lash is ready—you are slaves!"

And to others:

"Go crawl and grovel in the dirt! who knows but your masters may take pity!"

And each of these words, cold, yet fiery—calm, yet stormy, lashes the great popular commotion into huger waves, from which gleam bloodshot eyes, and over which rise threatening arms, clenched hands. The man in the red cloak moulds the common mind as he goes, with a master hand—he works it in his grasp like moistened clay: he laughs at it, and taunts it, and overwhelms it with contemptuous sarcasms, and pushes scornfully aside the menacing breasts, and stands the very impersonation of their thoughts and feelings, with a grim smile on his lips, a lurid fire in his eyes which makes him lord of them—lord of their hearts and arms.

The commotion ever rises higher, and the great wave, extending from the governor's palace to the capital, the whole length of Gloucester-street, surges to and fro, and breaks into a foam of cries and furious gestures everywhere. And still the bell tolls mournfully, and ever and anon rise those shouts which mount to the gathering clouds above.

But now another sound startles the multitude. A cannon roars from the palace, sending its hoarse sombre voice upon the wind which now begins to rise. And then a drum is heard.

The governor has set out from the palace for the capital, there to open the House of Burgesses. Before him ride his body-guard with drawn sabres, and the face of the old man is seen through the window of his splendid chariot, which is drawn slowly onward by six glossy horses, who toss their rosetted heads and push aside the muttering crowd with their chests.

The crowd mutters inarticulately: gazes sidewise at the cortège slowly passing.

The governor raises his head, and pointing with his white, jewelled finger through the window of the chariot, says to one of the gentlemen who ride with him:

"What is that bell?"

"They began tolling it upon the intelligence this morning, your Excellency."

The governor shakes his head and sinks back in his chariot, muttering, "Well, well, the die is thrown!"

The crowd mutter too, and with ever-increasing rage: the cavalcade is followed by groans and murmurs which are menacing murmurs.

So it continues all day: the chariot goes slowly back again under the now lurid sky, and disappears within the palace gates.

The crowd is increasing even yet: the windows of the houses are filled with the excited faces of women, who exchange whispers and wave their handkerchiefs to those they recognize in the tumultuous throng below.

That throng, like a forest trembling at the approaching whirlwind, moans and sighs and utters a crackling noise like grating boughs: a rumbling like breakers on the coast.

The Raleigh tavern is full of heads. Men pass to and fro, and a meeting is held in the Apollo room, where many words are uttered. History has spoken of the place, the words, the men.

Without, the tumult increases always as the night draws on.

The man in the red cloak is still passing from group to group, and when he leaves each group, it utters murmurs, menaces and curses; he is master of the storm, and revels in it.

On the great square especially the crowd is densest, and sweeps more irresistibly than elsewhere from side to side, swaying about and uttering hoarse cries. A dozen speakers, mounting one after another upon the temporary platform, near the centre, strive vainly to be heard.

The material storm rising in the lurid sky above, from which thunder begins to mutter, might permit them to be heard; the moral tornado is too furious.

Suddenly, a half silence falls upon the multitude, and they listen to a man wrapped in an old red cloak, whose face awes them: the time has come.

As he speaks, with awkward and slovenly gestures, in his rude, harsh voice, the multitude are silent; they only look at his eyes. Those eyes are fine. He rises in height; he thunders; he lightens: the crowd shudder, and rise up and shout.

"They are there at York!" he thunders, with a curling lip; "are you afraid?"

And, descending from the platform, he hears a roar which drowns the thunder overhead.

Yes, the blank stamps are in the vessel at the port of York, and fifty horsemen whirl out of the town. Hundreds of men follow on foot, shouting; they will have them; they will burn them here before the palace of the royal governor.

The man in the red cloak wraps himself up grimly and pushes through the crowd; he can wait.

He approaches the Raleigh; he raises his eyes: he sees standing before him a man of the people, holding a staff in his hand, and covered with dust. This man's eyes have the expression of a madman's; his face is pale, his lips are white. He gazes at the stranger; he scarcely hears him speak.

"Well met!" the stranger says; "see the storm which I spoke of!"

The wayfarer says nothing.

"You miss a great feast," the stranger goes on, grimly; "you are too happy in your mountain."

"I am there no longer."

"Your wife—"

"I have none."

And the face flushes passionately, and two bitter tears roll down the pale, wan cheeks.

"No wife!" the stranger says, looking at him.

"God took her to himself."

And bending down, he uttered a moan, and remained silent—pale, gloomy, and despairing.

"Rouse! rouse!" the stranger says, "it is not the time to grieve!"

The wayfarer looks at him, and his eyes make the stranger tremble.

"I am calm," he says.

"Come in here with me," says the stranger, "we must wait."

And they enter the Raleigh.

Night draws on, lurid and tempestuous; the sky is dark with clouds, from which issue thunder and lightning. The wind moans.

The crowd has not moved, and is almost silent, until a light appears approaching from the side of York.

They shout then, and surge backward and forward, tumultuously going to meet the light.

Through the press comes slowly onward a wagon, whose six horses foam at the mouth and pant, covered with sweat. They have galloped all the way from Yorktown.

The wagon pauses in the middle of the square, and is buried almost beneath the surge of men who throw themselves upon it.

The horses, unhitched hastily, are lashed, and disappear like shadows, but shadows which overthrew men as they ploughed their furious way into the darkness.

The wagon is rifled with the rapidity of lightning. The boxes containing the blank stamps are hurled out and piled into a mass. The crowd utters a hoarse shout, and the torch is applied to them.

The flame licks and clasps them, winding round and through the pile of half broken boxes. Then it soars aloft, and throws its glare upon the crowd, whose faces but now were concealed by the darkness—faces full of rage,—rude faces of the common people, who hear still that thunder of the stranger, louder than the storm about to burst.

Then it is that they see two figures on the platform; and they shout.

One is a man in a red cloak; the other younger, with a pale, fiery face, which makes them shudder. The latter speaks; the man in the red cloak listens.

The thunder roars, but it does not drown that stranger's wild voice, which sounds like a wail from the other world. The fire throws a crimson glare upon all faces; his is pale.

He strikes them with his burning words as with hot firebrands; he ploughs his way through the bosoms of the surging multitude with a tremendous, gigantic passion; he hurls upon them an eloquence which makes them shudder. He arraigns England at the bar of eternal justice and brands her; he lashes her with a whip of fire; he plunges the weapon into her breast, and the blood spouts hot and gurgling. The great multitude hold their breath—then roar.

The speaker sways to and fro, with his hair streaming from his brow, his neck bare, his eyes full of blood, his lips stained with a red foam.

He pours upon them a flood of passion which overwhelms them—he rides upon the wave of popular commotion like a whirlwind; he trembles, and they tremble with him; he shouts, and they utter a roar which drowns the storm.

He raises his clenched hands to heaven, and with an overpowering, terrible vehemence, which burns, and strikes, and obliterates, speaks of the grinding oppression of all ages;—facts glow and take vitality under his quivering hands; they blaze like the roaring flame before him.

He staggers with the gigantic grandeur of his passion; raves almost with his writhing lips, but with a madness which bends all down with its terrible, inexorable method. He totters from side to side, and again rises.

The multitude look at him with pale faces, then faces flushed with wrath, terror, and indignation; and every word he utters burns into them like a hot iron, leaving an ineffaceable impression upon every heart. He speaks the thoughts, the feelings, and the passions of them all.

And as he raises his pale brow to the storm, his fiery eyes, his bleeding lips, a sudden flash of lightning blinds all eyes with its terrible radiancy, lighting up tree and house, and all the great surging crowd; and then comes a crash of thunder like a thousand cannon, which seems to trample out the very fire, for the flame crumbles into gloom, and disappears.

Pale, overwhelmed, and staggering, his mouth filled with bloody foam, the speaker falls back fainting into the outstretched arms of the man in the red cloak, who holds him on his breast.

"Good!" murmured Patrick Henry, smiling grimly, "the Revolution is begun!"

CHAPTER XLVII.

IN WHICH THE AUTHOR OF THE MS. OMITS DESCRIBING FOUR WEDDINGS.

"I NEED not add to this history a description of the merry wedding parties which ere long filled three houses with merriment and rejoicing.

"Those particular scenes are much more agreeable to attend than to describe; and perhaps all description would only blur the picture of those jubilees, full of wild revelry, as were all such in the ancient colony and Old Dominion—indeed, are at the day we live in.

"Perhaps the saddest bridegroom was our friend the Captain, whose honest face could not look very cheerful when his brother's pale cheeks came to his memory, and when the *bon pere* was away. But he comforted himself with the thought that he would have both of them at 'Flodden'—the old man at least, certainly,—where the best chamber in the mansion was set apart for the old fisherman.

"Mr. Effingham, as we may imagine, was radiant with joy; and it is scarcely too much to say, that Clare was quite as happy. The sisters were married on the same day; and, at the Hall, Miss Alethea gave her hand to Mr. Jack Hamilton, almost at the same moment. That unconquerable bachelor was fairly conquered and enslaved.

"Our friend Lanky married Donsy soon afterwards, and the Captain kept his promise; and the happy young couple took up their abode at the cottage. Lanky often told his wife that he owed his success in gaining her affections to the advice of the Captain, which had led him to don those military accoutrements which had made such an impression upon her heart. But Donsy to the last denied that such was the fact; and was not even convinced when Lanky's pine-knot head was sawed argumentatively from a point due northeast to the opposite portion of the compass.

"Our comedy is now quite ended. Having listened for many hours to those ante-revolutionary voices speaking of themselves, and telling us what thoughts, and schemes, and hopes, and fears occupied them then, we may go out into the broad sunny world to-day, no worse for having heard those sincere utterances. The past has tried to speak, and the poor chronicler has written down what the low voice dictated. If there is any good in what he has placed on the page—a scene of conquered passion, or pure love, denying self, his hours have not been thrown away. And now, the history being ended, he will rest."

EPILOGUE.

It was one of those pure days which, born of spring, seem almost to rejoice like living things in the bright flowers and tender buds:—and she was failing.

All the mountain winds were faintly blowing on the smiling trees, and on the white calm brow of one who breathed the pure delightful airs of opening spring, before she went away to breathe the airs of that other land, so far away, where no snows come, or frost, or hail, or rain; but spring reigns ever, sublimated by the light which shines on figures in white garments round the central throne.

She heard those figures calling, calling, calling, with their low soft voices full of love and hope; calling ever to her in the purple twilight dying o'er the world; rejoicing every one that she was coming.

She looked upon the faces seen through mist around her, and besought them smiling, not to weep for her, but look to the bright land where she was going—for her faith was strong. She begged them to take tender care of the flower which lay but now upon her bosom, and not think of her. A voice had told her in the night that she was waited for: and now the sun was fading in the west, and she must go.

Alcestis-like she kissed them on their brows and pointed to the skies: the time had almost come.

She looked with dim faint eyes, as in a dream, upon that past which now had flowed from her and left her pure — she saw the sunset wane away and die above the rosy head-lands, glooming fast:—she murmured that her hope was steadfast ever; that she heard the angels; that they called to her, and bade her say farewell to all that was around her on this earth, for now the expected time had come.

The tender sunset faded far away, and over the great mountains drooped the spangled veil, with myriads of worlds all singing as her heart was singing now. She saw the rosy flush go far away, and die away, and leave the earth: and then the voice said Come!

She saw a cross rise from the far bright distance, and a bleeding form: she saw the heavenly vision slowly move, and ever nearer, nearer, brighter with the light of heaven. She saw it now before her, and her arms were opened. The grand eternal stars came out above—the sunset died upon her brow—she clasped the cross close to her bosom—and so fell asleep.

THE END.

813
C775vi
37293

Americans in Fiction

A series of reprints of 19th century American novels important to the study of American folklore, culture and literary history

THOMAS BAILEY ALDRICH
The Stillwater Tragedy

JAMES LANE ALLEN
A Kentucky Cardinal

GERTRUDE ATHERTON
Los Cerritos: A Romance of Modern Times
The Californians
Senator North
Aristocrats
The Splendid Idle Forties

ARLO BATES
The Puritans

OLIVER THOMAS BEARD
Bristling With Thorns

ALICE BROWN
Tiverton Tales
The County Road

FRANCIS H. BURNETT
Through One Administration

WILLIAM A. CARUTHERS
Kentuckian in New York, or the Adventures of Three Southerns
The Cavaliers of Virginia

CHARLES WADDELL CHESNUTT
The Conjure Woman
The Wife of His Youth; and Other Stories of the Colour Line
The House Behind the Cedars

KATE CHOPIN
Bayou Folk

JOHN ESTEN COOKE
The Virginia Comedians
Surry of Eagle's Nest
Mohun: or the Last Days of Lee and His Paladins
My Lady Pokahontas

ROSE TERRY COOKE
Rootbound and Other Sketches

MARGARET DELAND
John Ward, Preacher

THOMAS DIXON
The Leopard's Spots
The Clansman

EDWARD EGGLESTON
Roxy
The Faith Doctor

MARY HALLOCK FOOTE
The Led-Horse Claim

PAUL LEICESTER FORD
The Honorable Peter Stirling

HAROLD FREDERIC
Seth's Brother's Wife

MARY E. WILKINS FREEMAN
A New England Nun; and Other Stories
The Portion of Labor

HENRY B. FULLER
The Cliff Dwellers